Island Escapes

Island Escapes:
Seduction
at Sea

HEIDI RICE

NATALIE ANDERSON

SHERYL LISTER

MILLS & BOON

First Published in Great Britain 2021
by Mills & Boon, an imprint of HarperCollins*Publishers* Ltd,
1 London Bridge Street, London, SE1 9GF

www.harpercollins.co.uk

HarperCollins*Publishers*
1st Floor, Watermarque Building,
Ringsend Road, Dublin 4, Ireland

ISLAND ESCAPES: SEDUCTION AT SEA
© 2021 Harlequin Books S.A.

Vows They Can't Escape © 2017 Heidi Rice
Princess's Pregnancy Secret © 2018 Natalie Anderson
All of Me © 2015 Sheryl Lister

ISBN: 978-0-263-30278-3

MIX
Paper from
responsible sources
FSC™ C007454

VOWS THEY CAN'T ESCAPE

HEIDI RICE

With thanks to my cousin Susan, who suggested I write a romance with a female CEO as the heroine, my best writing mate Abby Green, who kept telling me to write a classic Modern/Presents, my best mate Catri, who plotted this with me on the train back from Kilkenny Shakespeare Festival, and to Sarah Hornby of the Royal Thames Yacht Club, who explained why having my hero and heroine spend a night below decks while sailing a yacht together round the Caribbean probably wasn't a good idea!

CHAPTER ONE

XANTHE CARMICHAEL STRODE into the gleaming steel-and-glass lobby of the twenty-six-storey office block housing Redmond Design Studios on Manhattan's West Side, satisfied that the machine-gun taps of her heels against the polished stone flooring said exactly what she wanted them to say.

Watch out, boys, woman scorned on the warpath.

Ten years after Dane Redmond had abandoned her in a seedy motel room on the outskirts of Boston, she was ready to bring the final curtain crashing down on their brief and catastrophic liaison.

So the flush that had leaked into her cheeks despite the building's overefficient air conditioning and the bottomless pit opening up in her stomach could take a hike.

After a six-hour flight from Heathrow, spent power-napping in the soulless comfort of Business Class, and two days and nights figuring out how she was going to deal with the unexploded bomb the head of her legal team, Bill Spencer, had dropped at her feet on Wednesday afternoon, she was ready for any eventuality.

Whatever Dane Redmond had once meant to her seventeen-year-old self, the potentially disastrous situation Bill had uncovered wasn't personal any more—it was business. And *nothing* got in the way of her business.

Carmichael's, the two-hundred-year-old shipping company which had been in her family for four generations, was the only thing that mattered to her now. And she would do anything to protect it and her new position as the majority shareholder and CEO.

'Hi, I'm Ms Sanders, from London, England,' she said to the immaculately dressed woman at reception, giving the false name she'd instructed her PA to use when setting up this meeting. However confident she felt, she was not about to give a bare-knuckle fighter like Dane a heads-up. 'I have an appointment with Mr Redmond to discuss a commission.'

The woman sent her a smile as immaculate as her appearance. 'It's great to meet you, Ms Sanders.' She tapped the screen in front of her and picked up the phone. 'If you'd like to take a seat, Mr Redmond's assistant, Mel Mathews, will be down in a few minutes to escort you to the eighteenth floor.'

Xanthe's heartbeat thudded against her collarbone as she recrossed the lobby under the life-size model of a huge wing sail catamaran suspended from the ceiling. A polished brass plaque announced that the boat had won Redmond Design a prestigious sailing trophy twice in a row.

She resisted the urge to chew off the lipstick she'd applied in the cab ride from JFK.

Bill's bombshell would have been less problematic if Dane had still been the boy her father had so easily dismissed as 'a trailer trash wharf rat with no class and fewer prospects,' but she refused to be cowed by Dane's phenomenal success over the last decade.

She was here to show him who he was dealing with.

But, as she took in the ostentatious design of Dane's new headquarters in New York's uber-hip Meatpacking District, the awe-inspiring view of the Hudson River from the lobby's third-floor aspect and that beast of a boat, she had to concede the meteoric rise of his business and his position as one of the world's premier sailing boat designers didn't surprise her.

He'd always been smart and ambitious—a natural-born sailor more at home on water than dry land—which was exactly why her father's estate manager had hired him that summer in Martha's Vineyard to run routine maintenance on the small fleet of two yachts and a pocket cruiser her father kept at their holiday home.

Running routine maintenance on Charles Carmichael's impressionable, naive daughter had been done on his own time.

No one had ever been able to fault Dane's work ethic.

Xanthe's thigh muscles trembled at the disturbingly vivid memory of blunt fingers trailing across sensitive skin, but she didn't break stride.

All that energy and purpose had drawn her to him like a heat-seeking missile. That and the superpower they'd discovered together—his unique ability to lick her to a scream-your-lungs-out orgasm in sixty seconds or less.

She propped her briefcase on a coffee table and sank into one of the leather chairs lining the lobby.

Whoa, Xan. Do not think about the superpower.

Crossing her legs, she squeezed her knees together, determined to halt the conflagration currently converging on the hotspot between her thighs. Even Dane's superpower would never be enough to compensate for the pain he'd caused.

She hid the unsettling thought behind a tight smile as a thirtysomething woman headed in her direction across the ocean of polished stone. Grabbing the briefcase containing the documents she had flown three thousand miles to deliver, Xanthe stood up, glad when her thighs remained virtually quiver-free.

Dane Redmond's not the only badass in town. Not any more.

* * *

Xanthe was feeling less like a badass and more like a sacrificial lamb five minutes later, as the PA led her through a sea of hip and industrious young marketing people working on art boards and computers on the eighteenth floor. Even her machine-gun heel taps had been muffled by the industrial carpeting.

The adrenaline which had been pumping through her veins for forty-eight hours and keeping her upright slowed to a crawl as they approached the glass-walled corner office and the man within, silhouetted against the New Jersey shoreline. The jolt of recognition turned the bottomless pit in her stomach into a yawning chasm.

Broad shoulders and slim hips were elegantly attired in steel-grey trousers and a white shirt. But his imposing height, the muscle bulk revealed by the shirt's rolled-up sleeves, the dark buzz cut hugging the dome of his skull, and the tattoo that covered his left arm down to his elbow did nothing to disguise the wolf in expensively tailored clothing.

Sweat gathered between Xanthe's breasts and the powder-blue silk suit and peach camisole ensemble she'd chosen twelve hours ago in London, because it covered all the bases from confident to kick-ass, rubbed against her skin like sandpaper.

The internet hadn't done Dane Redmond justice. Because the memory of the few snatched images she'd found yesterday while preparing for this meeting was comprehensively failing to stop a boulder the size of an asteroid forming in her throat.

She forced one foot in front of the other as the PA tapped on the office door and led her into the wolf's den.

Brutally blue eyes locked on Xanthe's face.

A flicker of stunned disbelief softened his rugged features before his jaw went rigid, making the shallow dent in his chin twitch. The searing look had the thundering beat of Xanthe's heart dropping into that yawning chasm.

Had she actually kidded herself that age and money and success would have refined Dane—tamed him, even—or at the very least made him a lot less intense and intimidating? Because she'd been dead wrong. Either that or she'd just been struck by lightning.

'This is Ms Sanders from—'

'Leave us, Mel.' Dane interrupted the PA's introduction. 'And shut the door.'

The husky command had Xanthe's heartbeat galloping into her throat to party with the asteroid, reminding her of all the commands he'd once issued to her in the same he-who-shall-be-obeyed tone. And the humiliating speed with which she'd obeyed them.

'Relax, I won't hurt you. I swear.'

'Hold on tight. This is gonna be the ride of your life.'

'I take care of my own, Xan. That's non-negotiable.'

The door closed behind the dutiful PA with a hushed click.

Xanthe gripped the handle on her briefcase with enough force to crack a nail and lifted her chin, channelling the smouldering remains of her inner badass that had survived the lightning strike.

'Hello, Dane,' she said, glad when her voice remained relatively steady.

She would *not* be derailed by a physical reaction which was ten years out of date and nothing more than an inconvenient throwback to her youth. It would pass. Eventually.

'Hello, *Ms Sanders.*'

His thinly veiled contempt at her deception had outrage joining the riot of other emotions she was busy trying to suppress.

'If you've come to buy a boat, you're all out of luck.'

The searing gaze wandered down to her toes, the insolent appraisal as infuriating as the fuses that flared to life in every pulse point en route.

'I don't do business with spoilt little rich chicks.'

His gaze rose back to her face, having laid waste to her composure.

'Especially ones I was once dumb enough to marry.'

CHAPTER TWO

Xanthe Carmichael.

Dane Redmond had just taken a sucker punch to the gut. And it was taking every ounce of his legendary control not to show it.

The girl who had haunted his dreams a lifetime ago—particularly all his wet dreams—and then become a star player in his nightmares. And now she had the balls to stand in his office—the place he'd built from the ground up after she'd kicked him to the kerb—as if she had a right to invade his life a second time.

She'd changed some from the girl he remembered—all trussed-up now in a snooty suit, looking chic and classy in those ice-pick heels. But there was enough of that girl left to force him to put his libido on lockdown.

She still had those wide, feline eyes. Their sultry slant hinting at the banked fires beneath, the translucent blue-green the vivid colour of the sea over the Barrier Reef. She had the same peaches-and-cream complexion, with the sprinkle of girlish freckles over her nose she hadn't quite managed to hide under a smooth mask of make-up. And that riot of red-gold hair, ruthlessly styled now in an updo, but for a few strands that had escaped to cling to her neck and draw his gaze to the coy hint of cleavage beneath her suit.

The flush high on her cheekbones and the glitter in her eyes made her look like a fairy queen who had swallowed a cockroach. But he knew she was worse than any siren sent to lure men to their destruction, with that stunning body and that butter-wouldn't-melt expression—and about as much freaking integrity as a sea serpent.

He curled his twitching fingers into his palms and braced his fists against the desk. Because part of him wanted to throw her over his knee and spank her until her butt was as red as her hair, and another part of him longed to throw her over his shoulder and take her somewhere dark and private, so he could rip off that damn suit and find the responsive girl beneath who had once begged him for release.

And each one of those impulses was as screwed-up as the other. Because she meant nothing to him now. Not a damn thing. And he'd sworn ten years ago, when he'd been lying on the road outside her father's vacation home in the Vineyard, with three busted ribs, more bruises than even his old man had given him on a bad day, his stomach hollow with grief and tight with anger and humiliation, that no woman would ever make such a jackass of him again.

'I'm here because we have a problem…' She hesitated, her lip trembling ever so slightly.

She was nervous. She ought to be.

'Which I'm here to solve.'

'How could *we* possibly have a problem?' he said, his voice deceptively mild. 'When *we* haven't seen each other in over a decade and I never wanted to see you again?'

She stiffened, the flush spreading down her neck to highlight the lush valley of her breasts.

'The feeling's mutual,' she said. The snotty tone was a surprise.

He buried his fists into his pants pockets. The last thin thread controlling his temper about to snap.

Where the heck did she get off, being pissed with him? *He'd* been the injured party in their two-second marriage. She'd flaunted herself, come on to him, had him panting after her like a dog that whole summer—hooked him like a prize tuna by promising to love, honour and obey him, no matter what. Then she'd run back to daddy at the first sign of trouble. Not that he'd been dumb enough to really believe those breathless promises. He'd learned when he was still a kid that love was just an empty sentiment. But he *had* been dumb enough to trust her.

And now she had the gall to turn up at *his* place, under a false name, expecting him to be polite and pretend what she'd done was okay.

Whatever her problem was, he wanted no part of it. But he'd let her play out this little drama before he slapped her down and kicked her the hell out of his life. For good this time.

Lifting her briefcase onto the table, Xanthe ignored the hostility radiating from the man in front of her. She flipped the locks, whipped out the divorce papers and slapped them on the desk.

Dane Redmond's caveman act was nothing new, but she was wise to it now. He'd been exactly the same as a nineteen-year-old. Taciturn and bossy and supremely arrogant. Once upon a time she'd found that wildly attractive—because once upon a time she'd believed that lurking beneath the caveman was a boy who'd needed the love she could lavish on him.

That had been her first mistake. Followed by too many others.

The vulnerable boy had never existed. And the caveman had never wanted what she had to offer.

Good thing, then, that this wasn't about him any more—it was about *her*. And what *she* wanted. Which was exactly what she was going to get.

Because no man bullied her now. Not her father, not the board of directors at Carmichael's and certainly not some overly ripped boat designer who thought he could boss her around just because she'd once been bewitched by his larger-than-average penis.

'The problem is...' She threw the papers onto the desk, cursing the tremor in her fingers at that sudden recollection of Dane fully aroused.

Do not think about him naked.

'My father's solicitor, Augustus Greaves, failed to file the paperwork for our divorce ten years ago.'

She delivered the news in a rush, to disguise any hint of culpability. It was not her fault Greaves had been an alcoholic.

'So we're still, technically speaking, man and wife.'

CHAPTER THREE

'YOU HAD BETTER be freaking kidding me!'

Dane looked so shocked Xanthe would have smiled if she hadn't been shaking quite so hard. That had certainly wiped the self-righteous glare off his face.

'I've come all the way from London to get you to sign these newly issued papers, so we can fix this nightmare as fast as is humanly possible. So, no, I'm not kidding.'

She flicked through the document until she got to the signature page, which she had already signed, frustrated because her fingers wouldn't stop trembling. She could smell him—that scent that was uniquely his, clean and male, and far too enticing.

She drew back. Too late. She'd already ingested a lungful, detecting expensive cedarwood soap instead of the supermarket brand he had once used.

'Once you've signed here—' she pointed to the signature line '—*our* problem will be solved and I can guarantee never to darken your door again.'

She whipped a gold pen out of the briefcase, stabbed the button at the top and thrust it towards him like a dagger.

He lifted his hands out of his pockets but didn't pick up the gauntlet.

'Like I'd be dumb enough to sign anything *you* put in front of me without checking it first…'

She ruthlessly controlled the snap of temper at his statement. And the wave of panic.

Stay calm. Be persuasive. Don't freak out.

She breathed in through her nose and out through her mouth, employing the technique she'd perfected during the last five years of handling Carmichael's board. As long as Dane never found out about the original terms of her father's will, nothing in the paperwork she'd handed him would clue him in to the *real* reason she'd come all this way. And why would he, when her father's will hadn't come into force until five years after Dane had abandoned her?

Unfortunately the memory of that day in her father's office, with her stomach cramping in shock and loss and disbelief as the executor recited the terms of the will, was not helping with her anxiety attack.

'Your father had hoped you would marry one of the candidates he suggested. His first preference was to leave forty-five per cent of Carmichael's stock to you and the controlling share to your spouse as the new CEO. As no such marriage was contracted at the time of his death, he has put the controlling share in trust, to be administered by the board until you complete a five-year probationary period as Carmichael's executive owner. If, after that period, they deem you a credible CEO, they can vote to allocate a further six per cent of the shares to you. If not, they can elect another CEO and leave the shares in trust.'

That deadline had passed a week ago. The board—no doubt against all her father's expectations—had voted in her favour. And then Bill had discovered his bombshell—that she had still technically been married to Dane at the time of her father's death and he could, therefore, sue for the controlling share in the company.

It might almost have been funny—that her father's lack of trust in her abilities might end up gifting 55 per cent of his company to a man he had despised—if it hadn't been more evidence that her father had never trusted her with Carmichael's.

She pushed the dispiriting thought to one side, and the echo of grief that came with it, as Dane punched a number into his smartphone.

Her father might have been old-fashioned and hopelessly traditional—an aristocratic Englishman who believed that no man who hadn't gone to Eton and Oxford could ever be a suitable husband for her—but he had loved her and had wanted the best for her. Once she got Dane to sign on the dotted line, thus eliminating any possible threat this paperwork error could present to her father's company—*her* company—she would finally have proved her commitment to Carmichael's was absolute.

'Jack? I've got something I want you to check out.' Dane beckoned to someone behind Xanthe as he spoke into the phone. The superefficient PA popped back into the office as if by magic. 'Mel is gonna send it over by messenger.'

He handed the document to his PA, then scribbled something on a pad and passed that to her, too. The PA trotted out.

'Make sure you check every line,' he continued, still talking to whomever was on the other end of the phone. He gave a strained chuckle. 'Not exactly—it's *supposed* to be divorce papers.'

The judgmental once-over he gave Xanthe had her temper rising up her torso.

'I'll explain the why and the how another time,' he said. 'Just make sure there are no surprises—like a hidden claim for ten years' back-alimony.'

He clicked off the phone and shoved it into his pocket.

She was actually speechless. For about two seconds.

'Are you finished?' Indignation burned, the breathing technique history.

She'd come all this way, spent several sleepless nights preparing for this meeting while being constantly tormented by painful memories from that summer, not to mention having to deal with his scent and the inappropriate heat that would not die. And through it all she'd remained determined to keep this process dignified, despite the appalling way he had treated her. And he'd shot it all to hell in less than five minutes.

The arrogant ass.

'Don't play the innocent with me,' he continued, the self-righteous glare returning. 'Because I know just what you're capable—'

'You son of a...' She gasped for breath, outrage consuming her. 'I'm not *allowed* to play the innocent? When you took my virginity, carried on seducing me all summer, got me pregnant, insisted I marry you and then dumped me three months later?'

He'd never told her he loved her—never even tried to see her point of view during their one and only argument. But, worse than that, he hadn't been there when she had needed him the most. Her stomach churned, the in-flight meal she'd picked at on the plane threatening to gag her as misery warred with fury, bringing the memories flooding back—memories which were too painful to forget even though she'd tried.

The pungent smell of mould and cheap disinfectant in the motel bathroom, the hazy sight of the cracked linoleum through the blur of tears, the pain hacking her in two as she prayed for him to pick up his phone.

Dane's face went completely blank, before a red stain of fury lanced across the tanned cheekbones. '*I* dumped *you*? Are you *nuts*?' he yelled at top volume.

'You walked out and left me in that motel room and you didn't answer my calls.' She matched him decibel for decibel. She wasn't that besotted girl any more, too timid and delusional to stand up and fight her corner. 'What *else* would you call it?'

'I was two hundred miles out at sea, crewing on a bluefin tuna boat—that's what I'd call it. I didn't get your calls because there isn't a heck of a lot of network coverage in the middle of the North Atlantic. And when I got back a week later I found out you'd hightailed it back to daddy because of one damn disagreement.'

The revelation of where he'd been while she'd been losing their baby gave her pause—but only for a moment. He could have rung her to tell her about the job *before* he'd boarded the boat, but in his typical don't-ask-don't-tell fashion he hadn't. And what about the frantic message she'd left him while she'd waited for her father to arrive and take her to the emergency room? And later, when she'd come round from the fever dreams back in her bedroom on her father's estate?

She'd asked the staff to contact Dane, to tell him about the baby, her heart breaking into a thousand pieces, but he'd never even responded to the news. Except to send through the signed divorce papers weeks later.

She could have forgiven him for not caring about *her*. Their marriage had been the definition of a shotgun wedding, the midnight elopement a crazy adventure hyped up on teenage hormones, testosterone-fuelled bravado and the mad panic caused by an unplanned pregnancy. But it was his failure to care about the three-month-old life which had died inside her, his failure to even be willing to mourn its passing, that she couldn't forgive.

It had tortured her for months. How many lies he'd told about being there for her, respecting her decision to have the baby. How he'd even gone through with their farce of a marriage, while all the time planning to dump her at the first opportunity.

It had made no sense to her for so long—until she'd finally figured it out. Why he'd always deflected conversations about the future, about the baby. Why he'd never once returned her declarations of love even while stoking the sexual heat between them to fever pitch. Why he'd stormed out that morning after her innocent suggestion that she look for a job, too, because she knew he was struggling to pay their motel bill.

He'd gotten bored with the marriage, with the responsibility. And sex had been the only thing binding them together. He'd never wanted her or the baby. His offer of marriage had been a knee-jerk reaction he'd soon regretted. And once she'd lost the baby he'd had the perfect excuse he'd been looking for to discard her.

That truth had devastated her at the time. Brought her to her knees. How could she have been so wrong about him? About *them*? But it had been a turning point, too. Because she'd survived the loss, repaired her shattered heart, and made herself into the woman she was now—someone who didn't rely on others to make herself whole.

Thanks to Dane's carelessness, his neglect, she'd shut off her stupid, fragile, easily duped heart and found a new purpose—devoting herself to the company that was her legacy. She'd begged her father for a lowly internship position that autumn, when they'd returned to London, and begun working her backside off to learn everything she needed to know about Europe's top maritime logistics brand.

At first it had been a distraction, a means of avoiding the great big empty space inside her. But eventually she'd stopped simply going through the motions and actually found something to care about again. She'd aced her MBA, learnt French and Spanish while working in Carmichael's subsidiary offices in Calais and Cadiz, and even managed to persuade her father to give her a job at the company's head office in Whitehall before he'd died—all the while fending off his attempts to find her a 'suitable' husband.

She'd earned the position she had now through hard

work and dedication and toughened up enough to take charge of her life. So there was no way on earth she was going to back down from this fight and let Dane Redmond lay some ludicrous guilt trip on her when *he* was the one who had crushed her and every one of her hopes and dreams. Maybe they had been foolish hopes and stupid pipe dreams, but the callous way he'd done it had been unnecessarily cruel.

'You promised to be there for me,' she shot back, her fury going some way to mask the hollow pain in her stomach. The same pain she'd sworn never to feel again. 'You swore you would protect me and support me. But when I needed you the most you weren't there.'

'What the hell did you need *me* there for?' he spat the words out, the brittle light in the icy blue eyes shocking her into silence.

The fight slammed out of her lungs on a gasp of breath.

Because in that moment all she could see was his rage.

The hollow pain became sharp and jagged, tearing through the last of her resistance until all that was left was the horrifying uncertainty that had crippled her as a teenager.

Why was he so angry with her? When all she'd ever done was try to love him?

'I wanted you to be there for me when I lost our baby,' she whispered, her voice sounding as if it were coming from another dimension.

'You wanted me to hold your hand while you aborted my kid?'

'*What?*' His sarcasm, the sneered disbelief sliced through her, and the jagged pain exploded into something huge.

'You think I don't *know* you got rid of it?'

The accusation in his voice, the contempt, suddenly made a terrible kind of sense.

'But I—' She tried to squeeze the words past the asteroid in her throat.

He cut her off. 'I hitched a ride straight to the Vineyard once I got back on shore. We'd had that fight and you'd left some garbled message on my cell. When I got to your old man's place he told me there was no baby any more, showed me the divorce papers you'd signed and then had me kicked out. And that's when I figured out the truth. Daddy's little princess had decided that my kid was an inconvenience she didn't need.'

She didn't see hatred any more, just a seething resentment, but she couldn't process any of it. His words buzzed round in her brain like mutant bees which refused to land. *Had* she signed the divorce papers first? She couldn't remember doing that. All she could remember was begging to see Dane, and her father showing her Dane's signature on the documents. And how the sight of his name scrawled in black ink had killed the last tiny remnant of hope still lurking inside her.

'I know the pregnancy was a mistake. Hell, the whole damn marriage was insane,' Dane continued, his tone caustic with disgust. 'And if you'd told me that's what you'd decided to do I would have tried to understand. But you didn't have the guts to own it, did you? You didn't even have the guts to tell me that's what you'd done? So don't turn up here and pretend you were some innocent kid, seduced by the big bad wolf. Because we both know that's garbage. There was only *one* innocent party in the whole screwed-up mess of our marriage and it wasn't either one of us.'

She could barely hear him, those mutant killer bees had become a swarm. Her legs began to shake, and the jagged pain in her stomach joined the thudding cacophony in her skull. She locked her knees, wrapped her arms around her midriff and swallowed convulsively, trying to prevent the silent screams from vomiting out of her mouth.

How could you not know how much our baby meant to me?

'What's wrong?' Dane demanded, the contempt turning to reluctant concern.

She tried to force her shattered thoughts into some semblance of order. But the machete embedded in her head was about to split her skull in two. And she couldn't form the words.

'Damn it, Red, you look as if you're about to pass out.'

Firm hands clamped on her upper arms and became the only thing keeping her upright as her knees buckled.

The old nickname and the shock of his touch had a blast of memory assaulting her senses—hurtling her back in time to those stolen days on the water in Buzzards Bay: the hot sea air, the shrieks of the cormorants, the scent of salt mixed with the funky aroma of sweat and sex, the devastating joy as his calloused fingers brought her body to vibrant life.

I didn't have an abortion.

She tried to force the denial free from the stranglehold in her throat, but nothing came out.

I had a miscarriage.

She heard him curse, felt firm fingers digging into her biceps as the cacophony in her head became deafening. And she stepped over the edge to let herself fall.

CHAPTER FOUR

WHAT THE—?

Dane leapt forward as Xanthe's eyes rolled back, scooping her dead weight into his arms before she could crash to earth.

'Is Ms Sanders sick?' Mel appeared, her face blank with shock.

'Her name's Carmichael.'

Or, technically speaking, Redmond.

He barged past his PA, cradling Xanthe against his chest. 'Call Dr Epstein and tell him to meet me in the penthouse.'

'What—what shall I say happened?' Mel stammered, nowhere near as steady as usual.

He knew how she felt. His palms were sweating, his pulse racing fast enough to win the Kentucky Derby.

Xanthe let out a low moan. He tightened his grip, something hot and fluid hitting him as his fingertips brushed her breast.

'I don't know what happened,' he replied. 'Just tell Epstein to get up there.'

He threw the words over his shoulder as he strode through the office, past his sponsorship and marketing team, every one of whom was staring at him as if he'd just told them the company had declared bankruptcy.

Had they heard him shouting at Red like a madman? Letting the fury he'd buried years ago spew out of his mouth?

Where had that come from?

He'd lost it—and he *never* lost it. Not since the day on her father's estate when he'd gone berserk, determined to see Xanthe no matter what her father said.

Of course he hadn't told her that part of the story. The part where he'd made an ass of himself.

The pulse already pounding in his temple began to throb like a wound. He'd been dog-tired and frantic with worry when he'd arrived at Carmichael's vacation home, his pride in tatters, his gut clenching at the thought Xanthe had run out on him.

All that had made him easy prey for the man who hadn't considered him fit to kiss the hem of his precious daughter's bathrobe, let alone marry her. He could still see Charles Carmichael's smug expression, hear that superior I'm-better-than-you tone as the guy told him their baby was gone and that his daughter had made the sensible decision to cut all ties with the piece of trailer trash she should never have married.

The injustice of it all, the sense of loss, the futile anger had opened up a great big black hole inside him that had been waiting to drag him under ever since he was a little boy. So he'd exploded with rage—and got his butt thoroughly kicked by Carmichael's goons for his trouble.

Obviously some of that rage was still lurking in his subconscious. Or he wouldn't have freaked out again. Over something that meant nothing now.

He'd been captivated by Xanthe that summer. By her cute accent, the sexy, subtle curves rocking the bikini-shorts-and-T-shirt combos she'd lived in, her quick, curious mind and most of all the artless flirting that had grown hotter and hotter until they'd made short work of those bikini shorts.

The obvious crush she'd had on him had flattered him, had made him feel like somebody when everyone else treated him like a nobody. But their connection had never been about anything other than hot sex—souped up to fever pitch by teenage lust. He knew he'd been nuts to think it could ever be more, especially once she'd run back to Daddy when she'd discovered what it was *really* like to live on a waterman's pay.

Xanthe stirred, her fragrant hair brushing his chin.

'Settle down. I've got you.' A wave of protectiveness washed over him. He didn't plan to examine it too closely. She'd been his responsibility once. She wasn't his responsibility any more. Whatever the paperwork said.

This was old news. It didn't make a damn bit of difference now. Obviously the shock of seeing her again had worked stuff loose which had been hanging about without his knowledge.

'Where are you taking me?'

The groggy question brought him back to the problem nestled in his arms.

He elbowed the call button on the elevator, grateful when the doors zipped open and they could get out of range of their audience. Stepping inside, he nudged the button marked Penthouse Only.

'My place. Top floor.'

'What happened?'

He glanced down to find her eyes glazed, her face still pale as a ghost. She looked sweet and innocent and scared—the way she had once before.

'It's positive. I'm going to have a baby. What are we going to do?'

He concentrated on the panel above his head, shoving the flashback where it belonged—in the file marked Ancient History.

'You tell me.' He kept his voice casual. 'One minute we were yelling at each other and the next you were hitting the deck.'

'I must have fainted,' she said, as if she wasn't sure. She shifted, colour flooding back into her cheeks. 'You can put me down now. I'm fine.'

He should do what she asked, because having her soft curves snug against his chest and that sultry scent filling his nostrils wasn't doing much for his equilibrium, but his heartbeat was still going for gold in Kentucky.

His grip tightened.

'Uh-huh?' He raised a sceptical eyebrow. 'You make a habit of swooning like a heroine in a trashy novel?'

Her chin took on a mutinous tilt, but she didn't reply.

Finally, score one to Redmond.

The elevator arrived at his penthouse and the doors opened onto the panoramic view of the downtown skyline.

At any other time the sight would have brought with it a satisfying ego-boost. The designer furniture, the modern steel and glass structure and the expertly planted roof terrace, its lap pool sparkling in the fading sunlight, was a million miles away from the squalid dump he'd grown up in. He'd worked himself raw in the last couple of years, and spent a huge chunk of investment capital, to complete the journey.

But he wasn't feeling too proud of himself at the moment. He'd lost his temper downstairs, but worse than that, he'd let his emotions get the upper hand.

'Stop crying like a girl and get me another beer, or you'll be even sorrier than you are already, you little pissant.'

His old man had been a mean drunk, whom he'd grown to despise, but one thing the hard bastard had taught him was that letting your emotions show only made you weak.

Xanthe had completed his education by teaching him another valuable lesson—that mixing sex with sentiment was never a good idea.

Somehow both those lessons had deserted him downstairs.

He deposited her on the leather couch in the centre of the living space and stepped back, aware of the persistent ache in his crotch.

She got busy fussing with her hair, not meeting his eyes. Her staggered breathing made her breasts swell against the lacy top. The persistent ache spiked.

Terrific.

'Thank you,' she said. 'But you didn't have to carry me all the way up here.'

She looked around the space, still not meeting his eyes.

He stifled the disappointment when she didn't comment on the apartment. He wasn't looking for her approval. Certainly didn't need it.

'The company doc's coming up to check you out,' he said.

That got her attention. Her gaze flashed to his—equal parts aggravation and embarrassment.

'That's not necessary. It's just a bit of jet lag.'

Jet lag didn't make all the colour drain out of your face, or give your eyes that haunted, hunted look. And it sure as hell didn't make you drop like a stone in the middle of an argument.

'Tell that to Dr Epstein.'

She was getting checked out by a professional whether she liked it or not. She might not be his responsibility any more, but this was his place and his rules.

The elevator bell dinged on cue.

He crossed the apartment to greet the doctor, his racing heartbeat finally reaching the finish line and heading into a victory lap when he heard Xanthe's annoyed huff of breath behind him.

Better to deal with a pissed Xanthe than one who fainted dead away right before his eyes.

CHAPTER FIVE

'WHAT I'M PRESCRIBING is a balanced meal and a solid ten hours' sleep, in that order.'

The good Dr Epstein sent Xanthe a grave look which made her feel as if she were four years old again, being chastised by Nanny Foster for refusing to go down for her nap.

'Your blood pressure is elevated and the fact you haven't eaten or slept well in several days is no doubt the cause of this episode. Stress is a great leveller, Ms Carmichael,' he added.

As if she didn't know that, with the source of her stress standing two feet away, eavesdropping.

This was *so* not what she needed right now. For Dane to know that she hadn't had a good night's sleep or managed to eat a full meal since Wednesday morning. Thanks to the good doctor's interrogation she might as well be wearing a sign with Weak and Feeble Woman emblazoned across it.

She'd never fainted before in her life. Well, not since—

She cut off the thought.

Do not go back there. Not again.

Rehashing those dark days had already cost her far too much ground. Swooning 'like a heroine in a trashy novel,' as Dane had so eloquently put it, had done the rest. The only good thing to come out of her dying swan act was the fact that it had happened before she'd had the chance to blurt out the truth about her miscarriage.

After coming round in Dane's arms, her cheek nestled

against his rock-solid shoulder and her heart thundering in her chest, the inevitable blast of heat had been followed by a much needed blast of rational thought.

She was here to finish things with Dane—not kick-start loads of angst from the past. Absolutely nothing would be achieved by correcting Dane's assumption now, other than to cast her yet again in the role of the sad, insecure little girl who needed a man to protect her.

Maybe that had been true then. Her father's high-handed decision to prevent her from seeing Dane had robbed them both of the chance to end their relationship amicably. And then her father had mucked things up completely by hiring his useless old school chum Augustus Greaves to handle the admin on the divorce.

But her father was dead now. And with hindsight she could see that in his own misguided, paternalistic way he had probably believed he was acting in her best interests. And the truth was the end result, however agonising it had been to go through at the time, *had* been in her best interests.

Who was to say she wouldn't have gone back to Dane? Been delusional enough to carry on trying to make a go of a marriage that had been a mistake from the start?

Nothing would be gained by telling Dane the truth now, ten years too late. Except to give him another golden opportunity to demonstrate his me-Tarzan-you-Jane routine.

She'd found his dominance and overprotectiveness romantic that summer. Believing it proved how much he loved her. When all it had really proved was that Dane, like her father, had never seen her as an equal.

The fact that she'd felt safe and cherished and turned on by the ease with which he'd held her a moment ago was just her girly hormones talking. And those little snitches didn't need any more excuses to join the party.

Much better that Dane respected her based on a misconception, even if it made him hate her, than that she encourage his pity with the truth. Because his pity had left her confidence and her self-esteem in the toilet ten years ago—and led to a series of stupid decisions that had nearly destroyed her.

She was a pragmatist now—a shrewd, focused career woman. One melodramatic swoon brought on by starvation and exhaustion and stress didn't change that. Thank goodness she wasn't enough of a ninny to be looking for love to complete her life any more. Because it was complete enough already.

Maybe there was a tiny tug of regret at the thought of that young man who had come to her father's estate looking for her, only to be turned away. But the fact that he'd come to the worst possible conclusion proved he'd never truly understood her. How could he *ever* have believed she would abort their child?

'I appreciate your advice, Doctor,' she replied, as the man packed the last of his paraphernalia into his bag. 'I'll make sure I grab something to eat at the airport and get some sleep on the plane.'

No doubt she'd sleep like the dead, given the emotional upheaval she'd just endured.

She glanced at her watch and stood up, steadying herself against the sofa when a feeling of weightlessness made her head spin.

'You're flying back tonight?' The doctor frowned at her again, as if she'd just thrown a tantrum.

'Yes, at seven,' she replied. She only had an hour before boarding closed on her flight to Heathrow. 'So I should get going.'

The elderly man's grave expression became decidedly condescending. 'I wouldn't advise catching a transatlantic flight tonight. You need to give yourself some time to recover. You've just had a full-blown anxiety attack.'

'A...*what*?' she yelped, far too aware of Dane's over-bearing presence in her peripheral vision as he listened to every word. 'It wasn't an anxiety attack. It was just a bit of light-headedness.'

'Mr Redmond said you became very emotional, then collapsed, and that you were out for over a minute. That's more than light-headedness.'

'Right...well, thanks for your opinion, Doctor.' As if she cared what 'Mr Redmond' had to say on the subject.

'You're welcome, Ms Carmichael.'

She hung back as Dane showed Dr Epstein out, silently fuming at the subtle put-down. And the fact Dane had witnessed it. And the even bigger problem that she was going to have to wait now until the doctor had taken the lift down before she could leave herself. Which would mean spending torturous minutes alone with Dane while trying to avoid the parade of circus elephants crammed into his palatial penthouse apartment with them.

She didn't want to talk about their past, her so-called anxiety attack, or any of the other ten-ton pachyderms that might be up for discussion.

However nonchalant she'd tried to be with Dr Epstein, she *didn't* feel 100 per cent. She was shattered. The last few days *had* been stressful—more stressful than she'd wanted to admit. And the revelations that had come during their argument downstairs hadn't exactly reduced her stress levels.

And, while she was playing Truth or Dare with herself, she might as well also admit that being in Dane's office had been unsettling enough.

Being alone with him in his apartment was worse.

She shrugged into the jacket she'd taken off while Dr Epstein took her blood pressure. Time to make a digni-fied and speedy exit.

'Where's my briefcase?' she asked, her voice more high-pitched than she would have liked, as Dane walked back towards her.

'My office.'

He leaned against the steel banister of a staircase leading to a mezzanine level and crossed his arms over that wide chest. His stance looked relaxed. She wasn't fooled.

'I couldn't scoop it up,' he continued, his silent censure doing nothing for the pulse punching her throat, 'because I had my hands full scooping up *you*.'

'I'll get it on my way out,' she said, deliberately ignoring the sarcasm while marching towards the elevator.

He unfolded his arms and stepped into her path. 'That's not what the doctor ordered.'

'He's not *my* doctor,' she announced, distracted by the pectoral muscles outlined by creased white cotton. 'And I don't take orders.'

His sensual lips flattened into a stubborn line and his jaw hardened, drawing her attention back to the dent in his chin.

She bit into her tongue, assaulted by the sudden urge to lick that masculine dip.

What the heck?

She tried to sidestep him. He stepped with her, forcing her to butt into the wall o' pecs. Awareness shot up her spine as she took a hasty step back.

'Get out of my way.'

'Red, chill out.'

She caught a glimpse of concern, her pulse spiking uncomfortably at his casual use of the old nickname.

'I will not chill out. I have a flight to catch.' She sounded shrill, but she was starting to feel light-headed again. If she did another smackdown in front of him the last of her dignity would be in shreds.

'You're shaking.'

'I'm *not* shaking.'

Of course she was shaking. He was standing too close, crowding her, engulfing her in that subtly sexy scent. Even though he wasn't touching her she could feel him everywhere—in her tender breasts, her ragged breathing and in the hotspot between her thighs which was about to spontaneously combust. Basically, her body had reverted to its default position whenever Dane Redmond was within a ten-mile radius.

'Unless you've got a chopper handy, you've already missed your flight,' he observed, doing that sounding reasonable thing again, which made her sound hysterical. 'Midtown traffic is a bitch at this time of day. No way are you going to make it to JFK in under an hour.'

'Then I'll wait at the airport for another flight.'

'Why not hang out here and catch a flight out tomorrow like Epstein suggested?'

With him? In his apartment? Alone? Was he bonkers?

'No, thank you.'

She tried to shift round him again. A restraining hand cupped her elbow and electricity zapped up her arm.

She yanked free, the banked heat in his cool blue gaze almost as disturbing as what he said next.

'How about I apologise?'

'What for?'

Was he serious? Dane had been the original never-give-in-never-surrender guy back in the day. She'd never seen him back down or apologise for anything.

'For yelling at you in my office. About stuff that doesn't matter any more.'

It was the last thing she had expected. But as she searched his expression she could see he meant it.

It was an olive branch. She wanted to snatch it and run straight for the moral high ground. But the tug of regret in the pit of her stomach chose that precise moment to give a sharp yank.

'You don't have to apologise for speaking your mind. But, if you insist, I should apologise, too,' she continued. 'You're right. I should have consulted you about…about the abortion.'

The lie tasted sour—a betrayal of the tiny life she'd once yearned to hold in her arms. But this was the only way to finally release them both from all those foolish dreams.

'Hell, Red. You don't have to apologise for that.'

He scrubbed his hands over his scalp, the frustrated gesture bringing an old memory to the surface of running her hands over the soft bristles while they lay together on the deck of the pocket cruiser, her body pleasantly numb with afterglow from the first time they'd made love.

She pressed tingling palms against the fabric of her skirt, trying to erase the picture in her head, but the unguarded memory continued to play out—one agonising sensation at a time. Goosebumps pebbling her arms from the warm breeze off the ocean…the base of her thumb stinging from the affectionate nip as he bit into the tender flesh.

'You sure you're okay? I didn't hurt you? You're so small and delicate…'

'I get why you did it,' Dane continued, as the erotic memory played havoc with her senses. 'You weren't ready to be a mom, and I would have been a disaster as a dad.'

He was telling her he agreed with her. Case comprehensively closed. But what should have been a victory only made the sour taste in her mouth turn to mud.

She *had* been ready to be a mother. How could he have doubted that? Didn't he *know* how much she had wanted their baby? And why would he think he'd make a terrible father? Was this something to do with all his scars, the childhood and the family he had never been willing to talk about?

Good grief, get real. You are not *still invested in that fairytale.*

The idiotic notion that she could rescue him by helping him to overcome stuff he refused to talk about had been the domain of that romantic teenage girl. That fairytale was part of her past. A past she'd just lied through her teeth to put behind her. This had to be the jet lag talking again, because it was not like her to lose her grip on reality twice in one day.

'I'd really like to settle this amicably,' she said at last, determined to accept his olive branch.

'We can do that—but you need to stay put tonight. You took a couple of years off my life downstairs, and you still look as if a strong breeze could blow you over.'

That searing gaze drifted to the top of her hair, which probably looked as if a chinchilla had been nesting in it. Awareness shimmered, the sharp tug in her abdomen ever more insistent.

'I feel responsible for that,' he said, the gentle tone at odds with the bunched muscle jumping in his jaw.

'I told you. I'm okay.' She couldn't stay. Couldn't risk becoming that poor, pathetic girl again, who needed his strength because she had none of her own. 'And, more importantly, I'm not your responsibility.'

'Think again,' he said, trampling over her resistance, the muscle in his jaw now dancing a jig. 'Because until I sign those papers you're still my lawfully wedded wife.'

It was an insane thing to say. But much more insane was the stutter in her pulse, the fluttering sensation deep in her abdomen at the conviction in his voice.

'Don't be ridiculous, Dane. We are not *actually* married and we haven't been for over ten years. What we're talking about is an admin error that you wouldn't even know about if I hadn't come to see you today.'

'About that…' He hooked a tendril of hair behind her

ear. 'Why *did* you come all the way to Manhattan when you could have gotten your attorney to handle it?'

It was a pertinent question—and one she didn't have a coherent answer for.

The rough pad of his fingertip trailed down her neck and into the hollow of her throat, sending sensation rioting across her collarbone and plunging into her breasts.

She should tell him to back off. She needed to leave. But something deeper and much more primal kept her immobile.

'You know what I think?' he said, his voice hoarse.

She shook her head. But she did know, and she really didn't want to.

'I think you missed me.'

'Don't be silly. I haven't thought of you in years,' she said, but the denial came out on a breathless whisper, convincing no one.

His lips lifted on one side, the don't-give-a-damn half-smile was an invitation to sin she'd never been able to resist.

'You don't remember how good it used to be between us?' he mocked, finding the punching pulse at the base of her throat. 'Because I do.'

His thumb rubbed back and forth across her collarbone, the nonchalant caress incinerating the lacy fabric of her camisole.

'No,' she said, but they both knew that was the biggest lie of all.

A wad of something hard and immovable jammed her throat as his thumb drifted down to circle her nipple, the possessive, unapologetic touch electrifying even through the layers of silk and lace.

The peak engorged in a rush, poking against the fabric and announcing how big a whopper she'd told.

She needed to tell him to stop. He had no right to touch

her like this any more. But the words refused to form as her back stretched, thrusting the rigid tip into his palm.

He dipped his head as his thumb traced the edge of her bra cup, rough calluses rasping sensitive skin as it slid beneath the lace. His lips nudged the corner of her mouth, so close she could smell coffee and peppermint.

'You were always a terrible liar, Red.'

She couldn't breathe. Couldn't think. Certainly couldn't speak.

So objecting was an impossibility when he eased the cup down to expose one tight nipple and blew on the sensitive flesh.

'Oh, God.'

Her lungs seized and her thigh muscles dissolved as he licked the tender peak, then nipped at the tip. She bucked, the shock of sensation bringing her hip into contact with the impressive ridge in his trousers. She rubbed against it like a cat, desperate to find relief from the exquisite agony.

He swore under his breath, then clasped her head and slanted his lips across hers. She opened for him instinctively and let his tongue plunder her mouth, driving the kiss into dark, torturous territory.

Her fingers curled into his shirt to drag him closer, absorbing his tantalising strength as the slab of muscle crushed her naked breast.

Her sex became heavy and painfully tender. Slick with longing. The melting sensation a throwback to her youth—when all he'd had to do was look at her to make her ready for him.

How can I still need him this much?

Her mind blurred, sinking into the glorious sex-fogged oblivion she'd denied herself for so long. *Too long.* Her tongue tangled with his, giving him the answer they both craved.

He kissed the way she remembered. With masterful

thrusts and parries joined by teasing nips and licks as he devoured her mouth, no quarter given.

The day-old beard abraded her chin. Large hands brushed her thighs, bunching the skirt around her waist until he had a good firm grip on her backside.

Excitement pumped through her veins like a powerful narcotic, burning away everything but the sight, the sound, the scent of him.

He boosted her up—taking charge, taking control, the way she had always adored.

'Put your legs round my waist.'

She obeyed the husky command without question, clinging to his strong shoulders. Her heartbeat kicked her ribs and pummelled her sex as their tongues duelled, hot and wet and frantic.

Her back hit the wall with a thud and the thick ridge in his trousers ground against her panties, the friction exquisite against her yearning clitoris.

Holding her up with one arm, he tore at her underwear. The sound of ripping satin echoed off the room's hard surfaces, stunning her until he found her with his thumb. She moaned into his mouth, the perfect touch charging through her system like lightning.

His answering groan rumbled against her ear, harsh with need. 'Still so wet for me, Red?'

Blunt fingers brushed expertly over the heart of her, then circled the swollen nub, teasing, coaxing, demanding a response. Everything inside her drove down to that one tight spot, desperate to feel the touch which would drive her over. The coil tightened like a vice and propelled her mindlessly towards the peak.

'Please...' The single word came out on a tortured sob.

Dane was the only man who knew exactly what she needed and always had.

Suddenly he withdrew his fingers, sliding them through

the wet folds to rest on her hip. Leaving her teetering on
the edge of ecstasy.

She panted. Squirmed. Denied the touch she needed.
The touch she had to have.

'Don't stop.'

He buried his face against her neck, the harsh pants of
his breathing as tortured as her own. 'Have to,' he grunted.

'Why?'

Her dazed mind reeled, her flesh clenching painfully
on emptiness. Desire clawed at her insides like a ravenous
beast as he left her balanced brutally on the sharp edge
between pleasure and pain.

'No *way* am I taking you without a condom.'

As the sex fog finally released its stranglehold on
her brain the comment registered and horrifying reality
smacked into her with the force and fury of an eighteen-
wheeler. The nuclear blush mushroomed up to her hairline.

Did you actually just beg him to make love to you?
Without protection?

If only there was such a thing as death by mortification.

This was now officially *the* most humiliating moment
of her life. The trashy novel swoon had merely been a
dress rehearsal.

She scooped her breast back into her bra, its reddened
nipple mocking her.

She had to get away from here. Sod the divorce papers.
She'd deal with them later. Right now saving herself and
her sanity was more important than saving Carmichael's.

CHAPTER SIX

DANE BREATHED IN the sultry scent of Xanthe's arousal, still holding on to her butt as if she were the only solid object in the middle of a tornado.

How could it be exactly the same between them? The heat, the hunger, the insanity?

He felt as if he'd just been in a war. And he was fairly sure it was a war he hadn't won.

What were you thinking, hitting on her like that?

He'd been mad. Mad that he'd shouted at her, mad that she'd collapsed in front of him, and madder still that he cared enough about her to be sorry. But most of all he'd been mad that he could still want her so much, despite everything.

The come-on had been a ploy to intimidate her, to make her fold and do as she was told. But she hadn't. She'd met his demands with demands of her own. And suddenly they'd been racing to the point of no return like a couple of sex-mad teenagers—as if the last ten years had never happened.

'Dane, put me down. You're crushing me.'

The furious whisper brought him crashing the rest of the way back to reality.

He drew in an agonising breath of her scent. Light floral perfume and subtle sin. And lifted his head to survey the full extent of the damage.

Her hair had tumbled down, sticking in damp strands to the line of her throat. A smudge of mascara added to the bluish tinge under her eyes, the reddened skin on her chin and cheek suggesting she was going to have some serious beard-burn in the morning.

He should have shaved. Then again, he should have done a lot of things.

She looked shell-shocked.

He had the weird urge to laugh. At least he wasn't the only one.

She pushed against his chest, struggling to get out of his arms in earnest.

'Stop staring at me like that. I have to leave.'

He let her go and watched her scramble away, trying to be grateful that he'd at least managed to stop himself from leaping off the deep end this time. The painful erection made sure he didn't feel nearly as great about that last-minute bout of sanity as he should.

She swept her hair back and bent to slip on the heels which must have fallen off at some point during their sex apocalypse, making it impossible for him not to notice how the slim skirt highlighted the generous contours of her butt. He tore his gaze away.

Haven't you tortured yourself enough already?

She pressed a hand to her forehead, glancing round—still struggling to calm down, to take stock and figure out what the heck had just happened was his guess.

Good luck with that.

'I should go.' She smoothed her clothing with unsteady hands and brushed a wayward curl behind her ear. It sprang straight back.

He planted his hands in his pants pockets and resisted the urge to hook it back round her ear a second time. Because look how that had ended the first time.

She was right. She should go. Before the urge to follow through on what they'd just started got the better of them.

Hitting on her had been a dumb move. What exactly had

he been trying to prove? That she still wanted him? That he was the one in charge? Or just that he was the biggest dumbass on the planet?

Because, whatever way you looked at it, that dumb move had stirred up stuff neither one of them was ready to deal with. Yet.

'You think?' he sneered, because their sex apocalypse wasn't just on *him*.

She'd made the decision to sneak back into his life and poke at something that had died a long time ago. And when he'd made that first dumb move, instead of telling him no she'd gone off like a rocket—giving him a taste of the girl he remembered which he wasn't going to be able to forget any time soon.

She glared at him, picking up on his pissy tone.

Yeah, that's right, sweetheart. I'm the guy you decided wasn't good enough for you. The guy you still can't get enough of.

'Don't you dare try to put this insanity on *me*,' she said. 'I didn't start it. And, anyway, we finished it before things got totally out of hand. So it's not important.'

Hell, yeah, it is. If I say it is.

'*We* didn't finish it,' he pointed out, because scoring a direct hit seemed vitally important. '*I* did.'

The flush scorched her skin and she blew out a staggered breath. 'So what? I got a little carried away in the heat of the moment. That's all.'

'A *little*?' Talk about an understatement.

Her lips set in a mulish line, the blush still beaming on those beard-scorched cheeks.

'It was a mistake, okay? Brought on by stress and fatigue and…' She paused, her gaze darting pretty much everywhere but his face. 'And sexual deprivation.'

'Sexual deprivation?' He scoffed. 'How do you figure *that*?'

She was going to have to spell that one out for him.

'I've been extremely busy for the past five years. Obviously I needed to blow off some steam.'

He should have been insulted. And a part of him was. But a much larger part of him wanted to know if she'd really just told him she'd been celibate for five years.

'Exactly how long has it been since you got to "blow off some steam"?'

Her eyes narrowed. 'That's none of your business.'

'That long, huh?' he mocked, enjoying the spark of temper—and the news that he'd been her first in a while—probably way too much.

He'd never sparred with her when she was a girl. Because she'd always been too cute and too fragile. It would have been like kicking a puppy. He'd always had to be so careful, mindful of how delicate she was. Back then he'd been terrified he'd break her, that his rough, low-class hands would be too demanding for all that delicate, petal-soft skin. So he'd strived hard to be gentle even when it had cost him.

But she'd given as good as she'd gotten a minute ago. And damn if that didn't turn him on even more.

The flush now mottled the skin of her cleavage, and suddenly he was remembering gliding his tongue across her nipple, her soft sob of encouragement as he captured the hard bud between his teeth.

His blood surged south. And he got mad all over again.

She'd been so far out of his reach that summer. But somehow she'd hooked him into her drama, her reality, made him want to stand up to her daddy, to fight her demons, to brand her as his and follow some cock-eyed dream. When she'd told him she was pregnant he'd been horrified at first, but much worse had been the driving need that had opened up inside him—the fierce desire to claim her and their child.

She'd convinced him she wanted to keep his baby. And that was all it had taken to finally tip him over into an alternative reality where he'd kidded himself they could make it work. That she really wanted to make it work. With him. A British heiress and a nobody from Roxbury. *As if.*

He'd spent years afterwards dealing with her betrayal, determined that no one would ever have the power to screw him over like that again—even after he'd finally figured out that she'd probably just been playing him all along so she could stick it to her overbearing daddy.

The thought that he could still want her so much infuriated the hell out of him. But he'd just behaved like a wild man, making it tough to deny.

He'd ripped off her panties, damn it. When was the last time he'd done something like *that*? Been so desperate to get to a woman he'd torn off her underwear? Hadn't even taken the time or trouble to undress her properly, to kiss her and caress her?

He might not be a master of small talk, but he had some moves. Moves women generally appreciated and which he'd worked at acquiring over the last ten years.

Until Xanthe had strolled back into his life and managed to rip away all those layers of class and sophistication and bring back that rough, raw, reckless, screwed-up kid. The kid he'd always hated.

She made a dash for the elevators.

'Hey, wait up!' He chased her down, grabbed her wrist.

She swung round, her eyes bright with fury and panic. 'Don't touch me. I'm not staying.'

He lifted his hand away. 'I get that. But I want to know where you're going.' He scrambled for a plausible reason. 'So I can get the papers delivered tomorrow.'

In person.

'You'll sign them?'

She sounded so surprised and so relieved he wondered if there was more to those papers than she was letting on. Because she *had* to know there was no way on earth he would want to contest their divorce—no matter how hot they still were for each other.

Focus, dumbass.

He shook off the suspicion. His objective right now was to make sure she didn't hightail it all the way back to London before he was finished with her.

This wasn't over. Not by a long shot. But he'd learned the hard way that it was better to retreat and work out a strategy rather than risk riding roughshod straight into an ambush.

Her old man and his goons had taught him that on the night he'd come to collect his wife—believing he had rights and obligations only to discover that promises meant nothing if you were rich and privileged and already over the piece of trash you'd married.

The anger surged back, fresh and vivid, but he was ready for it now, in a way he hadn't been earlier.

So had he been kidding himself that he was over what she'd done? That didn't have to be bad. As long as he dealt with it once and for all.

'Sure, I'll sign them,' he replied.

Once I'm good and ready.

She'd stirred up this hornets' nest, so he wasn't going to be the only one who got stung.

'Thank you,' she said, and the stunned pleasure in her voice crucified him a little. 'I'm glad we finally got the chance to end this properly. I didn't have—' She stopped abruptly, cutting off the thought, her cheeks heating.

'You didn't have what?'

What had she been about to say? Because whatever it was she looked stricken that she'd almost let it slip.

'Nothing.'

Yeah, right. Then why was her guilty flush bright enough to signal incoming aircraft?

'I hope we can part as friends,' she said, thrusting her hand out like a peace offering, the long slim fingers visibly shaking.

Friends, my butt.

They weren't friends. Or their marriage would not have ended the way it had. Friends were honest with each other. Friends were people you could trust. And when had he ever been able to trust *her*?

But still he clasped her hand, and squeezed gently to stem the tremor.

She let go first, tugging free to press the elevator button. She stepped into the car when it arrived, her eyes downcast. But as she turned to hit the lobby button their gazes met.

The muscle under his heart clenched.

'Goodbye, Dane.'

He nodded as the doors slid shut. Then he pulled out his mobile and dialled his PA.

'Mel? Ms Carmichael—' he paused '—I mean Ms Sanders, whose real name is Carmichael, is going to be stopping by any second to collect her briefcase. I want you to book her a suite at The Standard for the night and bill it to me. Then arrange a car to take her there.'

The place was classy, and only a few blocks away on the High Line. He wanted to know exactly where she was.

He didn't want any more nasty surprises. From here on in this was his game and his rules. And he was playing to win.

'Okay,' Mel said, sounding confused but, like the excellent assistant she was, not questioning his authority. Unlike his soon-to-be ex-wife. 'Is there anything else?'

'Yeah, if she kicks up a fuss...' He wouldn't put it past the new, improved kick-ass Xanthe to do the one thing guaranteed to screw up his plans. 'Tell her taking care of her accommodation is the least I could do...' He paused, the lie that would ensure Xanthe accepted his offer tasting bittersweet. 'For a *friend*.'

CHAPTER SEVEN

THAT EVENING XANTHE stood in front of the bathroom mirror in the corner suite her ex-husband had booked for her as a final gesture of 'friendship,' still trying to feel good about the outcome of their forced trip down memory lane that afternoon.

Tomorrow morning she would have the signed divorce papers in her hand, all threats to Carmichael's would be gone, and she and Dane could both get back to their lives as if Augustus Greaves and his shoddy workmanship had never happened.

Mission accomplished.

The only problem was she didn't feel good about what had happened in Dane's office and later in his apartment. She felt edgy and tense and vaguely guilty—thoughts and emotions still colliding in her brain three hours later, like a troop of toddlers on a sugar rush.

She smoothed aloe vera moisturiser over the red skin on her face which, fresh from a long hot bath loaded with the hotel's luxury bath salts, beamed like a stop light. If only she'd seen that warning before she'd let Dane devour her, because stubble rash was the least of her worries.

The memory of his rough, frantic handling sent an unwelcome shiver of awareness through her exhausted body. Firm, sensual lips subjugating hers, that marauding tongue plunging deep and obliterating all rational thought, solid pecs rippling beneath her grasping fingers, his teeth biting into her bottom lip and sending need arrowing down to her core...

She gripped the sink, her thighs turning to mush. *Again.*

She shivered, even though the bathroom's central air was set at the perfect ambient temperature. She needed to sleep. And forget about this afternoon's events.

But sleep continued to elude her.

She'd had some success in distracting herself for the first hour after Dane's driver had deposited her at the striking modernist hotel on Manhattan's High Line Park by doing what she did best—formulating an extensive to-do list and then doing it to death.

The first order of business had been to book herself on the evening flight to Heathrow tomorrow and bump herself up to first class. After today's 'episode' a lie-flat seat was going to be a necessity.

With her flight booked, she'd messed around for another thirty minutes selecting designer jeans, a fashionable T-shirt, fresh underwear and a pair of flats online from a nearby boutique and getting a guarantee that it would be express-delivered by tomorrow morning at 10 a.m. No matter how washed out she felt, at least she wouldn't have to *look* washed out, wearing her creased silk suit on the flight home.

Unfortunately while actioning her to-do list she'd got a second wind that she didn't seem able to shake—even after soaking for twenty minutes in the suite's enormous bathtub.

She just wanted to turn her brain off now and get comatose. But she couldn't. Maybe it was the jet lag kicking in? It was close to dawn now in the UK—the time she usually woke up to get ready for work and have her morning caffeine hit while sitting on the balcony of her luxury flat by the River Thames, allowing herself five minutes to enjoy the sun rising over Tower Bridge.

Her body clock had obviously decided that habit wasn't going to change, no matter what time zone she was in. Or how shattered she felt.

Unfortunately, being unable to sleep had given her far too much time to dissect all the things that had gone wrong this afternoon. Her fainting fit, the shocking revelation that Dane had assumed she'd aborted their child, but most of all her ludicrous reaction to Dane's come-on.

And she'd come to one irrefutable conclusion. When she got back to London she needed to look at options to get back in the dating game—because all work and no sex had clearly turned her into an unexploded bomb. She hadn't had a date in three years, no actual intimate contact in at least four, and she hadn't gone all the way since…

Xanthe watched the frown puckering her brow in the mirror deepen into a crevice.

Since the last time she'd made love to Dane.

No wonder she'd lost it with him. Her physical reaction to him had nothing to do with their past—or any lingering feelings—and everything to do with her failure to find another man with the same orgasm-on-demand capabilities as her ex-husband.

Since Dane, she'd always taken care of her own orgasms. At first she had put it down to some kind of perverse physical loyalty to the man who had abandoned her. Whenever another man touched her, her body had insisted on comparing him to Dane. Her failure to get aroused hadn't bothered her too much—in fact she'd begun to think it was a boon. After all, she never wanted to be a slave to her sex drive again—so in thrall to a guy's sexual prowess that she confused lust with love.

But apparently her sex drive was still a slave to *Dane's* sexual prowess.

Don't go there. It doesn't mean anything.

Dane wasn't unique. He didn't have some special mojo

that made her more susceptible, more in tune to his touch than to any other guy's. She just hadn't found the right guy yet—the right 'other guy' to hit all her happy buttons— because she hadn't been looking.

She'd got so used to taking care of her own business the loss hadn't become apparent until she'd walked into Dane's office this afternoon and had some kind of sexual breakdown. Triggered by Dane, who—in his usual in-your-face style—had decided to demonstrate exactly what she had been missing.

Of course she'd responded to Dane with all the restraint of a firecracker meeting a naked flame. She'd been running on stress and adrenaline for three days, and working herself to the bone for a great deal longer.

Dane had always known how to trip her switch, how to touch and caress and take her in ways that gave her no choice but to respond. And that obviously hadn't changed. But only because she'd been holding herself hostage for ten years...not exploring the possibilities.

After the trauma of their marriage, she had convinced herself in the last ten years that an active and fulfilled sex-life wasn't important. But clearly it *was* important—to her sense of self and her sense of well-being.

When she got back to the UK she was going to remedy that. Why not check out a few dating websites?

She shuddered involuntarily.

But until then she needed to get rid of all the sexual energy pumping around her system and stopping her from dropping into the exhausted sleep she so desperately needed.

She touched her fingertip to the tender skin on her chin, then trailed the nail down, inadvertently following the path Dane had taken three hours ago. Parting her robe, she sucked in a breath as the cool satin brushed over the tender skin of her nipple. Hooking the lapel round her breast to expose herself, she circled the ripe areola, still supremely sensitive from Dane's attentions. Her nipple rose in ruched splendour, the air cool against heated flesh. The gush of response between her thighs settled low in her abdomen, warm and fluid and heavy. She pinched the nipple, remembering the sharp nip of his teeth, and the coil of need tightened into a knot.

Untying the robe's belt, she let it fall open, revealing the neatly trimmed curls at the apex of her thighs, and spotted a small bruise on her hip. She ran her finger over the mark, remembering the feel of Dane's fingers digging into her skin as he boosted her into his arms.

'Wrap your legs round my waist.'

She cupped her aching sex, pressing the heel of her palm hard against her pelvic bone.

But as she closed her eyes all she could see was Dane's eyes staring back at her, the iridescent blue of the irises almost invisible round the lust-blown pupils, the hot look demanding she come...but only for him.

She parted the wet folds, but as she ran the pad of her finger over the tight bundle of nerves all she could feel were the urgent flicks and caresses of thick, blunt, calloused fingers.

'Always so damn wet for me, Red.'

His low, husky voice reverberated through her as she rubbed her clitoris in urgent, helpless strokes. She knew the right touch, the perfect touch to take her over quickly and efficiently. But this time the memory of Dane's fingers, firm and sure, mocked her battle for release, teasing and tempting her, taking her higher, and higher.

She panted. Not quite there yet. Never. Quite. There.

'Please, please...'

She slammed her palm down on the vanity unit and opened her eyes to see a mad woman staring back at her— hot, bothered and still hopelessly frustrated.

Every nerve-ending pulsated, desperate for release. A release that remained resolutely out of reach. Tantalising her senses…torturing her already-battered brain. A release she was very much afraid only Dane could give her.

The bastard.

Damn her ex-husband. Had he ruined her now for herself? As well as for every other man? How was that fair? Or proportionate?

She tied the robe with shaking hands, covering her nakedness. The flushed skin was screaming in protest, too sensitive now even for the silky feel of satin. She washed her hands and swallowed round the fireball in her throat, which was equal parts mortification and arousal. Cursing Dane and his clever, commanding caresses with every staggered breath.

She walked back into the bedroom of the suite and crossed to the phone. She would call down and ask for some sleeping pills. She hated taking any kind of medication, hated having her senses dulled, but if she didn't do something soon the toddlers in her head were liable to explode right out of her ears.

Whatever black magic Dane had worked on her sex-starved body this afternoon would be undone by a decent ten hours' sleep, and tomorrow evening she would be winging her way back across the Atlantic, the signed papers snug in her briefcase.

She was never going to see him again. Or feel his knowing fingers. Or watch his sexy I'm-gonna-make-you-come-like-an-express-train smile. And that was exactly how she wanted it. She was her own woman now. Or she would be again, once she was out of his line of fire.

A sharp rap at the door had her hesitating as she lifted the handset.

It took her tired mind a moment to process the interruption, but then she remembered. Her clothes. In typically efficient New York City style, the boutique had delivered them ahead of schedule.

Dropping the phone she crossed the room and flung open the door without bothering to check the peephole.

All the blood drained out of her head and raced down to pound in her already pouting clitoris. And the toddlers in her head began mainlining cocaine.

'Dane, what are you doing here?'

And why do you have to look so incredible?

Her ex stood on the threshold in worn jeans and a long-sleeved blue T-shirt covered by a chequered shirt. The buzz cut shone black in the light from the hallway, complementing the dark frown on his handsome face. Wisps of chest hair revealed by the T-shirt's V-neck announced his overwhelming masculinity. Not that it needed any more of an introduction.

With his broad shoulders blocking the doorway, his imposing height towering over her own five feet six inches in her bare feet and his blue eyes glittering with intent, he looked even more capable of leaping tall buildings in a single bound in casual clothing than he had in his captain of industry outfit.

'We need to talk.'

Flattening a large hand against the door, he pushed it open and strolled past her into the room before she could object.

'We've already talked,' she said, her voice as unsteady as her heartbeat as she gripped the lapels of the flimsy robe, drawing them over her throat in a vain attempt to hide at least some of the marks left by his kisses.

She squeezed her traitorous nipples under folded forearms to alleviate the sudden rush of blood which had them standing out against the satin-like torpedoes ready to launch.

Good grief, she was as good as naked, while he was

fully dressed. No wonder her heartbeat was punching her pulse points with the force of a heavyweight champ.

He turned, his size even more intimidating than usual as he stepped close. *Too close.* She took a step back, not caring if it made her look weak. Right now she *felt* weak. Too weak to resist her physical reaction to him. And that would be bad for a number of reasons. None of which she could recall, because her brain was packed full of cotton wool and rampaging toddlers tripping on cocaine.

'You shouldn't be here,' she said, wanting to mean it.

'What didn't you have?'

The terse question had the toddlers hitting a brick wall while the endorphin rush detonated into a thousand fragments of shrapnel.

'Excuse me?'

'You said, "I didn't have," and then you stopped. What were you about to say?'

'I have no idea.'

'You're lying.' Dane could see it in her eyes. The translucent blue-green was alive with anxiety as her teeth trapped her bottom lip.

Unfortunately he could also see she was naked under her robe. And his body was already riding roughshod over all sensible thought.

Blood charged into his groin, but he kept his gaze steady on hers. He'd spent the last three hours trying to convince himself that seeing her again would be nuts. Why not just sign the divorce papers, have Mel deliver them tomorrow and put an end to this whole fiasco?

But that one half-sentence, that one phrase that she'd left hanging kept coming back to torment him. That and the brutal heat that he had begun to realise had never died.

'I didn't have...'

Eventually he'd been unable to stand it any more. So

he'd walked the three blocks to the hotel. There was something she wasn't telling him. And that something was something he needed to know.

Maybe they meant nothing to each other now. But they had once, and not all his feelings had faded the way they should have. Which might explain why his libido hadn't got the memo.

He still wanted her, and it was driving him crazy.

The light perfume of her scent, the sight of her hair curling in damp strands to her shoulders, the moist patches making the wet satin cling to her collarbone, the trembling fingers closing the robe while he imagined all the treasures that lay beneath…

Damn it, Redmond. Concentrate. You're not here to jump her. You're here to get the truth.

He'd convinced himself that she'd got rid of their kid because she'd *had* to, because it had been the only way she could be shot of him, and he'd never questioned it, but in the last three hours he'd begun picking apart the evidence—and not one bit of it made any sense.

He'd always known Xanthe didn't love him, because no one *really* loved anyone else. But when had she ever given him any indication that she didn't want to keep their baby? Never. Not once. She had been the one who had insisted she wanted to have it when the stick had turned blue. She had been the one to say yes instantly when he'd suggested marriage. She had been the one who had kept on smiling every morning as she'd puked her guts up in the motel bathroom while he was left feeling tense and scared. And she'd been the one who had never stopped talking about the tiny life inside her. So much so, that she'd made him believe in it, too.

How could that girl have given up on their baby because of one dumb argument?

'I'm not lying,' she said. 'And you need to leave.'

The quiver of distress in her voice made a mockery of the spark of defiance in her eyes. He could see the war she was waging to stay strong and immune. Her back was ramrod-straight, and her chin stuck out as if she were waiting for him to take a shot at it.

Frustration tangled with lust.

Gripping her upper arms, he tugged her towards him. Her muscles tensed under his palms, the thin layer of smooth satin over warm skin sending sex messages to his brain he did not need.

'Tell me the truth, Red. What really happened to our baby? You owe me that much.'

A shudder ran through her and she looked away—but not before he spotted the flare of anguish.

'Please don't do this. None of it matters any more.'

'It does to me,' he said, and the feelings inside him—feelings he'd thought he'd conquered years ago—raced out of hiding to sucker-punch him all over again.

Hurt, loss, sadness, but most of all that futile festering rage.

Except this time the rage wasn't directed at Xanthe but at himself. Why hadn't he fought harder to see her? Why hadn't he made more of an effort to get past her father and his goons and find out what had really happened?

She kept her head down, but a lone tear trickled down the side of her face. Pain stabbed into his gut—a dull echo of the pain when Carmichael's goons had dragged him off the estate and beaten him until he'd been unable to fight back.

'Look at me, Xan.'

She gave a loud sniff and shook her head.

Cradling her cheek, he brushed the tear away with his thumb and raised her face to his. Her eyes widened, shadowed with hopelessness and grief, glittering with unshed tears.

And suddenly he knew. The truth he should have figured out ten years ago. The truth that would have been obvious to him then if he'd been less of a screwed-up, insecure kid and more of a man.

He swore softly and folded his arms around her, trying to absorb the pain.

'You didn't have an abortion, did you?'

He said the words against her hair, breathing in the clean scent of lemon verbena, anchoring her fragile frame against his much stronger one.

His emotions tangled into a gut-wrenching mix of anger and pain and guilt. How could he have got things so wrong? And what did he do with the information now?

She stood rigid in his arms, refusing to soften, refusing to take the comfort he offered. The comfort her old man had denied them both.

He swallowed down the ache in his throat. 'That sucks, Red.'

She drew in a deep, fortifying breath, her whole body starting to shake like a leaf in a hurricane. He tightened his arms, feeling helpless and inadequate but knowing, this once, that he was not going to take the easy road. She wasn't that girl any more—sweet and sunny and stupidly in love with a guy who had never existed—and up until two seconds ago he would have thought he was glad of it. But now he wasn't so sure.

His throat burned as she trembled in his arms and he mourned the loss of that bright, optimistic girl who had always believed the best of him when he had been unable to believe it himself.

CHAPTER EIGHT

'I'M SO SORRY, Mrs Redmond. There's no heartbeat and we need to operate to stop the bleeding.'

The storm of emotion raged inside her, the sobs she'd repressed for so long choking her as her mind dragged her back to that darkest of dark days. Lying on the hospital gurney, the white-suited doctor looking down at her with pity in his warm brown eyes…

Dane's hand stroked her hair. His heartbeat felt strong and steady through worn cotton, his chest solid, immovable, offering her the strength she'd needed then and been so cruelly denied. Tearing pain racked her body as she remembered how alone, how useless, how helpless she'd felt that day. And the horror that had followed.

She gulped for air, her arms yearning to cling to his strength as tears she couldn't afford to shed made her throat close.

Be strong. Don't cry. Don't you dare break.

He kissed her hair, murmuring reassurances, apologies that she'd needed so badly then but refused to need now. Then his hips butted hers and she felt the potent outline of him, semihard against her belly.

Arousal surged in her shattered body, thick and sure and so simple. Reaction shuddered down to her core.

Flattening her hands against the tense muscles of his belly, she pushed out of his arms and looked up to find him watching her, his expression grim with regret and yet tight with arousal. Reaching up, she ran her palms over his hair, the way she'd wanted to do as soon as she'd walked into his office.

Absorbing the delicious tingle of the short bristles against her skin, she framed his face and dragged his mouth down to hers. 'You're ten years too late, Dane. There's only one thing I want now.'

Or only one thing she could still allow herself to take.

His eyes flared and her body rejoiced. This was the one thing they had always been good at. She didn't want his pity, his regret, his sympathy—all she wanted was to feel that glorious heat pounding into her and making her forget about the pain.

His mouth captured hers, his tongue plunging deep, demanding entry. She opened for him, the heady thrill obliterating the treacherous memories.

Large hands ran up her sides under the robe, rough calluses against soft skin bringing her body to shimmering life. He crushed her against him, banding strong arms around her back, forcing her soft curves to yield to his strength. She draped her arms over his shoulders as he picked her up, carried her to the king-sized bed and dropped her into the centre. Parting the thin satin with impatient hands, he swept his burning gaze over her naked skin, the dark rapture in his eyes making her feel like a sacrifice already burning at the stake.

She reached for his belt, desperate to wrap her fingers round his thick length and make him melt, too. But he gripped her wrists and pinned her hands to the mattress above her head, leaving her naked and exposed while he was still fully clothed.

'Not yet,' he growled, the barely leashed demand in his gruff voice exciting in its intensity. 'Let me touch you first. Or this is gonna last about two seconds.'

She stopped struggling against his hold, the terse admission more gratifying than a thousand declarations of undying devotion. Lying boneless, she let her own hunger overwhelm her, frantic to feel the rush of release that would make her forget everything but this day, this hour, this moment.

It was madness, but it was divine madness—the perfect end to a disastrous day. She was sick of thinking about consequences, about her own troubled emotions and the implications of everything that had happened ten years ago. She was sick of thinking, full stop. And, however else Dane had failed her—as a husband, as a friend—he had never failed her as a lover.

Still holding her wrists, he bent to kiss her lips, his mouth firm and demanding, before trailing kisses down her neck, across her collarbone. She rose off the bed, his groan a potent aphrodisiac as he licked at one pouting nipple.

A soft sob escaped her as he ran his tongue around the areola and then suckled the hard bud, making it swell against his lips into a bullet of need. She moaned, low and deep, as he bit into the tender flesh. Hunger arrowed down to her core. Sharp and sure and unstoppable. And then he transferred his attentions to the other breast.

She panted, writhing under the sensual torture. 'Please, I need you...'

'I know what you need, baby,' he growled. 'Open your eyes.'

She did as he demanded, to find his striking blue gaze locked on hers. Bracketing her wrists in one restraining hand, he watched her as he found her wet and wanting. She lifted her hips, pushing into the unbearably light caress as the moisture released.

She couldn't think, couldn't feel, her skin burned as his playful strokes had the pleasure swelling and then retreating, tempting and then denying.

'Dane...' His name came out on a broken cry. 'Stop messing about.'

He barked out a harsh laugh, the fierce arousal in his face sending her senses into overdrive. 'You want me to use my superpower?'

'You know I do. You...'

Her angry words dissolved in a loud moan as he released her wrists to part her legs. Holding her open with his thumbs, he blew across the heated flesh. She bucked off the bed. The tiny contact unbearable.

She watched, transfixed, shaking with desire as his dark head bent and his tongue began to explore her slick folds. A thin, desperate cry tore from her throat as blunt fingers entered her, first one, then two, stretching her, torturing that hotspot deep inside only he knew would throw her over the edge.

She screamed, her fingers digging into his hair, urging him on as he set his mouth on her at last, suckling the swollen nub. She hurtled into glorious oblivion, exquisite rapture slamming into her as her senses exploded into a thousand shards of glittering light.

Dane lifted himself up, the lingering taste of her sweet and succulent, the need for release unbearable. She stared at him, her eyes wide, the sea-green dazed and wary, her body flushed with pleasure, her skin luminous.

Damn, but she was the most beautiful woman he'd ever seen. Even more beautiful than before. She'd lost that openness, that faith in him that had always scared the hell out of him, and now she had a million secrets of her own, but he could still zap her with his superpower.

The old joke made him smile—but the smile turned to a grimace as the insistent throbbing in his groin tipped from torment into torture.

If he didn't get inside her in the next two seconds he was liable to embarrass himself.

Dane located the condoms in the front pocket of his

jeans and grappled with his belt and shoved his pants down. He ripped open a foil packet and rolled on the protection. Grasping her hips, he lifted her up, then paused.

'Tell me you want this.'

Tell me you want me.

The pathetic plea echoed in his head and made him tense. This was about sex and chemistry, pure and simple. Raw, rough, elemental. He didn't need her approval. He just needed to be inside her.

'You know I do,' she said, bold and defiant.

He stopped thinking and plunged deep, burying himself to the hilt, then groaned, struggling to give her time to adjust before he began to move.

'You okay? You're so tight…' His mind reeled, remembering it had been a while for her. Five years at least. His heady sense of victory at the thought was almost as insane as the delirious wish to be able to take her without a condom.

Draping her arms over his shoulders, she lifted herself up to angle her hips and take him deeper. 'Just move.'

'Yes, ma'am,' he said, laughing.

She was his. She had always been his in the only way that really meant anything.

He drew out, thrust back, feeling her clench around him. The heat in his abdomen built into an inferno as he established a ruthless rhythm, determined to drive her over again before he found his own release.

He clung on to control, an explosive orgasm licking at the base of his spine as her soft sobs became hoarse cries and she reached the point of no return. Her muscles clamped tight, massaging his length as she hit her peak. He thrust once, twice, and collapsed on top of her, his brutal release violent in its intensity as his seed exploded into the sweet, shuddering clasp of her body.

CHAPTER NINE

'WELL, THAT WAS…' Xanthe struggled to breathe while being crushed into the mattress, the floaty, fluffy sensation fading fast to be replaced with all the aches and pains of not one but two mind-blowing orgasms.

Her brain knotted with the stupidity of what they'd just done.

He shifted, lifting his weight from her, and the sensual smile on his too-handsome face was both arrogant and strangely endearing.

'Awesome,' he supplied.

'Actually, I was going to say insane.'

He grunted out a strained laugh and rolled off her. Xanthe watched him sitting on the edge of the bed with his back to her as he bent to untie his boots and then kick his pants off the rest of the way.

'More like inevitable.' He took off his shirt and balled it up to drop it next to his jeans. 'Since we've both been primed for it since this afternoon,' he added, his voice muffled as he pulled his T-shirt over his head and dumped it on the pile of clothing.

Her throat clogged at the sight of his broad back, deeply tanned but for the whiter strip of skin on his backside and the now faded scars that stood out in criss-crossing stripes across his ribs. An echo of sympathy and sorrow and curiosity about those marks hit her unawares. She forced the feelings down, disturbed by the direction of her thoughts.

Dane's secrets were his own and always had been, and they were no concern of hers.

He stood up and strolled across the room, gloriously naked, his languid stride both arrogant and unashamed. Xanthe became transfixed by the bunch and flex of the gluteal muscles in his tight, beautifully sculpted butt cheeks. Her body hummed back to life—like one of those relighting candles people put on a birthday cake as a joke, with a flame that keeps flaring no matter how hard you try to blow it out.

She slipped under the sheets, far too aware of her own nakedness now. She'd always thought those candles were really annoying.

'What do you think you're doing?' she ventured, trying to sound stern.

He glanced back over one broad shoulder as he opened the bathroom door. 'Grabbing a shower.'

She hauled the sheet to her neckline to cover any hint of vulnerability. 'I don't remember inviting you to stay.'

He leaned against the door, thankfully shielding at least some of his more impressive assets and sent her a stern look that she suspected was much more effective than her own.

'I'm having a shower and then we're going to get to that talk.'

'I don't want to talk.' She ignored the raised eyebrow. 'All I want to do is sleep,' she protested.

And try to forget about the fact that Dane's position as her go-to guy for earth-shattering orgasms had not diminished in the least.

'Preferably alone,' she added for good measure.

Now that stallion had bolted out of the stable. Twice. She did not need a repeat performance.

'And you can,' he said. 'Once we're finished talking.'
'But…'

The door slammed behind him.

'I don't want you here,' she finished lamely as the power shower was switched on behind the closed door.

Oh, for—she swore, using a word that would have had Nanny Foster reaching for the soap.

The man was incorrigible. Domineering and dictatorial and completely contrary. Surely there could be nothing left to say about what had happened ten years ago? He'd figured out the truth, they'd jumped each other, had multi-orgasmic make-up sex…end of story.

If she were at full strength she would pick up the phone right now and call hotel security to have him thrown out. Even if it *would* be somewhat problematic explaining why they should be kicking out the man whose credit card details were on the room.

Unfortunately, though, she wasn't at full strength. She dragged her weary body out of the bed. If nothing else, the make-up sex had killed her second wind stone dead. She could happily sleep for a month now.

So she'd just have to go for damage limitation.

Grabbing a bunch of cushions off the sofa, she jammed them into the middle of the bed in case he got any ideas about joining her once he'd finished his shower.

And just in case *she* got any ideas…

She whisked his discarded T-shirt off the floor as the only nightwear option on offer—the hotel's satin robe had been about as useful as a negligee in a rugby scrum—and put it on to establish a second line of defence. The shirt hung down to mid-thigh, the sleeves covering her hands, and looked less enticing than a potato sack. Perfect.

Not so perfectly, it smelled of him—that far too enticing combination of washing powder and man.

She hauled herself back into the bed, trying not to notice the sexy scent as she prepared to stay awake for a few minutes more in order to give Dane his marching orders.

Curling into a tight ball with her back to the wall of cushions, she watched the winking lights across the Hudson River through the hotel's floor-to-ceiling glass walls, and stared at the corner suite's awe-inspiring view of the Jersey shoreline.

The buzz of awareness subsided into a relaxing hum and the tender spot between her thighs became pleasantly numb. She inhaled his scent, lulled by the sound of running water from the shower.

The thundering beat of her heart slowed as her mind began to drift. Her eyelids drooped as she floated into dreams of hot, hazy days on the water and muscular arms holding her close and promising to keep her safe.

For ever.

Dane sat in his shorts and concentrated on finishing off the last few bites of the burger and fries he'd ordered from room service, mindful of the soft snores still coming from the pile of bedclothes a few feet away.

What was he still doing here?

Xanthe had been dead to the world ever since he'd come out of the bathroom. He'd thought at first she might be faking sleep to avoid the conversation they still needed to have about why she'd lied to him in his apartment. Letting him believe she had terminated the pregnancy. Why the heck hadn't she just told him about the miscarriage then, instead of waiting for him to figure it out on his own?

But after ten minutes of watching her sleep, her slim body curled in the bed like a child and barely moving, he'd conceded that not only wasn't she faking it, but she wasn't likely to stir until morning.

Given that, he had no business hanging around. They weren't a couple. And he didn't much like hanging around after sex even when the woman he'd just had sex with was a casual date, let alone his almost-ex-wife.

But once he'd begun to get dressed he'd been unable to locate his T-shirt. After hunting for a good ten minutes, he'd finally spotted a blue cuff peeking out from under the bedclothes. A quick inspection under the covers had been enough to locate the missing shirt—and trigger a series of unwanted memories.

Xanthe in her wet swimsuit on the deck of the pocket cruiser, pulling on his old high school sweatshirt to ward off the chill after a make-out session in the water. Him grabbing one of his work shirts to throw over her as she raced ahead of him into the motel bathroom, her belly rebelling in pregnancy. And a boatload of other equally vivid memories—some mercilessly erotic, others painfully poignant.

That old feeling of protectiveness had struck him hard in the chest—and stopped him from walking out.

He'd messed up ten years ago. She was right. He hadn't been there when she needed him. But there was nothing he could do about that now. Except apologise, and she hadn't wanted his apology.

He knew a damn distraction technique when he saw one, and that was what she'd done—used sex and chemistry as a means of keeping conversation at a minimum.

He'd been mad about that once he'd figured it out in the shower, but he'd calmed down enough now to see the irony. After all, mind-blowing sex had always been *his* go-to distraction technique when they were kids together and she'd asked him probing questions about the humiliating scars on his back.

Dumping the last of the burger on the plate, he covered the remains of the meal with the silver hood and wheeled the room service trolley into the hall.

Uneasiness settled over him as he returned to the suite. He needed to leave. She could keep the undershirt. He had a hundred others just like it. He didn't even know what he was still doing here.

But as he approached the bed to grab his work shirt off the floor and finish getting dressed a muffled sob rose from the lump of bedclothes, followed by a whimper of distress.

Edging the cover down, he looked at her face devoid of make-up, fresh and innocent, like the girl he remembered. But then her brow puckered, her lips drew tight, and her hand curled into a tight fist on the pillow beside her head. Rapid movement under her eyelids suggested she was having some kind of nightmare as she stifled another sob.

His heart punched his ribcage and got wedged in his throat. He needed to go. But instead of heading for the door he crouched beside the bed and rested his palm on her hair. He brushed the wild curling mass back from her forehead, instinct overriding common sense.

'Shh, Red, everything's okay. Go back to sleep.'

She shook off his hand, her breathing accelerating as the nightmare gripped her. 'Please pick up the phone Dane... *Please.*'

The hoarse, terrified whimpers tore at his conscience, guilt striking him unawares. Awake, she'd been strong and resilient. But asleep was another matter.

He couldn't walk away. Not yet.

Tugging on his jeans and leaving the top button undone, he whipped back the sheets to discover a row of cushions from the couch laid out down the middle of the bed. A rueful smile tugged at his mouth.

What was the great wall of throw pillows supposed to keep in check? His libido or hers?

Digging the makeshift barrier out of the bed, he slung the cushions back on the couch. Climbing in behind her, he gathered her shaking body into his arms until her back lay snug against his chest, her bottom nestled into his crotch.

He ignored the aching pain as blood pounded into his lap, grateful for the confining denim while waiting for her laboured breathing to even out—the renewed rush of heat not nearly as disturbing as the rush of tenderness.

Holding her wrist, he laid his arm across her body, careful not to touch any part of her that would make the torment worse. But the memory of spooning with her like this, after they'd made love that final time ten years ago, came flooding back to fill the void. Except that time his hands had caressed the compact bump of her belly, his head spinning with amazement and terror at what the future would hold.

Tortured thoughts of what she'd endured without him rose to the surface.

Eventually she stilled, the rigid line of her body softening against his.

Obviously, some remnant of the misguided kid he'd once been still remained. Because a part of him wanted to stay and hold her through the night, in case she had any more nightmares. But he couldn't go back and erase what he'd done, and she wouldn't want him here when she woke up in the morning.

So he'd just stay for a short while—until he was sure she was okay. Then he'd leave and get Mel to send over the divorce papers in the morning. So she'd lied about the miscarriage? Did he really want to know why? Delving into her reasons now wouldn't serve anyone's purpose.

But as he listened to the comforting murmur of her breathing his body relaxed against hers and all his sound decisions drifted out into the night, shooting across the Hudson River, heading up towards the Vineyard and back into fitful dreams.

CHAPTER TEN

SOMETHING HEAVY BECKONED Xanthe out of sleep. Deep, drugging, wonderful sleep that made her feel secure and happy.

Her eyelids fluttered open and her gaze focused on a hand. A large tanned hand with a tattoo of a ship's anchor on the thumb was holding hers down on the pillow, right in front of her face. The hand looked male. Very male. And very familiar.

She blinked, struggling to bring her mind into focus, and realised that a male arm, attached to the male hand, lay across her shoulders. She drew in a deep breath, the scent of clean sheets and clean man reminding her of the good dreams that had danced through her consciousness before waking. She shifted, aware of the long, muscular body wrapped around hers, and his deep breathing made the hair on the back of her neck prickle.

Dane.

Thin strands of sunlight shone through the slatted blinds, illuminating the hotel room's luxurious furnishings as the events of the evening before crowded in and her abdomen warmed, weighed down by the hot brick in her stomach.

She stole a moment to absorb the comfort of being cocooned in a man's arms for the first time in… She frowned. For the first time in a decade.

Dane had always gravitated towards her in his sleep. She'd always woken up in his arms during the brief weeks of their marriage. It was one of the things she'd missed the most. And this time she didn't have the stirrings of morning sickness to cut through her contentment.

She had a vague recollection of nightmares chasing her, and then his arms and his voice lulling her back to sleep.

Holding her breath, she shifted under his arm and inched her hand out from under the much larger one covering it.

The rumble of protest against her hair froze her in place.

Long fingers squeezed hers, before his thumb inched down her arm, sliding the sleeve of the T-shirt down to the elbow—the T-shirt that was supposed to be protecting her from the thoughts making her belly melt.

'You playing possum?' A gruff voice behind her head asked.

'I'm trying to.' She sighed, annoyed and at the same time stupidly aroused.

She could feel the solid bulge against her bottom, the unyielding wall of his chest that was sending delicious shivers of reaction up her spine.

'Mmm…' he mumbled, sounding half-asleep as his hand lifted and then settled on her thigh.

His calloused caress had goosebumps tingling to life as he trailed his hand under the hem of the T-shirt and rubbed across her hip.

Awareness settled between her legs and she rolled abruptly onto her back to halt his exploration.

His hand rested on her belly as he rose up on one elbow to peer down at her. His short hair was flattened on one side, and the stubble on his chin highlighted that perfect masculine dimple. Amusement and desire glinted in the impossible blue. Her breath squeezed under her diaphragm.

He'd always looked so gorgeous in the morning—all rumpled and sexy and usually a little surly. He'd never been much of a morning person, unlike her. But he didn't look surly now. He looked relaxed and devastatingly sexy.

'I didn't plan to stay the night,' he said, by way of explanation. 'But seeing as I'm here…'

His hand edged down, that marauding thumb brushing the top of her sex. Her belly trembled in anticipation.

'This isn't a good idea,' she murmured, trying to convince herself to push his hand away.

Pressing his face to her neck, he nuzzled kisses along her jaw. 'Nope.'

The tremor of awareness drew her the rest of the way out of sleep and into sharp, aching need. He cupped her, slid his fingers through her slick folds, locating the knot of desire with pinpoint accuracy.

She gasped and rolled towards him, letting him lift the soft cotton shirt over her head and throw it away. He captured one aching nipple with his lips as his fingers continued to work their magic.

Memories assailed her of waking up just like this, with his hands and tongue and teeth beckoning her out of sleep and into ecstasy. She pushed back the rush of memory, the sapping tide of romanticism, until all that was left was the hot, hard demand of sexual need.

She desired Dane—she always had. But that was all it had ever been.

Reaching out, she cradled the bulge confined behind a layer of denim. 'Why are you wearing your jeans in bed?'

'Stop asking dumb questions,' he grumbled. 'And help me out of them.'

She didn't need any more encouragement. This was wrong, and they both knew it, but it didn't seem to matter any more. In a few short hours they will have declared the end of their marriage. And she wanted him here, now, more than she'd ever wanted any man. Just once more.

She released the button fly with difficulty, to find him long and hard beneath stretchy boxers.

'Take them off,' she demanded, pleased to hear the power, the assurance in her voice.

She was taking control. He couldn't walk all over her any more. And here was the proof.

But as he threw the covers back and divested himself of the last of his clothes she found herself feeling strangely vulnerable as he climbed over her, caging her in.

'Tell me exactly what you want, Red. I want to make you come so hard you scream.'

The words excited her beyond bearing. And terrified her, too. Reminding her of the boy who had once taken her to places no other man ever had.

She'd never been coy about sex, but she'd never been bold either—except with him.

Folding her hand around his huge length, she flicked her thumb across the tip, trying to regain control. Regain the power. Adrenaline rushed through her as his thick erection jerked against her palm.

His mouth took hers as his fingers delved into her hair and he angled her head to devour her. The scrape of his beard ignited tender skin…her tongue tangled with his.

He reached across her to grab a condom from the bedside table.

She took it from him. 'Let me.'

'Go ahead,' he said, relinquishing control.

The fire in his eyes was full of approval, and a desire that burned her to the core. No other man had ever desired her the way he had.

She fumbled with the foil packet, her skin flushing at his strained laugh.

He chuckled. 'You need more practice.'

She slipped the condom on, aware that she had never done this for another man. Determined not to let him know it. He wasn't special, He was just…filling a need. A need that she had neglected for far too long.

Her thoughts scattered, centring on his thumb as he began to stroke her again. Stroking her into a frenzy. One long finger entered her and she flinched slightly. Evidence of their rough coupling the night before was still present, still there.

'Hey…' He cupped her cheek, forcing her to meet his eyes. 'Are you too sore for this?'

His concerned expression had her heartbeat kicking her ribs. Bringing with it a myriad of unwanted memories. His rough hand holding her hair, rubbing her back as she threw up in the motel toilet. Those lazy mornings when the nausea hadn't hit and he'd taken her slowly, patiently, watching her every response, gauging her every need and meeting it.

'I'm fine,' she said, precisely because she wasn't.

Don't be kind. Please don't be kind. I can't stand it.

'Uh-huh.' He didn't look convinced. Holding her, he rolled, flipping onto his back until she was poised above him, her knees on either side of his hips.

'How about *you* take charge this time?' he said, and she felt her heart expand in her chest.

But then his thumb located that pulsing nub and every thought flew out of her head bar none. *She had never been in charge of her hunger for him.*

He coaxed the orgasm forth as she sank down on his huge shaft.

'That's it, Red. Take every inch.'

He held her hips, lifting her as she parted round the thick length, almost unable to bear the feeling of fullness, of stretching, but unable to stop herself from sinking down again to take more, to take him right to the hilt.

His harsh grunts matched her moans as she rode him, increasing the tempo. A stunning orgasm was racing towards her. Her mind reeled as his gaze locked on hers, encouraging, demanding, forcing her over that perilous edge as he gave her one last perfect touch.

She sobbed, throwing her head back, her body shattering as she came hard and fast. She heard him shout out moments later, his penis pulsing out his release as his fingers dug into her thighs.

She fell on top of him, her forehead hitting his collarbone with a solid *thunk* as her heart squeezed tight.

She closed her eyes, her staggered breathing matching the pounding beat of her heart as his large hands settled on her back and stroked up to her nape. Blunt fingers massaged her scalp.

He laughed, the sound low and deep and self-satisfied. Warning bells went off, but they sounded faint and unimportant, drowned out by the glorious wave of afterglow.

'How about…before we finalise our divorce…' his deep voice rumbled against her ear '…we treat ourselves to a honeymoon?'

She lifted herself off him with an effort. 'What are you talking about?'

'I've got a week's vacation coming.' He brushed his fingers down her arms, setting off a trail of goose pimples and reigniting those damn birthday candles. 'I was supposed to be heading to Bermuda this afternoon, for a sailing trip to Nassau. I could postpone it for a couple of days.'

For a split second her endorphin-clouded mind actually considered it. Being with him—escaping from the endless stress and responsibilities of her job, from all the pain and regret of their past. But then her heart jumped in her chest and reality crashed in on her.

This was *Dane*. The man who had always been able to separate sex from intimacy in a way she never had. Or at least not with him.

She didn't hate him any more. And he still had the ability to seduce her and turn her into a puddle of lust with a single touch, a single look. She couldn't risk being alone with him for another hour, let alone for another night.

'I don't think so,' she said.

She climbed off him and bent to retrieve his discarded T-shirt, suddenly desperate for clothing. But his hand clamped on her wrist. His face was devoid of the lazy amusement of a moment ago.

'Why not?'

He looked genuinely irritated by her refusal, which told her all she needed to know.

'Because I have a company to run. I'm CEO of Carmichael's now—I can't afford to take time off,' she finished, giving him the face-saving answer.

She couldn't tell him the real reason—that she didn't want to risk spending time alone with him. He'd think she was nuts. Maybe she *was* nuts.

She was stronger, wiser and older now, with a healthy cynicism that should protect her from remaking the catastrophic mistakes of her youth. But the new knowledge that Dane had only abandoned her because he'd thought she'd abandoned *him* left a tiny sliver of opportunity for those old destructive feelings to take hold of her emotions again—especially coupled with more mind-altering sex.

She didn't want to be that idiot girl again, and if anyone could sway her back into the path of destruction it was a juggernaut like Dane. And the worst of it was *he* would remain unscathed. The way he always had before. For him, sex was always just sex—and that hadn't changed, or he would never have suggested another night of no-holds-barred sex after the tumult of the last twenty-four hours.

But why wouldn't he when *he* didn't have to worry about stirring up old feelings because he had never loved her the way she'd loved him? He'd only suggested marriage because of the guilt and responsibility he'd felt over her pregnancy—and, however her father had interfered in their break-up, it was obvious their marriage had been doomed to failure.

Deep down, she would always be a romantic—an easy target for a man like Dane who didn't have a single soft or sensitive or romantic bone in his body.

He'd never let her in. Had never let his guard down during the whole three months they'd lived in that motel.

He finally let go of her wrist and she scooted to the edge of the bed to put on the T-shirt, feeling awkward and insecure, reminded too much of that romantic child.

'So you're running daddy's company now?'

She dragged the T-shirt over her head. 'It's not his company any more. It's mine.'

Or it would be as soon as she had Dane's signature on those divorce documents and the controlling 6 per cent of the shares could be released to her.

She swallowed down a prickle of guilt at her deception. Dane had no claim on Carmichael's—it was simply a paperwork error. A paperwork error that, once corrected, he need never know about.

'He hated my guts when we were kids...'

The non sequitur sounded casual, but she could hear the bite in his voice and knew it was anything but.

What did he expect her to say? That her father had been a snob and had decreed Dane unsuitable? How could she defend Dane without compromising herself and her decision to take on Carmichael's after her father's death? The company had meant everything to her father and she understood that now—because it meant everything to *her*. And if a small voice in her head was trying to deny that and assert that there was more to life than running a successful business, it was merely an echo of that foolish girl who had believed that love was enough.

'He didn't hate you,' she said. 'I'm sure he just thought he was doing what was best for me.'

Even as she said the words they sounded hollow to her, but she refused to condemn her father. He had loved her in his own way—while Dane never had.

'Did it ever occur to you that if I'd been able to see you that day, things might have turned out differently?' He raised a knee and the casually draped sheet dipped to his waistline.

His expression was infuriatingly unreadable. As always.

'I don't see how.' She hesitated, trying to force thick words out past the frog in her throat. 'And it worked out okay for both of us, so I have no regrets.'

She turned away from the bed, desperate not to be having this conversation. It would expose her. She didn't want him to know how hard it had been for her. How much losing him and their baby had hurt her at the time. And how much else it had eventually cost her.

But he reached over and snagged her wrist again. 'That's bullshit. And you want to know how I *know* it's bullshit?'

'Not particularly,' she said, far too aware of the way his thumb was stroking her pulse, hoping he couldn't feel it hammering in her wrist like the wings of a trapped hummingbird.

'Last night you had a nightmare about losing the baby,' he said. 'That's why I stayed. That's why I was here when you woke up. Maybe if I had been able to do that ten years ago, I wouldn't still need to do it now.'

Her pulse pummelled her eardrums. She wanted to ask him how he knew she'd been having a nightmare about the miscarriage. But she definitely didn't want to know how she'd given herself away in her sleep. She felt vulnerable enough already.

'You didn't need to stay. I would have been fine. I've had them before and...'

She realised her mistake when his expression hardened.

'How many times have you had them before?'

Too many.

'Not often,' she lied.

'That bastard.' His fury wasn't directed at her, but still she felt the force of his anger.

'It's okay. Really. I've come to terms with what happened.'

'Don't lie, Red.'

He hooked his thumb round her ear, brushing her hair back and framing her face. The gesture was gentle, and full of concern. Making her heart pulse painfully.

'You can lean on me—you know that, right?'

'I don't need to lean on you,' she said, denying the foolish urge to rest her head into the consoling palm and take the comfort he offered.

'What are you so scared of?' he said, cutting through the defences she'd spent ten years putting in place.

'I'm not scared.' How could he know that when he had never really known *her*? 'Why would I be?'

'I don't know—you tell me,' he said tightly. 'Why did you let me go on believing you had an abortion yesterday?'

She stiffened and pulled away from him. How could he still read her so easily?

'Why would I bother to correct you? I didn't think it mattered any more. It was so long ago.'

'Of course it matters. I deserve to know what really happened. Especially if you're still having nightmares because—'

'Why, Dane?' she interrupted. 'Why do you deserve to know? When you never wanted our baby the way I did?'

He tensed and something flashed over his face—something that might almost have been hurt. But it was gone so quickly she was sure she had misinterpreted it. Dane had never wanted the baby—that much she knew for sure.

'If you had, you would have demanded to see me,' she said, cutting off the painful thought. 'Instead of assuming I'd had an abortion.'

'I *did* demand to see you.' Temper flashed in his eyes. 'Your father had his goons throw me out.'

'He...*what?*' The breath left her lungs in a painful rush. Anguish squeezed her chest. 'Did they hurt you?'

She could still remember those men. They'd terrified her, even though her father had always insisted they were there to protect her.

His eyes narrowed, and the annoyed expression was one she recognised. If there was one thing Dane had always despised, it was anything remotely resembling pity.

'I handled myself,' he said.

She didn't believe him. At nineteen he'd been tough and muscular, and as tall as he was now, but he'd also been a lot skinnier, a lot less solid—still partly a boy for all his hard knocks. Four of those men against one of him would have done some serious damage.

She noticed the crescent-shaped scar cutting across his left eyebrow and knew it hadn't been there before—she'd once known every one of the scars on his body. The scars he would never talk about.

She pointed at the thin white mark bisecting his brow. 'Where did you get that scar?'

He shifted, avoiding her touch. She dropped her hand, aware of the heavy weight in her belly.

'I don't remember.'

He sounded unconcerned. But that guarded expression told a different story. He did remember—he just wasn't prepared to discuss it.

The hollow pain blossomed. Why was she pressing the point? Maybe because he'd held her last night, through her nightmare...making her feel weak and needy. And then made love to her this morning with such unerring skill, coaxing the exact response he'd wanted out of her.

He'd held all the power in their relationship and it was now brutally obvious he held it still.

'My father had no right to treat you that way,' she said. 'If you tell me what injuries you suffered I'll have my legal team work out suitable compensation.'

Paying him off suddenly seemed like the perfect solution. The only way to get herself free and clear of him and the emotions he stirred in her. Her only chance of acquiring the distance she'd surrendered so easily ever since walking into his office yesterday.

'Don't play the princess with me. I don't want your money. I never did. And I sure as hell don't need it any more.'

'It's a simple matter of compen—'

'You didn't do anything wrong,' he said, slicing through her objection. '*He* did. If anyone owes me an apology, it's him.'

'Well, he's been dead for five years. So you're not likely to get one.'

'I don't want an apology from a dead guy—what I want is for you to acknowledge what he did to us was wrong. Why is that so damn hard for you?'

She threw her hands up in the air. 'Fine. I agree what he did was wrong. Is that enough for you?'

'No. I want you to stay here with me.'

'What has that got to do with anything?'

'He split us up before we were ready. We've got a chance now to take some time to say goodbye to each other properly.'

His gaze flicked down her frame, and the inevitable flare of heat she felt in response made it doubly clear exactly what their goodbye was supposed to entail.

'We're both grown-ups now and we deserve to finish this thing right. Why can't you see that?'

Because I'm scared I might still care about you. Too much.

'I've told you—it's just bad timing.'

'Don't give me that. If you're running the company you can make time for this. But you won't. And I want to know why.'

'I won't because I don't *want* to spend time with you,' she shouted back, determined to mean it. 'If your ego can't accept that, that's your problem—not mine. We're over— we've been over for ten years.'

'Yet I can still make you come so hard you scream. And you haven't let another guy do that to you for five years. Five years is a heck of a long time.'

The blush flushed through her to the roots of her hair. His eyes went razor-sharp.

'What the…? Has it been *longer* than five years?'

How could he know that?

'I didn't say that.' She scrambled to deny it. Knowing she couldn't lie because he would read her like a book and know the truth instantly.

Dane had always been able to use her need for him against her. He'd never treated her like a wife when they were married. Had never been capable of opening up to her and sharing anything of himself with her. And she'd been so pathetically grateful for any sign that he cared about her at all, she'd found that romantic.

She knew the truth now, though—that his possessiveness, his protectiveness, hadn't been a sign of his love. It had simply been a sign of his need to claim ownership. If he ever found out that she'd never shared her bed with any other man but him, she'd be handing him a loaded gun.

'You don't have to say it,' he said. 'It's written all over your face.'

'Oh, shut up!' She stormed off, determined to lock herself in the bathroom before he discovered the humiliating truth and shot down the last remaining shreds of her composure.

His laugh followed her all the way into the shower cubicle.

Who knew Xanthe could be so cute when she was mad?

Dane let out a strained chuckle as she slammed the bathroom door behind her, then rubbed the heel of his palm over the ache in the centre of his chest. The choking feeling returned.

It shouldn't really matter to him that his wife hadn't slept with that many other guys, but somehow it did. It also shouldn't matter to him that she didn't want to hang out at the hotel for another night.

He wasn't a possessive guy, or a particularly protective one. But with Xanthe it had always been different. Because he'd been her first. And she'd once been pregnant with his child.

And seeing her have that nightmare, knowing it wasn't the only one she'd had, had affected him somehow. Made him feel guilty for not being there when she'd needed him, even though his head was telling him it wasn't his fault.

She'd been stressed and exhausted when she'd arrived in his office yesterday. Enough to face-plant right in front of him. And in that moment she had reminded him of the girl she'd been—the girl he'd felt so in tune with because of the way she'd been bullied by her father. That girl had always been trying to please a guy who would never be pleased. And now it looked as if she was still doing it.

That had to be why she'd worked herself into the ground to take on her old man's company. She'd never had any interest in it back then. He didn't doubt she was good at her job—she'd always been smart and conscientious, and it seemed she'd added a new layer of ball-buster to the mix since then. But if she enjoyed it so much why didn't she have a life outside it?

He knew how easy it was to lose sight of your personal life, your personal well-being when you were building a business. He'd done the same in the last few years. Hell, he'd only managed a couple of short-term hook-ups since they'd split. But his company had been his dream right from when he was a little kid and he'd hung around down by the marina to avoid his father's belt.

And he was a lot tougher than Xanthe would ever be. Because he'd been born into a place where you hit the ground running or you just hit it—hard.

He knew how to take care of number one. He always had. Because no one else had wanted the job. Xanthe had always been way too open, way too eager to please. And it bugged him that she was still trying to please a dead man.

He didn't like seeing that hollow, haunted look lurking behind the tough girl facade. And she was still his wife until those papers were signed.

After getting dressed, he picked up his cell phone and keyed in his attorney's number. He'd promised to sign the damn papers, but who said he had to sign them straight away?

'Jack, hi,' he said, when his attorney answered on the second ring. 'About those papers I sent over yesterday...'

'I had a look at them last night,' Jack replied, cutting straight to the chase as usual. 'I was just about to call you about them.'

'Right. I've agreed to sign them, but I—'

'As your legal counsel, I'd have to advise against you doing that,' Jack interrupted him.

'Why?' he asked, his gut tensing the way it had when he was a kid and he'd been bracing himself for a blow from his old man's belt. 'They're just a formality, aren't they?'

'Exactly,' Jack replied. 'You guys haven't lived together for over ten years, and two to five years separation is the upper limit for most jurisdictions when it comes to contesting a divorce.'

'Then what's the deal with telling me not to sign the papers?'

Jack cleared his throat and shifted into lecture mode. 'Truth is, your wife doesn't require your signature on *anything* to get a divorce. She could have just filed these papers in London as soon as she found out about the failure to file the original documents and I would have gotten a heads-up from her legal representative. That's what got me digging a little deeper—I got to wondering why she'd come all the way to Manhattan to deliver them in person and that's when I found something curious buried in the small print.'

'What?' Dane asked, the hairs on his neck standing to attention.

The fact that Xanthe hadn't needed to bring the documents over in person had already occurred to him. That she hadn't needed to bring them at all seemed even more significant. But the anxiety jumping in his stomach wasn't making him feel good about that any more.

'There's a codicil stating that neither one of you will make a claim on any property acquired after the original papers should have been filed.'

'Then I guess I can quit worrying about her trying to claim back-alimony.' He huffed out a breath. He was not as pleased with the implication that Xanthe had made a point of not wanting any part of his success as he ought to be.

'Sure, but here's the thing—it goes on to state all the assets that can't be claimed on. Why would she need to itemise those in writing? She'd have a hell of a legal battle trying to claim any of your property on the basis of a separation made years before your company even began trading. But that's when I got to thinking. What if it wasn't *your* property she was trying to protect but her own?'

'I don't get it. I couldn't make any claim on her property.'

Did she think he *wanted* her property? Her old man had once accused him of being a gold-digger. Of getting his daughter pregnant and marrying her to get his hands on Carmichael's money. Had she believed the old bastard? Was that why she'd let him go on believing she'd had an abortion? To punish him for something he hadn't done?

Anger and injured pride collided in his gut, but it did nothing to disguise the hurt.

'Turns out you're wrong about that,' Jack continued. 'You've got grounds to make a claim on her company. I just got off the phone with a colleague in the UK who checked out the terms of her father's will. A will that was written years before she even met you. One thing's for sure—it answers the question of why she came all the way over to Manhattan to get you to sign her divorce papers.'

As Dane listened to Jack lecturing him about the legalities and the terms of Charles Carmichael's will his stomach cramped and fury at the sickening injustice of it all started to choke him. The same futile fury he'd felt after the beating he'd taken all those years ago because he'd wanted to see his wife, to know what had happened to his child.

Each word Jack uttered felt like another blow he couldn't defend himself against. Suddenly he was furious with Xanthe as well as her old man. For making him feel like that again. Worthless and desperate, yearning for something he couldn't have.

She'd planned to play him all along by coming here. How much of what had happened in the last day had even been real? She'd said she didn't want to spend any more time with him. And now he knew why—because once those papers were signed she'd have the guarantee she needed that he couldn't touch her father's precious company.

She'd lied. Because she'd decided he didn't deserve the truth. She'd even accused him of not caring about their baby. And then…

He thought about her whimpers of need, those hot cries as she came apart in his arms. She hadn't just lied to him, she'd used his hunger for her against him. Turned him back into that feral kid begging for scraps from a woman who didn't want him. Then she'd slapped him down and offered to pay him off when he'd had the audacity to ask for one more night.

He signed off with Jack, then sat down and waited for her to come out of the bathroom. The bitterness of her betrayal tasted sour on his tongue.

The good news was he had more leverage now than he could ever have dreamt of. And he was damn well going to use it. To show her that *no one* kicked him around—not any more.

CHAPTER ELEVEN

I⊤ TOOK XANTHE twenty minutes to realise she could not hide in the bathroom for the rest of her natural life.

She'd faced a hostile board for five years and her father's stern disapproval for a great deal longer. She could deal with one hot as hell boat designer.

But even so she jumped when a knock sounded on the door.

'You still in there or have you disappeared down the drain?'

The caustic tone was almost as galling as the flush that worked its way up her torso at the low rumble of his voice.

'I'll be out in a minute.'

'A package got delivered for you.'

Her clothes.

Hallelujah.

She reached for the bolt on the door, then paused.

'Could you leave it there?'

With the hotel's satin robe somewhere on the floor of the suite and his T-shirt neatly folded to give back to him on the vanity unit, all she had to cover her nakedness was a towel.

'Why don't you order us some breakfast?' she added, trying to sound unconcerned. Because clearly he was not going to do the decent thing and just leave her in peace.

'You want the package—you're gonna have to come out and get it.'

Blast the man.

Grasping the towel tight over her breasts, she flicked back the bolt and opened the door. She shoved the T-shirt at him, far too aware of his spectacular abs peeping out from behind his unbuttoned shirt.

He took it, but lifted the package out of reach when she tried to grab it. 'Not so fast.'

'Give me the package,' she demanded, using her best don't-mess-with-me voice—the one that had always worked so well in board meetings but seemed to be having no impact at all on the man in front of her. 'It has my clothes in it. If you still want to talk we can talk, but I refuse to discuss anything with you naked.'

Because look how well that had turned out the last time she'd done it.

He kept the package aloft. 'If I give you this, I want a promise that you'll come out of there.'

She frowned at him, noticing the bite in his tone. Something was off. Something was *way* off—the muscle in his jaw was working overtime to keep that impassive look on his face.

'What's wrong?'

'Not a thing,' he said, his jaw as hard as granite. 'Except that you've been sulking for a good half hour.'

She hadn't been sulking. She'd been considering her options—very carefully. But she was finished with being a coward now. Better to face him and get whatever he had to discuss over with. Because standing in a towel with that big male body inches away was not helping.

She reached out for the package. 'Deal.'

He slapped it into her palm.

Whipping back into the bathroom, she locked the door and leaned against it. Something was most definitely wrong. Where had the wry amusement gone? That searing look he'd given her had been as hard as it was hot.

Blowing out a breath, she got her new clothes out of the

packaging. Sitting in the bathroom wouldn't solve anything. It was time to face the music and wrap this up once and for all.

Five minutes later she walked back into the suite, feeling a lot more steady with the new jeans and T-shirt and fresh underwear on. He'd donned his T-shirt and discarded the overshirt, but even covered, his pecs looked impressive as they flexed against the soft cotton while he levered himself off the couch.

She noticed the divorce papers on the coffee table in front of him. He must have had them couriered over. Relief was mixed with a strange emptiness at the thought that he'd already signed them. Which was, of course, ridiculous.

'Sorry to keep you waiting,' she said, polite and distant, even though her body was already humming with awareness. Clearly that would never change.

'Really?'

He still sounded surly. Maybe she should have come out a bit sooner.

She didn't dignify the question with an answer. Crossing the room to the coffee pot on the sideboard, she poured herself a cup to buy some time. Even after half an hour of prepping she didn't know what to say to him.

The tense silence stretched between them as she took a quick gulp of the hot liquid and winced. 'I see you still like your coffee strong enough to Tarmac a road,' she commented.

The unbidden memory made her fingers tremble. She turned to find him watching her.

'I don't know what you want from me, Dane. I've said I'm sorry for what my father did, for what happened. Obviously our break-up...' She paused, clarified. 'The way our break-up happened was regrettable. But I want to end this amicably. I can't stay in New York any longer.'

Because, however tempting it would be to indulge herself, let her body dictate her next move, she never wanted to be a slave to her libido again.

'That's why you came here? To end this amicably?'

It was a leading question. And, while it hadn't been the reason she'd boarded the plane yesterday morning at Heathrow, she felt an odd tightening in her chest at the thought of what they'd shared the day before and through the night. Stupid as it was, her heart skipped a beat.

Had she been kidding herself all along? Despite the implications for Carmichael's, she could have done this whole process by proxy. It would have been simpler...more efficient. But as soon as Bill had mentioned Dane's name to her she'd been bound and determined to do it in person. And she suspected her reasons were much more complex than the ones she'd admitted to herself.

How much had her coming here *really* had to do with the threat to Carmichael's? And how much to do with that grief-stricken girl who had mourned the loss of him as much as she had mourned the loss of their baby?

He had been the catalyst—the one who'd shown her she was more, *could* be more than her father had ever given her credit for. And, despite the shocks to her system in the last hours, she would always be grateful to have discovered that he hadn't abandoned her the way her father had wanted her to believe.

Placing the coffee mug back on the counter, she faced him fully. 'Honestly? I think I needed to see you again. And, as difficult as this has been—I'm sure for both of us—I'm glad I did.'

'Yeah?'

'Yes.' Why did he still sound so annoyed?

'Nice speech. I guess that's my cue to sign these?' He scooped the divorce papers up from the table. 'And then get out of your way?'

'I suppose…' she said, feeling oddly ambivalent about the papers, her pulse beginning to hammer at her collarbone.

He didn't just sound surly now. He sounded furious. And he wasn't making much of an effort to hide it.

'Tough, because that's not gonna happen.' He ripped the papers in two, then in two again, the tearing sound echoing around the room. Then he flung the pieces at her feet.

'Why did you do that?' She bent to pick them up, her heart hammering so hard now she thought it might burst.

Grasping her arm, he hauled her upright. 'Because I'm not as dumb as you think I am. I know what your phoney divorce papers are really for. To stop me claiming the fifty-five per cent of your old man's company he left to *your husband* in his will.'

'But…' Her knees dissolved. The blow was made all the more devastating by the look of total disgust on his face.

'You didn't come here to end a damn thing *amicably*. You came here to play me.'

'That's not true.'

But even as she said it she could feel the guilt starting to strangle her. Because when she'd come here that was exactly what she'd intended to do.

'Well, it is partially true. But that was before I found out…'

'You think you can lie and cheat and say and do whatever the hell you want to get your way? Just like your old man? Well, you're gonna have to think again. Because *no one* screws with me any more.'

There were a million things she could say in her defence. A million things she wanted to say. But her throat closed, trapping the denial inside her. She felt herself shutting down in the face of his anger. Wanting to crawl away and make herself small and invisible. The way she had whenever her father had shouted at her, had bullied and

belittled her, had derided her for being too soft, too senti-
mental, too much of a *girl*.

'I've got to hand it to you…the seduction was a nice
touch.'

Heat seared her to the core as his gaze raked over her,
as hot as it was derisive.

'You've certainly learned how to use that fit body to
your advantage.'

The contemptuous comment felt like a smack in the
face. Releasing the anger which had lain dormant for far
too long.

'How dare you imply…?'

Hauling herself out of his arms, she slapped him hard
across the face, determined to erase that smug smile.

His head snapped back on impact. And fire blazed in
her palm.

But her anger faded as quickly as it had come, the vol-
canic lava turning to ash as he lifted a hand to his cheek
to cover the red stain spreading across the tanned skin.
His eyes sparked with contempt, and his powerful body
rippled with barely controlled fury.

Shock reverberated through her.

He manipulated his jaw, then licked his lip, gathering the
tiny spot of blood at the corner of his mouth. The nonchalant way in which he had accepted the blow made her feel
nauseous. How many other times had he been hit before?

'So daddy's little princess finally learned how to fight
back,' he said, the fury in his tone tempered by an odd
note of regret.

The shock disappeared, to be replaced with weari-
ness and a terrible yearning to turn back the clock. What
were they doing to each other? She couldn't hate him any
more—it hurt too much to go there again.

But how could he have such contempt for her? Know
so little about who she'd been then and who she was now?

'Dane, I can explain. This isn't what it looks like.'

Except it was in some ways.

She reached for him, needing to soothe the blotchy mark she'd caused. He jerked away and brushed past her, heading for the door.

'It's *exactly* what it looks like.'

He opened the door, and part of her heart tore inside her chest. He was walking away from her again—the way he had once before. But she couldn't find the words to stop him, all her protests lodged inside her.

He paused at the door, fury still blazing in the ice-blue eyes. 'I never wanted your old man's money—or his crummy company. Which just makes it all the sweeter now that I can take a piece of it if I want to. Just for the hell of it. Don't contact me again.'

Xanthe collapsed onto the couch as the door slammed, her mind reeling and her whole body shaking.

She wrapped her arms around her midriff, taking in the unmade bed, the torn pieces of document on the carpet, the unfinished mug of black coffee. A gaping wound opened up in her stomach and threw her back in time to that dingy motel room in Boston. Lost and alone and terrified.

Tears squeezed past her eyelids as she sniffed back the choking sob that wanted to come out of her mouth.

If Dane followed through with his threat she might very well lose everything she'd worked so hard for in the last ten years. Even the *threat* of legal action would be enough to destroy her position as CEO. If the board ever found out she'd mismanaged this situation so catastrophically they would surely withdraw their support.

But far worse than the possibility of losing her job was that look of contempt as he'd accused her of being daddy's little princess.

Was that really what he'd thought of her all those years ago? That she was some spoilt little rich girl? Was that why he'd never trusted her with his secrets? Was that what he thought of her now, despite all she'd achieved?

And why did it sting so much to know he'd always thought so little of her?

She stood up and thrust shaky fingers through her hair, scrubbing away the tears on her cheeks.

No. Not again. She was not going to fold in on herself. Or let his low opinion of her matter.

Ten years ago stuff had happened that had been beyond their control. Her father's interference... The miscarriage... But there had been so much more they could have controlled but hadn't. And anyway the past was over now. Dane Redmond didn't mean anything to her any more.

Maybe she should have told him about the will as soon as she had discovered he hadn't abandoned her. She could see now that hadn't played well when he'd figured it out. But *he* was the one who had assumed she'd had an abortion, who had never trusted in her love, and *he* was the one who was threatening to take her company away from her. Why? Because she'd had the audacity to protect herself?

This was all about his bull-headed macho pride. Dane, in his own way, was as stubborn and unyielding as her father.

Well, she wasn't that timid, fragile, easily seduced child any more. And she was *not* going to sit around and let him crucify her and ruin everything she'd worked for.

She had the guts to stand up to him now. He was in for a shock if he thought this 'princess' wasn't tough enough to get him to sign the damn divorce papers and eliminate any threat to her company—even if she had to scour Manhattan to find him.

Four hours later, after a frantic trip to his offices and a fruitless interrogation of his tight-lipped PA, she discovered it wasn't going to be that easy.

Sitting in the first-class departure lounge at JFK, en

route to St George, Bermuda, she felt a knot of anxiety start to strangle her as she contemplated how she was going to stay strong and resolute and indomitable if she was forced to confront her taciturn and intractable ex-husband on a yacht in the middle of the Atlantic...

CHAPTER TWELVE

'THERE, ON THE HORIZON—that has to be it.' Xanthe pointed at the yacht ahead of them and got a nod from the pilot boat operator she'd hired that afternoon at the Royal Naval Dockyard on Ireland Island, Bermuda. She pushed back the hair that had escaped her chignon and started to frizz in the island's heat.

The punch of adrenaline and purpose had dwindled considerably since her moment of truth at the hotel the day before—now the snarl of nerves was turning her stomach into a nest of vipers. The boat sped up, skipping over the swell. She held fast to the safety rail. The sea water sprinkling her face was nowhere near as refreshing as she needed it to be.

At least her madcap chase to find Dane and confront him was finally at an end, after a two-hour flight from JFK, a sleepless night at an airport hotel in St George, scouring the internet for possible places he might have harboured his boat, and then a three-hour taxi journey criss-crossing Bermuda as she checked out every possible option.

She'd arrived at the Royal Naval Dockyard on the opposite tip of the island, the very last place on her list, at midday, with her panic starting to eat a hole in her stomach. The discovery that Dane had been there and just left had brought with it anxiety as well as relief at the thought of confronting him.

She gripped the rail until her knuckles whitened as the pilot boat pulled closer to the bobbing yacht.

At least her frantic transatlantic call to London at four that morning had confirmed Dane had yet to start any legal proceedings against her. So there was still time—if she could talk sense into him.

The gleam of steel stanchions and polished teak made the sleek vessel look magnificent as the blue-green of the water reflected off the fibreglass hull.

Her heart stuttered as she read the name painted in swirling letters on the side.

The Sea Witch.

The teasing nickname whispered across her consciousness.

'I'm under a spell...you've bewitched me, Red...you're like a damn sea witch.'

The muscles of her abdomen knotted as she tried to erase the memory of his finger circling her navel as he'd smiled one of his rare smiles while they'd lain on the beach at Vineyard Sound together, a lifetime ago, and he'd murmured the most—and probably the only—romantic thing he'd ever said to her.

Beads of sweat popped out on her upper lip as she spotted Dane near the bow, busy readying the boat's rigging. She'd caught him just in time. His head jerked round as the pilot boat's rubber bumpers butted the yacht's hull and the boat's captain shouted to announce their arrival.

She shook off the foolish memories and slung her briefcase over her shoulder. She had a short window of opportunity. She needed to get on board before Dane could object or the pilot boat's captain would realise the story she'd spun him about being a guest who had missed the sailing was complete fiction.

Grabbing hold of the yacht's safety line, she clambered

into the cockpit. She quickly unclasped her life jacket and flung it back to the pilot boat.

'I can take it from here—thank you so much!' she shouted down to the captain.

The man glanced at Dane, who had finished with the rigging and was bearing down on her from the other end of the boat. 'You sure, ma'am?'

Not at all.

'Positive,' she said, flinching when Dane's voice boomed behind her.

'What the *hell* are you doing here?'

She ignored the shout and kept her attention on the pilot boat's captain. 'I'll be in touch in approximately twenty minutes. And I'll double your fee if you leave us now.'

Dane didn't want her on board, which meant he would have to listen to reason. It wasn't much of a bargaining chip, but it was the only one she had.

'Okay, ma'am.' The pilot boat captain tipped his hat as his nervous gaze flicked to Dane and back. 'If you say so.'

The boat's engine roared to life. The captain had peeled the nimble vessel away from the yacht, obviously keen to avoid unnecessary confrontation, and was headed towards the marina when Dane reached her.

'Where is he going?'

She turned to face him. 'He's returning to the harbour and will come to pick me up once I give him the signal.'

Her rioting heartbeat slammed into her throat.

He looked furious, his face rigid with temper.

'Is this some kind of joke? Get off my boat.'

'No.' She locked her knees, forcing her chin up. 'Not until you sign the divorce papers.' She dumped the brief-case at his feet. 'I have a new set in there to replace the ones which fell victim to your temper tantrum at the hotel.'

His scowl darkened at the patronising comment, and

the punch of adrenaline she'd felt after he'd stormed out
on her returned full force. Bolstering her courage.

*That's right, you don't have the tiniest notion who you're
dealing with now.*

The slap of the sea against the hull and the cry of a
nearby seabird pierced the silence as the seconds ticked
by—seeming to morph into hours—and the rigid fury
rippling through him threatened to ignite. With his tall,
muscular body towering over her, and the dark stubble
covering his rigid jaw he looked more disreputable than a
pirate and a lot more volatile.

She forced herself to resist flinching under the contemptuous appraisal as his gaze scoured her skin. Okay, maybe
she'd underestimated the extent of his anger. But showing
him any weakness would be the height of folly, because
Dane would exploit it. The way he had exploited it once
before. When she'd been young and naive and completely
besotted with him.

His T-shirt was moulded to the wall of pecs in the
breeze, the pushed-up sleeves revealing his tattoo, which
bulged as he crossed his arms over his broad chest and
stared her down. The sweet spot between Xanthe's thighs
hummed, the unwanted arousal tangling with the punch of
adrenaline to make anxiety scream under her breastbone
like a crouching tiger waiting to pounce.

'What makes you think I won't haul you overboard?'

The ice-blue of his eyes made her brutally aware that
this was no idle threat.

'Go ahead and try it.' She braced herself, prepared for
the worse, bunching her hands into fists by her side. After
the last twenty-four hours spent chasing him across the
Atlantic she wasn't going to give up without a fight.

And, if the worst came to the worst, she could survive
the two-mile swim back to the marina…

If she absolutely had to.

* * *

What the ever-loving—?

Dane cut off the profanity in his head, desire already pooling in his groin like liquid nitrogen.

To say he was shocked to see Xanthe was an understatement of epic proportions. Maybe not as stunned as when she'd shown up in Manhattan to inform him they were still married. But close.

She was the only woman, apart from his mother, who had ever managed to hurt him. And while he knew she couldn't hurt him any more, because he was wise to her, he hadn't planned to test the theory. Especially on the vacation he had been looking forward to for months. Hell, *years*.

This was supposed to be a chance for him to get some much needed R & R. To enjoy the simplicity of being out on the water with nothing to worry about but keeping his course steady and the wind in his sails.

But as she stood in front of him, her lush hair dancing around her head in a mass of fire and those feline eyes glittering with defiance, he couldn't deny the leap of adrenaline.

When was the last time a woman had challenged him or excited him this much? Xanthe was the only one who had ever come close. But the girl he'd married was a shadow of the woman she was now.

They'd always been sexually compatible. But that firecracker temper of hers was something he'd only ever seen small glimpses of ten years ago—on those rare occasions when she'd stood up to him.

Unfolding his arms, he cracked the rigid line of his shoulders in a shrug and headed back towards the bow.

Big deal—she had more guts than he'd expected. He'd see how far that got her once she discovered he wasn't going to play ball.

Ducking under the mainsail, he set about untying the line he'd secured to the anchor chain and then pressed the button to activate the yacht's windlass.

'What are you doing?'

The high-pitched squeak of distress from over his shoulder told him she'd followed him.

'Weighing anchor,' he said, stating the obvious as he lifted the anchor the rest of the way into the boat, then marched back past her. 'You've got two minutes to call your guy before we head for open water.'

She scrambled after him. 'I'm not getting off this boat until you agree to sign those papers.'

He swung round and she bumped into his chest. She stumbled back to land on the bench seat of the cockpit, her cheeks flushed with a captivating mix of shock and awareness.

Arousal powered through his system on the heels of adrenaline.

'I'm not signing a damn thing.'

Taking the wheel, he adjusted the position of the boat until the breeze began to fill the mainsail.

'It's a four-day trip to the Bahamas, which is where I'm headed. With nowhere to stop en route. You want to be stuck on a boat with me for four days, that's up to you. Either that or you can swim back to the marina.'

He cast a look over his shoulder, as if assessing the distance.

'You're a strong swimmer. You should be able to make it by sunset.'

The mulish expression on her face was so priceless he almost laughed—until he remembered why she was there. To protect the company of a man who had treated him like dirt.

She glared back at him. 'I'm not budging until you sign those papers. If you think I'm scared of spending four days on a yacht with you, you're very much mistaken.'

The renewed pulse of reaction in his crotch at this ball-busting comment forced him to admire her fighting spirit. And admit that the fierce temper suited her.

Unfortunately for her, though, she'd chosen the wrong balls to bust.

The mainsail stretched tight and the boat lurched forward.

She gripped the rail, and the flash of panic that crossed her face was some compensation for the fiery heat tying his guts in knots as the yacht picked up speed.

'Yeah, well, maybe you should be,' he said, realising he wasn't nearly as mad about the prospect as he had been when she'd climbed aboard the yacht.

She'd chosen to gatecrash his solo sailing holiday and put them both into a pressure cooker situation that might very quickly get out of control. But if it did, why the hell should *he* care?

Doing the wild thing with Xanthe had never been a hardship. And seeing the unwanted arousal in her eyes now had taken some of his madness away, because it proved one incontrovertible fact. What had happened between them in that hotel room had been as spontaneous and unstoppable for her as it had been for him.

He wasn't going to sign her phoney papers because that would be the same as admitting she'd been right not to trust him with the truth back in Manhattan. That her father had been right not to trust him all those years ago, too.

Charles Carmichael had accused him of being a gold-digger, of being after the Carmichael money, and his daughter must believe it too or she wouldn't have tried to trick him into signing those papers.

He was a rich man now—he could probably buy and sell her precious Carmichael's twenty times over—but even as a wild-eyed kid, starved of so many things, he'd never asked for a cent from her *or* her old man.

Xanthe had been his once—she'd insisted she loved him. But even so a part of her had stayed loyal to her old man or she would have asked questions when her father had told her lies about him. She would have tried to contact him after the miscarriage. She wouldn't have let him go on believing she'd had an abortion up to two days ago. And she sure as hell wouldn't need any guarantee that he wasn't going to rip her off for 55 per cent of a company he had never wanted any part of.

If she wanted to spend the next four days pretending she was immune to him, immune to the attraction between them, so be it.

They'd see who broke first.

Because it sure as hell wasn't going to be him.

Exhaustion and nerves clogged Xanthe's throat as the boat bounced over the swell. She bit down on her anxiety as she watched the land retreat into the distance. She'd come all this way to reason with him—and argue some sense into him. And she'd do it. Even if she had to smack him over the head with a stanchion.

'I apologise for not telling you about my father's will.' She ground out the words, which tasted bitter on her tongue. Her ability to sound contrite and subservient, which was probably what he expected, had been lost somewhere over the Atlantic Ocean. 'I should have been straight with you once I knew you hadn't abandoned me ten years ago, the way my father led me to believe.'

He'd put his sunglasses on, and his face was an impassive mask as he concentrated on steering the boat—making it impossible for her to tell if her speech was having any impact.

The strong, silent treatment, which she had been treated

to so many times in the past, only infuriated her more, while also making greasy slugs of self-doubt glide over her stomach lining.

She breathed deeply, filling her lungs with the sea air. Stupid how she'd never realised until now how easily he had undermined her confidence by simply refusing to communicate.

She dug her teeth into her bottom lip.

Not any more.

She wasn't that giddy girl, desperate for any sign of affection. And she wasn't getting off his precious boat until she had what she'd come for: namely, his signature on the replacement documents she had stuffed in her briefcase so she could end their marriage and any threat of legal action.

She glanced past him, back towards the mainland. Her pulse skipped a beat as she realised the pilot boat had disappeared from view and that Ireland Island was nothing more than a haze on the horizon dotted by the occasional giant cruise ship.

She pulled in a staggered breath, let it out slowly. The plan had been to get Dane's signature on the divorce documents—not to end up getting stuck on a yacht with him for four days.

She'd expected him to be uncooperative. What she *hadn't* expected was for him to call her bluff. Somewhere in the back of her mind she'd convinced herself that once she got in his face he'd be only too willing to end this charade.

But as the spark of sexual awareness arched between them, and the hotspot between her thighs began to throb in earnest, she realised she'd chronically underestimated exactly how much of an arrogant ass he could be.

The one thing she absolutely could *not* do was let him know how much erotic power he still wielded.

'You don't want me here, and I don't want to be here.

So why don't we just end this farce and then we never have to see each other again?'

His gaze finally lowered to hers. The dark lenses of his sunglasses revealed nothing, but at least he seemed to be paying her some attention at last.

Progress. Or so she thought until he spoke.

'I don't take orders, Princess.'

The searing look was meant to be insulting, with the cruel nickname adding to her distress. Her anxiety spiked.

'Fine. You refuse to meet me even halfway...' She scooped the briefcase off the bench seat in the cockpit. 'I guess you're stuck with me.'

She headed below decks.

It wasn't a retreat, she told herself staunchly, simply a chance to refuel and regroup.

The cool air in the cabin's main living space felt glorious on her heated skin as she took a moment to catch her breath and calm her accelerated heartbeat.

But her belly dropped to her toes and then cinched into tight, greasy knots as her eyes adjusted to the low lighting and she took in the space they would be sharing for the next four days.

The yacht had looked huge from the outside, but Dane had obviously designed it with speed in mind. While the salon was luxuriously furnished in the best fabrics and fittings, and boasted a couch, a table, shelves crammed with books and maps, a chart table and a well-appointed galley equipped with state-of-the-art appliances, it was a great deal snugger than she had anticipated.

The man was six foot three, with shoulders a mile wide, for goodness' sake. How on earth was she going to fit in a space this compact with him without bumping up against that rock solid body every time the boat hit a wave?

And then she noticed the door at the end of the space,

open a crack onto the owner's cabin, where a huge mahogany carved bed took up most of the available space, its royal blue coverlet tucked into the frame with military precision.

A hot brick of panic swelled in her throat, not to mention other more sensitive parts of her anatomy. She swallowed it down.

Dane wouldn't be spending much time below decks, she reasoned. No solo sailor could afford to spend more than twenty minutes at a time away from the helm if they were going to keep a lookout for approaching vessels or other maritime dangers. And she had no plans to offer to share the load with him, given she was effectively here against her will—not to mention her better judgement.

Dumping her briefcase, she crossed into the galley and flung open the fridge to find it stocked—probably by his staff—with everything she could possibly need to have a five-star yachting vacation at his expense.

He'd accused her of being a princess, so it would serve him right if she played the role to the hilt.

It didn't matter if the living space was compact. It had all the creature comforts she needed to while away her hours on board in style until he saw reason. With Dane occupied on deck, she could use this as her sanctuary.

After finding a beautifully appointed spare berth, with its own bathroom, she cleaned up and stowed her briefcase. Returning to the galley, she cracked open one of the bottles of champagne she'd found in the fridge, poured herself a generous glass and made herself a meal fit for a queen—or even a princess—from the array of cordon bleu food.

But as she picked at her meal her heartbeat refused to level off completely.

How exactly was she going to dictate terms to a man who had always refused to follow any rules but his own?

A man she couldn't get within ten feet of without feeling as if she were about to explode?

Dane held fast to the wheel and scanned the water, blissfully empty and free of traffic now they'd left Ireland Island and the pocket cruisers and day trippers behind. He wheeled to starboard. The sail slapped against the mast, then drew tight as the boat harnessed the wind's power. He tipped his head back as *The Sea Witch* gathered speed. Elation swelled as the dying sun burned his face and the salt spray peppered his skin.

Next stop the Bahamas.

What had he been thinking, waiting so long to get back on the water?

But then his gaze dropped to the door to the cabin, which had been firmly shut ever since Xanthe had stormed off a couple of hours ago.

He imagined her sulking down there, and wondered if she planned to hide away for the rest of the trip.

The boat punched a wave and the jolt shimmered through his bones.

His heartbeat sped up. Her little disappearing act confirmed what he already knew—that he wasn't the only one who'd felt the snap and crackle of that insane sexual chemistry sparking between them when she'd arrived. The fact he was the only one prepared to admit it gave him the upper hand.

He sliced the boat across the swell and felt the hull lurch into the air.

She'd made a major miscalculation if she thought they would be able to avoid it on a fifty-five-foot boat, even if she planned to hide below decks for the duration.

Switching on the autopilot as the sun finally disappeared below the horizon, he ventured below—to find the salon empty and the door to the spare berth firmly shut.

But he could detect that subtle scent of spring flowers that had enveloped him two nights ago, when he'd been wrapped around her in sleep.

He rubbed his chin, feeling two days' worth of scruff. He imagined her fingernails scraping over his jaw. What was that saying about opposites attracting?

They were certainly opposites—him a 'wharf rat' who had made good and her the princess ballsy enough to run a multinational company, even if she *was* only doing it to please her old man. But the attraction was still there, and stronger than ever.

He wasn't going to push anything because he didn't have to. She would come to him—the way she had before. And then they'd see exactly who needed who.

He grabbed a beer from the fridge, a blanket from his cabin and the alarm clock he kept on hand to wake him up during the night while he was on watch. But as he headed back up on deck, ready to bed down in the cockpit, he spotted an artfully arranged plate of fancy deli items sitting on the galley counter covered in sandwich wrap. Next to it was an open bottle of fizz, with a note attached to it.

For Dane, from his EX-wife.
Don't worry, the princess hasn't poisoned it…yet!

He coughed out a gruff chuckle. 'You little witch.'

But then the memory of the meals she'd always had waiting for him in their motel room when he'd got back from another day of searching for work slammed into him. And the rueful smile on his lips died. Suddenly all he could see was those brilliant blue-green eyes of hers, bright with excitement about the pregnancy. All he could hear was her lively chatter flowing over him as he watched her hands stroke the smooth bump of her stomach and shovelled up the food she'd made for him in silence. Too scared to tell her the truth.

Heat flared in his groin, contradicting the guilt twisting in his gut as the crushing feeling of inadequacy pressed down on him.

That agonising fear felt real again—the fear of going another day without finding a job, the terror that had consumed him at the thought that he couldn't pay their motel bill, let alone meet the cost of Xanthe's medical care when the baby arrived.

Putting the beer back in the fridge, he chugged down a gulp of the expensive champagne and let the fruity bubbles dissolve the ball of remembered agony lodged in his throat.

Get a grip, Redmond.

That boy was long gone. He didn't have anything to prove any more. Not to Xanthe, not to himself, not to anyone. He'd made a staggering success of his life. Had worked like a dog to get to college and ace his qualification as a maritime architect, then developed an award-winning patent that with a clever investment strategy had turned a viable business into a multimillion-dollar marine empire—not to mention acing the America's Cup twice with his designs.

He had more than enough money now to waste on bottles of pricey fizz that he rarely drank. Getting hung up on the past now was redundant.

She'd thought she loved him once and, like the sad little bastard he'd been then, he'd sucked up every ounce of her affection—all those tender touches, the adoring looks, all her sweet, stupid talk about love and feelings.

But he wasn't that sad little bastard any more. He knew exactly what he wanted and needed now. And love didn't even hit the top ten.

He sat on deck, wolfing down the food she'd made for

him and watching the phosphorescent glow of the algae shine off the water in the boat's wake while a very different kind of hunger gnawed at his gut.

He didn't need Xanthe's love any more, but her body was another matter—because, whether she liked it or not, they both knew that had always and *would* always belong to him.

CHAPTER THIRTEEN

XANTHE STEADIED HERSELF by slapping a hand on the table the following morning and glared at the hatch as the boat's hull rocked to one side. How fast was he driving this thing? It felt as if they were flying.

Luckily she'd already found her sea legs which, to her surprise and no small amount of dismay, were just where she'd left them the last time she'd been sailing—ten years ago. With Dane.

The boat lurched again, but her stomach stayed firmly in place.

Don't get mad. That had been her mistake yesterday. She needed to save herself for the big battles—like getting him to sign the divorce papers. Provoking him was counterproductive.

After a night of interrupted sleep, her body humming with awareness while she listened to him moving about in the salon on his short trips below deck, she knew just how counterproductive.

Given the meteoric rise in the temperature during their argument yesterday, she needed to be careful. Knowing Dane, and his pragmatic attitude to sex, he wouldn't exert too much effort to keep the temperature down, even if it threatened to blaze out of control. So it would be up to her to do that for both of them.

Xanthe poured herself a mug of the strong coffee she'd found brewing on the stove and added cream and sugar, adjusting to the sway of the boat like a pro.

While she wasn't keen to see Dane, she couldn't stay down here indefinitely. Early-morning sunlight glowed through the windows that ran down the side of the boat. Each time the hull heeled to starboard she could see the horizon stretching out before them.

Her pulse jumped and skittered, reminding her of the days they'd spent on the water before, and how much she'd enjoyed that sense of freedom and exhilaration. Of course back then she'd believed Dane would keep her safe. That he cared about her even if he couldn't articulate it.

She knew better now.

Good thing she didn't need a man to keep her safe any longer.

She dumped the last of the coffee into the sink and tied her hair back in a knot.

She wasn't scared of Dane, or her reaction to him, so it was way past time she stopped hiding below deck.

Even so, her heart gave a definite lurch—to match the heel of the boat—when she climbed out of the cabin and spotted Dane standing at the wheel. On the water, with his long legs braced against the swell, his big capable hands steering the boat with relaxed confidence and his gaze focused on the horizon, he looked even more dominant and, yes—damn it—sexy. Her pulse jumped, then sank into her abdomen, heading back to exactly where she did not need it to be.

She shut the door to the cabin with a frustrated snap. His gaze dropped to hers. Her face heated at the thorough inspection.

'You finished sulking yet, Princess?' His deep voice carried over the flap of canvas and the rush of wind.

Her temper spiked at the sardonic tone. 'I wasn't sulking,' she said. 'I was having some coffee and now I plan to do some sunbathing.'

After a night lying awake in her cabin and listening

to him crewing the boat alone, she had planned to offer to help out this morning. She needed to get him to sign those papers, and she'd never been averse to good honest work, but his surly attitude and that 'princess' comment had fired up her indignation again.

She'd be damned if she'd let his snarky comments and his low opinion of her and her motives get to her.

Ignoring him, she faced into the wind, letting it whip at her hair and sting her cheeks. The sea was empty as far as the eye could see, the bright, cloudless blue of the sky reflecting off the brilliant turquoise water. She licked her lips, tasted salt and sun…and contemplated making herself a mimosa later.

Gosh, she'd missed this. Despite having the fellow traveller from hell on board, maybe this trip wouldn't be a complete nightmare. But as she reached to swing herself up onto the main deck, a bulky life jacket smacked onto the floor of the cockpit in front of her.

'No sunbathing, princess, until you put that on and clip yourself to the safety line.'

She swung round. 'I'm not going to fall off. I'm not an amateur.'

'How long since you've been on a boat?'

'Not that long,' she lied.

She didn't want him to know she hadn't been sailing since they'd parted. He might think her enforced abstinence had something to do with him.

'Uh-huh? How long is "not that long"? Less than ten years?'

She sent him her best death stare. But the hotspots on her cheeks were a dead giveaway.

'Yeah, I thought so,' he said, doing his infuriating mind reading thing again. 'Now, put on the PFD or get below.'

'No. There's barely a ripple on the water. I don't need to wear one.' He was just doing this out of some warped desire to show her who was boss. 'If it gets at all choppy I'll put it on straight away,' she added. 'I'm not an idiot. I have no desire to end up floating around in the middle of the Atlantic.'

Especially as she wasn't convinced he'd bother to pick her up. But she refused to be bullied into doing something completely unnecessary just so *he* could feel superior.

Instead of answering her, he clicked a few switches on the wheel's autopilot and headed towards her.

She pressed against the hatch to avoid coming into contact with that immovable chest again as he reached past her for the jacket. She got a lungful of his scent. The clean smell was now tinged with the fresh hint of sea air.

Hooking the jacket with his index finger, he dangled it in front of her face.

'Put it on. Now.'

Her jaw tightened. 'No, I will not. *You're* not wearing one.'

'This isn't a negotiation. Do as you're told.'

Temper swept through her at his dictatorial tone.

'Stop behaving like a caveman.' She planted her feet, all her good intentions to rise above his goading flying off into the wild blue Caribbean yonder.

Once upon a time she would have been only too willing to do anything he said, because his certainty, his dominance had been so seductive. Not any more.

The backs of her knees bumped against the seat of the cockpit as he loomed over her. Traitorous heat blossomed between her legs as she got another lungful of his exquisite scent. Fresh and salty and far too enticing.

'The hard way it is, then,' he announced, flinging the jacket down.

Realising his intention, she tried to dodge round him— but he simply ducked down and hiked her over his shoulder.

She yelped. Dangling upside down, eyeballing tight

male buns in form-fitting shorts, as she rode his shoulder blade.

Finally getting over her shock enough to fight back, she punched his broad back with her fists as he ducked under the boom and hefted her towards the hatch.

'Put me down this instant!'

He banded an arm across her legs to stop her kicking. 'Keep it up, princess, and I'm tossing you overboard.'

She stopped struggling, not entirely sure he wouldn't carry out his threat, and deeply disturbed by the shocking reaction to his easy strength and the delicious scent of soap and man and sea.

Damn him and his intoxicating pheromones.

He swung her round to take the steps. 'Mind your head.'

When he finally dumped her in the salon she scrambled back, her cheeks aflame with outrage.

The tight smile did nothing to disguise the muscle jumping in his jaw and the flush of colour hitting tanned cheeks. She wasn't the only one far too affected by their wrestling match.

'Are you completely finished treating me like a two-year-old?'

She absorbed the spike of adrenaline when his nostrils flared.

'You don't want to be treated like a toddler?' His voice rose to match hers. 'Then don't act like one. You want to go on deck, you wear the jacket.'

'Being stronger and bigger than me does *not* make you right,' she said, her voice gratifyingly steely…or steely enough, despite the riot of sensations running through her. 'Until you give me a valid reason I'm not wearing it. You'll just have to keep carrying me down here.' Even if having his hands on her again was going to increase the torment. 'Let's see how long it takes for that to get *really* old.'

She stood her ground, refusing to be cowed. This stand-off was symptomatic of everything that had been wrong with their relationship the first time around. She'd given in too easily to every demand, had never stuck up for herself. Never made him explain himself about anything—which was exactly how they'd ended up being so easily separated by her father's lies and half-truths.

Dane had threatened her company and refused to listen to reason, all to teach her a lesson about honesty and integrity—well, she had a few lessons to teach *him*. About respect and self-determination and the fine art of communication.

She wasn't a doormat any more. She was his equal.

'If you want me to wear it, you're going to have to explain to me why I need to when you don't. And then *I'll* decide if I'm going to put it on.'

He cursed under his breath and ran his hand over his hair, frustration emanating from him.

Just as she was about to congratulate herself for calling him on his Neanderthal behaviour, he replied.

'We're sailing against the prevailing winds, which means the swell can be unpredictable. I know when to brace because I can see what's coming. Without a jacket on you could go under before I could get to you.'

'But…that's…' She opened her mouth, then closed it again. 'Why didn't you just say that to start with?' she finally managed, past the obstruction in her throat.

He looked away, that muscle still working overtime in his jaw.

And the melting sensation in her chest, the sharp stab of vulnerability, gave way to temper and dismay. Why had it always been so hard for him to give her even the smallest sign that he cared? It was a question that had haunted her throughout their relationship ten years ago. It was upsetting to realise it haunted her still.

'You know why.'

His eyes met hers, the hot gaze dipping to brand the glimpse of cleavage above the scooped neck of her T-shirt. Heat rushed through her torso, darting down to make her sex ache.

He cupped her cheek, his thumb skimming over her bottom lip, the light in his eyes now feral and hungry. 'Because when I'm with you not a lot of thinking goes on.'

'Don't…' She jerked away from his touch, desperate to dispel the sensual fog. But it was too late. His compelling scent was engulfing her, saturating her senses and sending pheromones firing through her bloodstream.

Her breathing became ragged, her chest painfully tight, as arousal surged through her system.

'Quit pretending you don't want it, too,' he said as he watched her, the lust-blown pupils darkening the bright blue of his irises to black.

'I…I don't.' She cleared her throat, disgusted when her voice broke on the lie. 'We're not doing this again. That's not why I'm here.'

If they made love she was scared it would mean more than it should. To her, at least. And she couldn't risk that.

'Then stay out of my way,' he said. 'Or I'm going to test that theory.'

He walked away, heading back on deck.

'I'm not staying below decks for three days!' she shouted after him, gathering the courage that had been in such short supply ten years ago.

So what if she still wanted him? She couldn't let him control the terms of this negotiation. If she didn't speak out now she'd be no better than the girl she'd been then, ready to accept the meagre scraps he'd been willing to throw her way.

'I came here to save my company,' she added as he mounted the steps, still ignoring her. 'If you think I'm going to sit meekly by while you attempt to steal fifty-five per cent of it, you can forget it.'

His head jerked round, the scowl on his face going from annoyed to furious in a heartbeat, but underneath it she could see the shadow of hurt.

'I didn't want a cent from your old man when I was dead broke. Why the hell would I want a part of his company *now*?' he said as he headed back towards her.

She'd struck a nerve—a nerve she hadn't even realised was still there.

'Then why did you threaten to sue for a share of it?' she fired back, determined not to care about his hurt pride.

She had nothing to feel ashamed of. *She* wasn't the one who had stormed out of their hotel room claiming he was going to sue her just for the hell of it.

'I never said I was going to sue for anything,' he added. 'You made that assumption all on your own.'

'You mean…' Her mouth dropped open. Was he saying she'd come all this way and got stuck on a yacht with him for no reason? 'You mean you're *not* planning to take legal action?'

'What do you think?'

The concession should have been a relief, but it wasn't, the prickle of shame becoming a definite yank. She'd always known how touchy he was about her father's money, but how could she have forgotten exactly how important it had always been to him never to take anything he hadn't earned?

'Then why wouldn't you sign the divorce papers?' she asked, trying to stay focused and absolve her guilt.

How could she have known that his insecurities about money ran so deep when he'd never once confided in her about where they came from? If he'd simply signed the papers in Manhattan, instead of going ballistic, she never would have made the assumption that he intended to sue for the shares in the first place.

'And why won't you sign them now?'

'Your *phoney* divorce papers, you mean?'

'They're not phoney. They're just a guarantee that—'

'Forget it.'

He cut off her explanation, the scowl on his face disappearing to be replaced with something else—something that made no sense. He didn't care about her, he never really had, so what was there to regret?

'I'm not signing any papers that state I can't claim those shares if I want to.'

'But that's just being contrary. Why wouldn't you sign them if you don't want the shares?' she blurted out.

'I don't know,' he said, his tone mocking and thick with resentment. 'Why don't you try figuring it out?'

She didn't have to figure it out, though. Because it suddenly all became painfully obvious.

He expected her to *trust* him. In a way he'd never trusted her.

The searing irony made her want to shout her frustration at him, but she bit her lip to stop the brutal accusation coming out of her mouth.

Because it would make her sound pathetic. And it might lead to her having to ask herself again the heartbreaking question that had once nearly destroyed her.

Why had he never been able to believe her when she'd told him she loved him?

She refused to butt her head against that brick wall again—the brick wall he had always kept around his emotions—especially as it was far too late to matter now.

But then he touched her hair, letting a single tendril curl round his forefinger. The gentleness of the gesture made her heart contract in her chest, and the combination of pain and longing horrified her.

He gave a tug, making the punch of her pulse accelerate. And the yearning to have his mouth on hers became almost more than she could bear.

'Dane, stop,' she said, but the demand sounded like a plea.

She placed her palms on his waist, brutally torn as she absorbed the ripple of sensation when his abdominal muscles tensed under her hands.

'Don't push me, Red,' he murmured, his lips so close she could almost taste them. 'Or I'm gonna make you prove exactly how much you don't want me.'

For tantalising seconds she stood with desire and longing threatening to tear her apart. She should push him away. Why couldn't she?

But then he took the choice away from her.

Cursing softly, he let her go.

She watched him leave, feeling dazed and shaky. She'd fallen under Dane's sensual spell once before and it had come close to destroying her…because he'd always refused to let her in.

But until this moment she'd had no idea exactly how much danger she was in of falling under it again. Or that all those tangled needs and desires to understand him, to know the reasons why he couldn't love her or trust her, had never truly died.

Dane yanked the sail line harder than was strictly necessary and tied it off, his heart pumping hard enough to blow a gasket.

He reprogrammed the autopilot. The maritime weather report had said they were in for a quiet day of smooth sailing.

Smooth sailing, my butt.

Not likely with Xanthe on board.

He'd wanted to bring the princess down a peg or two

when she'd shown up on deck looking slim and beautiful and superior. He sure as hell wasn't going to let her
sunbathe in front of him while he took the wheel like a
lackey. Or that's how it had started. But the truth was he'd
wanted her to wear the PFD, had decided to insist upon
it, because he'd been unable to control the dumb urge to
make sure she was safe.

And as soon as he'd had her in his arms again, yelling
and punching as he carted her below deck, the desire to
have her again had all but overwhelmed him too... Then
he'd lost it entirely when she'd made that crack about him
wanting a piece of her precious company.

He hated that feeling—hated knowing she could still get
to him. Knowing that there was something about Xanthe
that could slip under his guard and make him care about
her opinion when it shouldn't matter to him any more.

Resentment sat like a lead weight in his stomach.

From now on there was going to be no more sparring
and no more conversations about their past. He wasn't
going to get hung up on why she hadn't been sailing for ten
years, even though she'd once been addicted to the rush.
Or waste one more iota of his time getting mad about the
fact she didn't trust him.

Their marriage was over—had been over for a long
time—and it wasn't as if he wanted to resurrect it.

Arousal pulsed in his crotch, adding to his aggravation.

He usually averaged five hours' sleep a night when he
was sailing solo, despite the need to wake up every twenty
minutes and check the watch. Last night he hadn't managed more than two. Because he'd spent hours watching
the stars wink in the darkness, thinking about all the stuff
that might have been, while waiting for the night air to cool
the heat powering through his body.

The only connection between them now was sexual,
pure and simple—an animal attraction that had never died.

Complicating that by sifting through all the baggage that had gone before would be a mistake.

So keeping Xanthe at arm's length for a little while made sense—until he knew for sure that he could control all those wayward emotions she seemed able to provoke without even trying.

He doubted they'd be able to keep their hands off each other for the three days they had left together on the boat—but he could handle the heat until she got one thing straight.

Sex was the only thing he had to offer.

CHAPTER FOURTEEN

'DANE, IS EVERYTHING OKAY?' Xanthe yelled above the whistling wind as she clambered on deck and clipped her safety harness to an anchor point.

The yacht mounted another five-foot wave as water washed over the bow and the rain lashed her face.

Their argument over the life jacket yesterday seemed like a distant memory now.

'Get below, damn it, and stay there!' he shouted back, wrestling with the wheel to avoid a breaking wave—which brought with it the danger of capsizing.

The squall had hit with less than an hour's warning that morning. Dane had woken her up from a fitful sleep to issue some curt instructions about how to prepare the belowdecks, given her a quick drill on the emergency procedures if they had to use the life raft, insisted she take some seasickness pills and then ordered her to stay below.

After yesterday's argument and the evening that had followed—with the tension between them stretching tight as they both avoided each other as best they could—the rough weather and their clearly defined roles this morning had actually come as a relief.

So she'd obeyed his terse commands without question, even while smarting at his obvious determination not to give her anything remotely strenuous to do. When it came to skippering the boat, he was in charge. It would be foolish to dispute that, or distract him, when all his attention needed to be on keeping them afloat.

Correcting his 'princess' assumptions could wait until they got through this.

But as the hours had rolled by and the storm had got progressively worse she'd become increasingly concerned and frustrated by his dogged refusal to let her help. Thunder and lightning had been added to the hazards aboard as the squall had moved from a force-four to something closer to a force-eight by the afternoon, but through it all Dane had continued to insist she stay below.

Rather than have a full-blown argument, which would only make things more treacherous with the visibility at almost zero, she'd kept busy manning the bilge pump, rigging safety lines in the cabin and locking down the chart table when the contents had threatened to spill out. All the while trying to stay calm and focused and zone out the heaving noise outside.

They'd come through the worst of it an hour ago. The torrential rain was still flattening the seas, but the winds were dying down at least a little bit. But two seconds ago she'd heard a solid crash and she'd rushed up on deck, no longer prepared to follow orders.

Relief washed through her to see Dane standing at the wheel, the storm sails intact. But her relief quickly retreated.

His face was drawn, his clothing soaked, his usually graceful movements jerky and uncoordinated. He looked completely shattered. She cursed herself for waiting so long to finally confront him about his stubborn refusal to allow her on deck.

He'd been helming the yacht for over five hours and hadn't slept for more than twenty minutes at a time since they'd left Bermuda two days ago because he'd been keeping watch solo.

Maybe it had been ten years ago, but she'd once been a competent yachtswoman because she'd learnt from a

master. She should take the helm. There weren't as many
breakers to negotiate now, visibility was lifting and a quick
survey of the horizon showed clear skies off the bow only
a few miles ahead.

'Dane, for goodness' sake. Let me take over. You need
some sleep.'

'Get back below, damn it!'

He swung the wheel to starboard and the boat heeled.
But as she grabbed the safety line she saw a trickle of blood
mixed with the rain running down his face, seeping from
a gash at his hairline.

Horror gripped her insides, and her frustration was consumed by panic. 'Dane, you're bleeding!'

He scrubbed a forearm across his forehead. 'I'm okay.'

Hauling herself up to the stern, she covered his much
larger hand with hers, shocked by the freezing skin as he
clung to the wheel.

'This is insane,' she said, desperate now to make him
see reason. 'I can *do* this. You have to let me do this.'

An involuntary shudder went through him, and she realised exactly how close he was to collapsing when he
turned towards her, his blue eyes bloodshot and foggy with
fatigue. Good grief, had he given himself a concussion?

'It's too rough still,' he said, the words thick with exhaustion. 'It's not safe for you up here.'

'It's a lot calmer than it was,' she said, registering the
weary determination in his voice. However stupidly macho
he was being by refusing to admit weakness, his determination to stay at the helm was born out of a desire to
protect her.

'At least go below and clean the cut,' she said, clamping down on all the treacherous memories flooding back
to make her heart ache.

The mornings when he'd held her head as she threw up
her breakfast in the motel bathroom…the intractable look

on his face when he'd demanded she marry him after the stick had gone blue…and the crippling thought of him battered and bruised by her father's bodyguards when he'd come back to get her…

Her gaze drifted over his brow to the scar that he'd refused to explain. She shook off the melancholy thoughts as blood seeped from the fresh injury on his forehead. She couldn't think about any of that now. He had a head injury. She had to get him to let go—at least for a little while.

'Seriously, I can handle this!' she shouted above the gusting wind, her voice firm and steady despite the memory bombarding her of another argument—the one they'd had the morning he'd left her…

She'd let him have the last word then, because she hadn't had the courage to insist she was capable of handling at least some of the burden of their finances. She'd been so angry about his attitude that morning, at his blank refusal to let her get a job.

But maybe it was finally time to acknowledge the truth of what had happened that day. *Of course* he'd had no faith in her abilities—because she'd had no faith in them herself. And he hadn't left her. He'd gone to find a job so he could support her.

He hadn't been able to rely on her because she *had* been weak and feeble, beaten down by her father's bullying. And her one show of strength—the decision to run off and marry Dane and have the baby growing inside her—had really been nothing more than a transference of power from one man to another.

Dane had made all the decisions simply because she'd been too scared, too unsure to make them herself. That Dane might have been equally scared, equally terrified, had never even occurred to her. But what if he had been? And what if he'd kept his feelings hidden simply to stop himself from scaring her?

'I'm not a princess any more, Dane!' she shouted, just in case he was still confusing her with that girl. She didn't want to argue with him, but she had to make him believe she could handle this. 'I'm a lot tougher than I look now,' she added.

Because I've had to be.

She cut off the thought. She could never tell him all the reasons why she'd been forced to toughen up because that would only stir up more of the guilt and recriminations from their past. Until she'd found herself alone in that motel bathroom she'd let him take all the strain. But she didn't need to do that any more.

'Please let me do this.'

She braced herself for an argument, keeping an eye on the sea, but to her astonishment, instead of arguing further, he grasped her arm and dragged her in front of him.

His big body bolstered hers and she felt the familiar zing of sexual awareness, complicated by a rush of emotion when his cold palms covered her hands on the wheel.

Tears stung her eyes and she blinked them away.

'You sure you can hold her?' he said, and the exhilaration in her chest combined with a lingering sense of loss for that complicated, taciturn boy who had taught her to sail a lifetime ago. And whom she had once loved without question.

She nodded.

He stood behind her, shielding her from the beating rain. She melted into him for a moment and the punch of adrenaline hit her square in the solar plexus, taking her breath away as she felt the boat's power beneath her feet.

When she'd been that frightened, insecure girl, scared of her father's wrath, always looking for his approval, Dane had given her this—the freedom and space to become her own woman. And she'd screwed it up by falling for him hook, line and sinker.

If this time with him taught her one thing, let it be that she would never do that again. Never look for love when what she really needed was strength.

'Go below! I've got this!' she shouted over her shoulder, trying to concentrate on the job at hand and not let all the what-ifs charging through her head destroy the simple companionship of this moment.

'I won't be long,' he said, and the husky words sprinted up her spine.

Giving her fingers a reassuring squeeze, he took a deep breath and stepped away, leaving her alone at the helm. He pointed towards the horizon.

'Head towards the clear blue. And avoid the breakers.'

She concentrated on the break in the storm line, scanning the sea for the next wave. 'Will do. Take as long as you need.'

Widening her stance, she let her limbs absorb the heel of the boat as it rode over the swell. The rain was finally starting to trail off. Arousal leapt, combining with the deep well of emotion, as she watched him unclip himself from the safety line and saw his shoulders fill the entryway before he disappeared below.

The boat rolled to the side and Dane's heart went with it, kicking against his ribs like a bucking bronco as he staggered into the salon, his head hurting like a son of a bitch, but his heart hurting more.

He shook his hands and the shivering racked his body as he stripped off the life jacket and the wet clothing with clumsy fingers and headed back to his cabin.

He didn't want to leave Xanthe alone up there too long. She'd always been a natural sailor, and he'd sensed a new toughness and tenacity in her now, a greater resilience than when they were kids together. But even so she was his responsibility while she was on the boat, and he didn't want to screw it up. *Again.*

He winced as shame engulfed him. He'd already put her at risk, sailing them both straight into a force-eight because he'd been too damn busy thinking about the hot, wet clasp of her body and trying to decipher all the conflicting emotions she could still stir in him, instead of paying the necessary attention to the weather report, the cloud formation and the sudden dip in air pressure.

They'd been lucky that it hadn't been a whole lot worse.

But he knew when he was beaten. He had to sleep—get a good solid thirty minutes before he could relieve her at the helm. Gripping the safety line she'd rigged, he made his way to the head, dug out a piece of gauze to dab the cut on his forehead, then staggered naked into the cabin.

Thirty minutes—that was all he needed—then he'd be able to take over again.

His eyes closed, and his brain shut off the minute his head connected with the pillow.

He woke with a start what felt like moments later, to find the cabin dark and the boat steady. The events of the day— the last few days—came back in a rush.

Xanthe.

He jerked upright and pain lanced through the cut on his forehead where he'd headbutted the boom. He cursed. How long had he been out? He'd forgotten to set an alarm before crashing into his berth. He looked up to see clear night through the skylight. Then noticed the blanket lying across his lap.

The blanket that hadn't been there when he'd fallen headlong into the bunk what had to be *hours* ago.

Emotion gripped as he pulled the blanket off.

Was she still on deck? Doing his job for him?

Ignoring the dull pain in his head, he pulled on some

trunks and a light sweater. Heading through the salon, he noticed the debris left by the storm had been cleared away and the film of water that had leaked in through the hatch onto the floor had been mopped up. His wet clothes hung on the safety line, brittle with salt but nearly dry.

The night breeze lifted the hairs on his arms as he climbed onto the deck. The helm was empty, the autopilot was on, the storm sails were furled and the standard rigging was engaged as the boat coasted on a shallow swell.

Xanthe lay curled up in the cockpit, out cold, her PFD still anchored to the safety line, her fist clutching the alarm clock.

His heart hammered hard enough to hurt his bruised ribs.

He cast his gaze out to sea, where the red light of a Caribbean dawn hung on the horizon, and struggled to breathe past the emotion making his chest ache.

She'd seen them through the last of the storm, then kept watch all night while he slept. How could someone who looked so delicate, so fragile, be so strong underneath? And what the hell did he do with all the feelings weakening his knees now? Feelings he'd thought he had conquered a decade ago?

Desire, possessiveness, and a bone-deep longing.

He'd convinced himself a long time ago that Xanthe had never really belonged to him. That what he'd felt for her once had all been a dumb dream driven by endorphins and recklessness and desperation. He didn't want to be that needy kid again. So why did this feel like more than just the desire to bury himself deep inside her?

He crouched down on his haunches, forcing the traitorous feelings back.

He was still tired—and more than a little horny after three days at sea with the one woman he had never been able to resist. It had been an emotional couple of days.

And the storm had been a sucker punch neither of them had needed.

He pressed his hand to her cheek, pushing the wild hair, damp with sea water, off her brow. She stirred, and the bronco in his chest gave his ribs another hefty kick.

'Hmm...?' Her eyes fluttered open, the sea green dazed with sleep. 'Dane?' she murmured, licking her lips.

The blood flowed into his groin and he welcomed it. Sex had always been the easy part of the equation.

'Hey, sleepyhead,' he said, affection and admiration swelling in his chest.

This wasn't a big deal. She'd done a spectacular job and he owed her—that was all. Unclipping her harness, he lifted her easily in his arms.

'Let's get you below. I can take over now.' The way he should have done approximately twelve hours ago.

He realised how groggy she was when she didn't protest as he carried her down the steps into the salon and headed to his own cabin.

He wanted her in his bed while he took charge of the boat. By his calculation they'd reach the Bahamas around twilight. They'd have to anchor offshore, and dock first thing tomorrow morning, but he intended to keep his hands off her for the rest of the trip. Even if it killed him.

Then he'd sign her divorce papers.

And let her go.

Before this situation got any more out of hand.

Sitting her on the bed, he crouched down to undo her jacket. She didn't resist his attentions, docile as a child as he pulled it off and chucked it on the floor. Her T-shirt was stuck to her skin, the hard tips of her nipples clear through the clinging fabric.

He gritted his teeth, ignoring the pounding in his groin. The desire to warm those cold nubs with his tongue almost overwhelming.

'How's your head?' she murmured sleepily.

He glanced up to find her watching him, her gaze unfocused, dark with arousal.

'Good,' he said, his voice strained.

She needed to get out of her wet clothes, grab a hot shower. But if he did it for her he didn't know how the heck he'd be able to keep his sanity and not take advantage of her.

'Have you got it from here?'

He tugged the clock out of his back pocket. Fifteen minutes before he had to check the watch.

'I should head back on deck,' he said, hoping she couldn't see the erection starting to strangle in his shorts. Or hear the battle being waged inside him to hold her and tend to her and claim her again...

Because he knew if that happened he might never be able to let her go.

Sleep fogged Xanthe's brain, as her mind floated on a wave of exhaustion. He looked glorious, standing before her in the half-light—the epitome of all the erotic dreams which had chased her through too many nights of disturbed sleep. Strong and unyielding... The raw, rugged beauty of his tanned skin, his muscular shoulders, the dark heat in his pure blue eyes, blazed a trail down to tighten her nipples into aching points.

She shivered, awareness shuddering through her.

She heard a strained curse, then the bed dipped and her T-shirt was dragged over her head. The damp shorts and underwear followed. Her limbs were lethargic, her skin tingling as calloused fingers rasped over sensitive flesh with exquisite tenderness, beckoning her further into the erotic dream and making her throat close.

'Red, you're freezing...let's warm you up.'

She found herself back in strong arms, her body weightless. But she didn't feel cold. She felt blissfully warm and languid, with hunger flaring all over her tired body as she stood on shaky legs.

Hot jets of water rained down on her head as strong fingers massaged her scalp. She breathed in the scented steam—cedarwood and lemon—her body alive with sensation as a fluffy towel cocooned her in warmth, making her feel clean and fresh, the vigorous rubbing igniting more of that ravishing heat.

Back on the bed, she looked into that rugged face watching her in the darkness, its expression tight with a longing that matched her own.

Struggling up onto her elbows, she traced a finger through the hair on his chest, naked now, down the happy trail through the rigid muscles of his abdomen to his belly button.

She heard him suck in a staggered breath, and the sound was both warning and provocation. Emotion washed through her as she stroked the heavy ridge in his pants and felt the huge erection thicken against her fingertips.

A hand gripped her wrist and gently pulled her away. 'Red, you're killing me,' he murmured, his low voice raw with agony.

She lifted her head, saw the harsh need that pierced her abdomen reflected in Dane's deep blue eyes. Drifting in a sensual haze, she let the uncensored swell of emotion fill up all the places in her heart that had been empty for so long.

'Stay with me.'

The words came out on a husk of breath, almost unrecognisable. Was that *her* voice? So sure, so uninhibited, so determined?

'I need you.'

A tiny whisper in her head told her it was wrong to ask, wrong to need him this much. But this was just a dream, a dream from long ago, and nothing mattered now but satisfying the yearning which had begun to cut off her air supply and stab into her abdomen like a knife.

'There's never been anyone else,' she said. 'Only you. Don't make me beg.'

Moisture stung her eyes—tears of pain and sadness for all those dreams that had been forced to die inside her, along with the life they'd once made together. If she could just feel that glorious oblivion once more all would be well.

Only he could fix this.

'Shh… Shh, Red…' Rough palms framed her face, swiping away the salty tears seeping from her eyes. 'I've got this. Lie down and I'll give you what you need.'

She flopped back on the bed, then bowed up, racked with pleasure as his tongue circled her nipples, firm lips tugging at the tender tips. Desire arrowed down. Sharp and brutal. Obliterating every emotion but want.

Moisture flooded between her thighs as blunt fingers found the swollen folds of her sex. Her breath sawed out, her lungs squeezing tight as the agony of loss was swept away by the fierce tide of ecstasy.

She bucked, cried out, as those sure, seeking lips trailed across her ribs, delved into her belly button, then found the swollen bundle of nerves at last. Sensation shot through her, drawing tight, clutching at her heart and firing through her nerve-endings, making everything disappear but the agonising need to feel him filling her again.

Large fingers pressed inside her and her clitoris burned and pulsed under the sensual torment. The wave of ecstasy crested, throwing her into the hot, dark oblivion she sought. She screamed his name, the cry of joy dying on her lips as she tasted her own pleasure in a hard, fleeting kiss.

'Now, go to sleep.'

She registered the gruff command, making her feel safe and cherished.

His hand cradled her face and she pressed into his palm, the gentle touch making new tears spill over her lids as she closed her eyes. A blanket fell over her and she snuggled into a ball, drifting on an enervating wave of afterglow.

And then she dived into a deep, dreamless sleep.

CHAPTER FIFTEEN

'Is that Nassau?' Xanthe called out to Dane, hoping the flush on her face wasn't as bright as the lights she could see across the bay, which had to be the commercial and cultural capital of the Bahamas.

A kaleidoscope of red and orange hues painted the sky where the sun dipped beneath a silhouette of palm trees and colourful waterfront shacks on the nearby beach.

She'd slept the whole day away. Her body felt limber and alive, well-rested and rejuvenated… Unfortunately that wasn't doing anything for her peace of mind as snatches of conversation from the hour before dawn, when Dane had come to relieve her on deck after her shattering stint at the helm, made her heart pummel her chest and her face burn with the heat of a thousand suns.

Had she actually begged him to give her an orgasm?

Yup, she was pretty sure she had.

And had she blurted out that he'd been the only man she'd ever slept with?

Way to go, Xanthe.

How exactly did she come back from that with any dignity? Especially as she could still feel the phantom stroke of his tongue on her clitoris?

He stopped what he was doing with the rigging and strolled across the deck towards her.

The fluid gait, sure-footed and purposeful and naturally predatory, put all her senses on high alert and turned the tingle in her clitoris to a definite hum.

'Yeah, the marina is on Paradise Island,' he said as he approached, his deep voice reverberating through her sternum. 'But we're anchored here till morning. It's too dangerous to try docking after sunset.'

The blush became radioactive as he studied her face.

'You slept okay?'

'Yes… Thank you.' Like the dead, for twelve solid hours.

The memory of him washing her hair, rubbing her naked skin with a towel and then blasting away all her other aches and pains made her heart jam her larynx.

'You're welcome.' His lips kicked up on one side, the sensual curve making the pit of her stomach sink into the toes of her deck shoes. 'Thanks for taking such good care of *The Sea Witch*,' he murmured.

Her knees trembled, her heart swelling painfully in her throat at the thought of how carefully he'd taken care of *her*.

Who was she kidding? This wasn't just about sex—not any more. Or at least not for her. The fear she thought she'd ridden into the dust kicked back up under her breastbone. She was falling for him again. And she didn't seem to be able to stop herself.

His gaze glided over the blush now setting fire to her cheeks.

'Is there a problem?' he asked.

She cleared her throat.

Backing down had never been the answer with Dane—she of all people ought to know that by now. Being coy or embarrassed now would be suicidal.

He'd left her feeling fragile and vulnerable and scared. Which almost certainly hadn't been his intention, because having her love him had never been part of Dane's agenda. She had to turn this around, make it clear that sex was the only thing they still shared… Or he'd know exactly how much last night had meant to her.

'Actually there is, and it has to do with your extremely altruistic use of your superpower,' she said, cutting straight to the chase.

His eyebrows hiked up his forehead.

'And how is that a problem?' he asked, but it wasn't really a question. The bite of sarcasm was unmistakable.

She'd annoyed him. This was good.

'Not a problem, exactly,' she said—as if she could dispute that, when he'd turned her into a quivering mess who had screamed his name out at top volume. 'But I would have been fine without it. I didn't need a pity orgasm.'

'A… A pity *what*?' Dane choked on the words as the tension in his gut gripped the base of his spine and turned his insides into a throbbing knot of need. 'What the *hell* are you talking about?'

'I didn't need you to take pity on me. When I said I wanted to make love to you, I planned to hold up my end of the bargain.'

'How?'

Anger surged through him. He'd been on a knife-edge all damn day, his emotions in turmoil, his hunger for her driving him nuts—but not nearly as much as his yearning to ask her to stay with him. Which was even more nuts. They'd grown up, gone their separate ways. They had nothing in common now—nothing that should make him want her this much. And now she was accusing him of… What?

He didn't even know what she was talking about. He'd given her the one thing he was capable of giving her without sinking them both any further into the mire. And she'd just told him she hadn't wanted that either.

'You were exhausted—barely awake,' he ground out. 'Because you'd been up all night doing *my* damn job for me.' Blood was pulsing into his crotch, making it hard for him to regulate his temper. Or his voice, which had risen to a shout they could probably hear back in Manhattan. 'You needed to sleep.'

Her cheeks flushed. 'So you decided to help me with that? Well, thanks a bunch. Next time I have insomnia I'll be sure to order up Dane's pity orgasm remedy.'

'You ungrateful little witch.'

Fury overwhelmed him. He'd wanted nothing more than to feel her come apart in his arms, make her moan and beg and say his name and *only* his name. But she'd been tired and emotional. And then she'd struck him right through the heart with that statement about him being the only one.

It had taken him a moment to figure out what she was telling him. But when he'd got it—when he'd realised he was the only guy she'd ever slept with—it had felt like watching his boat shoot across the finishing line of the America's Cup and being knifed in the gut all at the same time.

The burst of pride and pleasure and possessiveness had combined with the terror of wanting to hold on to her too much—throwing him all the way back to the grinding fear of his childhood. So he'd held back. He'd given her what she needed without taking what he wanted for himself.

And now she was telling him what he'd given her wasn't enough.

'Ungrateful?' She seared him with a look that could have cut through lead. 'Don't you get it? I don't *want* to be grateful. I'm not a charity case. I want to be your equal. In bed as well as out of it.'

He grabbed her arms, dragged her close. 'You want to participate this time? I don't have a problem with that.'

She thrust her hands into his hair, digging her fingers into the short strands to haul his mouth to within a whisper of hers. The desire sparking in her eyes turned the mossy green to emerald fire.

'Good, because neither do I,' she said, then planted her lips on his.

The kiss went from wild to insane in a heartbeat. The need that had been churning in his gut all day surged out of control as he boosted her into his arms.

He couldn't keep her, but he could sure as hell ensure she never forgot him.

Rough stubble abraded Xanthe's palms as her whole body sang the 'Hallelujah Chorus.' Her breasts flattened against his chest and their mouths duelled in a wild, uncontrollable battle for supremacy.

His tongue thrust deep, dominant and demanding, parrying with hers as wildfire burned through her system. She hooked her legs round his waist, clinging on as he staggered down to the cabin with her wrapped around him like a limpet.

Barging through the door, he flung her onto the bed. She lurched onto her knees, watching as he kicked off his trunks. The thick erection bounced free, hard and long and ready for her.

Everything inside her melted. All the anger and agony and the terrifying vulnerability was flushed away on a wave of longing so intense she thought she might pass out.

This was all they had ever been able to have. She had to remember that.

He grabbed the front of her T-shirt and hauled her up, ripping the thin cotton down the middle. His lips crushed hers, his tongue claiming her mouth again in a soul-numbing kiss. Drawing back, he helped her struggle out of the rest of her clothing, his groans matched by the pants of her breathing.

At last they were naked, the feel of his skin warm and firm, tempered by the steely strength beneath. Muscles rip-

pled with tension beneath her stroking palms. He cupped
her sex, his fingers finding the heart of her with unerring accuracy. She bucked off the bed, his touch too much
for her tender flesh. He circled with his thumb, knowing
just how to caress her, to draw out her pleasure to breaking point. His lips clamped to a nipple and drew it deep
into his mouth.

Sensations collided, then crashed through her. She
sobbed as the blistering climax hit—hard and fast and
not enough.

'I need you inside me,' she sobbed, desperate to forget about the aching emptiness that had tormented her
for so long.

He rose up, grasped her hips, positioned himself to
plunge deep. But as he pressed at her entrance he froze
suddenly. Then dropped his forehead to hers and swore
loudly. 'I don't have any protection. This wasn't supposed
to happen.'

His dark gaze met hers, and her brutal arousal was reflected in those blindingly blue eyes. She blurted out the
truth. 'It's okay. As long as we're both clean. I won't get
pregnant.'

'You're on the pill?'

The gruff assumption reached inside her and ripped
open the gaping wound she'd spent years denying even
existed. She slammed down on the wrenching pain. And
on the urge to tell him the terrible truth of how much she'd
lost by loving him.

Don't tell him. You can't.

'Yes,' she lied.

He kissed her, his groan of relief echoing in her sternum, feeding her own need back to her. Then he angled
her hips and thrust deep.

Her body arched, and the sensation of fullness was overwhelming as she struggled to adjust to the thick intrusion.

He began to move, driving into her in a devastating rhythm that dug at that spot inside only he had ever touched.

'Let go, Red. I want to see you come again. Just for me.'

The possessive tone, the desperation in his demand felt too real, too frightening. She'd given him everything once. She couldn't afford to give it all to him again.

'I can't.'

'Yes, you can.' He found her clitoris with his thumb. Swollen and aching.

The perfect touch drove her back towards the peak with staggering speed. Her whole body clamped down, euphoria driving through the fear. His eyes met hers, the intensity in their blue depths reaching out and touching her heart.

She gripped broad shoulders, the muscles tensed beneath her fingertips as she tried to shield herself against the intense wave of emotion. But it rose up anyway, shaking her to the core as her body soared past that last barrier to plunge into the abyss.

He shouted out, the sound muffled against her neck, as he emptied his seed into her womb.

She came to moments later, his body heavy on hers. The bright, beautiful wave of afterglow receded, to be replaced by the shattering feeling of an emotion she hadn't wanted to feel.

Lifting up on his elbows, he brushed the hair back from her brow. The shuttered look in his eyes made her shudder with reaction. The feeling of him still intimately linked to her was too much.

'Are you okay?' he said.

The wariness in his expression made her heart feel heavy. How could he protect himself so easily when she'd never been able to protect herself in return?

One rough palm caressed her cheek and she turned

away from it, feeling the sting of tears behind her eyelids at this glimpse of tenderness.

This was just sex for him. That was all it had ever been.

'Never better.' She pressed her palms against his chest, suddenly feeling trapped. And fragile. 'I need to clean up.'

He rolled off her without complaint. But as she tried to scramble off the bed firm fingers caught her wrist, holding her in place. 'Xan, don't.'

She glanced over her shoulder. 'Don't what?'

'Don't run off.'

He tugged her back towards him and slung an arm around her shoulder, and—weak and feeble woman that she was—she let him draw her under his arm until her head was nestled against his chest, her palm resting over his heart, which was still beating double time with hers.

His thumb caressed her cheek, and the rumble of his voice in her ear drew her in deeper. 'Why has there never been anyone else?'

She considered denying it. If he'd sounded smug or arrogant she probably would have, but all he sounded was guarded.

'I wish I hadn't told you that.' She sighed. 'It was a weak moment. Can't you forget it?'

'Nope,' he murmured into her hair.

It occurred to her that he probably didn't want *this* burden any more than he'd wanted any of the others she'd thrust upon him.

'If it's any consolation,' he said, his fingers threading through her hair as his deep voice rumbled against her ear, 'there hasn't been anyone important for me either.'

Her heartbeat hitched into an uneven rhythm. Ten years ago that admission would have had her bursting with happiness. She would have taken it as a sign. A sign that she meant something to him. Something beyond the obvious. But she wasn't that optimistic any more. Or as much of a pushover. And she couldn't risk letting herself believe again. Because it had already cost her far too much.

'I guess we've both been pretty busy...' She tried to smile, but the crooked tilt of her lips felt weak and forced.

'I guess,' he said.

The husky agreement let them both off the hook. Until he spoke again.

'That scar—low under your belly button. How did you get it?'

She stilled, unable to talk, struggling to stop her eyes filling with unshed tears.

'Was it the baby?'

The hint of hesitation in his voice made her heart pound even harder, emotion closing her throat.

She nodded.

His arm tightened.

She needed to talk about this. To tell him all the things she'd been robbed of the chance to tell him then.

Perhaps this was why it had always felt as if there was more between them? She clung to the thought. So much of their past remained unresolved. Maybe if she took this opportunity to remedy that they could go their separate ways without so many regrets?

All she had to do was get enough breath into her lungs to actually speak.

Dane's heart thudded against his collarbone. He could feel the tension in her body, her silent struggle to draw a full breath. He'd known it had been bad for her. He hadn't meant to bring all that agony back. But the question had slipped out, his desire to know as desperate as his desire to comfort her. And for once his anger at her father was nowhere near as huge as his anger with himself.

Whatever the old bastard had done after the fact, Dane

was the one who'd stormed out of that motel room and hadn't contacted her for days.

So when all was said and done it was down to him that he hadn't been there when she'd needed him. However much he had tried to put the blame on her old man.

'Can you talk about it?' he asked, the husk of his voice barely audible.

She nodded again and cleared her throat. The raw sound scraped over his temper and dug into the guilt beneath. When her voice finally came it wasn't loud, but it was steady.

'I have a scar because they had to operate. I was bleeding heavily and they…'

She hesitated for a moment, and the slight hitch in her breathing was like a knife straight into his heart.

'They couldn't get a heartbeat.'

Hell.

He settled his hand on her head, tugged her closer. The urge to lend her his strength impossible to deny, however useless it might be now.

'I'm so damn sorry, Red. I should never have insisted on marrying you and taking you to that damn motel. It was a dive. You would have been okay if you'd stayed on daddy's estate…'

She pulled out of his arms, her eyes fierce and full of raw feeling as she silenced him with a finger across his lips.

'Stop it!'

Her voice sounded choked. And he could see the sheen of tears in her eyes, crucifying him even more.

'That's not true. It would have happened regardless. And I wanted to be with *you*.'

He captured her finger, his heart battering his ribs so hard now he was astonished that it didn't jump right out of his chest.

'He was right about me, though,' he said.

'What was he right about?' She seemed puzzled—as if she really didn't get it.

'He called me a wharf rat. And that's exactly what I was.'

He pushed the words out, and tried to feel relieved that he'd finally told her the truth. The one thing he'd been so desperate to keep from her all those years ago.

'I grew up in a trailer park that was one step away from being the town dump. My old man was a drunk who got his kicks from beating the crap out of me, so I hung around the marina to get away from him until I got big enough to hit back.'

Even if the squalid truth about who he really was and where he'd come from could never undo all the stuff he'd done wrong, at least it would go some way to show her how truly sorry he was—for all the pain he'd caused.

'If that doesn't make me a wharf rat, I don't know what does.'

Xanthe clutched the sheet covering her breasts, which were heaving now as if she'd just run a marathon. Her mind reeled from Dane's statement. So it *was* his father who had caused those terrible scars on his back. She'd always suspected as much. Sympathy twisted in her stomach—not just for that boy, but for the look in Dane's eyes now that told her he actually *believed* what he was saying.

How could she have got it so wrong? She had believed his silence about himself and his past had been the result of arrogance and pride and indifference, when what it had really been was defensiveness.

'I'm sorry your father hurt you like that.'

And what did she do with the evidence that it still hurt her so much to know he'd been abused?

'Don't feel sorry for that little bastard,' he said. 'He didn't deserve it.'

Of course he did. But how could she tell him that without giving away the truth—that a part of her had never stopped loving that boy.

'My father called you a wharf rat because he was an unconscionable snob, Dane. It had nothing to do with you.' That much at least she could tell him.

'He loved you, Xan, and he wanted to protect you. There's nothing wrong with that,' he said with a weary resignation. 'If I could have...' His gaze strayed to her belly and the thin white scar left behind by the surgeon's incision. 'I would have protected our baby the same way.'

The admission cut through her, and emotions that were already far too close to the surface threatened to spill over.

God, how could she have accused him of not caring about their child when it was obvious now that he might have cared too much? Enough to blame himself for the things that her father—both their fathers—had done.

She bit down on the feelings threatening to choke her.

'That's where you're wrong. He didn't love me. He thought of me as his property.'

How come she had never acknowledged that until now? All those years she'd worked her backside off to please her father, to get his approval, never once questioning what he had ever done to deserve it.

'I was an investment. The daughter who was going to marry a man of *his* choosing who would take over Carmichael's when he was gone. My falling in love...having a child by a man he disapproved of and who refused to bow down to the mighty Charles Carmichael...they were the real reasons he hated you.'

Dane cupped her cheek, the cool touch making her heart ache even more.

'I guess we both got a raw deal when the good Lord gave out daddies.'

She let out a half laugh, and the tears that had refused to fall for so long threatened to cascade over her lids.

She settled back into his arms, so he wouldn't see them. 'The baby was a little boy,' she said, determined to concentrate on their past and not on their future, because they didn't have one.

'For real?'

She heard awe as well as sadness in his tone.

'I thought you should know.'

Their baby, after all, was the only thing that had brought them together. Surely this chance to say goodbye to him properly would finally allow them to part.

'I'm glad you told me,' he murmured, his fingers linking with hers, his thumb rubbing over her wrist where her pulse hammered.

She hiccupped, her breath hurting again, the tears flowing freely down her cheeks now.

'Hell, Red, don't cry,' he said, kissing the top of her head and gathering her close. 'It's all over now.'

She splayed her fingers over the solid mass of his pectoral muscles, feeling exhausted and hollowed out. Because she knew it *wasn't* over. Not for her. And she was becoming increasingly terrified that it never had been.

CHAPTER SIXTEEN

XANTHE WOKE THE following morning feeling tired and
confused.

Dane had woken her twice in the night. The skill and
urgency of his lovemaking had been impossible to resist.
He'd caught her unawares, that clever thumb stroking her
to climax while she was still drifting on dreams... She
stretched, feeling the aches and pains caused by the energy of their lovemaking.

Last night's revelations had been painful for them both,
but getting that glimpse of the boy she'd once known and
finally knowing more of what had haunted him felt important.

The boat swayed and she heard a bump. Glancing out of
the window, she could see the masts of another boat. They
had arrived at the marina on Paradise Island.

Getting out of bed, she slung on capri pants and one of
Dane's T-shirts and poured herself a cup of coffee from
the pot Dane had already brewed. As she loaded it up with
cream and sugar she tried to deal with all the confusing
emotions spiralling through her system.

She was in trouble. Big trouble. That much was obvious. And it wasn't just a result of last night's confidences,
the hot sex, or even the tumultuous day spent battling the
elements together. This problem went right back to her
decision a week ago to bring Dane those divorce papers
in person.

Every single decision she'd made since had proved

one thing. However smart and focused and rational and sensible she thought she'd become in the last ten years, and however determined never to let any man have control over her life, one man always had. And she'd been in denial about it.

But she wasn't that fanciful girl any more—that girl who had loved too easily and without discrimination. She was a grown woman who knew the score. She had to bring that maturity to bear now.

She poured the dregs of her barely touched coffee down the sink.

Taking a deep but unsteady breath, she headed up on deck. Dane stood on the dock, tall and indomitable and relaxed, talking to a younger man in board shorts and a bill cap. Her heart jolted as it had so often in the past, but this time she didn't try to deny the profound effect he had on her.

He'd shaved, revealing the delicious dent in his chin which she could remember licking last night.

She shook off the erotic thought.

Not helping.

Dane spotted her standing on the deck and broke off his conversation. His hot gaze skimmed down her body as he walked towards her.

'Morning,' he said.

'Hi.'

She stood her ground as he climbed onto the boat, the heat in his eyes sending her senses reeling.

'I should head home today,' she said, as casually as she could, and held her breath, waiting for any flicker of acknowledgement that what had happened last night was a big deal. 'I thought I'd check out the flights from Nassau.'

She silently cursed the way her heart clenched at his patient perusal.

'Why don't you stay for one more night?' he said at

last. 'I've got a suite booked at the Paradise Resort before I head back to Manhattan tomorrow.'

She sank her hands into the back pockets of her capri pants to stop them trembling and control the sweet hit of adrenaline kicking under her breastbone. What was making her so giddy? It was hardly a declaration of undying love.

'Why would you want to do that?' she asked, determined to accept the casual invitation in the spirit it was offered.

He gave her a long look, and for a terrible moment she thought he could see what she was trying so hard to hide—the panic, the longing, and all those foolish dreams which had failed to die.

But then his lips lifted in a sensual smile and heat fired down to her core. 'Because we've both been through hell in the last couple of days and I figure we've earned a reward.'

He touched a knuckle to her cheek, skimmed it down to touch the throbbing pulse in her neck. The snap and crackle of sexual awareness went haywire.

'I could show you the town,' he added. 'Nassau's a cool city.'

'But I don't have anything to wear,' she said, still trying to weigh her options.

This wasn't a big deal. After the enforced intimacy of the boat, the intensity of emotion brought on by the storm, not to mention the lack of sleep and the stresses and strains of what had happened so long ago still hanging between them, why shouldn't he suggest one more night of fun? After all, they'd had precious little fun in their acquaintance. She had to take this at face value. Not read more into it than was actually there.

'You're not going to need much,' he said, his smile loaded with sensual promise. 'I was kidding about showing you around. We probably won't get out of the suite.'

She laughed, the wicked look in his eyes going some way to relieve the tension. 'What happens to *The Sea Witch* once you've gone back to Manhattan?' She glanced back at the boat, feeling a little melancholy at the thought of leaving it.

He nodded towards the young man still standing on the dock. 'Joe's my delivery skipper—he'll take it back to Boston.'

His hand cupped the back of her neck, sending sensation zinging all over her body.

'Now, quit stalling—do we have a deal or don't we?'

She swallowed heavily, her heart thudding against her throat. She could say no. She probably *should* say no. But having his gaze searching her face, his expression tense as he waited for her answer... She knew she didn't want to say no.

The man was intoxicating...like a dangerously addictive drug. She needed to be careful—conscious of all the emotions that had tripped her up in the past—but she was a stronger, wiser woman now, not a seventeen-year-old girl. And while she was riding the high had there ever been anything more exhilarating?

He tugged her into his arms, his lips inches from hers, the fire in his eyes incendiary. 'Say yes, Red. You know you want to.'

'Yes,' she whispered.

His lips covered hers and she let the leap of arousal mask the idiotic burst of optimism telling her that this might be more than she'd hoped it could be.

'Slow down, Dane. I'm stuffed. I don't want to burst the seams on this dress.'

Xanthe tried to sound stern as Dane clasped her hand and led her past the quaint, brightly coloured storefronts of Nassau's downtown area. The colonnades and verandas announced the island city's colonial heritage, while SUVs vied for space on the tourist-choked streets with horse-drawn carriages.

After four days on the yacht, the four-course meal in the luxurious surroundings of a Michelin-starred restaurant had been sensational, but the truth was she'd barely managed to swallow a bite. The potent hunger in his eyes every time he looked at her had turned her insides to mush.

She'd been riding a wave of endorphins since their bargain on the boat—but was determined not to let his invitation get the better of her. Then something had shifted when he had appeared in their enormous suite at the resort on Paradise Island looking breathtakingly handsome in a dark evening suit and told her he was taking her out on a date.

After all the sex they'd shared the suggestion shouldn't have seemed so sweet. So intimate. So overwhelming. But somehow it had.

'And you bursting out of your dress is supposed to be a problem?'

His eyes dipped to the hem of the designer dress she'd picked from the array of garments he'd had sent up to their suite. The incendiary gaze seared the skin of her thighs, already warmed by the Caribbean night.

'It *is* on a public street,' she shot back, struggling to quell the erratic beat of her heart.

The evening had been a revelation in some ways—Dane had played the gentleman with remarkable ease—but it had been only more disturbing in others.

Because getting a glimpse into his life now, and seeing the level of luxury he could afford, had only made her more aware of how far he'd come. He'd always been tenacious and determined, but she couldn't help her fierce wave of pride at the thought of how hard he'd worked to leave that boy behind and escape the miserable poverty of his childhood.

She shouldn't have been surprised by the exclusiveness of the five-star resort hotel on Paradise Island, or by the lavish bungalow that looked out onto a private white sand beach and the sleek black power boat he'd piloted to take them into Nassau—especially after seeing the penthouse apartment Dane owned in Manhattan—but, like Nassau itself, which was a heady mix of old world elegance, new world commerce and Caribbean laissez-faire, Dane seemed like a complex contradiction.

His animal magnetism was not dimmed in the slightest by this new layer of wealth and sophistication. Even in an elegant tuxedo, the raw, rugged masculinity of the man still shone through. The tailored jacket stretched tight over wide shoulders now, as he led her back towards the dock where the speedboat was moored.

'I've always thought clothes are overrated,' he teased, helping her into the boat. 'Especially on you.'

He shrugged off the jacket and dumped it in the back of the boat, then tugged off the tie, too, and stuffed it into the pocket of his suit trousers.

'I don't care how damn fancy that restaurant is,' he said, and the vehemence in his tone was surprising. 'Nothing's worth getting trussed-up like a chicken for.'

'You didn't like the food?' she asked.

'The food was great—but it was way too stuffy in there.'

He smiled at her, and the glint of white against his swarthy skin was a potent reminder of the boy. Wicked and reckless and hungry—for so much.

But was he hungry for *her*? In anything other than the most basic way?

He switched on the engine and the boat roared to life, kicking at the soft swell as he directed the boat away from the dock and into the water.

She glanced back at the fading lights of Bay Street, the wind pulling tendrils of hair out of her chignon as Dane handled the powerful boat with ease. And tried not to let the question torture her.

She mustn't get ahead of herself—read too much into this night.

She was concentrating so hard on getting everything into perspective that she didn't register that they weren't returning to the resort until the boat slowed as it approached a beach on the opposite side of the bay. A cluster of fairy lights and the bass beat of music covered by the lilting rumble of laughter and conversation announced a bar in the distance.

Dane released the throttle and let the boat drift into a small wooden dock lit by torches. Jumping out, he secured the line.

'Where are we?' she asked accepting his outstretched hand as he hauled her off the boat.

'An old hang-out of mine,' he said as she stepped onto the worn uneven boards.

He tugged her into his arms. Awareness sizzled through her system, but alongside it was the brutal tug of something more. Something that made her feel young and carefree and cherished—something she had been certain she would never feel again.

'I'm taking you dancing,' he said.

'You…? Really…?' Her breath choked off in her throat, and the panicked leap of her heart was almost as scary as the thundering beat of her pulse.

Was this another coincidence? Like the name of the boat? Surely it had to be.

But the wonder of the only other time they'd been dancing echoed in her heart regardless. The dark shapes of the cars in the car park…the strains of a country and Western band coming from the bar where they'd been refused entry when they'd spotted Dane's fake ID… Dane's strong arms directing her movements as he'd shown her the intricate steps and counter-steps of a Texas line dance and they'd laughed together every time she stepped on his toes.

And the giddy rush of adoration as they eventually settled into a slow dance on the cracked asphalt.

She'd been so hopelessly in love with him then.

She tried to thrust the memory aside as he led her down the dock, and ignored the swoop of her heart as he swung her into his arms to cross the sand.

She let out a laugh, though, desperate to live in the moment. Was this fate, testing her resolve?

Surely it was just the Caribbean evening, the promise of dancing the night away with such a forceful, stimulating man again and all the hot sex that lay in their immediate future that was making her as giddy as a teenager.

Dane's thoughts and feelings were still an enigma. And *her* thoughts and feelings had matured. She mustn't invest too much until she knew more.

She clung on to her resolve as he held her close in the moonlight, igniting her senses as they bumped and ground together to the sound of the vintage reggae band.

But as he guided the boat back towards Paradise Island her heart battered her ribcage, and excitement burst inside her like a firework when he murmured, 'I hope that made up for our wedding night.'

So he had remembered that treasured memory of dancing in the parking lot, too.

As they entered the suite he banded an arm round her waist and hauled her into his body.

'That's got to be the longest evening of my life.'

Breathing in the scent of salt and cedarwood soap which clung to him like a potent aphrodisiac, she spread her hands over his six-pack, felt his abs tense as arousal slammed into her system. The way it always did.

Everything seemed so right this time, so perfect.

'I know,' she said.

His nose touched hers. 'I want to be inside you.'

The heat in his gaze burned away the last of her fears as her fingertips brushed the thick arousal already tenting the fabric of his trousers.

'I know.'

Gripping her fingers, he headed towards the bedroom, hauling her behind him.

And she let her heart soar.

Dane didn't question the frantic need driving him to claim her, possess her. Because he couldn't. Not any more.

The sight of her in the designer dress, its sleek material sliding over slender curves, watching the sultry knowledge in her mermaid's eyes, had been driving him wild all evening. And the last vestiges of the civilised, sensible guy he'd become had been blown to smithereens—the way they had been every day, one crucial piece at a time, ever since she'd marched into his office a week ago.

This hunger wasn't just lust. He knew that—had known it for days, if he was honest with himself. And for that reason he should just let her go. But he couldn't.

Because she was his—any way he could get her. And the desire to mark her as his, keep her near him, had become overwhelming.

He'd insisted on taking her out to dinner, then tortured them both with a slow dance at the Soca Shack to prove that he could hold it together. That this didn't have to mean more than it should. But he'd felt as if he were holding a moonbeam in his arms as she moved against him—so bright, so beautiful, and still so far out of reach—and it had finally tipped him right over the edge of sanity.

He slammed open the first door he came to—the bathroom suite. Swinging her round, he pressed her up against the tiles, filled his hands with those lush breasts. He sucked her through the shimmering silk of her gown, groaning against the damp fabric when he found her braless.

She bucked against him, her response instant and oh-so-gratifying when he tugged the straps off her shoulders, freeing her full breasts.

He kicked off his shoes and pushed down his pants, his gaze fixed on the ripe peaks of her breasts, reddened from his mouth.

She found his erection, but he dragged her hand away.

'Lose the dress,' he said as he tore off his shirt, and the gruff demand in his voice made the light of challenge spark in her eyes.

'I don't take orders,' she said, sounding indignant, but he could see the hot light of her lust. She understood this game as much as he did—even if it didn't feel like a game any more.

'Lose the dress or it gets ripped off.'

'Oh, for…'

She shimmied out of the clinging silk to reveal the lacy panties he adored. Palming her bottom, he lifted her onto the vanity unit, shoving her toiletries off the countertop. The bag crashed to the floor, scattering her stuff across the tiles.

Need careered through his system along with pain and possession—the same damn combination that had tortured him a lifetime ago.

She placed trembling palms on his chest. 'Dane, slow down.'

'In a minute,' he said, the need to have her, to claim her, powering through him like a freight train.

He ripped the delicate panties. And plunged his fingers into the hot, wet heart of her at last.

She sobbed, gasped and grasped his biceps. He stroked the slick flesh, knowing just how and where to touch her to send her spiralling into a stunning orgasm. He watched her go over, and the powerful emotion coiling inside him—part fear, part euphoria—made his erection throb harder against her thigh.

'You ready for me?' he demanded, barely able to speak as need tormented him.

She nodded, dazed. He sank into her to the hilt, the euphoria bursting inside him as she clasped him tight.

Yes. If this was the only way he could have her, the only way he could make her his, he was going to show her that this was one thing no other man would ever be able to give her.

She clung to his arms as he thrust hard and dug deep, her muscles milking him as she started to crest again. The hunger gripped him, as painful as it was exquisite. He shouted out as she sobbed her release into his neck. And his seed burst into the hot, wet grip of her body.

The wish that they could create another baby and then she'd *have* to be his was savage and insane. Just the way it had been all those years ago.

Reality returned as he came down, tasting the salty sweat on her neck, and the first jabs of shame and panic assaulted him. Hell, he'd taken her like an animal. He should have held back. He didn't want her to know how much he needed her.

He eased out of her. Felt her flinch.

'Did I hurt you?'

She was trembling. 'No, I'm fine.'

The words pulsed in his skull. Mocking him and making him ache at the same time. He forced an easy smile to his lips and turned on the hot jets of the shower. Steam rose as he checked the temperature.

'Let's get cleaned up.'

He dragged her under the spray with him. But as he washed her hair, feeling the strands like wet silk through his fingers, that need consumed him all over again. To hold her, to have her, to make her stay.

And the visceral fear that had lurked inside him for so long roared into life and chilled him to the bone.

'Is everything okay?'

Xanthe watched Dane leave the shower cubicle and grab a towel, feeling his sudden withdrawal like a physical blow.

He wrapped the towel round his hips. 'Sure,' he said, but he didn't turn towards her as he bent to pick up the toiletries scattered over the floor.

The joy that had been so fresh and new and exciting a moment ago, when he'd taken her with such hunger and purpose, faded. She turned off the shower and pulled one of the fluffy bath sheets off the vanity unit to wrap around herself, suddenly feeling exposed and so needy.

Had she completely misjudged everything? All the signals she'd thought he'd been sending her this evening that there might be more? That his feelings matched her own?

'I'll do it.' She stepped towards him to help pick up her toiletries, but he shrugged off her outstretched hand.

'I made the mess. I'll clean it up.' He placed the bag on the vanity unit, dumping the last of its scattered contents inside.

The strangely impersonal tone sent a shudder through her. She wrapped the towel tighter. Then lifted another towel to dry her hair.

'Where are the birth control pills?'

The clattering beat of her heart jumped into an uneasy rhythm at the flat question. 'Sorry?'

'Your pills? You said you were on the pill,' he prompted. 'I don't see them here.'

He'd checked her toiletries for contraceptive pills? Agony twisted in the pit of her stomach. Slicing through the last of the joy.

'I'm not on the pill.'

His brows arrowed down in a confused frown. 'So what type of birth control are you using?'

She could see the accusation in his eyes, hear the brittle demand in his voice, and all the blurred edges came together to create a shocking and utterly terrifying truth.

She'd been wrong—so wrong—all over again.

'I'm not using any,' she said.

'What the hell—?'

He looked so shocked she felt the hole in the pit of her stomach ripped open—until it was the same gaping wound that had crippled her once before.

He marched towards her and gripped her arm. 'What kind of game are you playing? Are you *nuts*? I could have gotten you pregnant again.'

She tugged her arm free, the accusation in his face cutting into her insides. How stupid she had been to keep this a secret. When it was the thing that had grounded her for so long. Stopped all those stupid romantic dreams from destroying her.

'I'm not going to get accidentally pregnant. Because I can't.'

She walked past him, suddenly desperate to get away from him. She needed to have some clothes on and to get out of here.

'Wait—what are you saying?' He followed her out of the bathroom and dragged her round to face him.

She thrust her forearms against him. 'Let me go. I want to leave.'

She tried to wrestle free, but he wouldn't let go.

'You need to tell me what you mean.'

She could feel the storm welling inside her, tearing at her insides the way it had for so many years while she'd struggled to come to terms with the truth. But she didn't want to break in front of him. She had to be in control, to be measured, not let him see how much this had dev-astated her when she told him the details—or he would know she'd fallen for him again. And the one thing she could not bear was his pity.

'I told you—I can't get pregnant.'

'Why can't you?'

The probing question was too much.

'What gives you the right to ask me that?'

'Hell, Red, just tell me why you can't have another child. I want to know.'

The storm churned in her stomach, more violent than the one they'd survived together, and tears were stinging her eyes.

'Because I'm barren. Because I waited too long in that motel room to call my father. I was sure that you would come for me. I was haemorrhaging. There was an infec-tion. Understand?'

She headed towards the lounge, frantic now.

'I need to leave. I should have left yesterday.'

This time she held back the tears with an iron will. Pity, responsibility, sex—those were the only things Dane had ever had to give. She could see that so clearly now.

'Why didn't you tell me?' His voice sounded strained.

'Because it happened and now it's over,' she said.

She got dressed while he watched. Grateful when he didn't approach her. She was stronger now. She could get through this. She wasn't the bright, naive girl she'd once been—someone who'd come close to being destroyed by her past. She could never let him have that power over her again.

Shoving the few meagre items she had brought with her into her briefcase, she turned to look at him.

He stood in the doorway, the towel hooked around his waist, his expression frozen and unreadable.

'You know what's really idiotic?' she said. 'For a moment there I thought we could make this work. That some-how we could overcome all the mistakes from our past, all the things we did wrong, and make it right.'

'What?'

He looked so stunned she hesitated—but only for a mo-ment. This was a ludicrous pipe dream. It always had been and always would be.

'It was a stupid idea,' she said. 'Like before.'

She wanted to be angry with him, so she could fill the great gaping hole in the pit of her stomach. But she couldn't. Because all she could feel was an agonising sense of loss.

'Damn it, Red. I'm sorry. I didn't mean to hurt you.'

He approached her and lifted his hand, but she stiffened and stepped back.

'Can't you see that just makes it even more painful?' she said.

He let his hand drop. His expression wasn't frozen any more. She could see confusion, regret, maybe even sad-ness, but she steeled herself against the traitorous wobble in her heart that made her want to believe they still had a chance.

She pulled the papers out of the briefcase. The papers she'd come all this way to make him sign in order to end their marriage, without ever realising that what she had really wanted to do was mend it.

'You expected me to trust you, Dane. And you got angry when I didn't. But despite all the confusion with these—' she lifted the papers and dropped them on the coffee table '—the truth is I do trust you. And I think I always did. Be-cause I never stopped loving you. That's why it's so ironic that you were never able to trust me.'

His jaw flexed. His gaze was bleak. But he didn't try to stop her again as she walked out the door.

She felt herself crumpling. The pain was too much. But

she held her body ramrod-straight, her spine stiff, until she climbed into a cab to take her to the airport.

She collapsed onto the seat, wrenching sobs shuddering through her body.

'You all right, ma'am?' the cab driver called through the grille.

'Yes, it's okay. I'm okay,' she murmured as she scrubbed away the tears with her fist and tried to make herself believe it.

She *would* be okay. Eventually. The way she had been before. Dane was a part of her past. A painful, poignant part of her past. She'd just forgotten that for a few days.

He'd never been a bad man. He had simply never been able to love her. Not the way she needed to be loved.

Once she was back in the UK—back where she belonged, doing what she loved—everything would be okay again.

But as they headed to the dock, and the boat to Nassau, even the promise of a fifteen-hour workday and her luxury apartment overlooking the Thames couldn't ease the lonely longing in her battered heart—for something that had only ever been real in her foolish romantic imagination.

CHAPTER SEVENTEEN

'BILL SAYS THEY'RE ready to sign off on the Calhoun deal. He's checked through the contracts and everything looks good.'

'Right. Thanks, Angela,' Xanthe murmured as she studied the small pleasure boat making its way up the Thames.

July sunlight sparkled off the muddy water, reminding her of...

'Is everything okay, Miss Carmichael?'

Xanthe swung round, detaching her gaze from the view out of the window of her office in Whitehall to find her PA studying her with a concerned frown on her face. The same concerned frown Xanthe had seen too often in the last two weeks. Ever since she'd returned from the Bahamas.

Get your head back in the game.

'Yes, of course.' She walked back to her desk, struggling to pull herself out of her latest daydream.

Everything *wasn't* okay. She wasn't sleeping, she'd barely eaten a full meal in two weeks, and she felt tired and listless and hollow inside.

Maybe it was just overwork. After the... She paused to think of an adequate word... After the *difficult* trip to the Caribbean, she'd thrown herself back into work as soon as she'd returned. She'd wanted to be busy, to feel useful, to feel as if her life had purpose, direction—all those things she'd lacked so long ago when she'd allowed herself to fall into love with Dane Redmond the first time.

But work wasn't the panacea it had once been.

She missed him—not just his body and all the wonderful things he could do to hers, but his energy, his charisma, the dogged will, even the arrogance that she'd once persuaded herself she hated. Even their arguments held a strange sort of nostalgia that made no sense.

Their trip had only been five days in total. Her life, her outlook on life, couldn't change in five days. This was just another emotional blip that she would get over the way she'd got over all the others.

But why couldn't she stop thinking about him? About the feeling of having his arms around her as she wept for their baby? The force field of raw charisma that had energised everything about their encounter and made everything since her return seem dull and lifeless in comparison?

And that look on his face when she'd told him of her foolish hopes… He'd looked astonished.

Every night since her return she'd lain awake trying to analyse that expression. Had there been disbelief there? Disdain? Or had there been hope?

Angela slipped a pile of paperwork onto the desk blotter. Then pointed at the signature field on the back page. 'You just need to sign here and here, and I'll get it back to Contracts.'

Xanthe picked up the gold pen she used to sign all her deals. Then hesitated, her mind foggy with fatigue and confusion. 'Remind me again—what's the Calhoun deal?'

She heard Angela's intake of breath.

When her PA finally spoke, her voice was heavy with concern. 'It's the deal you've been working on for three months…to invest in a new terminal in Belfast.'

Xanthe wrote her signature, the black ink swimming before her eyes, the tears threatening anew.

Good Lord, why couldn't she stop going over the same ground, reanalysing everything Dane had said and done? Trying to find an excuse to contact him again?

This was pathetic. *She* was pathetic.

The intercom on her desk buzzed. She clicked it on as Angela gathered up the documents and began putting them back into the file. 'Yes, Clare?' she said, addressing the new intern Angela had been training all week.

'There's a gentleman here to see you, Miss Carmichael. He says he has some papers for you. He's very insistent. Can I send him in?'

'Tell him to leave them outside.' She clicked off the intercom. 'Could you handle it, whatever it is, Angela? I think I'm going home.'

'Of course, Miss Carmichael.'

But as Angela opened the door Xanthe's head shot up at the low voice she could hear outside her office, arguing with the intern. Her mind blurred along with her vision at the sight of Dane striding into her office.

'Excuse me, sir, you can't come in here. Miss Car—'

'The hell I can't.'

He walked past Angela, who was trying and failing to guard the doorway.

'We need to talk, Red.'

Xanthe stood up, locking her knees when her legs refused to cooperate. A surge of heat twisted with a leap of joy, making her body feel weightless. She buried it deep. Shock and confusion overwhelmed her when he marched to the desk, his muscular body rippling with tension beneath a light grey designer suit and crisp white shirt.

'What are you doing here?'

Hadn't she made it clear she never wanted to see him again? Couldn't he respect at least *one* of her wishes? She couldn't say goodbye all over again—it wasn't fair.

Pulling a bunch of papers from the inside pocket of his suit, he slapped them down on the desk. 'I've come to tell you I'm not signing these.'

'Shall I call Security?' Angela asked, her face going red.

If only it could be that simple.

'That's okay, Angela.'

'I'm her husband,' Dane growled at the same time.

Angela's face grew redder. 'Excuse me…?'

'I'll handle this,' Xanthe reiterated. Somehow she *would* find the strength to kick him out of her life again. 'Please leave and shut the door.'

The door closed behind her PA as heat she didn't want to feel rushed all over her body and her heart clutched tight in her chest. She glanced down at the crumpled papers. Their divorce papers. The ones she'd tried to make him sign to protect her company.

'If you've quite finished bullying my staff, maybe you'd like to explain to me why you found it necessary to come barging in here to tell me something I already know.'

She'd had new papers drawn up as soon as she'd returned. Papers without the codicil.

'Dissolving our marriage is merely a formality now,' she said, trying to keep the panic out of her voice. She couldn't argue about this now—not when she was still so close to breaking point. 'In case your lawyer hasn't told you, I've filed new papers,' she added. Maybe this was simply a misunderstanding. 'There's nothing in them you should find objectionable. I trust you not to sue for the shares. You've got what you wanted.'

'I know about the new papers. I'm not signing those either.'

'But… Why not?' Was he trying to torture her now? Prolong her agony? What had she done to deserve this punishment?

'Because I don't want to,' he said, but he didn't look belligerent or annoyed any more. His features had softened. 'Because you matter to me.'

'No, I don't—not really,' she said, suddenly feeling desperately weary. And sad.

Did he think she wanted his pity? Maybe he was trying to tell her he cared about her. But it was far too little and way too late.

'Don't tell me how I feel, Red.'

'Then please don't call me Red.'

The sweet nickname sliced through all her defences, reminding her of how little she'd once been willing to settle for. And how she'd nearly persuaded herself to do so again.

He walked round the desk, crowding into her space. She stiffened and tried to step back, but got caught between the chair and the desk when his finger reached out to touch a curl of hair.

'I came here to ask you to forgive me,' he said. 'For being such a monumental jerk about pretty much everything.'

She drew her head back, her heart shattering, the panic rising into her throat. 'I can't do this again. You have to leave.'

Dane looked at Xanthe's face. Her valiant expression was a mask of determination, but the stark evidence of the pain he'd caused was clear in the shadows under her eyes that perfectly applied make-up failed to disguise. And he felt like the worst kind of coward.

He'd spent the last fortnight battling his own fear. Had come all this way finally to confront it. He had to risk everything now. Tell her the truth. The whole truth.

'I don't want to dissolve our marriage. I never did.'

It was the hardest thing he had ever had to say. Harder even than the pleas he'd made as an eight-year-old in that broken-down trailer.

'I love you. I think I always have.'

She stilled, the pants of her breathing punctuating the silence. The sunlight glowed on the red-gold curls of her hair. But then the quick burst of euphoria that he'd finally had the guts to tell her what he should have told her a decade ago died.

'I don't believe you,' she murmured. She looked wary and confused. But not happy. 'If you had ever loved me,' she said, her voice fragile but firm, 'you would be able to trust me. And you never have.'

He felt a tiny sliver of hope enter his chest, and he who had never been an optimist, nor a romantic, never been one to explain or justify or even to address his feelings knew he had one slim chance. And no matter what happened he wasn't going to blow it.

'I do trust you. I just didn't know it.'

'Don't talk in riddles. You didn't trust me over the miscarriage—you thought I'd had an abortion. And you didn't trust me not to get pregnant again. For God's sake, you even searched my toiletries.'

'I know. But that was down to me and stuff that happened long before I met you. I can see that now.'

'*What* stuff that happened?'

Oh, hell.

He might have guessed Xanthe wouldn't take his word for it.

He stood back, not sure he could explain himself with any clarity but knowing he would have to if they were going to stand any chance at all.

'You asked me once a very long time ago what happened to my mother.'

'You said she died when you were a child—like mine.'

He shook his head. How many other lies had he told to protect himself?

'She didn't die. She left.'

'What? When?'

Xanthe stared blankly at Dane as he ducked his head and braced his hands against the desk. She felt exhausted, hollowed out, her heart already broken into a thousand tiny fragments. He'd said he loved her. But how could she believe him?

'When I was a kid.' He sighed, the deep breath making his chest expand. 'Eight or maybe nine.'

'I don't understand what that has to do with us.'

He raked his fingers over his hair, finally meeting her eyes. The torment in them shocked her into silence.

'I didn't either. I thought I'd gotten over it. I missed her so much, and then I got angry with her. But most of all I convinced myself I'd forgotten her.'

'But you hadn't?'

He nodded, glanced out of the window.

Part of her didn't expect him to explain. Part of her wasn't even sure she wanted him to. But she felt the tiny fragments of her heart gather together as his Adam's apple bobbed and he began to talk.

'He hit her, too, when he was wasted. I remember she used to get me to hide. One night I hid for what felt like hours. I could hear him shouting, her crying. The sound of...'

He swallowed again, and she could see the trauma cross his face. A trauma he'd never let her see until now.

'She was pregnant. He slapped her a couple of times and went out again. To get drunker, I guess. When I came out she was packing her stuff. Her lip was bleeding. I was terrified. I begged her to take me with her. She said she couldn't, that she had to protect the baby. That I was big enough now to look out for myself until she could come back for me.'

His knuckles turned white where he held the edge of the desk.

'But she never did come back for me.'

Was this why he had always found it so hard to trust her? To trust anyone? Because the one person who should have stayed with him, who had promised to protect him, had abandoned him?

'Dane, I'm so sorry.'

Xanthe felt her heart break all over again for that boy who had been forced to grow up far too fast. But as much as she wanted to comfort him, to help him, she knew she couldn't go back and make things better now.

'Don't be sorry. It was a long time ago. And in some ways it made me stronger. Once I'd survived that, I knew I could survive anything.'

'I understand now why it was so hard for you to ever show weakness.'

And she *did* understand. He'd had to survive for so long and from such a young age with no one. His self-sufficiency was the only thing that had saved him. Why would he ever want to give that up?

'But I can't be with someone who doesn't need me the way I need them. It was like that with my dad. And it was the same way with us. I waited too long to call him that day because I didn't want to betray you.'

Her voice caught in her throat, but she pushed the words out. She had to stand up for herself. For who she had become. She couldn't be that naive, impressionable girl again. Not for anyone.

'I love you, Dane. I probably always will. You excite me and challenge me and make me feel more alive than I've ever felt with any other person. But I can't be with you, make a life with you, if we can't be equal. And we never will be if you always have to hold a part of yourself back.'

But as she opened her mouth to tell him to leave he took her wrists, first one, then the other, and drew her against him. He touched his forehead to hers, his lips close to hers, his voice barely a whisper. Tension vibrated through his body as he spoke.

'Please give me another chance. I loved that girl because

she was sweet and sexy and funny, but also so fragile. I thought I could protect her the way I could never protect my mom. And I love knowing that some of that cute, bright, clever kid is still there.'

He pressed his hand to her cheek, cradled her face, and the tenderness in his eyes pushed another tear over her lid.

'But don't you see, Dane? I can't be that girl any more. You walked all over me and I let you.'

He wiped the lone tear away with his thumb. 'Shh, let me finish, Red.'

The lopsided smile and the old nickname touched that tender place in her heart that still ached for him and always would.

'What I was going to say was, as much as I loved that girl, I love the woman she's become so much more.'

She pulled back, scared to let herself sink into him again. 'Don't say that if it isn't true.'

'You think I told you about my mom to make you feel sorry for me?'

She shook her head, because she knew he would never do that—he had far too much bullheaded pride. 'No, of course not. But…'

He touched his thumb to her lips. 'I told you because I want you to know why it's taken me so damn long to figure out the obvious. The truth is I was scared witless, Red. Of needing you too much. The way I'd once needed her. But do you know what was the first thing I felt when you walked into my office and told me we were still married?'

'Horror?'

He laughed, but there wasn't much humour in it. 'Yeah, maybe a little bit. But what I felt the most…' His lips tipped up in a wary smile. 'Was longing.'

'That was just the sex talking.'

His hands sank down to her neck. 'Yeah, I wanted to believe that. We both did. But we both know that's a crock.'

She ducked her head, but he lifted her chin.

'I love that you're your own woman now. That you're still tender and sweet and sexy, but also tough and smart enough to stand up to me, to never let me get away with anything. We're likely to drive each other nuts some of the time. I'm not always going to be able to come clean about stuff. Because I'm a guy, and that's the way I work. But I don't want to sign those papers. I want to give our marriage another chance. A *real* chance this time.'

'But I live in London and you live in New York. And we—'

'Can work anything out if we set our minds to it,' he finished for her. 'If we're willing to try.'

It was a huge ask with a simple answer. Because she'd never stopped loving him either.

'Except... I can't have children naturally. But I want very much to be a mother.'

'Then we'll check out our options. There's IVF, adoption—tons of stuff we can look at.'

'You'd be willing to do all that for me?' His instant commitment stunned her a little.

'Not just for you—for me, too. I want to see you be a mother. I always did. I was just too dumb to say so because I was terrified I wouldn't make the grade as a father.'

She sent him a watery smile, stupidly happy with this new evidence of exactly how equal they were. While she'd been busy nursing her own foolish insecurities she'd managed to miss completely the fact that he had some spectacularly stupid ones, too.

'Hmm, about that...maybe we should look at the evidence?' she teased.

'Do we have to?' he replied, looking adorably uncomfortable.

'Well, you're certainly bossy enough to make a good

father.' Her smile spread when he winced. 'And protective enough, and tough enough, and playful enough, too.'

She pressed herself against him, reached up to circle her arms round his neck, tug the hair at his nape until his mouth bent to hers.

'I guess we'll just have to work on the rest.'

'Is that a yes?' He grinned, because he had to be able to see the answer shining in her eyes through her tears. Her happy—no, her *ecstatic* tears. 'You're willing to give this another go?'

'I am if you are.'

His arms banded round her back to lift her off the floor. 'Does that mean we get to have lots of make-up sex?' he asked.

His hot gaze was setting off all the usual fires, but this time they were so much more intense. Because this time she knew they would never need to be doused.

'We're in my office, in the middle of the day. That would be really inappropriate.'

His grin became more than a little wicked as he boosted her into his arms. 'Screw *appropriate*.'

EPILOGUE

'YOU GRAB THAT ONE... I've got this one.'

Xanthe laughed, scooping up her three-year-old son, Lucas, before he could head for the pool while she watched her husband dive after their one-year-old daughter who, typically, had crawled off in the opposite direction.

Rosie wiggled and chortled as her favourite person in all the world hefted her under his arm like a sack of potatoes—very precious potatoes—into the beach house that stood on a ridge overlooking the ocean.

After facing their third round of IVF, almost two years ago now, she and Dane had embarked on the slow, arduous route to adoption. The discovery a few months later that Xanthe was pregnant, in the same week they'd been given the news that they'd been matched with a little boy in desperate need of a new home, had been like having all their Christmases come at once, while being totally terrifying at the same time.

They would be new parents with *two* children. But could they give Lucas the attention he needed after a tough start in life while also handling a newborn?

Xanthe could still remember the long discussions they'd had late into the night about what to do. But once they'd met Lucas the decision had been taken out of their hands. Because they'd both fallen in love with the impish little boy instantly. As quickly as they'd later fallen in love with his sister, on the day she was born.

'Mommy, I want to do more swimming,' Lucas demanded.

'It's dinnertime, honey,' Xanthe soothed as her son squirmed. 'No more swimming today.'

'Yes, Mommy—*yes*, more swimming!' he cried out, his compact body full of enough energy to power a jumping bean convention—which was usually a sign he was about to hit the wall, hard.

'Hey, I'll trade you.' Pressing a kiss to Rosie's nose, Dane passed her to Xanthe. 'You give the diaper diva her supper and I'll take the toddler terminator for his bath.'

Dane nimbly hoisted their son above his head.

'Come on, Buster, let's go mess up the bathroom.'

'Daddy, can we race the boats?'

'You bet. But this time I get to win.'

'No, Daddy, I *always* win.'

Lucas chuckled—the deep belly chuckle that Xanthe adored—as Dane bounced him on his hip up the stairs of the palatial holiday home they'd bought in the Vineyard, and were considering turning into their permanent base.

Dane had already moved his design team to Cape Cod, and was thinking of relocating the marketing and sponsorship team from the New York office, too. His business was so successful now that clients were prepared to come to him.

Xanthe allowed her gaze to drift down Dane's naked back, where the old scars were barely visible thanks to his summer tan, until it snagged on the bunch and flex of his buttocks beneath the damp broad shorts as he mounted the stairs with their son. The inevitable tug of love and longing settled low in her abdomen as her men disappeared from view.

Extracurricular activities would have to wait until their children were safely tucked up in bed.

Rosie yawned, nestling her head against Xanthe's shoulder, and sucked her thumb, her big blue eyes blinking owlishly. She cupped her daughter's cheek. The flushed baby-soft skin smelled of sun cream and salt and that delicious baby scent that never failed to make Xanthe's heart expand.

'Okay, Miss Diaper Diva, let's see if we can get some food into you before you fall asleep.'

After a day on the beach, trying to keep up with her daddy and her big brother while they built a sand yacht, her daughter had already hit that wall.

Ella, their housekeeper, arrived from the kitchen, as the aroma of the chicken pot pie she'd prepared for the children's evening meal made Xanthe's stomach growl.

'Would you like me to feed her while you take a shower?'

'No, we're good.' Xanthe smiled.

In their late fifties, and with their own children now grown, Ella and her husband John had been an absolute godsend when she'd gone back to work—taking care of all the household chores and doing occasional childcare duties while she and Dane concentrated on bringing up two boisterous children and running two multinational companies with commitments in most corners of the globe.

'Why don't you take the rest of the evening off? I've got it from here,' Xanthe added. 'That pie smells delicious, by the way.'

'Then I'll get going—if you're sure?' Ella beamed as Xanthe nodded. 'I made a spare pie for you and Dane, if you want it tonight. If not just shove it in the freezer.'

'Wonderful, Ella. And thanks again,' she said.

The housekeeper gave Rosie a quick cuddle and then bade them both goodbye before heading to the house she and her husband shared in the grounds.

As Xanthe settled her daughter in the highchair she watched the July sunlight glitter off the infinity pool and

heard wild whooping from upstairs. Apparently Dane and
their son were flooding the children's bathroom again during their boat race.

The sunlight beamed through the house's floor-to-
ceiling windows, making Rosie's blonde hair into a halo
around her head. Xanthe's heart expanded a little more
as she fed her daughter. To think she'd once believed that
her life was just the way she wanted it to be. She'd had
her work, her company, and she'd persuaded herself that
love didn't matter. That it was too dangerous to risk her
heart a second time.

Her life was a lot more chaotic now, and not nearly as
settled thanks to her many and varied commitments. They
had a house on the river in London, and Dane's penthouse
in New York, as well as this estate in the Vineyard, but
as both she and Dane had demanding jobs and enjoyed
travel they rarely spent more than six months a year in
any of them.

As a result, their children had already climbed the Sug-
arloaf Mountain, been on a yacht trip to the Seychelles and
slept through the New Year's Eve fireworks over Sydney
Harbour Bridge. Eventually she and Dane would have to
pick one base and stick to it, which was exactly why Dane
was restructuring his business and why she'd appointed
an acting CEO at Carmichael's in London, giving herself
more flexibility while overseeing the business as a whole.

But with Dane's nomadic spirit, her own wanderlust,
and their children still young enough to thrive on the adventure, they'd found a way to make their jet-set lifestyle
work for now.

By risking her heart a second time she had created a
home and a family and a life she adored, and discovered in
the process that love was the *only* thing that really mattered.

Rosie spat out a mouthful of food, looking mutinous as
she stuffed her thumb into her mouth.

Xanthe grinned. 'Right, madam, time to hand you over to your daddy.' She hauled her daughter out of the high-chair and perched her on her hip. 'He can read you a bed-time story while I feed your brother, and then rescue the bathroom.'

And once all that was done, when both her babies were in bed, she had *other* plans for her husband for later in the evening.

She smiled. Love mattered, and family mattered, but sometimes lust was pretty important, too.

'How do you feel about taking the munchkins to Mont-serrat next month?'

'Hmm...?' Xanthe eased back against her husband's chest as his words whispered into her hair and his hands settled on her belly.

The sun had started to drift towards the horizon, sending shards of light shimmering across the ocean and giving the surface of the pool a ruddy glow. She felt gloriously lan-guid, standing on the deck. The children were finally out for the count, and Ella's second chicken pot pie had been devoured and savoured over a quiet glass of chardonnay.

The adult promise of the evening beckoned as warm calloused fingertips edged beneath the waistband of her shorts.

'Montserrat? Next month?' he murmured, nipping at her earlobe. 'I've got to test a new design. Figured we could rent a house...bring Ella and John along to help out with the kids while we're working. We might even get some solo sailing time.'

She shifted and turned in his arms, until her hands were resting on his shoulders and she could see the dusk reflected in his crystal blue eyes.

'Sounds good to me,' she said. 'As long as we have a

decent internet connection I can handle what I need to on the Shanghai development.'

She pressed her palms to the rough stubble on his cheeks and sent him a sultry grin which made his expression darken with hunger.

'But right now all I want to handle is *you*.'

His lips quirked, his challenging smile both promise and provocation. 'You think you can *handle* me, huh?'

Large hands sank beneath her shorts to cup her bare bottom and drag her against the solid ridge forming in his chinos.

Arousal shot to her core, staggering and instantaneous. 'Absolutely,' she dared.

'We'll just see about that,' he dared back, as he boosted her into his arms.

She laughed as he carried her into the house, then took the steps two at a time to get to their bedroom suite. But after he'd laid her on the bed, stripped off her clothes and his, his gaze locked on hers and her heart jolted—she could see all the love she felt for him reflected in his eyes.

'You're a witch.' He trailed his thumb down her sternum to circle one pouting nipple. 'A sea witch.'

She groaned as he cupped her naked breasts.

'But you're *my* damn sea witch.'

She bucked off the bed as he teased the tender peak with his teeth.

'Perhaps you should use your superpower to make sure I never forget it,' she said breathlessly.

'Damn straight,' he growled, before demonstrating to her, in no uncertain terms, just how thoroughly she belonged to him, while she gave herself up to the passionate onslaught and handled everything he had to offer just fine.

* * * * *

PRINCESS'S PREGNANCY SECRET

NATALIE ANDERSON

To my family, for your patience, belief,
bad-but-good puns and supreme fun...

We are such an awesome team, and I am
so very lucky.

CHAPTER ONE

DAMON GALE STALKED the perimeter of the crowded ballroom, dodging another cluster of smiling women whose feathered masks neither softened nor hid their hunger as they stared at him.

He shouldn't have discarded his mask so soon.

Turning his back on another wordless invitation, he sipped his champagne, wishing it contained a stronger liquor. Women wanted more from him than he ever wanted from them. Always. While they agreed to a fling—fully informed of his limits—when it ended, recriminations and resentment came.

You're heartless.

He smiled cynically as the echo rang in his head. His last ex had thrown that old chestnut at him a few months ago. And, yes, he was. Heartless and happy with it.

And what did it matter? For tonight business, not pleasure, beckoned. Tonight he was drawing a line beneath a decades-old disaster and tomorrow he'd walk away from this gilded paradise without a backwards glance. Just coming back had made old wounds hurt like fresh hits.

But for now he'd endured the outrageously opulent entrance, navigated his way up the marble staircase and walked through not one but five antechambers. Each room was larger and more ornate than the last, until finally he'd reached this gleaming monstrosity of a ballroom. The internal balcony overlooking the vast room already brimmed with celebrities and socialites eager to display themselves and spy on others.

Palisades palace was designed to reflect the glory of the royal family and make the average commoner feel as inconsequential as possible. It was supposed to invoke awe and envy. Frankly all the paintings, tapestries and gilded carvings exhausted Damon's eyes. He itched to ditch his dinner jacket and hit one of the trail runs along the pristine coastline that he far preferred to this sumptuous palace, but he needed to stay and play nice for just a little while longer.

Gritting his teeth, he turned away from the lens of an official photographer. He had no desire to feature in anyone's social media feed or society blog. He'd been forced to attend too many of these sorts of occasions in years past, as the proof of the supposed strength of his parents' union and thus to maximise any political inroads they could make from their connections.

The bitterness of their falsity soured the champagne.

Fortunately *his* career wasn't dependent upon the interest and approval of the wealthy and powerful. Thanks to his augmented reality software company, he was as wealthy as any of the patrons in attendance at this palace tonight. But even so, he was here to make the old-school grace and favour system work for him just this once. Grimly he glanced over to where he'd left his half-sister only ten minutes ago. The investors he'd introduced her to were actively listening to her earnest, intelligent conversation, asking questions, clearly interested in what she was saying.

That introduction was all she'd agreed to accept from him. She'd refused his offer to fund her research himself and, while it irritated him, he didn't blame her. After all, they barely knew each other and neither of them wanted to dwell on the cancerous and numerous scars of their parents' infidelities. She had her pride and he respected her for it. But he'd been determined to try to help heal two decades of hurt and heartache caused by lies and deception, even in some small way, given his father's total lack of remorse. From the intensity of that discussion, it seemed his job was done.

Now Damon turned away from the crowds, seeking solace in solitude for a moment before he could escape completely.

Symmetrical marble columns lined the length of the room. On one side they bracketed doors to the internal courtyard currently lit by lights strung in the trees. But on the other side the columns stood like sentries guarding shadowy alcoves.

A wisp of blue caught his eye as he approached the nearest column and he veered nearer. A woman stood veiled in the recess, her attention tightly focused on a group of revellers a few feet away. Her hair was ten shades of blue, hung to her waist and was most definitely a wig. A feathery mask covered half her face like an intimate web of black lace. Her shoulders, cheekbones and lips sparkled in a swirling combination of blue and silver powder.

Damon paused, unable to ignore the way her long dress emphasised every millimetre of her lithe body, clinging to her luscious curves and long legs. Despite that sparkling powder, he could see the tan of her skin and it suggested she was more mermaid than waif. She definitely spent time in the sun and that toned body didn't come from sitting on a spread towel doing nothing.

She was fit—in all interpretations of the word—but it was her undeniable femininity that stole his breath. Her pointed chin and high cheekbones and perfectly pouted lips were pure prettiness and delicacy, while her bountiful breasts were barely contained in the too-tight bodice of her midnight-blue dress.

She hadn't noticed him as she stood still and alone, watching the crowd. So he watched her. Her mask didn't hide her emotions—while her intentions were not obvious, her anxiety was. Something about her stark isolation softened that hard knot tied fast in his chest and set a challenge at the same time.

He was seized by the desire to make her smile.

He was also seized by the urge to span his hands around her narrow waist and pull her close so he could feel the graceful combination of softness and strength that her figure promised.

He smiled ruefully as raw warmth coursed through his veins. Its unexpected ferocity was vastly better than the cold ash clogging his lungs when he'd first arrived. Perhaps there could be a moment of pleasure here after all, now his business was concluded and that personal debt paid.

He quietly strolled nearer. Her attention was still fixed on the people gathering in the glittering ballroom, but he focused on her. She hovered on the edge of the room, still in the shadow. Still almost invisible to everyone else.

Her breasts swelled as she inhaled deeply. He hesitated, waiting for her to move forward. But contrary to his expectation, she suddenly stepped back, her expression falling as she turned away.

Damon narrowed his gaze. He had his own reasons for avoiding occasions like this, but why would a beautiful young woman like her want to hide? She should have company.

His company.

He lifted a second glass from the tray of a passing waiter and stepped past the column into the alcove. She'd paused in her retreat to look over that vast room of bejewelled, beautiful people. The expression in her eyes was obvious, despite the mask and the make-up. Part longing, part loneliness, her isolation stirred him. He spoke before thinking better of it.

'Can't quite do it?'

She whirled to face him, her eyes widening. Damon paused, needing a moment to appreciate the layers of sequins and powder on her pretty features. She was so very blue. She registered the two glasses he was holding and darted a glance behind him. As she realised he was alone, her eyes widened more. He smiled at her obvious wariness.

'It's your first time?' he asked.

Her mouth opened in a small wordless gasp.

'At the palace,' he clarified, wryly amused while keenly aware of the fullness of her glittered lips. 'It can be overwhelming the first time.'

Fascinatingly a telltale colour ran up her neck and face, visible despite the artful swirls of powder dusting almost every inch of her exposed skin. She was *blushing* at the most innocuous of statements.

Well, almost innocuous.

His smile deepened as he imagined her response if he were to utter something a great deal more inappropriate. Her body captured his attention, and he couldn't resist stealing a glance lower.

Heat speared again, tightening his muscles. He dragged his gaze up and realised she'd caught his slip. Unabashed he smiled again, letting her know in that time-worn way of his interest. She met his open gaze, not stepping back. But still she said nothing.

Alone. Definitely unattached. And almost certainly on the inexperienced side.

Damon hadn't chased a woman in a long while. Offers from more than willing bedmates meant he was more hunted than hunter. He avoided their attempts to snare him for longer, bored with justifying his refusal to commit to a relationship. He had too much of what women wanted— money and power. And yes, physical stamina and experience. Women enjoyed those things too.

But the possibilities here were tempting—when she reacted so tantalisingly with so little provocation? Those too-blue eyes and that too-sombre pout were beguiling.

He'd barely expected to stay ten minutes, let alone find someone who'd rouse his playful side. But now his obligation to Kassie had been met, he had the urge to amuse himself.

'What's your name?' he asked.

Her pupils dilated as if she was surprised but, again, she said nothing.

'I think I'll call you "Blue",' he said leisurely.

Her chin lifted fractionally. 'Because of my hair?'

He had to stop his jaw from dropping at the sound of her husky tones. That sultriness was at complete odds with her innocent demeanour. She was as raspy as a kitten's tongue. The prospect of making her purr tightened his interest.

'Because of the longing in your eyes.' And because of the pout of her pretty mouth.

'What do you think I'm longing for?'

Now there was a question. One he chose not to answer, knowing his silence would speak for itself. He just looked at her—feeling the awareness between them snap.

'What should I call you?' she asked after a beat.

He lifted his eyebrows. 'You don't know who I am?'

Her lips parted as she shook her head. 'Should I?'

He studied her for a moment—there had been no flash of recognition in her eyes when he'd first spoken to her, and there was none now. How...*refreshing*. 'No,' he said. 'I'm no one of importance. No prince, that's for sure.'

Something flickered in her eyes then, but it was gone before he could pick it up.

'I'm visiting Palisades for a few days,' he drawled. 'And I'm single.'

Her lips parted. 'Why do I need to know that?'

That sultry voice pulled, setting off a small ache deep in his bones. He didn't much like aches. He preferred action.

'No reason.' He shrugged carelessly, but smiled.

Her lips twitched, then almost curved. Satisfaction seeped into his gut, followed hard by something far hotter. Pleasure. It pressed him closer.

'Why are you all alone in here?' He offered her the second glass of champagne.

She accepted it but took such a small sip he wasn't

sure that the liquid even hit her lips. A careful woman. Intriguing.

'Are you hiding?' he queried.

She licked her lips and glanced down at her dress before tugging at the strap that was straining to hold her curves.

Definitely nervous.

'You look beautiful,' he added. 'You don't need to worry about that.'

That wave of colour swept her cheeks again but she lifted her head. There was an assuredness in her gaze now that surprised him. 'I'm not worried about that.'

Oh? So she held a touch more confidence than had first appeared. Another shot of satisfaction rushed. His fingers itched with the urge to tug the wig from her head and find out what colour her hair really was. While this façade was beautiful, it was a fantasy he wanted to pierce so he could see the real treasure beneath.

'Then why aren't you out there?' he asked.

'Why aren't you?' Alert, she watched for his response.

'Sometimes attendance at these things is *necessary* rather than desired.'

'These "things"?' she mocked his tone.

'It depends who's here.'

'No doubt you desire these "things" more when there are plenty of pretty women.' She was breathless beneath that rasp.

But he knew she was enjoying this slight spar and parry. He'd play along.

'Naturally.' Damon coolly watched her over the rim of his glass as he sipped his drink, deliberately hiding his delight. 'I am merely a man, after all.' He shrugged helplessly.

Her gaze narrowed on him, twin sparks shooting from that impossible blue. 'You mean you're a boy who likes playing with toys. A doll here, a doll there...'

'Of course,' he followed her smoothly. 'Toying with dolls can be quite an amusing pastime. As can collecting them.'

'I'll bet.'

He leaned forward, deliberately intruding into intimate space to whisper conspiratorially, 'I never break my toys though,' he promised. 'I take very good care when I'm playing.'

'Oh?' Her gaze lanced straight through his veneer, striking at a weak spot he didn't know he had. 'If you say it, it must be true.'

Appreciating her little flash of spirit, he was instantly determined to take very great care...to torture her delightfully.

'And you?' he asked, though he already suspected the answer. 'Do you often attend nights like this?' Did she play with toys of her own?

She shrugged her shoulders in an echo of his.

He leaned closer again, rewarded as he heard the hitch in her breathing. 'Do you work at the hospital?'

Tonight's ball was the annual fundraiser and, while he knew huge amounts were raised, it was also the chance for hospital staff to be celebrated.

'I...do some stuff there.' Her lashes lowered.

Wasn't she just Ms Mysterious? 'So why aren't you with your friends?'

'I don't know them all that well.'

Perhaps she was a new recruit who'd won an invitation for this ball in the ballot they held for the hospital staff. Perhaps that was why she didn't have any friends with her. It wouldn't take long for her to find a few. Some surgeon would snap her up if he had any sense. Then it wouldn't be long before she lost that arousing ability to blush.

A spear of possessiveness shafted through him at the thought of some other guy pulling her close. Surprising him into taking another step nearer to her. Too near.

'Do you want to dance?' He gave up on subtlety altogether.

She glanced beyond him. 'No one is dancing yet.'

'We could start the trend.'

She quickly shook her head, leaning back into the shadows so his body hid her from those in the ballroom. Damon guessed she didn't want to stand out. Too late, to him she already did.

'Don't be intimidated by any of that lot.' He jerked his head towards the crowds. 'They might have the wealth but they don't always have the manners. Or the kindness.'

'You're saying you don't fit in either?' The scepticism in her gaze as she looked him over was unmissable.

He resisted the urge to preen in front of her like some damn peacock. Instead he offered a platitude. 'Does anyone truly fit in?'

Her gaze flashed up to his and held it a long moment. Her irises were such a vibrant blue he knew they had to be covered with contacts. The pretence of polite small talk fell away. The desire to reach for her—to strip her—almost overwhelmed him. Now *that* was inappropriate. He tensed, pushing back the base instinct. Damn, he wanted to touch her. Wanted her to touch him. That look in her eyes? Pure invitation. Except he had the feeling she was too inexperienced to even be aware of it.

But he couldn't stop the question spilling roughly from his lips. 'Are you going to do it?'

Eleni Nicolaides didn't know what or how to answer him. This man wasn't like anyone she'd met before.

Direct. Devastating. *Dangerous.*

'Are you going to do it, Blue?'

'Do what?' she whispered vaguely, distracted by the play of dark and light in his watchful expression. He was appallingly handsome in that tall, dark, sex-on-a-stick sort of way. The kind of obviously experienced playboy who'd never been allowed near her.

But at the same time there was more than that to him—something that struck a chord within her. A new—seductive—note that wasn't purely because of the physical magnetism of the man.

He captivated every one of her senses and all her interest. A lick of something new burned—yearning. She wanted him closer. She wanted to reach out and touch him. Her pulse throbbed, beating need about her body—to her dry, sensitive lips, to her tight, full breasts, to other parts too secret to speak of...

His jaw tightened. Eleni blinked at the fierce intensity that flashed in his eyes. Had he read her mind? Did he know just *what* she wanted to do right now?

'Join in,' he answered between gritted teeth.

She swallowed. Now her pulse thundered as she realised how close she'd come to making an almighty fool of herself. 'I shouldn't...'

'Why not?'

So many reasons flooded her head in a cacophony of panic.

Her disguise, her deceit, her *duty*.

'Blue?' he prompted. His smile was gentle enough but the expression in his eyes was too hot.

Men had looked at her with lust before, but those times the lust hadn't been for her but for her wealth, her title, her virtue. She'd never been on a date. She was totally untouched. And everyone knew. She'd read the crude conjecture and the jokes in the lowest of the online guttersnipes: *THE VIRGIN PRINCESS!!!*

All caps. Multiple exclamation marks.

That her 'purity' was so interesting and so important angered her. It wasn't as if it had been deliberate. It wasn't as if she'd saved herself for whichever prince would be chosen for her to marry. She'd simply been so sequestered there'd been zero chance to find even a friend, let alone a boyfriend.

And now it transpired that her Prince was to be Xander of the small European state of Santa Chiara. He certainly hadn't saved himself for her and she knew his fidelity after their marriage was not to be expected. Discretion was, but not that sort of intimate loyalty. Or love.

'Do you ever stop asking questions?' she asked, trying for cool and sophisticated for these last few moments of escape.

Wishing she could be as accepting as so many others who didn't doubt their arranged marriages. Because this was it. Tomorrow her engagement would be formally announced. A man she'd barely met and most certainly didn't like would become her fiancé. She felt frigid at the thought. But those archaic royal rules remained unchallenged and offered certainty. The Princess of Palisades could never marry a commoner. This disguise tonight was a lame leap for five minutes of total freedom. The only five minutes she'd have.

'Not if I'm curious about something.'

'And you're curious about—'

'You. Unbearably. Yes.'

Heat slammed into every cell. She couldn't hold his gaze but she couldn't look away either. His eyes were truly blue—not enhanced by contacts the way hers were—and hot. He seemed to see right through her mask, her carefully applied powder, her whole disguise. He saw the need she'd tried to hide from everyone.

She was out of place and yet this was her home—where she'd been born and raised and where her future was destined, dictated by duty.

'You have the chance to experience this…' he waved at the ballroom full of beautiful people '…yet you're hanging back in the shadows.'

He voiced her fantasy—reminding her of her stupid,

crazy plan. She'd arranged for a large selection of costumes to be delivered to the nurses' quarters at the hospital for tonight's masquerade. No one would know that one dress, one wig, and one mask were missing from that order. All done so she, cloistered, protected, precious Princess Eleni, could steal one night as an anonymous girl able to talk to people not as a princess, but as a nobody.

She could be no one.

And yet, when it had come to it, she'd swiftly realised her error. She'd watched those guests arrive. Clustered together, laughing squads of *friends*—the kind she'd never had. How could she walk into that room and start talking to any of them *without* her title as her armour? What had she to offer? How could she blend in when she hadn't any clue what to discuss other than superficial niceties? She'd ached with isolation, inwardly mocking her own self-piteous hurt, as she'd uselessly stared at all those other carefree, relaxed people having fun.

Privileged Princess Eleni had burned with jealousy.

Now she burned with something else, something just as shameful.

'I'm biding my time,' she prevaricated with a chuckle, drawing on years of practising polite conversation to cover her shaken, unruly emotions.

'You're wasting it.'

His bluntness shocked that smile from her lips. She met his narrowed gaze and knew he saw too much.

'You want a night out, you need to get out there and start circulating,' he advised.

Her customary serene demeanour snapped at his tone. 'Maybe that's not what I want.'

The atmosphere pulsed between them like an electrical charge faulting.

Heat suffused every inch of her skin. Now she truly was unable to hold his gaze. But as she looked down he reached out. The merest touch of fingers to her chin, nudging so she looked him in the eye again. She fought to quell the uncontrollable shiver that the simple touch generated.

'No?' Somehow he was even closer as he quietly pressed her. 'Then what do you want?'

That she couldn't answer. Not to herself. Not now. But he could see it anyway.

'Walk with me through the ballroom,' he said in a low voice. 'I dare you.'

His challenge roused a rare surge of rebellion within her. She who always did as she was bid—loyal, dutiful, serene. Princess Eleni never caused trouble. But *he* stirred trouble. Her spirit lifted; she was determined to show strength before him.

'I don't need you to dare me,' she breathed.

'Don't you?' He called her bluff.

Silent, she registered the gauntlet in his hard gaze. The glow of those blue eyes ignited her to mutinous action. She turned and strode to the edge of the alcove. Nerves thrummed, chilling her. What if she was recognised?

But this man hadn't recognised her and she knew her brother would be busy in the farthest corner of the room meeting select guests at this early stage in the evening. Everyone was preoccupied with their own friends and acquaintances. She *might* just get away with this after all.

'Coming?' She looked back and asked him, refusing—yet failing—to flush.

He took her hand and placed it in the crook of his elbow, saying nothing, but everything, with a sardonic look. The rock-hard heat of his biceps seeped through the fine material of his tailored suit and her fingers curled around it instinctively. He pressed his arm close to his side, trapping her hand.

He walked slowly, deliberately, the length of the colonnades. To her intense relief, he didn't stop to speak to anyone, instead he kept his attention on her, his gaze melting that cold block of nervousness lodged in her diaphragm.

It turned out she'd been wrong to worry about recognition. Because while people *were* looking, it was not at her.

'All these women are watching you,' she murmured as they drew near the final column. 'And they look surprised.'

A smile curled his sensual lips. 'I haven't been seen dating recently.'

'They think I'm your date?' she asked. 'Am I supposed to feel flattered?'

His laughter was low and appreciative. 'Don't deny it, you do.'

She pressed her lips together, refusing to smile. But the sound of his laugh wasn't just infectious, it seemed to reach right inside her and chase all that cold away with its warmth.

'There.' He drew her into the last alcove, a mirror of the first, and she was appallingly relieved to discover it too was empty at this early hour.

'Was that so awful?' he asked, not relinquishing her hand but walking with her to the very depths of the respite room and turning to face her.

Inwardly she was claiming it as a bittersweet victory. A date at last.

'Who are you?' She felt foolish that she didn't know when it was clear many others did. 'Why do they look at you?'

He cocked his head, his amusement gleaming. 'Why do *you* look at me?'

Eleni refused to answer. She was *not* going to pander to his already outsize ego.

His lazy smile widened. 'What do you see?'

That one she could answer. She smiled, relishing her release from 'polite princess response'.

'I see arrogance,' she answered boldly. 'A man who defies convention and doesn't give a damn what anyone thinks.'

'Because?'

She angled her head, mirroring his inquiring look. 'You don't wear a mask. You don't make the effort that's expected of everyone else.'

'And I don't do that—because why?' His attention narrowed—laser-like in its focus on her.

'Because you don't need to,' she guessed, seeing the appreciation flicker in his eyes. 'You don't want their approval. You're determined to show you don't need *anything* from them.'

His expression shuttered, but he didn't deny her assessment of him. Her heart quickened as he stepped closer.

'Do you know what I see?' Almost angrily he pointed to the mask covering most of her face. 'I see someone hiding more than just her features. I see a woman who wants more than what she thinks she should have.'

She stilled, bereft—of speech, of spirit. Because she did want more and yet she knew she was so spoilt and selfish to do so. She had *everything*, didn't she?

'So what happens at midnight?' That tantalising smile quirked his lips, drawing her attention to the sensuality that was such a potent force within him.

She struggled to remind herself she was no Cinderella. She was already the Princess, after all. 'Exactly what you think it will.'

'You'll leave and I'll never see you again.'

His words struck deep inside her—sinking like stones of regret.

'Precisely,' she replied with her perfectly practised princess politeness.

She shouldn't feel the slightest disappointment. This was merely a fleeting conversation in the shadows. Five minutes of dalliance that she could reminisce over a whole lot later. Like for the rest of her life.

'I don't believe in fairy tales,' he said roughly, his smile lost.

'Nor do I,' she whispered. She believed in duty. In family. In doing what was right. Which was why she was going to marry a man she didn't love and who didn't love her. Romance was for fairy tales and other people.

'You sure about that?' He edged closer still, solemn and intense. 'Then flip it. Don't do the expected. Don't disappear at midnight.' He dared her with that compelling whisper. 'Stay and do what you want. You have the mask to protect you. *Take* what you want.'

She stared up at him. He was roguishly handsome and he was only playing with her, wasn't he? But that was…okay. Intense temptation and a totally foreign sensation rippled through her. The trickle soon turned into a tsunami. From the deepest core of her soul, slipping along her veins to ignite every inch of her body.

Want.

Pure and undeniable.

Couldn't she have just a very little moment for herself? Couldn't she have just a very little of *him*?

He couldn't hide his deepening tension. It was in his eyes, in the single twitch of the muscle in his jaw as the curve of his smile flatlined. That infinitesimal *edge* sharpened. But he remained as motionless as the marble column behind him, hiding the ballroom from her view. Waiting, watching.

Take what you want.

That dare echoed in her mind, fuelling her desire.

She gazed into his eyes, losing herself in the molten steel. She parted her lips the merest fraction to draw in a desperate breath. But he moved the moment she did. Full predator—fast, powerful, inescapable—he pressed his mouth to meet hers.

Instinctively she closed her eyes, unable to focus on anything but the sensation of his warm lips teasing hers. Her breath caught as he stepped closer, his hands spanning her waist to draw her against him. She quivered on impact as she felt his hard strength, finally appreciating the sheer size of the man. Tall, strong, he radiated pure masculinity.

He took complete control, his tongue sliding along her lips, slipping past to stroke her. Never had she been kissed like this. Never had *she* kissed like this, but his commanding passion eviscerated any insecurity—and all thought. Lost to the sensation she simply leaned closer, letting him support her, pressing her into his iron heat.

Heavy, addictive power flowed from him to her as he kissed the very soul of her. His arms were like bars, drawing her against the solid expanse of his chest. A moan rose in the back of her throat and he tightened his hold more. She quivered at his defined strength—not just physical. It took mental strength to build a body like his, she knew that too.

Her legs weakened even as a curious energy surged through her. She needed him closer still. But his hand lifted to cup her jaw and he teased—pressing maddeningly light kisses on her lips instead of that explosive, carnal kiss of before. She moaned, in delight, in frustration.

At that raw, unbidden response, he gave her what she wanted. Uncontrolled passion. She clutched at him wildly as her knees gave out—swept away on a torrent of need that had somehow been unleashed. She didn't know how to assuage it, how to combat it. All she could do was cling— wordlessly, mindlessly begging for more. The intensity of his desire mirrored her own—she felt him brace, felt the burning of his skin beneath her fingertips as she touched his jaw, copying his delightful touch.

But now his hand stroked lower, pressing against her thigh. Breathless she slipped deeper, blindly seeking more. But she felt his hesitation. She gasped as he broke the kiss to look at her. Unthinking she arched closer, seeking to regain contact. But in the distance she heard a roaring. A clinking of—

Glasses. *Guests.*

Good grief, what was she *doing*?

Far too late those years of training, duty and responsibility kicked in. How could she have forgotten who and where she was? She could not throw everything away for one moment of *lust*.

But this lust was all-consuming. All she wanted was for him to touch her again—decisively, intimately, now.

Brutal shame burned from her bones to her skin. She had to get alone and under control. But as she twisted from his hold a long tearing sound shredded the unnatural silence between them. Time slowed as realisation seeped into her fried brain.

That too tight, too thin strap over her shoulder had ripped clear from the fabric it had been straining to support. And the result?

She didn't need to look to know; she could feel the exposure—the cooler air on her skin. Aghast, she sent him a panicked glance. Had he noticed?

Of course he'd noticed.

She froze, transfixed, as his gaze rested for a second longer on her bared breast before flicking back to her face. The fiery hunger in his eyes consumed her. She was alight with colour and heat, but it wasn't embarrassment.

Oh, heavens, no.

She tugged up the front of her dress and turned, blindly seeking escape.

But he drew her close again, bracketing her into the protective stance of his body. He walked, pressing her forward away from the crowd she'd foolishly forgotten was present. And she was so confused she just let him. Through a discreet archway, down a wide corridor to space and silence. He walked with her, until a door closed behind them.

The turn of the lock echoed loudly. Startled, she turned to see him jerkily stripping out of his dinner jacket with barely leashed violence. His white dress shirt strained across his broad shoulders. Somehow he seemed bigger, more aggressive, more sexual.

Appallingly desire flooded again, rooting her to the spot where she clutched her torn dress to her chest. She desperately tried to catch her breath but her body couldn't cope. Her lips felt full and sensitive and throbbed for the press of his. Her breasts felt tight and heavy and, buried deep within, she was molten hot and aching.

All she could do was stare as he stalked towards her.

All she could think was to surrender.

CHAPTER TWO

'SLIP THIS AROUND your shoulders and we can leave immediately.' He held the jacket out to her. 'No one will…' He trailed off as she stared at him uncomprehendingly.

He'd only been stripping in order to *clothe* her? To protect her from prying eyes rather than continue with…with…

Suddenly she was mortified. She'd thought that he'd been going to—

'No.' She finally got her voice box to work. 'No. That's impossible.'

Nervously she licked her lips. What was impossible was her own reaction. Her own *willingness*. Horrified, she stepped away from the temptation personified in front of her, backing up until she was almost against the wall on the far side of the room.

He stood still, his jacket gently swinging from his outstretched hand, and watched her move away from him. A slight frown furrowed his forehead. Then he shifted, easing his stance. He casually tossed the jacket onto the antique sofa that now stood between them.

His lips twisted with a smile as rueful as it was seductive. 'I'm not going to do anything.'

'I know,' she said quickly, trying and failing to offer a smile in return.

She wasn't afraid of him. She was afraid of herself. Her cheeks flamed and she knew a fierce blush had every inch of her skin aglow. Shamed, she clutched the material closer to her chest.

This had been such a mistake. More dangerous than she ever could have imagined. Her breathing quickened again. She was so mortified but so *sensitive*. She glanced at him again only to have him snare her gaze in his. He was watching her too intently. She realised that his breathing was quickened, like hers, and a faint sheen highlighted his sun-kissed skin.

'Are you okay?' he asked softly. 'I'm sorry.'

But he didn't look sorry. If anything that smile deepened.

But she also saw the intensity of the heat banked in his expression and something unfurled within her. Something that didn't help her resistance.

'It wasn't your fault,' she muttered. 'It's a cheap dress and it doesn't really fit that well.'

'Let me help you fix it,' he offered huskily. 'So you can get out of here.'

'I can make do.' She glanced at the locked door behind him. 'I'd better go.'

She knew there was another exit from the room, but it was locked by the security system. She couldn't use it without showing him she was intimate with the palace layout. He could never know that. Maybe she could drape the blue and purple hair of her wig over her shoulder to hide that tear.

'Trust me,' he invited gruffly. 'I'll fix your dress. Won't do anything else.'

That was the problem. She wanted him to do something. Do *everything* or *anything* he wanted. And that was just crazy because she couldn't set a lifetime of responsibility ablaze now. What made it worse was that he knew—why she'd moved to put not just space, but furniture between them.

'You can't get past them all with that strap the way it is now,' he muttered.

He was right. She couldn't get away from him either. Not yet.

So she stepped nearer, turning to present her shoulder with the torn strap. 'Thank you.'

Holding her breath, heart pounding, she fought to remain

still as he came within touching distance. The tips of his deft fingers brushed against her burning skin as he tried to tie the loose strap to the torn bodice. She felt it tighten, but then heard his sharp mutter of frustration as the strap loosened again.

She inhaled a jagged breath. 'Don't worry—'

'I'll get it this time,' he interrupted. 'Almost there.'

She waited, paralysed, as he bent to the task again, trying desperately to quell her responsive shiver to the heat of his breath on her skin but he noticed it anyway. His hands stilled for that minuscule moment before working again.

'There,' he promised in a lethal whisper. 'All fixed.'

But he was still there—too close, too tall, too everything. She stood with her eyes tight shut, totally aware of him.

'You're good to go.'

Good. She didn't feel like being good. And she didn't want to go.

She opened her eyes and saw what she'd already felt with every other sense. He was close enough to kiss.

She shook her head very slightly, not wanting to break this spell. 'It was a dumb idea. I shouldn't have come.'

She hadn't meant to tell him anything more but the secret simply fell from her lips.

'But you've gone to such trouble.' He traced one of the swirls of glitter she'd painted on her shoulder. His finger roved north, painting another that rose up her neck, near her frantically beating pulse, and rested there.

'You shouldn't miss out.' He didn't break eye contact as he neared, but he didn't close the half-inch between their mouths.

She had to miss out. That was her destiny—the rules set before she was even born. Yet his gaze mesmerised, making her want all kinds of impossible things. Beneath those thick lashes the intensity of his truly blue eyes burned through to her core.

'You'd better get back out there, Blue.' He suddenly broke the taut silence and dropped his hand. His voice roughened, almost as if he were angry.

'Why?' Why should she? When what she wanted was right here? Just one more kiss? Just once? Hot fury speared—the fierce emotion striking all sense from her. 'Maybe I can...' she muttered, gazing into his eyes.

'Can what?' he challenged, arching an eyebrow. 'What can you do...?'

She tilted her chin and reached up on tiptoe to brush her lips over his. Sensation shivered through her. This was right. This was *it*.

He stiffened, then took complete control. He gripped her waist and hauled her close, slamming her body into his. She felt the give of her stupid dress again. She didn't mind the half-laugh that heated her.

'You can do that,' he muttered, a heated tease as he kissed her with those torturous light kisses until she moaned in frustration. 'You can do that all you like.'

She did like. She liked it a *lot*.

Kisses. Nothing wrong with kisses. Her bodice fluttered down again, exposing her to him. Thank goodness. His hands took advantage, then his mouth. The drive for more overwhelmed her. Never had she felt so alive. Or so good.

She gasped when he lifted her, but she didn't resist, didn't complain. He strode a couple of paces to sit on the sofa, crushing her close then settling her astride his lap.

She shivered in delight as he kissed her again. She could die in these kisses. She met every one, mimicking, learning, becoming braver. Becoming unbearably aroused. Breathless, she lost all sense of time—could only succumb to the sensation as his hand swept down her body, down her legs. Slowly he drew up the hem of her dress. His fingertips stroked up her hot skin until he neared that most private part of her. She shivered and he lifted his head, looking deep into her eyes. She knew he was seeking permission.

She wriggled ever so slightly to let him have greater access because this felt too good to stop. Still watching her, he slid his hand higher.

'Kiss me again,' she whispered.

Something flared in his eyes. And kiss her he did, but not on her mouth. He bent lower, drawing her nipple into the hot cavern of his mouth while at the same time his fingertips erotically teased over the crotch of her panties.

Eleni gasped and writhed—seeking both respite from the torment, and more of it. No one had touched her so intimately. And, heaven have mercy, she liked it.

She caught a glimpse of the reflection in the mirror hanging on the opposite wall. She didn't recognise the woman with that man bending to her bared breasts. This was one stranger doing deliciously naughty things with another stranger—kissing and rubbing and touching and sliding. Beneath her, his hard length pressed against his suit pants. It fascinated her. The devilish ache to explore him more overtook her. She rocked against his hand, shivering with forbidden delight. She was so close to something, but she was cautious. He pulled back for a second and studied her expression. She clenched her jaw. She didn't want him to stop.

'Take what you want,' he urged softly. 'Whatever you want.'

'I…'

'Anything,' he muttered. 'As much or as little as you like.'

Because he wanted this too. She felt the tremble in his fingers and it gave her confidence. Somehow she knew he was as taken aback as she by this conflagration. She might not have the experience, but she had the intuition to understand this was physical passion at its strongest.

Her legs quivered but she let him slide the satin skirt of her dress higher. It glided all the way up to her waist, exposing her almost completely. Her legs were bared, her chest, only her middle was covered in a swathe of blue. She sighed helplessly as that hard ridge of him pressed where she was aching most.

She struggled to unfasten his shirt buttons; she wanted to see his skin. To feel it. He helped her, pulling the halves of his shirt apart. For a moment she just stared. She'd known he was strong, she'd felt that. But the definition of his tense muscles—the pecs, the abs—still took her by surprise. The light scattering of hair added to the perfection. He was the ultimate specimen of masculinity. She raised her gaze, meeting the fire in his, and understood the strength he was holding in check.

'Touch all you like,' he muttered, a guttural command.

She liked it *all*. Suddenly stupidly nervous, she pressed her palm over his chest—feeling the hardness and heat of him. But she could feel the thump of his heart too and somehow that grounded her. She read the desire in his eyes, intuitively understanding how leashed his passion was. That he, like she, wanted it *all*.

'Touch me,' she choked. Her command—and his reply—dislodged the last brick in the wall that had been damming her desire inside. She did not want him to hold back with her.

He caressed her breasts with his hands, teasing her as she rocked on him, rubbing in the way the basic instinct of her body dictated—back and forth and around.

'So good,' she muttered, savouring the pressure of his mouth, the sweep of his hands, the hardness of him under her. 'So good.'

It was so foreign. So delicious. Feverish with desire, she arched. Pleasure beyond imagination engulfed her as faster they moved together. Kisses became ravenous. Hands swept hard over skin. Heat consumed her. She moaned, her head falling back as he touched her in places she'd never been touched. As he brought her sensuality to life.

She heard a tearing sound and realised it had been the

crotch of her panties. They'd not survived the strength of
his grip. She glanced and saw he'd tossed the remnants of
white silk and lace onto the wide seat. Now she could feel
his hand touching her again so much more intimately.

'Oh.'

She dragged in a searing breath and gazed into his eyes.

'That's it, Blue,' he enticed her in that devilish whisper. 'Come on.'

She couldn't answer—not as his fingers circled, and
slipped along the slick cleft of her sex, not as they teased
that sensitive nub over and over and over. She bit her lip
as that searing tension deep in her belly tightened. She
rocked, her rhythm matching the pace of his fingers as they
strummed over and around her. He kissed her, his tongue
soothing the indent of her teeth on her lip, then stroking
inside her mouth in an intimate exploration of her private
space. Just as his finger probed within her too.

She tore her mouth from his and threw her head back,
arching in agony as she gasped for breath. He fixed his
mouth on her breast, drawing her nipple in deep. Pleasure
shot from one sensitive point to another, rolling in violent
waves across her body. She shuddered in exquisite agony,
crying out as she was completely lost to this raw, writhing bliss.

When she opened her eyes she saw he was watching her,
his hand gently stroking her thigh.

She breathed out, summoning calm and failing. Giddy,
she gazed at him, stunned by the realisation that she'd just
had an orgasm. She'd let him touch her and kiss her and
he'd made the most amazing feelings flood through her.
But the hunger had returned already and brought that special kind of anger with it.

That emptiness blossomed, bigger than before. There
was more to this electricity between them. More that she'd
missed. More that she wanted.

A chasm stretched before her. A choice. A line that, once

crossed, could never be reclaimed. But it was *her* choice. And suddenly she knew exactly how she wanted this one thing in her life to be. Within her control.

For this first time—for only this time—she wanted physical intimacy with a man who truly wanted her back. A man who wanted not her title, not her purity or connections. Just her—naked and no one special. This man knew nothing of who or what she was, but he wanted her. This was not love, no. But pure, basic, brilliant lust.

Just this once, she would be *wanted* for nothing but herself.

Almost angrily she shifted on him, pressing close again, kissing him. He kissed her back, as hard, as passionate. She moaned in his mouth. *Willing* him to take over. But he drew back, pressing his hand over hers, stopping her from sliding her palm down his chiselled chest to his belt.

'We're going to be in trouble in a second,' he groaned. 'Stop.'

She stared dazedly into his face as he eased her back along his thighs, almost crying at his rejection.

'I need to keep you safe,' he muttered as his hands worked quickly to release his zipper. 'One second. To be safe.'

She couldn't compute his comment because at that moment his erection sprang free. Never had she seen a man naked. Never had she *touched*. He reached into his trouser pocket and pulled out a small packet that he tore open with his teeth. Her mouth dried as she stared avidly.

Of course he was prepared. He was an incredibly handsome, virile man who knew exactly how to turn her on because *he* was experienced. He was used to this kind of anonymous tryst and he definitely knew how to make a woman feel good. And that was...*okay.*

As she tore her gaze away from the magnificence of him she caught sight of their reflections in that gleaming mirror again. The image of those two strangers—half naked and entwined—was the most erotic thing she'd ever seen in her life. Their pasts didn't matter. Nor did their futures. There was only this. Only them. Only now. She turned back to look at the overwhelming man she was sitting astride with such vulnerability—and with such desire.

Princess Eleni always did the right thing.

But she wasn't Princess Eleni tonight. She was no one and this was nothing.

'Easy, Blue.' He gently stroked her arm.

She realised her breathing was completely audible—rushed and short.

'Just whatever you want,' he muttered softly.

He wasn't just inviting her. He was giving her the choice, *all* the control. Yet his voice and his body both commanded and compelled her own and there was no choice.

This once. This *one* time. She wanted everything—all of him. She shimmied closer. The sight of his huge straining erection made her quiver and melt. She didn't know how to do this. She looked into his eyes and was lost in that intensity. And suddenly she understood.

She kissed him. Kissed him long and deep and softened in the delight. In the *rightness* of the sensation. She could feel him there beneath her. She rocked her hips, as she'd done before, feeling him slide through her feminine folds. His hands gripped her hips, holding her, helping her. She pressed down, right on that angle, every sense on high alert and anticipation. But her body resisted, unyielding.

She *wanted* this.

So she pushed down hard. Unexpectedly sharp pain pierced the heated fog of desire.

'Blue?' A burning statue beneath her; his breathing was ragged as he swore. 'I've—'

'I'm fine,' she pleaded, willing her body to welcome his.

'You're tight,' he said between gritted teeth.

'You're big.'

He filled her completely—beneath her, about her, within

her. The force and fire of his personality scalded her. Her breath shuddered as she was locked in his embrace, and in the intense heat of his gaze.

'Have I hurt you?' His question came clipped.

'No.' It wasn't regret that burned within her, but recognition. This was what she wanted. 'Kiss me.'

And he did. He kissed her into that pure state of bliss once more. Into heat and light and sparkling rainbows and all kinds of magic that were miraculous and new. Touching him ignited her and she moved restlessly, eager to feel him touching her again too. That fullness between her legs eased. Honeyed heat bloomed and she slid closer still to him. She sighed, unable to remain still any more. His arms tightened around her, clasping her to him as he kissed her back—exactly how she needed. *Yes.* This was so good, it had to be right. He shifted her, sliding her back, and then down hard on the thick column of his manhood.

He suddenly stood, taking her weight with no apparent difficulty. Startled, she instinctively wrapped her legs around his waist. He kissed her in approval and took those few paces to where that narrow table stretched along the wall. He stood at the short end and carefully placed her right on the edge of it, then slowly he eased her so she lay on her back on the cool wood. Her legs were wound around his waist, her hips tilted upwards as he braced over her, his shaft still driven to the hilt inside her. That mirror was right beside her now but she didn't turn her head to look again at those strangers; she couldn't. Her wicked rake claimed every ounce of her focus.

'This is madness,' he muttered. 'But I don't care.'

Nor did she. This moment was too perfect. Too precious. Too much to be denied.

His large hands cupped her, holding her as he pressed into her deeply, and then pulled back a fraction, only to push forward again. Again, then again, then again. Every time he seemed to drive deeper, claiming more and more of her.

And she gave it to him. She would give him everything, he made her feel so good. He gazed into her eyes and in his she saw the echo of her own emotions—wonder, pleasure, *need*.

She'd never been as close to another person in all her life. Not so passionately, nakedly close. Nor so vulnerable, or so safe. Never so free.

She kissed him in arousal, in madness, in gratitude. Trusting him implicitly. He'd already proven his desire to please her.

'Come again,' he coaxed in a passionate whisper. 'I want to feel you come.'

She wanted that too. She wanted exactly that.

He touched her just above the point where they were joined, teasing even as he filled her. She gasped as she felt the sensations inside gather once more in that unstoppable storm.

'You…please…' she begged incoherently as she feverishly clutched him, digging her fingernails into his flesh. She wanted him to feel the same ecstasy surging through her. She needed him on this ride *with* her. As she frantically arched to meet him she heard his groan. His hands gripped tighter, his expression tensed. She smiled in that final second. She wanted to laugh. She wanted to revel in it and she never, ever wanted it to end.

His face flushed as sensation swept the final vestige of control from his grasp. Pleasure stormed through her again, surging to the farthest reaches of her body. She sobbed in the onslaught of goodness and delight and his roar of satisfaction was the coda to her completeness.

Her eyes were closed. She could hear only the beating of her heart and his as they recovered. She was pinned by his weight and it was the best feeling on earth.

But then laughter rang out. Not hers. Nor his.

'What's in this room?'

Eleni snapped her head to stare at the door as someone on the other side tried the handle.

'Hello?'

More laughter reverberated through the wood.

Reality returned in a violent slam, evaporating the mist of delight. Suddenly she saw herself as she'd look to anyone who burst through that door—Princess Eleni of Palisades, ninety per cent naked, sprawled on a table with her legs around the waist of some stranger and his body ploughed deep into hers.

Sordid headlines smashed into her head: *shameless wanton...a one-night stand...the eve of her engagement...* There would be no mercy, no privacy—only scorn and shame. She had to get out of here. Aghast, she stared up at the handsome stranger she'd just ravished. What had she done?

Damon watched his masked lover's eyes widen in shock. Beneath the blue sparkled powder, her skin paled and her kiss-crushed lips parted in a silent gasp. This was more than embarrassment. This was fear. He was so stunned by her devastated expression he stepped back. She slipped down from the table and tugged at her crumpled clothing. Before he could speak someone knocked on the door again. More voices sounded out in the corridor.

Her pallor worsened.

'I'll get rid of them,' he assured her, hauling up his trousers so he could get to the door and deny anyone entrance to the room. He was determined to wipe that terror from her face.

He pressed a hand on the door. Even though he'd locked it, he couldn't be sure someone wouldn't be able to unlock it from the other side. He listened intently, hoping the revellers would pass and go exploring elsewhere. After a few moments the voices faded.

He turned back to see how she was doing, but she'd vanished. Shocked, he stared around the empty room, then stalked back to where she'd been standing seconds ago.

Only now did he register the other door tucked to the side of that large mirror. There were two entrances to this room and he'd been so caught up in her he'd not even noticed.

He tried the handle but it was locked. So how had she got through it? Keenly he searched and spotted a discreet security screen. Had she known the code to get out? She must have. Because in the space of two seconds, she'd fled.

Just who was she? Why so afraid of someone finding her? Foreboding filled him. He didn't trust women. He didn't trust anyone.

If only he'd peeled off that mask and seen her face properly. How could he have made such a reckless, risky decision?

Anger simmered, but voices sounded outside the other door again, forcing him to move. He glanced in the mirror at his passion-swept reflection. Frowning, he swiftly buttoned his shirt and fixed his trousers properly. Thank heavens he'd retained enough sense to use protection. But as he sorted himself out he realised something he'd missed in his haste to ensure that door was secure. The damn condom was torn. And more than that? It was marked with a trace of something that shouldn't have been there. He remembered when she'd first pushed down on him. When she'd inhaled sharply and tears had sprung to her eyes.

Uncertainty. *Pain.*

Grimly he fastened his belt. He'd been too lost to lust to absorb the implications of her reaction. Now his gut tensed as he struggled to believe the evidence. Had she given him her virginity? Had she truly never had another lover and yet let him, a total stranger, have her in a ten-minute tryst in a private powder room?

Impossible. But the stain of her purity was on his skin. His pulse thundered in his ears. *Why* would she have done something so wild? What was her motivation?

Hell, what had *he* been thinking? To have had sex with

a woman he'd barely met as fast and as furiously as possible? Almost in public?

But her expressive response had swept all sensible thought from his head. She'd *wanted* him and heaven knew he'd wanted her. He was appalled by his recklessness; his anger roared. But a twist of Machiavellian satisfaction brewed beneath, because he was going to have to find her. He was going to have to warn her about the condom. The instinct to hunt her pressed like the blade of a knife. She owed him answers.

Find her. Find her. Find her.

His pulse banged like a pagan's drum, marching him back to the busy ballroom. He even took to the balcony to scan the braying crowd, determined to find that blue hair and swan-like neck. But he knew it was futile. The midnight hour had struck and that sizzling Cinderella had run away, never wanting to be seen again.

Least of all by him.

CHAPTER THREE

'YOU LOOK PEAKY.'

Eleni forced a reassuring smile and faced her brother across the aisle in his jet.

'I have a bit of a headache but it's getting better,' she lied.

She felt rotten. Sleeplessness and guilt made her queasy.

'The next few weeks will be frantic. You'll need to stay in top form. They want the pretty Princess, not the pale one,' King Giorgos turned back to the tablet he'd been staring at for the duration of the flight.

'Yes.'

She glanced out of the small window. Crowds had gathered with flags and celebratory signs. She quickly dug into her bag to do a touch-up on her blush, thankful that the jet had landed them back on Palisades.

Giorgos had escorted her on a three-day celebration visit of Santa Chiara to meet again with Prince Xander and his family. Not so long ago she'd have inwardly grimaced at her brother's smothering protectiveness, but she'd been glad of his presence. It had meant she'd not been left alone with Prince Xander.

The Shy Princess captures the Playboy Prince...

Their engagement had captured the imaginations of both nations. Her schedule and the resulting media interest had been beyond intense these last few weeks. At least all the appearances had kept her too busy to think. But late at night when she was alone in her private suite?

That was when she processed everything, reassuring herself she was safe. She would never tell anyone and that man from the ball would never tell anyone. He didn't even know who she was. She didn't know his name either. Only his face. Only his body.

She shivered but forced another smile when her brother glanced at her again. 'I'm going to go to my hospital visit this morning,' she said brightly.

Giorgos frowned. 'You don't wish to rest?'

Always protective. And also, always frowning.

She shook her head.

It had been nothing more than a sordid physical transaction. A ten-minute encounter between strangers. And surely, *please, please, please*, she would soon forget it. Because right now the memories were too real. She relived every moment, every word, every touch. And the worst thing? She wanted it again, wanted more, wanted it so much she burned with it. And then she burned with shame. Tears stung at the enormity of her betrayal. She was now engaged to another man yet all she could think of was *him*, that arrogant, intense stranger at the ball.

Thankfully displays of physical affection weren't 'done' between royals so the few 'kisses for the camera' on her tour with Prince Xander had been brief—her coolness read by the media as shyness. In private her fiancé had seemed happy to give her the time and space to adjust.

It was Giorgos who had asked if she was going to be happy with Xander and who'd reassured her that her fiancé's 'playboy' status was more media speculation than solid truth. For a moment she was tempted to confess her dreadful affair, but then she saw the tiredness in the back of her brother's eyes. He worked so hard for his people.

And she couldn't bear to see his crushing disappointment. She remembered how Giorgos had teased her with big-brother ruthlessness and laughter. But how he'd aged a decade overnight when their father died. Under the burden of all that responsibility he'd become serious, distant and more ruthless, without that humour. She understood he was wretchedly busy, but he'd tried his best for her—sending people to educate her, protect her, guide her. He just hadn't had the time himself. And she could not let him down.

He believed Xander to be the right fit for her—from a limited pool of options—and perhaps he was. So she'd make the best of it.

For Giorgos.

But the thought of her wedding night repulsed her. As crazy as it was, that brief conversation with that stranger at the ball had engendered far more trust in her than any of the discussions she'd had with polite, well-educated, aiming-to-please but ultimately careless Prince Xander. She simply didn't want him like that. She shivered again as that cold, sick feeling swept over her.

'I don't want to miss a visit,' she finally answered as she rose to disembark the jet.

She needed to do something slightly worthwhile because the guilt was eating her up. Her brother nodded and said nothing more. If anyone understood duty before all else, it was he.

An hour later, as she walked the corridor towards her favourite ward, that cold queasiness returned.

'Princess Eleni?' Kassie, the physiotherapist escorting her to the ward, stopped.

From a distance Eleni registered the woman was frowning and her voice sounded distanced too.

'Are you feeling okay?'

Damon Gale was barely existing in a state of perpetual anger. He hadn't left Palisades without trying to find and warn his mystery lover there might be consequences from their time together. He'd described her to his half-sister Kassie, but she'd not been able to identify the woman either. No one could. None of his subtle queries had given any answers. Where had she disappeared to so quickly? Heaven knew, when he found her he was giving her a piece of his mind. But at night she came to him in dream after dream.

He woke, hard, hungry and irritable as hell. There was so much more they should have done. But now she was hiding. Not least the truth about who she was. Why?

He loathed nothing more than lies.

So this morning, weeks since that damn ball, he'd once again flown back to Palisades. Now he waited for Kassie at the hospital in her tiny office, looking at the clever pen and ink drawings of the child patients pinned to the noticeboard.

He heard a footstep and a low, hurried whisper just outside the door.

'Ma'am, are you sure you're feeling all right?'

That was Kassie. Damon's muscles tensed.

'I'm just a bit…dizzy. Oh.' The woman groaned.

He froze, shocked at the second voice. He *knew* those raspy tones. She spoke in his dreams. Every. Damn. Night.

'Do you need a container?' Kassie asked delicately.

'I had a bug a few days ago but I thought I was over it or I'd never have visited today,' the woman muttered apologetically. 'I'm so sorry. I'd never want to put any of your patients at risk.'

'They're a hardy lot.' Now Kassie's smile was audible. 'I'm more concerned about you. Are you sure I can't get a doctor to check you over?'

'No, please. No fuss. I'll quickly go back to the palace. My driver is waiting.'

Palace? Damon was unable to move. Unable to speak. His woman had known the security code to get through that second door in the palace. Did she work there? But she'd said she worked at the hospital. That was why he was back here again.

'Maybe you should rest a moment,' Kassie urged softly.

'No. I need to go. I shouldn't have come.'

Damon stood. Those words exactly echoed ones he'd heard that night at the masked ball. Those exact tones in that exact, raspy voice. It was *her*.

He strode across the room and out into the corridor. But

his half-sister had her back to him and she was standing alone. Damon looked past her and saw no one—the corridor ended abruptly with a corner.

'Who was that?' he demanded harshly.

Kassie spun, startled. 'Damon?' She blinked at him. 'I didn't know you were coming back again so soon.'

'I have another meeting,' he clipped. 'Who were you talking to?'

'I'm not supposed to say because her visits are strictly private,' Kassie answered quietly. 'But she wasn't feeling well today and left early.'

'Whose visits?' What did she mean by 'private'?

'The Princess.'

Damon stared dumbfounded at his half-sister.

Princess Eleni of Palisades?

Wasn't she the younger sister of King Giorgos, a man known for his protectiveness and control over everything—his island nation, his emotions, his small *family*. Hadn't he been the guardian of the supposedly shy Princess for ever?

Now the covers of the newspapers at the airport flashed in his mind. He'd walked past them this morning but paid little attention because they'd all carried the same photo and same headline—

A Royal Engagement! The Perfect Prince for Our Princess!

But the Princess was not perfect. She'd fooled around with a total stranger only a few weeks ago. And now she was engaged. Had she been rebelling like some wilful teen? Or was there something more devious behind her shocking behaviour? And, heaven have mercy, how *old* was she?

'What do you think was wrong with her?' he asked Kassie uneasily. He needed to get alone and research more because an extremely bad feeling was building inside him.

'I'm not sure. She was pale and nau—'

'Where did she go?' he interrupted.

Kassie was staring at him. 'Back to the palace. She visits my ward every Friday. She never misses, no matter what.' Kassie ventured a small smile. 'She doesn't seem your type.'

He forced himself to answer idly, as if this didn't matter a jot. 'Do I have a type?'

Kassie's laugh held a nervous edge as she shook her head. 'Princess Eleni is very sweet and innocent.'

But that was where Kassie was wrong. Princess Eleni wasn't sweet or innocent at all. She was a liar and a cheat and he was going to tear her to shreds.

Thank God he finally knew where and how he could get to her. He just had to withstand waiting one more week.

CHAPTER FOUR

IN HER BATHROOM Eleni stared at her reflection. Her skin was leached of colour and she felt sick and tired all the time. Wretched nausea roiled in her stomach yet again, violent and irrepressible. She'd been avoiding mirrors since the ball. She couldn't see herself without seeing those two strangers entwined...

It had been over a month since that night. Now she gazed at her breasts and held in her agonised gasp. Was it her imagination or were they fuller than usual? That would be because her period was due, right? But finally she made herself face the fact she'd been trying desperately to forget. Her period was more than due. It was late.

Two weeks late.

She'd been busy. She'd been travelling. Her cycle could be screwed up by nerves, couldn't it?

Frigid fear slithered down her spine as bitter acid flooded her mouth again. Because a lone, truly terrifying reason for her recurring sickness gripped her.

Surely it was impossible. She'd seen him put on that condom. She couldn't possibly be pregnant. That foul acid burned its way up into her mouth. She closed her eyes as tears stung and then streamed down her face. She needed help and she needed it now.

But there was no help to be had. She had no true friends to trust. Her childhood companions had been carefully selected for their families' loyalty to the crown and swiftly excised from her life if they'd slightly transgressed. There were acquaintances but no real confidantes and now most were in continental Europe getting on with their careers. Eleni had studied at home. It was 'safer'; it endorsed their own, prestigious university; it was what Giorgos had wanted. She'd not argued, not wanting to cause him trouble.

She was terrified of troubling him now.

But she was going to have to. Shaking, she showered then dressed. She quickly typed an email to Giorgos's secretary requesting a meeting for this evening. Her brother was busy, but Prince Xander was arriving from Santa Chiara tonight for a week's holiday with her. They'd be travelling to the outer islands to spend more time together. She was dreading it. She had to speak to Giorgos first. She had to tell him the truth.

Still incredibly cold, she grabbed a jacket and stuffed a cap in the pocket while her maid, Bettina, phoned for her car.

It was far later than when she usually went to the hospital, but she was desperate to get away from her suite where her maid was lining up sample wedding dresses from the world's top designers. The only thing she could do while waiting to meet Giorgos was maintain some kind of schedule. Given she'd left her visit so abruptly last week, she couldn't miss this week as well. She'd control the nausea and control her life.

Once she got to the hospital she asked Tony, her security detail, to wait for her outside. But she didn't go into the ward, and instead walked along the corridor to the other side of the building. She tugged on the cap and headed out to the private hospital garden. She needed to steel herself for the polite questions from the patients she'd come to help entertain. But she'd been lying all day, every day for the last few weeks and it was taking its toll. Telling people over and over again how excited she was at the prospect of marrying Prince Xander was exhausting. And horrible. But the bigger the lie, the more believable it apparently was.

She leaned over the wrought-iron railing, looking down at the river. She was going to have to go back and front up to Giorgos. Her gut churned, but it wasn't the pregnancy hormones making her nauseous now. How did she admit this all to him?

I'm sorry. I'm so sorry.

Sorry wasn't going to be good enough. She dreaded sinking so low in his eyes. Never had she regretted anything as much as her recklessness that night at the ball.

A prickle of awareness pressed on her spine—intuition whispered she was no longer alone. Warily she turned away from the water.

'You okay?' The man stood only a couple of paces away. 'Or are you feeling a little blue?'

The bitterness in that soft-spoken query devastated her. It was *him*. Her blood rushed and the edges of her vision blackened as she shrank back. Something grasped her elbow tightly, the pain pulling her from the brink of darkness.

'It's okay, I'm not going to let you fall.'

He was there and he was too close, with his words in her ear and his strength in his grip and his heat magnetic.

Oh, no. No.

'I'm sorry.' Eleni ignored the sweat suddenly slithering down her spine and snapped herself together.

He released her the second she tugged her arm back, but he didn't step away. So he was close. Too close.

'I don't know what came over me.' She leaned against the railing, unable to stop the trembling of her legs or the jerkiness of her breathing.

'Yeah, you do.' He leaned against the wrought iron too, resting his hand on the rail between them. Not relaxed. *Ready to strike.*

Tall, dark and dangerous, he looked like some streetwise power player in his black trousers, black jersey, aviator sunglasses and unreadable expression.

'There's no point trying to hide any more, Eleni,' he

said. 'I know who you are and I know exactly what your problem is.'

She froze. 'I don't have a problem.'

'Yeah, you do. You and I created it together. Now we're going to resolve it. Together.'

All strength vanished from her legs. They'd *created* it? The full horror hit as she realised he *knew*.

'I'm sorry,' she repeated mechanically. 'I don't know who you are and I don't know what you're talking about.' She willed her strength back. 'If you'll forgive me, I need to go.'

'No.' He removed his sunglasses. 'I won't forgive you.'

Her heart stuttered at the emotion reflected in his intense blue eyes. Accusation. Betrayal. Anger...and something else.

Something she dared not try to define.

She clenched her fists and plunged them into the pockets of her jacket, fighting the paralysis. 'I have to leave.'

'Not this time. You're coming with me, Eleni. You know we need to talk.'

'I can't do that.' Why had she thought it wise not to tell her security detail where she was going?

'Yes, you can. Because if you don't...'

'What?' She drew in a sharp breath as a sense of fatality struck. 'What will you do?'

Of course it would come to an ultimatum. The determination had been on his face from the second she'd seen him. He was livid.

'You come with me now and we take the time to sort this out, or I tell the world you're pregnant from screwing a stranger at the palace ball.'

His tawdry description of what they'd done stabbed. It hadn't been a 'screw'. It had meant more than she could ever admit to anyone.

'No one would believe you,' she muttered.

'You're *that* good at lying?' He was beyond livid. 'You

want this scandal dragged through the press? That you're going to marry a man without telling him that you're pregnant, most probably by another?'

She flinched at his cruelly blunt words but she latched onto the realisation that he wasn't *sure* the baby was his.

'You want the whole world to know that you're not the perfect Princess after all?' he goaded her relentlessly. 'But a liar and a cheater?'

'I've never been the perfect Princess,' she snapped back, defensive and hurt and unable to stay calm a second longer.

'Come on.' The softness of his swift reply stunned her.

Her heart thundered. He'd echoed the forbidden words from weeks ago. Heat flared. So wrong.

'I can't,' she reminded him—and herself—through gritted teeth. 'My fiancé is arriving in Palisades tonight.'

'Really?' He glared at her. 'That cheating life is what you really want?' His frustration seeped through. 'That's why you're standing by the river looking like you're about to throw yourself in? You're lost, Eleni.'

'You don't know what I am.'

He knew nothing about her and she knew as little about him—not even his damn name.

Except that wasn't quite true. She knew more important things—his determination, his strength, his consideration.

And *her* guilt.

'The one thing I do know is that you're pregnant and the baby very well might be mine. You owe me a conversation at least.'

He wasn't going anywhere and he was perfectly capable of acting on his threat, she knew that about him too. She tried to regain her customary calm, and decided to bluff. 'So talk.'

'Somewhere private.' He glanced up at the multi-storeyed hospital building behind her. 'Where we can't be seen or overheard.'

That made sense but it was impossible. She shook her head.

'My car is just around the corner,' he said, unconcerned at her latest refusal.

Her heart thudded. She shouldn't go anywhere alone with any man and certainly not this one.

'I'll go straight to the media,' he promised coolly. 'And I have proof. I still have your underwear.'

She was aghast; her jaw dropped.

'You *wouldn't*,' she choked.

'I'm prepared to do whatever is necessary to get this sorted out,' he replied blandly, putting his sunglasses back on. 'I suggest you walk with me now.'

What choice did she have?

She hardly saw where she was going as she moved back through the hospital, then to the right instead of the left. Away from her guard. Hopefully Tony wouldn't notice for a few minutes yet—in all her life she'd never caused trouble for him.

She slid into the passenger seat of his car.

'Five minutes,' she said just as he closed the door for her.

He was still laughing, bitterly, as he got in, locked the doors and started the engine. 'You might want to put on your seat belt, because it's going to take a little longer than that this time, sweetheart.' He pulled out into the road. 'We have a lifetime to work out.'

'Where are you taking me?' She broke into a cold sweat.

'As I said, somewhere private. Somewhere where we won't be disturbed.'

'You can't take me away from here.' Frantically she twisted in her seat, terrified to see the hospital getting smaller as they moved away from it.

'I know how quickly you can move, Eleni. I'm not taking the risk of you running from me this time.'

Surprised, she turned to face him.

'Relax.' He sent her an ironic glance. 'I'm not going to hurt you, Princess. We just need to talk.'

Sure, she knew he wouldn't hurt her physically. But in other ways? She tried to clear her head. 'You have the better of me. I don't even know your name.'

'So you're finally curious enough to ask?' His hands tightened on the steering wheel. 'My name is Damon Gale. I'm the CEO of a tech company that specialises in augmented reality. I have another company that's working on robotics. Most women think I'm something of a catch.'

Damon. Crisp and masculine. It suited him.

'I'm not like most women.' She prickled at his arrogance. 'And a lot of men think I'm a catch.'

'You definitely took some catching,' he murmured, pulling into a car park and killing the engine. 'Yet here we are.'

Eleni looked out of the car window and saw he meant literally. He'd brought her to the marina. 'Why are we here?'

'I need the certainty that you won't do one of your disappearing acts, but we can't have this argument in the front seat of a car and...' He hesitated as he stared at her. 'We need space.'

Space? Eleni's heart thundered as she gazed into his eyes. Beneath her shock and fear something else stirred—awareness, recognition.

This is the one I had. This is the one I want.

Suddenly that forbidden passion pulsed through every fibre of her being.

Unbidden. Unwanted. Undeniable.

CHAPTER FIVE

HE'D KNOWN HER eyes weren't that unnaturally intense indigo they'd been at the ball, but the discovery of their true colour had stolen a breath that Damon still hadn't recovered. They were sea green—a myriad of bewitching shades—and he couldn't summon the strength to look away.

She lies.

He reminded himself. Again.

The alluring Princess Eleni Nicolaides had used him and he couldn't possibly be considering kissing her. He'd not been completely certain before but he was now—she was pregnant. To him.

Grimly he shoved himself out of the car and stalked around it to open her door. Impatiently he watched the emotions flicker across her too-expressive face—wariness, curiosity, decision—and beneath those? Desire.

His body tightened. More than anger, this was possessiveness. So off-base. Rigid with self-control, he took her arm, steeling himself not to respond to the electricity that surged between them. It took only a minute to guide her down the steps and along the wooden landing to his yacht. She stopped and stared at it.

'Eleni,' he prompted her curtly. 'We need to talk.'

'You have to take me back soon.' She twisted her hands together. 'They'll be wondering where I am.'

'They can wonder for a while yet,' he muttered.

He hustled her past the cabin and through to the lounge. The windows were tinted so no one on deck could see them, and his sparse crew were under strict instruction to stay out of sight and work quickly. He remained in front of the only exit to the room. He couldn't be careful enough with her.

'Take off the cap.' He could hardly push the words past the burr in his throat, but he needed to see her with no damn disguise.

She lifted the cap. Her hair wasn't long and blue, it was cut to a length just below her chin and was blonde—corn silk soft, all natural and, right now, tousled.

'How did you figure out who I was?' she asked in that damnably raspy voice.

He shook his head.

Once he'd realised who his mystery lover was, he'd been lame enough to look online. But she was more perfect in the flesh. Tall and slender, strong and feminine, with those curves that caused the most base reaction in him. Her complexion was flawless and her sweetheart-shaped face captivating. But her beauty was a façade that apparently masked a shockingly salacious soul. He was determined to get to the truth.

'You knew I was going to be at the hospital,' she said after he didn't reply to her first question. 'How?'

Her fingers trembled as she fidgeted with the cap, but he'd not brought her here to answer *her* questions.

'Were you going to tell him?' he asked.

He glared as she didn't answer. She was so good at avoiding everything important, wasn't she?

He felt the vibration beneath the deck as the engines fired up. About time. Icily satisfied, he silently kept watching. Now she'd be tested. Sure enough, as the yacht moved she strode to the window.

'Where are you taking me?' she asked, her volume rising.

'Somewhere private.' Somewhere isolated. Triumph rushed at the prospect of having her completely alone.

'This *is* private. We don't need to move to make it more so.' Panic filled her voice and turned wide eyes on him. 'This is abduction.'

'Is it?' he asked, uncaring. 'But you agreed to come with me.'

'I didn't realise you meant...' She paled. 'I can't just *leave.*'

He hardened his heart. 'Why not? You've done that before.'

This was the woman who'd had sex with him when she knew she was about to announce her engagement to another man. Who'd then run off without another word. And who was now pregnant and concealing it—apparently from everyone.

The betrayal burned like no other. He hated being *used.* His father had used him as cover for his long-term infidelities. His mother had used his entire existence to promote her political aspirations—hell, she'd even told him she never would have had him if it weren't for the possible benefit to her career. His father had not only agreed, he'd expected Damon to understand and become the same. A parasite—using anyone and anything to enhance success. He'd refused and he'd vowed that he'd never let anyone use him again.

But Eleni had.

Yet that look on her face now was torture—those shimmering eyes, the quiver of her full lips.

Desire tore through his self-control, forcing him closer to her. Furious, he locked it down, viciously clenching his fists and shoving them into his trouser pockets. It was this uncontrolled lust that had got him into this mess in the first place.

It was insane. Once more he reminded himself he knew nothing of importance about her other than her shocking ability to conceal information. But as he watched, she whitened further. Whitened to the point of—

'Eleni?' He rushed forward.

'Oh, hell.' She pressed her hand to her mouth.

Oh, hell was right. He reached for a decorative bowl just in time.

* * *

Oh, no. No.

Eleni groaned but the sickness couldn't be stopped. Of all the mortifying things to happen.

'Sit down before you fall down,' he muttered.

'I'm not used to being on the water,' she replied.

'If you're going to lie, at least try to make it believable. It's well known you love sailing, Princess. Your illness is caused by your pregnancy.'

She was too queasy to bother trying to contradict him. What was the point? 'I need fresh air.'

'You need to stay in here until we're away from the island.'

'You can't be serious.' Aghast, she stared up at him. 'You're going to cause an international incident.'

'Do you think so?' He stared at her grimly. 'I think the spectacle is only going to get even more insane when they find out I'm the father of your unborn child.'

She closed her eyes and groaned. 'At least let me use a bathroom.'

'Of course.'

He guided her to a small room. He opened a drawer and handed her a toothbrush, still in its packet. She took it, silently grateful as he left her in privacy.

But he was just outside the door when she opened it again a few minutes later.

She walked back into the lounge just as a uniformed crew member was leaving. The man didn't say a word, didn't meet her eyes. He simply melted from the room.

'Who was that?' she asked.

'Someone extremely discreet and very well paid.'

He'd left fresh water in a tall glass and a few crackers on a plate. She turned away; there was no way she could eat anything right now.

'You're naive if you think he won't sell your secrets.'

The man had recognised her. It was only a matter of time before people came to her rescue.

'I've been betrayed before, Eleni. I know how to make my business safe.'

Eleni looked at the hard edge of Damon's jaw and wondered who had betrayed him. 'Your business?'

'My baby.'

Her blood chilled. 'So you planned this.'

There'd been a crew ready and waiting on this boat and no doubt he paid them ridiculously well. He'd gone to huge trouble to get her away from the palace. Maybe she ought to feel scared, she barely knew him after all, but she didn't believe she was in danger. Rather, in that second, the craziest feeling bloomed in her chest.

Relief.

His eyes narrowed. 'You know this isn't about rescuing you.'

His words hit like bullets. She shrank, horrified that he'd seen her *selfishness*. Guilt brought defensiveness with it. 'I don't need rescuing.'

His smile mocked. 'No?'

Damon was more dangerous than she'd realised. She couldn't cope with her reaction to him. It was as if everything else in the world, everything that mattered, simply evaporated in his presence. His pull was too strong.

But then she remembered he wasn't certain she was pregnant to *him*. Perhaps her way out was to convince him he *wasn't* the father. Then he'd return her to Palisades. She'd go to Giorgos. She should have gone to Giorgos already.

'I *can't* stay here,' she pleaded.

'Give in, Eleni,' he replied indifferently. 'You already are. The question is, can you be honest?'

Not with him. Not now.

But she burned to prove that she didn't need 'rescuing'—not from her situation, or from herself. He strolled towards her but she wasn't fooled by the ease of his movement. He was furious. Well, that made two of them.

'How many other possibilities are there?' he asked too softly, his gaze penetrating.

'Excuse me?' She tensed as he came within touching distance.

'Who are the other men who might be the father of your child?' He watched her so intently she feared he could see every hidden thought, every contrary emotion.

'Can you even remember them all?' he challenged.

She flushed at his tone, lost for words.

'You have sex with me at a ball within five minutes of meeting me,' he murmured, continuing his hateful judgment. 'You didn't even know my name.'

'And you didn't know mine,' she flared. 'And we used protection. So there you go.'

'But *I* wasn't engaged to anyone else at the time.'

That one hurt because it was truth. 'Nor was I,' she mumbled weakly.

'Not "officially".' His eyes were so full of scorn that she winced. 'But you *knew*. You knew the announcement was about to be made. You owed him your loyalty and you cheated.'

Damon was right, but he didn't know the reality of the marriage she faced. He'd never understand the scrutiny and crazy constraints she endured in her privileged world.

At her silence now, pure danger flashed in his eyes. She backed away until the wall brought her to a stop. Her heart raced as he followed until he leaned right into her personal space.

'So, how many others?' he asked again, too softly.

She'd brazen it out. Disgust him so he'd take her back to Palisades in repulsion. 'At least four.'

'Liar.' Slowly he lifted his hand and brushed the backs of his fingers over the blush burning down her cheekbones. 'Why won't you just tell me the truth, Eleni?'

His whisper was so tempting.

She lifted her chin, refusing to let him seduce her again. And at the same time, refusing to run. 'I don't have to tell you anything.'

'What are you afraid of?' he taunted huskily. 'The world finding out your secret? That Princess Eleni The Pure likes dressing up in disguise and doing it fast and dirty with a succession of strangers? That she can't get enough?'

Anger ignited, but something else was lit within as well. That treacherous response. She *had* liked it fast and dirty. With him. She closed her eyes but he tilted her chin back up, holding it until she opened them again and looked right into the banked heat of his.

'Are you ashamed of what happened, Eleni?'

Tears stung but she blinked them back. Of *course* she was ashamed. She couldn't understand how it had happened. How she could have lost all control and all reason like that. And how could her body be so traitorous now— aching for him to take that half step nearer and touch her again?

The intensity deepened in his eyes. A matching colour mounted in his cheekbones.

Hormones. Chemicals. That crazy reaction that she still couldn't believe had happened was happening again.

'You like it,' he muttered. 'And you want it.'

'And I get it,' she spat, reckless and furious and desperate to push him away. 'From whomever, whenever I please.'

'Is that right?'

'Yes,' she slammed her answer in defiance.

He smiled. A wickedly seductive smile of utter disbelief.

'You'll never know.' She was pushed to scorn.

'You don't think?' He actually laughed.

'Maybe I'm pregnant with my fiancé's baby,' she snapped. Reminding him of her engagement might make him back off. She *needed* him to back off.

His smile vanished. 'I don't think so, Princess.'

She stilled at his expression.

'You haven't slept with him,' Damon said roughly. 'I was your first, Eleni. That night with me, you were a virgin.'

She gaped, floundering in total mortification as he threw the truth in her face.

How had he known? How? She pressed against the cool wall, hoping to stop shaking.

'Why lie so constantly?' he demanded, leaning closer, the heat of his body blasting. 'You still have nothing to say?'

How could she possibly explain? She couldn't answer even her own conscience.

'There is nothing wrong with liking sex,' he said roughly. 'But there is something wrong with lying and cheating to get it.'

She trembled again, appalled by how aroused she was. She could no longer look him in the eye; he saw too much. She wanted to hide from him. From herself. Since when was she this wanton animal who'd forgo all her scruples simply to get a physical fix?

'Eleni.'

She refused to look at him.

But she couldn't escape the sensations that the slightest of touches summoned. He brushed her cheek with a single finger, and then tucked a strand of her hair back behind her ear. She stood rigid, desperate not to reveal any reaction.

'Let's try this again, shall we?' He leaned so close.

She bit the inside of her cheek, hoping the pain would help keep her sane, but she could feel his heat radiating through her.

'No lying. No cheating,' he murmured. 'Just truth.'

The tip of his finger marauded back and forth over her lips; the small caress sent shock waves of sensuality to her most private depths.

Her pulse quickened, but his finger didn't. Slowly he teased. Such pleasure and such promise came from a touch so small, building until she could no longer hold still. He teased until she parted her lips with a shaky breath.

He swooped, pressing his mouth to hers, taking advantage to slide his tongue deep and taste until he tore a soft moan from her. So easily. He wound his arm around her waist and drew her close, holding her so he could kiss her. Again. Then again.

After all these sleepless nights he was with her—with all his heat and hardness. She quivered, then melted against him. Immediately he swept his hand down her side, urging her closer and she went—her body softening to accommodate the steel of his.

With his hands and with his lips, he marauded everywhere now. Kissing her mouth, her jaw, her neck, he slid his hand across her aching breasts, down her quivering stomach, until he hit the hem of her skirt. He pushed under and up. High, then higher still up her thigh. Demanding—and getting—acceptance, intimacy, willingness. So quickly. So intensely. She curled into his embrace, then arched taut as a bowstring as he teased her.

'Eleni…' he whispered between kisses and caresses. 'How many lovers have you had?'

Unable to contain her need, she thrust against that tormenting finger that was so close, that was stirring her in a way that she could no longer resist. On a desperate sigh she finally surrendered her not so secret truth. 'One.'

He rewarded her with more of that rubbing designed to drive her insane. She couldn't breathe. Closer, *so* close.

'And how many times have you had sex?'

She shook with aching desire. With the need for him to touch her again. Just once. One more touch was all she needed. 'One,' she muttered breathlessly.

Her answer seemed to anger him again. He held her fast and kissed her hard. Passionate and ruthless, his tongue plundered the cavern of her mouth. He was dominant and claiming and all she could do was yield to his passion.

But the fires within him stoked her own. She kissed him back furiously, hating him knowing how aroused she was. But there was no controlling her reaction. No stopping what she wanted. And she *wanted. Now.*

It was at that moment, of her total surrender, that he tore his mouth from hers.

'How many men have kissed you like that?' he rasped.

She panted, her nipples tight and straining against her suddenly too tight bra. *'One,'* she answered, pushed beyond her limits.

'And how many men have kissed you liked that, but *here*?' His fingers pushed past the silk scrap of material covering her, probing into her damp, hot sex.

She gasped at the delicious intrusion. Her limbs trembled as release hovered only a stroke or two away. She gazed into his gorgeously fiery eyes, quivering at the extreme intimacy connecting them.

'Answer me, Eleni.' He ground out a brutal whisper.

'None.' Her answer barely sounded.

She registered his sharp exhalation but then he kissed her again. Somehow she was in his embrace, his body between hers. Heaven help her, she went with him to that sofa. She let him. Wanted him. But as he pushed her skirt higher and slid lower so he was kneeling between her legs she realised where this was going. A lucid moment—she gasped and shifted.

'Don't try to hide. I'm going to kiss you. There won't be even an inch of you that I haven't tasted. Every intimacy is *mine.*'

His blunt, savage words stunned her. Blindly she realised that his control was as splintered as her own. That he too was pushed beyond reason. Pleasure surged and she couldn't resist or deny—not him. Not herself.

She groaned at his first kiss, shocked at how exposed she felt and embarrassed by just how much she ached for his touch. It was like being taken over by a part of herself she didn't know was there. That lustful, brazen part. She flung her arm over her face, hiding from him. From herself. But there was no hiding from the sensations he aroused and the delight and skill of his mouth on her. His tongue. There. Right there.

She moaned in unspeakable pleasure.

'Look at that,' he muttered arrogantly in the echo of her need. 'You like it.' His laugh was exultant. 'You like it a lot.'

His attention was relentless. She arched again, pressing her hands against her eyes but unable to hold back her scream as a torrent of ecstasy tore through her. She shuddered, sweet torture wracking her body.

Then she was silent, suspended in that moment where she waited for his next move. For him to rise above her, to press against her, to take her. She ached anew to feel him. She wanted him to push inside and take her completely.

But he didn't. He didn't move at all.

She lay frozen, her face still buried in her arm as the last vestiges of that bliss ebbed. And then shame flooded in. Bitter, galling shame.

She twisted, suddenly desperate to escape. But he grasped her hips hard, prevented her moving even an inch.

'Stop hiding,' he growled savagely. 'There are things we must discuss.'

'Discuss? You think you discuss anything?' She threw her arms wide and snarled at him. 'You dictate.' He *bulldozed*. 'And you...you...'

'Take action.' He finished her sentence for her, as breathless and angry as she. 'And I'll continue to do so. And first up, you're not going to marry Prince Xander of Santa Chiara. You're going to marry me.'

CHAPTER SIX

'I'M NOT MARRYING YOU,' Eleni snapped, furiously shoving him. 'I'm not marrying anyone.'

'Right.' He lazily leaned back on his heels and sent her a sardonic look. 'That's why the world is currently planning party snacks for the live stream of the royal wedding of the century.'

She was sick of his smug arrogance. Awkwardly she curled up her legs to get past him and angrily pulled her skirt down, too mortified to hunt for her knickers. 'I wasn't going to go through with it.'

'Really?' He stood in a single, smooth movement, mocking her with his athletic grace. 'What was the plan?'

She loathed how inept he made her feel. How easily he could make her lose all control. How much her appallingly stupid body still wanted his attention. 'You have no idea how impossible it is for me to get away.'

'As it happens, I do have some insight into the technical difficulties.' His gaze narrowed. Hardened. 'So you were going to go through with it.'

She'd never wanted to but she'd known it was what was expected. Since she'd suspected her pregnancy her desperation had grown. She glared at him from the centre of the room. 'I didn't know what to do.'

'Why not try talking to him?'

She rolled her eyes. He made it sound so easy.

'Giorgos wouldn't listen.'

'Giorgos?' Damon's eyebrows shot up. 'What about the man you were supposed to marry?'

Who? Oh. He meant Xander. As if she could talk to him—she barely knew him.

'I'm guessing you don't love him. Prince Xander, that is,' Damon added sarcastically.

She turned away from Damon. Her heart beat heavy and fast and she perched on the edge of a small chair—far, far away from that sofa. 'Obviously not or I wouldn't have... done what I did with you.'

'Then why marry him?'

'Because it is what has been expected for a long time.'

'So it's duty.'

'It would benefit our countries...'

'Because a royal wedding is somehow going to magically smooth away any serious issues your respective countries may be facing?' He laughed derisively. 'And you'll throw in some rainbows and unicorns to make it all prettier and perfect?'

'You don't understand the subtleties.'

'Clearly not,' he muttered dryly. 'And was my child meant to be the fruit of this fairy-tale unity?' he demanded. 'When in reality she or he will grow up lonely in a house devoid of warmth and love with parents absent in every sense.'

Eleni stared, taken aback by his vehemence. And his insight.

'I'll never let my child be used that way.' His eyes were hard. 'I know the unseen impact of a purely political union and I'll do whatever it takes to ensure my kid doesn't endure that kind of bleak upbringing.'

'I'm not going to marry him,' she said in a low voice. 'I know I can't.'

'But if you don't marry someone, your child will be labelled a bastard. We might live in modern times, but you're a *princess* and there are certain expectations. What kind of life will your child have without legitimacy? Will she be kept cloistered in the shadows, even more stifled than you were? Look how well that turned out for you.'

She flinched. He saw too much and he judged harshly.

But the horrible thing was, he was right. She had to think of a better way. She leapt to her feet and paced away from him, twisting her cold hands together. She didn't want to involve *him*—he twisted everything up too much.

'I need to call Giorgos,' she said. It must be almost two hours since she'd left Palisades and her brother would be irate already.

'I agree.'

She spun on the spot. 'You do?'

'Of course. It'll be better if you're completely honest with him. Do you think you can be—or are you going to need help with that again?'

She flushed, remembering just how Damon had dragged the intimate truth from her only minutes ago. Now his biting sarcasm hurt and she felt sick enough at the thought of confessing all to her brother.

'What, you expect me to cheerily tell him I'm here of my own free will?' She flared. 'That you didn't bundle me into a boat and set sail for the high seas before I could blink?'

'The choice was yours.'

'What choice did you give me?' she scoffed.

'To speak the truth, or give you time. I think it was a reasonable choice.'

'It was blackmail. Because you're a bully.'

'You've already admitted you didn't know what to do. You couldn't figure a way out. Here it is and you're happy about it. Don't dramatise me into your villain.'

Eleni rubbed her forehead. Damon's words struck a deep chord. She'd been refusing to admit to herself how glad she was he'd stolen her away. She'd been unable to think up an escape and he'd offered one. She wasn't as much mad with him, but mad with herself for needing it—and for layering on complications with her wretched desire for him. Her emotional overreactions had to end.

She'd been too scared to admit to Giorgos how badly

she'd screwed up. But if she wanted her brother to treat her as an adult, she had to act like one.

'Okay.' She blew out a breath and turned to look Damon in the eye. 'I'm not sorry you took me away. You're right. I needed this time to think things through. Thank you.'

'How very gracious, Princess,' Damon drawled. 'But don't be mistaken. Like I said, this isn't a rescue. I'm not doing you a favour. I'm claiming what's mine. And I'm protecting it.' He picked up a handset from a small side table and held it out to her. 'Phone your brother.'

Eleni's hands were slick with sweat as she tapped the private number onto the screen.

'Giorgos, it's me.' She turned away from Damon as her brother answered his private line immediately.

'Eleni. Where are you?' Giorgos demanded instant answers. 'Come back to the palace now. Do you have any idea of the trouble you've caused?'

'I'm not coming back yet, Giorgos. I need time to think.'

'Think? About what?' Her brother dismissed her claim. 'Your fiancé is already here. Or had you forgotten that you're about to go on tour with him?'

'I can't do it, Giorgos.'

'Can't do what?' Giorgos asked impatiently.

Eleni closed her eyes and summoned all her courage. 'I'm pregnant,' she said flatly. 'Prince Xander isn't the father.'

Silence.

Seven long seconds of appalled silence.

'Who?' Giorgos finally asked in a deadly whisper. *'Who?'*

'It doesn't matter—'

'I'll kill him. I'll bloody— Tell me his name.'

'No.'

'Tell me his name, Eleni. I'll have him—'

'Call off the hounds, Giorgos.' She interrupted her brother for the first time in her life. 'Or I swear I'll never return.' Her heart broke as she threatened him. 'I will disappear.'

Her guilt mounted. Her horror at doing this to the brother she loved. But she pushed forward.

'It doesn't matter who it was. He didn't seduce me. I was a fully willing participant.' She screwed her eyes tight shut, mortified at revealing this intimacy to her brother, but knowing the way he'd assume she'd been taken advantage of because he still thought of her as an innocent, helpless kid. She needed to *own* this. 'I made the mistake, Giorgos. And I need to fix it. Tell Xander I'm sick. Tell him I ran away. Tell him anything you like. But I'm not coming back. Not yet. Not 'til I've sorted it out.'

'Are you with the bastard now?' Giorgos asked impatiently.

'I'm not marrying him either,' Eleni said.

She didn't catch Giorgos's muttered imprecation.

'This child is mine. Pure Nicolaides.' She finally felt a segment of peace settle in place inside.

This was what she should have done at the beginning. She had to make amends now—to all the people she'd involved. 'And please don't blame Tony for losing track of me. It wasn't his fault.'

'Your protection officer has no idea where you've gone. He's clearly incompetent. He has been dismissed.'

'But it's not his fault.' Eleni's voice rose. Tony had been with Eleni for years. He had a wife and two children. He needed the work. 'I told him—'

'Lies,' Giorgos snapped. 'But it *is* his fault that he lost track of you. His employment is not your concern.'

'But—'

'You should have thought through the consequences of your actions, Eleni. There are ramifications for *all* the people of Palisades. And Santa Chiara.'

Twin tears slid out from her closed eyes. She would make it up to Tony somehow. Another atonement to be made.

'How do I stop a scandal here, Eleni?' Giorgos asked.

She cringed. Was that what mattered most—the reputation of the royal family? But she knew that was unfair to Giorgos. He was trying to protect *her*. It was what he'd always done. Too much.

'I'm so sorry,' she said dully. 'I take full responsibility. I will be in touch when I can.'

She ended the call before her brother could berate her any more. She turned and saw Damon casually leaning against the back of the sofa as if he were watching a mildly entertaining movie.

'Did you have to listen in?' Angered, she wiped the tears away. 'You know they'll have traced the call.'

'And they'll find it leads to some isolated shack in Estonia.' He shrugged. 'I work in the tech industry, Eleni. They won't find us in the next few days, I promise you that. We're hidden and we're safe.'

'What, this is some superhero space boat that can engage stealth mode?' She shook her head. 'They'll be checking the coastline.'

'And we're already miles away from it and your brother knows you're not under duress. You've shocked him, Eleni. I'm sure he'll wait to hear from you. The last thing he'll want now is the publicity from mounting a full-scale search and rescue operation.'

She'd shocked Giorgos. Once he'd got past that, the disappointment would zoom in. She was glad she wasn't there to see it.

'There's one option we haven't talked about,' Damon said expressionlessly. 'It is early enough in the pregnancy for termination to be—'

'No,' she interrupted him vehemently.

She had such privilege. She had money. This child could be well cared for.

And it was *hers*.

That was the thing. For the first time in her life she had

something that was truly, utterly her own. Her responsibility. Her concern. Hers to love and protect. No one was taking it away from her. There was a way out of this if she was strong enough to stand up to her brother's—and her nation's—disappointment. And she was determined to be.

'I'm not marrying Prince Xander,' she said fiercely. 'I'm not marrying you. I'm not marrying anyone. But I *am* having this baby.' She pulled herself together—*finally* feeling strong. 'I have the means and the wherewithal to provide for my baby on my own. And that is what I will do.'

'Do you?' Damon looked sceptical. 'What if Giorgos cuts you off completely? How will you fend for yourself then?'

'He wouldn't do that.' Her brother would be beyond disappointed, but he wouldn't abandon her. She should have trusted him more, sooner.

'Even so, what price will you pay for one moment of recklessness?' Damon badgered. 'The rest of your life in disgrace.'

'I could step away from the spotlight and live in one of the remote villages.' She would ask for nothing from the public purse.

It was the personal price that pained her. She'd let her brother down in both public and private senses. But she would not let this baby down. She'd made her first stand, and now she had to follow through and not let Damon block her way either.

'So that's your escape neatly done,' he noted softly. 'But what price will my *child* pay if you do that?'

She flushed, unsettled by his cool sarcasm. He made it sound as if she was thinking only of herself, not her baby. But she wasn't. She'd understood what he'd said about a child growing up with all that expectation and wasn't this a way of removing that?

But he clearly considered that she'd been stifled and cloistered and, yes, spoilt. He thought her behaviour with him at the ball a direct consequence of that. Maybe he was right. That flush deepened. She loathed this man.

'I'm not marrying you,' she repeated. She *couldn't*.

The absolute last thing Damon Gale wanted to do was marry—her or anyone—but damn if her rejection didn't just irritate the hell out of him. What, was his billionaire bank balance not good enough for her spoilt royal self?

He'd sworn never to engage in even a 'serious' relationship. But the worst of all possible options was a 'politically expedient' wedding. Yet now he was insulted because, while she'd agreed to a political marriage once already, she was adamantly refusing his offer. Why? Because he wasn't a *prince*?

'I'll never let you use my baby for your political machinations.' He glared at her.

All she did was stick her chin in the air and glare back.

His body burned and he paced away from her. That damned sexual ache refused to ease. Heaven only knew why he wanted this woman. But it had been like this since the moment he'd first seen her at that ball. To his immense satisfaction, he'd had her—there and then. He'd immediately wanted more, but then she'd fled.

Now he'd finally found her again, yet within moments of getting her alone on his boat he'd totally lost control and done exactly what he'd promised himself he wouldn't. He'd touched her. Instead of verbally tearing her to shreds, he'd pressed his mouth to her until she'd warmed like wax in his hands. Pliable and willing and ultimately so wanton and gorgeous. It had taken every speck of self-control to not claim her completely there on the sofa.

He knew he could use this mutual lust to get the acquiescence to his proposal he needed, but he wanted more than her gasping surrender. He wanted her to accept that he was *right*. Poor little princess was going to have to marry a mere man. A man she wanted in spite of herself, apparently.

'What were you thinking at that ball?' He couldn't understand why she'd taken such a massive risk. Was it just lust for her too or had there been more to it? Had she been trying to sabotage that engagement? But to throw away her virginity?

'Clearly I wasn't. What were *you* thinking?'

He leaned back against the wall. He'd been thinking how beautiful she was. How something vulnerable in her had pulled him to her.

'I tried to find you because I realised the condom had torn, but you'd vanished from the ball like a—' He broke off. 'I was on a flight the next day. I came back several times, but couldn't find any information about you. I asked—'

'You asked?'

'Everyone I knew. No one had seen you there. You never went back into the ballroom.' He shook his head and asked again. 'Why did you do it?'

Her shoulders lifted in a helpless shrug.

He hesitated but in the end was unable to stop the words coming out. 'Did you even think of trying to get in touch with me?'

Her beautiful face paled. 'I didn't know your name. I wasn't about to run a search on all the guys who'd been at that ball. I couldn't risk anyone suspecting me. How could I tell anyone?'

'How hard would it have been to go through that guest list?' he asked irritably. 'To identify men between a certain age? To look at security footage? You could easily have found out who I was, Eleni. You just didn't want to.' And that annoyed him so much more than it should.

'If I'd tried to do that, people would have asked *why.*'

'And you didn't want them to do that, because you'd already made a promise to another man.' He ran his hand through his hair in frustration. 'I've seen those "official" photos. They weren't taken the day after you slept with me. They were taken before, weren't they?'

She couldn't look him in the eye. 'Yes.'

Damon's blood pressure roared. 'Yet you never slept with him.'

'You're going there again?'

'But you kissed him?' He pressed on, relentless in his need to make his point.

'You can watch it on the news footage.'

He had already. Chaste, passionless kisses. She'd looked nothing like the siren who had writhed in *his* arms and pulled him closer, begging him with her body. The Princess that Damon had kissed was hot and wanton.

'The only time you kiss him is when there are cameras rolling?' He moved forward, unable to resist going nearer to her. 'You don't kiss him the way you kiss me.'

She flung her head up at that. 'Are you jealous?'

So jealous his guts burned right now. 'He doesn't want you,' he said bluntly.

Something raw flashed across her face. 'What makes you say that?'

He stopped his progress across the room and shoved his fists into his trouser pockets. 'If he wanted you the way he ought to, then he'd have moved heaven and earth to find you already. But he hasn't found you. He hasn't fought at all.'

That engagement was a political farce, so he had no reason to feel bad about cutting in and claiming what was already his. They'd sacrifice a year of their lives in sticking it out in a sham of a marriage until the baby was born. That was the only solution. Lust faded and there sure as hell was no such thing as for ever. Princess Eleni here was just going to get over her snobbishness and accept her marriage, and her divorce. And that he was no prince of a man.

* * *

Eleni inwardly flinched at that kicker. Because there it was—the cold, unvarnished truth.

Her fiancé didn't want her. Her brother found her an irritant. She had no worthwhile job. And now that her 'purity' was sullied, she'd no longer be desired as a prince's wife anyway. 'I guess my value's plummeted now I'm no longer a virgin,' she quipped sarcastically.

'Your value?' Damon's eyes blazed. 'He shouldn't give a damn about your virginity.'

His anger surprised her. 'In the way you don't?'

A different expression cut across his face. 'Oh, I care about that,' he argued in a slow, lethal whisper.

'It was none of your business,' she said haughtily.

'You don't think?' He laughed bitterly. 'That's where you're so wrong. And who you sleep with is now my business too.'

'I'm. Not. Marrying. You.' She utterly refused.

'It won't be for ever, Eleni,' he assured her dispassionately. 'We can divorce easily enough in time, without destroying the union of two entire nations,' he added pointedly. 'I will retain custody of our child. You will go back to being a princess.'

'Pardon?' The air was sucked from her lungs.

'I'll raise our child alone, without the pressure of public life.'

'What?' She stared at him, horrified to read the utterly cool seriousness on his face. 'But I'm this child's mother. A child needs her mother.' If anyone knew that, she did.

There was a thick silence.

His expression shuttered. 'A child needs parents who want her. Who love her. And if they're together, they need to be in love with each other.' His words dropped like heavy stones into a still pond. 'While we want each other, we don't—and won't—love each other. This isn't some fairy-tale romance, Eleni. This is real. And we have a real problem to deal with. As adults.'

Not a fairy tale.

She knew theirs was a connection forged by nothing but lust and hormones. But now? What he'd just said came as a greater shock than any the day had brought so far.

He wanted to take her baby from her.

'You've had a long day. You must need something to eat.' He changed the subject easily, as if he hadn't just shaken her whole foundation.

'I couldn't...' She was too shocked to contemplate something so banal as food.

'Suit yourself.' He shrugged carelessly. 'You obviously need sleep to get your head together. But starting tomorrow we'll look at ensuring your diet is appropriate.'

Appropriate? What, he thought he was going to dictate every aspect of her life now?

'How lovely of you to care,' she said acidly.

'I care about my child.' He turned his back on her. 'I'll show you to your quarters.'

Silently she followed him along the gleaming corridor of the large yacht that was still steaming full-speed away from Palisades.

He stopped almost at the end. 'You're in here,' he said briefly, gesturing through the doorway. 'I'm in the cabin next door, if you decide you do need something.'

She didn't move into the room immediately; she was too busy trying to read him. Beyond the too-handsome features, there was intense determination.

A fatalistic feeling sank into her bones. There was no escaping, no getting away from what he wanted. And he didn't actually want *her*—only her baby.

But earlier she'd felt his hardness, his heat, she'd heard his breathlessness as he'd kissed her into ecstasy. Surely he'd wanted her? But he hadn't taken her. And he could have, they both knew that.

All of which merely proved that it had been just sex for him, while she'd thought it had been somehow special…

Strain tightened his features. 'I'm not going to kiss you goodnight,' he muttered. 'I'm too tired to be able to stop it from escalating.'

As if she'd been waiting for him to kiss her? Outraged, she snarled. 'You don't think I could stop it?'

'Maybe you could,' he said doubtfully. 'But I'm not willing to take the risk.'

She stepped into the cabin and slammed the door right in his face.

Not a fairy tale.

No. This was nothing less than a nightmare. She glanced angrily at the large, smooth bed. As if she were ever going to sleep.

CHAPTER SEVEN

'*ELENI.*'

The whisper slipped over her skin like a warm, gentle breeze. Smiling, she snuggled deeper into the cosy cocoon.

'*Eleni.*'

She snapped her eyes open. Damon was leaning over her, his face only a breath from hers.

'Oh…hey… What are you doing in here?' she asked softly.

'Making sure you're okay,' he answered, equally softly.

'Why wouldn't I be?' She'd been buried deep in the best sleep she'd had in weeks.

His smile appeared—the magnetic one that had melted all her defences that night at the ball. The one she hadn't seen since. 'Well, I was wondering if you were *ever* going to wake up.'

Why would he think she wouldn't? Had he been trying to rouse her for hours already? His smile diverted her sleepy thoughts onto a different track—had he been about to try waking her with a *kiss*?

Blood quickening, she clutched the sheet to her chest and tried to sit up.

'Easy.' He held her down with a hand on her shoulder. 'Not so fast.' He sat on the edge of her bed and pointed to the bedside table. 'I brought food and water. You must be hungry now.'

The dry crackers on the plate brought her fully awake with a sharp bump. This was no fairy tale. Damon had no thought of romance, only practicality—preventing her morning sickness from surfacing.

'Thank you.' She pulled herself together, determined

to be polite and battle him with calm rationality. No more emotional outbursts that only he drew from her. All she needed now was for him to leave.

But clearly he didn't hear her unspoken plea, because he watched her expectantly. With an expressive sigh she lifted the glass of water.

'You normally sleep this late?' Damon asked.

'What time is it?'

'Almost eleven.'

She nearly spat out the mouthful of water she'd just sipped.

That amused grin flashed across his face again. 'I take it you don't usually sleep in.'

Of course not. Never in all her life.

'Has anyone been in contact?' she asked, trying to distract herself from how infuriatingly gorgeous he looked in that old tee and jeans combo.

'You're asking if they've tracked you down?' He shook his head. 'Radio silence.'

She didn't quite know how to feel about that. 'Perhaps they're planning a rescue raid and are about to break in and arrest you,' she muttered acidly. 'Any second now.'

'You came willingly.' That evil amusement lit his eyes. 'More than once.'

Uncontrollable heat washed through her, threatening an emotional outburst. Eleni levered up onto her elbow and glanced about for her robe. It wasn't there. Of course. None of her wardrobe was. The clothes she'd worn yesterday were on the floor where she'd left them. She blushed, imagining the reprimand.

Lazy, spoilt princess.

Awareness prickled. She snuck a look at him from beneath her lashes.

'Got a problem, Princess?' The slightest of jeers, low and a little rough and enough to fling her over the edge.

'Yes,' she said provocatively. 'I don't have anything fresh to wear.'

His eyes widened and for the briefest of seconds his raw reaction to her was exposed. He wanted her still. She was too thrilled by the realisation to stop.

'Hadn't thought of that in all your evil planning, had you?' she purred.

But his expression blanked. 'Maybe I felt clothes weren't going to be necessary.'

'Oh, please.'

But he'd turned that desire back on her, teasing her when she'd wanted to test him.

'You love the idea.' He leaned closer, his whispered words having that warm, magnetic effect on her most private parts. 'And as we're going to be married, there's no need to be shy.'

Her reaction to his proximity was appalling but all she wanted now was to know he was as shattered as she.

'We're *not* going to be married.' She summoned all her courage and threw back the sheet, meeting his bluff with a fierce one of her own. 'But you want me to spend the day naked?'

As he stared, she fought every instinct to curl her legs up and throw her arms around her knees. Instead she stayed still, utterly naked on the soft white linen.

His gaze travelled the length of her body—lingering on those places too private to mention. She gritted her teeth so she wouldn't squirm. But as his focus trained on her breasts, she felt the reaction—the full, tight feeling as her nipples budded and that warmth surged low within. He looked for a long, long time—and then looked lower, rendering Eleni immobile in the burning ferocity of his attention. Her skin reddened as if she'd been whipped and the slightest of goosebumps lifted. It took everything she had not to curl her toes and die of frustration.

Finally, just when she'd felt she was about to explode,

he moved. Wordlessly he pulled his tee shirt over his head and held it out to her.

Desire flooded impossibly hotter still as she stared at his bared chest. Her senses ravenously appreciated his warm tan, the ridged muscles, that light scattering of hair arrowing down to—

'Put it on,' he snapped.

She snatched it from him. But if she'd doubted whether he wanted her as much as she wanted him, she now knew.

Just sex.

She forced herself to remember that this was just sex to him. But a trickle of power flowed through her veins.

He didn't move back as she got out of the bed—he just sat there, too close, his head about level with her breasts. So she stood in front of him—refusing to be intimidated.

The tee skimmed midway down her thighs and swamped her with a sense of intimacy as his scent and warmth enveloped her. Stupidly she felt as if she were more exposed than when she'd had nothing on. Her gaze collided with his—locked, and held fast in the hot blue intensity. She wanted him to touch her again. She wanted more of that pleasure he'd pulled so easily from her last night. She was almost mad with the need for it.

'Stop looking at me like that, Princess,' he said shortly.

The rejection stung. 'Don't call me Princess.'

'Why not?' he challenged almost angrily. 'It's who you are.'

'It's not all I am,' she answered defiantly. 'I don't want that to be all I am.'

She just wanted to be Eleni. She didn't want the reminder of who she *ought* to be all the time and of her failure to do her duty.

Hormones. It had to be the hormones. Here she was facing the biggest mess of her life, rupturing the royal connection of two nations, but all she wanted was for Damon to haul her close and kiss her again. She made herself walk to the door.

'Take me back to Palisades,' she said calmly, trying to sound in control.

'So now that you've used me to hide from your brother's wrath, you want to use your brother to protect you from me.'

She turned back and saw the bitterness of Damon's smile. 'That's not—'

'No?' He shook his head in disbelief. 'Sorry, Eleni, I'm not a servant who you can order around and who'll fulfil your every whim.'

'No?' she echoed at him angrily. His opinion inflamed her. She stalked back to where he still sat braced on the edge of her bed, his fists curled into the linen. 'But that's what you said I could do. You said I could take what I wanted from you.'

'That's what you really want, isn't it?' he asked roughly, reaching out to grab her waist and hold her in front of him. 'You want me to make you feel good again.'

She wanted it so much—because she wanted it *gone*. But she knew what he wanted too. He might not like her much, but he still wanted her.

'Actually,' Eleni corrected him coolly, 'now I'm offering that to you. Take what you want from me.'

If he did that, she was sure she'd be rid of this wretched, all-encompassing desire. It was too intense—she couldn't *think* for wanting him.

His mouth tightened as he stared up at her, insolence in his expression. 'Look at Princess Sophisticated,' he jeered through gritted teeth. 'What do you think you're doing? Trying to soften me up with sex?'

She froze at the anger now darkening his eyes. 'I just don't think this needs to be that complicated.'

'This couldn't be *more* complicated. And sex only makes

things worse.' He laughed unkindly. 'I'll have you again, don't you worry about that. But only once we've reached an agreement.'

He'd laughed that night too. When she'd had the most intense experience of her life, he'd *chuckled*. Her bold pretence fell, leaving angry vulnerability in its wake.

'You can seduce me until I scream,' she said furiously. 'But you can't make me say yes to *marrying* you.'

He stood, slamming her body against his as he did.

She gasped at the intense wave of longing that flooded her. But it roused her rage with it.

'You'll never get my total surrender.' She glared up at him, even as tremors racked her traitorous body as he pressed her against his rock-hard heat.

'And I don't want it,' he growled back, rolling his hips against hers in a demonstration of pure, sensual power. 'Lust passes.'

She hoped to heaven he was right. But his smug superiority galled her. 'You just have to know it all, don't you?'

But she didn't need another overprotective male trying to control every aspect of her life.

His gaze narrowed. 'I only want what's best for my baby.' He released her and stalked to the door, turning to hit her with his parting shot. 'We will marry. The baby will be born legitimately. And ultimately my child will live a safe, free life. With me.'

He slammed the door, leaving her recoiling at his cold-hearted plan. Shame slithered at her lame attempt to seduce him, suffocating the remnants of the heat he'd stirred too easily. He was too strong, too clinical when she'd been confused with desire. She was such a fool.

But that he truly planned to take her child horrified her. She had to fight him on that. She had to win.

Eleni snatched up her skirt. She marched out to the lounge to confront Damon again, only to catch sight of the large screen revealed on the wall. The sound was muted, but she recognised the image. Stunned, she stepped forward to look more closely.

Bunches and bunches of flowers and cards from well-wishers were placed at the gates of Palisades palace. The camera zoomed in on one of the bunches and she read the 'get well soon' message written—to *her*. Giorgos had taken her idea literally and told the world she was too unwell to embark on her tour with Prince Xander.

'There are so many.' She sank onto the nearest sofa.

'Why are you so surprised?' Damon walked forward and sat in the chair at an angle to her sofa, his voice cool. 'You're their perfect Princess.'

She rubbed her forehead. She was an absolute fraud and all those people were being kind when she didn't deserve it.

'It's not a total lie. You *don't* feel well,' he added gruffly.

'I've made a mess of everything.'

'So marry me. We'll live together away from Palisades until the baby is born.'

And then he was going to take her child from her.

Suddenly she broke; tears stung her eyes even as she laughed hopelessly. 'The stupid thing is, I don't even know for sure that I am pregnant.'

'Pardon?'

Of course she was pregnant. She knew it. She was late and there were all those other signs—morning sickness, tender breasts...

'Eleni?' Damon prompted sharply.

She sighed. 'I haven't done a test.'

He gazed at her, astounded. 'How can you not have done a test?'

'How could I?' She exploded, leaping back to her feet because she couldn't contain her frustration a second longer. 'How would I get a test without everyone finding out?' She paced, railing at the confines of the luxurious room and of the life she was bound by. 'I don't even do my own personal shopping—how can I when I don't even carry my own damn *money*?' She'd never shopped alone in all her life. She registered the dumbfounded amazement on Damon's face.

'I don't have any income,' she explained furiously. 'If I want anything I just ask someone and it arrives. Is that someone now you?' She gestured wildly at him. 'I don't have a money card, Damon. Or any cash. I've never needed it. I know that makes me spoilt. But it also makes me helpless.' It was beyond humiliating to be so dependent. 'It makes me useless.'

She flopped back down on the sofa and buried her face in her hands, mortified at the sting of fresh tears. So much for controlling her emotional outbursts.

'All this effort you've gone to, to steal me away might be based on one massive mistake.' She laughed bitterly at the irony. Wouldn't that just serve him right?

Damon hunched down in front of her, his hands on her knees. 'Eleni.'

His voice was too soft. Too calm.

'What?' She peered at him.

He studied her, his expression uncharacteristically solemn. 'Even if you're not pregnant, could you really marry him now?'

'Because I've spent the night on board a boat with another man and no chaperone?' She glared at him, hating that old-school reasoning and the expectation that she'd stay 'pure'—when no prince, no man, ever had to.

But Damon shook his head. 'Because you don't love him. You don't even want him.' He cocked his head, a vestige of that charming smile tweaking his lips. 'At least you want me.'

She closed her eyes. She *hated* him. And she hated how much she wanted him.

There was nothing but silence from Damon. She realised he'd left the room but a moment later he returned, a small rectangular box in his hand.

'You always have pregnancy tests on board?' Humiliation washed over her at her ineptitude.

'No. But as I suspected you were pregnant, I thought it might be useful.' So easily he'd done what she was unable to.

She snatched the box from his outstretched hand. 'I'll be back in a minute.'

CHAPTER EIGHT

DAMON GAZED DOWN at the distressed woman who'd word-lessly waved a small plastic stick at him as she returned to his sofa. The positive proof hit him—she truly had no clue. Her one escape plan had simply been to *hide* and now she was lost. Her lies yesterday had been those of an inexpe-rienced, overly sheltered girl trying to brazen her way out of a dire situation.

He grimaced—was he actually feeling sorry for her now? Fool.

She could be confident when she wanted and had strength when she needed it. She was *spoilt*, that was her problem. Utterly used to getting her own way and never having to wait. He gritted his teeth as he remembered the way she'd flung back her bed coverings and taunted him. So brazen. So innocent. So damned gorgeous he was still struggling to catch his breath.

But she was going to have to wait for that now. And so was he.

Never had he understood how his father could have com-pletely betrayed his mother. Why he'd risked everything he'd worked so hard to achieve. But now Damon understood all too well what could cloud a man's reason and make him forget his responsibilities and priorities.

Shameless lust. The age-old tale of desire.

He was not making the mistakes of his father. He was not abandoning his child to illegitimacy. But nor would he remain in a loveless marriage for years on end.

'You need to marry me, to protect the baby.' He tried to stay calm, but her repeated refusals were galling.

He'd never allow his child to be used for political manoeuvring. His baby would be raised in a safe environment with him. Their divorce would be better than being trapped in a home where the parents tolerated each other only for 'the look of it'.

Eleni paled.

'You know that, away from the palace, my child can have a normal life.' He tried to speak reasonably. 'Not hounded by press or burdened by duty.'

He saw her mouth tremble. He'd known this was how he'd get to her. She'd told him earlier—she didn't want to be *only* a princess.

'*I* can give this child everything,' she argued.

'Really? Can you give her complete freedom? With me, she can be free to do whatever she wants. Study whatever, live wherever. No pressure to perform.'

'And your life isn't in the public eye?' she queried sharply. 'Don't you billionaires get picked for "most eligible" lists in magazines?'

'When you're not a prince and therefore not public property, privacy can be paid for.'

'But this child will be a prince—or princess,' she pointed out, her voice roughening. 'And you can't deny this child his or her birthright.'

'The child can decide whether to take on a royal role when it's old enough.'

Eleni laughed at him. 'You think it's something you can just *choose*?'

'Why not?' Damon challenged her.

She shook her head. 'Giorgos would never allow it.'

'I don't give a damn what Giorgos wants.'

'But I do. Since our father died, he's been brother, father and mother to me and all the while he has that huge job. The hours he works—you have no idea...' She trailed off, pain shadowing her eyes.

Damon remembered when the King had died just over a

decade ago. His father had returned to Palisades for the funeral and taken an extra week to visit his long-term lover—Kassie's mother. Grimly Damon shoved that bitter memory aside. But he couldn't recall much about the Queen at all. He frowned at Eleni. 'Where's your mother?'

Eleni looked shocked. Then she drew in a deep breath. 'She died twenty minutes after giving birth to me.' Despite that steadying breath, her voice shook. 'So I know what it's like not to have a mother. And I know what it's like to have your parent too busy to be around to listen... I want to be there for my child. And I will be. In all the ways she or he needs. *Always.*'

Damon stared at her fixedly, ignoring her passion and focusing on the salient information. Her mother had died in childbirth.

He pulled out his phone. 'You need to see a doctor.'

Eleni gaped at him, then visibly collected herself. 'I'm not sure if you know how this works, Damon, but the baby isn't due for *months.*'

So what? She needed the best care possible from this moment on.

'Just because my mother died in childbirth, doesn't mean that I might have trouble,' she added stiffly.

'You need a basic check-up at the very least.'

'Because you don't trust me to take care of myself?'

Blood pounding in his ears, he ignored her petulance. Quickly he scrolled through his contacts to find his physician and tapped out a text asking him to find the best obstetrician he knew. Sure, women gave birth round the world almost every minute, but not always in full health and Eleni's news had caught him by surprise.

'I don't need cotton-wool treatment.' Her tone sharpened.

'I don't intend to give it to you,' he muttered, feeling better for having started the search. 'But I'm not going to ignore your condition either.'

'It's just pregnancy, not an *illness*,' she rasped. 'And I am sensible enough to ensure I get the best treatment when I get back to shore. Trust me, I don't want to die. But you can't make me see someone I don't want to see, nor stop me from doing the things I like.'

Looking at her was always a mistake—especially when she was passionate and vitality flowed from her glowing skin. Had people stopped her doing the things she'd liked in the past? He couldn't resist a tease. 'And what do you like?'

She glared at him, picking up the heavy innuendo he'd intended. 'Not that.'

He laughed even as a wave of protectiveness surged. 'Did you know some women have a heightened libido when pregnant?'

'I'm not one of those women.'

Her prim reply was undermined by the quickening of her breath. It spurred him to tease her more. 'No, you have the appetite of a nymphomaniac all the time.'

'I do not.'

'Yeah, you do.' He laughed again at her outraged expression. But that sensual blush had spread over her skin and sparks lit up her green-blue eyes.

There was no denying the chemistry between them. But he'd not realised just how inexperienced she was in all areas of life—not just the bedroom. Not to have access to cash? To have any normal kind of freedom?

Yes, she was spoilt, but she was unspoilt in other ways. She'd been too sheltered for her own good. And finally he could understand why. She was the precious baby who'd lost her mother far too soon. Raised by her bereft, too-busy father, and then a brother too young and too burdened to know how to care for a young girl and let her grow. All they'd wanted to do was protect her.

It was a sentiment Damon was starting to understand too well.

And now guilt crept in. He regretted the horrible scenario he'd painted—threatening to take her child from her. What kind of cold-hearted jerk was he?

But he'd been angered by her constant refusals and he'd lashed out, instinctively striking where it would hurt most. He drew in a calming breath. He'd win her acceptance with care, not cruelty.

'So it was the three of you, until your father died?' he asked, wanting to understand her background more.

'My father was a very busy man,' Eleni answered softly. 'He was the King—he had a lot to occupy his time. So for a long while it was Giorgos and me. He's a bit older, but he was always fun.' Her expression warmed briefly. 'When Father died, Giorgos took over.'

'Giorgos was young for that.'

'He is very highly regarded,' she said loyally.

'You're close.'

Her gaze slid from his. 'He has a big job to do. Back then he knew some of the courtiers didn't think he was old enough to handle the responsibility—'

'So he worked twice as hard to prove them wrong.' Damon smiled at her surprised look. 'It's understandable.'

She gazed out of the window. 'He's not stopped working since.'

And she was left lonely in her little turret in the palace. Damon saw how easily it had happened. She was loyal and sweet but also trapped and stifled.

'I'm supposed to marry a royal,' she said quietly. 'It's tradition. I know you think it's stupid, but it's how it's always been. I wanted to do the right thing for Giorgos.'

'Well, I'm not a prince and I never will be.' Damon took a seat. 'But won't it be easier to divorce me, a commoner, than cause conflict with two countries if you divorce your Prince?'

Her lips tightened. 'I'm not supposed to get divorced,' she said quietly. 'That's not part of the fairy tale.'

'Times change. Even royals live in the real world, Eleni. And they get divorced.'

She looked anywhere but at him. 'I barely know you.'

'Do you know Prince Xander?' Damon asked bluntly.

The shake of her head was almost imperceptible.

'Then what's the difference between marrying him and marrying me?' His muscles pulled tighter and tighter still in the face of her silence. The urge to go to her, to kiss her into acquiescence, made him ache. Despite her denial earlier he knew he could do it. All he'd have to do was kiss her and she'd be breathless and begging and he needed to get away from her before he did exactly that. He wanted to hear her say yes to him without that. 'Am I an ogre?'

'You want to take my child from me.'

'And you tried to deny the child was mine. I figure that makes us even.' He stood, unable to remain in the same room as her without succumbing to reckless action. 'Take your time to think about your options, Eleni. I'm in no rush to go anywhere.'

Why didn't she want to marry Damon? Eleni couldn't answer that honestly—not to him when she could barely admit the truth to herself. She'd never wanted anyone the way she wanted him. Her marriage to Xander would have been a loveless union. But safe compared to the tempestuous gamut of emotions Damon roused in her. She was terrified of what might happen to her heart if she stayed with him for long.

She scoffed at her inner dramatics. She needed to grow up and get a grip on her sexual frustration. Because that was all this was, right? Her first case of raw lust.

She turned off the large computer screen and foraged in the bookcase lining one of the walls, her thoughts circling around and around until her stomach rumbled and she realised how ravenous she was.

Quietly she left the room and found her way to a sleek

galley kitchen. No one was in there, thank goodness, because she was starving. She located the pantry, pouncing on an open box of cereal.

'You okay?'

'Oh.' She swallowed hastily as she turned. 'You caught me.'

He had been swimming, probably in the pool on deck. Eleni stared, fascinated by the droplets of water slowly snaking down his bronzed chest until they were finally caught in the towel he'd slung low around his hips.

'Not yet.' He walked forward. 'What are you doing that is so awful?'

Staring at your bare chest.

'I shouldn't have helped myself,' she mumbled. 'Eating straight from the packet.'

'That's not awful. That's survival instinct.' He reached into the box she was holding and helped himself to a couple of the cereal clusters. 'Don't you go into the kitchen at the palace?'

She shook her head, forcing herself to swallow.

'You just ask one of the servants?'

'What do you expect?' She bristled. 'I live in a palace and that comes with privileges.'

'But what if you wanted to just make a sandwich?'

'Then someone makes it for me.'

'You never wanted to make your own sandwich?'

'It's not my place to.' She refused to rise to his baiting. 'I'm not going to take someone's job from them.'

He looked at her as she snaffled another cereal snack. 'What would you have done if being a princess wasn't your place?'

'I studied languages and art history.' She shrugged. 'I'd probably teach.'

'But what would you have done if you could have chosen anything?'

Eleni sighed. 'My brother loves me very much but he is

very busy and most of my education was left to an older advisor who had ancient ideas about the role of a princess.'

'You're there to be decorative.'

'And quiet and serene—'

'Serene?' He laughed. 'You're a screamer.'

She sent him a filthy look.

'So?' He teased, but pressed the point. 'What would you have done?'

'I wanted to be a vet.' But she'd known it was impossible. The hours of study too intense when she had public duties to perform as well.

'A vet?' He looked taken aback.

'I like dogs.' She shrugged.

'You have dogs?'

'I had a gorgeous spaniel when I was younger.'

'So why not vet school? Did you not have the grades?'

'Of course I had the grades.' She gritted her teeth and turned away because she knew where he was going with this, so she didn't tell him she'd wanted to do Fine Arts first. Again she'd been denied—too frivolous. She was a princess and she had to remain demure and humble. But was hers really such an awful life to bestow upon a child? Yes, there were restrictions, but there was also such privilege. Couldn't she make it different?

'You know I can offer our child a level of freedom that you can't,' Damon said. 'Isn't that what you want, your child not to have to "perform" the way you've had to all your life?'

'I want the best for my child in every way,' Eleni said calmly. And she knew exactly what she had to do for her child now. Nothing was ever going to be the same. She sucked in one last deep breath. 'They're all going to figure out that I was pregnant when we married.'

He stilled; his gaze glittered. 'Either we lie and say the baby was born prematurely, or we say nothing at all.' He cleared his throat. 'The second option gets my vote.

There will always be whispers and Internet conspiracy theories but we rise above it with a dignified silence and carry on.'

She nodded. 'I understand what you're saying about giving our child freedom, but I'm its mother and I won't walk away from it. Ever.' She braced and pushed forward. 'If you're serious about doing what's best for our child, then you won't ask me to.'

He carefully leaned against the bench. 'So you'll marry me.'

'If we work out a plan. For after.' When their marriage ended, it needed to be smooth. 'I think there are precedents in other countries for a child not to take a royal title,' she said bravely. Giorgos would have a fit but she would have to try to make him understand. 'We can keep him or her out of the limelight and work out some kind of shared custody arrangement.'

Her heart tore at the thought, but her child had the right to be loved by both its parents.

'Then we'll work it out.' Damon looked out of the window.

'So now you've got what you wanted,' Eleni said.

He looked back at her. His blue eyes had darkened almost to black. 'And what's that?'

'Me. Saying yes.' She watched, surprised to see his tension was even more visible than before. 'What, you're not satisfied?'

'No.'

'Then what do you want?'

He took the two steps to bring himself smack bang in front of her. 'I want my tee shirt back.'

Desire uncoiled low and strong in her belly. 'But I'm not wearing anything underneath it.'

'Good.' His blunt expression of want felled her.

'Are you wearing anything under the skirt?' he asked roughly, gripping the hem of the tee.

She could barely shake her head. 'I thought you said this would only complicate things.'

'Now we're in agreement on the big issues, we can handle a little complication.'

He tugged the tee shirt up. She lifted her arms and in a second it was gone. She was bared to his gaze, his touch, his tongue.

She gasped as he swooped. There was no denying this. He desired her body. Fine. She desired his. Reason dissolved under sensual persuasion. He pressed the small of her back—holding her still, keeping her close, until he growled something unintelligible and picked her up to sit her on the edge of the bench. He pushed her knees apart so he could stand between them. Elation soared through Eleni.

This was what she wanted.

His kiss was nothing less than ravaging. She moaned as he plundered, his tongue seeking, tasting, taking everything and she did more than let him. She gave—straining closer. She wound her arms around his neck, arching and aching. His hands swept down her body, igniting sensation, sparking that deeper yearning. He slid his warm palm under her skirt. She trembled as he neared where she was wet and ready. His kiss became more rapacious still as he touched her so intimately, and her moan melted in his mouth. He lifted away only to tease her more—kissing the column of her neck, down to her collarbones and then to the aching, full breasts pointing hard for his attention.

But the nagging feeling inside wouldn't ease—resistance to this hedonism. It had been wrong before; it was still wrong now. She closed her eyes, turning her face to the side as heat blistered her from the inside out.

'Don't hide.' He nudged her chin. 'Let me see you.'

'I can't,' she muttered, desperately turning her face away.

He pulled back completely, forcing her to look into his eyes. 'You're not cheating. Your engagement is broken now.'

She was ashamed that he knew her desire for him had

overruled her duty and her loyalty. Her engagement to Xander had been a loveless arrangement, but Damon was right. She was an appalling person.

'This is nothing much more than what happened yesterday.' Damon tempted her again.

Wrong. It was so much more. If she let him in again, she wasn't sure she could cope. The passion was all-consuming, addictive and all she could think about at a time when she should be concerned with her family. With her duty. But she couldn't think clearly when she was within five hundred paces of this man.

And she doubted him. He'd wanted to find her after the ball only because he'd known there was a risk of pregnancy, not because he'd wanted more time with her. He was only taking advantage of the situation now—certainly it wasn't that he liked her.

But he'd *wanted* her when he *hadn't* known who she was. He wasn't going for the 'perfect Princess' that night, he'd wanted just *her*. There was something still seductive about that.

Damon was studying her too intently. It was as if he could strip back all her defences and see into her poor, inexperienced soul.

'Why didn't you tell me you were a virgin?' he asked softly.

There was no point holding back the truth now. 'Because you would have stopped.'

He expelled a harsh breath and framed her face with surprisingly gentle hands. 'You could have said you were inexperienced.'

'I was pretending I wasn't,' she muttered, mortified. The mask, the costume had combined to make her feel confident. He'd made her feel sexy and invincible. Unstoppable. 'I had a persona that night…now I don't.'

'Are you sure it was a persona?' Damon challenged. 'Or

was it the true you?' He skimmed the tips of his fingers down her neck until she shivered.

Was she that person? That woman who took such risks—and found such pleasure?

You want more than what you think you should have.

'There is nothing wrong with liking this, Eleni.' He tempted her to the point of madness.

'But I like it too much.' She confessed that last secret on the merest thread of a breath. 'It's not *me*. It scares me.'

That was why she'd resisted his proposal initially. The intensity of her desire for him terrified her.

His expression tightened. 'I scare you?'

'Not you. Me,' she muttered. 'I never behave like this. Like *that*.' She was appalled at how she'd behaved that night and since. All those outbursts? The waves of emotion? 'You were right. I lied. I cheated. I'm every bit that awful, spoilt person you said I was.'

Damon shifted away from her.

Eleni watched, suddenly chilled at the loss of contact. Her body yearned for the closeness of his again. But he'd switched it off. How could he do that so easily?

Hurt and alarm hit. She shouldn't have spoken so rashly. She shouldn't have stopped him because at least she could've been rid of the frustration that now cut deeper than ever.

'You need to be at peace before this happens again,' Damon said quietly—too damn in control. 'Then you won't need to hide. Then you can truly let go.'

She watched, amazed and horrified as he walked to the doorway. How, exactly, was she supposed to find peace when he was making the decision for her? When he was leaving her this...*needy.*

'I hate you,' she called. One last emotional outburst.

'I'm sure.' Damon glanced back with a smile. 'I'd never dream that you could love me.'

CHAPTER NINE

'I'M NOT WAITING for Giorgos to hunt me down like some fugitive. I want to go to him.' Eleni braced for Damon's response as she sat opposite him at the table the next morning.

She wasn't letting him make all the decisions any more. After the most desultory dinner, she'd spent the night mentally practising her confrontations with both Damon and Giorgos and it was time to put both plans into reality.

Damon arched a sardonic eyebrow. 'Good morning, fire-breathing warrior woman, who are you and what have you done with my meek fiancée?'

'I need to see him,' she insisted.

Damon's answering smile was uncomfortably wicked. 'The yacht turned around last night. We'll be back at Palisades in less than an hour. I've just let him know I have you.'

Eleni stared as his words knocked the wind from her sails.

'Well.' It was going to happen so much sooner than she'd expected. She puffed out a deep breath but it didn't settle her speeding heart. 'We might want to let him know I'm safe on board, otherwise he might try to blow up your boat.'

Damon chuckled. 'I thought Palisades was a peace-loving nation.'

It was, but when Damon's yacht entered the marina, Eleni's nerves tightened unbearably. Never before had she defied Giorgos's wishes and now the weight of his inevitable disappointment was crushing.

'I should handle him by myself,' she said to Damon

as she counted the number of soldiers waiting on the pier ready to escort her. It was a heavy-handed display of her brother's authority. 'I should have done that in the first place.'

Damon turned his back on the waiting men with an arrogant lift to his chin. Apparently he was unfazed by the latent aggression waiting for them. 'I'll stay silent if that's what you wish, but I will be beside you.'

Because he didn't trust her?

Except there was something in Damon's eyes. Something more than protectiveness and more than possessiveness. She turned away, not trusting her own vision. Because the last thing she deserved was tenderness.

The military men wordlessly ushered them into a car and drove them straight to the palace. The gleaming building felt silent, as if everyone were collectively holding their breath—waiting for Giorgos's explosion. For the first time in her life Eleni felt like a stranger in her own home. The only person not tiptoeing on eggshells was Damon. He casually strolled the endless corridors as if he hadn't a care in the world.

They weren't taken to either her private suite or to Giorgos's. Instead her brother's assistant led them to a formal room usually reserved for meetings with visiting Heads of State. Chilled, Eleni paused in the doorway. Giorgos grimly waited in full King mode—white dress uniform, jacket laden with medals and insignia, boots polished to mirror-like sheen. All that was missing was his crown.

'I've cancelled an engagement at the last minute. Again.' Giorgos fixed a steely stare on Damon.

But her brother's barely disguised loathing apparently bounced off as Damon blandly stared right back.

'You took advantage of an innocent,' Giorgos accused shortly. 'You seduced her.'

Was she invisible? Straightening her shoulders, Eleni stepped forward.

'Maybe I seduced him.' She clenched her fists to hide how badly her hands were shaking, but she was determined to take control of this conversation. *She* was having the input here, not Damon.

Her brother finally bothered to look at her, but as he faced her he became like a marble sculpture. Expressionless and unreadable.

'Damon and I will be married as soon as possible,' she said, determined to state her case before he tore her to shreds.

Giorgos continued to look unmoved. 'Last time we spoke you insisted you were not marrying either Prince Xander or Mr Gale.'

'I was upset,' she conceded coolly. 'But this is the best course of action, Giorgos.'

'He is not a prince. He has no title whatsoever.'

Of course her brother knew Damon's background already—he'd have had his investigators on it from the moment he'd gotten the message this morning. From Giorgos's frown, Damon's success mattered little to him. 'You know the expectations—'

'Change the law, create a new custom.' For the second time in her life Eleni dared to interrupt her brother. 'You're King. You have the power.'

'And should I abuse power trusted to me, for personal gain?'

'Is it personal gain, or would you simply be granting the same right that any other citizen in Palisades already has?' Why couldn't she have the right to choose for herself?

Giorgos's eyes narrowed. 'So I simply ignore centuries of custom and duty? I abandon all levels of diplomacy and the expectations of our important neighbours and alliances?'

'My personal life shouldn't be used for political manoeuvring.'

'So you got yourself pregnant instead of simply making that argument?'

She recoiled in shock and her anger unleashed. 'Of course I didn't. But would you be listening to me if I *wasn't* pregnant?'

Giorgos sent Damon the iciest look she'd ever seen. 'You know about our mother?'

'Yes. I will ensure Eleni receives care from the best specialists.'

Giorgos shook his head. 'Our doctor is ready to give her a check-up now.'

Eleni gaped. Did her brother think she was somehow incapacitated?

Damon answered before she could. 'I don't think that's necessary—'

'It is entirely necessary. She must be—'

'Stop trying to overrule each other.' Eleni interrupted Giorgos again, her heart and head pounding. 'My medical decisions will be made by *me*.'

'Dr Vecolli is already here,' Giorgos insisted.

'I'm not seeing Dr Vecolli.'

'He's been our family physician for twenty years.'

'Which is exactly *why* I'm not seeing him. He's like a grandfather to me. I would like to see a female doctor.' She glared as Giorgos frowned at her. 'What, do you think no woman can be a doctor, or is it just me you thought so incapable I couldn't even be trusted with animals?'

'I once wanted to be an airplane pilot.' Giorgos dripped cold sarcasm. 'But you *know* we cannot hold down a full-time job while fulfilling royal duty. It is impossible.'

'*Why?*' she challenged. 'Couldn't I be useful other than cutting ribbons and awarding prizes?'

'You're going to have your hands full with your baby, or had you forgotten that?'

Eleni flared anew at Giorgos's patronising tone. 'So while plenty of other mothers work, I can only be a brood mare? Do you think I'm that incompetent?' She was out-raged—and *hurt*.

'I don't think you're—' Her brother broke off and ran a hand through his hair.

'Why are we so enslaved by the past?' she asked him emotionally. 'Just because things have always been done a certain way, doesn't mean they always have to continue in that same way.' And she was more capable than he be-lieved her to be—wasn't she?

Giorgos was silent for a long moment. Then he sighed softly. 'Then how do you plan to manage this?'

'By marrying Damon. I'll have the baby and then…' She drew in a steadying breath. 'Beyond that, I don't re-ally know. But I don't want all those limitations on me any more. They're untenable.'

She braced for his response. She couldn't yet tell him her marriage had an end date already. One let-down at a time was enough.

Giorgos's expression revealed more now. But he didn't need to worry; this wedding wouldn't end the world.

'It could be leaked that Eleni was corralled into the wed-ding with Prince Xander.' Damon broke the tense silence. 'She was too afraid to stand up to you and the Prince. Pub-lic sympathy will be on her side if it is cast as a forbidden love story.'

She didn't deserve public sympathy.

'She fell in love with me during her secret hospital vis-its.' Damon embroidered the possible story. 'But you re-fused your consent for her to have a relationship with a commoner. She was so distraught she really did get sick. Only then did you realise how serious she was.'

Eleni winced at the scenario he'd painted. Did everyone need to know she'd been unable to stand up for herself? More importantly, it didn't do her brother justice.

'Do we need to make Giorgos sound such a bully?' She frowned.

Giorgos's eyes widened with an arrested expression.

'Prince Xander is still the injured party,' Damon continued after a beat. 'But it can be spun that they'd not spent much time together. Therefore her defection won't make him appear any less attractive.'

Eleni smothered her startled laugh. Damon was light years more attractive than Xander.

For a long moment Giorgos studied the painting hanging on the wall opposite him. With every passing second Eleni's heart sank—recriminations and rejection were inevitable.

'You might have met your match, Eleni.' Giorgos slowly turned to her, the wryest of smiles in his eyes. 'He won't curl round your little finger.'

'The way you do?' Eleni dared to breathe back.

'You will be married in the private chapel today.' Giorgos's steely seriousness returned. 'I will release a public proclamation together with a few photographs. You will not make a public appearance. Rather you will go away for at least a month.'

'Away?' Eleni was stunned at the speed of his agreement.

'You need to get your personal situation stable while this fluff is spread in the press.' Giorgos's sarcasm edged back. 'You'll go to France. I have a safe house there.'

'But the safest house of all is this one,' Eleni argued. She was not letting her brother banish her. Not when she had to get to grips with a husband she barely knew and to whom she could hardly control her reaction. Staying home would give her the space and privacy to deal with Damon.

'Remaining in Palisades would give Damon a chance to learn palace protocol and understand the expectations for our...*future*.' She glanced at Damon, fudging just how short their future together was going to be.

Damon shrugged but his eyes were sharp. 'I'm happy to hang here for a while if that's what you wish, Eleni.'

'I am scheduled to spend a few weeks at the Summer House,' Giorgos said stiffly. 'So that would work.' He turned icily to Damon. 'But understand that I will be watching you, even from there. I don't trust you.'

'Fair enough,' Damon answered equally coolly. 'If I were you, I wouldn't either.' He smiled as if he hadn't a care in the world. 'I'll not take a title, by the way. I'll remain Damon Gale.'

'While I'll remain Princess Eleni Nicolaides,' Eleni answered instantly.

'And the child will be Prince or Princess Nicolaides-Gale—we get it,' Giorgos snapped. 'Let's just get everything formalised and documented before it leaks. I expect you at the chapel in an hour. Both of you looking the part.'

Her brother stalked towards the door, his posture emanating *uptight King*.

'I'll send someone to the yacht to fetch a suit,' Damon drawled once Giorgos had left. 'I guess you'd better go magic up a wedding dress.'

She stared at her fiancé and clapped a hand over her mouth in horror.

'Don't worry.' Damon's satisfied smile turned distinctly wicked. 'You can wear as little as you like—I will not say no. That busty blue number you wore at the ball would be nice—'

Flushing hotly, Eleni swiftly walked out on him, desperately needing a moment alone to process everything. But her maid hovered at the door to her suite, the woman's expression alert with unmistakable excitement.

'Oh, Bettina. I'm sorry I've been away.' Eleni quickly pasted on a smile. 'And I'm not back for long.'

Bettina nodded eagerly. 'I have done the best I can in the last half hour. I've hung the samples so you can choose. There are nine altogether—from New York, Paris, and one from Milan.'

'Samples?' Eleni repeated, confused.

'The wedding dresses.'

Nine wedding dresses? Eleni gaped. If that wasn't being spoilt, she didn't know what was.

'Would you like to try them on?'

Eleni saw the sparkle in her maid's eyes and realised the fiction that Eleni was marrying her long-secret love had already spread. She drew in a deep breath and made her smile bigger. 'Absolutely.'

But her smile became a wide 'oh' as Bettina wheeled out the garment rack she'd hung the gowns on. And then Eleni surrendered to vain delight—at the very least she could look good on her wedding day.

The sixth option was the winner; she knew as soon as she stepped into it. It was exactly what she'd choose for *herself*—not as something befitting 'Princess Eleni'. The sleek dress with its svelte lines and delicate embroidery was subtle but sexy and she loved it.

As Eleni walked away from her maid, her suite and her life as she knew it, butterflies skittered around her stomach, but she determinedly kept her smile on her face.

She couldn't let the fairy-tale image fall apart just yet.

Giorgos stood waiting for her at the entrance to the private chapel. Her smile—and her footsteps—faltered as she saw his frown deepening. But this might be her only chance to speak to him privately.

'I'm sorry I let you down,' she said when she was close enough for only him to hear.

'You haven't.' Her brother held out a small posy of roses for her.

Tears sprang to her eyes as she took the pretty bouquet from him. 'Thank you,' she whispered.

He nodded, stiffly. 'Do you love him?' Giorgos suddenly asked.

The direct question stole her breath. For the first time that she could recall, her brother looked awkward—almost unsure—as he gazed hard at a spot on the floor just ahead of them.

She couldn't be anything but honest. 'I don't know.'

That frown furrowed his brow again. 'Make it work, Eleni.'

Then he held out his arm, that glimpse of uncertainty gone. She nodded, unable to speak given the lump in her throat, and placed her hand in the crook of his elbow.

As Giorgos escorted her into the chapel, Eleni caught sight of Damon standing at the altar. He was dressed in a stunningly tailored suit. He seemed taller, broader; his eyes were very blue. He claimed the attention of every one of her senses. Every thought. Her pulse raced, her limbs trembled. She tried to remember to breathe. She couldn't possibly be *excited*, could she? This was only part of the plan to secure her child's legitimacy and freedom. This was only for her baby.

But those butterflies danced a complicated reel.

It's just a contract. It's only for the next year. It doesn't mean anything...

But reciting her vows to Damon in the family chapel heightened her sense of reverence. Here—in front of her brother, in front of him, in this sanctuary and symbol of all things past and future—she had to promise to love him.

He's the father of my child.

She could love him only for that, couldn't she? It wasn't a lie.

But a whisper of foreboding swept down her spine and she shivered just as Damon turned towards her. She met his gaze, almost frozen by the enormity of their actions.

But Damon wasn't frozen. He had that slightly wicked expression in his eyes as he reached to pull her close.

The kiss sealing their wedding contract should have been businesslike, but he lingered a fraction too long. That heat coursed through her veins. She closed her eyes and in that instant was lost. Her bones ached and the instinct to lean into him overwhelmed her. Only at the exact moment of her surrender, he suddenly pulled away. She caught a glimpse of wildness in his eyes but then her lifetime of training took over. She turned and walked with him out of the chapel and into the formal throne room. There she dutifully posed for endless photos with Giorgos on one side of her, Damon on the other. She smiled and smiled and smiled. Perfectly Princess Eleni.

Her brother took her hand and bowed. 'You make a beautiful bride, Eleni.'

Because all that mattered was how she looked and how this arrangement looked to the world? But Giorgos's expression softened and he suddenly gave her a quick hug.

'Take care of yourself.' With the briefest of glances at Damon, her brother left.

A little dazed, Eleni gazed after him. It had been years since he'd hugged her. Her nerves lightened. The worst was over, right? Now she could move forward.

'Eleni.'

She turned.

Damon stood too close, too handsome, his expression too knowing. That little respite from inner tension was over as she realised the first night of her marriage lay ahead. The beginning of the end of the thing neither of them had wanted in the first place.

'We should take a couple of photos somewhere less formal,' Damon suggested.

Eleni shook her head as his glance around the ornate room revealed his less than impressed opinion.

'There's nowhere "less formal" anywhere in this palace,' she informed him with perverse pleasure.

'What about outside?' Damon eyed up the French doors that no one had opened in Eleni's life.

'That's locked,' she said.

Damon turned the handle and the door opened silently and easily on the hinge.

Of course it did.

He sent her a triumphant smile that did even more annoying things to her insides.

'You're the most irritating creature alive,' she grumbled.

'I know,' he commiserated drolly. 'But you still want me.'

'What are you doing?' she whispered, stalking outside to get away from him as much as anything.

'This is your palace, Eleni. You're allowed to run around in it, right?' He was still too close.

'You're…'

'What?' he challenged, arrogance in his eyes as he wrapped his arm around her waist, stopping her flight and drawing her close. 'What am I?'

Not good for her health.

Eleni half laughed, half groaned as she gave into temptation and leaned against him. But she refused to answer.

Damon retaliated physically. Magically. Reigniting those embers settled so slightly beneath her skin. The kiss banished the last butterflies and a bonfire burned, engulfing her body in a delicious torture of desire. This time he held nothing back, pulling her close enough for her to feel just how she affected him. Desire flared, compounded by the awareness that, this time, there was nothing to stop them.

Click. Click, click, click.

She put her hands on his broad chest and pushed, remembering too late there was a freaking photographer following them.

'I'm the Princess,' she muttered, mainly to remind herself.

But Damon kept her close with one arm around her waist and a light grip on her jaw. 'I didn't marry "the Princess".'

'Yes, you did.' There was no separating who she was

from what she was. She had to accept that and now he did too.

The photographer looked disappointed when Damon sent him away. As he left, thudding blades whirred overhead and she glanced up to see her brother's helicopter swiftly heading north.

'So now we're alone,' Damon said softly. 'And not a second too soon.'

She suppressed the shiver at the determination in his tone and gazed at the rings on her finger to avoid looking at him. He'd surprised her in the chapel, sliding an engagement ring on her finger as well as a wedding band.

'You don't like them?' he asked, inexorably escorting her towards that open French door.

On the contrary, she loved them, but she was wary of showing it. She couldn't quite make out his mood. Was he angry as well as aroused? 'How did you pick them so quickly?'

A grim smile briefly curved his mouth. 'I had just a little longer to prepare for our wedding than you did.'

Even so, his organisational skills were impressive. 'It's a sapphire?'

He shook his head. 'A blue diamond for my blue bride.'

Her heart knocked. The stone's colour was the exact shade of the dress she'd worn that fateful night.

'You still look blue.' He cocked his head curiously. 'Why? You have the support of your brother. Everything that mattered has been resolved. So why so sad?'

Because this wasn't going to last. Because for all the foolishness in the garden, this was as much of a charade as her wedding to Xander would have been. Because she was a romantic fool. Part of her had wanted real love on her wedding day.

You can't be a child any more, Eleni. You're having a child.

Unable to answer his demanding tone, she walked

through the palace towards her private apartment. There wasn't a servant or soldier to be seen, as if by some silent decree they knew to stay out of sight. And it was a good thing too. She'd seen the banked heat in Damon's eyes. She knew he wasn't about to show her any mercy.

Her pulse skittered, speeding up the nearer she got to her rooms. At the foot of the staircase he reached out and took her hand.

She tried to hide the quickening of her breath but she knew he could feel the slamming pulse at her wrist and she could see the tension tightening his features too.

He wanted and he would have. Because she wanted too. And maybe this 'want' would have to do. Maybe they could make this work. With the reluctant acceptance of her brother, with the physical attraction binding them, with the baby…maybe this could work *indefinitely*.

She paused at the top of the staircase, drawing in a deeper breath to try to steady her anticipation. Damon released her hand, only to swing her into his arms.

'What are you doing?' she whisper-shrieked, clutching his shoulders as he suddenly strode down the last corridor to her apartment. 'You're not carrying me over my own threshold?'

'Indulge me.'

Excitement rippled down her spine, feathering goosebumps across her skin at his intensity. 'I didn't think you'd be one for wedding traditions.' Her throat felt raspy as she tried to tease.

His grip on her tightened for a nanosecond, and then eased again.

'I was never getting married,' he said carelessly as he kicked the door shut behind them. 'But seeing as that vow has been torn up, I might as well make the most of it.'

She looked into his face as he set her down, wishing she could read his mind. 'Why didn't you want to marry?'

He hesitated for a split second. 'It's not in our nature to be with one person all our lives.'

Our nature, or just *his*? His warning stabbed deep, bursting the warm bubble of desire.

'You don't believe in monogamy?' she clarified, his harsh reality cooling her completely.

'No. I don't.'

So he would cheat on her.

He caught her shoulders, preventing her from walking away from him. 'I think it traps people into a perceived perfection that can't be maintained,' he said quietly, forcing her to meet his gaze. 'No one is infallible, Eleni. Certainly not me. Definitely not you.'

'I can control myself.' Rebellious anger scorched her skin. 'And I intend to keep the vows we just made.'

He smiled. 'Of course you do. And so do I. Until the time when we dissolve the deal. It is just a contract, Eleni. Nothing more.'

Her deeply ingrained sense of tradition and honour railed against that declaration. She'd stood in that chapel and she'd meant those vows. But for Damon, this was nothing more than a business proposition. So why had he carried her only a minute ago?

'But it is a contract with particular benefits,' he added.

'And you intend to make the most of those benefits?' She wasn't buying it.

'As much as you do. Or are you going to try to deny yourself because I've annoyed you?' His smile was all disbelief.

'I'm going to deny *you*.' This might be her wedding night but it made no difference. She wasn't sleeping with him now.

'I've made you angry.' His eyebrows lifted. 'You're very young, sweetheart.'

'No. You're very cynical.' She shoved his chest, but he only took two paces back from her. 'And I'm *not* a child.

Just because I haven't slept with half the world, doesn't mean I'm more stupid than you. Sex doesn't make you smarter. If anything it makes you more dense.'

'Come here, Eleni.'

What, he was going to ignore her argument and simply demand her submission just because he knew she found him sexy?

'Get over yourself.'

'You're saying no?' he asked, his early anger giving way to arrogant amusement. 'Because you're the one used to giving orders?'

'No, that's my brother,' she answered in annoyance. 'I'm the one used to standing in the corner doing what she's told.'

'Then why aren't you doing as you're told now?' He stood with his legs wide like some implacable pirate captain. 'Come here.'

The entrance vestibule of her apartment wasn't huge but it might as well have been the Grand Canyon between them.

'You come over here,' she dared, ignoring the pull of his attraction. 'I'm tired of being told what to do. I'm doing the telling this time.'

His eyes widened fractionally. For a long moment he regarded her silently. She could see the storm brewing in him and braced. Him walking closer was what she wanted. And what she didn't want.

'I'm not yours to boss around or *control*,' she said, touching her tongue to her suddenly dry lips but determinedly maintaining her bravado regardless. 'I'm going to do what's necessary. And *only* what is necessary.'

He took those two paces to invade her personal space again and swept his hand from her waist to her hip. 'This is necessary, Eleni.'

She turned her head away, her heart pounding. 'Not any more.'

'Because you're mad with me.' His lips brushed her cheek. 'Because I've ruined your belief in fairy tales?

There's only the real world, Eleni. With real complications and real mess.'

'And temporary desires,' she ended the lecture for him.

'That's right.'

'And you're feeling a temporary desire now?' she asked.

'Definitely.'

'Too bad.' She clamped her mouth shut.

He laughed again. 'You say you don't play games.' He gifted her the lightest of kisses. 'Say yes to me again, Eleni,' he coaxed, teasing too-gentle hands up and down her spine. 'Say yes.'

She glared at him for as long as she could but she already knew she'd lost. 'You're not fair.'

'Life isn't fair. I thought you knew that already.' He moved closer still, forcing her to step backwards until she was pressed hard between him and the wall. 'Say yes.'

She could hold out but it would only be for a little while. She wanted him too much. She had from the second she'd seen him that night. And it was just sex, right? Nothing to take too seriously. She might as well get something she wanted from this 'contract'.

'Yes.' It was always going to be yes.

His smile was triumphant but she swore she saw tenderness there too. Except it couldn't be that—he'd just told her this was only temporary. He brushed a loose tendril of hair back from her face.

'Don't pet me like I'm a good dog,' she snapped.

He laughed. 'Definitely not a dog. But very good. And very worth petting.' He put hands on her shoulders and applied firm pressure. 'Turn around.'

She met his gaze and sucked in a breath at the fire in his eyes. Wordlessly she let him turn her, surrendering this once.

'This dress is beautiful,' he said softly. 'But not as beautiful as the woman inside it.'

Eleni bowed her head, resting her forehead on the cool

wall. He undid the first button and pressed his lips to the tiny patch of bared skin. His fingers traced, then teased down to the next button. In only a heartbeat Eleni was lost in the eroticism—of not seeing him, but of feeling him expose her to his gaze, to his touch, to his tongue again, inch by slow inch.

Desire unfurled from low in her belly. Her body cared not for the complications and confusion of her heart and mind. Her body cared only for his touch, only for the completion he could bring her.

He teased too much. Too slow. Until she was trembling and breathless.

When her dress slithered to the floor in a rush he put firm hands on her waist and spun her to face him again. She'd worn no bra beneath the gown, so she was left with lacy panties, stockings, kitten heels and nothing else. His gaze was hot and suddenly she was galvanised, reaching out to push him to recklessness again. She wanted him as breathless, as naked—she needed to feel his skin against hers.

But she couldn't undo his buttons. She was too desperate for release from the tension that soared with every second she spent with him. His choked laugh was strained and he took over, swiftly discarding the remainder of his clothes until they lay in a tumble at their feet. For a second she just stared at him. And he at her.

Before she could think, let alone speak, he pulled her close again, as if he couldn't stand to be parted from her for a second longer. He devoured her—with his gaze, then his fingers, then his mouth. He kissed every exposed inch. Somehow they were on the floor and he was braced above her—heavy and strong and dominant. She gasped breathlessly, aching for him. But just at that moment, he lifted slightly away and she almost screamed in protest.

'What?' she snapped at him. Why was he stopping *now*?

His smile was both smug and twisted. 'I've had numerous lovers, Eleni, but you're the first one to run away afterwards.'

'Did I hurt your ego?' She half hoped so; that'd be payback for what he was doing to her now.

'You frustrated me. You still do.' A seriousness stole into his features. 'You know I don't want to hurt you.'

She understood frustration now. 'I'm not afraid.'

And he wasn't going to hurt her—he'd made it very clear that this was only this. Only lust. Only temporary.

'No?' He held fast above her. *So close.* 'You're not going to run away again?'

'Not while I'm this naked.' She sighed, surrendering to his seriousness. 'I can handle you.'

'Then no more hiding either,' he ordered, cupping her cheek. 'In this, hold nothing back.'

She was lost in the blue of his intense eyes. He wanted it all his way—acceptance that this was only sex. But at the same time he wanted everything from her. It wasn't fair. But it was life. And it was just them again.

'Okay.' She breathed. A wave of pleasure rolled over her as she accepted his terms. This total intimacy was finally okay.

Less than a second later he drove deep into her body. She cried out as he claimed her with that one powerful thrust. Trembling, she wrapped her arms around his muscular body. Maybe she couldn't handle him. She couldn't cope with how completely he took her, or how exquisitely he now tortured her by just holding still—his invasion total.

'Easy…' he muttered.

There was no easy. 'Please,' she begged, trying to rock her hips beneath him to rouse him into action. 'Please.'

She needed him to move—to take her hard and fast and break the terrible tension gripping her. Because this was too, too good and she was going insane with the desire for release.

'Damn it, Eleni.' He growled and rose on his hands, grinding impossibly deeper.

Passion washed over her. It felt so good she all but lost her mind in the fire that burned out of control so quickly. She was like dry tinder. With one spark the inferno licked to the bone. But suddenly, blessedly, he flared too. Ferociously he rode her. She moaned with every panting short breath until they bucked in unison. Waves of ecstasy radiated through each cell in her body with every one of his forceful thrusts. Fierce and fast she arched, taut and tight around him.

'Eleni.'

She loved the way he ground her name through his clenched teeth. Over and over he stroked her. She clenched her fists as the shuddering rush of pleasure started. Gasping for breath, she revelled in the floods of release as he shouted and thrust hard that one last time, pressing her flat against the wooden floor.

Her emotions surged as the waves of her orgasm ebbed. It was shocking how good he made her feel. How *shattered*. She didn't think she could possibly find the energy to stand, let alone smile. And she wanted to smile. More than that, she wanted him again. Already. She struggled to catch her breath before it quickened, but there was no reining in the rapacious desire that he'd unleashed within her. Only then she felt him moving—away.

Damon winced. Every muscle felt feeble. He'd meant to go more gently and ensure she was with him every step of the way. Hell, he'd meant to make her come first and more than once. But she'd provoked him, and he'd wanted her too much, until he'd taken her like this on the floor— unstoppable and unrestrained and so damn quick all over again.

He rolled onto his side to see more of her lithe, passion-slick, sated body. And this time she turned her head to look back at him. Letting him see her. Her green-blue eyes were luminous. His mouth dried as he read the craving within them. For all his teasing, he understood how much she wanted this. As much as he did. Something shifted inside—a warning that this was far too intense. But it was too late.

If he was any kind of a good guy he'd have wed her and then left her right alone, because, as he'd told her, sleeping together again would lead to complication and she was so inexperienced he didn't want to mess with her emotions. But he wasn't a good guy.

Not a prince, remember?

Fortunately he'd recovered from the whim to carry her into the apartment. That action had turned her soft skin pink, so he'd had to remind her of the reality of their situation. His words had snuffed the starry-eyed look from her face. Now all that remained was the flush of raw desire. Because that was all this was. Romance wasn't real. Love didn't last.

So, better him to be doing this with her than some other jerk, right? At least he was the one she wanted.

He was determined to please her. The sound of her sighs and the fierce heat of her hold were his ultimate reward. The intensity of their chemistry both angered and enthralled him. Now his exhausted body roared with renewed energy. He scooped her into his arms and stood. He'd ached to have her this close. To have her unable to say no to him, wanting and welcoming him—and only him.

He walked through the ornate lounge room, going on instinct to find her bedroom—a surprisingly simply decorated room. He was just so glad to see the bed. He placed her in the centre of it, gritting back the primal growl of victory. His skin tightened as his muscles bunched. Now they'd solved the problem of their immediate future, they could thrash this attraction that burned between them. An understanding of pleasure was the one thing he could give her. The enjoyment of what their bodies were built for, with no shame, no reticence and no regret. Just passion and play.

Satisfaction oozed as he started to tease that wild response from her again. He loved finally having her on the bed with all the time in the world to explore her properly. Her cheeks flushed, her eyes gleamed—dazed, passionate, willing.

He'd had her. He'd have her again. But something ached—something that was missing despite the almost intolerable ecstasy of the last orgasm they'd shared.

'Eleni.' He uttered a plea he hadn't meant to let free.

He'd coerced her into this marriage, but while she'd finally agreed—and accepted that it was only a contract—somehow he wasn't appeased. Not yet. Not even when he made her writhe uncontrollably. Not when she moaned again or when her hands sought to hurry him. Because he refused to be hurried. Not this time. He was slow and deliberate and determined to touch and taste and tease every last inch of her. But even when he'd done that, the nagging gap still irked.

Finally he allowed himself to invade her body with his own again. Helplessly groaning at the unbearable bliss, he locked into place. The driving need to get closer consumed him. He craved her heated softness and tight strength.

'Eleni.' He strained to stay in control.

'Yes.' Her sweet answer rasped over his desire-whipped skin and he drove deeper into her fire. Every muscle tensed as he fought the urge to give in already.

Too soon. It was too soon.

'Damon.' She tracked teasing fingers down his chest until he caught her hand and held it close and she whispered again. Sheer lust vocalised. 'Damon.'

His heart pounded. That was what he wanted. His name on her lips. Her eyes on his. Her body drinking his in. Her whole focus only on him. She arched, willing and sultry, and suddenly her enchanting smile was broken by her release.

'Damon!'

His name. *Screamed.*

A torrent of triumphant energy sluiced through every cell as the last vestige of his self-control snapped. He could no longer hold back, growling his passion as he furiously pounded his way closer. To her. To bliss. His world blackened as rapture hit and satisfaction thundered.

He had won.

CHAPTER TEN

DAMON QUIETLY PACED about the lounge in Eleni's apartment within the palace. His bags had been delivered before the ceremony yesterday and he drew out his tablet now.

The number of emails in his inbox was insane even for him and it wasn't yet eight in the morning. He clicked the first few open and grimaced at the capital letters screaming *CONGRATULATIONS!* at him.

Rattled, he flicked on the television, muting the volume so he couldn't hear the over-excited, high-pitched squeals of the presenters as they gushed about the surprise nuptials of Princess Eleni. A ticker ran along the bottom of the screen repeating the amazing news that she'd married a commoner—one Mr Damon Gale.

The piece they then played was about him. His business interests got a brief mention while his personal ones were explored in depth and all but invented. They focused on his upbringing, his family, his illegitimate half-sister...

He winced when he saw the media crews camped outside Kassie's small apartment in the village. But the horror show worsened in a heartbeat as his father flashed on the screen. Damon automatically iced his emotions—the response had taken him years to perfect. But the sensation of impending doom increased and he flicked on the audio to hear his father in action. Apparently John Gale was 'thrilled' that Eleni and his son Damon's relationship was finally public. His father didn't use her title as he talked, implying intimacy—as if he'd ever met her? But he wasn't afraid of using anyone to push himself further up the slippery pole of success; Damon knew that all too well.

He could hear his father's avaricious glee at the coup his son had scored.

'You must be very proud of Damon,' one reporter yelled.

His father visibly puffed up. 'Damon is brilliant. He inherited his mother's brains.'

Damon gritted his teeth. His father's false praise poked a wound that should have long healed. His parents were anything but normal. Narcissistic and concerned only with image, neither had hearts. Truth be told, nor did he. That was his genetic inheritance. No capacity for love. No capacity for shame. All his parents had was ambition. He had that too.

But he'd learned to define his own success. To make it alone, be the one in control, be the boss. His parents had been uninterested and absent at best, and abusive at worst, and they'd taught him well. Yeah, now he had the burning ambition not to need them or *anyone*.

'What about your daughter, Kasiani?' Another reporter jostled to the front. 'Is she also a friend of Princess Eleni's?'

His father didn't bat an eyelid at the mention of the daughter he hadn't seen in years and the reference to the women that he'd abandoned entirely—not just emotionally, but financially as well. Damon had actually been jealous of Kassie until he'd learned his father was truly fickle and incapable of any kind of decent emotion.

'I really can't comment further on Eleni's personal relationships.' He didn't need to comment further when the smug satisfaction was written all over his face.

Damon watched as his father walked past the reporter. But as the cameraman swung the camera to keep filming, Damon realised just where the interview had taken place—outside the terminal at Palisades airport.

Which meant his father was here. Now.

Damon muted the sound on the screen and strode from

Eleni's private apartment. He needed to speak to the palace secretary immediately.

'Mr Gale.'

Damon stopped mid-stride down the hallway as Giorgos's private secretary called to him.

'It's your father,' the secretary added.

'Please take me to him,' Damon said quietly.

John Gale had been shown to one of the smaller meeting rooms very near the entrance of the palace. Damon's appreciation of Giorgos's secretary increased and he nodded at the man as he stood back respectfully.

Drawing in a breath, Damon closed the door and faced the father he hadn't seen in five years. Not much had changed. Perhaps he had a little more grey in his hair, a few lines around his eyes, but he still wore that surface-only smile, neat suit and non-stick demeanour.

Damon didn't take a seat, didn't offer one to his father. 'Why are you here?'

'I wanted to congratulate you in person.'

The bare nerve of the man was galling.

'You're very quick off the mark. I haven't been married twenty-four hours yet.'

His father's smile stayed crocodile wide. 'I never thought you had it in you.'

'Had what in me?'

'To marry so…happily.'

'Happily?' Damon queried. 'You mean like you and Mother?'

'Your mother and I have a very successful arrangement.'

Yeah. An arrangement that was bloodless and only about making the most of their assets. 'And that's what you think this is?'

'Are you saying you're in love with her?' His father laughed. 'I'm sure you love the power and opportunity that come with her beautiful body.'

Revulsion triggered rage but Damon breathed deeply,

settling his pulse. He wasn't going to bite. His father wasn't worth it. But he couldn't help declaring the obvious. 'I'm not like you.'

His father frowned. 'Meaning?'

'You have at least one other child that you have done nothing for. You abuse people, then abandon them.'

His father's expression narrowed.

'How many others are there?' Damon asked bluntly.

'That was one mistake.'

Mistake?

'I saw you with her,' Damon said softly, knowing he'd regret the revelation but unable to resist asking.

'Who?'

'Kassie's mother.' Damon had followed him once, here in Palisades—the opulent island of personal betrayal had taken Damon on a swift bleak journey to adulthood and understanding. He'd seen his father kiss that woman with such passion. Damon had actually thought his father was truly in love. That he was truly capable of it and it was just that he didn't feel it for either Damon or his mother. 'Why didn't you leave us and stay with her?' He'd never understood it.

An appalled expression carved deeper lines in his father's face. 'I would never leave your mother.'

'Not because you love her,' Damon said. 'But because her connections were too important to your career. It was your arrangement.'

Because he was that calculating. That ruthlessly ambitious. That incapable of real love.

'Your mother and I make a good team. We understand each other.'

By turning blind eyes to infidelities and focusing on their careers. They'd used his funds and her family name. Connections and money made for progress in political circles. They'd had Damon only to cement the image of the 'perfect career couple'. Not because he'd actually been wanted, as his mother had told him every time he'd disappointed her. And that had been often.

'So you abandoned your lover and your daughter and refused to help when they were struggling because of the risk to your stupid career and supposedly perfect marriage.' Damon was disgusted.

'I offered her money but she was too proud to accept it. That was her choice.'

'You knew she suffered and you didn't go back.'

'What more could I have done, Damon?' his father asked. 'Was it my fault she chose to remain in that squalid little cottage?'

Damon understood it now—he'd realised the horrific truth when he'd learned how that woman had suffered for so long, so alone. His father had never loved Kassie's mother. He'd wanted her, used her and walked away when he'd had enough. When she'd refused his money his conscience was cleared and he'd considered himself absolved.

No guilt. No shame. No heart.

'It'll look strange if you don't invite us both here soon,' his father said, his callousness towards Kassie and her mother apparently forgotten already. 'Your mother would like to stay as a guest.'

'I'm never inviting either of you here,' Damon said shortly. 'How can you act as if we're close when we haven't seen each other in years?' Bitterness burned up his throat. He wanted the taint of the man nowhere near Eleni.

'We've all been busy.'

His father hadn't realised he'd been avoiding him? 'No. We have no relationship. You're not using this. You're not using me.'

'You can't get away from your blood, Damon.' John Gale laughed. 'You're my son. Just because we're more alike than you want to admit, doesn't mean it isn't so. You can't get away from who you are.'

He'd never wanted to be like either of his parents. They

were why he'd never wanted a serious relationship, let alone to marry. Why he'd wanted to build his company—his success—on his own terms. In isolation and not dependent on manipulated relationships.

'I might not be able to deny my blood, but I can deny you access to my wife and to our home,' Damon said coldly. 'You're not welcome here. You'll never be welcome here. I suggest you leave right now, before I have the soldiers throw you out.'

'Your wife's soldiers.'

'Yes.' Damon refused to let his father get a rise out of him. 'Don't come back. Don't contact me again. And don't dare try to contact Eleni directly.'

'Or?'

'Or I'll let the world know just *what* you are.' He'd strike where his father cared the most—his reputation, his image.

John's eyes narrowed.

'It will be much better for you to return to New York and whatever project it is you're about to launch,' Damon said lazily. 'And no more gleeful interviews mentioning Eleni and me. You're showing your lack of class.'

That blow landed and Damon watched as his father's complexion turned ruddy. After that, John didn't stick around and Damon slowly wound his way back up to Eleni's apartment. He'd done the right thing getting him out of the palace as quickly as possible. But his father's slimy insincerity stuck.

He didn't want it getting to Eleni. As soon as the baby was born he'd begin the separation process because she'd be so much better off without him. But he'd still be the Princess's ex-husband, the father of her child. Another prince or princess.

Too late he realised her life was now intrinsically tied to his. His gut tightened as he mulled the possible configurations of their futures and the fact that she would always be part of his world. In the cold light of day he realised he'd not 'won' anything at all.

Nor had she.

But he'd meant what he'd told her. Relationships never lasted. Not for anyone. And certainly not him. Never him. He refused.

He paused for a moment outside her apartment door to draw in a breath. Then he let himself in. It was too much to hope she was still in bed. She was dressed in a simple tee shirt and skirt and his wayward body tightened at the sight of her lithe legs.

'Where have you been?' she asked, sending him a sleepy smile, but her sea-green eyes were too searching for him to cope with.

'I have a company to run,' Damon said sharply, picking up his tablet and staring at it. Hard. 'I've neglected it long enough while tracking you down.'

Silence filled the room, tightening the invisible string connecting his eyes to her body and in the end he could no longer resist the tug.

A limpid look was trained on him. 'Perhaps you should have slept a little longer.'

He couldn't help but smile at that most princess-polite sass.

She wandered over to the window, affording him an even better view of her legs and the curve of her body. She had no idea of her sensuality.

'So what have you been working on that's caused your mood to…deteriorate?'

'It's not important.'

'It wouldn't have anything to do with your father, would it?'

He froze. 'Your palace spies have reported in already?'

'No spies. I saw a replay of the interview with him at the airport.' She turned to face him. 'Is he here?'

'He's already left.'

'You didn't want me to meet him?'

'No.' He didn't want to explain why. But he saw the wounded flash in her eyes. 'He's not a nice man.'

Her lips twisted. 'You don't need to protect me.'

'Yes, I do.' He huffed out a breath and glared at his tablet again, gripping it as if it were his life-support system.

His marriage to Eleni could be nothing like his parents' one. For one thing, it wasn't about to last. It wasn't about his career and never would be. It was about protecting his child. It was about protecting Eleni.

'Are you sure it's me you're protecting?' she asked quietly.

He glanced across at her. 'Meaning?'

'Your father...and you.' She looked uncomfortable. 'You're not close...'

'No.' Damon couldn't help but smile faintly. Definitely not close. 'I haven't had contact with him in almost five years.'

'None at all?'

He shook his head.

'He cheated on your mother.' She still looked super awkward. 'Kassie at the hospital...'

'Is my unacknowledged half-sister. Yes.'

'But you're in touch with her.'

'Yes.' He sighed and put the tablet down on the low table. 'My father isn't. My mother pretends she doesn't exist. Kassie is too proud to push for what she's owed.' He leaned back on the edge of the sofa, folding his arms across his chest. He'd had to find out what had happened. 'I once saw him with her mother,' Damon said. 'Years ago when we lived here in Palisades.'

'That must have been hard to see.'

Damon frowned at the floor. 'I couldn't understand why he didn't leave us for them when it was so obvious...'

'Did you ever ask him?'

About five minutes ago and his father had confirmed

what Damon had learned in later years. 'His career was too important. It was always too important to both my parents. The only reason they had me was to tick that box on their CV—happily married with one son...'

'But they must be proud of you.'

He laughed bitterly. 'Proud of a teenager who wasted his time making lame computer games?' He shook his head.

'But now you have a hugely successful company. More than one. How can they not be—?' She broke off and her expression softened. 'You shouldn't have had to "achieve" to get the support any child deserves.'

'I got more than my half-sister did,' he muttered shortly. 'He wouldn't even support them financially. Her mother died a long, slow, painful death. Kassie has been struggling since.'

'Is that why you got in touch with her?'

He nodded. 'But she wouldn't let me help her.' He rolled his shoulders. It still knotted him that Kassie had refused almost everything he'd offered. 'I can understand it.'

Sadness lent a sheen to Eleni's eyes. 'And your parents are still together.'

'Still achieving. Still silently seething with bitterness and unhappiness. Still a successful marriage. Sure thing.'

'He cheated more than once?'

'I expect so,' he sighed.

'So.' Eleni brushed her hair back from her face. 'That's why you made it clear our marriage is only to provide legitimacy for our baby. Why you think no relationship lasts.'

'As I said, a child shouldn't be raised in the household with unhappily married parents.' Unloving parents. 'We married for the birth certificate, then we do what's right. I didn't want this baby to be a tool for some political purpose. Not paraded as the future Prince or Princess or whatever. And I won't abandon it either.'

'I understand,' she said softly. 'I don't want that either.'

She bit her lip and looked down at the table between them. 'I'm sorry your parents…'

He held up a hand. 'It's okay. We all have our burdens, right?' She'd lost both her parents. She had expectations on her that were far beyond the normal person's. He shouldn't have judged her as harshly as he had.

'Damon?'

He glanced up at that roughened note in her voice.

Storms had gathered in her sea-green eyes. 'This baby was unexpected, unplanned…' she pressed a hand to her flat belly as she gazed across at him '…but I promise you I'll love it. I already do. I'll do whatever it takes to protect and care for it.'

'I know.' He believed her because she already was. He'd seen her stand up to her brother—knew that had been a first for her. And she was trying here, now, with him.

But somehow it made that discomfort within him worse. He wasn't like her. He didn't understand how she could love the child already. The truth was he didn't know how to love. He had no idea how to be a husband. He sure as hell had no idea how to be a father. When he'd first suspected she might be pregnant his initial instinct had been not to abandon his child. He was not doing what his father had done to Kassie.

But he had no idea how even these next few months were going to work. The tightness in his chest didn't ease. Disappointment flowed and then ebbed. Leaving him with that *void*. He ached for a real escape.

'Is that the photo Giorgos approved for release?' Eleni's voice rose in surprise.

He glanced at the muted screen still showing the number one news item of the world.

'Yes.' He cleared his throat. 'There's another with him in it as well, but this is the one the media have run with.'

'I can't believe he chose that one. It's…'

'What?'

'Informal.'

Damon knew why the King had chosen that particular picture. Eleni looked stunning with her skin glowing, her hair and dress beautiful…but it was that luminosity in her expression that was striking. While Damon was looking at her with undeniable desire, she was laughing up at him—sparkling, warm, delighted. This image, snapped in that moment in the garden, would sell the 'truth' of this fairy tale.

This image stole his breath.

But now another picture of him flashed on the screen—him at an event with another woman. Then another. Inwardly he winced. It seemed anyone who'd dated him in the past wanted their five minutes of fame now and had opened their photo albums to show off their one or two snaps.

'Wow, lots of models, huh?' Eleni muttered, her rasp more apparent. 'That's very billionaire tech entrepreneur of you.'

'It wasn't a deliberate strategy.' He stepped nearer to her, needing to touch her skin. 'They just happened to be at the parties.'

She subjected him to a long, silent scrutiny. 'You know my history. I don't know yours at all.'

'You mean lovers?' He grinned in an effort to shake off the prickling sensation her piercing greenish gaze caused. 'I've had a few. No real girlfriends. There's nothing and no one to trouble you.'

She didn't look convinced.

He shrugged. 'I'm busy with my work and I like to be good at it.'

The ugly fact was he was a hollow man—as success obsessed as his shallow parents. Just less visible about it. He liked to think he had a smidge more integrity than they did—by refusing to use other people to get to where he wanted to be. Utter independence was what he craved.

'Do you know I've got at least twenty new work offers

today purely because of my involvement with you?' he said a little roughly.

She lifted her eyebrows. 'And that isn't good?'

'*I* haven't earned these opportunities, Eleni.'

'Perhaps you could take advantage of them to enable other people to progress as well. To create jobs and other contracts—'

Her naive positivity hit a raw nerve. '*I* built my company from scratch.'

'And you don't want your association with me compromising your success story?' Her cheeks pinked. 'At least you had the choice to forge your own path. I'm one of the most privileged people on the planet and, while I am grateful for that, I'm also bound by the rules that come with it. I couldn't do what I want.'

And it seemed she still couldn't. He grabbed his tablet again and showed her the endless list of invitations and formal appearances the palace official had sent him. 'Is this amount normal?' he asked. 'Which would you usually decline?'

Her eyebrows shot up. 'None.'

None? He paused. 'There are too many requests here.'

Were they were trying to schedule her every waking moment? Damon wasn't having it.

'You don't say no.' The shock on her face said it all.

She really was a total pawn in the palace machine. Well, he wasn't letting them take advantage of Eleni, or her child, or him. Not any more.

'I'm okay with saying no,' he said.

'Well, I don't like to be perceived as lazy.' Her lips tightened. 'Or spoilt.'

And that was why Princess Eleni had always done as she was told—wore what was expected, said what was polite, did what was her duty. She'd obediently played her princess role perfectly for years.

Except when it had come to him. That night with him

she'd done what she *wanted*. She'd taken. And since then? She'd argued. She'd stood up for herself. She'd been everything but obedient when it came to him…

He didn't want that changing because she felt some misguided sense of obligation now she was married to him. Hell, she was likely to want to play the part of the 'perfect wife' but he wasn't letting it happen. For the first time in her life, he wanted Eleni Nicolaides to experience some true freedom.

'Why did you want to stay in Palisades rather than go to Giorgos's safe house in France?' he asked roughly.

She looked down. 'This probably sounds crazy, but it's actually more private here.'

'You're *happy* to be trapped inside the palace walls?'

She shrugged her shoulders. 'It's what I'm used to. I can show you how it works.'

He didn't need to know how it worked. He had a headache from all the gilded decorations already. 'I know somewhere even more private.' He rubbed his shoulder. 'I think we should go there.'

'You don't understand—'

'Yeah, I do. I know about the paparazzi and the press and the cell phones in every member of the public's hands. But my island is safe. It's secure. It's private.'

She stilled. 'Your island?'

She really hadn't done any research on him, had she? That both tickled him, and put him out.

'You have your island, I have mine.' He sent her a sideways grin. 'I'll admit mine isn't as big, but good things come in small packages.'

The look in her eyes was decidedly not limpid now. 'Are you trying to convince me that size doesn't matter?' she teased in that gorgeously raspy voice. 'Of course, I have no basis for comparison, for all I know I might be missing out—'

'You're concerned you're missing out?' He rose to her

bait, happy to slip back into this tease and turn away from the too serious.

'You tell me.' She batted her eyelashes at him.

This was the woman from that night at the ball—that playful, slightly shy, deliciously fun woman.

'Hell, yeah, you're missing out.'

Her mouth fell open.

'Come with me and I'll show you.'

Her lips twisted as colour flowed into her cheeks.

'It's in the Caribbean,' he purred.

She closed her mouth. 'That is also very tech billionaire of you.'

'Yeah. It is. So let's go there. Today.' He stood, energy firing. For the first time since seeing that damn screen this morning he felt good.

'But Giorgos—'

'But Giorgos what? We can let him know where we've gone.' He paused, waiting to see if she'd defy her brother's orders.

A gleam lit in her eye. Damon suppressed his smug smirk—seemed his Princess had unleashed her latent rebellious streak. He liked it.

'How long does it take to get there?'

CHAPTER ELEVEN

ELENI SAT ACROSS from Damon in one of the large leather recliners in his private jet and tried not to stare at him. Her face heated as she recalled what he'd done to her, what he'd encouraged her to do to him. Last night had been the first time she'd ever shared a bed. The first time she'd slept in a man's arms. She couldn't even *remember* falling asleep, only a feeling of supreme relaxation as she'd lain entwined with him.

'It's a long flight. You should rest while you can.' That wicked glint ignited his smile as if he knew exactly what she was thinking about.

'I need rest?'

'For the days ahead, yes.'

'Empty promises…threats…' she muttered softly.

He leaned forward and placed his finger over her lips. 'Don't worry. I'll make good on every one. When we're alone.'

'I see no cabin crew.' She blinked at him.

'You want them to hear you?' His eyebrows arched. 'Because you're not going to be quiet.'

'I can be quiet.'

'Can you?' He studied her intently, not bothering to add anything more.

Heat deepened and spread, heating her from the inside out. Every, single cell. Realisation burned. She was never going to be quiet with him.

'You're…' She couldn't think of her own name, let alone a suitable adjective this second.

'Good.' Looking smug, he leaned back in his seat and pulled his tablet out. 'I'm very good.'

'Full of yourself,' she corrected.

She couldn't sit for hours with nothing to occupy her except sinful thoughts. She burrowed in her bag and fetched out the paper and small pencil tin that she always had stashed. Sketching soothed, like meditation. And she'd spent so many hours with a pencil in hand, it was calming.

He didn't seem to notice her occupation. She became so engrossed in her work she lost track of time. When she glanced up she discovered he'd closed his eyes. She wasn't surprised; he'd had as little sleep as she. And he'd been worryingly pale when he'd returned to her apartment this morning after that meeting with his father.

With that downwards tilt to his sensual lips now, she understood that he was vulnerable too and much more complex than she'd realised. He'd been hurt. His parents' infidelities, their lack of support and interest. Their falseness.

Yet he'd grown strong. Now she understood his fierce independence and the fury he'd felt when he'd thought she'd somehow betrayed him. He didn't trust and she didn't blame him. He only wanted his child to avoid the hurt he'd experienced.

She looked down at the sketch she'd done of him and cringed. She'd never want him to see this—too amateur. Too embarrassing. She folded the paper over and put it in the small bin just as the pilot announced they weren't far from landing. Damon opened his eyes and flashed her a smile.

'It's just a short hop by helicopter from here,' he said as the plane landed.

'That's what you say to everyone you bring here?'

He met her gaze. 'You already know I never brought any of my women here. This is my home.'

'Heaven forbid you'd let any of them get that close.'

'Wouldn't want them getting the wrong idea.'

'I'm glad I "trapped" you into marriage, then, now I get to kick about on your little island.'

Damon grinned at her. Yeah, he couldn't wait for her to kick about. But he held back as Eleni gathered her small bag and stepped ahead of him to exit the plane. He'd seen her discard the drawing she'd been working on and he was too curious to let it go. On his way out he swiftly scooped up the paper and pocketed it. Given she'd been secretive and clearly hadn't wanted him to see it, he was going to have to pick the moment to ask her about it.

The helicopter ride was smooth but wasn't quick enough. He ached to get there—to his home. His own private palace. His peace.

He breathed out as they finally landed and he strode to the open-topped Jeep that he'd ordered to be left waiting for their arrival.

'Let me take you on a tour.' He winked at her. 'You can see exactly what kind of prize husband you've claimed for yourself.'

'You're not the prize. I am,' Eleni answered sassily as she shook her hair loose in the warm sunshine. 'It really is your island?'

'It's the company compound,' he drawled. 'We futuristic tech companies must have amazing work places for our staff. It's part of the image.'

'I didn't think you were a slave to any society's required "image". You're the man who doesn't care what anyone thinks of him, right?'

Right. *Almost.*

Reluctant amusement rippled through him. He liked it when she sparked up.

She stared as the pristine coastline came into clear view. He heard her sharp intake of breath. Now as he drove they could see a few roofs of other dwellings amongst the verdant foliage. He knew it was beautiful, but he was glad she could see it too.

'They live here all year round?'

'No.' He laughed that she'd taken him so seriously. 'It really is just my island. It was a resort, now it's not. My people stay for stints if they need to complete a big project, or to recharge their batteries. Every employee has at least six weeks a year here. Families can come too, of course.' He parked up by the main beach. 'Energy-wise it's self-sufficient, thanks to all the solar-power generation, and we grow as many supplies as we can.'

'So it's paradise.'

'Yeah.' Pure, simple luxury. 'There's no paparazzi. No media. No nosey parkers watching your every move. It is completely private.'

She glanced up into the blindingly blue—clear—sky. 'No drones? No spy cams everywhere?'

'No helicopters. No long-range lenses. No nothing. Just peace and security,' he confirmed, but grimaced wryly. 'And half my staff...but they'll be busy and you can do whatever you want, whenever you want.'

'With whomever I want?' she asked. There was an extra huskiness to her tone that made him so hard.

'No.' He reached across and turned her chin so she faced him. 'Only with me.'

She mock-pouted, teasing in that playful way he adored—demanding retribution of the most erotic kind. But after only a kiss he reluctantly pulled away. He couldn't bring her here and hurry her into bed. He could be more civilised than that.

'Come on,' he said briskly, getting out of the Jeep and pointing to the meandering path through the lush trees. 'I'll show you around the complex.'

Then he'd take her to his house and have her all to himself at last.

Eleni didn't want to blink and miss a moment. His island was like a warm jewel, gleaming with the promise of heat and holiday and indefinable riches. And with that total privacy, it was the ultimate treasure. A feeling of relaxation slowly unfurled through her body, spreading warmth and joy and such anticipation she could hardly contain it.

'This is the "den"—our main office here.'

She followed him into the large building. It was a large open space filled with desks, computers and space for tinkering and was currently occupied by five guys all standing round a giant screen.

'Going from left to right, we have Olly, Harry, Blair, Jerome and Faisal,' Damon said to her in a low voice. 'You have that memorised already, right?'

She smiled because, yes, she had.

'Guys,' Damon called to them. 'I'd like you to meet Eleni.'

Not *Princess*. Not *my wife*. Just Eleni. That different kind of warmth flowed through her veins again.

The men turned and shouts erupted. But not for her. It was pleasure that their boss had returned. One of the guys stepped to the side of the swarm around Damon to greet her.

'Nice to meet you, Eleni.' Olly's accent placed him as Australian.

The other men nodded, smiled and positively pounced on Damon again.

'Look, D—I know you're not here for work, but can I just run a couple things past you?' Faisal asked.

Damon was already halfway across the room, his gaze narrowing at the gobbledegook on the screen. 'Of course.'

All the men perked up but Eleni saw Olly and Jerome exchange a look and a jerk of the head towards her. The next second Jerome walked over.

'Eleni…' Jerome cleared his throat. 'Welcome. You must…ah…'

'I'm really happy to be here.' She smiled to put him at

ease. Eleni could make conversation with anyone. 'What is it you guys are working on?'

He led her to the nearest table that was covered in an assortment of electronics components and plastic figurines. 'We're designing a new visuals prototype and we need his thoughts on the latest version.'

'Visuals prototype?'

To his credit, Jerome spent a good five minutes explaining the tech to her and answering her questions. But it was obvious he was eager to talk to Damon too and in the end she put him out of his misery. 'Go ask him whatever it is you need to. I'm fine,' she laughed.

'Are you sure?' Jerome looked anxiously between her and Damon.

'Of course.'

He hurried away to join the conference around the screen. Damon stood in the centre, listening intently then quietly offering his opinion. The Australian was making notes on a piece of paper while Harry asked another question prompting another concise answer. It was evident they valued his every word and had missed his input. Everyone in the vicinity was paying total attention—to him. Eleni gradually became aware she was staring at him too. And for once no one was staring at *her*.

Blushing, she turned away and stepped outside to take in some fresh air. Her muscles ached slightly and a gentle feeling of fatigue made her sleepy. She leaned against the tall tree just outside the building and looked across at the beautifully clear water.

Ten minutes later Damon walked back to where she waited in the shade.

'Sorry,' he muttered as he reached to take her hand. 'That took longer than I realised.'

'It's fine. I enjoyed looking around.'

Damon sent her a speculative look that turned increasingly wicked the longer he studied her. 'What have you been thinking about?' he asked. 'You've gone very pink.'

The heat in her cheeks burned. 'Don't tease.'

'Oh, I'll tease.' He tugged on her hand and pulled her closer to him. 'But first let me show you the rest.'

'I think rest is a good idea.' She wanted to be alone with his undivided attention on *her* again. And right now she didn't care if that made her spoiled.

'There's a restaurant room,' he said.

Of course there was. Right on the beach, with a bar and a woman who waved and smiled at Damon the second she saw him. Eleni's spine prickled.

'Rosa will cook anything you want, as long as you want fresh and delicious.' Damon waved at the relaxed, gorgeously tanned woman and kept walking past.

'This place is just beautiful.' Eleni glanced back at the restaurant.

'Rosa is married to Olly, the guy with—'

'The beard.' Eleni sighed, stupidly relieved. 'The Australian.'

Damon grinned as if he'd sensed her irrational jealous flare. 'They live here most of the year round.'

'Lucky them.' She walked across the sand with him. 'Do you live here most of the year too?'

'Meetings take me away, but I'm here when I can be.'

Eleni could understand why; if it were her choice she'd never leave. But his marriage to her was going to make that problematic for a while. She had duties in Palisades that she had to perform.

'Where next?' she asked. 'Your house?'

'Not yet. You haven't seen the playroom.'

'Playroom?' she asked, startled.

He laughed and gave her a playful swipe. 'Not *that* kind of playroom.' He cocked his head. 'But now I know you're curious…'

'Shut it and show me the room.' She marched across the sand, cheeks burning.

It was a boat shed and it was filled with every water-sport toy imaginable—from surfboards, to kayaks to inflatables and jet skis. 'Okay, this is seriously cool.' She stepped forward to get a closer look.

'I knew you liked the water,' Damon said smugly. 'You swim, right?'

'Indoors at the palace,' she answered, checking out the kayaks stacked in racks up the wall. 'Giorgos had a resistance current feature installed so I can train each morning in privacy.'

'You don't swim in the sea?'

'With everyone watching?' She stared at him as if he were crazy. 'Rating my swimsuits every morning?' She shook her head. 'And he'd never let me on a jet ski.'

'No?' Damon's eyes widened.

'Safety issues.' She shrugged and straightened. 'And again, too many photographers.'

'You like to avoid those.'

'Do you blame me?'

'No.' He leaned against the door frame and sent her a smouldering look. 'I'm really good on a jet ski,' he said arrogantly. 'You can come with me.'

She crossed her arms and sent what she hoped was a smouldering look right back at him. 'Can I drive?'

'Sure. I have no problem with that.'

'But what if I want to go fast?' She blinked at him innocently.

'I think I can keep up.' He lifted away from the door frame and strolled towards her.

'You think?' Her voice rose as he stepped close enough to pull her against him.

'I think it's time you saw my house,' he growled.

'It's beyond time,' she whispered.

He guided her across the sand and up a beautifully main-

tained path through the well-established trees to the gorgeous building at the end.

An infinity pool—the perfect length for laps—was the
feature at the front. Comfortable, beautiful furniture was
strategically placed to create space for relaxation, conversation and privacy. The house itself was wooden, with two
storeys, and not monstrously huge but nor was it small.
Damon didn't speak as he led her inside—he simply let
her look around. It was luxurious, yes, but also cosy with
a sense of true intimacy. She didn't know why that surprised her, but it did.

He still said nothing, but smiled as if he sensed her appreciation. She took his outstretched hand and he led her
up the curling wooden staircase. She assumed it led to his
bedroom. Her heart hammered. A delicious languorous
anticipation seeped into her bones.

But while there were doors to other rooms on one side,
the room he drew her to wasn't for sleeping. It stretched
the length of the building. Unsurprisingly it was dominated
by symmetrical windows overlooking the sand, sea and
sky. A long table took up half the space. It was clearly his
desk, given the neatly stacked piles of papers and the writing utensils gathered in a chipped mug. A long seat took up
much of the remaining window space. A single armchair
stood in front of the large fireplace that broke up the floor-
to-ceiling bookshelves that covered the wall opposite the
windows. Books were stacked on every shelf. Books that
had clearly been read and weren't just there for the look
of it. This was more than his workspace. It was his think
space—his escape.

'I can see why you love it.' She stood in the middle of
the room and gazed from the intriguing space inside to the
natural beauty outside.

'Best view on the island.'

'The beauty is more than the view.' She noted the shades
for the windows, the pale warmth of the walls, the art that

he'd chosen to complement the space. 'The light is lovely,' she said softly. 'The colour. It must help you focus.'

'It's not a palace,' he said with a keen look.

'It's better than any palace.'

A small smile flitted about his mouth. 'So you like it?'

Intrigued that her opinion genuinely seemed to matter, she turned her back on the view to face him directly. 'Did you honestly think I wouldn't?' She wasn't that spoilt, was she?

'There's not a lot of gold leaf and crystal chandeliers.'

'Did you think I wasn't going to like it because there's no ballroom?' She felt slightly hurt. 'You don't need a ballroom—you have a beach.' She looked out across the water again. 'You're lucky to have a home, not a museum in which you live.'

She and Giorgos didn't own the palace, they were the guardians for the future of it, and for the people of Palisades. This small island was utterly Damon's and she had to admit she was a little jealous.

'You can stay here any time,' he said.

She sent him a crooked smile, rueful that he'd so clearly read her mind. She didn't want to think about the future yet. She just wanted to enjoy this freedom, in this moment. Enjoy him, while she had him.

'Thank you.' She faced him, determined to take the initiative, despite the mounting burn in her cheeks. 'So may I sit in the driver's seat?'

His focus on her sharpened. 'Meaning?'

Silently she just looked at him. He knew exactly what she meant already.

'Tell me,' he said softly—a combination of demand and dare. 'You can tell me anything.'

His easy invitation summoned that streak of boldness within her, just as it had that very first night. Something in him gave her the courage to claim what she wanted. The courage she got only with him. Only for him.

'I want to kiss you,' she muttered huskily and swallowed before continuing. 'The way you've kissed me.'

He stared at her so intently she wondered if he'd turned to stone.

'I dare you to let me,' she whispered.

'Is this what you've been thinking about?'

'All day,' she admitted with a slow nod.

His smile was as rueful—and as honest—as hers had been only moments earlier. He lifted his hands in a small gesture of surrender. 'That's why you drew this?' He held up a piece of paper.

She winced as she saw what he was holding. 'I put that in the rubbish.'

'Which was a shame.'

That he'd seen that drawing was the most embarrassing thing. Because it was him. Half nude. Heat flooded her. Mortifying, blistering heat.

'Why didn't you study Fine Arts?' he asked.

'It would have been arrogant to assume I had talent.' She hadn't been allowed.

'You do have talent.'

His words lit a different glow in her chest but she laughed it off. 'You're just flattered because I gave you abs.'

'I do have abs.'

'I don't usually draw...' She couldn't even admit it.

'Erotic pictures?' He laughed. 'What do you usually draw?'

'Dogs,' she said tartly.

'The pictures in Kassie's ward at the hospital are yours, right? You draw them for the children.'

He'd seen those? 'They're just doodles.' She shrugged it off.

'You're talented, Eleni.'

'You're very kind.' She bent her head.

He gripped her arms and made her look at him again.

'Don't go "polite princess" on me. Accept the compliment for what it is—honest.'

That fiery heat bloomed in her face again.

'Do you paint as well?'

'Sometimes, but mostly pen and ink drawings.'

'You're good, Eleni.'

'You promised me you were good,' she whispered.

A smile sparked in his eyes but he shook his head. 'You're trying to distract me.'

'Is it working?'

'You know it is. But why can't you take the compliment?'

Because it was too intimate. Too real. It meant too much. His opinion of her shouldn't matter as much as it did. But she didn't say any of that. She just shrugged.

'You have a lot to offer the world,' he said softly.

For a moment it was there again—that flicker of intensity that was different from the pure desire that pulled them together in the first place. This was something deeper. Something impossibly stronger. And she backed away from it.

'Stop with the flattery or I'll never leave,' she joked.

There was a moment of silence and she couldn't look at him.

'Where will you have me?' With those husky words he let her lead them back into that purely sensual tease. The easier, safer option.

'Here. Now.'

She walked, nudging him backwards. All the way to that comfortable armchair. She pushed his chest and he sat. She remained standing, looking down at him. He'd not had the chance to shave since their flight and the light stubble on his jaw lent him a roguish look. That curl to his lips was both arrogant and charming.

She leaned forward. 'Damon,' she breathed as she kissed him.

'Yes.' He held very still beneath her ministrations.

'You're irresistible.' She sent him a laughing look.

He chuckled. 'I'm glad you think so.' He tensed as she slowly undid his buttons. 'What a relief.'

'You don't seem very relieved.'

'I'm trying to stay in control.'

'Why would you want to do that?'

'I don't want to scare you.'

She laughed. 'You're no ogre.'

'I don't want you to stop,' he whispered.

'Why would I? I want you to lose control. You make me lose control all the time.'

'Eleni...'

'It's only fair,' she muttered. Not teasing.

'Fair? You know that's not how it works.'

A frisson of awareness reverberated through her body. Delight. Desire. Danger. That intensity flickered again. But she moved closer. Took him deeper. Stroked him harder. Doing everything she'd secretly dreamed of doing. She'd show him *not fair*.

He groaned. 'Don't stop.'

Pleased, she kissed him again and then again. His hands swept down her sides, stirring her to the point where she couldn't concentrate any more. She drew back.

'Stop touching,' she growled at him. 'It's my turn.'

He half laughed. She squeezed. Hard.

'Mine,' she said seriously—and for more than just this 'turn'.

He met her gaze. The blue of his eyes deepened as that something passed between them. No matter that she tried to dance past it, it kept curling back—entwining around them.

He lifted a hand, threading his fingers through her hair to cup the nape of her neck. 'Mine.'

His echo was an affirmation, not an argument. He was hers to hold. Hers to have. And yes, she was his too.

For now. Only for now.

She closed her eyes and let herself go—taking exactly what she wanted, touching in the way she'd only dreamed and never before dared. She liked feeling his power beneath her. Liked his vulnerability like this—letting her pleasure him.

'Eleni.'

She felt his power and restraint and fought to topple it. He curled his hands around the armrests and she heard his breathing roughen. His muscles flexed and she tasted salt as sweat slicked his skin.

'Eleni.'

She tightened her grip, swirling her tongue, and simply willed for him to feel it the same way she did—that unspeakable bliss. 'Let me make you feel good.'

That was what he did for her.

Spent and satisfied physically, a different need surged fiercely through Damon. He didn't want her doing this out of gratitude or pity. He lifted her onto his lap and cupping her chin, stared hard into her eyes—heavy-lidded, sea-green storms of desire gazed back at him. Dazed, yet seemingly seeing right into his soul.

Pure instinct drove him. He kissed her, slipping his hand under her skirt, skating his fingers all the way to her secret treasure. His heart seized as he discovered how hot and wet she was and satisfaction drummed in his heart. She'd not gone down on him from a sense of obligation; she'd almost got off on it. The least he could do was help her get the rest of the way. This thing between them had them equally caught. Her need—her ache—was his. Just as his was hers. She moaned as he flicked his fingers and pushed her harder, faster. He kissed her again and again, almost angry in the pleasure and relief of discovering her extreme arousal. It took only a moment and then she was there, pleasure shuddering through her body.

She was inexperienced, yet lustful. Her shy but unashamed sensuality felled him—he wanted to make it better and better for her. But there was no bettering what was already sublime. No beating the chemistry that flared so brightly whenever they came into contact.

He held her in his arms and stood, carrying her down the stairs to the comfort of his bed. In this one thing, at least, he could meet every one of her needs.

Again, again, and again.

CHAPTER TWELVE

'I THINK YOU can go a little faster than that.' Damon double-checked her life vest and then dared her.

'It's even more fun than I imagined.' Eleni smiled at him from astride the jet ski.

He grinned at the double-meaning glint in her eye. With wild hair and without a speck of make-up his Princess was more luminous than ever. With each moment he spent with her, he grew more intrigued. But he forced a laugh past the lump in his throat. 'Because you like fast.'

'I must admit I do.'

'Then why not see if you can beat me.'

Her eyes flashed again and he relished the way she rose to his challenge. He liked seeing her this happy. The one thing he could do was give her more moments of freedom before she returned to full-time royal life and that damn goldfish bowl she lived in.

He got on the other jet ski. 'Come on, we'll go to the cove.'

Her laughter rang out as she took off before he was ready. Grinning, he revved his engine and set out to hunt her down.

Two hours later Eleni sat on the beach suffused with a deep sense of contentment. The place was paradise—and Damon in paradise? Heartbreaking. He talked, teased, laughed. But she liked him like this too—just sitting quietly alongside her, relaxed and simply enjoying the feel of the sun.

Now she understood why he'd been unable to trust her initially. Why he didn't want his child caught between parents knotted together unhappily. But now that she knew, things had changed. Her feelings for him were deepening, growing, causing confusion.

She sat forward as a shiver ran down her spine. She didn't like the cold streak of uncertainty; she'd bring forward warmth instead. She sent him a coy look. 'I think I should go back to the house and have an afternoon nap.'

'Ride with me this time. One of the guys will come get the other jet ski later.'

He sped back to the main beach while she unashamedly clung, loving the feel of the wind on her face and the spray of the sea, taking the chance to rest before what was to come. But when they walked up to the house, he diverted to the staircase, turning to her with a smile on his face.

Eleni stood on the threshold and stared at the new desk that had replaced the window seat in Damon's office. It was angled, an artist's desk. A cabinet stood beside it, together with a folded easel. Boxes of art supplies were neatly stacked on the top of the cabinet and instinctively she knew that were she to open the drawers, she would most likely find more. Paper, paint, pens, pencils, pastels, ink, brushes, canvas—so many art supplies and a desk and chair that were not for Damon to use. But for her.

Her heart raced. 'When did you arrange this?'

Why had he arranged this? She stared at the beautifully set out equipment and then looked at him.

That gorgeous smile curved his mouth but he just shrugged. 'I unleashed one of the graphic designers in an art store in the States. He got in last night and set it up while we were out just now.' His gaze narrowed on her. 'Would it have been better for you to choose the supplies yourself?'

'No. No, this is…amazing. It's so much better than what I use at home.'

He nodded slowly. 'You don't spend money on it because—'

'It's just a hobby,' she answered quickly.

'But it's more than a hobby to you.'

She was unbearably touched that he understood how much she loved it. 'It's not going to bother you that I'm working here?'

Damon's smile faded, leaving him looking sombre, and suddenly that intensity flared between them. That silent pull of something that tried to bind them closer. 'I'm not going to tease you with the obvious answer because this is actually too important.' He reached out and cupped her face. 'I don't want you to sit in the corner and be decorative and silent. I like your company. And not just...'

He let the sentence hang and his smile said it all.

Eleni stared up at him, her own smile tremulous. He'd put her in his space—placed her desk next to his and drawn her close to his side. He wanted her near him. Eleni had never had such a gift.

'Thank you,' she said softly. 'I like your company too.'

When she woke the next morning Damon had already risen. She showered and put on a loose summer dress. She took some toast and fruit from the breakfast tray and climbed the stairs to see him. He glanced up from the book he was reading. In his white tee, beige trousers and bare feet, he was too gorgeous.

Even more so when that roguish smile lit up his eyes. 'I thought you might sleep in.'

Heat burned in her cheeks as she remembered the little sleep they'd stolen through the night. But she was determined to tease him every bit as much as he teased her, so she adopted her most princessy tone.

'I might take a nap later. You may care to join me then.' She gestured at her desk. 'I thought I'd take a look at my new toys, if that's okay.'

He shut his book with a snap and sent her a stern look. 'You ruined it with that last bit. You don't need my permission. You're free to do whatever you want.' He reached for another book on his desk. 'I'm not your King, Eleni. Not your master.'

She knew that. 'I was just trying to be polite.'

'You don't need to try to be anything with me, Eleni. You can just be yourself.'

She was self-conscious to start with, too aware of how near he was and nervous of making too much noise as she removed plastic wrap and opened packets. She'd never really shared space like this with anyone.

'I'm messy,' she said, glancing at the bottles of ink she'd opened to test out. 'Sorry.'

'That's okay. I'm messy too.'

That was a lie; his desk was immaculate. But as the morning progressed, the piles beside him began to grow. He read more than she'd have thought possible. He sent emails in batches, took video calls over the Internet. His focus didn't surprise her, nor his ability to recall facts or tiny facets of design and interface.

Rosa appeared with another tray of food—fresh, beautifully prepared and presented. Eleni was used to immaculate service but this was different. This was more intimate, more relaxed, more friendly. Just like the island itself. He had such privacy and freedom here. It was the perfect holiday escape for her.

But it was his reality. His life. The space he'd secured for himself to think and create and build.

He connected or disconnected from the rest of the world as he pleased. No wonder he'd looked so uncomfortable at the thought of spending serious time in the palace. It wasn't that he couldn't handle it, it was just that he didn't want to. He had other things to think about—fascinating things, much more meaningful to him than gallery openings and charity visits.

And he had history back in Palisades—bitter family history that hurt. She understood that, for him, attendance at glittering events was only to promote the fallacy of his parents' marriage. He thought everything about those evenings was false. But he was wrong.

They did important work. They had value too. She just had to help him understand it.

Lost in thought, she opened the drawers of the cabinet and selected a sheet of paper. She needed this time out to figure out their future. To accept it.

As she settled into her exploration of pen nibs and ink and the tin of beautiful pencils, time snuck away. When light glinted on the glass of water beside her desk, she looked up from the picture she'd fallen into drawing. To her surprise, the sun was almost at its zenith and she knew both the sand and the water would be warm. Her whole body melted at the thought.

'I just need to get this message sent and I'll go with you.'

Startled, she glanced over and met Damon's knowing gaze. He smiled at her and then looked down to his tablet, his fingers skipping over the keyboard.

She sat back, relaxing as she appreciated how hard he worked. People counted on him and he delivered. No wonder he'd become as successful as he had. An outlier—fiercely intelligent, gifted, and hard-working. But he liked to do things his way—in his place, in his time.

'It's looking good.' Damon rose and studied her page.

She chuckled and shook her head.

He pointed at the faint lines she'd drawn in. 'You've had training.'

'Well, drawing classes were quite an acceptable occupation for a young princess.'

'Until you wanted to get serious about it?' Damon was too astute.

Even she'd understood that it was impossible—as had her art professor. She still saw him sometimes. 'I used my interest to become knowledgeable about the art and antique treasures in the palace.' She stood and stretched, keen to get out to the warm sunshine. 'I like to take the tours sometimes.'

'As the guide?' Damon's eyes widened.

She nodded, laughing at his expression.

'No wonder they're always booked out so far in advance—they're all hoping to get on one of your days.'

'I don't commit to an exact timetable,' she admitted.

'Because you don't want to become an exhibit yourself.'

No. Trust him to understand that. And she hadn't wanted to disappoint people. She turned to get past him and head out to the beach.

'I don't see why it has to be only a hobby,' he said, still studying the incomplete drawing. 'You could sell them. People would buy them.'

Eleni laughed again. 'They'd sell only for the signature. There'd be no honest appraisal from anyone. Some fawning critics couldn't be objective for fear of offending the royal family while others would damn me to mediocrity for daring to think I could do something with skill.'

'You're afraid of what they think.' He sent her that stern look again. 'You don't need to give a damn, Eleni. You could sell them for charity. Imagine what you could raise.'

'But I do give a damn and so I raise money anyway. But I don't want this tied to that. This is my escape.' Just as this island was his.

'Then do it anonymously. We could find a dealer.'

'Or I could just do them for myself.' She sent him the stern look back. 'For my own enjoyment.'

'They'd bring joy to other people too,' he said charmingly.

'Flatterer.' She mock slapped him as she walked away.

'I have no need to flatter you when I already own your panties,' he called after her.

She stopped and swivelled to send him a *death* stare that time. 'Oh, that is—'

He threw back his head and laughed. 'True. It's true.'

* * *

Playing in the sea with Eleni was too much fun. She was so beautiful, lithe and, as he'd suspected that very first moment he'd seen her, strong. Now, as he sat on the sand beside her and let the sun dry his skin, satisfaction pooled within him. The same feeling that had crept up on him while she'd been seated beside him upstairs all morning.

But it was the quiet moments like these that unsettled him the most—when he felt too content.

Moments like these became too precious. And moments didn't last. Nor did marriages.

He stood, needing some space for a second to get them back to that light teasing. He turned and tugged her to her feet. He only had to whisper a dare and they raced back to the house. Play came so easy with her now she was free.

'How do you ever force yourself off this island?' she asked, breathless as he caught her.

'Actually we're leaving in the morning,' Damon muttered.

'What?' Her shocked query made him turn her in his arms so he could see her eyes.

'It's only twenty minutes by helicopter to the next island,' Damon quickly explained. 'There aren't many shops but...' He strode to a small cabinet in the lounge and retrieved a small purse that he tossed to her. 'Here. You can go wild, practise counting out the right currency before you hit the big cities.'

She caught the bag neatly with one hand but wrinkled her pretty nose. 'I don't want your money.'

'Well, until you earn your own I think you're stuck with mine, because I'm your husband and apparently that makes me responsible.' He sent her a deliberately patronising smile. 'I can give you an allowance if you'd like.'

The nose-wrinkle morphed into a full-face frown.

Chuckling, he backed her up against the wall. 'If our

positions were reversed, you'd do the same for me,' he whispered.

'Don't be so sure.'

'Oh, I'm sure.' Laughing, he kissed her.

But her lips parted and she didn't just let him in, she pulled him closer, hooking her leg around his waist, her towel dropping in the process.

'If you keep this up I'll get you a credit card, so you don't even have to count.' He rolled his hips against her heat, giving into the irresistible desire she roused in him.

'Payment for services rendered?' she asked tartly. 'Finally you've figured out I married you for your money.'

'I knew it.' He failed to claw back some semblance of sanity from the ultimate temptation she personified.

'It certainly wasn't for your charm.' She glared at him.

'Then spend every cent.' He smiled, loving the sparks in her eyes. Those few shops mainly stocked bikinis. The thought made his mouth dry. 'Meanwhile...' he stepped back and unfastened his shorts '... I was thinking you might want me to model for you.'

'You're...' Her gaze dropped and her words faded.

'You're not concerned about people taking photos?'

He shook his head as their helicopter descended. 'The people here appreciate the privacy of their visitors.'

To be frank, the island was barely larger than Damon's. There were only a few shops along the waterfront and, when Eleni saw this, her expressive features were a picture of mock outrage. He laughed, enjoying his little joke.

'They sell bikinis.' He held up his hands in surrender. 'I thought you'd love it.'

'You're the biggest tease ever.' She growled at him with a glint in her eye. 'You're the one who wants me to get the bikinis.'

'Have you ever bought a bikini before? All by yourself?'

'Actually I have. Online.'

'In the privacy of the palace.'

'Of course.'

'Well, you can cruise the whole mall here.'

She rolled her eyes.

'If you don't want to shop for skimpy little swimsuits, why don't you spend some coin and buy me an ice cream?' He dared her.

'Because you don't deserve it.'

She flounced off to the bikini store and he lazily loitered outside, watching her through the wide open doors as she browsed the racks. In less than five seconds she lost that faux indignation and relaxed. As she chatted to the woman serving behind the counter she relaxed even more and that gorgeous vitality oozed from her skin. His gaze narrowed as it finally clicked—*interaction* with others was what gave her that luminescence. The ability she had to be able to talk to anyone, and to put them at ease, wasn't just learned skill from being 'the Princess', it was a core part of *who* she was. Warm, compassionate. Interested. Caring.

So much more than him.

Now she'd stopped to talk to another couple of customers and she was positively glowing. One of the women was balancing a wriggling toddler in her arms. Damon watched as Eleni turned to talk to the child, who immediately stopped wriggling and smiled, entranced—as if Eleni was some damn baby whisperer. Of course she was—she had that effect on everyone, big and small. They stopped what they were doing and smiled when she came near. Because she was like a beautiful, sparkling light.

She was going to be such a great mother, given her truly genuine, generous nature. He narrowed his gaze as his imagination caught him unawares—slipping him a vision of how she was going to look when cradling their child in her arms. Primitive possessiveness clenched in his gut, sending a totally foreign kind of heat throughout his veins.

His woman. His baby. His world.

He blinked, breathing hard, bringing himself back to here, now, on the beach. Her body had yet to reveal its fertile secret—while her breasts were slightly fuller, her belly had barely a curve. But their baby was safe within her womb.

Despite the summer sun, a chill swept across his skin and he cocked his head to study her closer. The baby was safe, wasn't it? And Eleni. She was slim but strong, right? But icy uncertainty dripped down his spine—slow at first, then in a rush as he suddenly realised what he'd been too full of lust and selfish haste to remember.

Eleni's mother had lost her life in childbirth.

Damon felt as if some invisible giant had wrapped a fist around his chest and was squeezing it, making his blood pound and his lungs too tight to draw breath.

How could he have forgotten that? How could he have dragged her here to this remote island without seeing that damn doctor back in Palisades? He'd promised her brother that she'd get the best care, yet he'd been in too much of a hurry to escape his own demons to put her first. To put his child first.

He'd been thinking only of himself. His wants. His needs. His father had done that to Kassie and her mother. Now Damon was as guilty regarding Eleni and their unborn child.

How could he have neglected to tend to something so fundamental? He'd been so smug when he'd texted his assistant to find an obstetrician that day on the boat. As if he'd thought of everything—all in control and capable.

But he wasn't either of those things. Turned out he was less than useless—to not even have a routine check done before flying for hours out to somewhere this isolated? What the hell kind of father did he think he was going to make anyway?

He'd failed before he'd even begun. Both his wife and child deserved better. He huffed out a strained breath. At least seeing the truth now cemented the perfection of his plan. They'd be better off apart from him. He'd always known that, hadn't he? Wasn't that why he'd insisted on his and Eleni's separation in the first place?

This whole marriage and kids and happy-ever-after was never going to be for him.

Except, just for this little while on his island, he'd let himself pretend.

That he could have it all with her. Be it all for her.

But he couldn't.

Bitterness welled, a surging ball of disappointment within himself. For himself.

'Are you okay?' Eleni gave him a searching look as she joined him to stroll along the beach.

'Fine.' He flashed a smile through a gritted jaw and kept strolling along the beach, staring down at the sand.

But he wasn't and wasn't it typical that she'd already sensed that? She was too compassionate. Too empathetic.

'Did you spend up large?' He made himself make that small talk.

'Every cent.' She held up a carrier bag and shook it, a twinkle in her eye that he couldn't bear to see right now.

'Then let's go back,' he said briskly.

He sensed her quick frown but she simply turned and quietly walked alongside him.

Of course she did; that was Eleni all over—doing what was asked of her, knowing her place, unquestioning when she sensed tension.

It was how she handled Giorgos, how she handled the public and palace demands on her. And, apparently, it was now how she handled him.

It was the last damn thing that he wanted. He wanted impetuous, spontaneous, emotional Eleni who liked nothing more than to challenge him. But what he wanted no longer mattered. Because she was vulnerable and he didn't have the skills that she was going to need long term. He'd just proven that to himself. The lust they shared wasn't ever going to be enough and the sooner they separated, the better.

He was such a damn disappointment to himself—let alone to anyone else.

'I'm going to the workshop for a while,' he said the second their helicopter landed.

'Sure.'

He turned his back on that hint of coolness in her voice. The tiniest thread of uncertainty. Of hurt. He had to walk away to stop hurting her more. That was the point.

The guys were heads down, but he waved them away when he walked into the room. He'd rebalance in here. Get stuck in another of the projects. But while he could take in the info his team had sent him, he couldn't make it stick. The future kept calling—her pregnancy, the baby. What he was never going to be able to do for them both.

'Which do you want to go with?' Olly ventured over to Damon, showing him three designs for a new logo.

'I need to think about it.' Damon lifted the sheet displaying the three options, his gaze narrowing as he registered the colours. He wanted to do more than think about it. He wanted to ask Eleni. She had a better eye than any of them.

'I had a call from one of those futurist foundations,' Olly said as Damon headed to the door. 'They'd like you to speak at next year's gala.'

More like they wanted him to bring his beautiful Princess wife. He did *not* want her used that way.

'Next year?' Damon asked idly, still staring down at the sheet.

'They're planning well ahead of time. Futurists,' Olly joked.

Time. Damon walked out of the den. In time, according to Damon's plan, he and Eleni would be sharing custody but living separately. They'd be on their way to divorce already. She wouldn't be curled next to him in bed, or sitting at a desk at his side any more. And their child would be a few months old. Their tiny baby with its tiny heart would still be so vulnerable. His chest tightened. He had no idea how to provide the required protection. How did he protect Eleni? How did he give either of them what they needed when he hardly knew what that was? When he'd never had it himself?

Eleni had changed so much in the few days she'd had of freedom. He realised now how much more she needed. How much more she deserved. She was loving and generous and kind. She deserved someone who could give all that back to her tenfold.

She was going to be a far better mother to their child than his mother had been to him. She was open; she was generous. She was loving.

What did *he* have to offer her? She had a workaholic brother and no one else close in her life. She needed a husband who could offer her a warm, loving family. All he could offer were sycophantic grandparents who'd leech everything they could from the connection—and offer nothing. No warmth. No love.

Damon had money, sure. But King Giorgos would never let his little sister suffer financial hardship. There was nothing else he really had to offer her—other than orgasms and the occasional cheesy line that made her laugh. He didn't know how to be a good father, or a good husband. She deserved more than that. She deserved the best.

And he had to help her find that somehow. He owed her that much at least, didn't he?

He walked to the house, missing her already, wanting her advice on the decision he couldn't quite make, just wanting to be near her again. He found her at her desk—her new favourite place—clad in a vibrant orange bikini that was bold and cheerful and sexy as hell. She wore a sheer white shirt over it that hung loose and revealed a gently tanned shoulder. Her hair wasn't brushed into smooth perfection but looked tousled and soft and there wasn't a scrap of make-up on her glowing skin.

She looked beautiful and relaxed; he'd never seen her look happier. She was thriving, from so little. She should have so much more. More than he could ever give her.

Her welcoming smile pained him in a way he'd never been pained before.

'You're busy.' He hesitated, staying at a distance, trying to resist that fierce, fierce pull.

She deserves better.

'It's okay.' She put down her pen and turned her full focus on him. 'What did you want?'

He'd forgotten already. But her gaze grazed the paper he was holding.

'I just...' he glanced down at the images he held '... wanted your opinion on this.'

'My opinion?' she echoed softly.

'You have an artist's eye.' He gruffly pushed the words past the block in his throat. 'I wanted to know which you think is better.'

Eleni blinked, pulling her scattered wits together. He walked in here looking all stormy and broody and sexy as hell and then wanted her opinion on something he was clinging to as if it were worth his very soul?

'Are you going to let me see it?' She smiled but he didn't smile back.

He put the page on her desk. She studied the three designs that had been printed on it. That he valued her input touched her and it took her a moment to focus on what he'd asked her to do. 'I think this one is cleaner. It stays in the mind more.' She pointed to the one on the left. 'Don't you think?'

'Yes,' he said, nodding brusquely. 'Thank you.'

A defiant, determined look crossed his face as he stepped back from her. She stilled, trying to read all the contrary emotions flickering in his expression. He always tried to contain such depth of feeling, but right now it was pouring from him and she could only stare, aching to understand what on earth was churning in his head.

'What?' His lips twisted in a wry, self-mocking smile. 'I don't know why you're staring at me when you're the one with ink on her nose.'

'Oh.' Embarrassed, she rubbed the side of her nose with her finger.

He half snorted, half groaned. 'Come here,' he ordered gruffly, tugging a clean tissue from the box on his desk.

She loved being this close to him. Loved the way he teased her as he cared for her. She held ultra-still so he could wipe the smear from her face. He was so close, so tender and she ached for that usual teasing. But his eyes were even more intensely blue and his expression grave. He focused on her in a way that no one else ever had. He saw beyond the superficial layers through to her needs beneath. Not just her needs. Her gifts. He saw *value* in her and he appreciated it. That mattered to her more than she could have ever imagined. Suddenly, thoughtlessly, she swayed, her need to be closer to him driving her body.

'Eleni?' He gripped her arms to steady her, concern deepening the blue of his eyes even more. 'You okay?'

All the feelings bloomed in the face of the irresistible temptation he embodied—the capricious risk he dared from her with a mere look. But beneath it was the steadfast core of certainty. He'd caught her. Just as he'd caught her and held her close that very first night. Somehow she knew he'd always catch her. He was there for her in a way no one had ever been before. That spontaneous tide of emotion only he stirred now swept from her heart, carrying with it those secret words until they slipped right out of her in a shaky whisper of truth that she breathed between them.

'I love you.'

'I'M NOT SORRY I said that,' she said shakily, determined to believe her own words.

Impulsive. Impetuous. Spontaneous. *Stupid*.

Because he stood rigid as rock, his fingers digging hard into her upper arms and his eyes wide. But his obvious shock somehow made her bold. She could have no regrets. Not about this. Not now. So she said it again—louder this time.

'I've fallen in love with you, Damon.'

It felt good to admit it. Terrifying, but good.

His expression still didn't change. Just as it hadn't in the last ten seconds. But then he released her so quickly she had to take a step back to maintain her balance.

'You only think you're in love with me because I was your first.' He finally spoke—harsh and blunt. And then he turned his back on her.

That was so out of left-field that she gaped as he walked away towards his desk. 'Give me some credit.' She was so stunned she stormed after him and yanked on his arm to make him face her again. 'Even just a little.'

But he shrugged her hand off.

'Eleni, look…' He paused and drew breath. 'You've never felt lust before. You haven't had the opportunity until now. I'm just the first guy you've met who got your rocks off. But lust doesn't equal love. It never does.'

'Actually I do know that.' She wasn't stupid. And she didn't understand why he was lashing out at her. She was utterly shocked.

'Do you, Eleni?' He looked icier than ever. 'You've got freedom here that you've never had in all your life. I think you're confused.'

'Because I've been able to hang out at the beach without worrying about any photographers in the bushes? You think that's made me think I'm in love with you?' She couldn't believe he was saying this. 'I might not have had a million lovers, but I know how to care. I do know how to love.'

'No, you know how to acquiesce,' he said scathingly. 'How to do as you're told while suffering underneath that beautiful, serene exterior. While not standing up for yourself.'

'I'm standing up for myself now.'

He shook his head 'You're confused.'

'And you're treating me like the child my brother sees me as. You don't think I'm capable of thinking for myself?' Was he truly belittling her feelings for him? He didn't believe her and that hurt. 'This is real.'

'No, it isn't.'

'Don't deny my truth.'

'Eleni.' He closed his eyes for a second but then he seemed to strengthen, broadening his stance. He opened his eyes and his stark expression made her step back.

'I have used you. I have treated you terribly. You can't and don't love me.' He drew in a harsh breath. 'And I'm sorry, but I don't love you.' He seemed to brace his feet a bit further apart. 'We are only together now because you're pregnant.'

His words wounded where she was most vulnerable. Because underneath she'd known this had never been about *her*. He never would have sought her out again if he hadn't been worried about the contraception mistake that night. He'd never wanted to see her again—not just for her.

'This has only ever been for the baby,' she said softly.

'Yes. For its legitimacy and protection.'

'Yet you were happy to sleep with me again.'

His gaze shifted. Lowered.

He'd been happy to string her along. 'And Princess Eleni was an easy conquest because she was so inexperienced and frustrated it took nothing to turn her on…is that how this has been?' She couldn't bear to look at him now, yet she couldn't look away either.

'Eleni—'

'Maybe I was inexperienced and maybe I was starving for attention—' She broke off as a horrible thought occurred to her. 'Have you been laughing at me this whole time?'

Suddenly her skin burned crimson at the recollection of her unbridled behaviour with him. So many times.

'Never laughing.' His skin was also burnished. 'And I'm not now. But you *are* mistaking lust for deeper affection.'

She didn't believe him. She couldn't.

'So you don't feel anything for me but lust?' When he sat with her on the beach and they talked of everything and nothing? When they laughed about stupid little things?

There was a thin plea in her voice that she wanted to swallow back but it was too late. Maybe he'd been trying to keep his distance and now she'd forced him into letting her down completely. 'You don't think we could have it all?'

'No one has it all, Eleni. That's a promise that doesn't exist.'

'No. That's your excuse not to even try. It works out for plenty of people. Maybe not your parents—' She broke off. 'Is this what you learnt from them? Not to even try?'

'Yes.' He was like stone. 'I'm not capable of this, Eleni. Not marriage. Not for ever. Certainly not love.'

'You don't mean that.'

'Don't I?' He laughed bitterly. 'How can you possibly think you're in love with me?' He stalked towards her. 'I seduced you—an innocent. I knew you were shy that night. I knew you weren't that experienced. Did I let that stop me from taking you in a ten-minute display of dominant sex? No. It made it even hotter. But I got you pregnant. Then I kidnapped you. I forced you into marrying me. Tell me, how is that any kind of basis for a long-term relationship?' His short bark of laughter was mirthless. 'It will *never* work.'

'It wasn't like that.'

'It was exactly like that.'

No, it hadn't been. He was painting himself as a villain like in one of the games he'd once designed.

'You don't care about me at all?' She couldn't stop herself from asking it.

'Enough to know you deserve better.'

'Better than what—you?' She stared at him. 'You're more sensitive than you like to admit. More caring. You're kind to your employees, you've been kind to *me*.' She tried to smile but couldn't because this was too important and because she could already see he wasn't listening. And he certainly wasn't believing her. 'You're thoughtful, creative. And you think I don't mean it.'

'You only think you mean it.'

Could he get any more insulting? She'd prove him wrong. She glared at him. 'I know you don't want any part of royal life. You don't value what I am. So I will relinquish my title.'

'What?' He looked stunned—and appalled.

'I'll tell Giorgos that I want to live as a commoner. We could live anywhere then. Here, even. Maybe I could get a normal job, not just cut ribbons and talk to people. I could do something useful.'

He laughed.

Eleni chilled and then burned hot. He'd thrown it back at her—her love. Her proof. He was treating her as everyone else in her life had—as if she were a decorative but ultimately pointless ornament with no depth, no real meaning. No real value. When for a while there, he'd made her think he felt otherwise. That he saw her differently—that he thought she had more to offer. He'd shown her such caring and consideration. Hadn't meant that at all?

'Why won't you believe me?' she asked him, so hurt she couldn't hide. 'Are you too scared to believe me?'

He just stayed frozen. 'You don't mean it, Eleni.'

'Why is it so impossible to believe that I could love you?' She demanded his answer. Because she was certain this rejection came from fear. 'Or that I could want to give up everything to be with you?'

'So now you think there has to be something wrong with me because I don't want your love?' he asked cruelly. 'Maybe you suddenly want to give up your title because *you* don't like being a princess.'

'Poor me, right?' she said bitterly. 'I have to live in a castle and wear designer clothes and have all these things—'

'You're not materialistic,' he interrupted harshly. '*Things* aren't what you want. What you *want* is out.'

'No. What I want is *you*.'

He stared at her.

'I want you with me,' she carried on recklessly. 'At the palace. Not at the palace. I don't care. I just want you there wherever I am. I want to know I have you by my side.' She totally lost it. 'I don't care what companies you own or what tech you help create. I just want the man who makes me smile. Who laughs at the same things I do. The man who's passionate and who, usually, can think like no one else I've met.' She drew in a short breath. 'What I'm trying to do is put you first. Put you ahead of my brother. My family. My duties and obligations. Don't you get it? I want *you*.'

'I don't want that,' he said harshly. 'I don't want you like that.' His eyes blazed. 'I'm not in love with you, Eleni. Don't you understand that I'll *never* be in love with you? And you'll soon realise you're not in love with me.'

She sucked in a shocked breath as his total rejection hit like a physical blow.

Hadn't the first rejection been humiliation enough? No. She'd had to go on and argue. But the fact was he didn't want to love her. He never had.

All their time together had been nothing but a physical bonus while he put up with their marriage to make the baby legitimate. Eleni was simply a temporary side issue.

She'd mistaken his affection and amusement for a grow-ing genuine attachment, but the support he offered her was probably the kind he'd give any of his cool employees.

'I have to leave,' Eleni said dully. There was no way she could stay here with him now.

'You're going to run away?' he asked coldly. 'Because that's always worked so well for you in the past.'

No. She wasn't going to run away. In that one thing he was right. Running away never worked.

'This child is a *Nicolaides*.' She drew herself up tall. 'She or he will be royalty. And until Giorgos finally has a fam-ily of his own, she or he will be next in line to the throne after me. It seems there's no getting away from that. So I'm going to return to Palisades.' She was suddenly certain. And determined. 'That is where I belong.'

He stood very still. 'You won't see out these few months?'

If she hadn't believed that he didn't love her before, she did now. He had no emotion at all—no understanding of just how cruel that question was.

'I've just laid myself bare for you, Damon,' she choked. 'And you don't accept it. You don't accept me. You don't believe in me.' Her heart tore as she accepted *his* truth. 'You want me, but you don't love me. That's okay, you don't have to.' But bitterness choked her. 'One day, though, you are going to feel about someone the way I feel about you. And then you'll know. Because no one is immune, Damon. You're human and we're all *built* to feel.'

She stared hard at him as she realised what she'd failed to see before—and she hit him with it now. 'But what you feel most of is fear. That's why you hide away on your is-land paradise. Controlling every one of your interactions, having those brief affairs when you go to some city every so often. Keeping yourself safe because you're a coward. I get that your parents were less than average. I get that they hurt you. But don't use them as your excuse to back out of anything remotely complicated emotionally.'

She drew in a desperately needed breath. 'You don't think what I do has value—that I deserve more? Well, you're right, but not in the way you think. I help people. It may not be much, it may appear superficial, but in my role as Princess of Palisades I can make people smile. And I do deserve more. As a *person*. How can you possibly think I could stay here with you like this but not get all I need from you?' It would destroy her slowly and utterly.

The irony was *he* was the one to have shown her what she could have. What she'd hoped to have with him.

'You can't give me what I need, but I can't settle for less,' she said. 'So no, I won't "see out these few months". I can't stay a second longer than I have to.' Even though it was just about going to kill her to leave.

Eleni might never be loved personally. But as a princess she was. And that would have to do.

CHAPTER FOURTEEN

DAMON PACED ALONG the beach, waiting for her to finish packing. She couldn't leave soon enough. He'd spoken the truth. She didn't 'love' him. She was in 'lust'—with him a little, but mostly with the freedom he'd provided for her. It wasn't *him personally*. It was the situation. Any other man and she'd feel the same about him. It was only fate that had made Damon the one.

He clenched his fists, because she offered such temptation. She made him want to believe in that impossible dream. In her.

But it was better to end it now. The pain in her eyes had been so unbearable he'd almost had to turn away. He hadn't meant to hurt her. But she was inexperienced and naive and he realised now their divorce might hurt her more if they didn't part now. He didn't want to lead her confused emotions on.

She didn't look at him as she climbed into the helicopter that would take her back to his jet, and then to Palisades.

'I'll have rooms set aside for you,' she said regally. 'You may visit at the weekends, so we maintain the illusion of a happy marriage until after the baby is born.'

He *'may'*? His brewing anger prickled at her tone. 'And after?'

'You may visit whenever you want. I won't stop you from seeing the baby.'

Even now she was generous. His anger mounted more, but he contained it. She would care for their child better than he ever could. He understood that now. Because his father had been right—they were alike. Damaged. Incapable and frankly undeserving of love.

He couldn't damage Eleni or his child any more than he already had.

* * *

The sun and the sand mocked him. His team were abnormally quiet and left him alone. He stood it for only two days before summoning the jet. He needed to get further away. San Francisco. London. Berlin. Paris.

He wanted her. He missed her. But he did not love her. He did not know how to love. It was easy to stay busy in cities—to arrange endless, pointless meetings that filled his head with fluff. But people asked about the Princess and he had to smile and pretend.

She was better off without him.

His head hurt. His body hurt. His chest—where his heart should be if he had one—that hurt too. But he didn't have a heart, right?

Yet all he could think about was Eleni. He spent every moment wondering what she was doing. Whether she was okay. If she was smiling that beautiful smile at all.

She'd given, not taken. She'd offered him the one thing that was truly her own—her heart. He knew she'd never done that before. She'd been at her most vulnerable. And he'd rejected her.

But he'd had to, for her. Because he didn't deserve her love. He had no idea how to become the man who did. If she was freed from the marriage to him, she might find some other man to treat her the way she deserved. That would be the right thing to do.

Hot, vicious, selfish anger consumed him at the thought of someone else holding her. Of someone else touching her. Of someone else making her smile.

He didn't want that. He *never* wanted that.

He clenched his fist, emotions boiling into a frenzy. He had no freaking idea how to manage this. And that was when he realised—so painfully—how much he didn't want to let her go. He *never* wanted to let her go.

He logged into his computer, searching for somewhere to go and sort himself out for good. Far from Palisades.

Far from his own island that was now too tainted with the memories of her presence. He had to escape everything and pull himself together. But as he scrolled through varying destinations, his emails landed in his inbox.

There was one from the palace secretary.

Damon paused. It would probably be another schedule of engagements that they wanted him to approve or something. Unable to resist, he clicked to the email and opened it. But it wasn't a list. It was a concise couple of sentences informing him that Princess Eleni had seen the obstetric specialist of her choosing who'd written a brief report, the contents of which had been inserted into the email. In one paragraph it explained that the baby was growing at a normal rate. That the condition that had taken Eleni's mother was not hereditary. That the pregnancy posed no abnormal risk to her. That everything was progressing as it ought for both mother and baby.

His breath and blood froze. There was an image file attached to the email. Dazed, Damon opened it on auto. A mass of grey appeared. He looked at the arrow and markers pointing out a particular blob set in a darker patch in the middle of the picture. It was an ultrasound scan. It was his baby.

He tried to breathe but he just stared at that tiny, little treasure in the centre of his screen. It was there. It was real. It was happening. Heat swept through him in a burning drive to claim what was—

Mine.

Both hands clenched into fists.

Eleni.

The thought of her consumed him—her strength, her decisions, her role in all this. She was well. She was strong. She was safe. He ached to reach for her, ached to see her smile as she saw this picture—he just knew she'd smile at this picture. And the realisation rocked him.

Ours.

They had made this beautiful child *together*. That night she'd come with him and he'd claimed her and somehow in that insanely wonderful moment they'd created this miracle. It never should have happened—but it had. And Eleni was taking it on. She was doing her bit and she was doing it so damn well. And if he wanted to be part of that, *he* was the one who had to shape up. Seeing this now, reading Eleni's results, he realised just how much he wanted in and he burned with acidic shame. He'd missed so much already. He wished like hell he'd been there with her when she'd seen this doctor and when she'd had this scan. He should have been holding her hand for every damn second.

He bent his head, squeezing his eyes shut so he could no longer see the image on that screen. But the truth snuck in and stabbed him anyway. The fact was he had a heart. He really, truly had a heart and it hurt like hell. Because it was no longer his.

Eleni had it. It was all hers. He had to tell her. He had to apologise. He had to get her back. Groaning, he closed the picture file and read the doctor's report again. And again. Sucking in the reassurance that Eleni was healthy. Strong. Safe.

She'd asked if he was scared of love and at the time he'd refused to answer. He'd been utterly unable to. But now he faced the stark facts. He was terrified. Like a freaking deer in the headlights he'd simply frozen.

Frozen her out.

Where she'd been brave, proudly standing up to him, he'd been unable to admit, even to himself, how much he wanted her in his life. And when she'd unconditionally offered him everything she had, he couldn't believe her. No one had ever offered him that before.

Eleni had been right. He was a coward. He hid because it was easier. But in truth he was no better than his parents— putting all emotion aside for work. But she'd got under his skin and he'd been unable to resist—he'd taken everything she'd offered. He'd even convinced himself he was doing her a favour. He'd encouraged her to blossom and let all that sweet enthusiasm and hot passion out. He'd thought she'd needed freedom away from the palace. Freedom to take what she wanted—to ask for what she wanted.

And she had.

Eleni had offered him her love. And she'd asked for his in return.

But he'd rejected her. The worst thing he could have done was not take her seriously. Only he'd done even worse. He'd scoffed at her.

That hot streak of possessiveness surged through his veins as he clicked open that ultrasound image again. But he sucked in a steadying breath. He didn't get to be possessive, not without earning her forgiveness first. Not without begging to make everything better. And how did he get to her now she was back in that damn prison of a palace?

CHAPTER FIFTEEN

'ARE YOU SURE you're feeling up to this, ma'am?' Bettina asked Eleni carefully.

'That's what blusher is for, right?' Eleni answered wryly. 'And I still have quite the tan on my arms.' She forced a smile for her maid. 'I'm fine to go. It'll be fun. But thank you.'

She needed to fill in her day. She needed to feel *something*.

She'd been buried in the palace for almost a fortnight, hoping she'd hear from him. But she hadn't. She couldn't face drawing, couldn't face the pool. She'd tried reading. But her mind still wandered to him. She hated how much she ached for him.

He doesn't deserve me.

She tried to remind herself, but it didn't lessen the hurt. Hopefully this gallery visit would take her mind off him even for a few minutes. The fact that it was a children's tour was even better because children asked questions fearlessly—with no thought to privacy or palace protocol. It would be a good test. She'd have to hold herself together when they mentioned his name. And they would ask. They'd want to see her engagement and wedding rings. They'd want to see her smiling.

They expected a blushing, beyond happy bride.

Giorgos had sounded harried when he'd phoned, which was unlike him. And for whatever reason that he hadn't had time to explain, he was still residing at the Summer House and he'd asked if she'd attend the small gallery opening on his behalf. Of course she'd agreed. She'd been going insane staying inside. She needed to build a busy and fulfilling life. Then she could and would cope with the break in her heart.

But she'd appreciated the concern in Giorgos's voice. Just as she appreciated Bettina's quiet care. And her bodyguard's constant, silent presence.

She smiled as Tony opened the car door for her. 'It's nice to have you back.'

'Thank you, ma'am.'

'I promise not to disappear on you today,' she teased lightly, determined not to hide from the past.

'I understand, ma'am.' Tony's impassive expression cracked and he smiled at her. 'You won't be out of my sight for a second.'

'I understand and I do appreciate it.'

It was a beautiful late summer morning but she'd added a light jacket to complement the floaty-style floral dress she'd worn to hide her figure and deflect any conjecture and commentary. That suspicion would be raised soon enough. But preferably not today.

Twenty minutes later she stepped out of the car at the discreet side entrance of the new art space. She took a moment to accept a posy of flowers from a sweet young girl. But as she turned to enter the gallery she froze, her heart seizing. She blinked and moved as Tony guided her forward. But she glanced back as something caught her eye. For a second she'd thought she'd seen a masculine figure standing on the far side of the road—tall, broad, more handsome than Adonis…

Wishful, impossible thinking.

Because there was no man there now.

Releasing a measured breath, she walked with the small group of children through the new wing of the gallery, focusing her mind to discuss the paintings with them. But despite the easing of her morning sickness over the past few days, maintaining her spark during the visit drained her more than she'd thought it would. She was relieved when she saw Tony give her the usual signal before turning slightly to mutter into his mobile phone.

Damon had half expected soldiers to swoop on him and frogmarch him straight to the city dungeons, but the coast was clear and the path to the car easy. It was unlocked and he took the driver's seat, waiting for the signal. Anticipation surged as his phone rang. He could hardly remain still.

Finally the passenger door opened. He heard her polite thanks.

He started the engine. As soon as she'd got into the car and the door closed behind her, he pulled away from the kerb.

'Tony?' Eleni leaned forward in her seat.

'Damon,' he corrected, a vicious pleasure shooting through his body at just hearing her voice again.

He glanced up and looked in the rear-view mirror and almost lost control of the car in the process. She was so beautiful. But that soft colour slowly leeched from her skin as she met his gaze in the mirror and realised it truly was him. If he'd suffered before, he really felt it then. He'd killed her joy. The make-up stood out starkly against her whitened face. She'd had to paint on her customary vitality—her luminescence stolen. By him.

Her eyes were suddenly swimming in tears but she blinked them back. The effort she was expending to stay in control was immense. He hated seeing her this wretched. But at the same time, her distress gave him hope. His presence moved her. She hadn't forgotten him. Hadn't got over him.

He didn't deserve her.

'Why are you here?' She demanded his answer in the frostiest tones he'd ever heard from her.

All he wanted was to enfold her in his arms but he couldn't. She was furious with him and she had every right to be. He had to talk to her. Ask for forgiveness. Then ask for everything.

When he'd already rejected her.

He gripped the steering wheel more tightly as anxiety sharpened his muscles and he tried to remember where the hell he was going. Because this was going to be even harder than he'd imagined. And he'd imagined the worst.

'I'm kidnapping you.' He ground the words out, holding back all the others scrambling in his throat. He needed to get them somewhere that they could talk in private.

He glanced back at the rear-view mirror. Her emotion had morphed into cold, hard rage.

'I'm not doing this to Tony again,' she snapped, turning to look out of the window behind her to see if any cars were behind them. 'He'll be following. He doesn't deserve—'

'Tony knows you're with me,' he said quickly. 'So does Giorgos.'

She flicked her head back, her eyes flashing. 'So you planned this with everyone but me?'

He didn't want to answer more. He was only making it worse. Damn, it turned out he was good at that.

'This is *not* okay, Damon,' she said coldly.

'None of this is okay,' he growled, swerving around the nearest corner. 'And I can't wait—' He broke off and parked on one of the narrow cobbled streets.

'Can't wait for what?' she asked haughtily.

Eleni waited for his answer, trying to remain in control, but underneath her calm demeanour her heart was pounding and it was almost impossible to stop distress overtaking her sensibility. Damon was here. Not only that, he'd colluded with her brother and her bodyguard and she couldn't bear to think about *why*.

It mattered too much. *He* mattered too much.

But it was too late. He'd made his choice. He'd let her go. He'd let her *down*.

She refused to believe in the hope fluttering pathetically in her heart. This was too soon. She hadn't grown a strong enough scab over her wounds to meet him yet.

'Eleni.'

She closed her eyes. He couldn't *do* this to her.

One look. One word. That was all it took for her to want to fall into his arms again. She refused to be that weak. She couldn't let him have that power over her.

'Take me back to the palace,' she ordered.

He killed the engine. She watched, frozen, as he got out of the car and swiftly opened the rear passenger door. But before she could move he'd slid into the back seat with her and locked the doors again.

'Give me ten minutes,' he said, removing his aviator sunglasses and gazing intently at her. 'If you wish to return to the palace afterwards, then I'll take you there. I just want ten minutes. Can you give me that?'

She wanted to give him so much more already. But she couldn't. She'd been a fool for him already; she wasn't making that mistake again. 'What more is there to say, Damon? We want different things.'

'There's plenty more to say,' he argued shortly.

'Too late. You had your chance.' She glanced behind her, hoping Tony was less than a block away. But there was no car. No people.

'Ten minutes,' he pushed. 'I'm not letting you go until you listen to me.' He was silent for a moment. *'Please.'*

At that urgent whisper she turned back to face him. Starved of his company for days, she couldn't help drinking in his appearance now. He was studying her with that old intensity. Always he'd made her feel as if she were the only thing in the world that mattered.

Not fair. Not true. Not for him.

'Five minutes,' she answered flatly.

Only five. Because tendrils of hope were unfurling, reaching out, beginning to bind her back to him. That weak part of her wanted him to take her in his arms and kiss her. Then she might believe he was actually here. That he'd come back for her. But at the same time she knew that if he touched her, she'd be lost.

His smile was small and fleeting and disappeared the second he opened his mouth again. 'I'm so sorry, Eleni.'

Her heart stopped. Her breath died. She didn't know if she could take this. Not if he wasn't here to give her everything.

'Words said too easily,' she whispered.

'That night at the ball—'

'No,' she interrupted him furiously. 'We're not going back there. You're not doing this.'

'Yes, we are. It's where it all began, Eleni. We can't forget what's happened. We can't ignore—'

'You already have,' she argued. 'You already denied—'

'I lied,' he snapped back. 'Listen to me now. Please. That night was the most extreme case of lust I've ever felt,' he confessed angrily. 'And for you too. You know how powerful it was. How it *is*. You never would have let just any man touch you that way, Eleni. You never would have let just any man *inside*.'

She sucked in a shocked breath.

'I know I didn't want to admit it,' he said. 'But what's between us is something *much* more than that.' He gazed at her so intently, the blue of his eyes so brilliant it almost blinded her.

But she shook her head. Not for him, it wasn't.

'For me too,' he declared, rejecting her doubts. 'It was and is, Eleni. I've denied it for too long.' He bent closer, forcing her to look him right in those intense eyes. 'You were flirtatious, you were shy…so hot and so sweet.'

She winced. She couldn't bear for him to revisit her inexperience. Her naiveté. He'd thought she had nothing more than a teenage *crush* on him. He'd felt sorry for her.

'I belittled you when you told me your feelings,' he said.

'I didn't believe you. I couldn't…and I'm so sorry I did that to you.' Somehow he was sitting closer, his voice lower. His gently spoken words hit her roughly. 'I never should have let you go.'

'Why shouldn't you have?' She succumbed to the hurt of these last intolerably lonely days. 'You miss having my adoration? My body? My naive protestations of love?' She was so mortified. The imbalance was so severe. It was so unfair.

'Not naive.' He shook his head. 'Not you. *I'm* the ignorant one. I didn't know what love was, Eleni. I've never had someone give me what you've given me. And like the idiot I am, I didn't know how to handle it.' His gaze dropped. 'I don't know how to handle you or how I feel about you. It is so…' He trailed off and dragged in a breath. 'It's huge.' He pressed his fist to his chest. 'I was overwhelmed and I threw it away like it was a bomb you'd tossed at me.' His voice dropped to a whisper again. 'But the fact is, you'd already detonated my world. You took everything I thought I knew and turned it on its head. I thought I had it all together. The career. The occasional woman. The easy stroll through life. No complications. Every success was mine… but you made me *feel*.'

'Feel what?' she asked coldly, twisting her fingers together in her lap, stopping herself from edging anywhere nearer to him. She needed to hear him say so much more. She still couldn't let herself *trust*—

'Need,' he said rawly. 'Need to be with someone—to have you to talk to, to laugh with, to show everything, to hold, to just keep me company…to love…' He trailed off.

'So this is about *your* need?' She sent him a sharp look.

A harsh breath whistled out between his clenched teeth. 'I don't know how to be the kind of father that this baby deserves,' he gritted. 'I don't know how to be the kind of husband that you deserve. I have had awful examples of both and for a long time I believed…' Words failed him again.

Eleni didn't speak. She couldn't believe and it was becoming too hard to listen.

'I never imagined this would happen to me. And for it to be *you*?' He visibly paled. 'You deserve so much more than what I can give you.'

She shook her head, her rage surging. 'That's a cop-out, Damon.'

'You're a princess—'

'That's *irrelevant*,' she snapped.

'I don't mean your lineage. I mean in here.' He pressed his fist to his heart again but gazed at her. 'You're generous, loyal, loving, true…that's what I mean. You're not like other people—'

'I'm just like other people,' she argued fiercely. 'I'm human. *Most* people are loving and loyal, Damon. Most people are generous and honest.'

That was what he needed to learn and it crushed her that he hadn't learned it as he should have, that his life had been so devoid of normal family love.

'I'm nothing special,' she added.

'You're special to *me*!' he bellowed back at her. 'You're more generous, more loyal, more loving than anyone I've ever met and *all* I want is to be near you. You don't value yourself the way that you should.'

But she did now. She did, because of him. That was what he'd taught her. That was why she'd walked away from him. Because she knew what it was to truly love. And that she deserved more than he'd wanted to give her.

'Yes, I do,' she flung back at him brokenly. 'That's why I'm back in Palisades.' That was why she'd left him when it had almost killed her to do so. Because staying would have been an even more painful experience. She wasn't going to settle for less. Not now. Not from him. She couldn't exist settling for less from him. 'That's why I couldn't stay with you. Because I do need…'

The words stuck in her throat as the pain seeped out.

She knew he'd been hurt, but that he couldn't push past it for her? That hurt *her*.

He was staring into her eyes but his face blurred as her tears spilled—hot, fast, unstoppable, stupid tears.

'I'm so sorry, darling, so sorry I did this to you.' He reached out as she tried to turn away from him. His fingers were gentle as he captured her close and wiped the tears from her face. 'Please don't say I'm too late. It can't be too late. Because I love you, Eleni. Do you understand? I love you, I do.' He leaned closer as she remained silent. 'Eleni, please don't cry. Please listen to me.'

Her breath shuddered as she tried to still, needing to hear him.

His hands framed her face and he kept talking in those desperate hushed tones. 'Until you, I had no idea what love was—what it means, how to show it. And I want to love you, so much, but I don't know where to start. I don't know how to make this right. I'm begging you here, Eleni. How do I become the man you need?'

'You're *already* what I need,' she whispered hoarsely, so annoyed that he still didn't get it. 'You're everything I need. Just you. You're enough exactly as you are.' That was what he needed to learn too. 'And you have started.' She pushed past the ache in her throat. 'By showing up. By being here.'

By coming back for her.

He stared at her for a moment and then with the gentlest of fingertips he traced down her cheekbone. She struggled to quell her tremors at his tenderness.

'See? So generous,' he murmured, almost to himself. But then he cleared his throat and leaned that bit closer, his gaze fierce and unwavering. 'I love you, Eleni.'

Once again he said it. What she'd been too afraid to believe she'd really heard. And the words weren't whispered, they were strong, almost defiant.

He shook her gently. 'Did you hear me?'

* * *

Two more tears slowly rolled down her cheeks.

'I am so, so sorry it has taken me so long to figure it out. I miss you like—' He closed his eyes briefly but she'd already seen the stark pain. He opened them to stare hard at her. To try again. 'These past couple of weeks have been—'

That weak scab across her heart tore as he choked up in front of her. He couldn't find the words. She understood why—it was indescribable for her too.

'I know,' she whispered.

A small sigh escaped him. 'I don't deserve it, but please be patient with me. Talk to me. Talk like you did that hideous day you left me. I need your honesty… I just need you.'

She drew in a shaky breath, because she wanted to believe him so much. But she needed to understand. 'What changed? What brought you back?'

'Misery,' he said simply. 'I was so lonely and it hurt so much and I tried to escape it—you—but I couldn't. And finally I got thinking again.' He shook his head as if he were clearing the fog. 'I haven't been able to think clearly since that first second I saw you…it's just been blind instinct and gut reaction—equal parts lust and terror. I'd got *so* defensive and then, when I could finally think, I realised you were right. About everything. But I'd pushed you away. You're worth listening to, Eleni,' he whispered roughly, edging closer to her again. 'When you told me you loved me, I couldn't believe you… I was scared.'

'You don't think I was scared when I said it to you?'

The corner of his mouth lifted ruefully. 'You know my family doesn't do emotions. They do business connections. I want to do more than that, to be more…'

'You're more than that already. You just need to believe it.'

'I know that now. Because somehow, in all this, you *did* fall in love with me.' A hint of that old arrogance glinted in his eyes and his fingers tightened on her waist. 'You do love me.' His chin lifted as he all but dared her to deny it.

But she saw it in his eyes—the open vulnerability that he'd refused to let show before.

'Of course,' she said softly. 'I stood no chance.'

'Just as I stood no chance with you.' His hands swept, seeking as if he couldn't hold back from caressing her a second longer. 'And I'm afraid I can't let you go, Eleni. I can't live through you leaving me again.' He gripped her hips tightly. 'I'm taking you with me. I'm kidnapping you and I'm not going to say sorry for that.' Determination—desperation—streaked across his face.

At that raw emotion the last of her defences shattered.

'You're not kidnapping me.' She sobbed, leaning into his embrace. 'I choose to come with you.' Just as she'd chosen to be with him that first night. 'I choose to stay with you always.' She drew in a breath and framed his gorgeous face with her hands. 'I chose to marry you. I meant my marriage vows.'

'Thank God.' He hauled her into his lap with barely leashed passion. 'I love you. And I promise to honour you. Care for you...always.' He drew back to look solemnly into her eyes. 'It's not just a contract for me, Eleni.'

Her heart bursting, she flung her arms around his neck, kissing him with a hunger that almost overwhelmed her. 'I missed you so much,' she cried.

'Eleni.'

She heard the joy, the pure love in his voice. She felt it in his tender, fierce embrace and in the heat of his increasingly frantic kisses.

'I love you,' he muttered, kissing her desperately. 'I love you, I love you, I love you.'

It was as if he'd released the valve holding back his heart and now the most intense wave of emotion swamped her. Finally the veracity of *her* feelings could flow again. She had complete freedom to say what she wanted. To be who she was—who she'd wanted to be.

His lover. His beloved.

He held her so close, wiping away yet more tears that she didn't realise were tumbling down her cheeks. Opening her eyes, she saw a softness in his strong features that she'd not seen before. She trembled as she registered just how good this felt—how close she'd been to losing him. He'd been gone from her life too long. She needed his touch, his kiss, his hold—*now*.

'It's okay, sweetheart,' he soothed, kissing her again and again as she shuddered in his arms. 'It's okay.'

It was better than okay. It was heaven. And now she clung—unashamedly clung, needing to be so much nearer to him. 'Don't let me go.'

'Never again. I promise.'

But he'd hardly kissed her for long enough when he lifted his lips from hers and rested his forehead on hers, his breathing ragged. 'People are going to see us if we stay here too much longer…a palace car, illegally parked on the side of the road…'

'It doesn't matter.' Her voice rasped past the emotion aching in her throat. 'They know we're passionately in love.'

For real. Not just a fairy tale for the press. She ached to have him again completely.

He read her expression and groaned with a shake to his head. 'We can't be that reckless. And I'm crushing your pretty dress.' He lifted her from his lap, puffing out a strained breath. 'You're Princess Eleni, and this isn't right for you.'

She stilled, a thread of worry piercing her warmth. 'You don't like the palace.'

'I can learn to like it.' He brushed back her hair. 'I can learn a lot, Eleni. I can become the man you need. We can make it work.'

'You're already the man I need. You just need to stay—'

'Right by your side.' He met her gaze with utter surety in his. 'I know.'

Her eyes filled again. 'Where were you planning to drive me to?'

'Back to the boat.' A wry grin flitted across his lips. 'There aren't that many ways to kidnap a princess from Palisades. Damn palace is a fortress.'

She chuckled.

'But the treasure that was locked in there...' His old smug smile resurfaced. 'That's my treasure now.'

'And you're going to keep it?'

'Oh, I am. For always.'

'Then what are you waiting for? Let's get to the marina.'

His face lit up and then tightened in the merest split of a second. 'You can't imagine how much I need you—'

'Actually I think I can,' she argued breathlessly.

His laugh was ragged. 'You're hot and sweet, Eleni.' He swiftly climbed over to the driver's seat and started the engine.

'So, Giorgos and Tony were in on this?'

'I'm afraid so.' He drove quickly, confidently. 'You didn't stand a chance.'

'No?' she asked archly as he pulled into the park by the yacht.

'Believe it or not...' Damon got out of the car and opened her door '...they want you to be happy.'

'And they think being with you means happiness for me?'

'Does it?'

She stepped out of the car and reached up to stroke his face, seeing that hint of vulnerability flicker in his eyes once more. 'It does now, yes.'

He swiftly turned. 'We need to get on board. Now.'

'Are we going to sail off into the sunset?' She was so tempted to skip.

'Not for ever.' He winked at her. 'Palisades needs its Princess but I'll admit I'm going to push for part-time status.' He suddenly turned and swept her into his arms. With that gorgeous effortlessness he carried her across the boardwalk, onto the boat and straight into the bedroom. 'Because she'll be busy with her baby. And meeting the needs of her husband. And she'll be busy drawing and being creative with all the other things she's not let herself take the time for until now.' He paused, holding her just above the bed. 'Does that sound like a good plan to you?'

'It sounds like a brilliant plan.'

It was only moments until they were locked together. He was so close and she stared into his beautiful eyes.

'Take what you want from me, my beautiful,' he muttered. 'Anything and everything I have is yours.'

'I have your body,' she murmured. 'I want your heart.'

'It only beats because of you.' He laced his fingers through hers. 'I wasn't alive until I met you. You're everything to me. I love you, Eleni.'

'And I love you.' She wrapped around him, letting him carry them both into that bliss.

'Too quick,' he groaned, and gripped her hips tightly, slowing her.

Amused and beyond aroused, she tried to tease him. 'But what does it matter? We can go again, now we have all the time in the world.'

'Yes.' Those gorgeously intense eyes focused on her with that lethal desire and her heart soared as he answered. 'We have for ever.'

* * * * *

ALL OF ME

SHERYL LISTER

For Brandi

Chapter 1

Karen Morris stood off to the side in the Sapphire Room, one of the cruise ship's private dining rooms, smiling as her best friend approached. "Girl, you look so beautiful." Janae Simms had just exchanged wedding vows with popular R & B artist and producer Terrence "Monte" Campbell.

Janae smoothed a hand over the bodice of her white chiffon strapless A-line gown with a beaded motif accent at the hip. "Thanks."

"So, how does it feel to be a married woman?"

"I never thought I'd be this happy."

"Yeah. If that smile gets any wider, you'll be competing with the sun."

Janae giggled and looped her arm in Karen's. "I'm so glad you're my friend."

"Me, too."

"Come on. You need to help me eat some of my cake. We'll have a chance to talk more over lunch Monday."

"Lunch? Aren't you and Terrence going to be a little busy this week?"

Janae smiled and wiggled her eyebrows. "We'll be plenty busy, but he has to rehearse for his show that's on Wednesday night." He was one of several performers on the weeklong jazz cruise. "So, are we on for lunch?"

"Definitely."

After she ate a small piece of cake, Janae's brother Devin asked Karen to dance. Then she enjoyed dances with Janae's other two brothers and father. She started toward her table only to be pulled back to the floor by Donovan Wright, Terrence's best man and manager. By the time the short affair concluded, her feet were killing her.

Janae came up behind her. "Karen, we're leaving now. What time do you want to meet on Monday?"

She grinned and glanced over to where Terrence stood watching them. "Maybe you should be the one to decide. Your new husband looks like he's ready to eat you up."

"The feeling is mutual. How about one o'clock?"

"That'll work. I'll meet you at the entrance to the buffet." They spent another minute talking and then Karen said, "Enjoy your wedding night."

"I plan to," Janae said with a wink.

Karen smiled and shook her head, recalling how the two had met. She had practically dragged Janae to Terrence's—or Monte, as he was known in the music world—concert. What started as a backstage meet and greet after the concert had ended in marital bliss for her friend. She briefly wondered if she would get her own fairy-tale ending, then shoved the thought aside. *The only thing I'm focusing on is having a good time for the next week. Good music, good food, fabulous islands...me time.*

Janae's parents and Terrence's grandparents had elected not to cruise, so Karen stayed behind with Janae's brothers to see them off. She followed the family back down the hallway leading to the ship's entrance, where they would disembark. As they said their goodbyes, male laughter drew her attention.

She turned to see three men standing nearby, engaged in a lively conversation. All three were good-looking, but one in particular piqued her interest. He stood a few inches taller than his companions, with broad shoulders and the muscular build of a professional athlete. Her gaze lingered over his smooth golden brown features—close-cropped dark hair, chiseled jaw and full lips curved in a slight smile. The man was a serious piece of eye candy. Her gaze traveled over his body, then back up to his face to find him watching her with quiet intensity. Her heart rate kicked up a notch. Embarrassed that he had caught her staring, she quickly turned away. Moments later, she couldn't resist another peek.

Suddenly, he paused with the drink halfway to his lips and swung his head in her direction. His smile inched up, and he saluted her with his drink. Her breath stalled in her lungs.

"Karen?"

"Huh, what?" She tore her gaze away and tried to focus on what Janae's mother was saying. "I'm sorry. What did you say, Mrs. Simms?"

She chuckled. "I asked if you were going to miss your students this week."

"I love my little darlings, but I plan to enjoy a week without lesson plans and mediating 'he said, she said' arguments."

After a few minutes of polite conversation and a round of hugs, Karen wound her way around the ship toward her suite. Several men called out greetings and offered to buy her a drink, and one propositioned her for more, but she ignored them all. A vision of Mr. Eye Candy worked its way into her mind and she pushed it away, reminding herself that she was taking a break from men and focusing on herself and her career goals.

Damian Bradshaw half listened to his friends as they once again listed all the reasons why this cruise was a good idea. The cruise was an annual event, and they had invited him several times over the years, but he always declined. Troy Ellis slung an arm around his shoulders. "Man, you can't tell me you're not looking forward to some fun aboard a luxury cruise. Good music, good food, exotic ports—"

"And a ship full of fine, single women," Kyle Jamison cut in. "Mmm, mmm, mmm," he said, staring after a group of women walking by and smiling at them. "See what I mean? Damian, this is exactly what you need to get back in the groove."

"Who says I want to get back in the groove?" Damian muttered.

Troy dropped his arm and shook his head. "It's been five years, Damian. When do you think you'll be ready to move on?"

Damian clenched his jaw. He didn't need to be reminded how long it had been since he lost his wife. He had lived every one of those moments without her, counted every second since she'd died from a freak accident. He had no desire to open his heart to the possibility of pain again. "I have moved on."

Kyle crossed his arms and pinned Damian with a glare. "Have you really? You're one step up from a recluse. You're either at the office, at the gym or locked in your house. You probably don't even remember how to date."

"We have a lot to do at the office," Damian countered. The three friends co-owned a consulting firm and traveled around the country providing safety training to schools and corporate groups.

"All of which our dynamic office assistant, Delores, can handle until we get back. He's right, Damian," Troy said softly. "It's time. Joyce wouldn't want you to live the rest of your life alone." He grinned. "And, since we know you've been out of the game for a while, we'll be more than happy to offer you some pointers on how to attract a woman," he added, trying to lighten the mood.

Damian chuckled. "Yeah, I bet."

"We need to get this party started right. I'm going to get a drink," Kyle said.

Troy nodded. "Good idea. Let's go."

"I'll wait for you guys."

"You want me to bring you something?" Troy asked.

"Yeah. Bring me a beer." He watched them saunter off and flirt with two passing women.

He leaned against the railing, shoved his hands into his pockets and contemplated his friends' words. He hated to admit it, but they were right. He'd immersed himself in his job, staying at the office way past normal hours, working out at the gym to the point of exhaustion, then going home to an empty house and losing himself in thoughts of what could have been, what should have been. Damian rarely did anything that could be considered fun and hadn't thought about taking a trip. Even when Joyce was alive, she preferred a quiet evening at home to going out or leaving town, so they'd never traveled far. When they did, they only went on occasional weekend getaways.

He took in his surroundings. Boarding passengers streamed past him, their animated chatter and excitement filling the air. He couldn't remember the last time he had taken a real vacation. Maybe he needed this cruise after all.

"Here you go."

He accepted the beer from Troy. "Thanks."

Kyle held up his bottle. "I'd like to propose a toast. To a week of great music and endless pleasures."

"Hear, hear!" Troy said.

They looked at Damian expectantly. Sighing, he clinked his bottle against theirs, then tilted it to his lips.

Kyle smiled. "Now, the first lesson when picking up women is to find one who wants no attachments beyond the week and is just out for a good time."

"Usually, she'll be with a group of women, make eye contact and check you out from head to toe," Troy added.

Kyle nodded. "She'll find a way to cross your path at least twice, be wearing an enticing little number and give you a smile that says she's up for whatever you want."

"If you're interested, return her smile but don't approach her right away." Troy leaned closer. "Continue to flirt from a distance, maybe send her a drink. You know, heighten the desire."

"Now you're ready to make your move," Kyle said, clapping Damian on the shoulder.

"And, because we knew you wouldn't, we slipped a couple boxes of condoms into your bag," Troy finished with a smug smile. "Think about it, this'll be the perfect way to make that first step back into the land of the living."

"I'm thirty-three years old. I don't need you to tell me how to approach a woman," Damian gritted out. Kyle and Troy laughed. "What?"

"Man, you've been out of the game so long you wouldn't know what to say, even if she held up a sign saying 'Unattached and Available.'" Kyle paused thoughtfully. "Actually, you never really dated at all, since you and Joyce sort of hooked up in college."

He skewered Kyle with a look.

"You know I'm right. Yeah, you dated a few women back then—and I use the term *dated* loosely—but you and Joyce always circled back to each other."

Rather than responding and risk knocking Kyle out, he took another swig of his beer.

"Lay off Damian, Kyle. Give the brother a chance. We've only been on the boat for forty-five minutes, and we haven't even left the dock yet."

"Yeah. Lay off. I'm perfectly capable of deciding whether I want a woman or not." Though he mostly subscribed to the "or not" category. He had gone out a few times since his wife's death, but never progressed past a couple of dates and a few chaste kisses.

Kyle gave him a sidelong glance. "You sure? Because I can't have you embarrassing me and ruining my reputation with some lame pickup lines."

Damian shook his head and laughed, giving in to Kyle's wack sense of humor. "Man, I don't know how we've been friends all these years."

"Hell, you need somebody to keep you straight. Leaving you to your own devices, we might find you living as a monk with no sense of humor." They all laughed.

"Whatever."

Out of his periphery, he noticed a woman staring his way. She was standing in a group with two older couples, a younger couple and two other men. Their eyes locked, and he felt a kick in the gut. An embarrassed expression crossed her face, and she turned away. He willed her to look his way again, wanting to know if he'd imagined the spark of awareness. When she finally glanced back, he felt it again. A slow grin made its way over his face, and he saluted her with his bottle.

"Earth to Damian." Troy waved his hand in front of Damian's face.

Damian jerked back. "What?"

"Are you listening? What are you looking at?"

"Nothing," he murmured. He idly sipped his drink while scanning the woman from head to toe. She had flawless mocha skin and a strikingly beautiful face. The strapless gray dress she wore clung subtly to her lush curves and gave way to long, toned legs and stirred a desire he had never experienced, or at least hadn't experienced in a long time. He frowned, not liking the direction of his thoughts.

"Whoa. Hold up. I *know* you're not staring at the woman in the gray dress," Kyle said. "Didn't you hear anything I just said?" He shook his head. "Nah, bro, don't even go there. Nothing about her says 'I just want a good time.'

She has *permanent* and *keeper* stamped all over her. She's standing with old people, for goodness' sake!"

Damian ignored Kyle and continued to observe the woman as she hugged the older couples and then weaved her way through the crowd. A few men tried to stop her, but she shook her head and kept walking. One man couldn't seem to take no for an answer and reached out to grab her. He handed his bottle to Troy.

"I'll be right back." He moved with determined strides toward the woman.

As Damian approached, he heard the man say, "Hey, beautiful. How about you keep me company this week? I promise to show you a good time."

Clearly he'd had too much to drink if his slurred voice was any indication.

"No, thanks." She gasped sharply when the man grabbed her around the waist and pulled her to him.

"Aw, come on."

A scowl settled on her beautiful face. "You have about one second to remove your arm or—"

"You heard the lady," Damian interrupted. "I'm sure you don't want your cruise to end before the boat leaves the dock." The man spun around and opened his mouth to speak, but obviously thought better of it. Damian towered over the man by a good six inches and outweighed him by forty pounds of pure muscle.

The man dropped his arm, muttered something about stuck-up women and took off down the corridor.

Damian glanced at the woman who barely reached his shoulder in her heels. "Are you okay?"

"I… Yes. Thank you. Although I could have handled it."

He chuckled in faint amusement. "I have no doubt about that. Would you like an escort to your room, or will you be all right?"

"I'll be fine. Thanks again."

"My pleasure. Perhaps I'll see you again."

"Perhaps."

Damian followed the sway of her hips until she was out of sight, then made his way back over to where his friends waited.

"Please don't tell me you made a move on that woman," Kyle lit into Damian as soon as he returned.

"Give it a rest, Kyle. I saw a guy harassing her and just made sure she was okay. I didn't even get her name."

"What do you mean you didn't get her name? Man, you're more out of practice than I thought," Troy said with a laugh.

Damian rolled his eyes. "Shut up, Troy. Like I said before, I don't know why I still keep you guys around. I have plenty of time to find out her name…if I want to."

Troy's eyebrows shot up. "Sounds like you're interested."

He glanced over his shoulder in the direction she had gone, then faced his friends. "Maybe." Up close, she was even more beautiful, and damn if he wasn't attracted to her. As Kyle noted, everything about her shouted *relationship*, not *fling*. But he wasn't looking for either, or was he? At any rate, things were starting to look up. Coming on this cruise might not have been such a bad idea after all, especially if he got a chance to spend a little time with his mystery lady. Yep, things were definitely looking up.

Karen felt the heat of her rescuer's gaze on her back, but she refused to turn around. The man was positively scrumptious with a rich, deep voice that poured over her like warm melted chocolate. From a distance she hadn't been able to discern the color of his eyes, but with him standing so near, she could see the green flecks in his light brown eyes—eyes that reflected friendliness and something else she couldn't identify. He didn't seem like the usual guy on the prowl. She shook her head to clear her thoughts. Why did she even care? She didn't.

Or at least, that was what she told herself.

Chapter 2

Karen entered her cabin, locked the door, dropped down in the closest chair and kicked off her shoes. If she didn't care, why was her heart beating faster? And why did the prospect of seeing him again send a shiver of excitement down her spine? She pushed off the chair and went to change into more comfortable clothing to get ready for the muster drill.

She searched for him at the drill and during dinner, and experienced a twinge of disappointment at not seeing him. Devin and Donovan had invited her to hang out with them for the evening listening to a couple of performances. She particularly enjoyed the performance by Eric Darius. The young saxophonist had a way of infusing jazz and funk that had everyone in the room on their feet dancing, including her. By the time she made it to her room that evening, Karen was beyond exhausted. Rather than take Friday off, she had worked the full day and then taken an overnight flight to Florida. She slept as much as she could on the plane and had taken a short nap this afternoon, but the lack of sleep had taken its toll. She showered and brushed her teeth within fifteen minutes and crawled into bed. The lulling movement of the ship relaxed her, and she drifted off to sleep quickly.

When she woke up the next morning, Karen felt no more rested than she had the night before. Images of a sexy stranger had kept her tossing and turning all night.

Instead of going to the dining room for breakfast, she opted for a muffin and coffee from room service. After dressing, she went out on the balcony. Miles and miles of deep blue water stretched out before her, and a slight breeze blew across her face.

She would have to thank Terrence again for the suite. He insisted on paying for her room as a thank-you for bringing Janae to the concert that night. She smiled, thinking about how reluctant Janae had been about dating a superstar, but Terrence had proven himself more than worthy of her love and devotion.

Although happy for her friend, she couldn't stop the pang of sadness that hit her. Automatically, Karen's thoughts shifted to her spineless, cheating ex-boyfriend. One minute they had been looking at wedding rings, and the next she was reclaiming her single status. She'd given him her love and almost two years of her life, but obviously, it hadn't meant anything. The old pain and anger rose to the surface, and she drew in a deep breath. She had given Andre Robertson enough of her time and energy and didn't intend to waste another second on his trifling behind. She glanced out over the water once more before going inside.

Today was a new day, and she looked forward to all the activities and concerts. And, despite the lecture she had given herself about not getting involved with another man, she couldn't help hoping she crossed paths with the gorgeous hunk again.

Grabbing her book and sunglasses, Karen left her room. She meandered around the ship for a while, then went out to the deck. She found an empty spot at the railing and braced her forearms on the dark, polished wood. This trip was exactly what she needed to clear her mind. She stood there a few minutes longer and noticed someone vacate a lounger near the pool. She quickly claimed it. Pushing her sunglasses higher up on her nose, she leaned back, closed her eyes and took a deep, cleansing breath. Opening her eyes again, she stared up at the cloudless blue sky and smiled. The sun shone and warmed her skin, funky jazz blared from speakers and people all around her danced and laughed. She felt the stress melt from her body as she picked up her book.

Karen was so engrossed in the characters that she jumped when a hand touched her shoulder. Her head snapped up. A man stood next to her wearing swim trunks and holding a drink in his hand. She guessed him to be in his late fifties. He had on an ill-fitting toupee and really should have put on a shirt.

"You look like you could use some company," he said, leering at her with a gap-toothed smile that made her skin crawl.

Keeping her features neutral and trying not to cringe, she said, "I'm just fine reading my book *alone*."

He continued as if she hadn't spoken. "I think we could have a good time together. I'd be remiss in my duties as a man to let a beautiful woman like you sit here all alone."

She barely stifled an eye roll. "Thanks for your concern, but I'd like to get back to my book." She picked up the book and started reading, hoping he would get the hint and move on.

Finally, he walked away. *Good grief. I must be attracting every loser on this ship!* First the man in the hallway, now this guy. She took a discreet glance around to make sure he was gone. When she didn't see him, Karen sighed in relief and shook her head. She turned back, and her gaze collided with the man who had invaded her dreams. He stood in the pool staring at her, his hazel eyes twinkling with amusement. The corners of his mouth kicked up into a sexy smile, and her pulse spiked. Someone bumped him and he looked away, breaking the connection. She shook herself and turned her attention back to the book.

After reading the same page three times, Karen gave up all pretense of trying to read. Her eyes strayed back to the pool and searched until she spotted him again. Hidden behind her shades, she studied his broad shoulders, his sculpted chest and arms and the strong lines of his handsome face. He started across the pool, and she was fascinated with his powerful strokes and by the play of muscles in his back as he swam. *Have mercy!* She stared until he disappeared from her vision. Dropping her head, she once again tried to concentrate on her novel.

She had finally managed to get back into the story when a shadow fell over her. She immediately thought Mr. Toupee had returned but went still when she heard the low, sexy voice.

"I see you're still fighting off the masses."

Karen's head popped up. It was *him*. Her mouth went dry. Rivulets of water ran down his golden chest and sculpted abs before disappearing beneath his black trunks. The wet trunks clung to muscled thighs and drew her attention to the impressive bulge resting at his groin. He wiped at his face with a towel, glanced down and chuckled, bringing her out of her lustful thoughts. Gathering herself, she said, "Um, something like that." His heated gaze burned a slow path from her face, lingered at her breasts and continued down to her exposed legs and back up. Her breath caught.

"Maybe you should find yourself a bodyguard."

"Are you applying for the position?" she asked flirtatiously.

His brow lifted. Before he could answer, one of the men she had seen him with yesterday called out to him. He held up a hand, signaling for them to wait, then turned back to her and angled his head thoughtfully. "You never know."

"Hmm, interesting."

"You have no idea." Blessing her with another heart-stopping smile, he said, "I'll see you around."

"That man is too fine," she mumbled to herself as he sauntered off. Karen had no idea what had gotten into her, flirting with him like that. But she couldn't help herself. Something about the man fascinated her. She had always been bold by nature, and when she was growing up, her mouth had gotten her into trouble more times than she could count. Her mother often said, *Karen, one of these days your mouth is going to write a check your butt can't cash!* She wondered if this might be one of those times.

Damian was still chuckling when he reached Troy and Kyle. He couldn't remember the last time he'd flirted with a woman, but their verbal play stimulated him and filled him with newfound energy. A bodyguard? He'd be more than happy to guard every inch of her sexy body.

"Damian, didn't we have this discussion yesterday? You need to find a woman who just wants a one-night stand. Don't waste your time. She's not interested," Kyle said.

"She's not interested? How do you know she's not interested?" She had seemed to enjoy their exchange as much as he did.

Kyle threw his hands up in exasperation. "Trust me, she's not. Remember—relationship, permanent, keeper? *Not* a cruise-week hookup."

"Kyle, you haven't even spoken to the woman." Damian turned to Troy. "I guess you have something to say, too?"

Troy held up his hands in surrender. "Hey, I've decided that you're a lost cause. You've smiled more in the last twenty-four hours since meeting her than you have in the last twenty-four months. Any woman who can draw you out of your funk that fast…I say go for it."

He shot a glare at Kyle, then clapped Troy on the shoulder. "Thanks."

Kyle folded his arms across his chest. "Don't say I didn't warn you."

"Your warning is duly noted," Damian drawled. "I'm going to shower. I'll meet you guys at the grill in half an hour," he called over his shoulder as he headed for his room.

Once there, he stripped, turned on the shower and stood under the warm stream. While he was washing, his thoughts wandered back to the woman on the deck. Yeah, she did make him smile, and laugh, too. He frowned. He hadn't even thought to ask her name. Again. "I've really been out of the game a long time," he muttered, shaking his head. *Next time,* he promised himself.

Karen woke up Monday morning, read over the list of ship activities and found a morning Zumba class. She didn't make it to the gym as often as she liked, but so far, things were still holding firm. Since she planned to enjoy herself over the week, she figured she might as well offset some of those calories by taking the exercise class. She arrived on the crowded deck just as the class began, found a spot near the edge and jumped into the routine. Halfway through the session, she had second thoughts about her choice. The muscles in every part of her body burned, and she could barely catch her breath.

"Lord, have mercy! I don't know what I was thinking, interrupting my sleep for this torture session," the woman next to her said, breathing heavily. "You can best believe I'm not doing it again. I'm gonna need an extra cocktail later on to make up for this."

Karen let out a tired laugh. "I hear you."

When class ended, Karen trudged back to her room and collapsed on the bed with a loud groan. Knowing she needed to shower, she lay there awhile longer, then dragged herself up and into the bathroom. In the shower, she let the hot water stream over her aching muscles until they loosened up. After washing up, she slipped on a robe and pulled out her novel.

When she glanced up and checked the time, she realized it was almost time to meet Janae. Karen discarded the robe and put on her red halter dress. She used the flat-iron to style her chin-length hair so that the strands fell in soft layers, framing her face. She told herself she wasn't taking extra care with her appearance just in case she ran into Mr. Eye Candy again, but she knew it was a lie. At the last minute, she slicked her lips with gloss, stepped into her jeweled sandals and left.

Janae was already waiting when she arrived.

"Girl, I can't believe you beat me here," Karen said. "Your sexy husband let you out of his sight?"

"Barely," she answered with a chuckle. "He told me the rehearsal wouldn't last more than a couple of hours and that he'd find me as soon as he finished."

"Well, let's not waste time. I'm starving, and I *know* you need to eat. Gotta keep up your strength." They burst out laughing and headed to the buffet.

There were so many offerings that Karen had a hard time choosing what to put on her plate. She settled on a mixed green salad, baked tilapia with lobster cream and smoked Gouda macaroni and cheese topped with panko bread crumbs. She placed the plate on a table, then went back for a drink.

"I see you got the tilapia, too," Janae said when she returned.

"That lobster cream smelled heavenly, and I couldn't resist." They ate in silence for a few minutes before Karen asked, "Do you miss San Jose and teaching?" Janae had taught a special education class at the same school where Karen taught, but she'd recently relocated to Los Angeles, where Terrence lived.

"Not too much. So far, I like LA. Some days I miss teaching, but Terrence turned one of the rooms in the house into an art studio, and I've been painting."

"Girl, those landscapes are breathtaking. I know you don't like the spotlight, but have you thought any more about a gallery showing?"

"You know me too well. Terrence has been great keeping the tabloids out of our business, so it hasn't been as bad as I thought. But, to answer your question, I have thought about it. I actually have an appointment with a gallery director when we get back—someone Terrence's grandmother knows."

Karen's eyes widened. "Oh, my goodness. Are you serious? That's fantastic. You know I'll be at your first show."

"She has to like the pieces first."

"Please. She's going to love them. I'm so happy for you." Karen's and Janae's family had been trying to convince Janae to pursue an art career for years.

Janae shrugged. "We'll see. Enough about me. What's going on? You mentioned something about Andre. I thought you guys broke up a few months ago."

She set her fork down on the plate and expelled a harsh breath. "We did. Before I left Friday, he called wanting to talk."

"Did you talk to him?"

"No. I let it go to voice mail. I don't have anything to say to him. He was the one who decided I wasn't good enough for him and sought out someone more to his liking, so…anyway, I've decided to put men on the back burner and focus all my attention on getting into administration. Hopefully, an opening will come up soon."

"You told me about that." Janae angled her head. "With all the programs you put in place last year for the fourth-grade team, I can see you as a school principal. Didn't you present district wide?"

She chuckled. "Yeah. But maybe I should start as an *assistant* principal or counselor first."

"You know, you can have a relationship and still pursue your goals."

"Look who's talking. If I remember correctly, you were the same way before you met Terrence. Weren't you always saying, 'I have my teaching and painting and that's enough'?"

Janae pointed her fork at Karen. "And *you* were the one telling me to get back out there and try again after Lawrence and Carter. Now I'm giving you back your own *good* advice." She waved a hand. "You're on a cruise ship with dozens of fine men, and I'm sure at least one of them will be more than happy to help you jump back into the saddle, so to speak."

Karen's mouth gaped. "What happened to shy little Janae? Being with Terrence has got you acting all wild."

Janae laughed. "Hey. What can I say? The man knows how to—"

Karen held up a hand. "Stop. I do not need to hear this. You know I've loved Monte his entire career, and it's hard enough not having lustful thoughts about him as it is without hearing details regarding his sexual prowess. The man is downright sexy."

"Actually, if I remember correctly, your description of him went something like rich milk chocolate skin, dark brown eyes, full, sexy lips framed by a goatee and over six feet of rock-hard muscle."

"I can't believe you remember that," she mumbled. "Anyway, now that you've ruined my fantasy, I'll just have to concentrate on work. Besides, I haven't met anyone who comes close to being that fine." As the words left her mouth, an image of the man she had met the first day popped into her mind, along with a strange sensation that had her heart pumping. She wondered if he was married.

He had been with two other men and she didn't see any women, but that didn't mean anything. What if he was single? Karen glanced around the room. With hundreds of people on the ship, she'd be lucky if she saw him again. Sighing softly, she resumed eating.

"There are plenty of handsome men roaming around here." Janae folded her arms. "As a matter of fact, I don't think you'll have a problem finding someone to spend time with."

Karen arched an eyebrow upon seeing the sly grin on Janae's face. "Really? And what makes you think that?"

"For one thing, I noticed several guys watching you when you were fixing your plate." A smile played around the corners of her mouth. She leaned forward and whispered, "For another, there's a positively gorgeous specimen of a man headed this way."

Karen whipped her head around, and her gaze collided with the man who had invaded her dreams for the past two nights. He looked good, wearing a pair of black linen shorts with a matching button-down shirt and black leather sandals. The muscles in his arms and calves were on prominent display, flexing with every movement. *Mouthwatering.* Her heart thudded in her chest as he came closer and stopped at their table.

"Good afternoon, ladies." He fixed his stare on Karen. "We meet again," her dream hunk said with a wink. "Any more problems?"

Janae leaned back in her chair and gave Karen a sidelong glance. A smile tugged at her lips.

Karen cut her a quick look, then said, "No. None."

"Glad to hear it." He stood there a moment longer, as if he wanted to say more. Finally, he stuck out his hand. "I don't think we've been properly introduced. I'm Damian."

She reached for his hand. "Karen." His large hand engulfed her smaller one. Warmth spread up her arm and through her body. She withdrew her hand and pulled her gaze from his. "This is my best friend, Janae."

He nodded politely and shook Janae's hand. "Hello."

"Nice to meet you, Damian."

"Well, I don't want to interrupt your lunch, but I just wanted to make sure Karen hadn't had any more trouble."

"Oh, you're not interrupting," Janae said. "Have a seat." She pushed back from the table and stood. "I'll be right back. I want to check out the dessert table."

Karen stifled a laugh when Janae mouthed, *Yummy*, behind his back. She looked up to where Damian still stood, seemingly waiting for an invitation to sit. She pointed to the empty chair next to her. "Please have a seat, Damian." *A strong name for a tall, strong-looking brother.*

He folded his body into the chair, and they both fell silent for a few moments.

He chuckled nervously. "It's been a while since I've been in the company of such a beautiful woman. I'm way out of practice and not real sure what to do anymore."

She laughed. "Well, no time like the present to find out."

He nodded. "So, are you traveling with a companion? I noticed the men you were with."

"If you're asking whether I'm single, the answer is yes, I am. Those were Janae's brothers. And you?"

"Same." He paused. "Would you like to join me for dinner this evening?"

"I'm sorry. I've already made plans."

His face fell.

"But I'm free tomorrow night."

A smile lit his face. "Marcus Johnson is performing tomorrow night. Would you like to go with me to the concert?"

Karen hesitated. She had planned to attend the show anyway and didn't want to go alone. But she was supposed to be taking a break from men, and in her head, she listed all the reasons why she should tell him no. However, something about Damian had captured her attention. Why not throw caution to the wind and have a little fun? Besides, after this week, she'd never see him again. "I'd love to."

He came to his feet. "Great."

"What time is the show?"

"It starts at eight, but I'll get there early to save us a seat."

"Sounds good. I'll meet you there."

"I'll be waiting. Enjoy the rest of your day, Karen." He pivoted and sauntered off.

"Okay." She slowly lowered her trembling hand to her lap and stared after him, remembering how good he looked from the back in those swim trunks—broad shoulders, tapered waist and tight, muscled butt. That sexy stroll had several women stopping to watch. She smiled. Tomorrow, he would be all hers.

"So I guess you won't be instituting that dating hiatus after all," Janae said, dropping into her chair.

"I might be willing to make an exception just for him," she said absently, still staring at Damian's retreating back.

"Wow. That must be a new record for the shortest dating hiatus ever."

Karen slowly turned her head and glared.

Janae checked her watch. "It lasted all of…four and a half minutes."

"Ha-ha. So you got jokes now." She tried to hold on to her scowl, but lost the battle when Janae started laughing. They laughed so hard, people at nearby tables turned to stare. When they were finally able to regain some semblance of calm, Karen said, "I haven't laughed that hard in a long time. I really miss hanging out with you."

"Yeah, so do I." Wiping tears of mirth from her eyes, Janae asked, "What did Damian mean by you having trouble? Did something happen?"

"Not really. On the way to my room after seeing your parents off, some drunk fool tried to grab me, talking about keeping him company for the cruise. I was two seconds from knocking him on his butt when Damian intervened. He even offered to walk me to my room. Then yesterday, he happened to be at the pool when another jerk tried to hit on me."

"Hmph. Fine and a gentleman. Are you guys going to meet up soon?"

She smiled and nodded. "We're going to Marcus Johnson's show tomorrow night."

"You go, girl. And if he turns out *not* to be a gentleman, we can toss him overboard."

They shared another laugh, remembering the time Karen had said the same thing about Terrence when he first showed an interest in Janae. But something told her that Damian was every bit the gentleman she thought him to be.

Damian couldn't keep the smile off his face as he left the dining room. Karen. He had thought about her all night but figured he probably wouldn't see her again so soon. He couldn't remember the last time he had anticipated going on a date so much. Excitement hummed in his veins, something no other woman in the past five years had been able to elicit. He made his way out to the deck, where an up-and-coming band was playing.

I wonder if she'll wear something like that red dress. He hoped so. The tasteful halter dress revealed the smooth skin of her back and shoulders, reminding him of whipped chocolate mousse. A vision of him trailing his hands and mouth along the expanse of her neck, shoulders and back flooded his mind, sending an unexpected jolt of lust to his groin, and shocking him in the process.

The parts of him he thought had died with his wife suddenly roared to life, followed by an immediate stab of guilt. His chest tightened. Damian threaded his way through the crowd crammed on the deck, moved to the railing and stared out over the water. His guilt was irrational, he knew, but he couldn't help following the flash of memories as they arose. The music and voices faded as his mind traveled back to Joyce.

He had taken her under his wing and helped her adjust to a new school after she moved in with her grandparents across from his house when they were fifteen. Her father's job had relocated to another state, and rather than uproot Joyce, her parents had allowed her to stay in North Carolina and finish high school. Their relationship had just sort of developed over time, and what started as friendship gave way to a gentle love ending in marriage. Pain settled in his chest. He would never forget the day he came home from work and found her unconscious at the bottom of the stairs. She had sustained a severe brain injury in the fall and died two days later.

He squeezed his eyes shut to block out the memories. He drew in a long breath and released it slowly. Damian repeated the process until the pressure in his chest eased. He had been grieving for five long years. Karen's face shimmered in his mind's eye. Joyce would always hold a place in his heart, but she was gone now. Maybe it was time for him to stop merely existing and actually start living. Someone bumped him, shattering his reverie. Slowly the music and voices came back into focus. People all around him clapped, danced and sang along with the band.

He glanced up to the sky, smiled softly and let the music seep into his soul. Today was a new day, a new beginning with a beautiful and intriguing woman in his future, and he planned to enjoy both.

Chapter 3

Karen and Janae had a little while longer to hang out before it was time for Janae to meet Terrence, so they sat in on a question-and-answer session with a jazz artist.

"Is Terrence doing a Q & A, too?"

"Yes. The show is Wednesday night, and he'll do the Q & A and autograph signing the following afternoon. Knowing Terrence, he'll probably sing a couple of songs, too. We're going to do a little sightseeing when we get to Nassau earlier in the day, then get back in time for the session."

"You guys aren't getting off in Grand Turks tomorrow and Jamaica on Wednesday?"

"No. He doesn't want to be too tired for the concert, so we'll hang out in the room. But he promised we'd take a trip to Jamaica soon."

Karen chuckled. "Locked in an exquisite suite aboard a luxury cruise with his new bride, yeah, I'm sure he'll be *well* rested."

"I'll go easy on him," Janae said with a laugh. "Are you coming?"

"Of course I'm coming to the show."

"Hmm. You might be otherwise preoccupied," she said with a smirk.

"I don't think so. If we happen to hit it off, he's welcome to join me, but I'm not missing that show. And you tell Terrence…well, Monte, I'd better get my autographed CD."

Janae laughed. "I'll make sure to pass the message along. It's really good."

"Wait. You've already heard it?" At Janae's grin, she frowned and folded her arms. "See, you just ain't right. I thought I was your BFF."

"You are. Gotta go find my hubby, before he comes looking for me." She gave a little wave and started off.

Karen stared with her mouth hanging open. "I am so going to get you, you little traitor!" she called after Janae. "You weren't even a big fan of his until I dragged you to that concert."

Janae just laughed and kept going.

Karen shook her head and headed for her own room.

Once the ship reached Grand Turks the following day, Karen disembarked only long enough to take a picture in front of the welcome sign and pick up a souvenir. Back in her room, she pulled out her novel and read on the balcony until it was time to leave for dinner. Knowing she wouldn't have time to change between dinner and the concert, she toyed with putting on something else.

Standing in front of the mirror, Karen glanced at her profile and decided against it. The turquoise halter dress was similar to the red one she'd worn the day before and made her look and feel sexy. She smoothed down her hair and touched up her makeup. Satisfied with her appearance, she picked up her small black leather cross-body purse with a braided jewel and leather strap and left.

Devin had insisted she have dinner with him and Donovan, so she wouldn't have to eat alone. Tonight, Janae's oldest brother and his wife, along with two of Terrence's other friends, joined them. During dinner, she laughed and conversed, but her thoughts were never far from Damian. Sure, the man gave new meaning to good-looking, but she hadn't come on this ship for some meaningless fling. Her goals were clear: see her best friend get married and refocus on her career. However, if that were truly the case, why had she agreed to meet him tonight? *Because I'm drawn to him in a way I can't explain.*

Nervousness took hold, and she took a huge gulp of her wine. By the time dinner concluded, she had downed two glasses, hoping they would calm the marbles rolling around in her belly. They didn't. She stood to excuse herself and had to endure Devin's inquisition. She used to think Janae was kidding about his overprotectiveness. Now she knew better. After assuring him she didn't need him to check out her date, Karen made a quick getaway.

A crowd had already gathered by the time Karen arrived at the theater. How in the world would she find Damian? She had no clue where to begin. She scanned the left side, squinting in the jam-packed space. Taking a step farther into the room, she leaned forward to see if he was sitting on one of the lower levels. A warm hand circled her waist, and she turned to give the offender a blistering retort, but froze when she heard the seductively familiar voice.

"Looking for someone?"

She turned slowly. Good grief. Every time she saw the man he looked better and better. Tonight he wore tailored dark trousers and a silk pullover that emphasized his well-defined arms, chest and abs. "Hey. I didn't see you." The heat from his body pressed against her ignited a slow burn. A shiver passed through her. She eased out of his embrace before she was tempted to do something crazy, like reach up and run her hands all over him to see if those muscles felt as firm as they looked. "Where are we sitting?"

Damian cupped her elbow and gently steered her to where he had seats saved near the front.

"Wow. How did you get such great seats?"

He chuckled softly. "It's our first date. I wanted to impress you, so I got here early."

First? The tone of his voice and the intensity of his gaze suggested there would be more than one date if he had anything to say about it. "Well, consider me impressed." The lounge had a mixture of theater chairs, semicircular booths for six or eight, tables with chairs and love seats for two. Of course, he had chosen the love seat. If it unnerved her how close he stood, she had no idea how she would manage to get through one or two hours with him sitting so near.

Damian gestured her to the seat, then sat next to her. He turned and reached for her hand. "Karen, I want to thank you for agreeing to come tonight." He lifted her hand to his lips and placed a soft kiss on the back.

Karen stifled a moan at the feeling of his warm lips against her skin and melted into the seat. "Um. Thank you for asking." She imagined those same lips trailing a path up her arm, over her shoulders…

Get it together, girl, an inner voice snapped, shattering the vision.

"And I'm *really* glad you have on another dress like that red one you were wearing yesterday. You look absolutely stunning."

"It's one of my favorites."

"Now it's one of mine."

Typically, she had no problem engaging in a little harmless flirtation with men, but Damian was messing with her equilibrium. Even with the lights low, she saw the fire in his eyes, and the flirty comeback poised on her tongue died a swift death. Earlier he had mentioned being out of practice with women. If he defined this as "out of practice," what would he be like *with* practice?

He leaned over to say something else, but before he could open his mouth, the lights went down in the theater, Marcus Johnson came up on the stage and the music began. *Thank goodness.* She needed a minute. If she had any doubts that he had more than a passing interest in her, the look in his eyes cleared it up. He was definitely interested. Just some casual fun, someone to pass the time with—that was what she told herself. She hadn't planned on this. She hadn't planned on *him*. And Lord help her, she was interested in him, too.

She glanced down at his long fingers tapping out the song's rhythm on his thigh. He had large hands, making her speculate about the size of certain other parts. Her pulse jumped. *Karen Lynette Morris, you stop it right now!* she chastised herself. *Get your mind out of the gutter.* Karen reached up and discreetly wiped the moisture gathering on her forehead. She needed to get a grip. She was sitting here fantasizing about a man she'd met two days ago, or actually yesterday. Whenever. The point was, she had no business thinking about him in those terms. She pushed the sensual thoughts to the back of her mind and focused on the music, letting the smooth piano jazz sounds take over.

Soon, Karen found herself rocking to the beat along with everyone else. She and Damian shared a smile, their heads bobbing in time with the music. By the time the concert ended, she felt more relaxed and in control.

"He's really good," she said as they filed out with the crowd. "I don't have any of his CDs, but I'm definitely adding him to my collection."

Damian nodded. "Marcus is very good. I have a couple of his CDs." Once they made it to an open area, he pulled her to the side. "It's still early, and I'm not ready for the evening to end. How about we go check out the club? Do you like to dance?"

"I do, but I haven't in a while." She checked her watch. It was only ten. "Sure. Let's do it." He reached for her hand and entwined their fingers as if it was the most natural thing to do. She felt the same heat as she had when they shook hands at lunch.

They heard the music as they rounded the corner. Damian immediately pulled her onto the dance floor. Karen swayed her hips in time with his, her eyes glued to every move he made—slim waist, washboard abs, muscular thighs and arms. She loved dancing, and it had been a long time since she allowed herself to be free and uninhibited. After a few up-tempo grooves, the music changed to a ballad. He moved closer and wrapped his arms around her waist, bringing her flush against his hard body.

She trembled when his hand came in contact with her bare back. Any calm she previously felt fled. His fingers moved slowly across the exposed area, searing a path on her skin. She glanced up to see his gaze locked on hers. Karen's breath caught, and her heart hammered in her chest. His eyes darkened, the green flecks more evident. His gaze drifted to her mouth, then back up to meet her eyes. She wanted him to kiss her. They'd only been together a few hours, yet the only thing on her mind was having his lips on hers. She turned away and rested her head on his shoulder, hoping he didn't see the longing in her eyes.

Damian couldn't stop the rampant desire flowing through his body. Sensations coursed through his veins, the likes of which he'd never experienced. Holding Karen in his arms and running his hands over the smooth expanse of her bare skin—it was softer than he anticipated—had him on the verge of doing something totally out of character, like tossing her over his shoulder and carting her off to the nearest bed. Her gloss-slicked lips appeared soft and inviting, and he wanted nothing more than to taste and nibble on them. Before she dropped her gaze, he read the same thing in her dark brown eyes.

The guilt he had felt earlier rose, but he pushed it down, reminding himself those feelings had no place here. He wasn't married anymore or in a relationship. He was free to explore this attraction between him and Karen. Damian closed his eyes, held her closer and inhaled the seductive scent of her perfume, letting the powerful sensations take over. He liked the way she fit in his arms, as if she belonged there. Though the thought scared him, he couldn't move away. He wanted to hold her this way all night.

As if by some unspoken communication, the DJ played three slow songs in a row. Damian offered up a silent thank-you and tightened his arms around her. Too soon, the music changed again. Karen lifted her head and stepped out of his embrace, and he instantly missed the closeness.

"Can I get you something to drink?" he asked.

"Yes, please."

He quickly claimed the table a couple had just vacated, and she sat. "What would you like?"

"A cosmo."

"Coming right up." He squeezed in at the black-and-white marble bar and gave their order. Several minutes later, he returned, drinks in hand. Damian placed her drink on the table in front of her and then sat in the chair across from her.

"What did you get?"

"Jack and Coke." His brow lifted when she took a long drink from the glass. "Good?"

She nodded and tilted the glass to her lips again before setting it on the table with a trembling hand.

He chuckled inwardly, thinking she might want to slow down. He picked up his own glass and took a small sip. "What brings you on the cruise? Vacation?"

"My best friend got married before the ship left on Saturday. Her new husband is performing, so they decided to make it part of their honeymoon."

"The woman you were with yesterday?" She nodded and he said, "I wish them many happy years together." A memory of his wedding day flashed in his head. "Who's the lucky guy?"

"Maybe you've heard of him. R & B singer and producer Monte."

"Really? I know of him. I once heard he planned to never marry."

"So did I. But Janae is the sweetest person I know, and I guess he couldn't resist."

"Is that why you were dressed up when I saw you?"

"Yes. What about you? Are you on vacation?"

"I guess you can say that." He laughed. "Actually, my two friends guilt-tripped me into coming. They bought the ticket and then asked if I was going to waste their money and accused me of not being a good friend." Karen laughed—a low, throaty sound that made his heart jump.

"That's wrong." She leaned forward with laughter shining in her eyes. "Were you being a bad friend?" she asked teasingly.

"Probably," he admitted. "I've turned down every offer to take a trip together for the last several years."

"Well, I'd say you redeemed yourself by coming on the cruise. You should be off the hook for at least a *month*."

Damian laughed. "Good point. I'll make sure to tell them that." They laughed together again, and then silence fell over the table. He hadn't laughed with a woman in a long time and enjoyed the easy rapport they seemed to be developing. He covered her hand with his. "I still wasn't too keen on coming, even after we boarded…until I saw you. I'm looking forward to whatever this week brings."

"So am I."

They finished their drinks, both lost in thought.

He gestured toward the dance area. "Are you ready to hit the dance floor again?"

"Let's do it."

He rose, assisted Karen from the chair and trailed her as she dipped in time with the beat out to the dance floor. She raised her arms in the air and danced with reckless abandon, her sensual movements sending bolts of white-hot desire shooting through him. Damian sucked in a sharp breath and tried to will his body calm. They danced to a few more songs. Then he suggested taking a walk.

Karen fanned herself. "Whew. I haven't danced like that in ages. And definitely not in these shoes."

He glanced down at the sexy jeweled sandals and her red-painted toenails. "But they look amazing."

"Thanks. Shoes are my weakness. I needed an extra bag just for them."

He shook his head and chuckled. Come to think of it, the shoes she had had on that first day were just as sexy. "You have good taste." They came to an exit. "Are you okay to walk on the deck for a little while? We won't stay long."

"Sure. I could use the fresh air."

He held the door open and let her precede him, then led her over to an empty spot at the rail. Neither spoke for several minutes. Damian studied her as she stared out into the black night—the shimmering glow of her skin bathed in the moonlight, the serene expression on her face. Their attraction had been instant and strong. Why her? And why now? He didn't think he would ever allow himself to get close to another woman, but in less than twenty-four hours, Karen had proven him wrong. She fascinated him. Called to him. Made him laugh and feel alive for the first time in years.

She looked up at him. "Penny for your thoughts."

"I was just thinking about you. Us. How much I'm enjoying your company."

She smiled. "You're not so bad yourself."

Damian reached up and stroked a finger down her cheek

and lowered his head. He hovered close enough for their breaths to mingle, waiting, seeking permission. She hesitated for a brief moment, then tilted her head upward. He touched his mouth to hers, once, twice. Her lips parted beneath his, and he slid his tongue inside. He hadn't kissed a woman like this in a while—five years to be exact—but it didn't take long for him to catch up. She tangled her tongue with his, and he groaned deep in his throat. He turned, leaned against the rail, widened his stance and pulled her between his legs.

Karen wrapped her arms around his neck, grabbed the back of his head and held him in place. Damian had no problem with that. He had no intention of letting go—not until he got his fill—which in his estimation might take all night. He angled his head and deepened the kiss. His hands roamed down her back, cupped her bottom and brought her flush against his erection. He wanted her to feel what she was doing to him. They stood there with their mouths fused for who knows how long until she shivered. He gave her one last kiss, then lifted his head.

"Cold?"

"A little," she said, shivering again.

He rubbed up and down her arms, leaned down and placed a soft kiss on her lips. "Let's get you inside."

She nodded.

Taking her hand, he led her back inside. "May I see you to your room?"

"I'd like that."

Her swollen, moist lips and passion-filled eyes tempted him beyond reason. "Lead the way." They walked to the elevator hand in hand. Luckily, no one else boarded, because he really needed to kiss her again, and he couldn't wait one more second. As soon as the doors closed, he backed her against the wall and slanted his mouth over hers. All too soon the distinctive chime sounded, signaling the elevator had reached her floor. Reluctantly, Damian ended the kiss.

He followed her down the hall until she stopped at a door, unlocked it and pushed it open.

She stepped inside and stared up at him. "Would you like to come in for a few minutes?"

Hell yeah, I want to come in. Leaning against the door frame, he said, "I'd better not. What are your plans for tomorrow? Are you going into Jamaica?"

She nodded. "I'm taking one of the tours to Dunn's River Falls, and it includes lunch afterward at a popular restaurant."

"Mind if we spend the day together? I really enjoy being with you."

"I don't mind at all. I booked the tour at eleven. Tomorrow night I'm going to Monte's show. He had seats reserved for us, but I can ask Janae to see if he can get another one, if you want to go."

"If you won't be tired of my company by then, I'd love to. How about we meet for breakfast in the morning?"

"Sure. I'll wait for you by the buffet entrance at eight-thirty."

"Sounds like a plan." Damian wanted to kiss her again but didn't trust himself to stay in control. He was having a hard enough time standing close to her without touching her. She took the decision out of his hands when she pulled him down for a kiss that stole his breath.

"Thanks for a wonderful evening, Damian. I'll see you in the morning."

He kissed her softly. "Good night, Karen. Sweet dreams."

She backed into the room and closed the door softly. He stood with his hand on the door.

Damian wanted to make love to her.

The realization shook him to his core. Not so much that

he had the urge, but how strongly he felt it. He had been celibate for five years by choice because he hadn't found a woman who excited him. Karen more than excited him. She intrigued him like no other woman before. Including his late wife.

He hadn't accepted her invitation tonight, but if she offered tomorrow, he wouldn't turn her down. And he would be prepared.

Chapter 4

Damian went back to the deck, gripped the railing and gulped in a lungful of crisp ocean air. The startling depth of his desire for Karen had thrown him for a loop. How could he want a woman so much? And in such a short time. He could still smell her intoxicating perfume, feel her silky skin beneath his fingers and taste the sweetness of her kiss in his mouth. As much as he wanted to take Karen up on her offer, he needed to step back and gain some perspective. His mind said things were moving too fast, but his body argued they weren't moving fast enough. Even now his heart hadn't returned to a normal pace, and his erection throbbed with desire. Damian was tempted to go back and knock on her door. He hadn't accepted her invitation tonight, one, because he felt it was too soon, and two, he didn't have any protection. Troy and Kyle mentioned they had left him some condoms, and he made a mental note to check his bag when he returned to his room.

He remembered he needed to sign up for the tour in Jamaica and glanced down at his watch. Leaving the deck, he retraced his steps and searched out the tour desk, hoping it hadn't closed. Luckily it hadn't, and there were three spaces available for the eleven o'clock tour. He was too wound up to sleep and made his way to the piano bar, where an up-and-coming artist was playing. Damian claimed a stool at the circular bar, signaled the bartender and ordered a Coke.

"Thanks," he said, accepting the glass. Although his body had calmed considerably, his mind continued to race with thoughts of Karen.

"Excuse me. Is this seat taken?"

His head came up. A woman stood next to him wearing a white low-cut skintight bodysuit and offering a come-hither smile.

"Be my guest." He gestured to the stool, then went back to his drink.

She slid onto the stool, purposely leaning close enough to brush her breasts against his arm.

Damian pretended not to notice. He didn't want to give the woman any indication he might be interested. She tried making small talk, and he remained courteous, but after a few minutes began to think he should have gone to his room.

"So, does that empty left hand mean you're not married?"

He stared down at his hand. He'd finally stopped wearing his ring a year ago, and the tan line had faded completely, as if nothing had ever been there. "No, I'm not."

She scooted closer. "Are you looking to be?"

"No."

"Are you sure? A handsome guy like you looks like he should be married." Her hand skimmed his thigh, sliding upward. He clamped his hand down on hers and jumped from the stool. "I think I'm going to call it a night."

Her gaze raked over him. "Want some company?"

"No, thanks. Enjoy the cruise." He turned on his heel and strode out of the lounge. Damian scrubbed a hand down his face. While he didn't mind an assertive woman, overaggressiveness turned him off. He hadn't gone far when a hand touched his shoulder.

He groaned inwardly, thinking the woman had followed

him. Glancing over his shoulder, he was relieved to see his friends.

"Well, well. For somebody who didn't want to come on this cruise, you sure have been busy," Kyle said.

"What's up?"

Troy folded his arms across his chest. "That's what we want to know about you. We haven't seen you all day."

Kyle laughed. "My man D has jumped back into the game at full speed. I saw the woman in the catsuit. Hot! Curves for days. She basically handed herself to you on a platter."

"I wasn't interested."

"Is that because you're more interested in the woman you were dancing with earlier?" Troy asked.

"Damn, were you guys following me around or something?"

Troy shook his head. "No. We went looking for some fun and just happened to see you while we were dancing. She's the same woman you were staring at the first day?"

He nodded. "We're spending the day together in Jamaica tomorrow, then going to Monte's performance tomorrow night."

"I guess you didn't need our help after all," Kyle said with a laugh. He lowered his voice. "Those condoms are in the small inner pocket of your duffel bag...in case you were wondering."

Yeah, he *had* wondered. "Are you guys going into Jamaica?"

"Yeah," Kyle answered. "You think you can tear yourself away from your new friend long enough to hang with your *old* friends once we get to the Bahamas?"

He really wanted to spend as much time with Karen as possible since they had limited time together. However, even though they worked together, he had neglected his friendship with Kyle and Troy, and they did pay for the cruise. "Yeah, man."

They said their goodbyes, and Damian continued to his room. Once there, he showered and crawled into bed. An hour later, he lay awake with thoughts of Karen filling his head. Where was she from? What did she do? Did she feel the chemistry between them as strongly as he did? He planned to get the answers to those questions and more. Turning over, he made himself comfortable and closed his eyes. Morning couldn't come soon enough.

Karen untangled herself from the sheets and groaned. Another dream. Her pulse raced, and her breathing came in short gasps. It was the second one she'd had tonight, and seemed so real she would swear Damian lay beside her with his lips pressed against the hollow of her neck. She hadn't been able to get his kisses out of her mind, or the feel of his hands sliding over her bare back and hips.

Scooting off the bed, she went into the bathroom and splashed some water on her face in an effort to cool off. She walked back into the room, opened the curtain slightly and leaned against the door frame. The sun had already begun its ascent, breaking through the early gray morning with streaks of red, orange and pink. Her mind lingered over every detail since she had met Damian, from their flirting at the pool and the uncertainty in his voice when he asked her out, to his solicitous manner during the concert and the possessive way he'd held her while his mouth plundered hers.

She wanted him. Bad. So much that she had invited him into her room last night, something she would never do with a man she'd just met. Maybe the effects of the alcohol she'd consumed had lowered her inhibitions. No. It was the man, plain and simple. But he hadn't accepted her invitation, and Karen wondered why, when he clearly seemed to be as into her as she was into him, not to mention the huge erection she'd felt pressed against her belly.

Maybe she had read more into what was happening between them, or maybe he thought her too aggressive. She sighed softly. Whatever the case, she needed to apologize. She didn't want Damian to think she made a habit of inviting strange men into her room.

Pushing away from the sliding glass door, Karen went to get ready for breakfast. She dug out her black swimsuit. The sexy cutout one-piece had crisscrossing straps across the back, but aside from that, left her back and sides bare, and tied at the hips. She put it on and slipped into a black crochet cover-up. Grabbing her tote, she added her waterproof camera, a change of clothes, towel, comb, brush and wallet, then sat on a chair to fasten the straps on her flat sandals. She picked up the tote and room key and left.

Karen searched the dining room for Damian and spotted him waving. She started in his direction, then halted her steps when he came toward her wearing a black tank exposing his strong muscular shoulders and arms, black swim trunks and sandals. An involuntary moan slipped from her lips. The man exuded masculinity in waves. It would be harder than she thought to keep her desire under control. As she came closer, his gaze traveled over her, stopped at her breasts and then slid lower, just below her stomach. His eyes darkened with desire, sending a rush of heat directly to her core.

"Morning," Damian said, dipping his head to kiss her cheek.

His soft, warm lips lingered on her cheek, and a shiver passed through her. "Good morning. Have you been waiting long?"

"No. Just a few minutes." He led her to the table. "Why don't you leave your bag here and go fix your plate? I'll get mine when you come back."

"Okay." Karen surveyed the buffet and filled her plate with a small amount of scrambled eggs, potatoes with onions and peppers, two strips of crisp bacon and a slice of toast, then got a glass of orange juice. She placed her plate on the table, and Damian shook his head. "What?"

"That's all you're eating?"

She glanced down at the plate. "Yes, why?"

"I can still see half of your plate."

"I may go back for more."

He nodded, leaned down close to her ear and whispered huskily, "By the way, you're killing me with that outfit. Makes me want to cancel the tour." His mouth curved in a wicked grin, he winked and walked off.

The timbre of his voice and accompanying look turned her legs to jelly. Karen managed to pull out her chair and drop down in it before she collapsed. She fanned herself and took a long sip of juice.

Damian returned to the table with his plate piled high— French toast, scrambled eggs, potatoes, bacon, sausage and fruit.

"You can go back for more, you know. That's why they call it a buffet."

He paused with the saltshaker in his hand. "What? I don't have that much."

"Whatever you say," she said with a laugh, and forked up a portion of potatoes.

He wiggled his eyebrows. "I have a healthy appetite. What can I say?"

Her belly fluttered with the double meaning. She propped her chin in her hand and leaned forward. "So do I."

"That's good to know," he murmured.

Damian tried to concentrate on his breakfast. Their verbal exchange, combined with the revealing black cover she wore over her bathing suit, had him hard as a steel beam and he was tempted, once again, to drag her to the nearest bed and find out just how healthy of an appetite she had. He had never engaged in this type of sensual play with his late wife—she had been very reserved when it came to sex. But he knew things would be different with Karen. He sensed a passion and fire in her that he eagerly wanted to explore. He forced his thoughts elsewhere and finished breakfast.

"Are you ready to head out?" he asked when her plate was empty.

"Yes."

He stood, slung his backpack over his shoulder and helped Karen. More than one man turned when she walked by. Damian moved closer and placed a possessive hand on the small of her back. Sending a lethal glare at one man who was staring a little too long, he guided her toward the ship's exit.

The ship's coordinator checked off their names, gave them colored wristbands and directed them to a waiting van.

"Damian," Karen started, once they were en route, "I want to apologize about last night."

"For what?"

"The whole room invitation thing. I've never done anything like that before," she mumbled, and turned to stare out the window.

He turned her face back toward his. "You don't have to apologize. If it helps any, I really wanted to accept your invitation, but I didn't want to come on too strong."

He placed his arm around her shoulders, kissed her forehead and pulled her closer. They rode the rest of the way in silence. After reaching the park and getting water shoes, he suggested they rent a locker. Damian stripped off his shirt, placed it in his bag and put it in the locker.

"If you—" His eyes widened, and his mouth fell open.

Karen had taken off the cover and stood clad in a bathing suit that left every inch of her velvety brown back and sides bare. The sight almost dropped him to his knees. A man passing by whispered, *"Dayuum!"* while staring with his jaw unhinged. Damian couldn't blame the man, because she was a vision of beauty. He let his gaze roam lazily over every delectable curve.

She placed her tote in the locker and faced him. "Were you going to say something?"

He stared at her with confusion, then realized she had asked him a question. He shook his head. "I'm sorry. What did you ask?"

"I thought you were going to say something."

For the life of him, he couldn't remember one word. "Nothing. You look *amazing*."

She slowly looked him up and down. "So do you."

It's going to be a long day. He closed the locker and reached for her hand. "We'd better get going."

At the base of the fall, a vendor asked if they wanted their picture taken.

"Yes. Take two." He wanted a memory of this trip with her. The photographer took the pictures of them together, then one of them separately.

"You can view the pictures on your way out and buy if you like," the man said.

Once they started the climb, Damian took a picture of Karen using the waterproof camera she'd brought along. Instead of linking hands and climbing with the others, they chose to leisurely climb to the top, stopping to linger in some of the pools along the way. Unable to resist, Damian came up behind Karen, wrapped his arm around her and trailed kisses along the smooth flesh of her neck and shoulders. She moaned softly. Turning her in his arms, he transferred his kisses to her jaw and nibbled on her lush bottom lip until her lips parted. He kissed her hungrily. Her hands came up and circled his neck.

"I can't get enough of kissing you," he managed to say huskily against her lips before kissing her again.

"Damian," she whispered, her body trembling.

He pressed his lips to her temple, squeezed his eyes shut and tried to slow his galloping heart. Damian had never been so tempted by a woman in his life and certainly hadn't ever lost control this way. He opened his eyes, eased back and released her. Giving her one last kiss, he took her hand and gestured her forward. "Come on, baby. Let's keep going."

Karen didn't know how he expected her to climb anything after kissing her senseless. Her legs felt like rubber, her heart raced and her mind was a jumbled mess. She took a moment to collect herself before climbing the next step. They moved at a good pace for a while, and she stopped along the way to take a few pictures to show her students. After taking the last shot, she turned and lost her footing.

Damian tightened his grip on her waist. "Careful, sweetheart."

The low timbre of his voice in her ear and the heat of his touch wreaked havoc on her nerves. She sucked in a shaky breath. "I'm good." She glanced up. "We're almost at the top."

Once they reached the top, she turned and looked down with her arms spread. "That was great. I can't wait to get back and see the pictures."

He nodded. "I'm glad you allowed me to tag along. How about we get changed, stop and pick up the pictures, then get back to the van? It'll be leaving shortly for lunch."

"Okay." They retrieved their belongings from the locker and headed to the changing facilities.

"I'll wait for you over by the lockers," Damian said.

She nodded and watched his sexy stroll until he disappeared. "Mmm, mmm, mmm."

Inside, Karen stripped off her soaked bathing suit, dried off and dressed in shorts and a tank top. She combed out her wet hair and secured it back into a ponytail. She met Damian, and they returned the water shoes, paid for the pictures and boarded the van taking them to the restaurant.

"You didn't have to pay for the pictures, Damian," she said once the van pulled off.

"Think of it as my way of saying thank you. I can't remember the last time I enjoyed myself so much. I'll never forget it," he said, holding her eyes with an intensity that made her insides tremble.

"Neither will I." She stared down at the picture of them in her hands. At least she would have something to remember him by when the cruise ended. But for some reason, the thought of never seeing him again caused a churning in her stomach.

Chapter 5

Karen and Damian entered the open-air restaurant known for its jerk chicken and placed their order. They laughed and talked about everything from the Jamaican sights and weather to music and politics—everything except themselves—while waiting for their food. It took a while for it to arrive, but it was well worth the wait. She bit into the spicy, crispy chicken, and an involuntary moan slipped from her lips.

Damian lifted an eyebrow and chuckled. "Good?"

"Oh, yes. Don't take my word for it. Try it yourself."

He picked up a piece of chicken from his plate and tried it. Nodding, he finished chewing. "Mmm, it is good."

They ate in silence for several minutes. She scooped up some of the rice and peas, loving the subtle peppery flavor.

"Did you enjoy climbing the falls?" he asked between bites.

"Loved it."

"Are you always this adventurous?"

She shrugged. "I'll try anything once. Well, except bungee jumping. *That* will not be happening."

He threw his head back and roared with laughter.

"What? All I can think about is that cord snapping, along with my neck."

Still chuckling, Damian picked up his drink and took a sip. "That's not on my list, either, though I never quite thought about it like that."

"What about you? Do you like adventure?"

"I used to," he answered softly. His voice held a hint of sadness.

"Any reason why you don't anymore?"

He smiled faintly. "Working too hard, I guess."

"Well, I'm glad you decided to join me," she said, trying to lift his mood. "Sounds like you need to get out more."

Holding her gaze, he said, "Maybe. I haven't had this much fun in ages." He covered her hand. "I'm looking forward to much more."

"So am I."

They continued eating, and then he asked, "So, Karen, what do you do?"

She paused with the fork in her hand. The last man she had dated didn't think teaching met the standards of a successful career. What would Damian think? Karen halted her thoughts. She didn't care what anyone thought—she loved teaching. "I teach."

"Really?"

She stilled. "Is there something wrong with teaching?"

"Not at all. I think teachers are hardworking, dedicated and severely underpaid."

Relaxing, she laughed. "Me, too."

"What grade do you teach?"

"Fourth."

He shook his head. "You must have the patience of a saint."

"Some days it's a struggle, but I love it."

"I'm sure you're a phenomenal educator."

"Thanks. What about you?"

"I work for a consulting firm."

Before she could question him further, the driver indicated it was time to leave. They discarded the remnants of their lunch, followed their group out and rode the short distance back to the ship. As they boarded and made their way to the elevators, Karen tried to cover a yawn.

"Tired?"

"A little." She checked her watch—two-thirty. "Oh, by the way, you're good to go on the concert tonight if you still want to."

"You still offering?" Damian pushed the elevator button.

"I am. The show starts at eight." She got in the elevator, and he followed.

"Thanks. What're you going to do until then?"

"Shower, wash my hair and probably take a nap. Are you going to meet your friends?"

"I'll probably relax for a little while, then see if I can find them."

The elevator opened, and he followed her to her room. She unlocked the door and then turned back.

"I'll pick you up at seven-thirty. Is that all right?"

"That's fine."

"See you in a little while." He bent low and placed a gentle kiss on her lips. "Sleep well." Then he was gone.

After showering and taking a short nap, Damian went in search of Troy and Kyle and found them in the casino playing blackjack.

Troy looked up from his cards. "What's up? I see you got our message. I was wondering if you'd show up."

"How long you guys been playing?"

"Long enough to lose damn near all my money," Kyle grumbled, turning over his cards and showing another busted hand.

Damian laughed. "I'm glad I got here when I did. I need to keep my money."

"Please, you have almost as much money as Midas."

"Yeah, right. And you don't? Kyle, you have more money than Troy and I put together."

"That's because Kyle is a miser," Troy said and signaled the dealer to give him another card.

"It's called managing your money properly," Kyle said, mimicking the nasally tone of their high school economics teacher.

They looked at each other and broke out in laughter. Back in high school, they had teased Mr. Cornwell and laughed behind his back, but the three friends had taken the man's words to heart, made some lucrative investments and were now financially well-off. Doing this had also given them the freedom to start their own business when they were ready for career changes.

"How was Dunn's River Falls?" Kyle asked.

Damian smiled, remembering how good Karen looked in her swimsuit, how smooth her skin felt and how much he liked kissing her. "Great."

"That good?"

Damian nodded.

Troy lifted an eyebrow. "You're not planning to back out on us tomorrow, are you?"

"Nah, man. But I am going with her to Monte's show tonight. Front row, reserved seats. Remember when we saw her dressed up that first day?"

"Yeah," they both answered.

"Karen's best friend had just gotten married to Monte. So he reserved some seats."

Kyle threw down another busted hand. "I think I've lost enough money for one day." He stood. "Let's go listen to some music and grab something to eat, and then Damian can tell us all about *Karen*."

They filed out of the casino and caught a performance in the atrium. There was no room on the main floor, so they ended up going to the next level. Afterward, over an early dinner, they lamented the fact that so many great singing artists, like the one they'd just heard, were going the independent route. With radio stations and music companies looking for quick money, the market seemed to be flooded with cookie-cutter mediocre talent.

The conversation turned to Karen. "I don't know much about her, except that she's a teacher," Damian said.

"Did you tell her you used to teach?" Troy asked before forking up a piece of steak.

"No. I just told her I work for a consulting firm."

"Good move," Kyle said, toasting Damian with his wineglass. "You don't need to divulge all your secrets to somebody you probably won't see again."

"Hmm." For some reason, the knowledge that he might not see Karen again after this week bothered him, but he decided not to share that piece of information with his friends. He wanted to learn more about her. One week wouldn't be nearly enough time for him to uncover all he needed to know. But it was a start. He checked his watch and realized he had less than an hour to change before meeting Karen. He finished his meal and stood. "What time do you want to meet in the morning?"

Troy shrugged. "Say breakfast at eight, and we leave around nine?"

"Okay. What are we doing?"

Kyle and Troy shared a smile. Kyle said, "You just need to bring a couple of changes of clothes. We plan to have a good time."

Damian divided a wary gaze between the two men. "What are you two up to?"

"Just want you to enjoy yourself," Troy answered. He chuckled. "We may never get you out of the house again, so we have to pack it in while we can."

Though Troy had said the comment in a teasing manner, Damian couldn't stop the guilt that arose. They had been friends since middle school, and Damian could always count on the two of them to have his back no matter what. "I'll be ready."

In his room, Damian changed into tailored slacks, a silk polo and loafers. Thinking he might not get back until late, he filled his oversize backpack with the clothes he'd need for tomorrow's excursion and placed it on a chair. He pulled the duffel bag from the closet and searched for the condoms. He found them, tore off a few and put them in his wallet. Taking a quick look at his watch, he picked up the card key, slipped it into his pocket and left to pick up Karen.

When she opened the door, he could only stare.

"Hey, come on in. Let me grab my purse." She walked a few steps, slipped her arms into a sheer cover-up, turned back and chuckled. "Damian, are you coming in?"

Shaking himself, he followed her. "Sorry. Every time I see you, you take my breath away." She wore another sexy dress paired with matching sandals.

She smiled. "Thanks. You look pretty good yourself." She slung a purse over her shoulder. "I'm ready."

So was he.

In the elevator, Karen closed her eyes briefly and drew in a deep breath. The heat in Damian's eyes threatened to incinerate her. The chemistry between them increased exponentially each time they were together, and she didn't know how much longer they'd last before the intense desire overtook them. She glanced up to find his eyes fixed on hers. His gaze drifted to her mouth, and she subconsciously licked her lips, remembering the warm slide of his tongue against hers. Just as he reached for her, the ding of the elevator sounded.

Damian leaned close to her ear and murmured, "To be continued." He wrapped a hand around her waist and steered her around the crowd waiting to board, down the hall toward the theater.

Karen tried to put some space between them, but he held firm to her, the warmth of his strong fingers penetrating the silky material of her top. Just like earlier, his touch did things to her insides and made her have visions of the two of them naked and writhing in a bed. She pushed the dangerous thoughts from her head and kept walking. They met Janae coming from another direction.

The two women embraced. "Hey, Karen," Janae said. "Nice to see you again, Damian."

"Same here. Congratulations on your marriage."

"Thanks. How was Jamaica?"

Karen smiled. "Good."

"Very good," Damian reiterated.

Janae divided a speculative glance between Karen and Damian, then threw a look at Karen that said she wanted details.

Ignoring the look, Karen said, "Dunn's River Falls was great. You and Terrence will have to go when you come back."

"Is that so?" she asked with a smile. "Maybe we will."

They joined the line of people entering the theater. "Do you know where we're sitting?"

"Donovan said he'd be waiting near the front." As soon as they were seated, Janae leaned over and whispered, "What's going on with you and Damian?"

She looked over to where Damian stood talking to Donovan, and then back to Janae. "We're enjoying each other's company, that's all."

"Hmph. Girl, the way he looked at you when I asked about Jamaica said he was enjoying more than that. I think he likes you."

"I like him, too. He seems nice."

"Nooo, I mean he *really* likes you."

Karen waved a dismissive hand. "Please, we just met."

Janae shook her head. "Okay, Miss In Denial. Mark my words, the man is interested in far more than just hanging out with you for this week."

"He's just… I don't know."

"Sounds a lot like the way I was feeling about Terrence when we first met." She laughed. "You do remember what happened the first time we went to Terrence's concert, don't you?"

She stared, confused.

"One of us ended up married."

"What does that have to do with me and Damian? You and Terrence are in love."

"We didn't start off that way. Remember when we used to talk about how sensual *Monte's* music and lyrics were?"

"Yeah?"

"All I'm going to say is this new music is even more so. And the fireworks between you and Damian are enough to supply an entire Fourth of July celebration. Mark my words, there are going to be a lot of couples behind closed doors tonight, including y'all." She gave Karen a knowing look when Damian took his seat, and then leaned back with a smug smile.

Karen didn't comment. She knew exactly what Janae meant. In the past, music had been part of the foreplay when she and Andre made love. Her attraction to Damian far exceeded that of her ex, and it wouldn't take much for her to lose control—music or not. She hazarded a glimpse his way and found him seemingly deep in thought. He frowned briefly, and a shadow flickered across his face. *I wonder what that was about.* His voice broke into her thoughts.

"You're frowning. Is something wrong?"

"No," she said hastily. "Just thinking. It's nothing."

He studied her a moment. "You sure?"

"Yes." She reached down and gave his hand a reassuring squeeze.

He lifted it and placed a lingering kiss on the back. Smiling, he laced their fingers together and trained his eyes on the stage.

Karen turned and met Janae's smiling face.

Janae mouthed, *I told you.*

Soon the lights dimmed, and Monte hit the stage and greeted the audience. "Before we get started, I'd like my beautiful wife to join me."

Gasps and expressions of shock flooded the room. "Did you know he was going to do this, Janae?" Karen asked.

She nodded. "Yes. He promised it would be the only time." Janae stood, and Donovan escorted her to the stage.

While holding Janae's hand, Monte sang a beautiful ballad he had composed just for her, expressing the depths of his love. He looked at her with such emotion that it brought tears to Karen's eyes. She wondered how it would feel to have a man look at her that way.

A tear slid down her cheek. Damian gently wiped it away with the pad of his thumb before she could react. The tender and sweet gesture caught her by surprise, and the tears came faster.

Damian draped his arm around her shoulders and pressed a kissed to her temple. "Are you all right?"

"Yes," she said, sniffing. "I'm just happy for Janae, and the words to the song are so beautiful."

"He must love her a lot."

"He does, and she loves him just as much."

He stared at her for a lengthy minute with a strange look on his face before turning his attention back to the stage.

She wiped away the lingering tears, grateful that she hadn't worn mascara or eyeliner. She and Janae shared a smile when Janae returned; then Karen tuned in for the rest of the show. Monte sang a mixture of the old and new, and she found Janae's description of the new music quite accurate. He could have titled it *The Ultimate Make-Out CD*. By the show's end, she noticed more than a few couples snuggling closer.

Karen and Damian said their goodbyes to Janae, and he convinced her to take another walk. Outside, they strolled hand in hand along the deck, neither speaking. She marveled at how comfortable she felt with him. In the short time since she'd met him, he'd impressed her as a gentleman. He had a great sense of humor and a way about him she couldn't put into words that drew her as no other man had before. Why couldn't they have met under different circumstances? He stopped walking abruptly.

"Karen, I…" He wrapped his arm around her and pulled her into his embrace at the same time his head descended.

He kissed her with a potency that weakened her knees. She slid her arms around his neck and held him in place as his hands moved slowly up and down her back, caressing and teasing. His lips left her mouth and skated along her jaw before claiming her mouth again. At length, he lifted his head but didn't release her. She read the question in his eyes, knew what he was asking. She came up on her toes and kissed him.

Reaching for his hand, Karen led him back to her room. When they reached it, she slid the key in, unlocked the door and glanced back at Damian. Once they crossed the threshold, she knew there would be no turning back.

Chapter 6

Damian shut the door behind him and took a cursory glance around the suite. He noted an end table, a sofa and a small bistro-like table with two chairs on one side of the room. But what held his attention was the king-size bed on the opposite side of the room. Karen removed the top she had worn over the dress, then tossed it and her purse on the sofa. She wrung her hands together and looked everywhere except at him.

He placed his hands on her shoulders and turned her to face him. "Second thoughts?"

She shook her head hastily. "No."

"Are you sure? Karen, we don't have—"

She placed her finger on his lips. "I'm sure."

He captured her hand, kissed the center of her palm and wrist, then trailed kisses along her arm up to her shoulder. Moving closer, Damian tilted her chin, flicked his tongue against the corners of her mouth and nibbled on the lush fullness of her bottom lip.

"Damian," Karen said on a breathless sigh.

Hearing his name whispered from her lips spiked his arousal. Her mouth parted slightly, and his tongue found hers. He plunged deep, swirling and feasting on the sweetness like a starved man. His hands moved down her back, over her hips and around to gently knead her firm breasts. She trembled beneath his touch, fueling his passion, and the kiss intensified. Her hands came up to stroke the nape of his neck, and he groaned deep in his throat.

Karen tore her mouth away, breathing harshly.

Running his fingers lightly over the exposed area above her breasts, he asked, "Do you know how beautiful you are?" He bent and replaced his fingers with his tongue, the scent of her seductive perfume filling his nostrils and arousing him further. He had fantasized about being here with her like this almost from the moment they met. Damian swept her in his arms, covered the short distance to the bed in three strides and deposited her in the center. He kicked off his shoes and climbed onto the bed.

"You wear the sexiest shoes," he murmured. He lifted her leg, placed a lingering kiss on her ankle, undid the strap and slid the shoe off. He lifted her other leg and repeated the gesture.

She moaned softly, and the sound almost snapped his control. He closed his eyes to steady his breathing and maintain control. It had been five long years since he'd been intimate with a woman, and he was close to exploding.

Starting at her feet, he caressed and kissed his way up her body. He pulled her into a sitting position, reached behind her neck and released the clasp on her dress. The material fell away, pooling at her waist. Karen leaned back on her elbows and lifted her hips so Damian could slide the dress down and off, leaving her clad in a very sexy strapless purple lace bra and matching bikini panties. His breath stalled in his lungs. "Exquisite," he murmured while skimming his fingers over her hip. He left the bed, draped the dress over a chair and feasted his eyes on her loveliness. He pulled his shirt hem from his pants.

Karen scooted to the edge of the bed and stood. "Allow me."

He stood still while she eased the shirt up and over his head, then laid it on top of her dress. Her hands moved over his chest and stomach, electrifying him in the process. His breaths came in short gasps, and his muscles contracted beneath her touch. She moved her hand lower and stroked him through his slacks. His knees almost buckled, and he released a guttural moan. Damian endured the sweet torture a moment longer, then took a step back and undid his belt.

Karen followed his move, pressed a kiss to his chest and said, "I got this, baby." She unbuttoned his pants and lowered the zipper, and they dropped to the floor. She kneeled down for him to step out and added them to the pile of clothes. Standing, she eyed him seductively and smiled. "Very impressive."

He chuckled softly, wrapped his arms around her and nipped at her ear. "You think so?"

"Absolutely. With this body, you could grace every month in a hunk calendar. Did you play sports?"

He eased back and twirled her slowly. "I don't know about that, but you..." He shook his head. "Definitely. And yes, I played basketball in high school and college." He kissed her. "No more talking. Right now I need you naked and in my arms."

"Then what are you waiting for?"

In the blink of an eye, he had her naked and on the bed. Damian removed his underwear, crawled onto the bed and lowered himself onto her. He shuddered from the pleasure of feeling their bodies skin-to-skin. He kissed her with a hunger that both excited and frightened him, and she returned his kiss, giving as good as she got. He kissed his way down to her beautifully formed breasts and captured a chocolate-tipped nipple between his lips. He laved and suckled first one, then the other. He charted a path down the front of her body with his hand and slid two fingers into her slick, wet heat until she was writhing and moaning beneath him.

Karen leaned up and skated her tongue over his jaw, neck and shoulder. Her hands ignited an inferno in his body as they traveled down his back.

Damian was nearing the end of his control. He withdrew his fingers, slid off the bed and searched for his wallet. He took the condoms out, tore one off and tossed the other ones onto the nightstand. After rolling it on, he moved over her, grinding his body against her. They both moaned. "It's been a while, so I'm apologizing up front if things go a little fast the first time. But I promise to make it up to you."

"I'm holding you to that."

He shifted his body and eased into her warmth until he was buried to the hilt. He held himself still, savoring the feeling of her tight walls surrounding him. "You feel so good, baby," he whispered against her lips at the same time he started moving inside her.

"Mmm. So do you."

He closed his eyes and let the sensations take over as he kept up the relaxed pace.

Karen wrapped her legs around his waist and pulled his mouth down on hers, their tongues tangling and dancing.

Damian lifted her hips as he plunged deeper and faster. Her whimpers and cries of passion excited him in a way he had never experienced and couldn't explain. He gritted his teeth, feeling her nails biting into the skin on his back, but didn't slow.

"Damian!" She arched off the bed and screamed his name. Her body shook, and her inner muscles contracted, clamping around him like a vise.

He threw back his head and exploded in a rush of pleasure that tore through him like a crack of lightning. His eyes slid closed, he groaned her name and shuddered above her as the spasms racked his body. She reached up and stroked the sides of his face. He opened his eyes, and when their eyes connected, he felt it—a little tug on his heart. This was more than just sex. Damian dismissed the thought, leaned down and kissed her tenderly. He rolled to his side, taking her with him, and held her snugly against his body. After several minutes, their ragged breathing returned to normal.

Karen basked in the contentment she felt in Damian's arms. Her body still hummed with desire. Even now, as his hand idly stroked her hip, she could feel her passions rising again. Then his caresses became more purposeful, and her breathing increased. He lifted her leg over his and trailed his hand along her inner thigh and up to her core, where she was already wet. She moaned when his fingers slipped inside and began stroking her. He probed deeper, and she moved her hips in time with his rhythm. "Yes, yes, *yes*," she chanted. His fingers moved faster and faster. Her breaths came in short gasps, and her legs trembled. She arched her head back, closed her eyes and bucked against his hand, crying out wildly as an orgasm ripped through her. Before she could recover, he rotated his fingers and did *something*. Her eyes flew open, her body went rigid and she came again, seized by a rush of sensation so intense she thought she might pass out. As she lay gasping for air, Damian lowered his head and kissed her. She moaned against his mouth and circled her arm around his neck.

He withdrew his fingers, rolled over and grabbed another condom. He tore open the package, and she took it from him. Sitting up, Karen straddled his thighs and rolled the condom slowly over his engorged shaft.

He sucked in a sharp breath. "Sweetheart, what are you doing to me?"

She smiled seductively. "Getting ready to go for a little ride. You mind?"

His eyes lit with desire. "Not at all. Ride on."

She held his gaze as she lowered herself inch by exquisite inch until he was embedded deeply within her. She shuddered, reveling in the way he filled her completely. Karen ran her hands over the strong, muscular planes of his chest and abdomen. The sun had darkened his golden skin to a warm bronze. Leaning down, she flicked her tongue against his lips. With lightning speed, Damian grasped the back of her head and crushed his mouth to hers, kissing her with an eroticism that made her head spin.

"Mmm. You're something else," he said.

She braced her hands on his shoulders and whispered against his lips, "You might want to hold on."

He chuckled low and sexy. "Show me what you've got, baby."

Karen lifted off him until only the tip of his shaft remained. Holding his gaze, she slowly lowered back down and rotated her hips in a figure-eight movement. She repeated the motion several times. The look of pure ecstasy on Damian's face was like nothing she had ever seen and turned her on even more. He kneaded her breasts, pushed them together and leaned up to take the sensitive peaks of her nipples in his mouth, sending jolts of pleasure to her core.

"No more teasing," he growled, gripping her hips, lifting the lower part of his body off the bed and thrusting deep.

She caught his driving rhythm and rode him hard. He pounded into her, and their cries of passion filled the room. Soon desire unlike anything she had ever known consumed her, and she flung her head back and screamed his name.

He tightened his grip on her hips and thrust faster. Damian tensed, and then his body bucked beneath hers as he shouted her name.

Karen collapsed over his chest and felt the rapid pace

of his heart matching hers. "I don't think I can move," she moaned.

His hands glided over her sweat-slicked skin. "Fine by me. I happen to like where you are right now."

So did she…a little too much. Gradually their breathing slowed and she drifted off.

Damian awakened hours later and stared down at the woman cuddled next to him with the sheets twisted around their lower bodies. His gaze lingered over her exposed naked body bathed in the morning sunlight peeking through the partially open curtains. He couldn't get enough of her. After that second round, their first attempt to shower had ended with her hands braced against the wall as he entered her from behind. Then they wound up in one of the chairs before showering again and falling asleep.

Something was happening between them—something more than sex. He had felt it when they made love and during their conversations. Troy had been right. Damian couldn't remember the last time he had smiled and laughed so much. He and Karen had a lot of things in common—everything from music to sports to food. Though they talked, they hadn't let their guards down enough to discuss more personal topics. Other than what she revealed to him over lunch, he still didn't know much about her. Had she been married before? What did she like to do outside the classroom?

Over the past two days, the parts of him that had lain dormant for so many years surfaced and burst free. When he was younger, he had hiked, sailed, danced, laughed and enjoyed life. Karen was the first woman who seemed to possess the same zeal for life as him. The other women he dated wouldn't have been caught dead doing any activity that required more than lifting a wineglass to their lips. The other thing that crossed his mind was her calm-

ing presence. For as long as he could remember, he'd be
lucky if he slept for more than two hours at a time. Last
night he had slept five hours straight without any of the
restlessness that usually plagued him.

Damian glanced over his shoulder at the clock. He still
had a couple of hours before meeting his friends. He eased
out of her embrace, slid off the bed and headed for the
bathroom. She stirred for a moment and then turned over
and settled down. While in the bathroom, he found a new
toothbrush and toothpaste in a gift basket on the counter. After finishing, he returned to find Karen awake and
propped on her elbow. She had pulled the sheet up, covering her amazing body.

"Good morning," he said with a smile. "Did you sleep
well?"

"Good morning. I did. How about you?"

"It was the best sleep I've had in a long time."

She stared at him curiously, then asked, "Are you done
in the bathroom?"

He nodded. His eyes were riveted to her lush curves as
she passed him, and his body reacted in kind. He was sitting up in bed with the sheet draped across his lower body
when she returned.

Flipping the cover back, he patted the space next to
him. "Come join me." She scooted next to him, and he
wrapped his arms around her. Damian tilted her chin and
kissed her. "Now, that's a good-morning kiss."

"Mmm, I agree."

"Are you going to be busy tonight with your friends?"

"We didn't really make any concrete plans. Why?"

"I want to have dinner with you," he said while nibbling on the shell of her ear. "We only have a couple of
days left on the cruise, and I want to spend as much time
with you as I can."

"In that case, okay."

"Seven good for you?"

"Absolutely."

Damian lowered his head and kissed her again. He had only meant it to be gentle—a kiss sealing the date—but the moment he touched her lips, he was lost. He tumbled her backward on the bed and deepened the kiss while his hands roamed possessively over her body.

"Don't you need to meet your friends?" Karen murmured against his lips.

"Mmm-hmm. I have plenty of time for them. Right now I just want to concentrate on you and this beautiful body of yours."

He reached for the last condom on the nightstand, quickly sheathed himself and slid into her sweet warmth. He wanted to take his time, but the way her muscles tightened around him and the sound of her calling his name in that sexy voice were his undoing. Afterward, they both collapsed against the pillows trying to catch their breath.

"That was…" she started.

"Yeah, I know. Beyond incredible," he finished as he laced their fingers together. Everything about this woman turned him on, and he wouldn't mind staying this way for the rest of the day. He wondered what Troy and Kyle would do if he backed out of their excursion.

"What are you thinking about?"

He laughed softly. "I was trying to come up with an excuse to back out on my friends."

"I don't think that's a good idea."

He rolled his head in her direction. "Tired of my company already?"

"Not at all. I was thinking you just got out of the doghouse for being a bad friend. It would be a shame for you to be back in so soon."

Damian stared at her in disbelief, then laughed heartily. Soon they were both laughing hard. "Wow. I don't know if

I should be offended or not. I've never been with a woman who *wanted* me to go out with the guys."

Still chuckling, she said, "Don't be. I just happen to think good friends are hard to come by, and it's important to spend time with them when you can."

He quieted, thinking about her words. "Yeah. I agree. So do you plan to go ashore?"

"Yes. Janae and Terrence are making an appearance, and we're all going to lunch. Beyond that, I have no idea what we're doing."

He sat up and swung his legs over the side of the bed. "I guess I should probably get moving." He stood, retrieved his clothes and dressed quickly. He would shower once he got back to his room. But first he glanced back at Karen spread out on the bed looking sexy as hell—wild hair, kiss-swollen lips—with the sheet barely covering her body. She made an alluring picture. It was all he could do not to climb back into that bed.

She obviously interpreted his thoughts because she said, "Stop looking at me like that and go meet your friends."

Busted, he dropped his head. He leaned down and kissed her. "I'll see you tonight, sweetheart."

She gave him a tiny wave and smiled. "Bye. Have fun."

He stood there a minute longer, willing his feet to move. Finally, he forced himself to leave. Giving her one last look, he reluctantly opened the door and left with every detail about her imprinted on his brain.

Damian strolled down the corridor toward the elevator. He smiled. Yeah, he would enjoy the day with his friends, but his night—that would belong to Karen.

Chapter 7

"I wasn't sure you'd show up," Troy said when Damian set his plate on the table and lowered himself into the chair across from Troy.

"Believe me, I thought about canceling," Damian muttered, spreading strawberry jam on his biscuit. In his mind, he replayed last night and this morning. His groin throbbed in remembrance of Karen riding him. Kyle's laughter broke into his thoughts.

"You're daydreaming, bro. It must have been a helluva night."

"It was." They ate in silence for a few minutes.

"You're really feeling Karen?" Troy asked, forking up some scrambled eggs on his plate.

"I like her."

Troy raised an eyebrow. "You like her? That's it? As much time as you're spending with her, that's all you're gonna say?"

Damian shrugged. "It's only been a couple of days, so yeah, that's all I'm saying." He wasn't ready to share his feelings because he didn't quite understand them himself. They stared at him. "What?"

Kyle drained his glass of orange juice and shook his head. "You must really like her if you were thinking about canceling." He cocked his head to the side. "Out of curiosity, what made you decide not to cancel?"

"Karen. She said good friends are hard to come by and that I should take advantage of the time."

"Sounds like a wise woman." They finished breakfast, and Kyle checked his watch. "We should get going."

They all rose from the table and grabbed their backpacks. "You're still not telling me what we're doing?" Damian asked.

"We're gonna have some fun. That's all you need to know." Troy clapped him on the shoulder. "It'll be like old times when we used to go hiking or motorcycle riding."

Ten minutes later, the three men headed into town. They stopped to do a short tour of the Atlantis Resort and ended up engaging in a car race on the Raceway, which Kyle won and couldn't stop bragging about.

"It was only one race, and you *barely* won," Damian said.

"The fact remains, I won. I knew that tactical driving course would come in handy someday." Kyle was a former police detective.

"That wasn't tactical driving. That was cheating. If you hadn't cut me off, I would've won."

Kyle laughed. "Like I said, *tactical* driving."

"Whatever," Damian muttered. "What else are we doing?"

"We're taking a short hop over to one of the private islands to do some snorkeling," Troy answered.

They were shuttled to the dock area, where Troy had chartered a boat. The ride lasted less than an hour, and Damian could only stare at the island's lush beauty—endless blue sky, powder-white sand and warm turquoise water. "This is amazing. How did you guys find out about this place?"

"My old buddy from the force, Joshua, told us about it," Kyle answered. "He came with us four years ago. Troy and I come back every time we cruise this way." He gestured around. "See all this beauty you've been missing?"

He surveyed the area again. "Yeah." Four years ago would have been the first time they invited him to join them on the cruise. Back then nothing could pull him out of the deep funk he'd been in. The only thing he had wanted was to make it through the day.

Troy seemed to sense what was going though his head. "You're here now, so let's have some fun."

They headed over to one of the three buildings on the beach, where they were outfitted with snorkeling equipment. For the next two hours, they explored the depths of crystal-clear waters and saw a variety of plant and animal life. Once they finished, the three men returned the equipment, showered and ate lunch at the small beachfront grill. There were about a dozen people inside, so it didn't take long to get their food. Damian took his friends' suggestion and ordered the steamed fish, baked macaroni and cheese, and potato salad. Troy ordered a side of johnnycake— a slightly sweet-flavored bread. Lifting their glasses of planter's punch, they toasted to friendship and dug in.

"Oh," Damian said, "this is good."

"Told you," Troy said around a mouthful of macaroni and cheese. "This mac and cheese is better than my mama's." He glanced up and pointed his fork at Damian and Kyle. "And if either one of you two clowns mentions that to her, I'll kick your asses."

Damian grinned. "Man, I'm three inches taller, outweigh you by a good thirty pounds and, unlike you, work out regularly. It'll be no contest."

"Hell, I'll just shoot you," Kyle tossed out with a shrug.

They looked at each other and laughed. The trash-talking continued throughout the meal, and Damian realized how much he had missed hanging out with his friends. He downed the last of his drink, wiped his mouth and

tossed the napkin on his empty plate. Leaning back in
the chair, he groaned. "I haven't eaten like this in ages."

"Me, either," Kyle said. "Let's snag one of those loungers
or a hammock and let this food digest."

The men dragged themselves over beneath large palm
trees. Troy collapsed onto a lounger, while Damian and
Kyle chose hammocks. The temperatures hovered near
eighty, and the peaceful surroundings immediately relaxed Damian. His mind automatically shifted to Karen.
He wondered whether she was still on the island or back
on the ship. He continued to be in awe of their chemistry
in and out of bed. He would love to have her next to him
cuddled in the hammock. His eyes slid closed, and with a
smile on his face, he drifted off.

Troy's voice startled him and interrupted an incredible
dream he was having about Karen.

"Damian. Wake up."

His eyes popped open, and he ran a hand over his face.
"What time is it?"

"Five."

He sat up so quickly he almost tumbled out of the hammock. Coming to his feet, he glared at Troy and Kyle.
"What?" His heart started to pound in alarm. "The ship
is supposed to leave at five."

Kyle climbed out of the hammock near him, yawned and
stretched. "We know. We're staying overnight and catching up with the ship tomorrow in Key West."

Damian cursed. "Why didn't you tell me that?" he roared.

"Man, calm down. We just wanted you to experience a
little Caribbean nightlife before we head back," Kyle said.

Troy frowned. "We didn't think it would be a big deal."

"Well, it is a big deal," Damian said through clenched
teeth. "I told Karen we'd have dinner tonight." He paced
back and forth, imagining what kinds of thoughts would
run through her mind when he didn't show up at her door

as promised. He stopped pacing, dropped down in a nearby lounger and cradled his head in his palms. All his plans... gone.

"Sorry, man. We didn't know," Troy said softly, regret coloring his words.

Damian met Troy's gaze and heaved a deep sigh. "I know."

"I'll be happy to talk to Karen when we get back tomorrow and tell her it was our fault," Kyle added.

A member of the crew came over to let them know it was time to leave. Collecting their belongings, they followed the man back to the boat, boarded and made the short trip in silence. Then they hailed a taxi to transport them to the hotel where they would spend the night. The lavish hotel had every amenity imaginable, along with activities for the single crowd unmatched by any other hotel. However, the only thing on Damian's mind was Karen and how he would convince her to continue what they had started beyond the cruise.

Karen slept for another hour after Damian left, then got up and took a long soak in the Jacuzzi. Her muscles were a little sore from the intense workout they'd had. She leaned her head against the towel she'd rolled up and relaxed under the powerful jets.

A smile played around the corners of her mouth. The man knew his way around a woman's body, and she was glad to be on the receiving end. She remembered him saying it had been a while since he was intimate with a woman and briefly wondered why. Had he gotten his heart broken, too? Although they were only enjoying each other's company for the duration of the cruise, she wouldn't mind keeping in touch with him. They seemed to have several things in common, and most important, he hadn't ridiculed her career choice. Karen didn't know whether he was on the same page, but she thought she might casually bring it up over dinner this evening.

She completed her bath, dressed and went to meet her friends. Only Donovan and Terrence's two other friends, Audrey and Brad, had arrived at the designated meeting spot.

"What's up, Karen?" Donovan said, leaning down to kiss her cheek.

"Hey, Donovan."

"Terrence and Janae are going to be a few minutes late."

"Surprise, surprise," she said with a laugh. She spoke to Audrey and Brad. "Are you guys enjoying the cruise?"

"Most definitely." Audrey stared at her husband, her blue eyes shining with love. Brad brushed his hand across her cheek and placed a tender kiss on her lips.

"All right, you two, knock it off," Donovan muttered. "You're as bad as Terrence and Janae."

Karen laughed, but inside she wished a man looked at her with the love Brad had for Audrey. The look in Damian's eyes when he wiped her tears at last night's show surfaced in her mind. For a split second, she felt something, thought she saw something other than their obvious physical attraction. *Probably just my imagination and wishful thinking.* Devin's voice broke into her thoughts.

"Morning, everybody." There was another round of greetings. "I guess we're waiting for the newlyweds, *again*?"

"Yep," she said. The group chatted amiably for several minutes before Karen spotted Janae and Terrence approaching. "It's about time."

"Sorry. We sort of lost track of time," Terrence said with a sheepish grin.

Karen met Janae's smiling face and nodded knowingly. "Uh-huh."

"Now that Mr. and Mrs. Campbell have graced us with their presence, let's get this party started," Donovan said.

Karen took pictures as they walked through the Welcome Center to downtown Nassau. "The kids are going to love these photos." They entered a small shop.

"Girl, I know. Are you getting any souvenirs?" Janae asked.

She nodded. "I picked up something for them in Jamaica."

"You bought something for all thirty-four students?"

"I did. I have such a good class this year. They've been working hard, and their test scores show it. So I decided to reward them."

"And *that's* why you're the favorite teacher at the school…and why Nikki is always trying to one-up you."

"Please don't remind me about that woman." Nikki Fleming taught another fourth-grade class, and for the past two years had tried to undermine Karen at every turn. If Karen suggested a strategy to improve test scores or ways to engage the students, Nikki made it her business to come up with a reason why it couldn't work. "I don't know what her problem is. She's gotten even worse this year, if that's possible."

"Maybe she'll get an offer to teach in another state," Janae said wryly.

"I should be so lucky. I'd settle for one in another district," she said, following the group out of the crowded shop and into another one.

In the fourth shop, she found a cute wrap skirt and a T-shirt. She conversed with Janae and Audrey, but her mind kept straying to Damian and secretly hoping she would run into him while on the island. They had lunch in a restaurant recommended by Donovan and Terrence that served local specialties. Karen ate conch fritters, cracked lobster, potato salad and plantains, and washed it all down with a mango daiquiri.

"I'm so full. I think I need a nap now," she said with a groan.

Audrey laughed. "I hear you." She pointed to the guys, who were still stuffing their faces. "I don't know how they eat all this food."

"If I ate like that for just one day, I'd gain ten pounds," Janae said.

"Amen, sister." Karen and Janae raised their hands for a high five, and all three women fell out laughing.

"It's a good thing there are only two more nights on this cruise. Otherwise I might be needing a new wardrobe," Audrey said. "Hmm…"

"You ain't said nothing but a word, Audrey. All I need is an excuse. This one here," she added, eyeing Janae, "is no fun when it comes to shopping."

Janae rolled her eyes. "Please. That's because you get out of control whenever we go shopping. Five hours in a mall is just plain crazy."

"Five hours of nothing but shopping is like pure heaven," Audrey said, sighing wistfully. "Karen, let me know the next time you come to LA. Girl, I know all the great shopping spots—sales like you wouldn't believe."

Karen rubbed her hands together with glee. "Count me in."

"I'll pass," Janae said.

"Oh, come on, Janae," Karen pleaded. "It'll be so much fun."

"I don't think so."

"Tell you what. Karen, you and I can swing by and pick her up halfway through the day. We'll even feed her first."

"Audrey, two hours of shopping is my limit." Janae held up two fingers. *"Two."*

"Yes!" Karen tapped her chin thoughtfully. "I need to check my calendar to see which weekend I can fly down."

Once the guys finished eating, everyone headed over to

the beach. Audrey and Brad excused themselves and left to take a walk. A group of fans recognized Terrence, and he stopped to sign autographs with Donovan and Devin playing bodyguard.

Janae pulled Karen off to the side. "So how are things going with Damian?"

"Fine, I guess." Karen didn't know how to describe her feelings toward Damian. This was supposed to be nothing more than enjoying the company of a nice guy while on the cruise. Instead her feelings had taken on a life of their own.

"What does that mean?"

"I don't know. He's a really nice guy, and I like him."

"That's a good thing."

"I didn't count on liking him this much. He's an absolute gentleman, a great conversationalist, and makes me lose my mind with his kisses."

Janae raised an eyebrow. "That good, huh?"

"Girl, yes. He is beyond amazing. Said it had been a while since he'd been with a woman, but if that's his definition of being out of practice..."

"Sounds like you two hit it off pretty well. Might be something worth exploring."

Karen frowned. "I don't think so. I don't even know where the man lives."

"You do realize this is the twenty-first century. There's email, texting, Skype—"

"Ha-ha, Ms. Smarty-Pants. I know that." She shrugged. "But it's not something we've talked about. For all I know, he may not want anything past this week."

"Well, you never know unless you ask."

"True." Admittedly, Karen would like to see where things could go between them, but she didn't want to set herself up for disappointment.

They hung out at the beach for a while longer and then

headed back to the ship to give Terrence time to prepare for his Q & A session.

Later, after the session, Karen stood in line with the others to purchase and get her CD signed. Donovan told her she didn't have to wait, but she didn't feel right about cutting the line. To her surprise, Terrence told her the CD was on the house.

He handed her a CD, stood to take a picture with her and whispered, "I already signed this special one for you. I'll always be grateful to you for bringing Janae to the concert. I can't imagine my life without her. If you ever need anything, let me know."

She hugged him. "Aw, you're so sweet. Tell you what, if I get lucky enough to meet a special guy, you sing at my wedding and we'll call it even."

"Deal." He grinned. "I saw the guy you were with. Should I be getting a song ready?"

Karen laughed. "You might want to hold off on that. Like I told your wife, I have no idea where the man lives."

"Janae and I started as a long-distance relationship," he pointed out.

She ignored his comment. "You have a long line of people waiting."

He chuckled. "Okay. I can take a hint. See you later. We're celebrating tomorrow night. Janae will fill you in."

"All right."

Karen went back to her room and took a short nap. Eating all that good food and being in the sun had drained her. When she woke up, she still had a couple of hours before dinner with Damian. Picking up her novel off the nightstand, she slid the balcony door open and stepped outside. She stared out over the water as the boat moved farther away from Nassau.

They had one last stop in Key West tomorrow before reaching Miami the following day. The week seemed to

have flown by and went much better than she had anticipated. Nowhere in her wildest dreams did she ever think
she'd meet a man like Damian. Would he want to continue
what they had started or relegate her to his past? Sure, they
had several things in common and got along great in and
out of bed, but would that be enough?

She released a heavy sigh. Everything was going great
until things moved past the physical to the emotional.
And this is why I shouldn't let my feelings get involved.
Karen lowered herself into one of the cushioned chairs and
opened the book. She tried concentrating on the words, but
her mind kept wandering to dinner with Damian. After
sitting there for nearly an hour, she closed the book, got to
her feet and went inside to shower. She dressed, styled her
hair and applied light makeup. The closer it got to seven,
the more nervous she became.

When seven o'clock came and went, her nervousness
turned to concern. The phone rang and she snatched it up,
hoping it was Damian.

"Hey, girl," Janae said when Karen answered.

"Hey."

"I wanted to let you know that some of Terrence's mu-
sician friends are throwing us a party tomorrow night. It's
going to be in the Sapphire Room again at eight. You're
welcome to bring Damian. Are you guys getting together
tonight?"

"We were supposed to go to dinner, but I haven't heard
from him."

"What time was dinner?"

"Half an hour ago."

"Maybe he lost track of time with his friends. I'm sure
he'll be there."

"Maybe." But she wasn't convinced.

"Well, I'll let you go in case he's trying to call. I'll see
you tomorrow."

"All right." Karen placed the phone in the cradle.

As the minutes and hours ticked off, she realized Damian wasn't coming. She never thought he'd be the type of man to do something like this, but she was wrong. Again. She changed into her pajamas and crawled into bed, vowing not to let her guard down ever again.

Chapter 8

Damian could hear the music and laughter floating through the open French doors leading to his balcony. Kyle and Troy had tried to get him to join them, but he couldn't be bothered. What he wanted was to be with Karen. He rose from the chair he had been sitting in for the past hour and stepped out onto the balcony. Folding his arms across his chest, he tilted his head back and closed his eyes. He had only come on the cruise to get his friends off his back. He never intended to meet a woman, much less form an instant connection with one—a connection that he seemed to have no control over. Did she feel it, as well?

Tonight he had planned to fill in all the gaps, starting with her last name and where she lived. He shook his head, not believing he hadn't even asked her last name. Damian didn't care where she lived, as long as she agreed to keep seeing him. He wanted to tell her that he shared her passion for teaching and the joy of seeing new minds come alive. He still would…if he got the chance. Would she accept his apology? Even if she did, it was no guarantee she'd want to continue what they had started. A knock on the door interrupted his thoughts. He went back inside, crossed the spacious suite and opened the door to find Troy and Kyle standing there. Damian stepped back and waved them in.

"What are you guys doing here? I thought you'd be well into the night action by now."

"Yeah. Me, too," Kyle said. "But it's hard to have a good

time knowing you're up here miserable." He dropped down on a sofa, stretched out and flung an arm across his face.

Troy took a seat in a chair, and Damian sat across from him in a matching one. "I feel bad about making you miss your dinner with Karen. To make it up to you, I chartered a seaplane for tomorrow."

"I'll pitch in for the cost," Damian said.

Troy waved him off. "Nah, man. Don't worry about it since it was our fault. We should've asked you if you had plans, knowing how much time you two have been spending together."

"Is this thing serious between you two?" Kyle asked.

"I can't say it's serious, but I feel something for her I've never felt with any other woman."

Kyle brought his arm down and rolled his head in Damian's direction. "Even Joyce?"

Damian hesitated before answering quietly, "Yes." He'd asked himself the question and knew the answer, but saying the word out loud made him feel as though he was betraying Joyce.

Troy regarded him for a moment. "We figured as much."

"What does that mean?"

"Damian, we never thought…"

"Thought what?" Damian asked when Troy trailed off.

"We always wondered whether Joyce was the right woman for you. And after seeing you with Karen—"

Damian jumped up from the chair. "What the hell does that mean?"

"It means," Kyle started, coming to a sitting position, "that you and Joyce seemed more like best friends than lovers."

"Are you saying I didn't love my *wife*?" Damian exploded.

Kyle blew out a harsh breath. "Calm down, man. No,

that's not what I'm saying. Can you sit down, please? I'm getting a crick in my neck."

He plopped his six-foot-four-inch frame in the chair, crossed his arms and glared at Kyle.

"I know you loved Joyce, but were you *in* love with her—that deep, passionate kind of love that makes you lose your mind?"

Damian didn't answer. He and Joyce had shared a close friendship and trusted each other. And there were other reasons that factored into their marriage—reasons he'd never shared with anyone. No, they didn't have a passionate love, but he did love her.

"It's the kind of love that when you look at her, your only thought is how much you want to be with her."

"Sort of like the way you look at Karen," Troy said.

Damian frowned. "What, you're a mind reader now?"

"We've known each other for over twenty years. I'm sure you'd be able to see the same thing in Kyle or me. Look, Damian, Joyce was a sweet girl, and we all loved her, but it seemed as if you stopped living once you two married."

"We didn't expect you to hang out with us like you had before, but you never accepted the invitations even when Joyce was invited," Kyle added. "We don't want to see the same thing happen again."

He had never stopped to think about how cut off they'd been from life. His wife hadn't been much of a people person, and he hadn't wanted her to be uncomfortable, so he started declining invitations from his friends and family until, gradually, the invitations stopped. Damian remembered his own mother mentioning something similar a time or two.

"And you think that if I'm with Karen, I'll do the same thing again." He divided his gaze between the two men. Neither answered, but their expressions told all, and he felt his anger rising. "First of all, you're acting like I'm planning to get married right now, which I'm not. Second, Karen and Joyce are two different women."

"Look, we're not trying to upset you," Troy said. "But we're brothers. And when one of us is hurting, it affects us all. We've been worried about you, man. This week is the first time in a long while that you've been relaxed and almost happy like you used to be. I can't even imagine how hard it was to lose Joyce. But I just don't want you to go back to being the same way after this week is over."

Damian sat quietly as he digested Troy's words. Yeah, it had been hard, but honestly over the past few months, he'd begun to feel restless, as though he was ready to move on. He'd even gone on dates, but hadn't found a woman who stirred his interest. Until now.

"You used to be the one we could always count on for a good laugh." Kyle chuckled, as if remembering.

"You guys have always had my back. Though I may not have said it lately, I do appreciate it." Damian shook his head. "Not sure how much I appreciate all this advice, though," he said wryly.

"Hey, that's what friends and *brothers* do," Kyle said pointedly.

Damian nodded. "I realized this week that I miss having fun," he confessed. "I can't go back to being alone all the time."

"What if things don't work out with Karen?"

Once again, the thought of not being able to give their relationship a chance didn't sit well with him. "Even if they don't, I'm going to try to get out more."

"My boy is back!"

"Shut up, Kyle." But Damian was grinning as he said it. The three friends spent the evening catching up and reminiscing about old times. Damian enjoyed himself but anxiously awaited morning so he could get back to the ship…and Karen.

As soon as he'd boarded the ship the next day, Damian went to Karen's room but got no answer. He spent more than an hour searching the deck and various places for her, before concluding that she might have gone ashore. His friends agreed and convinced Damian to have lunch and wait for the ship to leave before resuming his search. When the ship pulled out of the dock, Damian strode urgently down the hallway toward her room, hoping to catch her before dinner. He stopped at her door and knocked. When she didn't answer, he knocked again.

"Karen? It's Damian."

He needed to find her and explain. Damian knew she was probably upset with him and wondered if she was in the room and refusing to answer. No. She wasn't that kind of person. An elderly couple stopped at the room across from hers, and the man eyed Damian warily. Moving away from the door, Damian trudged back the way he had come and took the elevator to the main dining restaurant and started his search again.

There had to be more than a thousand people on this cruise. Everyone seemed to be out milling around and enjoying their last night, which made looking for Karen more difficult. He ended up back on the deck staring out over the water, thinking about what would happen when he found Karen. In a perfect world, they'd exchange personal information and then… Realistically, life never went according to plan, and he had to wrap his mind around the possibility that she'd say no. However, the chemistry between them remained strong, and he'd use that as his starting point. But he had to find her first.

It was nearly midnight when Damian decided to try

knocking on Karen's door again. At the last moment, he scribbled a note, leaving his number and asking her to wait for him in the morning before disembarking, just in case she hadn't returned. He took the elevator to her deck and moved quickly down the corridor.

He stopped at her door and took a deep breath. Raising his hand, he knocked softly. No answer. He knocked harder and called out to her.

"It's a little late to be going around knocking on folks' doors, don't you think, son?"

Damian spun around to find the elderly gentleman he'd seen earlier that evening—the last time Damian came to the door—standing in his doorway wearing a pair of striped flannel pajamas.

"Either the young lady isn't in, or she's sending you a message."

Damian lowered his head in embarrassment. "I apologize for disturbing you, sir."

The man regarded him silently and nodded. He smiled knowingly and said, "I hope things turn out for you."

"So do I," he said. "Again, my apologies."

The man nodded once more and closed his door softly.

Damian pulled the note out of his pocket, slid it under the door, then made his way back to his room to pack. He tossed and turned for hours, finally drifting off near dawn. It seemed as if he had just closed his eyes when a loud bang next door startled him. He groaned and glanced over at the clock. *Eight.* He cursed under his breath and jumped off the bed. Snatching back the curtains, he saw buildings and realized they were pulling into port.

He quickly showered and dressed. Praying she hadn't left, he hurried to Karen's room. His anxiety mounted as two elevators passed because they were full. When he finally got to her room, Damian's heart nearly stopped. The door stood open, and the housekeeper's cart blocked the entry. *I'm too late.* He peeked in the room, knowing she was gone, but wanting to be wrong.

Sighing heavily, he trudged to his room. Kyle and Troy stepped out into the hall as he reached the door. Before they could ask, Damian shook his head, opened the door and grabbed his bags.

"Let's go." He walked off.

They disembarked and took a shuttle to the airport. After they arrived and went through security, Damian dropped into a chair to wait. Thankfully they had a morning flight, as he had no desire to sit around for hours. When the time came, he boarded the plane, settled into the seat and closed his eyes.

Had Karen gotten the note? Or was she—as the gentleman last night put it—sending him a message? The whys and what-ifs continued to attack him, and as the plane lifted off, he was left with wondering, once again, what could have been.

Chapter 9

Karen received a warm welcome back when she walked through the school office early Monday morning and her students greeted her with squeals, laughter and hugs. It was just the lift she needed after spending another restless night thinking about Damian. Last night, when she reached into the tote bag and took out the two books, the photo of her and Damian from Dunn's River Falls slipped out. She had lingered over every detail of his face and body—wet, sun-browned, smooth skin with those swim trunks plastered against him, hazel eyes and that killer smile.

Why couldn't she have stuck to her promise to stay away from men? They only brought on heartaches and headaches. Karen couldn't bring herself to throw the picture out and, after much inner debate, had placed it in the nightstand drawer. As much as she wanted to think of Damian as a fling, she knew, in those few short days, he had become more. But she'd never see him again and prayed his memory would fade soon.

Bringing herself back to the present, she hugged as many students as she could. "Okay. Let's line up." The students quickly got in line, and she led them to the classroom.

Karen took care of attendance and lunch count, then went over the daily schedule.

"Ms. Morris?" a student called. "Did you take any pictures?"

"Yes. As soon as everyone is quiet, I'll show you a few,

and then we'll have journal writing." She had downloaded some of the pictures onto a flash drive. Once the students settled, she turned the lights off and projected the pictures she'd taken onto the screen. They oohed and aahed as each picture filled the screen. Afterward, she turned the lights back on. "All right. Today in your journals I want you to tell me about your favorite vacation. Remember to do your best writing—letters on the line, spaces between words and correct capitalization and punctuation."

The day went by in a blur. She waited until the students were ready to leave before handing out the souvenirs. By the time the last student left, Karen was exhausted but glad to be back doing what she loved. She was putting the last of the books on a shelf when she heard a voice behind her.

"Hey, Karen."

"Hey, Melissa." Melissa Tucker was the school psychologist. Karen often helped her lead the conflict management group.

"Girl, I've been waiting all day to talk to you. I want to hear about that cruise." She took a seat on the edge of a desk.

Karen told her all about the wedding, Jamaica and the Bahamas.

"That sounds heavenly. So, did you meet any hot guys while you were there?" she asked slyly.

"I was there to see my best friend get married and relax, not meet guys." Karen walked over, sat at her desk and shut down her computer. The last thing she wanted was a reminder of the *hot guy* she had met.

Melissa came and stood in front of the desk, scrutinizing Karen with an intensity that almost made her squirm in the chair. She braced both hands on the desk. "Oh, my goodness! You met somebody, didn't you?"

"I just told you—"

"Please. It's written all over your face. Now spill it."

Karen sighed heavily. "His name is—well, *was* Damian."

"Ooh, does he look as fine as that name suggests?" Melissa asked with a grin.

"Finer," she admitted. She told Melissa how she'd met Damian, about the time they spent in Jamaica and their subsequent night together.

"Sounds like you had a great time with a great guy."

"Yeah, that's what I thought, too…until he stood me up and went MIA." She shrugged. "Anyway, it's no big deal. I'll probably never see him again, and we had fun while it lasted. He was just someone to pass the time with on the cruise, that's all."

"Well, at least you weren't bored," Melissa said with a laugh.

Karen's mind traveled back to dancing in the club, climbing the falls and snuggling in Damian's arms. "No, not at all." She waved a hand. "Enough of that. What's going on?"

"I know you heard about Priscilla. It's such a shame about her husband." Priscilla Mitchell, the school principal, had been absent the two days before Karen left for Janae's wedding, and suddenly retired the following week after her husband's involvement in a head-on collision. He would need full-time care for the foreseeable future.

"I heard, and it is. I'm going to miss her. She took me under her wing when I first came here." Karen had a special place in her heart for the woman who had mentored her when Karen started teaching eight years ago. They had developed a natural rapport, and the woman became a surrogate mother to Karen.

Melissa angled her head thoughtfully and wagged a finger at Karen. "You should think about applying for the position. They're going to fill it pretty quickly, I'm sure.

Until then, we're sharing a vice principal from one of the middle schools."

"What? I don't know," Karen said skeptically.

"Why not? You have your master's, and your concentration is in administration. You also have your counseling certificate. I think you'd be great."

"Hmm. Maybe." She had been thinking about going the administrative route. This might be the opportunity she was looking for. She unlocked a drawer, pulled out her purse, slung it over her shoulder and stood. "I'll think about it. Right now I'm going home. It's been a long day."

"I hear you. I'll be right behind you. Oh, I almost forgot, you and I will be going to a safety training next month."

"Is this something new?" Karen asked as they walked toward the front office.

"It's a two-day train-the-trainer type of thing. With all the shootings and mess going on in the schools, Priscilla wanted to make sure we have the best emergency preparedness program available. Plus, a lot of our stuff is really outdated. She heard about the company from her sister, who lives in Georgia. So she asked the superintendent about it, and he approved it. There'll be two people from each school in the district to serve as first responders or points of contact." She leaned closer and lowered her voice to a whisper. "Nikki was *not* happy when she wasn't chosen. She was even more pissed when Priscilla chose you, especially since you were on the cruise."

Karen shook her head. "I don't know why that woman has it in for me. I've never done anything to her."

"Except be a great teacher," Melissa said.

Karen rolled her eyes. "Isn't that supposed to be the goal of all teachers?"

"One would think so."

Not wanting to discuss Nikki Fleming further, Karen

returned to their previous conversation. "When is the training again?"

"Monday and Tuesday of the week before Thanksgiving. But they'll be coming back to spend about a week here doing assemblies for the kids and parents, checking out our current plan and helping to revamp it if necessary. You and I will work with them."

"What about my class?"

"From what I understand, most of the meetings will be before or after school."

"Great. There goes my free time."

"Hey, if we're lucky, at least one of the trainers from DKT Safety Consultants will be fine and sexy, as opposed to old and wrinkled and smelling like Bengay." Melissa wrinkled her nose.

Karen laughed. "Only you, Melissa. Only you." In her mind, old was safer. She didn't need fine and sexy.

"What? I need some male stimulation in my life. It's been too long. And you never know, one of them might help you get over your cruise-ship fling."

She grunted. "No, thanks. I'll pass." Besides, it would take *some* man to help her get over Damian.

Damian sat in his office staring out the window. He had been back to work a week, and memories of Karen plagued him day and night. No matter who he was talking to or what he was doing, visions of her danced around the edges of his mind. At night when he closed his eyes, he could see her face and hear her laughter. And sometimes he'd swear he could smell her intoxicating fragrance. He tried working out at the gym—pushing himself far beyond his limits—thinking if he were tired enough, he'd be able to sleep. Damian's old sleeping patterns had returned, and he found himself up prowling half the night.

Several times over the week he asked himself why he

hadn't camped out at her door instead of leaving a note. But he knew the answer. He didn't want to risk her rejection. More than once, he wondered whether they kept missing each other or if she had chosen not to answer her door, as well as not to respond to his note. What if she hadn't felt the connection as deeply as he had, or worse, she'd moved on? Somehow, in those few short days, Karen had made an impact on him. On his heart. And he had no idea how to deal with that, especially since there was the possibility that he would never see her again. Again he asked himself, why her? Why now? And would their paths ever cross again? Damian rotated his chair toward the door upon hearing a knock.

"What's up, Kyle?"

Kyle handed him a sheet of paper. "Here's the schedule for November and December. There's going to be a little more back-and-forth because of the holidays."

Damian accepted and scanned the sheet. "California?"

Kyle smiled. "Yep. West Coast. We're branching out. The first week and a half we'll be in LA and San Diego—just a couple of schools and a company wanting emergency preparedness training."

Damian glanced back at the sheet. "Looks like we're going to be spending more time in the Bay Area." There were schools in Oakland, San Francisco and San Jose. Some wanted one- or two-day train-the-trainer workshops, and others wanted that in addition to a full-scale school site overhaul. "We start there before Thanksgiving and go back in December," he murmured.

"I haven't been to Cali in a while. We'll have to schedule some fun time."

"I'm all for a change of scenery." Damian was tired of looking at the same walls every day. Although they wouldn't leave for another three weeks, maybe the trip would help him forget Karen.

"How've you been since we've been back? Are you still thinking about Karen?"

"Yeah, man. I can't get her off my mind. I don't know… there's just something about her."

"What's her last name?"

"I have no idea."

Kyle gave a shout of laughter. "What do you mean you don't know? You spent what…two, three days together, and you don't know her last name?"

"I know it sounds crazy, but we seemed to talk about everything except ourselves. I don't even know where she's from or where she lives." He gave Kyle a sidelong glance. "You used to be a detective. Can't you use some of that legendary expertise I keep hearing about to help me out?"

Kyle leaned against the door frame and folded his arms across his chest. "A detective…yes. God…no. Last time I checked, He was the only one who's all-knowing. Now, if you had a last name, and possibly the state, I may have been able to help you out." He chuckled. "Man, how could you not get the woman's last name? That's like Dating 101."

"At first, it didn't matter—you know, dinner and nice conversation." He hadn't planned on anything past the first night, didn't count on the explosive chemistry between them or the passion she ignited in him.

"Obviously, you didn't count on falling for Karen," Kyle said, reading Damian's mind.

"No. I didn't."

"Maybe this was a sign that you're ready for love again." He pushed off the wall. "See you later."

"Later."

Damian stayed way past closing. He made it home in record time, parked in the garage and entered the house, not bothering to turn on the lights. He knew every square inch with his eyes closed. His footsteps echoed loudly on the wooden floors in the otherwise silent space. In his upstairs bedroom, Damian shrugged out of his jacket and tossed it on a chair. He dropped down heavily on the side of the bed and removed his shoes.

His gaze strayed to the nightstand, where he had placed the photo of him and Karen taken in front of the falls. They looked good together. He picked it up, and his body automatically reacted as he remembered the heated kisses they'd shared while they climbed, opening a floodgate of memories. This time, instead of fighting them, he let them come—the texture of her velvety smooth skin beneath his hands, the sweetness of her kiss as their tongues danced and the scorching passion they shared that left him wanting more.

But it wasn't only about the physical connection. She stimulated him intellectually and enjoyed some of the same things he did. He studied the picture. He thought keeping busy would help him forget her, but Karen wasn't the type of woman a man could easily forget. Truth be told, he didn't want to. Although he had no idea how he would accomplish it, Damian hoped to find her again.

The next three weeks seemed to crawl by, and Damian was more than ready for the trip when the day came. As he packed, the phone rang and he activated the speaker on the cordless phone.

"Do you have me on that speaker, Damian?" his mother asked when he answered.

He sighed. "Yes, Mom. I have to pack, and it's easier than me trying to hold the phone."

"I hate that thing," she muttered.

He stifled a groan. He loved his mother, but he didn't have time for this today. He needed to be at the airport in two hours. "I know, Mom. What's going on?"

"Nothing. You've been back from that cruise over three

weeks. I thought you would've called me by now to tell me about it. Well?"

"Well, what?" he asked as he stuffed socks and underwear in the suitcase.

"Did you enjoy yourself?" she asked with an impatient sigh.

Loaded question. "It was fine." He went to the closet, took down four suits and put them in his garment bag.

"Damian, are you still there?"

"I'm here, Mom."

"I didn't hear you."

"I said it was fine. Great music and food, beautiful islands." And one extraordinary woman.

"Sounds like fun. Did you meet any nice girls? I'm sure there were plenty available."

Before he could fix his mouth to lie, "yes" tumbled out. He slapped a hand across his forehead.

"Really?" she asked excitedly. "What's her name, and when will I get to meet her?"

Damian sat down on the bed and picked up the phone, deactivating the speaker. "Her name is Karen, and probably never."

"Oh, that's too bad. I was hoping you'd find someone. I want you to be happy. You deserve to fall in love."

"What does that mean?" When she hesitated, he said, "Mom, what are you saying?"

"I'm simply saying I want you to find someone special."

"What about Joyce? Are you saying I wasn't in love?"

"No, honey. Joyce was a wonderful girl. I loved her like a daughter, but I just want you to be happy."

"Thanks, Mom." First his friends, and now his mother.

She hesitated. "Sweetheart, I know all about that promise you made to Joyce's grandmother."

His stomach dropped. He had never told anyone about that. "If she wanted to interfere in her granddaughter's life, that was her prerogative, but I made sure Lillian knew, in explicit detail, how I felt about her interfering in my son's life. Meddling old biddy," she grumbled. "I was two seconds from stopping that wedding. You and Joyce both deserved to find that special someone, and Lillian, with her selfish and manipulative ways, messed that up."

Joyce's grandmother had been diagnosed with terminal cancer and only had a few months to live. She extracted a promise from Damian to look out for Joyce, saying she could go to her grave a happy woman knowing her granddaughter would be taken care of. He knew what the woman was asking. Initially, he had no intention of being manipulated into marriage, but her rapid decline and the sadness in Joyce's eyes pushed him over the edge. It wasn't as if he and Joyce didn't get along. They were best friends, and he loved her. "I can't believe you knew all this time and never said anything. So what made you change your mind about stopping the wedding?"

"Your father. He reminded me that you were a grown man and could make your own decisions. That we raised you to be God-fearing, respectful and honorable, and you were all of those things."

"Remind me to give Dad a big hug the next time I come to visit. Mom, I don't want you to think that I wasn't happy with Joyce. I was. I loved her."

"I know, and I'm glad. Do you think you'll ever want to try marriage again?"

"For a long time I didn't, but now…"

"Does this have anything to do with the woman you met on the cruise?"

"Yes." He told her about the days he spent with Karen, how much he enjoyed being with her and about the mishap. "She probably thinks I stood her up, and I didn't get a chance to tell her what happened."

"Well, I'm sure if you gave her a call, she'd be willing to listen."

"I don't have her number. We sort of never got around to last names and exchanging personal information. I had planned to do all that at dinner."

She laughed. "No last name and no phone number? That must have been *some* attraction."

He cleared his throat. "Um…Mom, I need to get going."

Still chuckling, she said, "Okay. Keep me posted on any potential daughters-in-law. I need some grandchildren. How long are you going to be gone?"

It was definitely time to hang up. "Close to three weeks. I'll be home for Thanksgiving, then head west again for another two or three weeks. I'll call you when I get back."

"All right. Give my love to Kyle and Troy, and you boys be safe. Love you, baby."

"Love you, too, Mom."

Three hours later, he was on his way to California.

They spent the first half of the week in San Diego conducting workshops on emergency preparedness in the workplace, and the remainder of that week and the following one in LA schools. Last night they had flown to San Jose and were now setting up in the hotel's conference room for the school training that would begin in two hours. Troy came in as Damian filled a cup with coffee from a table at the back of the room. The hotel had also provided bagels, muffins and fruit.

He took a sip of the hot brew. "Is Delores here yet?" She and Laurie, the other office assistant, alternated taking care of the administrative duties when they traveled. Laurie had done the first half.

Troy was filling his own cup. "Yeah. She stopped at the ladies' room first."

Damian powered up his laptop at the front of the room,

then lowered the projection screen. He fished his flash drive out of the bag and brought up his presentation. After hooking up the projector, he went through the slides to make sure everything was in order.

"Morning, Damian," Delores said.

"Morning, Dee. How was the flight?"

"Not bad. Kyle is picking up the handouts from the business center right now. Do you need anything before I start setting up?"

"No. Thanks." He thoroughly enjoyed his job. Keeping kids safe was a priority for him. Everyone had their roles and performed them to perfection. Troy handled the business side of things—contracts, payments and such—while he and Kyle tag-teamed with the presentation. Damian focused on bullying and communications training, while Kyle handled the security, emergency preparedness and response training.

He was finishing up his coffee when the first participants arrived. Soon the room filled with people talking in small groups and taking advantage of the continental breakfast. Damian glanced down at his watch and caught Kyle's attention. They believed in starting and ending on time. He picked up one lapel microphone and handed Kyle the other one, before clipping the mic to his suit jacket and the battery to his belt. He tested it and then, satisfied, he turned to the crowd.

"If everyone would take a seat, we can get started. We have a lot of material to cover today." He waited for them to find seats and settle in before continuing. "My name is Damian Bradshaw, and this is Kyle Jamison. We're from DKT Safety Consultants and will provide you with the information you need to keep your schools safe from the inside out." He paused. "How many of you are from high schools?" Hands went up. "Middle schools?" A few more hands were raised. "Elementary schools?" Almost half the people in the room raised their hands.

Damian pushed the button for the first slide. "Let's talk about bullying. Thirty-three percent of elementary students report being frequently bullied, and twenty percent of kindergartners. It peaks in middle school, which is often the worst period for victims of bullying." He gave more statistics and launched into a discussion of the seriousness of cyber-bullying.

He scanned the room to let his words sink in. He opened his mouth to speak, and his heart stopped and then started up again. In the middle of the room sat Karen. *His* Karen.

Damian promptly lost his train of thought, and it took everything in him to stand there, when all he wanted to do was rush back to where she sat, sweep her into his arms and kiss her the way he had been fantasizing about for the past month.

Excitement filled his heart. Their eyes connected, and she gave him an icy stare. But he didn't care. All he cared about was that he'd found her.

Chapter 10

The moment Damian opened his mouth to speak, Karen's head snapped up. She'd recognize that sexy drawl anywhere. Thankfully, she was already sitting, because the way her body trembled, she doubted she'd be able to stand. What on earth was he doing here?

Their gazes fused, and his eyes widened in surprise. The corners of his mouth inched up in a brief smile before he continued with his presentation. Not wanting him to know how much he affected her, she met his stare with a frosty one. As soon as he turned away, Karen lowered her head and breathed in deeply in an effort to slow her pounding heart. He wore a dark suit that caressed his tall frame as if it had been made expressly for him. With his height, build and that black-magic voice, he commanded the room with ease. Every woman had her eyes glued to him. She forced down the surge of jealousy that rose within her.

"Are you okay?" Melissa whispered.

No! She nodded quickly and tried to focus on the information and not the timbre of his voice. She tried not to remember how it sounded close to her ear. She glanced down to read the note Melissa slid in front of her.

Did we get lucky or what? Those brothers are fine, fine, FINE! And they'll be coming to the school after the holiday for at least a week to work CLOSELY with us. And isn't it funny that his name is Damian, too? Just like the guy on your cruise. What are the odds?

Yeah, what *were* the odds? Karen reached for the pitcher of water and poured herself a glass. Her hands shook so badly, she barely avoided a spill. Bringing the glass to her lips, she took a hasty sip. She had to see him not only these next two days, but another week after the holiday, too. She managed to get through the morning and felt a sense of relief when he announced the lunch break. Karen had hoped she and Melissa could make a quick getaway, but Melissa had other plans.

"Hold on a minute, Karen. I want to speak to somebody before we leave. I'll be right back."

She groaned inwardly. Searching the room, she spotted Damian and one of his friends she remembered from the cruise talking with a small group of people. She kept one eye on him and the other on Melissa, hoping the woman would hurry up. Her shoulders fell in disappointment when someone else snagged Melissa's attention. Karen glanced quickly to the front to make sure Damian was still there. Panic flared in her gut upon not seeing him. And then behind her, she felt him before she heard him.

"I never thought I'd see you again," he said softly.

She slowly turned to find him staring at her with a blazing desire that sent heat skittering down her spine. "It doesn't matter."

"Yes, it does."

"Why? You obviously found something else to occupy your time." She cut him off as he started to speak. "You don't need to explain. We had a great time, but it was nothing more than a physical attraction. We got caught up in our surroundings and acted on it. It happens. No regrets. So let's leave it at that and be professionals."

His jaw tightened, and his nostrils flared. "Is that what you think?" His tone was hard.

She lifted her chin defiantly, but he didn't give her a chance to answer.

"You're wrong. Give me a chance to explain."

"There's no need. What we shared is over. If you'll excuse me, I need to get some lunch." She stepped around him and rushed over to where Melissa stood talking. "Excuse me. Melissa, we'd better get going. We only have an hour."

Finally, Melissa said her goodbyes. On the way out, Karen noticed Damian watching her with a grim expression. She had never considered how she would respond if she ever saw him again. Part of her wanted to turn cartwheels, but the other part was decidedly wary and reminded her that he stood her up.

During lunch, she toyed with the food on her plate and thought about her encounter with Damian. He seemed upset by her description of their time together as insignificant. Could he possibly have thought of it as more? Should she have given him a chance to explain what happened? No. She was just imagining things. Clearly, she was the only one who considered their time special. The one who, despite her protests, wanted more.

Several times during lunch, she started to mention it to Melissa, but changed her mind. Karen wanted to keep their prior relationship a secret, especially since she and Damian would have to work together. When they returned from lunch, she lingered in the bathroom until it was time for class to start. And she left as soon as he dismissed class.

Karen did the same thing the second day, hoping to avoid another confrontation. With Kyle leading most of the presentation, Damian stood off to the side. He appeared to be listening, but every time she glanced his way, he was staring at her.

During a group activity, he came to her table. "How's everything going? Do you have any questions?" He leaned close to read the answers the group had come up with and brushed his hand across her shoulder. Their eyes met. "Looks very good." With one more pass of his hand, he moved on to the next table.

That simple touch had stimulated every nerve cell in her body, forcing her to remember just how good it had been between them. She didn't know what kind of game he was playing, but she wanted no part of it. At the end of the day, she made up an excuse about not feeling well to Melissa and all but fled the hotel.

The saving grace was that she had the rest of this week and the next before seeing him again. She needed some distance.

Damian unclipped the microphone and placed it on the table. It was Friday evening, and their last conference before the Thanksgiving holiday. He shut down the computer and packed up everything. An image of Karen floated in his mind. A smile curved his lips. He still couldn't believe he'd found her. At first her cold demeanor put him off, but he'd caught her looking his way more than once. And for a split second, he saw it—desire. The same desire that had overtaken them on the cruise that night.

His plan had been to invite her to dinner at the end of the second day, but she lit out of the room as if it were on fire. Since then, there had been back-to-back conferences for the rest of the week. Tomorrow would be his last night in town before heading home, and he didn't intend to leave without seeing her again.

After packing up their equipment, Delores, Kyle, Troy and Damian ended up at a nearby restaurant suggested by the hotel staff. Over dinner, they discussed how the conferences and workshops had gone, as was their practice.

In their opinion, there was always room for improvement, and they strove to give their clients 100 percent. When they got back to the hotel, Delores went up to her room. She had a morning flight home. Troy excused himself to answer a phone call.

"Everything all right, Damian?" Kyle asked. "You're pretty quiet tonight."

"I'm fine. I need a favor."

"What's up?"

Damian pulled a card out of his pocket and handed it to Kyle. "You said you needed more than a first name. I did one better."

Frowning, Kyle took the card and read, "'Karen Morris. San Jose, California.'" He seemed puzzled for a moment, then his eyes widened in recognition. "Is this…? It can't be. How did you…?"

"She was at the conference Monday and Tuesday."

"Damn. I don't believe it." He grinned. "Did you talk to her?"

"For a minute. She's pretty pissed. Wouldn't give me a chance to explain. But I'm not leaving until I talk to her." He gestured toward the card. "I need an address and phone number. Sooner rather than later."

"You sure you want to do this? It sounds like she's not interested in starting up again."

"More sure than I have been about anything in a long time."

Kyle nodded and tapped the card against his finger. "Then I'll find her."

"Thanks. It's been a long week. I think I'm gonna head up and relax."

"I hear you. I'll probably do the same."

They got Troy's attention and motioned that they were going upstairs. He nodded. Damian and Kyle walked over to the bank of elevators and pushed the button.

Kyle laughed and shook his head. "I still can't believe you found your girl."

"Imagine how I felt. I lost my train of thought and was grinning like an idiot. It's a good thing I know that presentation like the back of my hand. Otherwise it would have been pretty embarrassing."

The two men stepped into the elevator when it arrived, and they rode to their floor. "I'll let you know when I have the information," Kyle said before they went into their separate rooms.

"I'm counting on it." Damian closed his door behind him and kicked off his shoes. Stripping, he went into the bathroom and turned on the shower. Twenty minutes later, clean and relaxed, Damian padded across the room to stand in front of the window. Looking out over the city, he vividly recalled Karen's warm smile and infectious laughter. Had she missed him as much as he had missed her? And how would she react when he showed up at her house?

After standing there for who knows how long, he crossed the room and stretched out on the bed. He picked up the remote, turned the television to a sports channel and watched highlights until his eyelids grew heavy. Damian clicked off the TV, turned off the lamp and slid beneath the covers, falling into a restless sleep.

Two hours later, he was wide-awake. He flipped through the television channels and caught the last thirty minutes of an old movie. Still unable to sleep, he pulled on a pair of sweatpants, a Carolina Panthers T-shirt and his tennis shoes. Damian stuck his wallet and room key in his pocket and went downstairs to the bar. He didn't want any alcohol, and coffee would definitely keep him up. In the end, he settled for a cup of decaf. He slowly sipped the steaming liquid and tried to keep his mind from speculating on how long it would take Kyle to find Karen's address. Time was running out. Although he'd be back after the holiday, he couldn't wait that long. He finished his coffee, walked wearily back to his room and fell across the bed.

Damian woke up the next morning fully clothed. His first inclination was to call Kyle, but he resisted the urge. Instead he pulled out his laptop and checked his emails. He deleted the junk mail and then clicked on one from his mother. She wanted to let him know that a woman who had come into her art studio asked whether he had remarried, and suggested that her niece might be perfect. He shook his head and quickly replied: No, thanks.

Done with the emails, he opened his presentation and made a few minor changes based on feedback and questions that were asked over the past two weeks. His cell phone chimed, and he snatched it up. He opened the text from Kyle, and he felt his heart thumping in his chest upon seeing Karen's address and phone number. He sent back a text: I owe u one. Damian saved the file and shut down the computer.

All hopes Karen had of distancing herself from thoughts of Damian were dashed, as Melissa spent the remainder of the week at school gushing about how handsome the trainers were. She brought them up at every turn, putting Karen in a foul mood. When Friday arrived, she packed up and left soon after her students.

She spent a quiet evening reading until her eyes would no longer stay open. Placing the book on her nightstand, she turned off the lamp and scooted down beneath the covers. It seemed as if she had just closed her eyes when the phone rang. She glimpsed over her shoulder and read the blurry numbers on the clock. *It is seven-thirty on a Saturday morning.*

"You have got to be kidding me," she said with a groan, rolling over and blindly reaching for the cordless. "Hello."

"Happy birthday to you, happy birthday to you, happy

birthday, darling daughter, happy birthday to you!" her
parents' chipper voices sang, her father's slightly off-key.

She sat up. "Hey, Dad. Hey, Mom. Thanks."

"We wanted to catch you before you started your day,"
her mother said. "Are you doing anything special?"

"Nope. Just some cleaning."

"That's no fun," her dad said. "You should at least have
a special meal."

"I may take myself out to dinner or something. How
are you guys?"

"Just fine. Can't wait to see you at Thanksgiving."

"Me, too, Dad." Although her parents lived less than
an hour away in Oakland, Karen's schedule often kept her
from making frequent visits. "I'll probably drive down
Wednesday and stay until Saturday."

"Sounds good, baby. You can get your birthday present when you come."

"Okay. Thanks, Mom. I love you guys."

"Love you, too," they chorused.

Karen disconnected and lay back looking at the ceiling. *No sense in trying to go back to sleep.* Truthfully, she
wasn't too excited about her birthday this year. It would be
the first year since college that she had celebrated alone.
She allowed herself another fifteen minutes for her pity
party, then, determined to make the best of the day, got up,
showered and dressed in comfortable sweats and a T-shirt.

Over the next hour, many of her family members, including her favorite cousin and grandmother, called with
happy birthday wishes. As usual, her grandmother asked
if Karen was dating. Her thoughts instantly went to Damian. She asked herself for the hundredth time if she had
done the right thing by not hearing him out. She reassured
herself she had done the right thing, and that some things
were best left in the past. But seeing him again brought

back every caress, every kiss and the emotional connection they shared on the cruise.

Somehow, Karen had to find a way to keep from falling for him.

Chapter 11

Karen had just finished cleaning the bathroom when the phone rang again. Every time it rang, she tensed, thinking Andre might be on the other end. He'd called several times wanting to talk, but she always let it go to voice mail. She toyed with changing her number but didn't want to deal with the hassle. Smiling, she answered the phone.

"Hey, girl," she said to Janae.

"Happy birthday!"

"Thanks."

"What are you doing today?"

"Nothing much. I'm cleaning right now."

"Girl, that's no way to celebrate your birthday. You should be living it up."

She laughed. "Melissa was busy and my best buddy ran off, got married and moved to the other side of the state. So who am I supposed to be living it up with?"

"I know. I'm sorry I deserted you," Janae said contritely.

"I guess I could make the drive to my parents', but I'll be seeing them next week."

"Or you could do the next best thing."

"What's that?" Her doorbell rang. "Hang on, Janae. Someone's at my door." Karen walked down the short hallway leading to her front door and peered through the peephole but didn't see anyone. The bell rang again, but she couldn't see the person. Irritated, she snatched the door open. Her mouth dropped.

"The next best thing would be for your best friend to fly up and spend your birthday with you," Janae said, spreading her arms wide.

Karen screamed, and the two women laughed and hugged and cried. "Come in. Oh, my God! I can't believe you're here. I'm so happy to see you. Where's Terrence?" she asked, leading Janae into the living room and offering her a seat on the couch. She started to ask how Janae got in but remembered Janae had the gate code.

"He's at home. He sends birthday greetings."

"How long are you staying?"

"Just until this afternoon."

"I wish you were staying longer."

Janae nodded. "Me, too. Now, you need to change clothes. We're going out."

"Where?"

"Don't worry about it, Ms. Nosy. We're going to celebrate. Just dress casually."

Karen changed into jeans and a navy scoop-neck tee. She slid her feet into black ballet flats, picked up her purse and met Janae in the living room. "I'm ready. Did you rent a car?"

"Something like that," Janae said with a secret smile.

She followed Janae out to the parking area and stood speechless when she saw a limousine. "I don't believe it," she whispered.

Janae grinned. "Terrence thought your day should be special, and I agree."

Karen shook her head. "I'm so glad I dragged you to that concert."

"So am I."

On the way, Janae told Karen about her appointment with the art gallery director.

"How did it go?"

"She said she was excited about my work. She has a

show coming up in December with the theme Great Escapes, and I have some pieces that would fit."

"Oh, my goodness!" Karen screamed. "That is *fantastic*. I knew she would love them. So, how does it feel?"

"Exciting, amazing, overwhelming. I'm scared to death."

"I'm so proud of you, Janae. You know I'm coming. How many pieces is she allowing?"

"Since I'm a new artist—five, with another five available just in case. If they sell well, she'll let me do more for the next series."

"Make sure you email me the dates and times."

"I will. The first showing is sometime around mid-December."

"I'll come down early so we can go shopping. Gotta have you looking good."

"Oh, no," Janae groaned.

Karen laughed. "Hey, you know me. Any excuse to shop. Ooh, Audrey might want to come, too."

"*Great*. I'm telling you now, whatever we don't have in two hours, we're not buying. So you'd better think power-shopping."

"Yeah, yeah, I know."

The driver stopped in front of Burke Williams Day Spa a short while later. "We always said we would come here one day," Karen said.

Janae nodded. "Yes, we did. Let's go get pampered."

The driver opened the back door and assisted them out of the car. "I'll be waiting for you ladies. Enjoy."

They thanked him and entered the spa. The receptionist greeted them, then gave them a locker key and a tour. The spa was decorated in an old-world Moroccan theme with deep, rich earth tones, columns and arches. Karen and Janae changed into thick robes and spa sandals. They relaxed by the fireplace in the lounge, sipping warm tea and nibbling on fresh fruit while waiting for their treatments to begin. They privately enjoyed a massage and facial, then met up in the nail-care room for a manicure and pedicure. Afterward, they changed and sat in the lounge.

"This is the best birthday present ever," Karen said with a satisfied sigh, leaning her head against the back of the sofa. "I'm so relaxed I could fall asleep right here."

"I hear you. I needed that massage. I ordered lunch from a local restaurant, and it should be delivered shortly."

"You thought of everything. Thank you so much for this. I was feeling sorry for myself this morning."

"What's going on?"

"First of all, I thought I'd have to spend my birthday alone. Second, I went to a safety training conference Monday and Tuesday, and you'll never guess who the presenter was."

"Who?"

"Damian."

Janae bolted upright on the couch. "*What?* Damian, as in *Damian* from the cruise?"

"The one and only. I couldn't believe it."

"Did you guys have a chance to talk?"

"Briefly. I told him we should just move on and leave things the way they are."

"And he said?"

"For a minute, I thought he seemed upset, but I'm sure it's just that he's probably not used to women turning him down."

"I don't know, Karen. But I guess it doesn't matter now since he's gone back to wherever he lives."

"His consulting firm is based out of North Carolina, and he'll be back the week after Thanksgiving for at least a week working at the school revamping the safety program and doing assemblies for the staff, parents and kids."

"Wow. I can't believe all this has happened since I saw

you a month ago. I guess you really did need that massage. So what are you going to do?"

"I don't know. Seeing him brought back everything from the cruise, and it's not going to be easy to ignore him when we have to work together. I've got a week to figure out how to deal with him." Her mind warned her that he was another man looking for a good time, but her body didn't care and wanted her to throw caution to the wind. Right now she couldn't tell which part of her had the upper hand.

Karen's cell buzzed. She frowned at the display, not recognizing the number. "Hello."

"Karen, it's Damian."

"Damian?" Her stunned gaze met Janae's amused one.

"Or not," Janae said with a wry chuckle.

Karen skewered her with a look. "What do you want, Damian?"

"I need to talk to you, Karen."

"I don't think—"

"Please, baby. Just give me fifteen minutes."

Why couldn't she resist this man? Sighing heavily, she said, "Fine. Fifteen minutes."

"Thank you. I'll see you in a couple of hours."

She gave him the information he'd need to get into the complex and disconnected. She rested her head on the back of the sofa and groaned. "He's coming over."

"I heard," Janae said. "At least you'll know why he stood you up."

"I guess."

She and Janae ate lunch quickly, and then the limo dropped Karen back at her place before taking Janae to the airport. Karen nervously paced while waiting for Damian to arrive.

Damian parked in an uncovered spot marked for visitors and sat in the car for a good ten minutes. Finally, he got out and walked across the lot. A limo pulled up in front of him, and the back window came down.

"Hello, Damian."

He stared at the familiar-looking woman and searched his brain for a memory. Smiling, he said, "Janae, right? You're Karen's friend from the cruise."

She nodded.

"It's good to see you again."

"Same here." She eyed him for a moment. "You must care about Karen a lot to try to find her."

"I do. I had no intention of leaving town without seeing her," he responded.

She smiled, seemingly satisfied by his answer. "Well, good luck. You're going to need it."

He chuckled softly. "Thanks."

The limo started off, then stopped again. Janae leaned out the window. "Oh, by the way, today is Karen's birthday. Thought you might like to know."

Damian grinned and stared after the limo as it drove off. Too bad he hadn't had that information beforehand.

He walked rapidly to her door, hesitated a beat, took a deep breath and rang the doorbell. His heart started pounding when he heard the rattle of a chain and the door opening. "Hey."

"Hi."

"May I come in?"

She hesitated for what seemed like forever in his mind, then finally stepped back. They stood there for a lengthy minute staring at each other, neither speaking. He took in the sight of her dressed in a pair of jeans and a pullover top. The outfit accentuated every luscious curve that he remembered. He dragged his gaze up to her face, met her hostile glare and questioned whether he had made the right decision in coming.

Karen opened the door wider, then turned and walked

away, leaving him to follow. He closed the door and trailed her as they passed through a cozy living room and ended up in the kitchen. She gestured to a chair at the wooden table. "Have a seat."

He removed his jacket, draped it over the back of the chair and sat. She wrapped her arms around her middle and nervously chewed on her lip. He hated the mistrust he read in her eyes. "How've you been?"

"Okay. You?"

"Miserable as hell without you."

Her eyebrow lifted a fraction. "Um…can I get you something?"

"Yes." Without stopping to question his actions, he reached out, tugged her down onto his lap and kissed her. She resisted for a split second before he heard her soft sigh of surrender. Shifting her until she straddled him, he deepened the kiss as his hands traced a path up her thighs and over the curve of her hips.

"Damian," she whispered against his lips.

The way she called his name made him lose all reason. He threaded his hand through her hair and held her head in place as he kissed her greedily, his tongue thrusting deep. Breaking off the kiss, Damian rested his head against hers. "I'm sorry."

Her eyes snapped open. She lifted her head and met his eyes.

"That wasn't supposed to happen. I—"

"Let me up!" She struggled in his arms, but he held firm. "Let me go. I'm not playing these games with you."

He released a deep sigh. "Will you just stop squirming for a minute and let me finish?"

Realizing her efforts to leave his lap were futile, she stopped and glowered at him.

He shook his head and chuckled softly. "What I was trying to say is that wasn't supposed to happen until we talked. But somehow, I seem to lose control each and every time I'm near you. I need you to know why I missed dinner. That I didn't hook up with some other woman on the cruise."

His confession deflated some of her anger. "You didn't?"

"No. We took a boat to one of the private islands to snorkel and have lunch, or so I thought. However, Kyle and Troy neglected to tell me they made plans for us to stay in the Bahamas and rejoin the cruise at the last port. By the time I found out, I had no way of contacting you or getting back to the ship before it left."

"Oh."

"Believe me, I was *not* happy. As soon as we boarded the ship the next day, I came to your room. But you didn't answer then…or the other three times I knocked. I think the couple across the hall thought I was stalking you." He paused. "So now you know. Why didn't you wait for me like I asked?"

"What are you talking about?"

"I left you a note."

"I never saw the note, Damian. I thought you found someone else."

He stroked her face. "Oh, baby. I'm so sorry. I couldn't even look at another woman after meeting you. We spent two days and one incredible night together. And I don't know about you, but I thought something special was happening between us."

"So did I. Now what?"

"That depends on you. I'd like to pick up where we left off and get to know each other. I want to know what makes you happy and what makes you cry. What your favorite food is, what you like to do when you're not teaching and everything else. What do you think?"

She smiled. "It sounds really good, but how are we going to manage that when, if I'm not mistaken, you live in North Carolina?"

His brow lifted. "We live in the twenty-first century. I'm sure we can figure something out. So what do you say?"

"I don't know, Damian. Even with technology, you're still on the other side of the country."

"True, but I really want to get to know you, and I'll do whatever it takes."

"How about we just go out while you're here and see where things go?"

It wasn't the answer he wanted, but it was a start. "I can work with that." He kissed her, long and slow. The kiss went from sweet and gentle to hot and all-consuming in an instant. He stood, placed her on the table, pulled the sweater over her head and removed her bra. Cupping her breasts in his hands, he reacquainted himself with their feel and taste before running a worshipping hand down her belly to unbutton and unzip her jeans.

"Ease up a little, baby," he told her as he pulled them and her panties off. "So beautiful." She looked sexy, leaning back on her elbows with her legs spread. So sexy, in fact, he had to taste her. Damian reclaimed his chair and hooked her legs over his shoulders. He kissed his way up her inner thighs until his face was buried in her lush sweetness. He pressed the tip of his tongue to her warm, moist center, swirling and teasing and grazing her clitoris. Her hips flew off the table, and she let out a strangled moan. He lifted her hips in his hands and slid his tongue inside her, stroking deeper and faster. Her legs began to quiver uncontrollably, and he didn't stop until she exploded around him, screaming his name.

"Happy birthday, baby." Carefully lowering her legs, he stood and quickly removed his clothes.

* * *

Happy birthday? How did he know it's my birthday? Karen lay on her kitchen table, gasping for air, spasms racking her body. So much for that little speech she'd made about moving on. Something about the way Damian kissed and touched her melted her insides, and she wanted him buried deep inside her. In a matter of seconds he stood before her, gloriously naked and his condom-sheathed shaft fully erect. Her core pulsed in anticipation. "Make love to me, Damian."

"You don't know how much I've wanted to hear those words, sweetheart." He spread her legs wider, stepped between them and eased inside, throwing his head back and growling softly.

He started moving, and it was so blatantly erotic that she was already on the verge of another orgasm. Karen opened herself wider, taking him in deeper. "Don't stop."

"I won't ever stop," he murmured.

Their lovemaking changed from slow and sensual to fast and wild. He thrust deep with rapid strokes, and she arched up to match his rhythm. A torrent of sensations coursed down her nerve endings, and she came in a blinding climax. Damian rode her hard, and moments later, he erupted with a hoarse cry of pleasure.

"Karen. Sweet, sweet Karen," he said, lifting her into his arms and kissing her tenderly. He collapsed onto the chair and held her close, the rapid pace of his heart beating against hers.

She wrapped her arms around his neck and laid her head on his shoulder. How could this one man touch the very essence of her so effortlessly? It was going to take everything within her to keep things strictly physical. She could not fall for him, not when he would be leaving for good after another week. Her eyes drifted closed as their hearts and breathing gradually slowed.

He stood with her in his arms, and a wicked grin covered his mouth. "Let's go take a shower. I really enjoyed that last time. And since it's your birthday, I have a few more *gifts* for you."

Karen laughed and pointed in the direction of her bedroom.

An hour later, Karen walked Damian to the door. They were both smiling. "By the way, how did you know it was my birthday?"

"I saw Janae as I came in, and she told me."

She shook her head and smiled.

"I'll be back at seven to pick you up for your birthday dinner." He kissed her.

"I'll be ready." She gave him a tiny wave and closed the door behind him. She danced back down the hallway to the kitchen and let out a loud, "Yes!" While she rinsed the few dishes in her sink and put them in the dishwasher, she replayed the afternoon in her mind. The man was magical when it came to lovemaking, and she still couldn't believe he had found her. He apologized for going behind her back to get her number and address—he'd enlisted Kyle's help— but told her he didn't want to leave town without seeing her and explaining what had happened. Karen wasn't mad at him. This birthday was turning out to be one of the best ever, she mused.

As soon as she finished in the kitchen, she headed to her closet to find something to wear for their dinner date tonight. The temperatures had dropped by at least ten degrees since last week, and it now felt more like late-fall weather.

After searching for fifteen minutes, she settled on her cream wool pants, chocolate-brown scoop-neck blouse and open-front cream cardigan. Karen sat down on the bed and smiled. She still couldn't get over the fact that Damian had come to her house, or that they had made love again.

Now that things were straightened out between them, she wasn't ready for him to go home tomorrow.

Another thought crossed her mind. They had to work together when he came back. How was she going to keep her hands off him or act as if she didn't know him? They'd need to talk about it tonight.

Chapter 12

Damian arrived at seven with two dozen pink roses in a crystal vase. "Happy birthday, sweetheart."

"Thank you. They're beautiful." First his determination to apologize, and now the flowers. He was making it difficult for her to keep her emotions in check. She directed him to place the vase on a table in the living room, then followed him out to his rental for the drive to the restaurant.

He'd chosen an expensive steak house, and they conversed quietly while dining on course after course of some of the best food Karen had eaten in a long time. As they finished dinner, she broached the subject that had been on her mind all afternoon. "Damian, how are we going to do this when you come back?"

His brow lifted. "Do what?"

"This. Us. We're going to have to work together at the school."

"We're going to do just what we're doing now." He covered her hand with his. "But it's going to be hard to keep my hands to myself," he added with a look that communicated exactly what he meant.

She snatched her hand back. "Damian, I'm serious."

"And I'm not? Karen, I don't intend to hide our relationship. I'll make sure not to compromise you in front of the students, but I need to be able to touch you, hold your hand or kiss you. I don't work for the school, so there's no reason why we can't see each other openly."

He was right, but she still felt a little uncomfortable and told him so.

"Fine," he said with a sigh. "If I'm going to be on lock-down, I need to have at least one little bitty kiss every day, Ms. Morris. So you need to figure out how to make it happen."

She laughed. "Damian Bradshaw, are you pouting?"

He frowned. "Men don't pout."

She shook her head. "Speaking of jobs, how long have you been doing safety training?"

"Only about three years."

"I would have thought it was much longer. You're a natural. What made you choose this line of work?"

A shadow crossed his face. "I wanted to keep kids safe. I used to be a high school chemistry teacher and also coached the boys' varsity basketball team."

"You were a teacher?" she asked with surprise. No wonder he thought teachers were dedicated.

He smiled and nodded. "I had this student, a senior named Torian Williams. He was brilliant—wanted to become a biochemist and was a star point guard on our team. Torian had been offered both academic and athletic scholarships from at least three schools. And he had a great sense of humor." Damian chuckled and shook his head. Then his smile faded. "I noticed him acting strange for a couple of days—not his normal upbeat self—and tried to find out if anything was wrong. I'd heard rumors about him being bullied, but I didn't know how bad things were. I told him I'd be around if he wanted to talk about anything. He made an appointment to come see me after school but never showed."

Karen was almost afraid to ask. "What happened?"

"An hour later, I got a call saying he had committed suicide—hung himself."

She gasped softly. "Oh, Damian. I'm so sorry."

"Kyle was one of the detectives on the case. They found Torian's cell phone, and someone had sent five hundred texts over two days telling Torian that he was worthless and that nobody wanted him, not even his parents."

"The text bombing you talked about at the training?"

"Yes. His mother was a drug user and, unless she needed something, couldn't be bothered with her son. Father was never in the picture. I just wish he had come to talk to me," he said emotionally.

His eyes reflected pain, and she squeezed his hand. "I'm sure Torian knew you cared about him. But why leave teaching? You obviously have a passion for it."

"I wanted to be able to do something on a larger scale. Hopefully we're making a difference."

"Well, you're already making a difference in my life," Karen said, changing the subject and wanting to erase the sadness in his face.

He brought her hand to his lips. "As you have in mine, sweet lady."

The passion in his eyes and seriousness in his voice made her breathing go short. *Oh, Lord. He's going to make me fall in love with him.* "You coached basketball? With your height, I'm surprised you didn't pursue that as a career."

"I tore my ACL as a junior in college. Even though my knee healed and I played my senior year, I didn't want to take a chance of a repeat injury. I still play for recreation and occasionally coach in a community league."

She was finding more and more to like about this man.

"Do you want to get dessert?" Damian asked, holding up the menu.

"No, thanks. But if you want something, feel free."

He tossed the menu on the table and signaled the waiter. "What I want for dessert isn't on the menu. Since you're going to be rationing out kisses when I get back, I have to stock up before I leave tomorrow."

Heat pooled between her legs, and she clamped them together to stem the rush of sensations. He paid the bill and escorted her out of the restaurant. On the drive back to her place, she pondered what else he might stock up on. Whatever he had in store, she was ready, and planned to do a little stocking up herself.

Damian barely let Karen open the door to her condo before he lifted her in his arms. He kissed her with a hunger that bordered on obsession. His feelings for this woman intensified by the minute. Without breaking the kiss, he carried her to the living room and sat on the couch with her in his lap. He fed himself with her kisses, explored the scented column of her neck and caressed her soft breasts.

As much as he wanted to make love to her again, he couldn't. He had an early-morning flight and would miss it for sure if they went anywhere near her bedroom. So he contented himself with just kissing her until it was time for him to leave. Pressing one last kiss to her lips, he leaned his head against hers, closed his eyes and held her against his heart.

"I don't want to leave you, but I have to go," Damian said with a heavy sigh.

Karen lifted her head. "I know."

He trailed a finger down her cheek. "I'm going to miss you."

She smiled. "I'm going to miss you, too. Thank you for making my birthday one of the best I've had."

"My pleasure. I only wish I knew about it sooner so I could have planned something more." He stood and placed her on her feet, then took her hand and walked to the door. "I'll call you when I get home tomorrow."

"Okay. Have a safe trip."

He dipped his head for one more kiss and slipped out the door. Driving back to the hotel, Damian took some time to dissect the riot of emotions swirling around in his gut. This was more than a physical attraction. He tried to pinpoint when it happened, but somehow, it seemed as if the feeling had always been there. Could he have started falling for her that first day on the ship when she smiled at him, or the night he held her in his arms on the dance floor? Was it after the first mind-blowing kiss or the night of explosive passion they shared? From the moment he'd seen her, he felt different. She had touched him on all levels—physically and emotionally. He parked in the hotel lot, cut the engine and leaned his head against the headrest. Now that he had acknowledged his feelings, the next week was going to be pure torture. But when he returned, his mission was clear—get her to fall with him.

"Man, you've been smiling for the past two days," Troy said, lounging in the doorway of Damian's office Monday morning.

"Is something wrong with me smiling?" Damian shifted his gaze from the computer screen as he sat answering emails and, yes, smiling. He and Karen had talked for over two hours last night after he got home. A little while ago, he had sent her a text telling her how much he looked forward to seeing her again and, in explicit detail, what he planned to do when he saw her. Her response had sent a jolt directly to his groin and had him contemplating searching airlines for a flight out tonight.

"Not at all. I'm glad things are working out with Karen. I am curious about something, though." He entered the office, closed the door and sat in a chair across from Damian. "This thing with Karen…are you sure it's not some kind of rebound affair?"

Damian leaned forward and pinned Troy with a glare.

"Hell no! It's been five years. I know Joyce isn't coming back, and it's not like I haven't dated other women. Karen is not a replacement for Joyce. She never could be. They're two very different women. Karen makes me feel like I've been given a new lease on life. She's... I...I don't know." He leaned back and pinched the bridge of his nose.

"Sounds like you might be falling in love with her."

"I don't know. Maybe. But we're only going to be in California another week, so it may come to nothing." He blew out a long breath. "All I know is I have deep feelings for Karen that I've never experienced with any other woman."

"Including Joyce?"

Damian nodded and waited for the guilt to rise. To his surprise, it didn't happen, and he realized his heart was truly ready to love again.

Troy shrugged. "It happens to some people like that." He chuckled. "For others, they have to be dragged into it kicking and screaming."

Damian laughed. "Are you in the kicking-and-screaming category?"

"No. I'll have no problems settling down with the right woman. Now, Kyle, on the other hand..."

They both laughed harder. "Definitely." Kyle loved his bachelor status and often said he didn't plan on settling down anytime soon.

"So, have you told Karen how you feel?" Troy asked when he stopped laughing.

"No. I just figured it out myself."

"Have you told her about Joyce?"

"Not yet, but soon." He was afraid Karen would have the same thoughts Troy had, that she was a substitute for another woman. Damian hoped he'd find the right words by the time he returned to California.

He and Troy talked a few minutes longer before getting back to work. He only had today and tomorrow to get everything ready, because they were closing the office for the holiday. Thinking about the holiday made Damian remember the conversation he'd had with his mother that morning. Since their conversation a few weeks ago, she'd been sending him emails and texts suggesting the "perfect woman." Once again, he reiterated that he wasn't interested in any of her potential candidates and threatened to leave Thanksgiving dinner if one showed up. All of his problems would be solved if he just told her about Karen, but he decided to wait until he was sure their relationship stood on solid ground.

He leaned back in the chair and drummed his fingers on the desk. What would his parents think of Karen? He sat up and rotated the chair toward the computer. He'd have his answer soon enough if things progressed the way he hoped.

Damian worked steadily over the next two days, staying late both nights. As a result, he didn't have a chance to talk to Karen. By the time Wednesday morning rolled around, he missed her more than he would ever have thought. He sat in his favorite chair on the screened-in porch sipping a glass of orange juice. He had purchased the house a year ago as a first step in moving toward the future. Painstakingly, he had boxed up all of Joyce's things and donated them to charity, only keeping a few precious mementos. The move proved to be the right one because there were too many memories in the house they shared, keeping him stuck in a place of grief and misery that he couldn't escape.

His thoughts shifted back to Karen. He wanted to hear her voice. The three-hour time difference made it only seven in California, and he knew she was probably sleeping in and enjoying her vacation. He stared out the wall of windows, finally seeing the sun peeking through the clouds. The temperatures here were at least thirty degrees cooler than in California.

He ran upstairs and grabbed a sweatshirt, then reached for the keys to the shed and left through a side door. Now that he had some free time, Damian figured it would be a good time to prune the tree in his backyard. It took him over two hours to complete the task and clean up. He put away the ladder and saw, locked the shed and went inside for a hot shower. As soon as he got dressed, he called Karen.

"Hey, sweetheart," he said when she answered.

"Hey, Damian. Are you working?"

"No. The office is closed for the rest of the week. What time are you going to your parents'?"

"Actually, I just got here. My cousin Deborah and I are going to hang out before the rest of the family arrives tomorrow. We haven't seen each other in a few months. What about you?"

"Unless my mother calls with a long to-do list—which she usually does—I won't go over until tomorrow."

She laughed. "What about your father?"

"Oh, she has a whole other one for him," he answered with a chuckle. They quieted for a moment. "I'm missing you, girl."

"I miss you, too, and can't wait for you to get back on Sunday. Didn't you promise me something?" she asked seductively.

"Yeah, I did. And if you keep talking like that, I might just hop on a flight tonight."

"Promises, promises."

"So you like to tease. We'll see if you can back it up."

"Oh, I can back it up."

She gave him a play-by-play of what to expect, and Damian's body reacted with lightning speed. "I think we need to get off this phone."

"What?" Karen asked innocently.

He laughed softly and shook his head. "Just wait until I get back. It's gonna be you and me."

"Mmm. I can't wait for that. I'll call you tomorrow."

They said their goodbyes, and Damian stretched out on the bed, trying to bring his body under control. He had been in a state of arousal since they'd exchanged those texts a couple of days ago, and he prayed that the next four would pass quickly.

Karen disconnected and smiled. Something about Damian brought out the naughty girl in her. With all the chemistry they had, it would take a herculean effort to remain professional and cordial around him at the school.

"Karen Morris, who in the world are you talking to on the phone like that?"

She jumped and whirled around. "Deborah! Girl, you almost gave me a heart attack. You can't be sneaking up on people like that." She engulfed Deborah in a hug. "You look good."

"Thanks. I feel like I've been gone forever. It's good to see you, cuz." The two cousins had grown up as close as sisters. Deborah was part of a small dance company and had been traveling for the past several months. "And you didn't answer my question. Were you and Andre talking naughty? I figured he'd be here with you."

Karen frowned. "No!" Deborah flinched. "Sorry. I forgot you've been gone, and we haven't talked in a while. Andre and I broke up a few months ago."

"Oh, sweetie, I'm so sorry. What happened?"

Karen waved her off. "It's fine. He decided that we weren't socially matched." She told Deborah about what happened at his mother's dinner party. Estella Robertson had never made it a secret that Karen didn't measure up to her standards, but Karen never thought she would go so far as to invite another woman to dinner—one whom her son had obviously been dating, handpicked by Estella—and seat her directly across from Andre and Karen. Karen had noticed the coy smiles and intimate gestures throughout the meal and had planned to confront him about all that, but he saved her the trouble. His response: "Well, we have more in common and travel in the same circles."

"Girl, I know he didn't. I would've put my foot up his highfalutin ass." She cocked her head to the side. "Then who were you talking to?"

"His name is Damian Bradshaw. I met him on the cruise when Janae got married last month."

Deborah raised a perfectly sculpted eyebrow. "Really? I've been gone way too long." She hooked her arm in Karen's. "Come on. I need details, and don't leave *anything* out."

Laughing, they cut through her parents' kitchen and out to the backyard as Karen told all. Later, as she settled in for bed, thoughts of Damian filled her mind. Deborah echoed Janae's sentiment that Damian's feelings had to be strong for him to go to such lengths to track Karen down. Though she was beginning to have deep feelings for him as well, she still planned to proceed with caution.

But each and every time she saw him, all her warning systems seemed to take a hike. Snuggling beneath the covers, she sighed. *One day at a time.*

Chapter 13

Karen had enjoyed spending time with her family for Thanksgiving, but she was glad to get back home. Damian had sent her a text letting her know what time his plane would arrive the following evening. Her heart raced at the thought of seeing him again. She loved the way his eyes sparkled when he laughed, loved the way he gave her his full attention when she talked, loved the passion he had for his job. And she loved that she could be herself with him. How had he gotten to her so quickly? It went without saying that the physical aspects of their relationship were off the charts. However, she began to doubt whether things would work out, especially with them living so far apart. Karen couldn't go through another broken heart. Until she was reasonably sure they were on the same page and had a good chance of making it, her feelings would remain a secret.

In anticipation of the extra time she would have to spend on the safety project, she used much of her Sunday doing lesson plans—something she typically did after school—and going over the notes she had taken at the conference. She and Melissa planned to meet tomorrow to outline the suggestions and questions to present to Damian and Kyle when they got together on Tuesday. When she finished, Karen picked up the mail that had accumulated while she was away and went through the stack.

Her heart almost stopped when she saw an envelope

from the school district office. She opened it with shaky fingers and pulled out the sheet of paper. Her heart raced as she read the words. They thanked her for applying, were impressed with her credentials and congratulated her on making the list. "Yes!" Her heart pounded with excitement. Then another thought occurred to her. If she got the job, how would she and Damian make their relationship work? Becoming principal meant staying put for at least two or three years. There was no way she'd turn down this job, and she was sure he wouldn't want to give up his career, either. *Great. One more thing to worry about.*

Late that evening, her cell chimed, indicating a text message. She picked it up and pushed a button.

Damian: Something came up. Won't make it over to-night.

Karen: No prob. C u at school. Everything ok?

Damian: Fine.

She tossed the phone on the bed, and another wave of disappointment washed over her. With nothing left to do, she packed her school tote, showered and went to bed.

The next morning, Nikki met Karen in the office.

"I heard you applied for Priscilla's job."

Karen glanced up from the memo she was reading but didn't respond.

"I don't think you're the right fit for this school, so I threw my name in the hat. Unfortunately for you, I've been teaching longer, which gives me the upper hand. And you know what they always say—it's not what you know, but who you know."

Karen mentally counted to ten. What she wouldn't give to be able to slap that smug smile off Nikki's face. "Is there a point to this conversation, Nikki?"

"I'm just trying to keep you from being disappointed when I get the job," she said nonchalantly.

"I wouldn't be so sure about that. Like you said, it's all about *who* you know." Karen refused to let this crazy woman intimidate her.

A look of uncertainty flashed briefly in Nikki's face before she stiffened her shoulders. "We'll see about that." She snatched the papers from her mailbox and stormed out.

Karen chuckled and went to make copies. This was not the way she wanted to start her week after enduring a sleepless night thinking about Damian's cryptic text.

She managed to make it through the day without encountering Nikki again and thought she was home free until Nikki barged into Melissa's office in the middle of Karen and Melissa's meeting that afternoon.

"May I help you, Nikki?" Melissa asked coolly. "Karen and I are discussing student concerns in our conflict management group."

"I have students in that group and should be included in the meetings."

"As there are no clear and present dangers involved, the information is deemed confidential. But I'll be sure to let you know if something comes up," Melissa added with an icy smile.

Karen glimpsed over her shoulder to see Nikki's tight-lipped glare.

"Karen, I do hope you don't have any more frivolous vacations planned for the rest of the school year," Nikki tossed out bitterly. "I wouldn't want anything to get in the way of you getting that principal position."

Karen met the woman's gaze unflinchingly. "If you're referring to attending the beautiful wedding of my best friend aboard a luxury cruise ship, I don't have anything planned. My students' welfare is very important to me, so I'm rarely absent. However, if something comes up, I have more than enough leave time. I'm sure it won't affect my chances, but thanks for your concern."

Sending Karen and Melissa a scathing look, Nikki turned and stormed out, closing the door with more force than necessary.

Karen and Melissa smiled and shook their heads.

"She does not want to start messing with me," Melissa said, rolling her eyes.

"I just hope this isn't a sign of things to come with her. Let's finish up so I can go home."

They worked for another thirty minutes before calling it a day. Tomorrow morning would be the first meeting with Damian and Kyle, and Karen was anxious to see how things would play out with her and Damian working together. Thoughts of Damian and his text message had stayed in the back of her mind all day. He hadn't sent her any other messages or called. By the end of the evening, she still hadn't heard anything from him, which compounded her worry. She tried to rationalize that his silence might be due to him preparing for the safety overhaul, but in the back of her mind, she had a nagging suspicion that something wasn't right.

Her suspicions were confirmed the moment she saw him the next morning. The spark in his hazel eyes was missing, and his demeanor had changed—still professional, but almost...sad.

"Morning, ladies. Not sure if you remember, but I'm Kyle Jamison, and this is Damian Bradshaw. We have a lot of ground to cover in the next several days, so let's get started. Damian will start walking the perimeter, and I'll take any questions before you have to get to class. Then we'll meet again this afternoon."

"See you this afternoon," Damian said. His eyes held

Karen's for the briefest of moments before he slipped out the door.

Something had happened between their last conversation and now. She had no idea what, but she intended to find out.

Clipboard and pen in hand, Damian went to the school's front entrance gate and noted the types of locks. He had exited the office as quickly as he could. He tried to put on a good face, but she obviously saw right through it. Seeing the hurt and confusion in Karen's eyes only increased his feelings of remorse. How could he explain the occasional bouts of grief that attacked him? This time had been particularly hard because on Sunday he'd actually forgotten that the day marked five years since Joyce's death. It wasn't until Kyle mentioned he would understand if Damian needed him to handle the first few days of the trip that Damian remembered. The anguish of that fateful day rose strong, and overwhelming sadness consumed him. But for the first time, he realized the grief didn't change what he felt for Karen—that the feelings could coexist.

He recalled someone in one of the few grief sessions he attended saying it was possible. However, at the time, he hadn't believed it. He also recalled several men sharing that some of the women they had dated after losing their wives felt they were competing and didn't want the men to mention their past spouses, or had difficulty dealing with the random attacks of grief. And that was the crux of his problem. He worried that Karen would feel the same way, and he had no clue how to go about broaching the conversation. The last thing he wanted was to hurt her.

Damian stopped to jot down notes about possible entry points at the back of the playground, then continued walking. What if she couldn't handle his past and changed her mind about them dating? Laughter and shouting drew him out of his thoughts. He turned to find children streaming onto the playground. He glanced at his watch. School would start in ten minutes. He wound his way back to the office, and a tall, good-looking woman who looked to be in her midthirties, wearing a wide smile, stopped him.

"Hello," she said, extending her hand. "I'm Nikki Fleming, one of the fourth-grade teachers. Thank you so much for coming. This place needs an overhaul, and I know you're just the man to do it."

Damian lifted an eyebrow and extracted his hand when it seemed that the woman wouldn't let go. "It's nice to meet you. We'll do everything we can to ensure that your students and staff have a safe school environment." She moved closer, and he took a step back.

"If you need any suggestions, just let me know."

"Thank you. I'd better get started. Have a nice day." He stepped into the office he and Kyle would be using and closed the door.

Kyle chuckled. "Man, you've been in hibernation for five years, come out for six weeks and have a dozen women falling all over you."

Damian shook his head, pulled out a chair and sat. "I'm not in the mood."

"How you holding up? I know the last couple of days have been rough."

"Yeah, but not for the reasons you're thinking." He gestured to the stack of folders on the table. "We have a lot to do. We'll talk later."

Kyle picked up a folder and opened it. "Maybe you should talk to Karen first. I saw the look on her face."

"Maybe," Damian murmured, picking up another folder. With the mixed signal he'd given Karen earlier, he wouldn't blame her if she told him to get lost.

He and Kyle worked steadily over the next three hours reviewing the school's existing emergency preparedness plan and flagging any possible gaps, stopping only for lunch before resuming the task. As the end of the day neared, the less his mind focused on the mounds of paperwork in front of him and the more it centered on Karen. Melissa joined the two men shortly before the bell rang. By the time Karen arrived and he took in her wary gaze, Damian wasn't any closer to figuring out how to proceed.

"I know it's been a long day for you ladies, so—" Damian began.

"Very," Karen said, cutting him off and pinning him with a look.

His jaw tightened. "We'll try to keep it to no more than a couple of hours," he finished, hearing the censure in her voice. He understood it and took full blame. They hadn't spoken since Sunday evening, or technically Thanksgiving, since a text didn't count as conversation. Their eyes held, and then she smoothly shifted her gaze to the notepad in front of him. Taking the hint, he and Kyle went through their preliminary findings.

"I noticed that all the gates are locked once school starts and all visitors have to come through the office. Has there ever been any training for the office staff on how to handle someone who is denied entrance?" Kyle asked.

"I don't think so," Melissa answered. "I can go ask the secretary, if you want. She's been here for fifteen years." At his nod, she stood and left the room.

Continuing with his questioning, Kyle turned to Karen. "What about teachers? When did you last have any preparedness training?"

"Aside from last month, I don't know of any and I've been here six years. We have the fire drills, but that's about it."

Melissa returned and relayed that the office staff had never been trained.

Damian added that to his list. "Mrs. Mitchell allotted

Friday's entire staff development day for training. If they haven't been already, I'd like the office staff to be included. Janitors, too. I know we developed lockdown procedures during the training. Has this been disseminated?"

"Yes," Melissa answered. "Karen and I distributed the information the day we came back."

"Good. The staff should be familiar with the procedures by Friday's session."

The group continued for another hour, and Damian was pleasantly surprised by the suggestions Karen made and incorporated them into his notes. He noticed Karen glancing up at the clock and checked his watch. Once Kyle finished speaking, he said, "How about we call it a day? It's almost five. We've made some good progress, and I'm sure you ladies have other things to do this evening." Although he said the words to both women, his gaze never strayed from Karen's.

They agreed to skip tomorrow's morning meeting and just meet in the afternoon. He and Kyle stood when the women did.

"You guys are great," Melissa said, passing them on the way out. "See you tomorrow."

When Karen came around the table, he wanted to say something…anything…but the words stuck in his throat.

"See you later." She slid a folded piece of paper across the table where he stood and walked out.

He was almost afraid to open it, but curiosity got the best of him. Picking it up, he opened it and read: *My house, 7:00p. Whatever it is, we need to work it out—one way or another. K.* For the first time in three days, he allowed himself a small smile.

Later that night, while she was rummaging in the refrigerator for the makings of a chef salad, Karen's thoughts shifted to Damian. She had never been one to let things build up and do nothing, hence her inviting him over to talk tonight. One way or another, the relationship needed to be settled. A thousand and one scenarios of why he was acting so strange crossed her mind, but she pushed them away and concentrated on her dinner.

While eating, she checked her personal email and clicked on one from Deborah. She had flown to New York the day after Thanksgiving with her theater company. Karen laughed at her cousin's rant about the cold and snow. She typed back: Hey, you always said you wanted to be on Broadway, so suck it up, and hit Send. Her phone rang, and her heart rate kicked up. She snatched it up.

"Hey, girl. Sorry I couldn't talk to you last week," Janae said when Karen answered.

She relaxed. "Hey. No problem. How was dinner?"

"It was wonderful. My parents and Terrence's grandparents acted like they'd known each other forever. How was yours?"

"Good, except my grandmother started in on her campaign to marry off all her grandkids again."

Janae laughed, then turned serious. "Have you heard any more from Damian since he came over on your birthday?"

"Are you sitting down?"

"I am now. What happened?"

Karen gave her the details about his first visit, their decision to see each other and his subsequent pulling away. "I don't know what to think. Everything seemed fine when we talked last week, and now…"

"He seemed like such a nice guy. I never pegged him for the wishy-washy type. What are you going to do?"

"I passed him a note asking him to come over tonight so we can try to work it out or…not."

"I hope he does and has a good reason for acting so

strange, especially since it was his idea for you guys to keep seeing each other."

"So do I—" Karen stopped midsentence when the doorbell rang. "I have to go. I think he's here."

"You'd better call and tell me *everything*. Oh, yeah, before I forget, the art show is going to be the weekend before Christmas. Don't forget to call me."

"I won't."

Karen disconnected and went to the front door. After a deep breath, she opened the door. Her heart rate sped up again. "Hey. Come on in." Karen stepped back for him to enter.

He leaned down and brushed a kiss across her lips. The contact was brief, but it seared her nonetheless. "Can I take your jacket?" He took it off and handed it to her. The jacket still held his warmth and smell, and she resisted burying her nose in it. She hung it in the front closet and led him to the living room. "Do you want something to drink or eat?"

"No, thanks."

She sat on the sofa, and he lowered himself beside her. For the longest time, he just sat with his head lowered and said nothing. "Damian, what's going on? Did you change your mind about us?" He lifted his head and Karen held her breath, waiting for his response.

He shook his head. He seemed to struggle with words, and she asked again, "Then what is it?"

Finally, he spoke in a voice so low, she had to lean closer to hear him. "Sunday marked five years since my wife died."

Wife? Karen had no idea what she had expected him to say, but this was not it. She sat in stunned silence for a moment, then covered his hand with hers. "I'm so sorry." She wanted to ask him a million questions, but the agony reflected in his face made her wait until he was ready to talk.

* * *

Since reading her note, Damian had tried to come up with a gentle way to tell her, but in the end, he just said it. The look on her face had gone from guarded to shock in a blink. He brought the hand covering his to his mouth and placed a soft kiss on the back. "I'm sorry for not calling and for sending that text, but I didn't know how to explain." He closed his eyes briefly to gather his thoughts. "It's not as bad or frequent as it used to be, but sometimes the grief comes out of nowhere."

"Tell me about her."

It was his turn to be shocked. The last woman he'd gone out with told him she didn't want to compete with his dead wife and didn't understand why he hadn't gotten over it after all this time. Karen squeezed his hand reassuringly. "Her name was Joyce, and I met her when I was fifteen." Damian told her about taking her under his wing, their growing friendship and subsequent marriage.

"How long were you married?"

"Twenty-one months. I came home from work late one afternoon and found her lying unconscious at the bottom of the stairs. She was just lying there...so still. She'd hit her head and sustained a severe brain injury." He felt his emotions rising and that deep, searing gut pain as if it were happening all over again. "She woke up briefly, then slipped into a coma. I stayed there all day and night waiting for her to wake up—praying, hoping—but she never did. Two days later, she was gone," he finished in an agonizing whisper. Damian didn't realize he was crying until Karen reached up to wipe away his tears.

She wrapped her arms around him and held him tight. "I'm so sorry, baby."

Her words and the way she held him shattered the remaining thread of control he'd held on to for five long years, and he cried in her arms. And she cried with him, whispering that she would be there for him.

Gradually, their tears stopped, but he continued to hold her in the silence. Damian couldn't believe he had broken down like that. He had cried at Joyce's funeral, but not like this. This time it felt as though his soul had been cleansed.

Several minutes passed before Karen asked, "Do you still love her?"

"If you're asking whether I'm still *in* love with her, the answer is no. She'll always hold a place in my heart and I will treasure those memories, but it doesn't diminish or change what I feel for you. I've been ready for some time and was lucky enough to meet a classy and unique woman who I can move forward with into a beautiful new life." He kissed her tenderly and rested his forehead against hers. "Thank you for coming into my life." He drew her closer. Now that he had shared his past, albeit not the way he had planned, he wanted to know about hers. "What about you? Have you ever been married?"

"No, but I came close. One minute we were looking at wedding rings, the next my career choice didn't fit with his high-society family and friends."

Damian leaned away and stared at her disbelievingly. "You're kidding me, right?"

"Nope."

A memory surfaced in his mind. When they were eating lunch in Jamaica, she had tensed and almost seemed reluctant to answer when he asked her about her job. Now he understood why. He listened as she told him about the conversation she'd overheard and about the other woman. He shook his head. "Sweetheart, that man is a fool. I know that's what you were probably thinking at first tonight, but please believe that I would never do that to you. You're very special to me."

"Please don't. We dated for over two years, and his betrayal hurt me."

"I promise I will never cheat on you." Her vulnerability gave him pause because she was always so self-assured. Her ex must have really done a number on her. "Do you still see him?"

"Since I've been back from the cruise, he's been calling and even showed up at the school wanting to get back together."

He went still.

"He's out of his damn mind if he thinks I'm taking him back."

"I'm glad to hear that because he's not getting you back. If he harasses you again, let me know. Kyle knows how to get a restraining order. He used to be a detective."

Karen sat up. "Do you think that's necessary?"

"Probably better than me kicking his butt if I catch him even looking your way."

She chuckled. "I never would have figured you for a brawler."

His shoulder lifted in a careless shrug. "Only when necessary." Damian didn't usually start fights, but he didn't back down from them, either.

They sat awhile longer, and as much as he didn't want to leave, both of them had to get up in the morning. Besides, he was emotionally drained and needed some time to process everything. He removed his arm from around her shoulders and sat up.

"Are you all right?"

"Yeah. I'd better leave. It's getting late, and I know you have to prepare for your kids." He stood and pulled her up. "Walk me to the door." When they got to the door, he turned and wrapped his arms loosely around her waist.

"Are we good now?" Karen asked.

"Since I was the one who kind of messed things up, you tell me."

She angled her head and smiled. "Yeah, we're good. So I guess that means you'll be wanting that daily little bitty kiss."

"You'd better believe it. I'll see you tomorrow." He slipped into his jacket, bent to kiss her and stepped out into the night.

Truth be told, he wanted more than just that little kiss. Sitting across from her today, even with things not straightened out between them, Damian wanted to strip her naked, kiss every spot on her beautiful body, then lay her on the table and make love to her until neither of them could move. He didn't know how long he was going to be able to last without having more than a few minutes each day with her.

An idea came to him, and he smiled. He just had to get through the rest of the week.

Chapter 14

Karen sat in her classroom the next morning finishing her lesson plan. After Damian had left last night, she was too mentally exhausted to do anything except shower and go to bed. She tapped the pen against her chin, still shocked by what he'd shared with her. *A widower at twenty-eight years old.* Never in a million years would she have guessed that as the reason for his behavior. The mess she had been through with Andre didn't hold a candle to what Damian had suffered. She couldn't imagine going through something like that at such a young age. Just thinking about it, she felt tears stinging her eyes.

The fact that he had felt comfortable enough with her to reveal his story in that way floored her. And when he broke down and cried in her arms, she was a goner. At that moment, Karen fell hopelessly in love with him. She still planned to tread lightly because, even though Damian said he was no longer in love with his late wife, he might never be able to give his heart completely to another woman.

Glancing up at the wall clock, she completed the task and made sure she had copies of the graphic organizers the students would need to start their book reports. She found that the sheets—broken down into introduction, body and conclusion—helped the students arrange their thoughts and notes in a logical way and made it easier for writing. The bell rang, and she walked out to meet her students where they lined up.

She passed Damian on the playground. "Morning," she said with a smile. Just the sight of him made her pulse race.

"Good morning."

"Did you sleep well? You look a lot better than yesterday."

A soft smile curved his mouth. "I did, and thank you. I hope you did, too."

"Yes. Very well."

"I'll see you later," he said and sauntered off. She stared after him until he disappeared. When she turned back, Nikki stood across the way with her arms folded, frowning. *This woman better not say anything to me.* Karen kept walking toward the playground.

After a morning filled with journal writing, math, library and music, Karen was more than ready for lunch. She sat with the other fourth- and fifth-grade teachers laughing and discussing the antics of the students. On her way out, Karen ran into Melissa, who was bubbling with excitement about another chance to meet with Damian and Kyle, and even suggested inviting them to dinner. Karen was having a hard enough time keeping her hands off Damian during those after-school meetings and didn't want to spend any more time in a "working relationship" than she had to. Not ready to disclose her personal relationship, she made up an excuse and said her goodbyes.

When school ended, Karen packed up and headed for the office, admittedly a little excited herself.

"So, Karen, you seem to be quite friendly with Mr. Bradshaw," Nikki sneered, stepping into Karen's path. "I wouldn't waste my time if I were you. Someone like him is probably used to being with women who, how shall I say it, have a few more lines on their résumés. Besides, you wouldn't want anyone to think the teachers working here behave in an unprofessional manner, especially one trying to become a principal."

Karen clamped her jaw tight to keep from saying something that might get her into trouble. "I need to get to my meeting." She stepped around her and strode down the hall. Melissa and Damian were already waiting when she arrived. Kyle came in a minute later.

"You okay, Karen?" Melissa asked with concern.

She nodded quickly. "Yes. Let's get started." Damian's expression said he didn't believe her, but she cut him a look that said, *Don't ask.*

They pored over policies, and Karen realized that, with all the technological advances, Melissa had been right. Some of the policies were obsolete. The subject turned to parent involvement.

"We've done this in several districts across the country, and by far, the lowest turnout is always from the parents. I would think they'd be interested in knowing what the school is doing and how they can help ensure their kids' safety." Kyle let out a frustrated sigh. "If either of you have ideas, I'm all for it."

Melissa gestured toward Karen. "This is Karen's area of expertise. I swear she's the only teacher here who gets almost one hundred percent parent participation with conferences, class parties, field trips…everything. When I taught, I'd be lucky if half my parents showed up to anything."

"Don't hate," Karen said.

Chuckling, Kyle said, "By all means, please share."

"I go out of my way to talk to my parents and make them feel they're part of the learning circle. I praise them when their children are doing well and support them when they're not. Once a month, I invite the parents in before school to have coffee or tea and a muffin—something I like to call 'Coffee Chat'—and ask me any questions. It's worked well for the past two years."

"So all we need to do is promise some food, and we'll raise participation," Damian drawled.

"Hey, it works for police officers, so I don't see why it won't work for parents," Kyle said.

They came up with a slogan, designed a flyer and made copies for the teachers to send home tomorrow. They finished stuffing mailboxes and called it a day. Melissa left to pack up, and Kyle excused himself to the bathroom, leaving Damian and Karen alone.

"How about I walk you to your car?" Damian asked.

"I'd like that."

He took her tote out and lifted it into her trunk. After closing it, he folded his arms. "When you came in this afternoon, you looked upset. What happened?"

"It was nothing. Just Nikki getting on my nerves, as usual."

"Nikki?"

She nodded. "She's another teacher here."

"Why would she—"

"She's been a pain in the butt since I've been here, even more so since we've both applied for the principal position."

"You're applying for the principal's job here?"

She nodded. In the back of her mind, she wondered again how they would make their relationship work in the long run if she got the position. She couldn't see either of them giving up their careers.

"That's great. I hope you get it."

He said that now, but what about later? "We'll see. Let's talk about something else."

"Sure," he said with a grin. "Don't you owe me something?"

"What?" Karen asked, trying to hide her smile. He reached out, gently pulled her into his arms and covered her mouth in a scorching kiss. She moaned and slumped against him. Where in the world did a man learn to kiss like this? His kisses stole her reasoning and made her forget her name.

"I don't think one kiss is going to do it for me, baby," he murmured, trailing kisses over the curve of her jaw and neck before claiming her mouth again.

"Damian," she whispered against his lips, "we have to stop."

"I know." He kissed her once more, then dropped his arms. Taking her hand, he opened the car door and closed it after she climbed in. "Buckle up and text me when you get home. I'll call you later."

His voice was strained, and she could see desire burning in his eyes, not to mention the huge bulge at his midsection. "Okay." She started the car and drove out of the lot, peeking in her rearview mirror to see him standing in the same spot.

Damian watched until Karen's car disappeared around the corner...and until his erection went down before going back inside. The weekend couldn't come fast enough. *Two more days.* He could do that. Luckily, his plans were coming together nicely. All he needed now was for Karen to go along with them.

"I don't think kissing falls under your scope of duties," a voice behind him said.

Damian's hand froze on the office doorknob, and he whirled around to see the same teacher who'd tried to make a pass at him the first day step out from the side of the office building. "Excuse me?"

"Don't try to play games, *Mr. Bradshaw*," she sneered. "I know what I just saw." She folded her arms, and a malicious gleam filled her eyes. "I did some research on your company—pretty impressive credentials and not one complaint. It would be a shame for that trend to change." Nikki angled her head thoughtfully. "I wonder what the superintendent would say if he found out the company he hired is doing more than overhauling safety."

"Ms. Fleming, my personal life is none of your concern."

"Is that so? I'm sure Karen's told you about applying for the principal position here. It would be a shame for her to be disqualified for unprofessional behavior."

He clenched his teeth. "I don't do well with threats," he said in a deceptively soft tone. "You might want to remember that." Damian left her standing there and entered the office without another word.

After packing up and walking Melissa out, he and Kyle headed back to the hotel. They parted at their rooms and made plans to meet up in an hour for dinner in the hotel's restaurant. Inside his room, he paced angrily. *The audacity of that woman!* He stopped pacing, remembering what Karen had said about being upset with Nikki and wondering if the woman had made the same threat to Karen. Damian started pacing again, torn over whether he should tell Karen or not.

He had to tell her. He didn't want her to be blindsided by whatever Nikki was planning.

He sat at the desk and checked his email, clicking on one from Troy. Troy had sent the information Damian needed for the surprise weekend getaway he was planning for Karen. He sent back a thank-you message, logged off and left to meet Kyle. Over dinner, they discussed their upcoming schedule and the progress they'd made this week.

"I see your woman wasn't shooting daggers at you today. Did you guys straighten things out?" Kyle asked as they finished their meal.

"Yes." Damian hesitated before adding, "I told her about Joyce."

Kyle froze with his glass at his lips. He slowly lowered it to the table. "Everything?"

Damian nodded.

"Including what happened on Sunday?"

Damian nodded.

"What did she say?"

"She asked me to tell her about Joyce." Damian related their conversation. "Then she told me she'd be there for me," he finished. His heart squeezed with the memory of that moment.

"I'm really happy for you, Damian. Karen's a great woman. Are you prepared for a long-distance relationship?"

"I am. Troy is letting me use his time-share in Vegas this weekend. It's killing me being so close to her and acting like we're just friends."

Kyle laughed. "Then you'd better stop looking at her like she's your favorite dessert, because everybody's going to know."

"That bad?"

"Yeah, bro. You got it *bad*." Kyle leaned back in the chair. "If I didn't know better, I'd think you were in love with Karen."

Damian stared into his drink.

"I take it by your silence that I'm right. Don't you think you need a little more time to decide whether you love her? You haven't known her that long."

"The length of time doesn't matter. I know better than anyone else that sometimes today is all you have."

"True dat, my brother." Kyle lifted his glass in a toast.

"Thankfully, we only have a few more days left before hitting the next school."

"Too bad. I'm enjoying myself."

He lifted an eyebrow. "Melissa?"

Kyle nodded slowly. "I like her. She's smart, confident, and on top of that—fine as hell."

Damian shook his head. "Nah, man. Don't even go

there. Mixing business with pleasure is bad news, especially if all you're looking for is a one-night stand. Melissa is a nice woman, and I don't want to see her hurt."

"I'm not going to hurt her. And you don't seem to have a problem mixing the two."

"My situation is different. I knew Karen beforehand, and I'm not looking for a one-nighter. I'm telling you, Troy will kill you if you mess with the business. We've worked hard, and I don't want to see our reputation trashed because you couldn't keep your pants zipped."

"I *said* I'm not going to hurt her," Kyle said through clenched teeth.

Damian sighed. "Look, if you're feeling her, that's great. Just make sure your intentions are honorable. Understood?"

Kyle drained the rest of his drink and stood. "Yeah." He reached into his wallet, withdrew some bills and tossed them on the table. "I'm going up."

Before he could respond, Damian's cell buzzed. "What's up, Troy?" He frowned, and Kyle paused.

"You tell me."

"What does that mean?"

"I got a call from someone at the school district insinuating there is more going on than safety training, specifically some inappropriate sexual behavior with employees."

"What?" Damian roared, drawing stares from nearby diners. He lowered his voice. "That's bullshit and you know it," he said through clenched teeth.

Kyle lowered himself into the chair and mouthed, *What's going on?*

"I'm going to my room, and I'll call you back," Damian said to Troy, and disconnected. Drawing in a deep breath to rein in his anger, he stood and added some bills to the table. "Someone called the school district contracting and HR department and said we're engaging in inappropriate sexual behavior with employees."

Kyle stared.

"I'll explain upstairs." They exited the restaurant and took the elevator back to Damian's room. Once there, he called Troy and put him on the speaker.

"What the hell is going on, Damian? I know you and Kyle aren't messing around—" Troy said before Damian could utter a greeting.

Kyle cut him off. "You know that's not the case, but I am curious about who would say that."

"I know what it's about," Damian said. "There's a teacher at the school who, from what I gather, has it in for Karen. She happened to see me kiss Karen this afternoon when I walked Karen to her car *after school* when all the students were gone. Karen is applying for the principal position, and Nikki threatened to expose us. My guess is that she's going for the same position and will do anything to discredit Karen."

"This is a mess," Troy said. "Are you sure that's all? We've got a great reputation, and I don't want it trashed. Kyle, you aren't messing around, are you?"

Kyle looked at Damian, who answered, "No, he's not. Do you want me to call the district office tomorrow?"

"No. I'll take care of it. I am going to have to explain that you and Karen are dating."

"By all means, please do. There are no rules against us seeing each other. Anything else?"

"No. I'll update you tomorrow."

Damian ended the call and pinched the bridge of his nose. "I can't believe that woman," he muttered.

"Is that the woman who introduced herself to you, sounding like she was offering more than just a hello?" Kyle asked.

He nodded and told Kyle about the confrontation.

"And you were worried about my interest in Melissa."

"Don't start." He shook his head. "I need to call Karen and tell her."

"Good luck with that. I'll see you in the morning."

When Kyle left, Damian removed his shirt and shoes, then sat on the bed. Picking up his cell, he called Karen.

"Hello."

"Hey, baby. I miss you. I wish you were here with me."

"I hear you. It's getting harder and harder to sit in those meetings pretending I don't know you."

"It's not working for me, either. So, what are you going to do with the rest of your night?"

"Right now I'm going to take a long, hot bubble bath. Then I'm going to hop into bed and read for a little while."

He groaned. "I didn't need to know all that." An image of her naked, soap-slicked skin flashed in his mind, and Damian waged a war within himself whether to hang up, jump in his car and drive over.

Karen laughed. "Hey, you asked."

"I guess," he grumbled. "I need to talk to you about something."

"What's going on?" she asked with concern.

"Nikki saw us kissing this afternoon and called your school district's office." He told her about the confrontation between him and Nikki.

"What?" she practically yelled. "We can't do this, Damian. We have to stop seeing each other. I can't jeopardize my career, and you can't, either."

"Calm down, Karen. We aren't doing anything wrong. We can't let this woman intimidate us."

"That's easy for you to say. You're going back to your cushy little office in North Carolina, but I have to work with her. Our reputations are on the line. Don't you know that this could spell disaster for your company? Her little stunt could ruin your business."

"Not when her claims are baseless. I'm not that concerned, because she's lying. Nothing inappropriate is going on, and you know it."

"Well, I am concerned. I can't risk her doing something to ruin my chances of getting that principal position."

"What does that mean, Karen?"

"Maybe we need to back off a bit—starting now," she answered softly.

"Baby, wait—" He heard a soft click in his ear and cursed under his breath.

Needing to expend some energy, and to keep himself from charging over to Karen's apartment, he changed into shorts, a T-shirt and his running shoes and went down to the hotel's gym. He got on the treadmill, started at a slow jog and increased the pace until he was at a full sprint, hoping the exertion would cool the fury racing through his body. He wasn't worried about Nikki. He'd told the woman all she needed to know and had no doubt Troy would take care of the issue.

As he adjusted the incline, his mind went back to Karen. Somehow, in the short time he'd known her, she had woven herself into the very fabric of his being, and he found himself wanting to wake up beside her each morning. Damian stumbled with that realization. He wanted her in his life permanently. He had spent a month thinking he would never see her again, and if Karen thought he was going to back off, he had news for her.

Now that he had her back, he'd be damned if he let a lie tear them apart.

Chapter 15

Damian met Karen at her car the next morning. "What are you doing here so early?" she asked, glancing around the lot to make sure no one saw them. She figured after their conversation last night, he would keep his distance.

"I couldn't wait to get my kiss."

Apparently not. "Damian, we can't—"

He cut her off with a scorching kiss, inhaling the words right off her tongue. "Yes, we can."

She pushed against his chest and backed out of his hold. "I won't jeopardize my job."

"Karen, I keep telling you we aren't doing anything wrong. I'm sure there are several married teachers in this district. When I taught, we even had one couple at the same school." He took her tote from the trunk, gestured toward the office and followed her across the lot.

Inside, after greeting the office staff and checking her mailbox, Karen reached for the tote.

"I got it." He moved it out of her reach.

She looked up at Damian's face. His mouth curved in a sensual smile, and his eyes held a wicked gleam. Her body heated. "Damian…"

"I'm just going to walk you to your classroom, that's all."

She eyed him, not believing him for one second. Shaking her head, Karen led him out the back door. As soon as they entered her classroom and she closed the door,

Damian snaked an arm around her waist and pulled her against his body.

"Damian, we—" She moaned as he slid his tongue between her parted lips—teasing, tantalizing and leaving her breathless. What was it that made him so irresistible?

"School doesn't start for forty-five minutes, and students aren't allowed on campus for another twenty-five," he murmured against her lips, before covering her mouth again.

Karen locked her hands around his neck and pressed closer to him. His hands roamed down her back to her hips. She was quickly losing control and gently pushed against his chest. "I…I need to get some things ready."

Still holding her, he said, "I know. Honey, I would never do anything to risk your job. Please believe that. But I also won't be intimidated by a jealous woman and her lies."

She believed him, but this just added to her growing list of worries, and she was seriously contemplating cutting her losses before getting in any deeper. Damian kissed her again, and the thoughts flew right out of her mind.

"What are you doing this weekend?"

"I don't have anything planned. Why?"

"Would you spend it with me? With everything going on, I think we need to get away for a couple of days."

"I don't know."

"Please, baby," he said, peppering her face with kisses. "Come away with me."

Karen sighed heavily. "Fine."

"Good. I need you to pack a bag for the weekend and be ready to leave Friday at five. The teachers' training ends at three, so that should give you plenty of time. How does that sound?"

"It sounds wonderful. Where are we going?"

"I'd like to surprise you. The only thing I will say is it involves a plane ride."

She smiled. "Okay."

"What are you doing for lunch?"

"I have yard duty."

Damian groaned.

She laughed softly. "How about dinner at my place tonight? Is six-thirty okay?"

"Kyle and I have to do some planning for tomorrow's training later tonight, so it's perfect."

She reached up to wipe the gloss from his lips. "See you later."

"We'll only meet for a short time after school. Do you need me to bring anything tonight? I don't want you to go through too much trouble."

"No. I have everything."

He nodded and left the room.

Karen rounded her desk and slumped down in the chair. "That man is too tempting."

While her computer booted up, Karen made sure she had all the supplies for the art project. She had borrowed one of Janae's ideas for foil art. After gathering everything, she went back to her desk to check emails. She opened one from Human Resources letting her know her interview had been scheduled for the next day. The three o'clock time meant she would miss the last half hour of the training. She'd pack for her weekend tonight, just in case the interview ran longer than anticipated. She responded to a parent, logged off, then left to meet her students.

The morning seemed to fly by, and the students' foil butterflies turned out well. Karen had them put away the markers and place their pictures on a back counter. She directed them to wash their hands and line up for lunch. Having yard duty left her fifteen minutes to eat a quick bite and make a list of groceries she needed to pick up for dinner. She took a picture of the project and attached it to a text message to Janae. Grabbing her radio, she went out to the playground as the students exited the cafeteria.

"Walk, please," she called out. "Make sure your lunch containers are in the right bucket and not on the ground."

She tightened her jacket around her. Although the sun shone, it did nothing to warm her in the midfifties temperatures. Karen spoke to another teacher on the way to check the bathrooms. For some reason, the kids always left the water on or slid beneath the stalls to lock the doors.

As Karen made her way to the basketball courts after clearing the bathroom, Nikki stepped into her path.

"I had my interview this morning, and they were very impressed. That job is as good as mine. I plan to make a few changes around this place and implement some of my own programs."

Karen seethed. Nikki had been trying to undermine Karen at every turn, and she never understood why. The suggestions implemented had made all their jobs easier. And, with what Damian had shared last night, it was taking some serious restraint not to knock Nikki flat on her butt. "Well, I'll just wait until a formal announcement is made before I offer up any congratulations."

Nikki opened her mouth to say something, and an alarm went off.

This wasn't the same alarm used during fire drills. Then Karen remembered the memo stating there would be a lockdown drill—the first one with the new procedures. Karen's radio beeped, and Melissa's voice came over the line.

"Lockdown with intruder."

The other two teachers joined Karen and Nikki, and they frantically waved the children over while asking what was going on.

Sensing their nervousness and remembering what she'd learned from the workshop, Karen took charge. "Let's calm down and get the children lined up on their class numbers. Bev, can you take Lena's class? Joe, you take Liz's. Follow the lockdown procedures we distributed a couple of weeks ago." They nodded and hurried off. Out of her periphery, she spotted Damian striding urgently toward them, but she turned her attention back to getting the students to safety. "Nikki—"

"Who put you in charge? I don't have to take orders from you. Anyway, it makes more sense for everyone to go inside the cafeteria. It'll be easier to account for the kids." Nikki tried to call the other teachers back.

"I don't have time to argue with you, Nikki," Karen snapped. "Take Mr. Colston's class and get to your room. I'll take Sheila's class." She quickly walked to where the students were lined up. Nikki followed, still arguing about where the students should go.

Damian met them at the line.

"Nikki, did you not read the memo and lockdown procedures Melissa and I brought back from the training?" Karen asked with exasperation.

"Need help?" Damian asked, dividing his gaze between the two women.

"Yes," Nikki answered. "I'm trying to tell her that the best place for the students is in the cafeteria, but she acts like she knows everything."

"In this case, Karen is correct. I'm sure you received the lockdown procedures. The students need to be in the classroom with the doors locked, lights off, blinds closed and windows covered. Have them sit on the floor away from the door and windows," Damian said. "Please escort your students *now*." He left to gather some straggling students.

Nikki stomped off with the two classes, but not before shooting daggers Damian and Karen's way. "Wait until the superintendent hears about this."

Karen and Damian got the children secured in the classroom, and Karen had them read in an effort to keep them calm and quiet. Nikki's threat of going to the superintendent worried Karen, giving her second thoughts about her decision to keep seeing Damian.

"I heard the end of Nikki's threat, and I know you're worried. Don't be. Everything will work out," he whispered.

She stared up at his reassuring gaze and nodded. She wanted to believe everything would work out with their relationship, but between Nikki's threat and the possibility that Karen might get the job, she didn't see how it could ever happen. Deep in her heart, Karen felt she was only a few days away from another heartbreak.

It seemed like forever as they sat waiting. Finally, the all-clear signal sounded, and Kyle's voice came over the speaker.

"I want to congratulate the teachers and staff for a job well done on following the procedures for an intruder lockdown. We'll use some time during the staff development workshop to provide specific feedback and answer any questions. Again, great job."

When Kyle finished, Damian said, "I need to get back to the office. I'll see you after school."

Nodding, she waited until he left to give instructions. The other teacher came to take her students back, and Karen spent the next several minutes answering questions as best she could about the drill. She made sure the students knew how proud she was of how they handled themselves. They were still pretty antsy, so she put in a movie instead of having them do the writing assignment she had originally planned. There were only forty-five minutes left in the school day anyway.

After dismissal, Karen met Damian, Kyle and Melissa in the office. They spent the first part of the meeting discussing what happened. Damian and Kyle reported on what they had observed from staff, as did Melissa.

"I'd like to hear your thoughts, as well," Kyle added, gesturing toward Karen.

"With this being new, I think the teachers handled themselves very well. After being reminded about the newly implemented procedures, everyone took charge and moved the students to safety. Well…except one person, of course."

Damian recounted the confrontation he witnessed.

"Please don't tell me she stood out there arguing. What if this hadn't been a drill? Someone could've gotten hurt," Melissa said with annoyance.

"So I can expect this teacher to be very vocal tomorrow?" Kyle asked.

"Exactly," Melissa answered, sharing a knowing look with Karen.

Kyle cut the meeting short so he and Damian could work on the presentation. With the impromptu drill, they needed to alter some material.

Karen tried to hide her disappointment, knowing her dinner plans were about to be canceled. She went back to her class to retrieve something she'd left and found Damian waiting beside her car when she came out.

"I take it you're going to need a rain check on dinner."

"Yeah. I'm sorry."

"Don't be. You have a job to do."

"I'll make it up to you this weekend."

"I'm looking forward to it. Oh, before I forget, my interview is tomorrow at three, so I have to leave early."

A smile lit his face. "I know you won't need it, but good luck." He leaned down and brushed a kiss across her lips. "I'll call you tonight."

"All right."

He held the door as she got in and stood there until she backed out. As she drove, Karen's thoughts traveled back once again to the latest confrontation with Nikki, her threat to call the superintendent and what would happen if Karen were selected for the position. She couldn't see having a long-distance relationship for two or three years. One of them would have to make a life-altering sacrifice.

She forced the thoughts from her mind, not wanting to think about it. For now, she would concentrate on enjoying her time with him and looking forward to their weekend.

Chapter 16

Karen's heart beat double time in her chest when she opened the door Friday evening to Damian. Excitement filled her with the prospect that they would have the entire weekend together. She'd had a difficult time paying attention during the training earlier that day, especially when they were paired up for one of the tabletop crisis scenarios. Even Melissa had noticed and asked her about it. "Hi. Come on in."

"Hey, baby," Damian said, bending to kiss her cheek. "How did the interview go?"

"It went well. They'll make the decision next week."

"I'm confident you'll get it. Are you ready?"

"Yes. My bag's right here. Let me grab my jacket and purse and we can go."

Turning her way once they were seated in the car, he brushed the back of his hand over her cheek. "I've been waiting all week to have you to myself."

Karen gave him a winning smile and ran her hand up his thigh. "And now that you have me?"

He sucked in a sharp breath and grabbed her hand before it reached its destination. "Baby girl, you're playing with fire."

"I'm not afraid of a little heat. Are you?"

Damian pulled her into an intoxicating kiss. "Just wait until later. I'll show you *heat*." He drove out of the complex toward the airport.

Karen collapsed against the seat and tried to control the rapid pace of her heart. One kiss, and he had her body on fire. When her heart rate finally slowed, she opened her eyes and focused on the passing scenery, trying to guess where they might be going and how long it would take to get there. They ran into traffic but made it to the airport and through security with twenty minutes to spare.

"Las Vegas?" she asked, looking at the sign above the gate.

He nodded. "I really wanted to take you to my home, but we'd end up spending most of our time in airports, so Troy let me use his time-share. It's far enough that we can have some privacy, but close enough to maximize our time."

She had wondered if they were going to North Carolina and wanted to ask if he still lived in the same house he had shared with his wife, but she held on to the question. If and when the time came, she'd find out, although she wasn't sure how she felt about it. Yes, he'd said he was no longer in love with his late wife, but Karen knew that some people who'd lost a spouse had a hard time letting go of their past lives and kept everything from pictures and furniture to clothes—almost like a shrine. Was Damian one of those people? A touch on her arm cut into her thoughts.

"Karen?"

She smiled up at him. "Sorry, just daydreaming. What did you say?"

"I asked if you were okay with going to Vegas."

"Yes. I've never been at this time of year."

The flight was short. After they deplaned, he secured a car and drove to a property just off the Strip. They checked in, and he led her up to a beautiful two-bedroom suite with expensive decor and lavish amenities, including a Jacuzzi large enough for two people.

"Wow. This is amazing," Karen said as she went from room to room. "Have you stayed here before?"

"It's my first time."

"Well, be sure to thank your friend."

"I'll do that. Are you hungry?"

"Starving." It was after eight, and she hadn't eaten since lunch. She glanced around the lush accommodations once more, excited to get their weekend started.

Damian deposited their bags in the bedroom, then handed her the restaurant listing. "What looks good? We can choose something off the list or go to one of the hotels on the Strip."

She scanned the list and handed it back. "Let's hit the Strip."

They headed back down to the car and, after a short drive, ended up at the Cheesecake Factory in Caesar's Palace. Afterward, they strolled hand in hand through the Forum shops. Karen stopped to study the Fountain of the Gods for a minute before continuing. He glanced up at the way the ceiling had been artfully disguised to give the feeling of daylight despite it being past ten in the evening.

"Are you ready to head back?" he asked.

"Yes, but let me find a bathroom first."

"Okay. I'll wait for you by the big fountain."

Damian watched her hips as she disappeared into the crowd. He placed his hands in his pockets and continued on the path toward the Fountain of the Gods. Passing Tiffany, he ducked in on a whim.

"May I help you, sir?" a friendly saleswoman asked, coming toward him.

"Just browsing."

"Let me know if you need anything."

"Thanks. I will." He wandered around the store, peeking in the cases filled with pendants and bracelets. A case of engagement rings caught his attention, specifically an emerald-cut three-stone engagement ring set in platinum that would look amazing on Karen's finger. His heart rate kicked up a notch. Was he really thinking about marriage again?

The saleswoman appeared at his side. "Would you like to see something?"

"Yes, please."

She moved behind the counter and removed the ring he indicated. "This is a great choice. It's just under three carats. I'm sure the lucky lady will love it."

The moment Damian held the ring, he knew with all certainty he wanted to get married again...but only to Karen. He glanced at the tag. The price didn't matter. She was worth every penny, and he'd been investing and saving wisely over the past five years. He searched for an accompanying band and, with the saleswoman's help, settled on a channel-set band with vertical baguette diamonds.

"Do you know the size?"

He studied the woman's hand. "May I see your hand?"

She stared at him questioningly but extended her hand.

He entwined their hands, closed his eyes for a moment, then released her hand. "Your hand is about the same size as hers. What size is your ring finger?"

The woman chuckled. "Ah, seven. Can't say I've ever had a ring measured this way before." She reached into the case. "You're in luck. I have both the engagement ring and band in that size."

Smiling, he reached into his pocket for his wallet and handed her his credit card. A minute later, Damian exited the shop with the ring tucked safely in his pocket. He made it to the fountain just as Karen appeared. He slung an arm around her shoulders, and they started back to the hotel.

The short drive was accomplished in less than ten minutes. He was anxious to have her in his arms, and as soon as he opened the door to the room, he hauled her against his chest and covered her mouth with his. Lifting Karen in his arms, he kicked the door closed and took determined strides toward the bedroom. He laid her in the center of the bed, followed her down and continued to kiss her, absorbing her essence into his very cells. Fighting for control, he broke off the kiss and slid off the bed. He had plans.

"I'll be right back."

Karen lay in the middle of the bed, every molecule in her body tingling. Never had she been with a man who inflamed her body with one touch the way Damian did. The man was the total package—kind, caring, intelligent and handsome—and had a way about him that made the sanest woman lose her mind. And she was in deep.

She heard the sound of water running, and a short time later, he came back to the bed, cradled her in his strong arms and carried her to the bathroom.

Her loud intake of breath pierced the silence. He had lit candles and placed them on the sink and around the edge of the huge tub, casting a warm glow throughout the space. He'd interspersed rose petals between the candles.

"Do you like it?"

"Like it? I *love* it." She tightened her arms around him and kissed him softly. "Thank you. It's beautiful."

Damian let her slide down his body until her feet hit the floor. He undressed them both, then gently lifted her into the tub. "Is the water okay? It's not too hot?"

Sinking down under the water, Karen sighed contentedly. "No. It's perfect."

He climbed in behind her and sat on the step. "Scoot closer."

She did, and he began to massage her shoulders. Her head dropped forward, and she moaned. "That feels so good." He kept up the ministrations until she was limp as a noodle.

He moved down the step and pulled her between his

legs. Picking up the washcloth, he added bath gel and circled the cloth across her shoulders, over her back and around to her breasts. Damian dropped the towel and used his hands to gently knead and stroke her breasts and the sensitive peaks of her nipples. His hands slid beneath the water to her center, where she was already pulsating. Karen brazenly widened her legs to give him full access and arched against his exploring fingers. She groaned in protest when he removed them.

Damian kissed her hair. "Don't worry, sweetheart. I'll give you everything you want." He washed them up, stood and helped her up. "Watch your step." Picking up thick towels, he dried them off and led her to the bedroom. He pulled back the covers.

She climbed in, moved to the center and watched as he put on a condom. She opened her arms, and he fell into them. Karen palmed his face and brought her mouth up to his, trying to communicate what she was feeling.

He tore his mouth away and rested his forehead against hers, breathing harshly and trembling above her. He lifted his head, and their eyes connected. "I love you, Karen."

Her eyes widened in surprise.

He dipped his head and took her mouth in a kiss so achingly tender, tears leaked from the corners of her eyes.

"I love you so much."

He guided himself into her, inch by incredible inch, and started a gentle rocking motion, gyrating his hips in slow, insistent circles. Every movement reached deeper and deeper, touching the very core of her soul. "Damian, I love you, too."

His movements stopped and he stared down at her, his hazel eyes blazing with desire. An expression of relief spread over his face. "Thank you." Kissing her, he began thrusting again, whispering tender endearments.

They moved together in a sensual rhythm until she

felt something burst within her. Karen came with a soul-shattering intensity as wave after wave of ecstasy washed over her.

Damian stiffened, arched and cried her name, groaning long and low. His body shook violently and collapsed on top of her briefly before rolling to his side, taking her with him. He brushed back the strands of her hair off her face and kissed her.

She sank into his comforting embrace and closed her eyes, sucking in air as spasms of delight continued to rocket through her body. Her breathing and heart rate gradually returned to normal. She vaguely remembered him pulling the sheet up over them before drifting off to sleep.

When Karen woke up the next morning, she was alone in bed. Her mind immediately went back to the gentle yet passionate way Damian had made love to her last night. She bolted upright. *He said he loved me!* She wasn't sure what shocked her more: the fact that he loved her or her own declaration of love. Although she hadn't intended to tell him so soon, what other response could she have given him, other than the truth? She flopped back against the pillows. Did he really love her, or was it just something he'd blurted out in the throes of passion? Then there was the issue of his wife. Would Karen be a substitute for the one he had lost? The way he behaved and the things he said told her no, but she didn't want to set herself up for the possibility of having her heart broken again.

"You're frowning. That can't be good."

Karen rolled her head in the direction of the door, where Damian stood leaning in the archway wearing jeans, a long-sleeved pullover shirt and black boots. "Good morning."

He pushed off the wall and came toward her. "I thought it was until I saw that expression on your face." Damian took a seat on the side of the bed. "What's going through that beautiful head of yours?"

"Last night… Look, I know people say things when they're caught up in the moment, and—"

"And you think my saying I love you was a result of us being 'caught up in the moment.'"

She nodded.

He cocked his head to the side. "I meant what I said, Karen. Think back to when I said the words."

She remembered him carrying her to the bed, kissing her…and telling her *before* they made love.

He brushed his lips across hers. "Karen, I do love you. I know you may think this is all happening quickly—because it is. But also know that Joyce has been gone for five years now. Let me assure you that you are *not* a substitute for her. I fell in love with your intelligence, your zeal for life and your beauty—inside and out. I love everything about you."

Tears welled in her eyes. "I love you, Damian."

He raised an eyebrow and leaned back. "You sure? Because if memory serves me correctly, you were the one shouting 'I love you' in the throes of passion."

Karen's mouth gaped. *"What?"* She grabbed a pillow and hit him across the head.

"Hey!" he said with mock outrage. "I'm just saying." Laughing, he snatched the pillow from her and pulled her across his lap, covers and all. "You are so good for me."

She rolled her eyes and tried to conceal a smile. "Whatever."

He smacked her playfully on the butt and placed her back on the bed. "I'll let you get dressed so we can get some breakfast." Damian leaned over and kissed her cheek, rose to his feet and walked out.

Still smiling, she threw the covers back and slid off the bed. Her bare feet were silent on the carpeted floor as she padded to the bathroom, stopping to pick out an outfit. Thirty minutes later, dressed for the cool weather in jeans and a sweater, Karen pushed her feet into a pair of low-heeled ankle boots. She got her jacket out of the closet, picked up her purse and went to meet Damian. He stood looking out of the living room window, but he turned at her approach.

His gaze slowly traveled down her body and back up. "Ready, beautiful?"

"Yes." She followed him out and down the hall to the elevator. "Where are we going?"

"No idea. I'm sure we can find a breakfast buffet or something. I figured we'd start in the hotels on the Strip, unless you have someplace specific in mind."

"No. That works."

The elevator arrived, and they rode the fifteen floors down. He helped her into the car, slid in on the other side and drove down Las Vegas Boulevard. He parked in the Bally's parking lot, reasoning that it was a good midpoint. They settled on a breakfast spot and went sightseeing after.

Hours later, Damian played and won a few hands at blackjack. Karen, who had never been lucky, won two hundred and fifty dollars when Damian put ten dollars in a slot machine for her. They ended the evening with the Eiffel Tower Experience at the Paris Hotel. From the glass elevator ride and breathtaking views, to the man holding her protectively against his heart, she couldn't have asked for anything more.

Time seemed to accelerate, and before she knew it, they were back in San Jose and he was pulling into her complex. Both were quiet, lost in thought. He got out, grabbed her bag off the backseat and came around to help her. Their steps were slow; they were seemingly trying to delay the inevitable. She opened her door, and he deposited her bag inside.

"I'm not going to come in."

She nodded in understanding.

Damian bent and breathed a kiss over her lips. "I love you. See you tomorrow." He turned and ambled down the walkway.

She closed and locked the door. Picking up her bag, she shuffled down the hallway to her bedroom. Karen set the bag on a chair and lowered herself on the bed, suddenly feeling very alone. They had two more days before he moved on to another school, and a week before he went back to North Carolina. After this amazing weekend, things had changed between them—their relationship had deepened, and she didn't know how she would handle him being so far away.

Her fears about their relationship magnified. By the time he left for home, she'd have an answer on the principal position. Karen wanted this position, but she wanted Damian, too. Were they on borrowed time? She sighed and stood. For now, her immediate worry was how to keep her feelings hidden when she saw him tomorrow at school. Especially with all the drama Nikki was determined to cause.

Chapter 17

Karen breezed into the school office Monday morning, spoke to the receptionist and made her way to the teachers' lounge area. She stopped short upon seeing Damian, along with Kyle and two other teachers. He stood there pouring a cup of coffee. No matter what he wore, the man looked scrumptious. It was the first time she had seen him casually dressed at school. They had student assemblies this morning, and he mentioned that everyday attire seemed to be less intimidating for the kids. Kyle was similarly dressed in jeans and a pullover shirt.

She went around the corner to check her mailbox and came back to the lounge. Just as Karen entered, Nikki swept past her and latched on to Damian's arm. It took everything within Karen to ignore the infuriating woman.

"Mr. Bradshaw, I'm glad I caught you before school starts," Nikki all but purred. "I wanted to know if you and Mr. Jamison plan to incorporate my suggestions into the new plan."

"We'll review all the staff suggestions," Damian said. "You'll receive a copy of the policies once they're finalized."

Karen seethed inside, but to Damian's credit, he smiled but didn't show any reaction to the obvious flirting.

He turned Karen's way with another smile. "Morning, Ms. Morris. How was your weekend?"

Giving him a dazzling smile in return, she said, "It was wonderful. And yours?"

His smile inched up higher. "It was the best weekend I've had in years," he replied, searing her with his gaze.

Her nipples tightened, and her core pulsed. "Um…that's great. I'll see you later." She turned and fled.

Melissa intercepted Karen on her way out. "Can I talk to you a minute?"

"Sure," she said, trailing Melissa to her office.

Melissa closed the door, placed a hand on her hip and narrowed her eyes. Pointing a finger at Karen, she asked, "What the hell is going on with you and Damian? And don't try to tell me it's nothing. At the training on Friday, I picked up some serious vibes between you two, and that little show a minute ago… Girl, the way he looked at you, I expected your clothes to melt right off you."

Karen dropped into a chair and ran a hand across her forehead. "It's him."

"Him who?" Melissa asked, puzzled.

"Damian…from the cruise."

Melissa slapped a hand over her mouth. "No way," she whispered.

"Yeah. Way. When I saw him the first day of that training, I almost fainted."

"This is so unbelievable."

"Tell me about it."

"So, are you, like, a couple now?"

"For now."

"That is so cool. What do you know about his friend Kyle? He has the smoothest walnut-brown skin and most kissable lips I've ever seen. Those neatly done twists and pierced ears give him that sexy-with-a-dangerous-edge kind of look, don't you think? Ooh, and don't get me started on that body. Did you see how his shirt is clinging to all those muscles?"

Karen laughed and stood. "I don't know anything except they've been friends since they were kids."

"Well, now that you have the inside track, maybe you could hook a sister up."

"You are truly crazy, Melissa. On that note, I'm outta here."

"One more thing. You'd better watch your back. If I picked up on those vibes, Nikki has, too. She's looking for any little thing to make you look bad."

"I know. She's already tried." At Melissa's curious expression, Karen told her about the confrontations between Karen, Damian and Nikki.

"I hope you're not letting that witch interfere in your relationship. Damian is right. There are no rules against what you're doing."

"I know, but we'll see." She'd caught Nikki's gaze as she left the lounge. The woman had sent Karen a look that, if looks could kill, would have had Karen at the nearest mortuary purchasing a burial plot.

That afternoon the secretary called her room and asked Karen to stop by her desk after school. *Hmm. She's never done that before.* She hung up, still curious, and went back to her students. When school ended an hour later, she dismissed her class and went to the secretary's desk.

"Hey, Terri."

"Hi, Karen." Terri handed Karen an envelope. "This came for you from the district office, marked urgent." She glanced over her shoulder, leaned forward and lowered her voice. "One came for Nikki, too. I hope she didn't get the job. She acts like she knows everything and doesn't know squat," Terri added, rolling her eyes. "Are you going to open it?"

"No. I think I'll wait until I get home." She tapped the envelope against her other hand, not sure she wanted to see the contents. "Thanks. I'll see you later."

Damian caught Karen as she made it to the classroom. "Hey. Everything okay? You look upset."

"Just a little nervous." She held up the envelope.

His eyes lit up, and his mouth curved in a wide grin. "Is that what I think it is? Aren't you going to open it?" he asked eagerly. "I know just how we can celebrate."

Karen wished she could muster the same enthusiasm. She'd been working toward an opportunity like this her entire career, but somehow, the moment felt bittersweet.

"Baby girl, you're killing me with the suspense."

She chuckled. It was hard not to get caught up in his excitement. Taking a deep breath, she opened it and removed the sheet of paper. Her heart beat erratically in her chest as she read the words. "I don't believe it," she whispered. "I got it." She shook her head. "I got the job."

Damian whisked Karen off her feet and swung her around. "Yes! I knew it." He stopped, lowered her to the floor and gave her a long, drugging kiss. "Congratulations, sweetheart. I'm so happy for you."

On one hand, she was ecstatic about reaching one of her career goals ahead of the timetable she had set for herself. On the other hand, she didn't know what to do about her and Damian. Surely he would tire of sporadic visits over a long period, and in the back of her mind Karen would always wonder if he'd found another woman to occupy his time with. She couldn't go through that again

"We can go out to dinner and celebrate. Let's invite Kyle and Melissa…" He trailed off, and his brow knitted. "What's wrong? Aren't you happy?"

"Yes, but…"

"But what? You told me this was part of your dream."

"It is, but…but I didn't think about… It never occurred to me…" She turned away.

He turned her back to face him and placed his hands on her shoulders. "Talk to me, Karen. What's going on?"

She stared up at him, trying to choose her words. "It's just, I never imagined meeting someone like you and now…now this changes things."

His brow lifted. "What things?"

"Us."

"Why would it change things between us?"

"I plan to be in this position at least two years."

"Yeah. And?"

"Come on, Damian. You don't honestly believe this relationship can last two or three years long-distance. I know you've thought about it."

"Why not? We can do it if it's what we both want."

Karen folded her arms. "So what happens if there are weeks or months when we can't see each other?"

"We deal with those times as they come." Damian angled his head. "Karen, what's this about? Are you having second thoughts about us? I thought we already talked about the distance thing."

"No, I don't want to stop seeing you, but I also don't want to wonder if you're seeing someone else when we're not together."

He heaved a deep sigh. "Baby, I love you. I would never cheat on you."

As much as she wanted to believe him, thoughts of Andre's betrayal leaped to the forefront of her mind. Although she loved Damian, she couldn't take that chance again.

"Honey, this is your day. Let's go out and celebrate tonight, and we can talk about it later."

She shook her head and smiled ruefully. "I'm not really in the mood to celebrate right now. I think I just want to go home." She packed up her belongings and rushed out of the room with Damian on her heels.

He didn't say anything as they passed through the office. When she made it to the car, he gently caught her arm. "Karen, wait a minute. Listen to me."

"I worked too hard for this position to give it up." Her voice cracked.

"I'm not asking you to give it up. I would never do that."

"I know that and I love you, but I just don't think this is going to work." She couldn't ask him to give up his career, either. His mouth settled in a grim line, and her heart broke at seeing the pain reflected in his face, knowing she was the cause.

"Karen—"

"It not that I don't trust you, Damian, but I… I don't know. I just…" She opened the back door, tossed in her stuff and closed it. She opened the driver's door and hopped in, but he held on to the door, preventing her from closing it. "I'm sorry."

"Sweetheart, let's talk about this. I know we can come to some kind of compromise that'll work for both of us."

She shook her head and bit her lip to keep from crying. "I'm so sorry," she whispered, pulling the door shut. Karen started the engine, backed up and drove out of the parking lot without looking back. The tears she'd held at bay now came in full force, clouding her vision and echoing the tears in her heart.

What the hell just happened? Damian couldn't believe how quickly things had spun out of control. One minute he was planning to spend the evening with Karen celebrating her promotion, and the next he was starring in the horror film of his life. He stood there confused and replaying the scene in his head. Had she just ended their relationship? He understood her being apprehensive; so was he. He had never been in a long-distance relationship, but he loved Karen, was proud of her and would never ask her to sacrifice her career. And no, he didn't want to give up his career, either. But he figured they'd discuss the situation and come to an agreement. Still stunned and cursing under his breath, he stomped back to the office. In the small conference room, he braced his hands on the table and tried to stop the growing ache in his heart.

"You all right?" Kyle asked, entering.

"Karen just received a letter appointing her principal of this school."

"Hey, that's great! We should celebrate."

"No." He gave Kyle a rundown on what had happened.

Kyle shook his head. "Wow. She ended it just like that? I'm sorry, man."

"So am I. Let's go."

They said goodbye to the secretary. Damian's disappointment and anger hadn't cooled during the ride back to the hotel, and probably wouldn't until he talked to Karen. As soon as he reached his room, he called her, but she wouldn't pick up. He paced back and forth. *"Dammit!"* How could she just toss their relationship aside? And why did she believe the worst? He stopped pacing. The answer came to him immediately—her ex. He knew the only thing on Karen's mind when she mentioned being worried about him cheating was history repeating itself. It all boiled down to trust. She had trust issues—contrary to what she voiced—but they'd just spent an entire weekend together and he'd told her, as well as shown her, that he loved her. Or so he thought. How could she believe he would jump into another woman's arms the first time her back was turned?

His cell rang, and he jabbed the button. "What!" he barked into the receiver.

"I certainly hope this isn't the usual way you answer the phone," came the soft reply.

He ran an agitated hand over his face. "Sorry, Mom," he mumbled. "Bad day."

"I'll say."

"Did you need something?"

"I haven't talked to you since the holiday, and you seemed distracted when you were here. I wanted to see how you were. Obviously, there's something going on. Well, it's nothing having a good woman can't cure."

"Not today, Mama, okay?" he said quietly. He didn't have the energy to fend off another of her matchmaking schemes.

"Mama? You only call me that when something's wrong. What's going on, Damian?" she asked, concern evident in her voice.

Damian stopped pacing and lowered himself wearily on a love seat. He tried to come up with a plausible excuse, but his mother knew him and could tell just by the sound of his voice if he was lying. He had never been able to fool her, and had stopped trying long ago. He also realized that regardless of the fact that he was a grown man, Gwendolyn Bradshaw would hop on the first plane leaving North Carolina if she thought Damian was in trouble. She had always been protective of him growing up, and even more so in the past five years. "I met a woman, Mom."

"Honey, is this about you feeling guilty? You have nothing—"

"No, that's not it. I'm fine."

"Oh, Damian. Sweetheart, I'm so happy to hear that," she said emotionally. "I've been so worried about you." She paused. "Wait. Then what's the problem?"

"Remember the woman I told you about from the cruise?"

"Yes."

"She lives here in San Jose and happened to be part of the first training session we conducted."

She laughed. "That had to be the shock of a lifetime."

"You can say that again." He gave her the details of what had occurred since then, ending with what had happened earlier.

"I'm sorry, honey," his mother said. Her voice softened. "Karen sounds like a lovely woman. Your father and I can't wait to meet her."

"She's amazing, and I wanted you guys to meet her, but it probably won't happen," he said resignedly.

"Damian Anthony Bradshaw, I've never known you to shy away from going after what you want. So don't you dare start now."

Damian grimaced. He hated when she called him by his full name.

"If you love her as much as you say, go after her."

"I do love her."

"Yes! I can't wait to tell your father. I'm finally going to get some grandchildren," she sang.

He groaned. "I have to go, Mom."

"When are you coming home?"

"We leave Saturday afternoon."

"Okay. Be safe."

"We will." He disconnected and tapped the phone against his knee. His mother was right. All his life, Damian had pursued his goals with the tenacity of a dog after a bone. Some things came easy, others required hard work, but he hadn't failed yet. And he didn't plan to now.

Karen dragged herself out of bed the next morning and stumbled to the bathroom. She had no desire to go to work today, even with her new promotion. At least Damian wouldn't be there. She stared at her reflection in the mirror. Her throat felt raw and her head hurt, but her eyes weren't as puffy as they had been the night before, thanks to the cold compresses she had applied.

He had called as soon as she got home yesterday, but she didn't pick up. Karen had spent the rest of the evening vacillating between hoping he'd call again and wanting to just end things now. She didn't want to invest any more of her heart, only to have it shattered later. North Carolina was a long way from California, and anything could happen during those weeks, or possibly months, when their schedules prevented them from connecting. She moved her head too quickly, intensifying the pounding, and groaned. Emotionally, she was a wreck.

Forcing herself to get moving, she dressed. Her stomach was still in knots, so she skipped breakfast and made the drive to school. Karen wanted to bury herself under the covers and avoid everyone, but that wasn't possible. She had a job to do. At school, she received many congratulations—except Nikki, of course—and started the transition from teacher to principal.

She spent the next two days moving into her new office and saying goodbye to her teary-eyed students. She reminded them that she wasn't leaving the school and would see them on the playground. Karen also invited them to visit her. Although her days were busy, Damian always found his way into her thoughts. Nights were worse. With nothing to occupy her mind, visions of him and the times they spent together plagued her.

Melissa burst into Karen's office Wednesday afternoon. "Is it true?" she asked excitedly. She had been off campus yesterday and most of today.

Karen waved her hand around the office and nodded. "Yep."

"I'm so happy for you!" She grabbed Karen in a tight hug. "Look at you. Principal, a fine man who loves you… Girl, you are on a roll."

A deep pain settled in the middle of Karen's chest at the mention of Damian, but she pasted a smile on her face. "Seems like it. Hopefully, I can follow in Priscilla's footsteps and continue to make this a great school."

"Girl, please. Priscilla is going to be so excited to know you're leading the school. I'm going to call her this afternoon." Melissa posed thoughtfully. "Although I wouldn't be surprised if she already knew."

"You're right about that. We never could keep a secret from her."

Melissa lowered her voice. "Did you know that Nikki went over to the superintendent's office and bad-mouthed you after the drill?"

"I had no idea, but she did threaten to do it that day before stomping off."

Melissa chuckled. "Well, it certainly backfired. After the superintendent saw Damian and Kyle's detailed report, *including* Nikki not following procedures, he told her she lacked the discipline and leadership needed from a school principal and all but tossed her out."

"Are you serious? How do you know all this?"

"His secretary and I have been friends for years, and she called to ask if I knew Nikki. Apparently, Nikki was pretty nasty, demanding to see the superintendent and ignoring protocol." She lowered her voice conspiratorially. "You didn't hear this from me, but that little stunt, along with those lies she told regarding DKT behaving inappropriately, just cost Little Miss High-and-Mighty her job."

Karen could only shake her head.

"Hey," Melissa said. "How about we go out to dinner and celebrate your promotion with the four of us—you, me, Damian and Kyle? I know a great place."

The last thing Karen needed or wanted right now was to see Damian. "Their schedule is pretty hectic for the next few days. And they'll be leaving at the end of the week."

"Oh, please. You can't tell me Damian won't make time to celebrate with his girlfriend."

"Maybe we can do it later. Right now I have a ton of things to do, and so do they."

Melissa opened her mouth to speak, and her cell rang.

She glanced down at the display. "Karen, I have to take this. I'll see you later."

Karen nodded, grateful that she had been spared from sharing the details of their breakup. Melissa's call took longer than expected, and Karen left before Melissa came back. Luckily, Melissa had to deal with a crisis at another school for the rest of the week, so they hadn't been able to discuss the dinner again. It was a short reprieve, Karen knew. At this point, she would take anything she could get.

By the end of the week, not seeing or being with Damian had Karen out of sorts. He hadn't called in three days. But why would he? Getting into her car Friday afternoon, she leaned against the headrest and let out a deep sigh. She missed his kisses and the way he made love to her, but mostly, she just missed sitting and talking with him. She dismissed the thoughts because they only made her feel worse.

Karen started the car and drove home. Once there, she kicked off her shoes, stretched out on the couch and massaged her temples, hoping to ease the tension. *Finally, the week is over.* Her cell rang, and her stomach clenched. She dug it out of her purse, checked the display and connected.

"Hey, Janae."

"Karen? What's wrong? Girl, you sound terrible."

"Gee, thanks."

"Must be all those late nights with Damian," Janae said with a giggle. "How is he?"

"I don't know."

Janae paused. "Ah…did I miss something? Last time I talked to you, didn't you say he told you he loved you?"

"Yes."

"Then what happened?"

"I got the job as principal."

"What?" Janae shrieked. "Oh. My. God. That is *fantastic*! Wait. What does that have to do with Damian?"

"There's no way this relationship is going to survive the distance between us for two or three years."

"What are you talking about? You guys are already doing it."

"Yeah, but as a teacher, I figured it would be easier to move around if I wanted to. Now…I can't pass up this opportunity, and he's not going to want to give up his job."

"Did he ask you to turn it down?"

"Of course not, but I can't ask him to sacrifice his career, either."

"Did he say he wouldn't?"

"No. He said we could talk about a compromise."

"Then what's the problem? From what you told me about that Vegas weekend, I think Damian is fully committed to the relationship. Give him a chance. I'm sure you both can figure something out. Have you talked to him since then?"

"No. He called once when I got home that day, but I let it go to voice mail."

"I really think you should talk to him. Good men don't grow on trees, and I wouldn't be so quick to toss him over. I'm sure there's no shortage of women looking for a man like him. How long is he going to be in town?"

"He leaves tomorrow."

"Promise me you'll talk to him if he calls."

"We'll see."

"Don't let him get on that plane without talking to him. You'll regret it. Promise me, Karen."

"Fine. I promise." So what if her fingers were crossed. "I need to go lie down. My head is killing me."

"All right. Keep me posted."

"I will. Tell Terrence hello."

"Okay."

Karen ended the call and tossed the phone onto the table in front of her. She stretched out on the couch, closed her eyes and massaged her temples again. After about half an hour, she sat up and started toward the bathroom to get something for her head. The doorbell rang. Snatching the front door open, she found Damian standing there. She felt a sense of déjà vu.

"May I come in?" he asked.

She stepped aside. He brushed past her and went to the living room. She closed the door and took a moment to compose herself, then followed him.

He gestured to the space next to him on the couch. "We need to talk."

She chose the chair instead and waited for him to speak.

Damian expelled a deep sigh. "Karen, I don't want to lose what we have. I realize you've been hurt before, but I'm not like him. I'm in this for the long haul and, like I said, would never cheat on you. Didn't you hear anything I said last weekend? You're the only woman I want. I love you. I gave you everything—my love and my trust—all of me, and I hope you feel the same. We can work through this. Trust me."

Yes, she felt it. "I can't give you what you want. We'll be on opposite sides of the country, and I can't expect you to…" Her heart squeezed and she trailed off, not able to finish the statement. "Maybe if we still feel the same way in a few months—"

His eyes pleaded with her. "Baby, you don't mean that."

She wanted to give in, but her heart was at stake, and she couldn't take the chance. Karen stood and wrapped her arms around her middle. Tears misted her eyes. "I can't," she whispered. "Please don't make this any harder."

"So that's it? Didn't you tell me you loved me?" Anger clouded his expression. "I'm not *him*," he gritted out. "Don't punish me for something he did. Don't punish us."

Karen heard the words but couldn't talk around the lump in her throat. She averted her eyes.

He slowly got to his feet, came to stand in front of her and tilted her chin. "My plane leaves tomorrow around one." Damian placed a solemn kiss on her brow. "I know we had something special, and I think it's still there, but I can't force you to change your mind." He gave her a look of patented regret, spun on his heel and walked out of her house, out of her life.

The click of the front door closing seemed to magnify in the space, symbolizing finality. Karen stood rooted to the spot, silent tears coursing down her cheeks, as she tried to convince herself that she had done the right thing.

Chapter 18

Damian slid behind the wheel of the car, leaned his head back and closed his eyes. Knowing she didn't trust him shattered his heart into a million pieces. He reached into his pocket, pulled out the small Tiffany box and opened the lid. The brilliant stones caught fire in the sun and glittered all around him. Every day since purchasing the ring, he had imagined sliding it onto Karen's finger and, later, her walking to meet him at the altar, where they'd pledge their love to each other for all time.

He snapped the lid shut and shoved the box back in his pocket. He started the engine and gripped the steering wheel. Some things weren't meant to be, and it was time he accepted that fact.

He drove back to the hotel for what would be his last night in California. He paced the confines of his room and wondered for the hundredth time how he and Karen had gotten to this point. A week ago, his world shone as bright as those diamonds; now it was as dark as the approaching night.

His cell buzzed. Damian glanced over to the table where he had left it, thinking maybe Karen had changed her mind, but knowing in his heart she hadn't. Walking across the floor, he picked it up and read a text from Kyle asking if he was ready to head downstairs for dinner. Truthfully, he had no appetite, but sent a message back in the affirmative.

Minutes later, Damian opened the door to Kyle. "Hey."

"How did it go with Karen?"

"It didn't."

Kyle blew out a long breath. "I don't know what to say. I thought for sure you two would be able to straighten out your differences. I'm sorry, man."

No sorrier than Damian was. They didn't exchange another word until they were settled in a booth at the back of the restaurant. Both ordered beers.

While perusing the menu, Kyle asked, "What happened?"

He glanced up from the menu. "In a nutshell, she doesn't trust me."

"Why? You haven't had any problems with the distance so far."

"I guess she never gave it much thought until now. All she sees is history repeating itself. Her ex cheated on her. Actually had the woman over to his mother's house at the same time he was dating Karen. It didn't help that I stood her up on the cruise and was still coming to terms with falling in love again. Now that she's committed to this position, she believes I'll get tired of the back-and-forth and start seeing someone else during the times we're apart."

Kyle shook his head with disgust. "Her ex was an ass. But this situation is completely different."

"I explained that, but she still didn't believe me."

The waitress approached with the drinks and took their food order. "Your food should be here shortly," she said with a smile, retrieving the menus and walking away.

"What are you going to do?"

Damian shrugged. "Nothing left to do. I can't force her to be with me."

"No, but you said you loved her. You're going to give her up just like that?" Kyle said, snapping his fingers.

"What do you want me to do, Kyle? I told her we could work out a way for us to be together. I promised her I would never cheat on her. She doesn't trust me, and she won't even try," he gritted out. He propped his elbows on the table and dropped his head in his hands. The ache in his chest intensified, and he struggled to draw in a breath. Lifting his head again, he said, "Look, I don't want to give Karen up, but—" He halted his speech to gain control of his emotions. "I love her, but right now there's nothing I can do about it."

Kyle nodded.

Their food arrived, but Damian couldn't summon an appetite. As a result, he left half of his meal on the plate and was more than ready to go up to his room when Kyle finished. They made plans to check out at ten-thirty and then parted.

Damian showered and packed. He picked up the ring and placed it in his carry-on bag, not wanting to take a chance on its being lost or stolen in his luggage. He only had fifteen hours left—fifteen hours to know whether the woman he loved would come to him.

After spending another restless night, he dragged himself to a sitting position and glanced at the clock—eight-thirty. He checked his cell to see if Karen had texted or called. Frustrated and disappointed, he tossed the covers aside and went to stand in front of the window. The gloomy picture outside matched his mood. *Four and a half hours.* Over the next two hours, he made preparations to leave. At exactly ten-thirty, he surveyed the suite one last time to ensure that he hadn't left anything and tried to accept the fact that she wasn't coming and they were over.

Karen rolled over Saturday morning and groaned. She scooted up against the headboard and pulled the covers tighter to ward off the chill. In less than twenty-four hours her world had collapsed. She'd lost the man she loved. Damian's words kept coming back to her: *"I would never*

cheat on you... I love you... You're the only woman I want."
Every time she closed her eyes, she saw his tortured gaze
and began to wonder if she'd made a mistake. In trying to
protect her heart, she hadn't considered his.

Deep down inside Karen knew Damian was not the
same kind of man as Andre, yet she had treated him like
one and the same. Damian had protected her from the first
day they met, never ridiculed her job and was happier than
she was about her promotion. Her heart hammered fast and
furious in her chest. *What have I done?*

The past four days without him had been pure hell. She
loved him, and suddenly the thought of not having him
in her life was almost too much to bear. Her conversation
with Janae popped into her head, along with her friend's
warning: *"Good men don't grow on trees, and I wouldn't
be so quick to toss him over. I'm sure there's no shortage
of women looking for a man like him."*

She'd be damned if she was going to hand over her good
man. Karen had to go to him. He had said his plane didn't
leave until one. The clock on her nightstand read ten forty-
five. She snatched up her cell and scrolled through the
contacts until she came to the number of the hotel where
he was staying.

"Yes, can you please connect me to Damian Bradshaw's
room?" Karen said as soon as the hotel clerk answered.

"One moment please."

"Come on, come on," she mumbled under her breath.

The clerk came back on the line. "I'm sorry, but Mr.
Bradshaw just checked out."

No, no, no. "Thank you." She hung up, threw off the
covers and dashed to the bathroom.

She brushed her teeth, washed her face and dressed in
ten minutes. Grabbing the brush, she slicked her hair back
and slid on a headband. After sticking her feet in a pair of
running shoes and grabbing her jacket, purse and keys, she

sprinted out to her car. Karen stuck the key in, gunned the engine and sped out of the complex toward the airport. She didn't have a clue what she would say, but she couldn't let him leave without at least telling him she loved him. On the drive, she realized she didn't know the airline or terminal. Engaging her Bluetooth, she called Janae.

"Hey, Janae. I don't have time to explain, but I need you to go online and tell me which airline has a flight out of San Jose to Charlotte, North Carolina, today leaving around one."

"Is this about Damian?"

She choked back a sob. "Yes. I messed up, and he's leaving."

"Okay. Hang on." Janae paused. "There's a Delta flight leaving at one-twenty."

"Thank you," Karen breathed.

"Now go get your man."

"I owe you."

"That's what friends are for. Later."

Fifteen minutes later, Karen parked in the daily lot outside Terminal A and ran across the street. She searched frantically for several minutes at the counters and around the lower level. Her heart sank upon not seeing him. And there was no way to get through security without a ticket.

Pacing and rubbing her hand across her forehead, she muttered over and over, "Think, Karen, think." She stopped and made a beeline for the counter. Maybe she could have him paged. Halfway there, she saw him and Kyle walk through the far doors, and her heart lurched.

"Damian! Damian!" she screamed, running toward him and not caring about the people staring at her.

He whirled around, and their eyes locked. His face was unreadable, and her steps slowed until she was standing in front of him.

"Hey, Karen," Kyle said. "I'll wait for you over by the

café, Damian." He gave Karen an encouraging smile and sauntered off.

She and Damian stood in strained silence. "Hi," she finally said.

"Hey."

She wrung her hands, not knowing how to begin.

"Why are you here?"

"I owe you an apology, Damian. I should've talked to you, tried to work it out, and I should have believed that you're a man of your word."

He cocked his head to the side. "And you do now?"

"Yes. I'm so sorry."

Damian paused, then nodded. "Apology accepted." He turned to walk away.

"Wait," she called anxiously, latching on to his arm.

He tensed.

"Please, wait."

He slowly faced her.

She dropped her hand. He didn't plan to make things easy for her, and she guessed she deserved it. "I love you, Damian, more than anything. And I do trust you."

He placed his hands on her shoulders. "Is that all?"

"No. I'm ready."

He moved his hands down to her waist and pulled her closer, a smile tugging at his lips. "Ready for what?"

She took a deep breath. "To give you what you want."

"And what's that?"

"Everything. My love, my trust…all of me. I know it's not going to be easy, but I need you in my life."

He hauled her against the solid wall of his chest and wrapped her in a crushing hug.

"I love you, Karen. I love you, baby. I didn't think you'd come. We'll do whatever it takes to make this work."

Tears of relief sprang from her eyes.

He leaned back, and she saw the sheen of tears in his

eyes. Keeping one hand around her waist, he used the other one to tip her chin up. "Promise me you won't ever push me away again."

"I won't," she cried.

Damian lowered his head and covered her mouth in a tender but heated kiss. He peppered her face with kisses before claiming her mouth again and telling her how glad he was that she came.

Karen held him tight, not wanting him to leave.

"I don't want to leave you," he whispered against her ear.

"I wish you didn't have to go."

"Come home with me."

She jerked back. "Come home with you? What? When?"

"Now."

"Now?" She searched his face. "Are you serious?"

"Very. I want you to meet my parents."

She glanced down at the oversize sweatshirt and old pair of jeans she had hastily thrown on and shook her head vehemently. "I can't go with you. I don't have a ticket, clothes…"

"I'll get you a ticket, and we can shop for everything you need."

"But—"

He put his finger on her lips. "Please. I want them to meet you."

"I don't know. This is crazy." But at the same time, she didn't want to be away from him. Then there was the curiosity about his house. "I have to go to work on Monday."

"Give me twenty-four hours, baby girl. That's all I'm asking." He unleashed that captivating smile on her, and she caved.

"Okay." The words were barely off her tongue when he grabbed her by the hand and dragged her over to the line to purchase a ticket. Everything happened so fast, her head spun.

"You okay?"

"It's just that everything is going so fast. I'm trying to catch up, that's all."

They reached the counter, and he pulled out his travel documents. Luckily, there were seats available. She handed over her driver's license, and a minute later she had a ticket. She would return on a 5:00 p.m. flight tomorrow. Smiling, they went through security and proceeded to the gate. When the time came to board, Karen was surprised to find herself seated in first class. She hadn't bothered to look at the ticket, but guessed with Damian's and Kyle's height, they definitely wouldn't be comfortable in coach.

Damian reached down for her hand. "You good, baby?"

She smiled and snuggled closer. "Better than good."

Two planes, a taxi and over seven hours later, Damian opened the door to his house and moved aside so she could enter. Given the late hour, she could only tell that the house was brick and had a nice porch.

He set his bags down in the foyer. Bending, Damian swept her up in his arms and strode purposely from the room and upstairs. "It's late. Let's go get comfortable. You can see the house tomorrow. We'll put your clothes in the washer tonight and go shopping in the morning."

"I don't have anything to sleep in." She had bought a toothbrush, toothpaste, comb, brush and deodorant in one of the airport shops.

"You won't need anything tonight. I'll keep you warm," he said, pressing a wall switch and entering his bedroom. He placed her on her feet.

She laughed. He was right. "Very nice," she said, turning in a slow circle. Dark, heavy furniture dominated the space with a huge bed as the focal point, decorated in soft gray hues.

"Come on. You can get your shower first."

She followed him into the bathroom done in gray and black marble.

He turned on the water and placed towels on the counter. "I'll bring you a shirt." He left and returned with a black T-shirt. "Enjoy."

"Thanks." She closed the door behind him, undressed and stepped into the heated space. She washed up, careful not to wet her hair, and contemplated her whirlwind of a day. At best, she figured they'd patch things up with a promise to visit in a couple of weeks. She never dreamed she would hop on a plane to go home with him or meet his parents. He promised to show her the house tomorrow, and Karen couldn't help being apprehensive. So far, nothing in his bedroom indicated the presence of his late wife, but would that hold for the rest of the house?

Chapter 19

While Karen showered, Damian went downstairs to retrieve his bags and turn off the lights. He still couldn't believe she had come. His heart had filled to near bursting when he heard her calling out to him, and it was all he could do to stand there. But he needed to hear her say the words, to tell him she trusted him and believed in him—in them. Back in his bedroom, he placed his suitcase in a corner and his carry-on bag on a chair. Unzipping an inside pocket, he took out the jeweler's box, clutched it in his palm and offered up a prayer of thanks. With any luck, the ring would end up exactly where it should be.

He walked down the hallway to a second bathroom and showered. When he returned, Karen was just coming out of the bathroom. Like any man, he got a thrill from seeing her in his shirt. He stood nearly a foot taller than her, so the shirt went almost to her knees.

She held up her clothes. "Can I put these in the washer?"

"Follow me." He led her back downstairs to the laundry room and waited while she started the washer, then carried her back upstairs.

He pulled the covers back on the bed and made a mental note to thank his housekeeper for changing the sheets. Damian placed Karen on the bed, climbed in and pulled her into his arms. He groaned with contentment.

"I'm so glad you came," he said, brushing a kiss across her lips. "So glad."

"Me, too."

He kissed her again and set about showing her just how happy he was.

Damian woke up the following morning, braced on his elbow and watched Karen sleep. Twenty-four hours ago, he thought he'd have to live without this remarkable woman. He wanted her by his side for always and didn't know how he was going to let her go this afternoon.

"Karen." He nuzzled her neck. "Wake up, sleepyhead. Time to get moving."

Her eyes fluttered, then opened slowly. "Mmm, morning. What time is it?"

"Morning. Just after eight. We have a lot to pack in before you leave."

She buried her face in his chest. "I wish I didn't have to go."

"So do I, baby. We have a couple of workshops scheduled this week. Otherwise I'd go back with you. The earliest I can fly down is Friday."

Karen groaned. "I'm going to LA on Friday. Janae is having her first art showing that night."

"Can you bring a guest?"

She lifted her head, and a smile lit her face. "You'll come to LA with me?"

"Sweetheart, I'll follow you anywhere. Do you still want to go shopping? Your clothes are on the bench at the foot of the bed."

"Yes. I can't meet your parents wearing a sweatshirt and old jeans."

He laughed. "You look beautiful in anything, and my parents won't care. If it'll make you more comfortable, I'll dress the same way."

"It doesn't. So let's go. You don't introduce somebody to your parents dressed like a hobo off the streets." She flipped the covers back, hopped up and grabbed her clothes off the bench. Still muttering under her breath, she cut him a look, went into the bathroom and slammed the door.

Damian fell back against the pillows and howled with laughter. When she was done dressing, they toured the house. He started with the two other upstairs bedrooms before heading down to the lower level and stopping first at his home office. He watched Karen wander around the room, then over to his desk. He held his breath, waiting for her response, when she picked up the small picture of Joyce. He had a few more photos, the banner Joyce had made for him when he got his first teaching job and the locket he'd given her when she graduated from college, all in a box kept in the hall closet. Everything else was gone.

"She's beautiful," Karen said.

"She was." He waited for her to say something else, but she replaced the picture and followed him out.

Damian escorted Karen through a formal living room with expensive but comfortable-looking furniture, a spacious gourmet kitchen and a large family room with leather furniture and a huge flat-screen television mounted on the wall. He went left and into a beautiful screened-in porch that looked lived-in.

"This is lovely. You must spend a lot of time here. I know I would." There were three walls of windows, two loungers and a small table between matching oversize chairs in front of a fireplace. It was the ultimate relaxation space.

"I do. It's the biggest reason I purchased the house."

Scanning the area, she wondered if he had spent hours out here with his late wife.

As if he had interpreted her thoughts, he said, "I bought it a year ago." He wrapped his arms around her. "You're the first woman who's been here."

She glanced over her shoulder at him, then turned back toward the windows. "Was it hard to leave your old house?"

"At first, yes. After a while, I felt like I was starting to suffocate and I couldn't pull myself out of it. I went to counseling for a while and realized I had been trapped in the same cycle of grief for four years. Moving helped tremendously. I even went out on a few dates." He turned her in his arms. "But no one made me want to try to love again until you. Don't ever think you're a substitute for another woman. You could never be one." He kissed her tenderly. "I love you, Karen."

Coming home with him had been the right decision. She needed to hear those words from him—needed reassurance of her place in his life. "I love you, too."

"Let's go get some breakfast."

Damian drove them to a local restaurant, grateful that they'd hurdled that issue. While eating, they talked, laughed and began the discussion of their long-distance relationship commitment. An hour later, he pulled into the mall parking lot. It didn't take her long to find what she needed. Karen added a tote bag and carried everything to the register. He overrode her protests to pay and placed his credit card on the counter.

"This impromptu trip was my idea, so it's only fair that I cover any expenses," he reasoned. They engaged in a stare-down until she finally relented.

"Fine, you win."

He gave her a quick kiss. "Thank you." He signed the receipt, picked up the bags and escorted her back out. "We'll go home so you can change, then head over to my parents'."

He drove home and carried her bags inside. Upstairs in his bedroom, he watched her pull out a curling iron, makeup and a host of other things. He shook his head. "Honey, we're not going to dinner at the White House, just over to my parents'."

"I know, but I want to look nice."

"What you're wearing is fine."

She placed her hands on her hips. "Damian Bradshaw, I am *not* wearing—"

He held up his hands in surrender. "Okay, okay. I'll wait for you on the porch."

"I won't be long." She gathered up her haul and went into the bathroom.

Damian's heart raced with excitement. He never thought he would risk his heart again—the pain of losing had been too much. Since meeting Karen, he realized the pain of not having her in his life outweighed everything else. He couldn't wait to introduce her to his parents.

Karen surveyed herself one last time. She wanted to look especially nice for his parents. Would they like her? Or would they compare her to his first wife?

When she toured the rest of the house, she saw that he kept only one small picture of Joyce in his office—nothing like the shrine Karen had envisioned. But Joyce was a beautiful young woman, and Karen couldn't help wondering how his parents would feel about him marrying again. She took a deep breath and tried to still the butterflies fluttering in her belly. She placed her stuff in the tote bag, turned off the light and made her way to the porch.

Damian stood facing the window with his feet braced apart and his arms folded across his chest, seemingly deep in thought. She crossed the floor and touched his arm. "You okay?"

He wrapped an arm around her shoulders and dropped a kiss on her hair. "I'm good. You look beautiful."

"Thanks. I'm ready, if you are."

On the way over, she wondered again how they would make the relationship work. "How are we going to do this, Damian?"

Damian's gaze slid to hers briefly, then back to the road. "Do what?"

"This. Us."

They came to a red light, and Damian reached over and covered her hand. "Baby, like I told you over breakfast, we *will* figure out what'll work best for both of us. Relax."

"Okay." She resumed watching the passing scenery. A few minutes later, Damian pulled into the driveway of a one-story brick ranch-style house on the corner with a circular driveway. She saw a smaller attached structure and asked about it.

"My mom has an art studio. It's connected to the house through a breezeway."

"An art studio? That sounds so cool."

"Yep."

"What type of art does she do?"

"Sculptures. I'm sure she'll give you a tour if you ask."

Just then, a tall, slender woman with the same golden-colored skin as Damian opened the front door. "Did your parents know you were bringing a guest?"

"Nah. I wanted to surprise them."

"I am so going to kill you, Damian. You're gonna give them a heart attack."

Damian laughed, hopped out and came around to her side.

He helped her out of the car and she whispered, "You'd better be right." He kissed her, and she saw his mother's eyes widen. Karen groaned and let him lead her up the walkway.

"Hey, Mom," he said, bending to kiss her cheek.

"Hi, sweetheart. Welcome back. And who is this lovely young woman?" she asked with a warm smile.

"Mom, I want you to meet Karen Morris. Karen, this is my mother, Gwendolyn Bradshaw."

"It's very nice to meet you, Mrs. Bradshaw," Karen said, extending her hand.

"I'm so happy to finally meet you, Karen," she said, ignoring Karen's hand and pulling her into a warm embrace. "Please come in. Louis is going to be so tickled to meet you."

Karen followed her through the foyer and large living room to an even larger family room, where a walnut-colored older version of Damian sat watching a basketball game.

"Louis, this is Damian's girl, Karen," Mrs. Bradshaw said.

He rose to his feet swiftly and engulfed her in a bear hug. "Welcome, Karen. It's nice to meet you. Make yourself comfortable."

"Thank you. It's nice to meet you, too."

He turned to Damian and pulled him into a rough hug. "Welcome back, son." His parents traded secret smiles.

When they were comfortably seated, Mrs. Bradshaw said, "Karen, tell me about yourself."

"I teach fourth grade."

Damian cleared his throat, and she smiled at him. "Actually, I've just been appointed principal."

"Congratulations. That's wonderful."

They spent another hour with his parents—his mother insisted on fixing an elaborate lunch—getting to know one another, and leaving no doubt in Karen's mind that she wouldn't be standing in the shadow of another woman. When the time came for Karen to leave, Damian's parents walked them out and again expressed their happiness. She waved at them until they were out of her sight. On the drive to the airport, she and Damian spoke very little, both reluctant to part. He parked in the lot and walked her inside.

He kissed her deeply. "I love you so much."

"I love you, too." She turned and started to walk away,

but Damian held on to her hand. "I can't leave if you're holding my hand. You have to let go."

"I can't let you go."

She chuckled. "What do you mean you can't let me go? I have a plane to catch and work to go to in the morning."

"I can't let you go—not without you agreeing to be my wife."

"Wait!" She gasped and stared at him in shock. "What did you…? Your *what*?"

Damian dropped to one knee in front of her. "Karen, I never thought I'd be able to give my heart again, but then you came along. Your presence calms me, your touch comforts me and your love reminds me what's most important each day. When I look at you, I know the love we share will continue to grow. You mean everything to me. Marry me. Let me give you all of me from this day forth."

Tears began to fall before he could finish and ask the question. "Yes, I'll marry you." She lowered to her knees to match him. "And I want to give you all of me."

He reached into his bag and pulled out a small box from Tiffany. Her eyes widened like saucers when she saw the ring nestled inside. He slid it on her finger. It fit perfectly. "Oh. My. God. It's *amazing*," she whispered through her tears. She launched herself at him, knocking him to the floor. "I love you, Damian."

Laughing, he said, "I love you, too."

They lay on the floor kissing until he said, "If you don't let me up off this hard floor, you're going to miss your plane."

She groaned and buried her head in his chest. Someone tapped her on the shoulder, and she looked up to see a smiling Kyle. Karen sprang up, hearing the clapping and whistling.

"I can't wait to show Troy this video," Kyle said with

a laugh, holding up his cell. "That was some proposal. Congratulations."

Her mouth fell open. "What? How did you…?" She narrowed her gaze at Damian. "Did you do this?"

He smiled and shrugged. "I wanted proof, just in case you changed your mind."

She shook her head. "I don't know what I'm going to do with you, Damian Bradshaw."

He laughed. "Hey, you're stuck with me now, for better or worse."

She glanced down at the ring on her finger, then back up at him. "Yeah, I am, huh?"

He kissed her once more and held her tightly against him. "You'd better go. Call me when you get home. I love you."

Holding him tight, she whispered, "I will. I love you, too." Karen released him and then walked away while she still could.

The trip home seemed much longer, but the knowledge that she would see Damian the following weekend and the exquisite ring on her finger made it bearable. She giggled to herself. *Grandma can scratch me off her matchmaking list.* She couldn't wait to see her parents' faces when she told them.

She and Damian still had a lot to work out, but Karen felt confident about their future together. She stared, once again, at the ring on her finger and knew she would love him forever.

Epilogue

One year later

"So, how does it feel to know in less than thirty minutes you'll be a married woman?" Janae asked, coming into the room where Karen waited for the wedding to begin.

"I'm so excited, I can barely stand it."

"This dress is spectacular."

Karen walked over to the mirror and ran her hand down the front of the strapless beaded gown with a sweetheart neckline, lace-up back and trumpet skirt. "I fell in love with this dress the moment I saw it."

"I think Damian's going to fall in love with it, as well." Janae wiped a hand across her forehead.

Noticing the slight frown on Janae's face, Karen turned from the mirror. "Are you okay?"

Janae waved her off. "I'm fine. Just a little light-headed and queasy."

"Janae? What are you telling me?" Janae paused, and Karen called her name again.

Finally, she smiled faintly and said, "You're going to be a godmother."

Karen's eyes filled with tears, and she hugged her friend. "I am so excited for you and Terrence."

"Thank you. But today is all about you. Don't go ruining your makeup with all this crying," she said, laughing. "No tears allowed."

Karen pulled a tissue from the box sitting on the counter, handed Janae one and turned back to the mirror. She dabbed at the corners of her eyes, being careful not to smudge the mascara and liner.

"So, are you ready to admit I was right?" Janae asked.

"What are you talking about?"

"Remember Terrence's concert on the cruise? I reminded you about what happened the first time we went to his concert—one of us ended up married. I told you to be careful because it would happen again, and you didn't believe me."

She laughed. "I totally forgot about that, but I guess you were right. I'm *really* glad you were right." She thought about all that had happened since the first day she saw Damian on the cruise and realized it had all been leading to this moment. What began as a cruise-ship fling would end in a lifetime of love and happiness. He was everything she could want and more, and she couldn't wait to start their life together.

Over the past year, even with the times apart, she and Damian had grown closer. Karen had settled well into her job as principal, even more so with Nikki gone. As Melissa had predicted, all Nikki's lies and drama had cost her her job. Karen's mind went back to her soon-to-be husband. After much discussion, she and Damian had decided to live in San Jose for at least another year, and then reexamine their options. A knock sounded on the door, and Melissa entered.

"I think it's time," she said with a smile. "Your dad is on his way."

Karen shared one more hug with Janae and Melissa, and they left just as Karen's father entered.

"Ready to go, angel girl?"

"I am, Daddy."

She linked her arm with his, and he escorted her out to where Damian awaited.

Damian paced the length of the floor in the room, waiting for his wedding to start. He didn't remember being this nervous last time.

"You're about to wear a hole in the floor, and I don't think the pastor would be pleased," Kyle teased. "Sit down. You're making me dizzy."

Troy laughed. "What's the problem? You've done this before."

"I know, but not like *this*." He couldn't explain it, but this time felt different.

"Are you having second thoughts?"

"No, nothing like that. I can't wait to make Karen my wife." He stopped. "Are you sure you guys are okay with me working from San Jose?" They had agreed to use Skype for most of their meetings, and Damian would join them at the conference sites, only coming to the North Carolina office when necessary. Troy had insisted on hiring someone part-time to do some of the local workshops to give Damian extra time with Karen. Kyle's younger brother had completed his final tour in the military and agreed to house-sit until Damian and Karen moved back.

"Damian, we've gone over this ten times." Kyle put his hands on Damian's shoulders. "Relax, man. It's all good."

Wiping beads of perspiration off his forehead, he nodded. "I know. I know. Do you have the ring, Troy?"

Troy threw up his hands. "Lord, please let this man hurry up and get married so he can drive someone else crazy."

"I'm not that bad," Damian grumbled.

Kyle and Troy shared a look and said, "Yeah, you are."

The three men burst out laughing and turned at the sound of the door opening.

The minister entered. "Are you ready, son?"

"Definitely," Damian answered.

"That's what I like to hear. Let's go meet your bride."

Damian, Troy and Kyle followed the minister to the sanctuary and the candlelight ceremony began. Janae and Melissa looked beautiful in their dresses, as did the little flower girl—one of Karen's young cousins. The ring bearer, another one of her family members, walked solemnly down the aisle and took his place next to Damian.

He glanced over to the mothers sitting in the front row. Both had tissues and were wiping their eyes. He'd had an opportunity to talk with William and Rhonda Morris and found them to be warm and caring people. Damian assured them he would always love and protect their daughter. They expressed their joy in gaining him as a son, and he felt blessed to have them as in-laws.

The doors opened, and when he saw Karen standing at the back holding her father's arm, he thought his heart would beat out of his chest. Beautiful didn't come close to describing how she looked in the strapless white dress that shimmered with every step. It took everything he had not to rush down the aisle. Kyle must have sensed his urgency because he placed a staying hand on Damian's arm.

"Easy, man."

It seemed to take forever for her to reach him, and when she did, Damian took her hand, brought it to his lips and kissed the back. He mouthed, *I love you*, and turned toward the minister. They repeated their vows, and Monte sang the song he'd sung for Janae on the cruise. Just like the last time, it moved Karen to tears. Throughout it all, he never took his eyes off her. At long last, he heard the words he had been waiting for.

"I now pronounce you husband and wife. Damian, you may kiss your bride."

"Finally," he breathed.

Karen reached up and gently touched his face. "This is the happiest day of my life. I love you very much, Damian."

"And I love you more." He gently wiped away her tears and lowered his head for their first kiss as husband and wife. He tried to convey just how much he loved her in the tender but passionate kiss.

Applause sounded all around them, but he kept right on kissing his wife.

Kyle elbowed him. "All right, that's enough. Save it for tonight."

Reluctantly, he lifted his head. They filed out along with the bridal party, then came back to take pictures. Damian noticed the subtle touches and heated looks Kyle and Melissa were trading and shook his head.

After taking pictures, they got into the back of a limousine waiting to take them to the reception hall.

Damian pulled Karen onto his lap. "So, Mrs. Bradshaw, are you sure you're okay with delaying our honeymoon?" School would resume on Monday, and Damian and Kyle had three scheduled conferences in San Francisco.

"Yes, Mr. Bradshaw. Although I do expect you to make it up to me."

"I know just the thing," he murmured, placing kisses along the column of her neck.

"Oh? And what might that be?"

"A cruise."

"Ooh, that sounds like fun. You owe me two nights anyway."

He chuckled, and their lips met again in a deep, provocative kiss that held the promise of more to come.

That first day, Kyle had said she had *permanent* and *keeper* stamped all over her, and he had been right. Karen was a definite keeper. Damian had been given a second chance, and he intended to love and cherish her for the rest of his life.

* * * * *

LET'S TALK
Romance

For exclusive extracts, competitions
and special offers, find us online:

- facebook.com/millsandboon
- @MillsandBoon
- @MillsandBoonUK

Get in touch on 01413 063232

For all the latest titles coming soon, visit
millsandboon.co.uk/nextmonth

JOIN US ON SOCIAL MEDIA!

Stay up to date with our latest releases, author news and gossip, special offers and discounts, and all the behind-the-scenes action from Mills & Boon...

 millsandboon

 millsandboonuk

 millsandboon

It might just be true love...

The Green A

The Green Alternative
Guide to Good Living

Edited by PETER BUNYARD
and
FERN MORGAN-GRENVILLE

With illustrations by Richard Willson

Methuen London

First published in Great Britain 1987
by Methuen London Ltd
11 New Fetter Lane, London EC4P 4EE
© 1987 Ecoropa Ltd
Printed in Great Britain
by Richard Clay Ltd,
Bungay, Suffolk

British Library Cataloguing in Publication Data

The Green alternative : guide to good living.
  1. Conservation of natural resources
  I. Bunyard, Peter   II. Morgan-Grenville,
  Fern   III. Ecoropa
  333.7'2   S936

  ISBN 0-413-60280-X
  ISBN 0-413-42440-5 Pbk

Ecoropa is a trans-European group concerned with ecological
threats of all kinds. It aims to inform by the issue of leaflets
and publications and membership is open to all.

Contents

Acknowledgements

We are very grateful to the following for their help and contributions:

Professor Frank Barnaby, Hugh Barton, Dr Paul Blau, Peter Bunyard, Dr Marcus Colchester, David Condon, Barry Cooper, The Very Rev A. H. Dammers, Dr Joan Davis, Derek Eastmond, Paul Ekins, Jeremy Faull, Warwick Fox, Roger Franklin, Ros Fry, Tony Gibson, Herbert Giradet, Edward Goldsmith, Nicholas Hildyard, Dr Donna Lee Iffla, Sandy Irvine, Dr Brian John, Colin Johnson, Stanley Johnson, Nicholas Kollerstrom, Satish Kumar, Dr Peter Mansfield, John Madeley, Dr Arabella Melville, Richard Meyer, Christopher Milne, Fern Morgan-Grenville, Helena Norberg-Hodge, Dr Miriam Polunin, Jonathon Porritt, Christopher Retallack, David Rothenberg, Diana Schumacher, John Seymour, Mukkat Singh, Sedley Sweeny, Colin Sweet, Dr James Thomson, Dr Bob Todd, Colin Trier, Peter Wilkinson.

We are also grateful for the help of many organisations, including the Council for the Protection of Rural England, the *Ecologist*, Friends of the Earth, Greenpeace, Survival International, the Town and Country Planning Association, the Nature Conservancy Council, ScotRail, the Centre for Alternative Technology and the Urban Centre for Appropriate Technology.

The editors are indebted to Methuen and in particular to Ann Mansbridge and Alex Bennion for their invaluable work.

To our children
and their children
that they may have an earth to inherit

Preface

Catastrophe is not new to the world. The Black Death killed one-third of the population of Europe in the fourteenth century; earthquakes have destroyed whole cities; drought and famine have brought civilisations to an end. Even predictions of a coming Armageddon are not new: they are found in many religions. So what is different about our present situation?

We believe that the difference lies in the scale of the threat to the planet itself, through environmental destruction. This threat is largely created by man himself, whose enormous capacity for destroying already weakened systems is the factor which makes the position so grave.

Piecemeal solutions are not enough. Unless we recognise the danger, and stand united to withstand the forces of destruction, the world as we know it may finally perish.

It is against this belief that this book was commissioned by Ecoropa.

What does Green mean?

It means, quite simply, concern for life on earth. Not just concern for one's own family or friends, for a community or the whole human race, but concern for the process of life itself and everything that nurtures and sustains that process. One can only care for other people by caring for the earth.

Everything depends on this: our quality of life, our ability to serve others or to fulfil our own potential, the very capacity of the human race to survive. To be Green means to have that understanding at the forefront of one's ideas and actions.

Introduction

Our world is in crisis, yet in Britain we do not suffer tragedies on the scale of an Ethiopian famine, nor have we experienced anything like the poisoning by pesticide of thousands of Indians at Bhopal. For us, life goes on much as we have come to expect. Other than occasional feelings of pity for disaster victims, should we mind what happens elsewhere? Surely we cannot be held responsible for the Sahara's remorseless advance, for the chopping down of tropical rain forests, or the misuse of chemicals in the Third World?

If the world were made up of isolated fragments there might be some justification for us to ignore problems on other continents. But through trade and communications, whatever we do, make, or desire has an effect on peoples and species of all kinds, however far removed from our temperate island.

Chains of fast-food hamburger shops in America can, albeit unwittingly, wipe out an Amerindian tribe that had survived many thousands of years in the tropical rain forests of the Amazon; equally, British imports of uranium to fuel nuclear power stations and supply fissile material for our warheads destroys the ancestral home of Australian Aborigines and helps reinforce South Africa's determination to claim Namibia. When we cut down a forest, we may not only be changing lives but also global climate; that we lose not just the forest but a whole range of species whose importance in holding together the living fabric of our earth is barely suspected. We are becoming aware of the climatic dangers of soaring carbon dioxide levels in the atmosphere as a result of our massive burning of fossil fuels. But carbon dioxide is only one of the gases that we release into our environment, each one of which, alone or in combination, is interfering with the natural systems that have evolved and developed over millions of years and is causing modern disasters like acid rain, the dying of our temperate forests and the death of fish in lakes and waterways, particularly in the northern hemisphere.

Those spectacular space shots of earth, with its swirling clouds, its sapphire seas, brown and green lands, are portraying an exceedingly delicate balance of natural forces which, left to themselves, achieve a life-supporting equilibrium. We inhabit a natural world of amazing beauty, of extraordinary complexity, much of it too easily disrupted by our onslaughts and interference. Many of us are undoubtedly concerned at the awful spectre of nuclear war. Yet it is the terrible attrition we are causing to our natural systems that poses the most certain threat to survival.

We must learn that nothing happens in isolation: tackling the symptoms but not the root cause today may create a worse problem tomorrow. Whether we like it or not we are part of nature and we are dependent on the stability of nature for our own survival. We cannot afford to sweep our problems under the carpet: in nature absolutely nothing is 'out of sight'. We can no longer with impunity dump our poisons into the seas; we dare not, if we wish to have a future, continue pouring the oxides of carbon, nitrogen and sulphur into the skies. We must stop now the destruction of the tropical rain forest, stop before we rip out the last hedge or poison our seas with radioactive discharges. And we must begin seriously to reckon the huge ecological cost of forcing our lands to produce mountains and lakes of inferior quality food by methods that not only cannot be sustained but degrade, destroy and pollute the environment.

The slide toward environmental collapse is already well advanced: that is hardly any longer in dispute. But can we do anything, or are the problems too overwhelming?

The activities of all individuals of the biological world have created our living planet. So we, as individuals of the human race, can begin to put our own lifestyles in order. The sum of our activities will create a harmony of existence that fosters life, rather than destroys it. We, the writers of this book, believe that the key is personal change – a gradual shift in the way we live, the way we spend our money, the food we eat, the things we do and the things we want. Whenever we spend money we are exercising a vote for or against extinction; in terms of survival there is usually a right and a wrong thing to buy – no matter what it is. There is too a right and wrong way of doing things. It is people's actions which will decide the kind of future we will have – or indeed whether we have any future.

This book is therefore addressed to all those who wish to stop contributing to the collapse of the environment, who wish to live within the ecological constraints of nature and who want to help pioneer the way forward towards ways of living which are sustainable.

In this book we have posed questions relating to different aspects of daily life, the sort of questions that have been troubling us. For some questions there are no easy answers. For instance eating too much sugar is bad for us, certainly at the level of consumption now found in Britain, but Caribbean countries depend on sugar exports for their economic survival.

Many people equate 'green living' with a tedious puritanical approach to life, with a whole lot of 'must nots'. But that is a total misconception. For instance, we suggest eating food that has no additives. Not only is such food *not* a penance, it has 'taste', and is highly nutritious.

We have tried to encompass most aspects of living, from food to politics, from energy to education in our book. All are interrelated, indeed our hope is that the book will help to create an overall outlook on life that is creative and responsible.

Our beautiful planet is threatened – not just by chemical, biological or nuclear war – but quite simply by the way we live. It is up to each of us to adapt to the crisis. This book is an attempt to put us on the right road. Survival itself is at stake.

Is our earth really threatened by some ecological catastrophe of our own making? Surely the earth is far too resilient for that?

Only in the last decade has it begun to be scientifically credible that we could gradually render the world uninhabitable. In fact mankind has been changing the face of the earth for thousands of years. However, since the industrial revolution the pace of change has accelerated sharply, particularly since the Second World War. Our economy has become heavily dependent on finite resources such as petroleum: indeed road and air traffic have multiplied many times in the past couple of decades as a result of our having a cheap, accessible and convenient fuel. This opening-up of the world through the mass transport of people and goods is having dramatic effects everywhere, including on the ecosystems – those communities of living organisms within a particular environment – of Antarctica and the tropical forests that up to now have survived more or less intact. We are now clearing natural vegetation at an unprecedented rate – some 200,000 square kilometres of virgin rainforest are falling to the axe, fire and massive dam schemes every year. At this rate we will have totally destroyed such forests by the middle of the next century.

And by releasing gases from vehicle exhausts, power stations, waste incineration, and manufacturing industry into the atmosphere through our growing needs for energy and transport, we are fundamentally altering the chemistry of the air. Acid rain, heating up of the earth's surface and climate changes are all likely consequences. And we are now well aware of the dangers of radiation releases from nuclear power stations.

We have intensified food production by using a whole range of chemicals, many of which – such as nitrogen fertilisers which can lead to cancer – are potential toxins to us and to other organisms, including those important to our welfare. We are using our rivers, lakes and the sea as sewers. Factory ships have in many instances decimated populations of fish to the point where their recovery is uncertain.

If the dying of our European forests is anything to go by we have now altered our environment to the point where entire ecosystems are packing up. Ultimately the earth is resilient: life *will* go on, but without us and without many of the animals and plants that have been an integral part of our time here.

Introduction

Is there anything we can do? Or have we really gone too far?

We simply do not know whether we have damaged the earth's regenerative processes beyond repair: our time perspective is too short to see beyond normal fluctuations. Confronted by a cold winter, we start wondering whether we are beginning an ice age; a long summer drought makes us think about predictions that too much carbon dioxide in the air is heating up the world. In the physical and living world, nothing is truly static and small swings one way or the other are part of regulatory processes. But as we remove large chunks of our natural environment, and flood others with a potent mix of chemicals, we erode the capacity of the system to deal with interference. The result may be that we are causing a sudden, sharp change to a different pattern – one to which we may find it hard, if not impossible, to adapt.

Although we are definitely beginning to cause catastrophic change to the environment, we may still have time to avert the worst effects. But we need to act now. We must become more aware of what we are doing, then perhaps at least self-interest will cause us to modify our behaviour.

Haven't we already started modifying our behaviour enough? Our industries are far less polluting and we have introduced a lot of laws to protect the environment.

It is absolutely true that industry has begun to learn how to use low- and non-waste technologies that produce less pollution. Moreover, far more is recycled than ten years ago: for instance 40 per cent of world steel is manufactured from scrap, needing only 15 to 20 per cent of the energy used for manufacturing from virgin ore: Thus, industry no longer causes the same amount of visible pollution as it did in the past.

On the other hand, the emphasis in manufacturing has switched to the production of complex chemical compounds; these are not only toxic in themselves but their manufacture produces other toxins like the isocyanate of the Union Carbide factory in Bhopal in December 1984 which killed about

Introduction

2,500 people and injured about 200,000. Many of these products are pesticides, and as such are purposefully distributed into the environment around us.

In fact industry is not solely to blame for environmental problems. A consumer society which demands such luxuries as cars, imported foods and holidays abroad with hundreds of millions criss-crossing the globe every year, and which seeks change for its own sake, is a major disruptive force in the world.

The growth of world markets and the attempt to satisfy demand as competitively as possible have led to intense exploitation of lands that traditionally were treated with great care. The net result is that more land is being eroded and losing its fertility than ever before in human history. All too rarely is reclamation feasible.

If we were to balance the improvements to our environment against the losses, we would find that the processes of destruction now far outweigh those of conservation and reclamation.

1 Conservation and nature

Since 1945: 125,000 miles of hedgerow have been lost in the UK (enough to go round the world five times at the equator)

95 per cent of permanent hay meadows have been lost

80 per cent of chalk downlands have been lost

60 per cent of heathlands have been lost.[1]

Loving the countryside does not necessarily lead to caring for it, but it is no good crying alone about destruction. On revisiting a bluebell wood and finding it a smooth green field of young wheat, it is no good cursing the farmer, protesting to friends that everything is being ruined, yet doing nothing else.

There are many organisations for buying wild and beautiful places and preserving them, for nurturing endangered species, for minimising the impact of modern development, but these organisations are almost helpless when it comes to saving an unremarkable, but much loved, wild place. Unless the area is exceptional enough to be bought by one of the charities, or receive a preservation order when designated a Site of Special Scientific Interest (SSSI), it falls outside the remit of most large organisations. This leaves only us, as individuals, to save threatened places. Almost always *someone* knows of imminent destruction before it happens or in its early stages. If we act immediately, through lobbying local councils and rallying support amongst the community, we may be able to save areas of beauty for ourselves and the rest of humanity.

It is no good our mourning to each other the loss of a tree that has stood for two hundred years, or a chestnut or hazel grove, coppiced for centuries, or a barn crumbling on the edge of a village. We must confront the forces of destruction – the unscrupulous developers, the road builders, the less enlightened planners, the buriers of nuclear waste. We must not say to our children, 'When I was your age that meadow was a carpet of wild flowers', but must be able to say: 'I saved that carpet of wild flowers and the wild life that depends upon it for you, and your children.' We must also make our own contributions by creating our own natural areas. Nature will continue to generate her own beauty long after the despoilers are gone, long after their monuments to insensitivity have fallen down: if we let her.

Isn't conservation an élitist activity, against the wishes of the masses?

Few British people remain untouched by some aspect of the beauty and interest of the countryside. In a recent public opinion poll[2] people were asked which were the three most important benefits to be gained from the countryside. 'Landscape/scenery' was top of the poll with 69 per cent, compared with 'wildlife' at 54 per cent and 'farming and food production' at 43 per cent. In a poll conducted in 1983,[3] 21 per cent said they would seriously consider switching their vote to a party which gave a commitment to reducing wastage of natural resources. When asked which things made a valuable contribution to the overall quality of life, 53 per cent mentioned 'attractive countryside', compared with 51 per cent who mentioned 'unpolluted atmosphere' and 35 per cent for 'access to a car'.

In 1985 a survey carried out for the Countryside Commission showed that 84 per cent of the population visited the countryside for recreation and almost everyone said they would like to go more frequently. This demonstrates that the conservation and protection of the wider countryside (not just those areas specifically set aside for recreation) serves a very broad social purpose and is not the exclusive concern of a few dedicated conservationists. One reflection of this strong public opinion has been the growth, over the past decade, in the membership of the non-government environmental organisations in Britain – like the Town and Country Planning Association, the Council for the Protection of Rural England, Friends of the Earth, Greenpeace and the Conservation Society – from 600,000 to over 3 million.

It is becoming increasingly clear that present agricultural and forestry industries, while presently serving the financial interest of those currently employed in them, are working against the interests of the land. When the land – ultimately the source of all wealth – deteriorates, it will clearly be those closest to it who suffer most. Conservation is about accepting that land is a common heritage, that everyone has a right to enjoy it and everyone has a responsibility to ensure that we live off only the interest from it, not the capital.

How important is wildlife to the well-being of the planet?

One answer was that of Chief Seattle, of the Divamish Indians, when the US government was forcing the purchase of his tribe's land in 1855:

> We do not own the freshness of the air or the sparkle on the water. How then can you buy them from us? Every part of the earth is sacred to my people, holy in their memory and experience. We know that the white man does not understand our ways. He is a stranger who comes in the night, and takes from the land whatever he needs. The earth is not his friend, but his enemy, and when he's conquered it, he moves on. He kidnaps the earth from his children. His appetite will devour the earth and leave behind a desert. If all the beasts were gone, we would die from a great loneliness of the spirit, for whatever happens to the beasts happens also to us. All things are connected. Whatever befalls the Earth, befalls the children of the Earth.

On a totally practical level, wildlife literally offers lifelines. For example, in a typical rainforest 1,400 plant species are believed to be potential cures against various cancers, at least 1,650 known tropical forest plants have potential as vegetable crops and one in four medicines in the West owes its origins to plants or animals in tropical rainforests.

3

The Green Alternative

Are we properly protecting our countryside?

We have strict planning controls for housing in the UK. It would be neither illogical nor unjust to have equally strict control on how land is developed for farming. At present farmers are allowed great freedom and are encouraged to exploit their land to their best financial advantage. Consequently in this country far too little land is cultivated (whether intentionally or not) in a way that benefits other creatures. The establishment of national parks and Sites of Special Scientific Interest is a step in the right direction. But it is only a very small step and many others must be taken before we have achieved a land and resource distribution that is fair to all species.

Are our national parks properly protected? How does the protection in the UK compare with other EEC countries?

If present destruction continues, we risk losing the richness and variety of our open 'wilderness' areas. Our finest scenery is threatened by the mining industry, which is keen to expand its opencast operations. It is also clear that recent intensification of farming and forestry has contributed to the erosion of much semi-natural vegetation in the uplands through ploughing, drainage, liming and burning and spraying. Intensive farming has also caused much of the dereliction and removal of stone walls and hedgerows; the loss of vernacular buildings and the building of huge, ugly, obtrusive new ones in unfortunate materials; intrusive farm roads scarring whole mountain sides; the taming of streams and marsh and the insensitive location of large blocks of alien coniferous forest.

Current legislation does not give our national parks the protection they need, and the legislation which does exist is inadequately applied. Planning applications within a national park have virtually the same rate of approval as those outside. Members of planning committees seldom have any knowledge of vernacular architecture and are often motivated by considerations other than the protection of these national parks. The UK compares badly with our European neighbours where, although some countries have similar

4

problems of local vested interests, there are stronger controls and national parks are 'wilderness' areas to a much greater extent.

What about Areas of Outstanding Natural Beauty?

AONBs enjoy virtually no protection and their designation as such is of dubious value.

Are Sites of Special Scientific Interest adequately protected?

Sites of Special Scientific Interest are areas designated by the government's statutory wildlife body, the Nature Conservancy Council, in which landowners, farmers and foresters are prohibited from carrying out 'potentially damaging operations'. In the UK there are 4,000 SSSIs covering between 6 and 8 per cent of the country's land.

They do not, however, afford total protection. Firstly, if a farmer threatens to do such works, the Nature Conservancy Council is obliged to offer him a 'management agreement' including compensation for 'profits forgone', even though those profits mainly derive from public subsidies in the form of agricultural grants and price support. Compensation payments of over £250 per acre per year are known in some places. This in fact means that the costs of agricultural support are transferred from the agricultural budget to the meagre conservation budget. The public is thus faced with the provocative spectacle of agricultural operations subsidised gratuitously in several ways with public money and causing environmental problems which can only be averted by use of further public funds to the small number of potential beneficiaries. One estimate suggests that it could cost up to £42.8 million per annum to protect SSSIs by this method. The compensation arrangements must be reformed and the subsidy element, both agricultural and forestry, removed from the calculations. And there will continue to be conflict while agricultural and forestry policies are opposed to environmental imperatives.

Secondly, SSSIs continue to be damaged and destroyed by

'development' pressures, i.e. roads, industrial and residential building, etc. It seems inexcusable that irreplaceable and nationally important sites are destroyed by things like car parks and roads, where alternative locations are almost always available.

Should farmers be fined heavily for offences against 'protected' sites, flora and fauna?

Where the powers exist, the fines are probably adequate. But outside the relatively small number of 'élite' SSSIs there is no way the local community can protect well-known and well-loved landscape features and wildlife habitats. It is essential that a new power is brought in so that a local council can stop a farmer carrying out such acts as hedge-removal or pond-filling, or a forestry company blanketing a wild open landscape with non-native conifers. Environmental groups such as the Council for the Protection of Rural England (CPRE) have termed this mooted power the 'Landscape Conservation Order'. After all, while the land may be held by a few, the landscape belongs to everyone.

The CPRE have just established a 'hot-line' for people to ring if they have identified a woodland or hedgerow tree threatened with removal (*hedges* are not covered by the tree preservation orders – TPOs). They suggest that people should first try and contact the Tree Officers of their local borough or district council to see if a TPO exists which can be enforced. Emergency TPOs can sometimes be made pending confirmation by the Local Planning Committee. If all else fails, ring David Condon at CPRE on 01–235 9481. The hot-line operates only during office hours at present.

You can also contact the local press, call the police, or get friends to stand around the tree while you try to persuade the landowner to change his or her mind.

How old are our hedges?

They have been with us a long time. There are field patterns in Cornwall dating back to the Bronze Age and archaeological remains are frequently associated with hedges: a Bronze Age hoard was found in one hedge bank. In Norfolk there are hedges following Roman field patterns and Caesar described hedge-laying in his *Gallic Wars*. *The Anglo-Saxon Chronicle* of AD 547 mentioned that King Ida of Northumbria created a hedge around a new town, and in medieval times hedges marked manorial boundaries which often became the parish boundary. Farmers also planted hedges to fence out the kings' deer. Between 1460 and 1600, and 1740 and 1830, hedges were planted to enclose land. In the first decade of the sixteenth century John Spencer, a grazier of Warwickshire, not only double-hedged his fields but planted acorns in his hedges to provide fuel and timber for the poor. It is believed that half of the hedge and walled landscape of England was established between the Bronze Age and the seventeenth century. In many counties, where the open-field system never caught on, the hedged field pattern was already in place before the Parliamentary Enclosures Acts of the Georgian period.

Generally speaking, the more species a hedge contains, the older it is. A rough guide is one woody species per century. So a hedge with nine different shrubs can be about 900 years old, though this dating method depends on the local geology. Some very old hedges carry woodland flowers like the blue-bell, woodruff and early purple orchid. Such hedges are believed to be relict strips of 'wildwood', the wood that grew up 7,000 years ago after the last ice age and out of which our ancestors carved fields.

Are hedges still being ripped up?

Hedgerow loss is continuing at an alarming rate and has increased in counties previously not seriously affected (e.g. Yorkshire and Warwickshire) according to the government's own countryside watchdog, the Countryside Commission.[4] A 1984 study by CPRE's Suffolk branch showed that hedgerow loss still continues, even in that long intensively farmed county, but the hedges now being removed are those on farm boundaries and along roads (inter-field hedges having largely disappeared in Suffolk already). An earlier study by the Institute of Terrestrial Ecology, using air-photographs, showed that of around 500,000 miles of hedge existing in England and Wales in 1946–7 some 140,000 miles had been removed by 1974; and all but 20,000 miles of this loss was attributable to farming, i.e. 4,000 miles removed by farming operations every year. Hedgerow trees have also suffered a dramatic decline – not just through removal but also by unsympathetic hedge-trimming, the use of mechanical flails, etc .

Hedges, perhaps more than anything else, provide the essential character of the British countryside, each region having its own distinctive shape and species. Hedges are the bones of the British landscape – and the famous 'patchwork quilt' effect depends on them.

Do hedges protect wildlife?

A high proportion of our plants and animals depend on hedges: 40 types of birds, including blackbirds, thrushes and linnets; and 250 species of flowering plants and ferns, including the wild rose, honeysuckle, bryony, primrose, violet, wild hops and lords and ladies. They not only provide home and cover for wildlife but also a vital link between populations in woods and other marginal areas, thus preventing genetic isolation.

Apart from wildlife, aren't hedges a waste of land?

Hedges benefit the farmer directly in a number of ways. They can improve milk and meat yields by giving shelter to dairy cattle and sheep, and they improve crop production for the same reasons. They are cheaper than fences in the long run. They harbour beneficial predators, such as ladybirds and lacewings, that destroy pest insects; they provide a useful source of timber; they promote shelter and cover for game; and they help prevent soil erosion.

Hedges were planted for good reasons and, in the long

term, the failure to retain more hedges may prove to have been a costly mistake for agriculture.

The British Trust for Conservation Volunteers, an independent body, trains and uses people skilled in hedge-laying and planting. Agricultural policy should be designed to encourage the use of such people in agriculture rather than encouraging the use of labour-saving machinery including flailing machines.

'Since 'e took down all 'is 'edgerows, he says
that 'alf 'is topsoil 'as blown onto George's farm,
so as 50 acres of it now belongs to 'im.'

Why are hedges being destroyed?

While grants are no longer being offered directly for hedge removal, hedges are being destroyed as a direct result of the financial incentives offered to farmers. An important part of the Common Agricultural Policy (and previous national policy) is to guarantee farmers artificially inflated prices for crops. For example, the price of wheat is occasionally 100 per cent more than its world market price. There is widespread agreement that higher crop prices have been responsible for much of the damage in the countryside over the past three or

9

four decades because high prices are a strong incentive for 'reclamation and land improvement' – which includes grubbing out hedges and replacing them with yet more agricultural produce.

Shouldn't all farm land have some natural buffer area around it to protect watersheds and the environment?

A recent Soil Association report[5] showed the damage of spray-drift to wildlife on field edges. And the Game Conservancy is currently demonstrating the benefits to farmers of leaving a clear swathe of at least six metres in width – unsprayed – around field margins. The numbers of butterflies and 'polyphagous predators' (i.e. aphid-eaters) are found to increase significantly and within a few years there is a substantial increase in grey partridge chick survival.

However, there is a wider principle at stake. The 'buffer zone' approach implies that it is fine to give 95 per cent of farmland regular doses of artificial fertilisers, herbicides and nitrates while giving the remaining 5 per cent some form of buffer or sanctuary. At a deeper level, the 'health' of the land and its beauty may be seen to be synonymous and farmers will foster an organic approach to the land, developing an increasing sensitivity to the rural environment as a whole.

Do agrochemicals cause long-term harm to wildlife?

Insecticides have accounted for the deaths of countless millions of wild animals, especially during the dark days of the late 1950s, with unknown consequences on species viability. The organochlorines – the chlorinated hydrocarbons such as DDT, dieldrin, aldrin and the more lethal eldrin – are highly persistent, accumulating in the individual's fatty tissues. From there they can be released during times of stress, thus endangering the life of the organism when it is at its most vulnerable. Organochlorines have been found to cause eggshell thinning, especially in birds of prey. Although organochlorines such as DDT are now banned from use in the

USA, they are still used in Britain and, to a much greater extent, in Third World countries.

The other main group of pesticides comprises the organophosphates or organophosphorus compounds which block enzymes associated with nerve-impulse transmission. Although extremely toxic, such compounds tend to break down over a period of a few days and therefore do not have the persistent effects of the organochlorines. None the less, when sprayed, organophosphate compounds affect many organisms other than those for which they are meant. Fish, for instance, are extremely vulnerable to the run-off of such pesticides.

Wildlife, including essential soil organisms such as earthworms, is seriously affected by the use of agrochemicals, including herbicides such as 2,4,5 T and paraquat. In general, pests are more readily able to develop resistance to pesticides than are their predators, and a consequence of agrochemical use is to unbalance predator–prey relationships.

In some parts of the world, such as Central America, crops like cotton are sprayed as many as forty times during the growing season, with up to 75 per cent of the spray drifting off target and contaminating cattle and humans. Efforts are now being directed to integrated pest management in which break (or alternating) crops are introduced and some form of biological pest control applied. Good husbandry can do much to reduce pest infections.

Badgers are said to provide a reservoir of bovine tuberculosis so that cattle become infected. Is the Ministry of Agriculture, Fisheries and Food (MAFF) right to exterminate badgers in known disease areas?

Badgers were implicated in spreading bovine tuberculosis in Switzerland in the 1950s, but the evidence was only circumstantial. Meanwhile in Britain, through the rigorous testing of cattle after the Second World War and the slaughter of diseased and 'reactor' animals, TB was reduced from as much as 40 per cent in the 1930s, when it caused some 2,500 human deaths each year, to less than 1 per cent by 1960. However, certain areas in the South-West and Gloucestershire were found, on continued testing, to have a higher reaction rate than elsewhere in the UK. The badger was implicated after one was found dead with TB on a Gloucester farm in 1975. As a result MAFF embarked on a campaign to clear the badger from areas where bovine TB was proving difficult to eradicate.

Since 1975 some 20,000 badgers have been gassed, suffocated, snared, cage-trapped and shot. Badgers, unlike cattle, are not live-tested but are killed first and more than 90 per cent of those killed have been found to be totally free of TB. Despite the intense campaign against the badger in the affected areas there has been little change in the reactor incidence among cattle. Moreover, in areas where badgers have not been disturbed the disease has declined of its own accord. Some critics of the badger-killing believe that the recalcitrant problem among cattle is caused by the stress imposed on a modern dairy herd with demands for very high milk production under crowded conditions.

A government commission under the chairmanship of Professor George Dunnet of Aberdeen University has now reported that the MAFF campaign can no longer be justified, there being insufficient evidence of a link between TB in badgers and in cattle. A West Country farmer is suing MAFF for having exterminated badgers on his land, thus creating a void which he fears may be filled by TB-carrying badgers.

Why are barn owls vanishing from Britain?

Barn owls have declined alarmingly for a variety of reasons, many being killed by traffic, which in recent years has increased in volume and speed. Barn owls habitually hunt along hedgerows and this habit frequently takes them along and across roads at a dangerous height and in poor light at dusk. A second reason is the decline in hedgerows with consequent reduction in available prey, such as short-tailed voles. Additionally, barn owls' roosting and nesting sites are destroyed as people convert old barns into holiday homes or demolish them. Like other birds of prey, barn owls are also particularly vulnerable to a build-up of chlorinated hydrocarbon pesticides derived from their prey species.

The organochlorines are not 'biodegradable'. Being synthetic, they are not broken down by bacteria or in the bodies or organisms that ingest them. An insect that has ingested a sub-lethal dose may be eaten by an insectivorous bird to which the small dose is passed and stored. If the bird is in turn eaten by a predator, the accumulating dose is again passed on. The effect of such cumulative poisons is thus shown most dramatically at the top of food chains, as has been amply demonstrated in recent years, especially, for example amongst predators such as the peregrine falcon, in which eggshell thinning and death of the chicks has decimated the population.

Current woodworm treatments often kill bats. Is there anything we can do about this?

Most householders have, at some time, to deal with an infestation of woodworm (whether in furniture, an outbuilding or loft, or a whole house) involving spraying or injecting a woodworm killer.

The majority of these preparations still contain the organochlorine insecticides dieldrin or Gamma HCH, and we should be aware of the consequences of using these substances. The organochlorines are not only poisonous to insects, but they are toxic to human beings, especially children, causing headaches and allergic reactions in sensitive subjects even when used in a remote part of the house. Bats have been severely affected by the spraying of lofts and outbuildings, and swifts and house martins nesting in eaves have been killed.

Permethrin is a synthetic form of an alkaloid found in pyrethrum (a natural plant extract long favoured by organic gardeners). It is biodegradable and not cumulative. It has a longer active life and is less toxic to mammals than the organochlorines.[6] The use of permethrin in woodworm fluids instead of organochlorines was slowly adopted by manufacturers so that now thirteen of the major companies can offer this alternative, either as a solvent or emulsion. But to date manufacturers seem disinclined to advertise it in any way, and a customer has to be very persistent to be able to buy it or to ensure its use in a treatment contract.

Now that safer alternatives are available, the conservation movement must press for total government banning of the use of organochlorines in woodworm treatment. When treatment of woodworm, repairs or alterations are planned in any building used by bats, advice must be sought from the Nature Conservancy Council to conform with legislation. They will also give free advice on how to get rid of bats where they are not wanted, visiting when asked and identifying bat types. They publish useful guides about bats,[7] give lists of chemicals safe for use in bat roosts[8] and also give the names of companies making safe chemicals.

And what about chemicals used in other products, like anti-fouling for boats?

Tributyl tin-based (TBT) anti-foulings were first introduced in the 1960s, became market leaders in the early seventies and completely replaced the relatively less toxic copper-based paints by the late 1970s.

They are attractive, convenient and effective but their side effects on marine biology are devastating. Less than one teaspoonful of TBT in 20 million gallons of water is sufficient to stop the growth of phytoplankton, the essential basis of marine life.

Until recently, the case against organo-tin paints centred on their apparent tendency to stunt the growth of the pacific oyster which today forms the basis of commercial oyster fisheries in Britain. The evidence against organo-tin compounds is, however, accumulating. Research establishments across the UK are daily documenting additional evidence clearly illustrating the toxicity of TBT. In early 1985 William Waldegrave, then junior Environment Minister, told readers of *Yachting Monthly* that he had 'seldom been faced with clearer scientific evidence of the need for environmental action, and fast'.

Yet despite Waldegrave's concern and France's three-year-old ban on TBT paints, Britain, following an intensive campaign by the paint manufacturers, has decided to move slowly. From January 1986 only the worst paints, of which more than 7.5 per cent is organo-tin will be banned. Since most anti-fouling paints on the market already meet the 7.5 per cent limit, this ban will have little or no effect.

Since there are proven alternatives to organo-tin-based paints, there is no possible justification, commercial or recreational, for not banning this indiscriminate poison from British coastal waters.

There is considerable illicit trading in wild animals. Is there anything we can do to protect them?

CITES (Convention on International Trade in Endangered Species) was drawn up in 1973 with the intention of identifying endangered species and protecting them from international exploitation. It can only be as successful as the will of the member countries allows.

Short-term trade benefits to some poor economies have to be offset against the longer term scientific, humanitarian and tourist benefits of a rich natural environment. Local poverty is exploited by unscrupulous traders, while governments turn a blind eye to revenue created from rich consumer countries. At its fifth biennial meeting in Buenos Aires in 1985, the secretariat of CITES reported that 'illegal trade is flooding into EEC countries' through the weak points (France, Italy and Germany), and that Hamburg is known to be a major conduit through which endangered species enter the EEC. It is up to civilised peoples to stamp on this trade, both by supporting all existing legislation and by ensuring that the collecting of animals (whether for zoos, petshops or animal experimentation) is carried out under strict licence.

Should there be an international agency to oversee zoos and give licences?

Some countries already have their own regulating bodies and it is unlikely that an international agency, as such, could work. Zoos need control but this is best imposed by the profession itself – which fully recognises the need to impose general standards of husbandry, display, breeding and conservation in many of the poorer establishments or, failing that, makes sure they close down. This is an area where ignorance of practical zoology and animal husbandry causes over-sentimental attitudes. Animals in cages are an emotive subject and certainly some are not suited to such a life. Even though certain species appear to thrive and live longer than in the wild, such cannot be a true measure of their well-being.

Many people argue that zoos are iniquitous institutions, which cause animal suffering both during the capture of wild animals and from the captivity itself. In Britain, recent legislation on the depth of pools in dolphinariums is a result of public concern over the very short life span of dolphins and killer whales in captivity. It may be that the depths required will cause many dolphinariums to close.

On the other hand, the role of zoos has changed dramatically in recent years from the traditional one of collecting animals for the sake of variety and keeping them in cages. Some zoos now try to create an impression of the animal's natural environment, and to educate the public about the behaviour and characteristics of their species. Some zoos also try to conserve endangered species through 'captive breeding' and setting up species survival plans. In the case of some species, notably the Arabian Oryx, the animals are reared in captivity until sufficient numbers can be released back into the environment to re-create a wild population. Or, if an environment is being destroyed, certain rare species may be collected for breeding in zoos in order to save them. Such new roles for zoos may provide some justification for their existence.

Are we being too sentimental over whales?

Sentimentality over whales has been overtaken by stark realities. The Blue whale, protected since 1966 – seventeen years after scientists rang warning bells about its declining numbers – has not recovered its stock despite twenty years of protection. As one species of whale was exploited to the brink of extinction, so the whalers turned to the next largest whale. Thus, the Blue, the Sei, the Humpback and the Fin whales have all had to be protected – the ultimate acknowledgement of bad management of the stocks. Now the tiny Minke whale is bearing the brunt of the slaughter. How long will it be before it too becomes too rare to find? Whales – and seals and dolphins – are extremely well adapted animals, highly intelligent and very sociable. Whales communicate over huge distances with sophisticated 'sonar'. They have taken 50 million years to evolve. Is it right that they should be wiped out in a few decades of furious slaughter?

Certain whale species, for instance the sperm whale, depend for their food on krill, which is made up of countless millions of larval crustacean forms. The Russians in particular have now sent specially designed factory ships to the Antarctic to harvest krill for human and livestock consumption. We may well over-harvest the krill, however, and disturb irreparably the balance of the Antarctic environment.

How protective of whales is the International Whaling Commission?

Over the last fifteen years the International Whaling Commission has imposed quotas, for certain species, which, had they been low enough to protect the whales, would have resulted in a limited number of whales being taken each year (much as we would have regretted it!) without jeopardising the stocks. The reverse has proved to be the case. The quotas have been systematically reduced in a lame attempt to safeguard stocks and have always proved too little, too late. A complete halt to whaling, as finally agreed by the International Whaling Commission, would not have been necessary had the quotas been sufficiently low. Agreement to end commercial whaling by 1 January 1986 was reached, but Russia, Japan and Norway have objected to the ruling and Greenpeace was forced to take the US government to court for failing to introduce fishing sanctions against any nation refusing to abide by the IWC rulings.

The Green Alternative

The case was won and now Japan faces a choice: either to stop whaling or to lose $2 billion worth of fishing products in US waters. Russia will stop if Japan stops. Norway has seen the writing on the wall by accepting 'protected' status for the stock of Minke whales it hunts. The era of commercial whaling is almost over, although Iceland and Korea are still trying to use whaling for 'scientific purposes' as a cover for continued commercial whaling operations. But the bloody business of whaling is rapidly approaching an overdue demise.

And seals?

Scientists have now come to the conclusion that no matter how many seals are killed, the amount of fish available to us is not increased. The truth is that mankind is responsible for the decline in fish stocks by over-fishing the seas for decades. Even today, factory fleets are literally 'hoovering' the seas, decimating complete shoals of fish in a matter of days. Moreover, it has now been shown that seals often prefer to eat fish species which were not commercially exploited at the time of the large seal culls. As far as the by-products are concerned, it must be remembered that 95 per cent of the carcasses of the 250,000 two-week old seal pups clubbed to death every year in front of their mothers on the Canadian ice-floes are left to rot on the ice. Their skins are used for trivia such as fur trimming on coats, purses, slippers and even turned into miniature replicas of their former owners – trinkets to be sold to tourists. If we are to kill seals, it cannot be simply for a 'luxury' trade – nor for reasons which don't stand up to scientific scrutiny, and certainly not because they are eating 'our' fish.

Couldn't we save on trees by using hemp, straw and other plant by-products for paper-making?

One edition of the *New York Times* is said to consume fifteen acres of a standing forest twenty years old. Over the course of one year, therefore, 15 × 365 acres (5,475) would be required; so to maintain production of this newspaper alone, an area twenty times this size would have to be set aside. Steps might be taken to preserve the forests by greatly reducing the use of paper in all spheres and re-cycling what we do use; and as communications of all sorts become more and more a matter of electronics, paper should be much less in demand.

Alternatives to timber for paper-making are not really feasible, however. A great deal of straw is burned up by farmers at harvest time because it does not pay them to bale it and sell it to the stock-rearing areas as bedding; it would cost as much to transport it (a very bulky load) from farms to the paper mills. In some countries alternatives to timber are being used – for example, bamboo in India, kenafe in South-East Asia and hemp in Italy and other countries. But all these alternative crops can provide us with only limited quantities of paper. Furthermore, the use of certain products – such as bamboo in India – is having a devastating effect on the environment and on the livelihood of people who have traditionally depended on bamboo for building materials and for the wildlife they sustain.

A much greater threat to forests than the manufacture of paper is the felling of vast areas of primeval woodland for timber and to produce arable land. It is here that conservationists must persuade governments to call a halt. The clear felling of forests not only uses up an irreplaceable asset, but causes wholesale erosion and the rapid loss of humus and fertility. The short-term profits of today become the deserts and famines of tomorrow.

How much forest is left in Britain, and how much in the rest of Europe?

The spread of agriculture, of cities, of transport systems and of industrial development decimated European forests. By the end of the nineteenth century Britain, then Europe's most industrialised nation, had reduced its forest cover to about 6 per cent of the total land area, although reafforestation by the Forestry Commission and commercial forestry groups has now raised that to nearly 9 per cent. West Germany, by comparison, has nearly 30 per cent forest cover, France over

The Green Alternative

20 per cent, Belgium 18 per cent, Norway 24 per cent and
Denmark 10 per cent. Only Ireland and the Netherlands have
a lower percentage than Britain. Sweden and Finland are
both very forest-rich and are major timber exporters. All
other Western European countries are timber importers and
Britain is at the top of the league, importing 92 per cent of her
timber requirements.

What's wrong with the Forestry Commission and commercial forestry groups covering slopes with conifers?

The land surface of England, Wales and Scotland was
covered with mixed deciduous woodlands after the last ice
age. Birch, hazel, ash, oak, beech, lime, poplar, willow, elm,
alder and pine recolonised the bare land, and these mixed
forests harboured a great variety of plant and animal life.
When they gave way to farming the thick layer of leafmould
they had accumulated was a valuable store of fertility on
which crops and farm animals thrived. But the conifer plantations planted in the last seventy years or so, mostly on hilly
land, do not enrich the soil. On the contrary, they rob it of
nutrients – making any future farming there extremely difficult. Conifer monocultures – be they spruce, larch, fir or pine
– also harbour a very limited variety of other life forms.

Up to 50 per cent of our ancient semi-natural woodlands
have been destroyed in the last thirty or forty years. Of this,
70 per cent were destroyed by intensive conifer forestry
operations, either directly by the Forestry Commission itself
or indirectly through grants and tax concessions to private
interests.

Much of the new conifer afforestation is taking place in the
wild open uplands – vital recreational areas which have
unique ecosystems. The Nature Conservancy Council
estimates that one-third of these upland habitats have been
destroyed in recent decades, including some in national
parks. In addition, afforestation in the uplands provides
fewer jobs than the agriculture it replaces.

After planting, the original moorland fauna and flora
are reduced, at best, to the plantation rides and margins.

Run-off from the plantation then leads to acidification of streams, rivers and lakes. Furthermore, chemical sprays, increasingly being used in intensive forestry, provide further problems.

A new scheme for broadleaf, deciduous planting was introduced in 1985, but it offers little encouragement for the maintenance and management of existing woodlands. The policy is still rather narrowly aimed towards timber production, at the expense of the environment. A more adaptable system of aid to woodland managers is needed in order to reconcile conservation, recreation and local employment needs with timber production priorities.

In what other ways are conifer plantations bad for the soil?

Firstly, conifers tend to acidify the soil. The pH value (at pH 7 the acids and alkalis are in balance) of soil in a typical spruce plantation is usually below 4; while that of a beechwood is often higher than 6. Secondly, afforestation with conifers often requires the soil to be ploughed deeply, the soil turned over and piled up in ridges on which the saplings are planted. The ditches between ridges cause rapid water run-off from hillsides. This further depletes the land of plant nutrients, making it less suited for subsequent agricultural use or, indeed, afforestation after the first timber harvest.

Why so many conifers? And how many?

Conifers grow fast and yield more usable timber per acre than virtually any other type of deciduous tree. We also consume their wood more than any other sort – for paper, planks, furniture and all kinds of construction materials – and because the trees tend to be straight they are more easily processed in modern timber mills. Conifer forests yield an annual return on investment of between $1\frac{1}{2}$ and 2 per cent, low by 'normal' industrial standards but higher than deciduous forests. In the last decade or so nearly 40,000 acres of British countryside were planted with conifers every year, mostly on hilly ground and usually on sheep farms bought up for this purpose. In some places this has significantly reduced rural employment because this type of forestry requires so few workers.

Is there no hope for a revival in planting deciduous trees?

In Britain grants are now available from several bodies, including the Forestry Commission and the Countryside Commission, for landowners who want to plant broadleaf trees on their land. This policy has been in operation since the demise of the elm. Farmers are encouraged to plant broadleaf trees of their choice on land which is difficult to use for modern agriculture; such trees are reckoned to enhance the beauty of the landscape though not to be of major commercial benefit. Some farmers are now interested in certain kinds of willows, poplars and beeches for producing firewood on a commercial scale. On the Continent, particularly in France, large-scale planting of hardwood trees is part of forestry policy. This is done on public and private land and is considered of economic as well as environmental benefit.

What about the importance of trees and hedgerows in preventing soil erosion?

Trees and hedges prevent soil erosion and rapid water run-off. The web of roots holds the soil in place and the leaf mould that accumulates acts like a sponge, soaking up moisture. 'Healthy' and well planted forests up in the hills are generally of great benefit to farming communities in the valleys below, and the loss of mountain and hilltop forests in Mediterranean countries such as Italy and Greece has led to massive erosion problems and the disappearance of rivers during the dry season. In places where permanent pastures are difficult to maintain it is crucial to prevent erosion, preferably with mixed forests. Even in countries like Britain the loss of forests in the hills has resulted in soil loss, though permanent grass cover does provide some protection.

Conservation and nature

What effect do industrial gases have on trees?

There are now over 3,000 gases reaching the atmosphere from our modern factories. These polluting gases react with each other in ways which are still not properly understood, enhancing each others' toxicity to plant organisms, notably long-lived ones such as trees. Acid rain damages leaves, bark and the roots of trees and leaches out beneficial minerals like calcium and magnesium, whilst releasing into the soil aluminium, cadmium, lead and mercury which are toxic to root systems. Sulphur dioxide also causes damage to trees in the form of dry deposition. Ozone is produced in the atmosphere as a result of nitrous oxides (from power station and vehicle exhausts) reacting with oxygen in the presence of sunlight. This low-level ozone is highly toxic to trees, impairing their ability to photosynthesise. Without question the enormous damage now apparent in forests throughout Europe and North America is due to the impact of our industrial civilisation.

What is really happening to the forests of Europe?

The Black Forest in south-west Germany is exposed to air pollution from the new industrial centres of eastern France and from the Stuttgart area. Damage to trees here has reached a level which makes it unlikely that much of the Forest will survive into the next century. Government statistics suggest that fir trees in the area have become an endangered species, and spruce trees are considered to be largely beyond recovery. Damage to broadleaf trees, too, has reached alarming proportions. In West Germany half the forests have been found to be visibly sick, according to a 1984 government survey, and serious damage to forests and trees is being reported from *all* countries in Europe. Air pollution is blamed as a primary cause, which is further amplified by secondary-disease organisms such as insects, fungi and bacteria.

The Green Alternative

Has the damage to European forests gone too far to be remedied?

In areas which are continuously exposed to toxic levels of air pollution forests are now beyond recovery. In some parts of the Black Forest even saplings die off shortly after being planted. Acidity is not always the cause, but even when it is, forests cannot be limed like lakes or farmland and cannot stand the shock of a sudden increase in pH. Acidification of the soil also leads to destruction of soil life, including earthworms, which in turn makes it more difficult for trees to extract nutrients from the ground. The accumulation of heavy metals (such as lead, mercury and cadmium) in the soil as a result of industrial and traffic pollution also has long-term effects which are almost impossible to remedy. In West Germany 7 per cent of the country's soil is now contaminated with heavy metals beyond the point where it should be used to grow crops for human consumption.

Is the CEGB correct in its analysis that the cause of forest dieback has still to be properly identified?

It is clear that forest dieback in Europe and North America is a complex problem. One eminent researcher in Germany has proposed the theory that trees are damaged and killed because of stress and that air pollution is just one of a number of causes. All researchers agreed, however, that without air pollution at present levels the forests of Europe would not be in the shocking state that they are. It is clear that the emissions from power stations seriously weaken trees, making them less able to withstand extreme weather conditions and attacks by secondary-disease organisms. Trees evolved to grow in unpolluted air and the CEGB's policy of refusing to treat flue gases certainly contributes to keeping the air over Europe polluted.

Conservation and nature

There has been increasing concern about tropical forests. Why do we need them?

Half the world's forests are tropical rain and monsoon forests, covering some 11 million square kilometres. True rainforest, requiring between 80 and 400 inches of rain a year (2,000 to 10,000 mm) covers a total of some 4.5 million square kilometres. It lies mainly in a girdle around the equator, extending roughly 10 degrees north and south, and therefore accounts for no more than 8 per cent of the earth's land surface, yet biologically rainforests comprise extremely active and diverse ecosystems. With many millions of species of plants and animals still to be discovered in them scientists estimate that such forests harbour up to half of all the species to be found on earth. They are also responsible for one-third of the earth's biological activity; hence a considerable proportion of the earth's metabolic cycle – of photosynthesis and of respiration – takes place in the tropics. The biologist Harald Sioli, ex-director of the Max-Planck Institute of Limnology, calculated in 1971 that the Amazon Basin, through photosynthesis, produces approximately 50 per cent of the oxygen added to the earth's atmosphere annually and consumes about 10 per cent of the gaseous carbon in the atmosphere.

The tropical forest is an extremely important component of global climate. Enormous quantities of water are evapotranspired into the atmosphere on both sides of the equator, which serves to cool the tropics and transfer heat towards the polar regions. If tropical forests are destroyed, world climate patterns will be disrupted.

So what is the threat to the tropical forests?

Although temperate forests and those in semi-arid lands have been cleared for agriculture and their timber used for construction, firewood and paper-making, tropical forests are increasingly under threat. They are now clear-felled for timber, and razed and burnt for agriculture and cattle ranching. They are stripped bare to expose the minerals locked in

25

the soils (for instance aluminium, iron and manganese as well as gold, copper and diamonds) or they are flooded in giant hydroelectric schemes as in Brazil and other Latin American countries.

More than 200,000 square kilometres of primary tropical rainforest are being destroyed each year.[9] Between 1950 and 1980 timber logging increased nearly twenty fold from 4 million cubic metres to 70 million cubic metres, and today commercial logging damages some 45,000 square kilometres every year. There is relatively little replanting and reclamation and the secondary forest, although of use to the timber merchant, is species poor and a far cry from the exuberance of intact primary forest.

Fuelwood-gatherers are responsible for the destruction of 25,000 square kilometres, and the cattle-rancher for another 25,000 square kilometres, mostly in Latin America. Meanwhile, the slash-and-burn peasant who tries to grow cash and subsistence crops on atrociously poor soils, and usually has to move on after a couple of years, probably destroys as much as 160,000 square kilometres of primary forest each year. In general such peasants, who have little or no tradition of living in tropical rainforests, are the victims of government policies and of highly inequitable land distribution.

The total destroyed each year is equivalent to some 2 per cent of all the tropical forest coverage and at that rate all the

primary forest will have gone within fifty years. Worse, in some parts of Latin America and South-East Asia, deforestation is increasing. The extent of cleared land in the Amazon of Brazil, for instance, increased from 28,600 square kilometres in 1975 to more than 77,000 square kilometres in 1978.

Aside from the loss of species, many of which are of potential use to man as medicines, food and spice crops and genetic stock against plant diseases, does it matter if all the tropical forests go?

Most tropical forests grow on lateritic soils which consist of a thick layer of soil from which most if not all dissolvable minerals, including those essential for healthy vegetation growth, have been washed out, and from which most organic matter has disappeared through rapid decomposition. Lateritic soil is particularly high in aluminium and iron, the former mineral being particularly toxic to plants. Rainforests have therefore evolved extraordinarily efficient symbiotic mechanisms to recycle minerals. In forests on the poorest tropical soils, trees form a dense root mat just below the soil surface which functions as a filter to prevent nutrient leaching; this depends on abundant fungal *mycorrhizae*, which make a bridge between the root and dead vegetation ensuring direct cycling that bypasses the soil. In general, the agricultural systems introduced into what was tropical rainforest cannot replicate such natural recycling methods, and the nutrient status of the ecosystem rapidly declines. Nor can it easily be improved by adding fertilisers as these are rapidly washed out in the rains.

With their shallow root mats and lack of tap roots, tropical rainforests need abundant rain. They also generate rain because of the rapid recycling of much of the rainfall – most scientists agree that at least 50 per cent, and possibly as much as 75 per cent, of the rainfall may evaporate and transpire into the atmosphere. The moist clouds are then carried by the prevailing winds further over the forest until the saturation of the air reaches the point when rain falls.

According to Eneas Salati of Brazil, the Amazon Basin,

encompassing 5 million square kilometres, receives 12 trillion (million million) tonnes of rainwater each year of which 6.5 trillion tonnes are evapotranspired and 5.5 trillion tonnes are discharged into the river system that drains into the Amazon Basin.

What happens to the moisture in the atmosphere?

The rain-bearing clouds over the equator are pulled high by the tropical sun into the troposphere and move towards the respective poles. Enormous energies are contained in the warm moist air on account of the latent heat carried by water vapour. That latent heat is released during precipitation: indeed the circulation of moist air from the tropics towards the poles is a vital mechanism in the transfer of tropical heat to more temperate regions.

Less moisture in the convection system means that less energy and less heat will be transferred towards the higher latitudes. This would fundamentally affect climate. Less moisture carried in the air, together with changes in the degree to which sunlight is reflected off the earth's surface by different vegetation patterns may well contribute to desertification and to a generalised cooling of higher latitude areas.

Is there a connection between the tropical atmosphere and the atmosphere over Europe?

Over the past fifteen years atmospheric chemists have learned that the atmosphere is a far more complicated system than a survey of the main constituent gases indicated. Trace gases, many of them involving photo-oxidation reactions, are now seen to play a major role in chemical transformations in the atmosphere, generating such phenomena as acid rain. The tropical atmosphere, which receives the most sunlight – some $2\frac{1}{2}$ times that received at the Poles – is particularly important in such transformations. Yet man's intervention is dramatically changing the chemistry of the tropical atmosphere, which may affect both climate and the rate of acid deposition.

So what is happening?

Not only are carbon dioxide and monoxide generated when the rainforest is cut down, but its replacement by cattle ranches and rice paddies is increasing the levels of methane by $1\frac{1}{2}$ to 2 per cent each year. Termites too, are another source of methane – and their populations are bound to increase as felled trees are left to rot. Under the oxidising conditions found in the tropical atmosphere the methane is also converted to carbon dioxide. Thus the destruction of the tropical forest is adding to the build-up of carbon dioxide in the atmosphere and to the 'greenhouse' effect by which heat from the sun is trapped close to the earth's surface.

The consequences for global climate are so grave that we must do our utmost to persuade those countries with tropical forests to protect them from misguided use and mismanagement. The world must understand the dangers of a deforested planet, and as individuals we should inform ourselves about the tropical ecosystem and its interaction with the remainder of the planet.

But surely, given our separation from such areas there's not much we can do?

Various suggestions have been made as to how to protect the rainforest. For instance, both the World Ecological Areas Programme (WEAP) published in the *Ecologist* in 1980 and Professor Ira Rubinoff's[10] proposal for an International Tropical Moist Forest Reserve System indicated ways in which the international community could compensate countries with such forests for leaving them alone, or employing benign management strategies such as those used by indigenous tribal peoples. A small *per capita* tax paid to a central international fund by developed countries with a *per capita* gross national product of at least $1500 per annum would yield as much as $3 billion annually.

The Green Alternative

But apart from paying some tax is there anything I can do as an individual?

A major problem is that governments see such virgin areas as useful space in which to shove landless peasants or even slum-dwellers. Indonesia, for example, intends to ship millions of Javanese to its other islands, including Sumatra and Timor, as part of a *Transmigration Programme* supported by the World Bank and other Development Agencies. The real purpose of this is to 'Javanise' the entire area at the expense of both the forests and the indigenous people, who in Timor at least are resisting.

We should lobby parliament and voice concern that our money, via taxes, is being used to perpetrate policies that are ultimately destructive.

But those crowded in the more densely populated islands like Java need somewhere to go. Why shouldn't they be helped to move to other islands where there's land?

Transmigration makes hardly a dent in the area of greatest poulation pressure: while Java's population has risen by more than 55 million in fifty-five years and is now increasing by 1.5 million people per year, only some 3 million have been transmigrated. Half a million people are supposed to be moved each year, but even that programme is running into severe difficulties because of the poverty of soils of much of the resettled areas left after the forest has been chopped down.

In fact, Java has some of the archipelago's richest soils, capable of sustaining a dense population, but more than 30 per cent of the best land is in the hands of 1 per cent of the population.

And what about Latin America?

In Latin America, government-sponsored schemes, often backed by the Development Banks and Overseas Aid, aim at resettling landless peasants in 'virgin areas', which actually often already harbour indigenous tribes. Such settlement schemes are doubling deforested areas in parts of Brazil every two years.

Catherine Caufield[11] points out that 'Brazil has 2.3 acres of farmland per person, which is more than the United States, the world's greatest exporter of food. Taking potential farmland into account, but still leaving aside Amazonia, each person in Brazil could have 10 acres. Instead, 4.5 per cent of Brazil's landowners own 81 per cent of the country's farmland and 70 per cent of rural households are landless.'

But if the World Bank and other development agencies like our own Overseas Development Administration come to realise that the schemes they promote do not work as intended, won't they withdraw their support?

The development banks and other agencies have been more concerned in meeting the requests of governments than with keeping an eye on the projects they are supposedly supporting. The World Bank itself has more than $15 billion a year to lend.

Besides massive irrigation schemes that money has been used for road-construction projects and increasingly for colonisation schemes, as in Indonesia and Latin America. Roads driven into the jungles are the initial cut that leads to a festering wound of ill-conceived development. Colombia is a case in point.

The World Bank helped fund a major colonisation scheme in Colombia's Amazon region at La Caqueta. Its own evaluation of that scheme is as damning as any:

> After deforestation and the planting of crops or pasture formation, erosion has increased and threatens to devastate large areas. Rainfall now runs off the Cordillera more rapidly, causing rivers in the project area to flood and erode during the rainy season and to run dry the rest of the year. Some claim that the weather itself is changing in the area, with less rainfall occurring. . . . The government itself is considering a reforestation programme to pay peasants for planting trees. . . . If

some radical reduction in erosion . . . is not brought about . . .
it appears that damage in the project area may be great.[12]

**But don't these agencies have qualified staff to tell them the
risks associated with their projects?**

The World Bank, for instance, receives details of several
hundred new potential projects each year, yet it only has a
handful of staff to evaluate the environmental implications.

**Countries with tropical forest are increasingly exporting
produce from their once forested areas, including beef and
timber. If we consumed only our own products would it help
conserve these forests?**

Individual actions undoubtedly add up, especially when they
are highly publicised. On the timber-importing side, Friends
of the Earth (UK) are campaigning to get the importers into
Britain of tropical woods to try to ensure that such timber is
obtained from licensed 'concessions' with proper management practices and reforestation schemes. FOE has also
asked the UK timber trade to put aside 1 per cent of its
tropical hardwood profits to ensure sustainable management
of the forests. How much influence the importers have on
those extracting the wood is questionable, but at least it might
be a step in the right direction.

We, as consumers, can help by trying to use our own
indigenous hardwoods whenever possible, tied in to a
campaign for the planting of more hardwoods in Britain so
that we too can build up sustainable forests.

What is the value of the tropical timber imports?

According to the UN Food and Agriculture Organisation, the
United Kingdom imported $442 million worth of tropical
timber in 1981 against $1,994 million by Japan and $581
million by the United States. Although the UK is one of
Europe's main importers of tropical hardwoods clearly any
campaign to reduce worldwide consumption must embrace
Japan. Meanwhile Japan, using giant chipping machines,

each one of which can 'eat' its way through 5 hectares of forest a day, is consuming entire hillsides of tropical forest in Papua New Guinea. The chipped wood is used for paper-making and for the packaging of goods for export from Japan. By buying goods from Japan packaged in that way, we are therefore inadvertently helping to deforest tropical regions.

And cattle?

Already the once-rich rainforests of Costa Rica and other parts of Central America have been decimated so that our beefburger chains can lay their hands on cheap beef. With advice from the FAO, which ignored the true nature of much of Amazonian soils, Brazil has cleared at least 3000 square kilometres each year.

Instead of giving this land to the millions of wretchedly poor subsistence farmers, as was proclaimed publicly, the Brazilian government through its agency SUDAM – Superintendency for the Development of the Amazon – apportioned out large chunks of land at giveaway prices for cattle-raising. Ranches of some 2,000 square kilometres began to dot the landscape, sweeping away Indian tribes and peasants, usually by force. The multinationals were soon on the scene – the Swift Armour Company, the Italian chemical company Liquigas, Volkswagen, Deltec International, and the King Ranch of Texas. The World Bank and the Inter-American Development Bank then provided substantial loans for the construction of meat-processing plants and for improving cattle-raising in Brazil. And while more meat was being exported from Brazil and Latin America than ever before, in those same countries *per capita* consumption of meat was actually falling.

And what about hydroelectric schemes in Latin America?

The Amazon carries one-quarter of all the world's fresh water, and the rivers of Brazil's Amazon Basin could generate the equivalent of 100 large nuclear power stations – more than double the projected future electricity demand in Brazil.

The intention is to develop one-fifth that amount by the year 2000.

By then as much as one-sixth of Brazil's Amazon region will, according to plans, have been transformed into an integrated industrial zone, with the development of mining, metal-processing, forestry, agriculture, cattle-ranching and human settlements. The now complete Tucurui Dam on the Tocantins river is one of some twenty dams which will convert that river into a giant lake 2,000 kilometres long, flooding several thousand square kilometres of forest, some containing the Amazon's most productive Brazil nut trees.

The rising waters of the Tucurui Dam are inundating some seventeen towns and villages, requiring the resettlement of some 15,000 people, not counting the many thousands more who are squatters in the area without any rights. Three Indian reservations are affected, one being completely flooded. The dams will exacerbate disease in the area, particularly malaria, and there are fears that the reservoir could harbour Schistosoma – the agent of Bilharzia.

Can we do anything to stop such projects?

Criticism of large dam projects from scientists, politicians, let alone from the people displaced, is increasing. The World Bank is now aware of some of the drawbacks of such schemes, and if it continues to support them it will undoubtedly bring upon itself mounting disapproval.

We must make our own voices heard through, for instance, informing our MPs, since it is our taxes which help fund development agencies.

Has man ever learnt to live in harmony with the tropical rainforest?

Tribal people have adapted themselves remarkably to the rainforest. In fact, they have actually adapted the rainforest to their own needs. They know which plants and animals will provide them with food, with medicines, with poisons for hunting and hallucinogens, but they also know what size of clearing best regenerates into forest after use. They do not simply abandon their garden plots once the fertility has gone but, in Brazil at least, encourage vegetation species which will attract game and therefore act as reserves for hunting. They are true managers of their environment.

In destroying forest for short-term gains we will soon have wiped out both the rainforest and the people who, through thousands of years of experience, know best how to use it and live in it.

Huge numbers of people travel all over the world. Does tourism affect the environment?

Tourism is a major worldwide activity, generating foreign exchange earnings and often having considerable impact on the environment and on the way of life of the host population. Cheap travel has opened up the world. People are no longer just visiting the crowded resorts of the industrialised countries – they are crowding off to the wilderness and other remote places to enjoy nature 'in the raw', as well as peoples whose traditions and cultures still capture the spirit of a pre-industrial age. The Galapagos, with its bizarre flora and fauna, the Himalayas and even equatorial tropical forests are now part of the tourist circuit for those who can afford a more enriching experience.

Today, hardly anywhere in the world remains exempt from the tour operator's desire to open up new markets. Equally, with up to 5 per cent, and more than 30 per cent in some instances, (as in Barbados and the Seychelles), of their gross domestic product arising out of tourism, most countries are very willing to exploit and develop their natural and man-derived resources for tourists' benefit.

The rate of growth of tourism since the Second World War has been phenomenal. International arrivals worldwide alone increased between 1945 and 1980 from 25 million to some 280 million. Overall, tourism is responsible for some 3,000 million movements per year, 90 per cent of which take place within a country. Not surprisingly, receipts have gone up accordingly – in those countries affiliated to the World Tourism Organisation, they rose from US$6.9 billion in 1960 to some $100 billion by 1982. Tourism is growing by 5 per cent per year, so will have doubled before the year 2000, partly fed by the growing number of people in the world who have 'paid leave'.

Surely such a growing and enormous tourist trade is bound to have far-reaching environmental and social consequences?

Too often in the past the inflow of tourists, coming *en masse* during the holiday season, overloaded the resort's system, leading to water shortages, sewage problems, electricity cuts and overcrowding. But with the development of competition and choice, tourists have tended to become more discerning, requiring better value for what in effect is an extremely important portion of their working lives. Less and less will they accept overcrowded beaches, shoddy hotels, inadequate facilities, noise and pollution.

Tourists are therefore drawn further and further into the unspoilt areas of the world, with varying impacts on those areas. Some areas have a greater tolerance than others. In a wildlife park in Africa, for instance, different species have different tolerances of human interference; the difficulty is to assess exactly when and by how much they are being affected. Lions apparently mind less than cheetah, yet it is the cheetah that is a greater draw. In an Australian resort, large crowds were drawn to watch the migration of penguins down to the sea each evening and arc lights and watching stands were brought in. The result was that the breeding pattern of the birds was severely disrupted.

Over the past fifteen years mountains, particularly the Himalayas, have been subjected to increasing pressure from tourists. Although they are by no means entirely to blame, the many thousands of tourists who now follow the trails though the Himalayan valleys are contributing to rapid environmental destruction in the region, where there are extremely sensitive ecosystems. Little attempt has been made to assess the impact. The incursions into the Himalayas have also brought peoples such as the Ladakhis abruptly into

contact with modern values and Western civilisation; in fact
the visitors are often the unwitting destroyers of those very
same traditions and customs that they have come so far to see.

Too many tourists can also cause irreversible damage to
natural ecosystems, resulting in the loss of wildlife and
habitats. Uncontrolled access to the coral reefs in the Indian
Ocean, whether by snorkellers, scuba divers or boats, has
caused great damage. The pulverising of coral by boat moor-
ings and trampling is one danger; another is the gathering of
mementoes. The result has been not only the loss of attractive
species, such as the triton conch, but the disturbance of the
entire ecosystem. For example, the ravaging of coral by the
crown-of-thorns starfish may be a result of the removal of the
triton conch, which feeds on the starfish and controls its
population.

**Doesn't the money brought in by tourism benefit the local
communities?**

Undoubtedly the revenue brought in through tourism can be
used for the restoration of monuments and religious sanctuaries; and it may also serve to keep traditions alive, although
the real meaning may be lost as the younger generation get
caught up in the cash economy and in emulating the lifestyle
of the visitors. The rise of delinquency, vandalism, crime and
prostitution have all been associated with tourism and usually
such consequences are ignored when evaluating the tourist
potential of a site.

What can we do to make tourism manageable?

The concept has arisen that tourism should be subject to
environmental planning and management, taking into
account the local population which too often has had to
accept a large influx of tourists without having had any voice
in such a development.

The carrying capacities of vulnerable environments can be
increased considerably through educating and informing the
visitors of the fragility and delicate nature of the world they

are to enter, through strict laws to prevent the taking of trophies, and through the provision of protected walkways and mooring facilities. A system of control over tour operators may also be essential. Once the carrying capacity of an area has been established, various strategies can prevent it being exceeded. For instance, counter-attractions can be created to take the pressure off vulnerable areas.

Given the extent of today's tourism it is inevitable that it will have considerable environmental impact; the approach must be to reduce that impact as much as possible while using the growing awareness of the tourist about the world in which he lives to help protect these natural and human resources which are threatened by his presence.

Therein lies the paradox of tourism – it is a direct result of our industrialised age, and yet it could prove the means by which sensitive parts of the world are saved from further destruction – though only if tour operators and host countries co-operate in adopting an ecologically conscious policy toward tourist developments. It is up to individual tourists to encourage such policies and themselves to be acutely aware of their own impact – social, cultural and ecological – when exploring the world.

2 Pollution of the environment

Industrial activity has always caused pollution. From the early days of the industrial revolution up to the end of the Second World War smoking chimneys were a sign of progress, of high employment and profits. Today, even though most Western industrialised countries control soot and fly ash from boilers and furnaces, gases are still emitted, some toxic and noxious, their consequences for the environment as grave as the more visible smoke and fumes from older industry. Ironically, building stacks some 400 feet high to carry the gases away from the local environment has exacerbated the pollution problem by ejecting the gas plume high enough in the atmosphere to undergo photochemical change, contributing to the acid rain problem. Enormous plumes of industrial gases travelling from USSR industry in Siberia and back over Western Europe can be traced high over the North Pole. Conversely, the gases discharged from Britain's power stations are carried in the prevailing winds over the North Sea to Scandinavia where, Swedish and Norwegian scientists say, they contribute to the acidification of lakes and rivers.

In both Norway and Sweden tens of thousands of square kilometres of fresh water are now either fishless or nearly so through acidification. Equally serious, the topsoil in southern Scandinavia is nearly ten times more acid than it was fifty years ago. Sweden has now resolved to reduce its own sulphur dioxide and nitrogen oxide emissions from power stations and industrial sources, and by 1995 expects them to be down by two-thirds to 30,000 tonnes per year, compared with 100,000 tonnes in 1978. At present Sweden receives some six times more sulphur from other countries than it generates. In addition to the acidified lakes and rivers in Scandinavia, some 7 million hectares of Europe's forest – an area equivalent to one-third of the United Kingdom – show signs of damage, with at least 250,000 hectares dying or dead.

As Friends of the Earth point out, the Protocol targets

accepted by other EEC countries could be met in Britain at reasonable cost using conventional desulphurisation technology. With the Wellman Lord system of flue gas desulphurisation, EEC targets could be met by 1995 at a cost of £1.432 billion – adding 3 to 4 per cent to electricity costs over ten years.

Nevertheless we are still abysmally ignorant as to the precise mechanism of either acidification or *Waldsterben* – the death of the trees. In both instances, complex photochemical reactions are at play in the atmosphere, but what is increasingly certain is that the sum of our industrial activities lies at the root of the problem, through upsetting natural nutrient cycles. Certainly the British approach to pollution control is much to blame (particularly that of 'discharge, disperse and dilute'), for we have assumed that as long as the chimney stacks are tall enough, and the discharge pipes into the sea and estuaries long enough, the environment will do the rest for us, taking our pollutants away from our shores and hopefully diluting them sufficiently by the time they reach anyone else's.

While no one can seriously deny any longer that gas emissions over land are important in causing acid rain, new potential sources of gas pollution have come to light with the discovery of massive algal blooms in the North Sea. It seems that fertiliser run-off, sewage effluent from cities and the discharge of nutrient-rich detergents are combining to make the sea, in particular the North Sea, into a breeding ground for certain kinds of algae. Like polluted lakes, seas are becoming eutrophied, and the result is the release of large quantities of gases such as dimethyl sulphide which through photo-oxidation changes brought about by intense sunlight in the atmosphere convert into sulphur dioxide and acid rain.

Today a great deal of pollution can be avoided by using new technologies. Fluidised-bed combustion boilers which use limestone mixed with the fuel to capture sulphur and which operate at temperatures low enough to prevent the formation of nitrogen oxides are proving economically worthwhile, particularly since their thermal efficiency is better than conventional boilers such as those used by the Central Elecricity

Generating Board (CEGB) in its power plants. Similarly many industries, historically major polluters, have now found ways to control their emissions as well as to recycle by-products. Instead of classic and expensive 'end of pipe' treatment, the new processes are 'low or non-waste technologies'. The USSR, for instance, uses 90 per cent of the slags from iron and steel manufacture for road-making aggregates, for cement and ceramic manufacture and for fertilisers. Increasingly too, the dusts generated during manufacture are recycled for their metal content while the top gases from pressurised plant furnaces are used to generate electricity.

We should no longer tolerate the casual disposal of wastes, whether they are discharged into the atmosphere or dumped either in the sea or in landfill sites. However carefully planned, landfill sites leak dangerous pollutants and in time can contaminate groundwater supplies.

Modern industrialised societies now depend on the products of the chemical industry. Man-made fabrics and fibres, pharmaceuticals, fertilisers, pesticides, paints, building materials, as well as chemicals for industrial processes, are just some of the 60,000 chemical compounds in common use. Several hundred of these are hazardous, either because of their toxicity to living organisms, including man, or because of their high inflammability or potential to explode. Industry has always claimed that its products are more beneficial than harmful and it is rare for cost/benefit analysis to go against a planning application for a new manufacturing process or product. And where do we draw the line? For example, the flame-retardant tris (2,3-dibromopropyl) phosphate has saved lives and reduced burns, yet it is probably carcinogenic. Who then should assess the risks of proceeding with manufacture – the industry, governments or the public?

Through such laws as the US Toxic Substances Control Act (TSCA) or the Sixth Amendment to the EEC Directive on the Classification, Packaging and Labelling of Dangerous Substances, industrialised countries force industry to test its products before manufacture or marketing, and then have those tests approved by government. Compliance with the US TSCA could cost chemical manufacturers as much as

500,000 US dollars for each new product, but perhaps we *should* be limiting the number of synthetic chemicals to which we are exposed? We must also remember that live organisms, particularly mammals, are used as guinea pigs for the testing, and many of them suffer miserably as a result.

An important way of reducing the impact of our consumer society on the environment is through recycling, which we, as consumers, must help to make work. Wilton, New Hampshire in the United States has, rather than levy rates for rubbish disposal, organised a recycling dump in which the town's people sort their rubbish into different categories and take it to the town dump, from where it is sold; for instance organic material is converted into compost and sold for horticulture. The Wilton dump has proved a great success and is certainly a model that councils in Britain should consider following.

Recycling has become economically imperative to industry as the costs of basic resources, including energy, have risen. In industrialised countries recycling scrap metal accounts for 45 per cent of steel production, saving the equivalent of 1.5 barrels of oil for every tonne recycled. More spectacularly, some 7.7 barrels of oil equivalent can be saved per tonne of recycled copper and nearly 30 barrels per tonne of aluminium. Calculations by the aluminium industry in the UK indicate that the cost of recycling aluminium is approximately £300 per tonne compared with £900 per tonne for extracting it from primary sources. In the US, where some 60 billion cans are produced each year, nearly 50 per cent of all aluminium is recycled. At present the US has some 6,000 locations for collecting cans. In the UK, where some 3½ billion cans are produced each year, less than 1 per cent of all aluminium is recycled and there are no collection points for cans. Using waste paper can save as much as 60 per cent of the energy required for making paper from fresh pulp and also save trees. In OECD countries the recycling of wastes has increased industry's profit margins by as much as 40 per cent.

With tighter anti-pollution legislation, some 'dirty' manufacturers take their industries to countries with cheap resources and labour, where control is far more lax. Most industry opposes harmonisation agreements, in which uniform pollution-control standards are applied between trading partners, protesting that countries with pristine environments and different climatic conditions have a greater capacity for absorbing pollutants and neutralising them. Such unscrupulous shortsightedness has led to a fearful toll on human health. Diseases such as Minamata disease – methyl mercury poisoning, which led to incurable brain damage and distorted development among the fishing community of Minamata in Japan during the 1960s – have now been exported to Thailand through the establishment of polluting industries. The same pattern is being followed in other developing countries. Chad, for instance, has offered to take nuclear waste from industrialised countries.

The problem of double standards – one for the highly industrialised countries, the other for developing countries – is clearly a vexed one, especially during a period of economic recession. A copper mining company in Arizona, complying with US regulations, shut down because it could no longer compete on the world market – one-fifth of the total costs of copper mining in the US are absorbed by pollution control. Yet over the border in Mexico, where pollution control is minimal, the mines still operate, and to add insult to injury, send their noxious plumes floating over into the United States.

Some Euro MPs, campaigned vigorously for strict minimal standards, aiming for uniformity in process and product standards to protect the environment better and allow fairer competition. Unfortunately, the interests of individual industries come first, both for the government taxing profits and for those seeking employment who believe that a job takes priority over a clean environment.

If we are concerned about acid rain and atmospheric pollution shouldn't we opt for nuclear power?

It helps nobody – and least of all the environment – to substitute one severe form of pollution for another. The pro-

The Green Alternative

nuclear loby promotes the idea that nuclear power is safe and clean, but since there is no such thing as a safe dose of radiation and no acceptable method of radioactive waste disposal, the Green attitude to nuclear power must be absolutely firm – namely that it is totally unacceptable in a civilised and caring world.

If we are forced to burn fossil fuels in the foreseeable future what do we do about acid rain and atmospheric pollution?

Some 60 per cent of Britain's sulphur emissions come from its coal-fired stations, none of which have had any means of entrapping sulphur. Some European countries have embarked on various schemes to reduce sulphur emissions – France, for instance, levies a charge on such emissions from thermal installations of more than 50 megawatts capacity. But until September 1986, Britain's Central Electricity Generating Board, with government support, obdurately refused to install any flue gas desulphurisation, claiming that such measures would add at least 12 per cent to electricity bills. However, in September 1986 the British government announced that the CEGB would spend £600 million over the next decade to reduce sulphur emissions from three major coal-fired power stations, Drax B, Fiddler's Ferry and probably West Burton. They have pledged to reduce SO_2 levels by 30 per cent by the end of the century. This does not mean that Britain has joined the 30 per cent club, because levels of coal combustion have fallen anyway due to less demand. Yet Japan has found the means to entrap more than 90 per cent of its sulphur emissions, including those from oil refineries as well as power stations.

Besides control of power station emissions, we can reduce toxic emissions from motor vehicle exhausts and increase the efficiency of all appliances burning gas, coal, wood or oil. Opinion polls show that the public is prepared to pay the extra cost for a cleaner and safer environment. All that is needed to solve the acid rain problem is political will and firm legislation.

Pollution of the environment

In view of sulphur dioxide (SO₂) pollution shouldn't we welcome opportunities to reduce our use of oil and coal?

There are perfectly sound reasons for cutting back on all forms of energy use, and indeed Britain can only benefit in the long run from a reduction in coal and oil consumption and from a sensible conservation of fossil fuel stocks. However, we should always be aware of the wider implications of a change in energy strategy. We have already seen the terrible social and economic consequences of a ruthless government campaign to reduce coal-mining capacity and develop an electricity generating system based primarily on nuclear power. If oil and coal production is cut back too sharply some reserves will, in effect, be 'sterilised' from future use. On the matter of SO_2 pollution, the problem could be eased by a greater dependence on low-sulphur coals for power-station use. Increased fuel-burning efficiency (for example involving fluidised-bed combustion) and the use of flue-gas 'scrubbers' can also reduce SO_2 pollution dramatically, as has already been demonstrated in countries like Sweden.

Shouldn't we believe the government when it says that it has gone a great way to solving the SO₂ problem?

Every year some 3 million tonnes of SO_2 are emitted from UK chimney stacks. British industry long ago learned to eject toxic substances at high velocity and to high altitudes, ensuring that 76 per cent of emissions cross the North Sea into northern Europe before coming to earth as acid rain. The European Convention on Long Range Transboundary Air Pollution binds its members to achieve a 30 per cent reduction in SO_2 emissions (based on 1980 levels) by 1995. In 1983 Britain refused to join the 'thirty per cent club', because the government claimed that Britain had already reduced its sulphur emissions by 25 per cent since 1980, and it has consistently refused to implement the recommendations of the Royal Commission on Environmental Pollution and of the Select Committees of both Houses of Parliament that the 30 per cent target should be met and that the CEGB (the major acid rain culprit) should reduce its SO_2 emissions by 60 per cent by 1993. In fact, British SO_2 emissions have fallen largely because of the economic recession and the changing nature of British industry. The British measures announced for the reduction of SO_2 emissions by 30 per cent by the end of the century must be welcomed as a small first step.

It is difficult to understand why Britain has adopted its entrenched position on this issue. Maybe the government is playing a dangerous game, waiting for the acid rain issue to become such a political 'hot potato' that it can suddenly and joyfully announce that a major programme of nuclear power expansion is the 'real' solution.

How much hazardous waste is produced in Britain?

No one knows for certain. According to the Hazardous Waste Inspectorate, a non-statutory body set up by the Department of the Environment in 1983, 4.4 million tonnes of hazardous waste were generated in England and Wales in 1983. The Confederation of British Industry (CBI) told the 1985 Commission on Environmental Pollution, which was investigating waste-management practices in Britain, that some 12 per cent of the estimated 100 million tonnes of industrial waste generated every year could be described as 'toxic or dangerous'. If the CBI is correct, then approximately 12 million tonnes of waste are hazardous.

What are the environmental dangers of hazardous waste?

The disposal of hazardous wastes has already resulted in gross pollution problems at numerous sites throughout the industrial world. The most notorious *known* dump site is at Love Canal, near Niagara Falls in the USA. Abandoned chemical wastes caused the wholesale contamination of a housing estate near Niagara Falls from which several hundred residents had permanently to be evacuated.

Does Britain have any Love Canals?

We do not know – *largely because no one has looked*. The
Department of the Environment (DOE) has no inventory of
abandoned dumps – and, more incredibly, it has no intention
of compiling one. The danger, as one member of a recent
Select Committee of the House of Lords pointed out, is that
we are living 'in a minefield for which we have lost the chart'.
A limited DOE survey was carried out in 1975, which
revealed fifty-three problem sites, several of which are still

'It's nice to know that we're top
of the league in something, anyway.'

used for the disposal of highly toxic wastes. In 1985, a desk study by the independent consultancy firm ECOTEC estimated that 'approximately 600 landfills may present a hazard'. Nonetheless, the DOE insists that the probability of Britain experiencing a major environmental disaster involving hazardous wastes is minimal.

What about other European countries?

Every major industrial country in the EEC except Britain has surveyed its old dumps and found many problem sites. In Denmark 100 sites are threatening groundwaters or surface waters. Germany has closed over 6,000 dumps, 800 of which are threatening water supplies. In Amsterdam 10,000 drums of toxic wastes were discovered buried beneath a rubbish dump; within 6 months 4,000 other illegal dumps had been discovered.

But surely today's landfills are run to the highest standards?

No. The Hazardous Waste Inspectorate has said about current disposal practices: 'A significant number of landfill operators appear ignorant of the technical and scientific research that underpins the controlled landfill disposal of hazardous wastes . . . disposal site licence conditions are, in some cases, wilfully breached without attracting effective enforcement action by the Waste Disposal Authorities.'

Are there any examples of groundwater pollution by chemicals in Britain?

Yes – but the DOE claims they are isolated cases.

Is that claim justified?

No. There is no record of any major landfill in Britain receiving a full hydrogeological survey prior to 1975 – some old landfills are therefore likely to have been sited (albeit unwittingly) over vulnerable aquifers. Even today, hydrogeological surveys are seldom carried out and many landfills are not regularly monitored for groundwater pollution. In the absence of such monitoring, what grounds have we for believing that Britain has avoided the problems now being encountered in *every* other country where landfill is being practised?

But surely landfills can be lined with clay and other materials to make them leak-proof?

Liners do not work in the long term. It is now known that some hazardous wastes – particularly industrial solvents – can transform even clay soils into sieves. Experiments in America reveal that clay exposed to the chemical naphtha is 730,000 times more permeable than when it is exposed to water.

Synthetic liners are just as likely to leak as clay liners. In 1980, Peter Montague of Princeton University studied four supposedly 'secure' landfills in New Jersey. All the landfills were double-lined. At one site, where the liners consisted of hypalon (a tough polymer material, reinforced with nylon), the primary liner leaked 124 gallons a day within four months of being installed. All three other sites also leaked.

The US Environmental Protection Agency has now said that all landfills should be regulated 'on the assumption that migration of hazardous wastes and their constituents and by-products . . . will inevitably occur'.

Is it true that other countries have banned the use of landfills?

Several countries have banned the use of 'dilute and disperse' sites – i.e., unlined sites where wastes are allowed to migrate out of the tip into the underlying soils on the assumption that they will be rendered harmless through microbial activity. In France, only sites with a 5-metre thick base of impermeable material are permitted to take special wastes. Similar regulations are in force in Germany.

In the US, all new landfills are now required to have 'a liner to prevent the migration of wastes to soils and surface waters'. In addition, a leachate collection system is obligatory (leachate is the polluting liquid that accumulates at the base of a landfill) and the dumping of liquid wastes in landfills is only permitted at 'facilities with liners and leachate collection and removal systems'.

Only twelve sites in Britain are lined. In effect, the vast majority of Britain's landfills would not be permitted to operate in either France, Germany or America.

Landfill sites are becoming scarce and expensive. Why aren't more sensible alternatives being tried, such as waste-derived energy production?

Local councils have a statutory responsibility to collect and dispose of domestic refuse. Although waste-derived energy is preferable to landfill disposal, refuse incinerators, RDF (refuse-derived fuel) plants and methane converters all have high investment costs, whereas landfill tipping is considered cheaper even if it leads to long-term environmental problems. Because of the shortage of landfill sites some councils such as Avon and the London borough councils have to 'export' their waste by road transport to other counties where sites are available. Transport costs are not added to the collection and disposal figures; this gives false comparisons of the commercial viability of energy from waste as opposed to landfill.

Why does the British government allow 'dilute and disperse' sites?

Britain justifies its reliance on 'dilution and disposal' by citing a single study, conducted in the mid-1970s which concluded: 'Sensible landfill is realistic and an ultra-cautious approach to landfill of hazardous and other types of waste is unjustified.'

Only 19 sites out of 5,000 were studied (that is, less than 0.4 per cent) and only 15 were examined in depth – hardly a 'statistically significant' sample. Of the sites surveyed, 2 were discovered to be causing water pollution problems.

What about incineration? Isn't this a safe method of disposal?

High-temperature, controlled incineration is *potentially* the most effective method of disposal available today: not only does it reduce the volume of waste for ultimate disposal, but it also reduces the toxicity of that waste. Moreover – and this makes it a critical weapon in the arsenal of responsible waste disposal – it can be used to treat a wide range of 'difficult' wastes, including organic solvents, chlorinated hydrocarbons, distillation residues and oily wastes.

But incineration is not without problems. Its safety depends on complex technology which demands the highest standards of management. To ensure the complete degradation of a waste to a non-toxic form, it is not enough to put the waste into a white-hot oven. The oven must have reached the right *temperature* (1200°C in the case of PCBs – polychlorobiphenyls used, for instance, in transformers), the waste must be left to burn for sufficient *time* to ensure complete combustion, and there must be adequate *turbulence* within the oven to ensure that the waste is well mixed with oxygen and thus evenly burned.

If the 'three Ts' of incineration – temperature, time and turbulence – are not taken into account when designing and operating an incinerator, then the incineration process can go badly awry. Certain British incinerators, such as ReChem at Pontypool, Wales, have been heavily criticised in this respect.

Why? What can go wrong?

Not only does incomplete combustion result in some of the original waste remaining unburned, but it also causes new compounds to form. Known as Products of Incomplete Combustion, or PICs, these new compounds can be even more toxic than the wastes from which they are formed. Researchers in Canada, America, Holland, Switzerland and Sweden, for example, have found that municipal incinerators (which burn household rubbish, usually at temperatures around 800°C) release significant quantities of dibenzofurans and dioxins, both highly toxic breakdown products of chlorinated wastes. Dibenzofurans and dioxins have also been found in emission from high-temperature incinerators, as have some twenty-two other organic compounds – the vast majority of which have still to be identified by chemists, let alone assessed for their effects on human health or the environment.

Does the chemical treatment of drinking water make it properly safe?

In treating water, the authorities are primarily concerned with destroying those organisms which might cause stomach upsets – or, worse still, cholera. But the chemicals used to treat water are also a potential threat to health. Certain natural organic substances, for example, are now known to react with the chlorine used to disinfect water supplies to form compounds known as trihalomethanes (THMs). Several THMs – chloroform is an example – are suspected human carcinogens. For that reason, treatment plants in America are required to use granulated activated carbon to remove THMs from drinking water. In Germany, the government limits the concentration of THMs in drinking water to 25 micrograms per litre – a level which is exceeded in several parts of Britain – and many German treatment plants are now using ozone instead of chlorine as a disinfectant. In Britain, however, the Water Research Council argues that 'it is more important to continue proven methods of disinfection than to take action to reduce concentrations of chlorinated organics that are in any case very low'.

Are THMs the only chemical pollutants in our water to pose a health threat?

Other chemicals such as tranquillisers and contraceptive hormones which have passed through the human body have also been detected in 'cleaned' water. Little is known about the effects of the 1,200 or so other micropollutants which have been discovered in drinking water. In 1975, the World Health Organisation reviewed 289 of the organic compounds commonly found in drinking water and found that no toxicological data of any sort existed for over half of them. More recently, in 1981, the Water Research Council reported that 'most' of the 343 organic compounds it had identified in drinking water 'have never been evaluated in terms of safety'. Among the compounds which the WRC detected were several known or suspected carcinogens – notably, chloroform, benzene, trichloroethylene and carbon tetrachloride.

We are poisoning the seas with our wastes, aren't we?

Highly acidic iron-rich waste is the legacy of the titanium dioxide industry whose production process was shown by Greenpeace to be one of the most polluting. To produce just 1 tonne of titanium dioxide (a harmless white pigment used in paints) you automatically produce 6 tonnes of potentially toxic waste. The iron component of the waste blankets the sea-bed, devastating bottom-dwelling communities. The acid causes abnormal behaviour in fish and acts synergistically with the iron component to lower the resistance of pelagic, or free-floating, species to disease.

It has been estimated that 50 per cent of certain species of fish caught in the North Sea are affected by chemical-waste dumping every year. The UK currently dumps 75 per cent of all industrial waste into the North Sea (over 80 million tonnes/year) and 98 per cent of all the sewage sludge.

The seas are so big, why should we worry about chemical and waste dumping?

In the early 1950s, it was discovered that toxic substances which were barely detectable in the general environment had accumulated to alarming levels in species at the top of the food-chain. One of the best documented cases of such 'bio-magnification' was the wholesale contamination of the aquatic food-chain in Clear Lake, California, after the spraying of DDD, a close chemical relative of DDT. Levels of DDD in the water were as low as 0.02 ppm (parts per million); plankton and other microscopic organisms feeding in the lake, however, had accumulated residues at 4 ppm; fish eating the plankton further concentrated the pesticide to levels as high as 20 ppm; and grebes feeding on the fish were found to be contaminated with 160 ppm – 8,000 times the level of DDD present in the lake – with the result that thousands died.

But surely in the open sea, wastes are dispersed so effectively that biomagnification is not a problem?

At Garroch Head off the Firth of Clyde, where most of Glasgow's sewage sludge and industrial waste is dumped, dispersal is so minimal that the dump is officially classified as an 'accumulative site'. The concentration of heavy metals on the sea bed in the immediate vicinity of the dump is now so high that the Royal Commission has called Garroch Head 'a sacrificial site'.

In Liverpool Bay, too, the dispersal of pollutants is minimal. Although levels of such contaminants as PCB and DDT fluctuate widely from year to year, 1976 tests revealed that the level of PCB in the livers of cod was as high as 9.5 ppm – almost twice the level which would render the fish unfit for human consumption in the United States. Levels of mercury are also very high. In fact, Hugh Neilson, a senior civil servant at the Ministry of Agriculture, Fisheries and Food (MAFF), told the Gregson Committee in 1981 that Liverpool Bay is now widely regarded as the area 'where the dirtiest fish in terms of some toxic compounds are found in the whole of Europe'.

The Irish Sea is also heavily polluted with PCBs, heavy metals, radionuclides such as caesium and plutonium, and other contaminants and, according to Martin Holdgate, chief scientist at the DOE, 'this sea is likely to be one of the most contaminated in Western Europe'.

But no fish are killed by these levels of pollution, are they?

Maybe not, but many fish suffer from 'sub-lethal' pollution. Sub-lethal pollutants do not kill outright but can instead induce a wide range of delayed long-term disorders – genetic damage, behavioural defects, fine lesions, reduced fertility and even sterility. Perhaps, because sub-lethal marine pollution is so insidious – and so 'un-newsworthy' – it has generally received little attention from the major national and international agencies concerned with pollution control. None the less, in the long-term, the effects of sub-lethal pollution may well be more damaging to the marine environment than pollutants which are *acutely* toxic. And predators higher up the food chain – including ourselves – are bound to concentrate such sub-lethal pollutants even more.

Even the Thames has got fish in it again, so surely we are now quite capable of cleaning up water?

We've cleaned up some rivers and lakes fairly successfully, particularly where a 'natural' load – i.e., mainly human wastes – caused the problem. Organic material in sewage used to make an unsightly mess in rivers, depleted oxygen and devastated fish life. Water treatment plants have indeed taken care of those nutrient wastes without much of a problem.

Lately, however, the main load of pollutants consists of chemicals, which come in via diffuse sources, like agriculture and are less easily removed by water treatment plants. These chemicals do not always create conspicuous pollution, like the frothing of streams and rivers which has been cleaned up over the past ten or fifteen years.

The pollutants now being encountered – chemicals of varying toxicity to humans and ecological systems – are sometimes hardly seen and generally only detectable by chemical analysis. Their invisibility means that they do not command the attention they should. In this respect they are rather like radioactivity, a concealed threat; their presence is usually detected only after damage has occurred, for instance at Love Canal, and Minamata.

How can we help to preserve clean water at home?

Use soap and soap flakes instead of detergents. If you cannot totally do without them use biodegradable products; some 40 per cent of the phosphate pollution of our water comes from conventional detergents. Economise on the use of clean water, for instance having showers instead of baths. Install an economy flush.

Another sort of pollution is wasteful packaging. Can this be avoided? What damage does it do to the environment?

The total energy used to produce all the packaging in the UK is equivalent to roughly 5 per cent of total energy consumption. Packaging of all types cost about £3,300 million in 1982, equivalent to £3.10 per week for each of the 20.5 million households. This was roughly 24 per cent of household income. The amount of packaging used is increasing, although the energy used has been reduced by more energy-efficient methods of production.

Packaging also uses non-renewable raw materials and accounts for 28 per cent by weight of domestic dustbin contents and a great deal more by volume. This causes further fuel consumption and environmental pollution through land-fill dumping, and costs the householder more in the form of rates.

Buy unwrapped goods when possible and avoid plastic bags and one-way bottles, beverages in cans (especially aluminium cans). Return bottles and use bags made from natural fibres. Sort out household litter and put glass and paper in special containers for collection. Leave dangerous waste such as batteries, drugs, and poisons in the places assigned to take them.

Isn't a lot of the packaging forced on us a waste of resources and energy?

Yes. A shopper has to distinguish between packaging for hygiene and transportation, and packaging designed solely to sell the product. Food producers or manufacturers often see packaging as a necessary cost in their budget. But packaging manufacturers see the package as *the* product and it is in their interest to extend its applications wherever possible, even if the final result is that the raw materials and energy, having served their purpose, end up as waste. The UK packaging industry employs some 75,000 people and has a *£4,000 million* annual turnover.

'Here's to Junkfood International and Paperchase Packaging Inc. – another ten years of profitable cooperation.'

Aluminium packaging consumes roughly 10 per cent of the total UK usage, most of the rest going to make aeroplane bodies and tanks. Tins account for about 6 per cent of total steel production, while paper and board packaging consumes 45 per cent of UK timber production.

The total primary energy required to produce all metal, glass and plastics packaging in the UK is estimated at about 2 per cent of the annual national energy consumption. Some 1,500,000 tonnes of oil is consumed annually by the UK plastics packaging industry in terms of raw material and energy. Paper and board packaging (44 per cent of which is imported) uses another 3 per cent, making a total of 5 per cent in all. This is a substantial amount in terms of energy as well as wasted resources.

After the energy crisis of the early 1970s, packaging companies have made considerable efforts to make more efficient use of energy. Since 1978 the energy used to produce and distribute an aluminium can, for example, has been reduced by an estimated 25 per cent. In the United States, where aluminium can collection and recycling is increasingly successful energy costs and pollution are being cut substantially.

Can we derive energy from waste?

So far eleven councils in Britain have set up energy-from-waste plants which convert 1,893,000 tonnes of waste to fuel. Japan already has 63 such plants, and countries such as Germany, Denmark, Holland and Sweden are following suit. However, it is important that the conversion plant is situated near a sizeable market for the energy, whether it be electricity, hot water, gas or fuel pellets. Although some councils do not appear to know exactly how much they spend on waste disposal, the 1985 figures are estimated at between £28 and £35 per tonne so that any energy derived from conversion is an added bonus. Income from reclaimed materials is only 0.44 of gross expenditure.

England and Wales dispose of 500 million tonnes of waste per year, and about £575 million is spent in the UK each year on refuse collection and disposal. Government figures estimate that the equivalent of 8,500,000 tonnes of coal would be available from waste-derived fuel, but only 6 per cent of this is actually converted. The total financial gain would be equivalent to £400 million per year in energy terms.

If there are no recycling centres in your area or schemes to convert waste into energy, tell your local council about the financial benefits of such schemes. Contact the chairman of the council committee responsible for waste management in your area and ask what plans there are for recovering energy from waste, write to your MP asking why Britain is throwing away millions of pounds of potential energy. Send your question and the reply to the local press.

For further details contact the Warmer Campaign (see list of addresses on p. 351).

Are bottle banks really cost-effective?

Bottles made from cullet (broken glass) are second-best substitutes for re-usable bottles, but the saving of cullet is preferable to simply throwing it away. Every tonne of glass recycled is one tonne less rubbish to be collected and disposed of. Glass accounts for approximately 10 per cent of all domestic refuse by weight and it is quite feasible for 1½ million tonnes of glass to be collected in bottle banks each year. The collection, treatment and delivery of cullet requires 78 per cent less energy per tonne than the quarrying, processing and transport of raw materials such as sand, limestone and soda ash. There is also a 20 per cent reduction in fuel consumption per tonne of glass when cullet replaces virgin raw materials in the melting process.

Can plastic be recycled?

Yes, but of the 50 million tonnes used worldwide each year (18 million in Europe alone) only about 20 per cent is recycled. This could be considerably increased as new plastic recovery techniques are developed.

The main way to recycle plastic at present is by shredding and granulating. Thermoplastics are recyclable, whereas thermosettings such as bauxolites are not. Some plastics release dangerous toxic substances when heated. Other plastics, like PET (polyethylene terephthalate) bottles, can be recycled provided that metal and other harmful plastic materials are not introduced, and that they can be collected in sufficient quantities. PET is increasingly used instead of glass because of its cheapness. PET bottles, like most other plastics, are not biodegradable and cannot be re-used. They can be recycled and made into various commodities from saucepan cleaners to duvet fillings and insulating kapok, but unfortunately most end up in the dustbin.

As a result of pressure from consumers and environmentalists, the Italian government has decided to ban all non-biodegradable plastic packaging materials, containers and plastic bags from January 1990 to reduce litter and disposal costs. This will affect the UK exports of these goods and may ultimately lead to a change of policy towards recycling. However, many people believe that the manufacture of biodegradable plastics is inappropriate, since this may cause new forms of pollution to soil and water, and feel that all throw-away plastics should be recycled.

Polycondensed plastics like nylons, polyesters and polyurethanes can be chemically recycled and about 90 per cent of the contents recovered where remelting is not possible. Much shrinkwrap can be recycled provided that the chemicals used are standardised. However, where different varieties of plastic are mixed in a product recycling gives poor results. Simplifying the number of plastics used and coding the type by the manufacturer would add to the efficiency of sorting and recycling.

Small recycling plants are now considered economically feasible because supply and demand can be locally matched and the plant worked to full capacity with a constant flow of inputs. In fact, some small enterprises in the UK are now using discarded plastic, such as sheets used to cover silage on farms, to manufacture products such as floor or wall tiles. However, larger plants have proved less successful because of seasonal and regional fluctuations.

Air pollution too can be a problem. Are there any serious forms of indoor pollutants?

Some of the more common pollutants to be found in indoor air are gases and vapours, floating particles, water vapour, fibres, carbon dioxide, dusts, carbon monoxide, aerosols, nitrogen oxides, spores, formaldehyde, bacteria, the highly radioactive gas and carcinogenic radon, viruses, organic vapour, dust-mite faeces and tobacco smoke. Indoor pollutants may arise from a number of sources, such as building materials, air conditioning systems, furnishings, activities within the building and the occupants themselves, as well as from underground or airborne toxins from outside.

Indoor pollution may even increase with efficient insulation. As houses become draught-free, pollutants, when they

occur, tend to build up. The Building Research Establishment is currently investigating optimum pollution control
methods and ventilating standards. For further information
contact the Building Research Establishment (see p. 344).

What about radon accumulation in our houses?

Radon gas is the result of the radioactive decay of uranium.
Uranium is naturally present in the earth's crust in concentrations of a few parts per million, and so the sub-soil continuously gives off small amounts of radon. In normal circumstances this is harmless.

In the vicinity of large accumulations of uranium, however,
radon can be a killer. In the UK, houses built on spoil from tin
mines in Cornwall which are rich in pitchblende were found to
contain radon doses of up to 23.7 millisieverts/year compared
with a national average of 7.1 mSv/year. In the USA, houses
near nuclear power stations have been found to contain radon
gases which give a total exposure to the population equivalent
to 455,000 chest X-rays per year, according to official
estimates increasing the risk of lung cancer by 13 per cent.
Radon has also long been known to be a major health hazard
to uranium miners.

The gas decays into elements such as radioactive bismuth
and polonium which can adhere to dust particles and be
inhaled. Outdoors, radon gas disperses quickly, but indoors,
especially in well-insulated houses, radon can easily build
up.

Various methods have been tried unsuccessfully to prevent
radon seepages into houses, including vapour barriers in
floors, air-cleaning systems, ventilating buildings with heat
exchangers, sealing walls with epoxy resin or pumping the
radon directly out of the soil. Good underfloor ventilation is
probably the best way of dispersal but it is worth noting that
many insurance companies do not cover for radon
contamination.

The Green Alternative

What pollution do cars cause?

At present a medium-size car travelling one kilometre will release 6.5 grammes of nitrogen oxides at 130 km per hour, 4.1 g NO_x at 100 km/h and 2.5 g NO_x at 80 km/h. It is clear that our driving habits greatly influence the harmfulness of motor vehicles. Indeed, the enormous number of cars on the roads and the great distances we cover are presenting a major environmental problem. We are burning fuel as if nothing mattered except our mobility. Much could be done to make our cars less polluting, but even when this is achieved we will still need to make much more frugal use of our cars or else the environment will remain permanently damaged by their onslaught.

There are also more than 3000 people killed each year on Britain's roads. And another 3000 people die from lung cancer after a lifetime of inhaling car exhaust emissions. The main carcinogen seems to be hydrocarbons such as benzo(a)pyrene, which is also the carcinogen in cigarette smoke. According to a study by the US National Resources Defence Council, at least 12 per cent of lung cancers originate from exposure to car exhausts, evidenced by the rapidly rising cancer rate among people living and working in large congested cities. People who drive a lot in their occupations have a 30 per cent higher than expected rate of lung cancer. Meanwhile those living away from roads have 15 per cent lower cancer rate than average.

Can anything be done about those harmful hydrocarbons?

Motor vehicles are a main source of nitrogen oxides and hydrocarbons. In the United States, Japan and Australia three-way catalytic converters are already used to help control emissions of the main exhaust pollutants, carbon monoxide (CO), hydrocarbons and nitrogen oxides (NO_x). The emissions standards in those countries are now some four times more stringent than those operating in Western Europe, where under the current EEC Vehicle Emissions Directive some 67 grams of CO, and 20.5 grams of hydrocarbons and NO_x can be emitted per test compared with 16 grams of CO and 4.6 of hydrocarbons and NO_x in the United States.

So what's the problem in EEC countries? Why not use the technology if it's available?

Britain, 'the dirty man of Europe', has again blocked any improvement in exhaust emissions by stating that it will not implement the EEC Directive if manufacturers are then required to fit catalytic converters. Britain says that internal combustion technology is developing towards the concept of the lean-burn engine which uses 10 to 15 per cent less fuel than present engines but also releases lower carbon monoxide and nitrogen oxide emissions. However, hydrocarbon emissions are unimproved and in order to control these simple oxidation catalysts would have to be fitted to engines.

William Waldegrave, the Environment Minister, having stated in March 1985 that 'We would like to see lean-burn technology combined with a simple oxidation catalyst' had already changed his mind by January 1986 when he admitted[1] that the UK government had no commitment to implement the Directive. Meanwhile, the Greater London Council Scientific Branch[2] made it clear that in London the European Community's limit for nitrogen oxide (NO_x), the World Health Organisation guidelines for carbon monoxide (CO) and GLC guidelines for ozone were being exceeded. What then of the government's statement that 'clear air is now a fact in our city centres . . . and motor vehicle emissions have been curbed'?

Have EEC regulations on exhaust emissions gone far enough?

These regulations are clearly a compromise to suit commercial interests and to appease the environment lobby. Catalytic converters which are in use in the USA and Japan and which dramatically reduce noxious gases from the exhausts of cars are still not a statutory requirement in Europe. They can only be used on cars run on lead-free petrol and that is still not widely available. The 'lean-burn' engine which car manufacturers are now developing will make our cars cleaner, but by the time they have become the norm our environment will be in a still more degraded state.

Britain's dispute with its European partners over the Directive means that for the time being, at least, pollution control of motor vehicle exhaust here is non-existent. Britain is also holding out against any pollution control for small cars, of less than 1.4 litres engine size. Therefore should agreement be reached on medium and large cars, that will still leave some 50 per cent of the car population in Britain without controls. Under such circumstances cars with the smallest engines will be producing twice as much pollution per mile as cars with the largest engines and five times as much pollution per gallon of petrol consumed. Should traffic on the roads increase as projected by the Department of Transport, then even were the Directive implemented for large and medium size cars, by the year 2000 pollution from cars could be as bad as ever.[3]

Would speed limits help reduce pollution?

They undoubtedly would. The problem is us, the consumers. Indeed, when the Federal Swiss and German governments suggested imposing speed limits to reduce nitrogen oxide production, they met with a storm of protests from motorists at the attempt to curtail their freedom to travel at speed.

Do diesel engines cause different pollution from petrol engines?

The emissions from diesel and petrol engines differ because of the engine designs and fuels and additives that each can use. Whereas the petrol engine requires spark-plugs, the diesel engine has a higher compression ratio so that fuel injected at the right moment is spontaneously ignited. Diesels can utilise various fuel types and quality, including petroleum-based, coal-derived and vegetable-oil fuels. Spark-ignition engines in contrast require a highly refined (i.e. high octane) fuel with very rigid specifications. At present, lead is added to increase the octane rating, although we shall phase this out over the next few years. The diesel vehicle has no lead in its fuel and produces much less carbon monoxide, local concentrations of which are associated with long-term health effects.

Nitrogen oxides, a possible cause of acid rain, are produced by both types of engine, depending mainly on combustion chamber temperature and the use of a catalytic converter in the exhaust. Diesels produce fewer hydrocarbons, but the ones they do produce contain a certain harmful chemical class of compounds known as aromatics. Diesel engines are also notorious for producing smoke. They produce very fine invisible soot particles that are so small they can penetrate deep into the lung. These have a huge surface area to which other organic molecules easily adsorb.

Does the source of a crude oil and the quality of the fuel produced from it affect vehicle emissions?

Concentrations of sulphur compounds in crude oil vary between different areas of the world. For example, Middle East oil has more sulphur than North Sea oil; however, sulphur can be removed during refining. A more serious matter is that many fuel oil sources to which the world may turn in future, such as tar sands or coal, have a much higher aromatic content than the crude oil now being extracted. Furthermore, a decline in the use of heavy fuel oil for electricity generation and heating oil, matched by increased demand for the lighter fractions of transportation fuels, has resulted in increased catalytic cracking of heavier fractions of crude oil distillate in conversion refineries. This process greatly increases the aromatic content, particularly of diesel fuel. Increased aromatic content also lowers the cetane number (a measure of the combustibility of a fuel), which at present is legally a minimum of 50 in Britain. However, the petroleum industries are pressurising the government to lower the cetane number, thus increasing the aromatic content of fuel.

How does the aromatic fraction affect diesel exhaust emissions? What are the health hazards associated with them?

Of particular concern is a specific group of aromatic compounds known as polycyclic aromatic hydrocarbons (PAHs) which include several potent and well-known carcinogens such as benzo(a)pyrene (BaP). Not only have carcinogens such as BaP been identified in diesel exhaust, but analysis of exhaust particles has shown these to be mutagenic. The chemistry within a combustion chamber is complex; it appears that the amount of PAHs in the exhaust is partly determined by aromatic concentration within the fuel, but PAHs may also actually be formed in the engine under some conditions. Used engine crankcase oil also contains PAHs scavenged from the combustion chamber, which has also been found to be mutagenic in tests. Extended oil change in some new models of both petrol and diesel increases the problem, and anyone handling used sump oils should do so with care.

Some manufacturers are now selling 30 per cent more small diesel cars which might present a problem if emissions are not more rigorously controlled. However, in the end by far the greatest problem is the sheer number of vehicles on the road.

Are people exposed to PAHs only through exhaust fumes?

No. We are exposed to PAHs through all kinds of combustion, from bonfires and municipal incineration of refuse, to wood-burning stoves and coal fires. Smoking of food, or charring, such as in a barbecue, produces PAHs. But by far the most significant exposure comes from smoking cigarettes.

The opponents of nuclear power have grossly overestimated the danger to human health of radiation, haven't they?

In early November, 1983 the Yorkshire Television film 'Windscale – Nuclear Laundry' was shown nationally. It claimed that childhood cancer rates in the villages close to Britain's nuclear reprocessing plant at Windscale (since renamed Sellafield) were some ten times higher than the national average. The government, in order to investigate these claims, ordered an inquiry under the chairmanship of Sir Douglas Black. In July 1984 Sir Douglas Black published the findings of his committee.

Far from the Black Report absolving Windscale from any connection with childhood leukaemia in Cumbria, it actually increased fears of a link. Sir Douglas concluded that there was an excess of cancers in the village of Seascale, that exposure to radiation was the only known cause of the disease in children, that they lived in a very radioactive environment as a result of the Windscale discharges and that no other environmental cause could be established. Because of the politically sensitive nature of the issue, however, he was required to give a 'qualified assurance' to the people of Cumbria, which he did and which was the most reported outcome of the Report. When Greenpeace gave evidence to the committee, Sir Douglas himself told Greenpeace that the primary objective of the Inquiry was to reassure the public of Cumbria, whereas the public were led to believe that the objective was to prove, or disprove, any causal link.

Greenpeace had for long been concerned about radioactive discharges into the Irish Sea from Windscale, and in November 1983 tried unsuccessfully to cap the waste pipeline from the reprocessing plant. While its divers were there, however, they found themselves in the middle of radioactive crud which caused their Geiger counters to go off scale. As a result of that unlawful discharge the beaches for twenty miles on either side of the plant had to be closed to the public for six months. Greenpeace failed to give an assurance that they would not make another attempt to cap the pipeline and were fined £50,000. The fine was then reduced and quickly paid off through public donation. British Nuclear Fuels were taken to court by the Public Prosecutor and fined £10,000 for the unlawful discharge.

The Green Alternative

Why not dump nuclear waste at sea?

The UK should not dump nuclear waste at sea on the assumption that dumping is safe: there is no definitive proof that it is. Should dumping later be found to be unsafe, we could never decontaminate the Atlantic. The international governing body, the London Dumping Convention, requires nations to ensure that dumping is safe *before* going ahead and that a comparison be made between land and sea options. But neither of these requirements has been met to date. Today, nearly forty years after the UK began dumping, a scientific review is finally underway, but we still cannot guarantee that scientists will have sufficient information available to make a definitive assessment.

In fact, the UK policy on nuclear waste has always been one of disposal and dispersal into the environment, as shown by the dumping at sea of packaged waste since 1949 and the discharge of 2.2 million gallons of contaminated waste every day from the Sellafield reprocessing works into the Irish Sea. Now that the government has been forced to adopt a more responsible attitude to radioactive waste, with the suspension of dumping in the Atlantic and the reduction of Windscale discharges, primarily as a result of pressure from organisations such as Greenpeace, radioactive waste will inevitably build up on land.

Nevertheless, for the time being it is preferable to store the waste above ground where it can be monitored and retrieved. But the volumes of waste generated in the future will be considerable, especially if we keep building nuclear plants. In fact, reprocessing spent nuclear fuel generates hundreds of times its original volume as waste without any acceptable method of dealing with it. We are storing up trouble for ourselves and future generations by committing ourselves to a nuclear programme, yet we could switch off all the nuclear plants tomorrow and still have enough generating capacity for our needs.

Pollution of the environment

Have we contaminated the Irish Sea with plutonium for ever?

Plutonium is an unavoidable by-product of the nuclear industry. More than 250 kilos of plutonium now lie on the sediments in the Irish Sea, discharged through the Sellafield pipeline. We know that a millionth of a gramme of plutonium inhaled will cause lung cancer. Instead of staying locked in the sediments as scientists predicted, plutonium is being remobilised from the sea bed and, by the action of tides, currents, the sun and the wind, is contaminating not only the Cumbrian coast and beaches but the very air people breathe, and is infiltrating and settling in the houses in which they live.

Plutonium has been detected tens of miles away from the point of discharge at Sellafield. It remains dangerous for a quarter of a million years and in effect the Irish Sea has been polluted for ever. This scandalous situation arose from a 'deliberate and controlled experiment' by the Sellafield authorities since the 1950s. Tragically, because we know so little about the effects of plutonium, especially on children, it may be years before we can assess the damage. It was only in 1982 that the authorities admitted that their assumptions about plutonium had been wrong and that, once ingested, plutonium finds its way into the blood stream five times more readily than they had first thought.

Surely we now know enough about plutonium to discharge at safe levels?

In every other country in the world, except France, discharges of plutonium into the environment are virtually outlawed. In Japan, for example, less than one curie* a year is permitted to be discharged. In the UK, Sellafield has been permitted to discharge up to 6000 curies a year. Although the levels are now down to about 300 curies and will be reduced to about 20 in 1991, even these levels would not be allowed

* One curie is equal to 37,000 million atomic disintegrations per second.

anywhere else in the world. Meanwhile, the authorities can legitimately claim that they are 'only' discharging a small percentage of their authorised levels and, in the event of an accident, the company can avoid prosecution because even an accidental release of several thousand curies will still be within the 'legal' limit.

3 Agriculture

It is surely one of the great ironies of our time that our farmers scarcely eat their own produce. Indeed, what better symbol of the growing detachment of our civilisation from the living process that sustains it than a television advertisement of the farm worker who gets back to his breakfast after the morning milking and there, on the table in front of him, with all its connotations of farm freshness, stands a packet of a famous brand of cereal. In modern farming the farm worker is increasingly isolated from the soil he is tilling; he sits encased in his tractor cab, either with ear muffs to shut out the noise or with radio blaring, and what goes on behind the tractor has more to do with the wonders of technology than with the wisdom of countless generations of his predecessors. Meanwhile, the farmer has become less concerned with husbanding natural resources than with manipulating purchased inputs in the form of artificial fertilisers, chemical sprays and animal feedstuffs. The soil, instead of being treated as a living substrate, has become a factory floor.

The industrialisation of agriculture and food production has had profound effects on society. It has eliminated the need for a large workforce on the land and a single man is now expected to manage on his own the farming of more than 40 hectares (100 acres), where traditionally between five and ten would have found employment. And because farm equipment is now manufactured by giant companies rather than by local firms many others in the countryside have also been made redundant. Overall the industrialisation of agriculture has eroded rural life.

Petroleum has become the key to most modern farming. Its products provide fuel for ever-increasing amounts of machinery; it forms the basis of most chemicals used on the land, including fertilisers, herbicides or pesticides, and it has become essential for the transport of farm produce from one part of the country, and indeed of the world, to another.

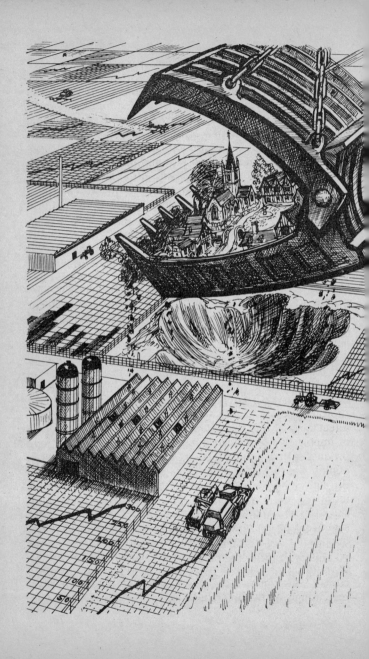

Agriculture

The mechanisation of agriculture has proceeded apace since the 1950s. In Britain in the 1920s the average energy input per hectare was 42 kilowatt-hours per year (one kilowatt-hour is 1,000 watts of energy used for one hour, or one unit of electricity). Then only 6 per cent of farms had electricity, their combined consumption being 25 gigawatt-hours (one million kilowatt-hours). Today the energy input per hectare has increased 60 fold and combined electricity consumption to more than 100 times its 1920 level. Clearly food production in energy terms has become an inefficient process. Moreover, all that energy poured into mechanisation is proving to be destructive to the land. Soil erosion in the UK, especially in the grain-growing parts of the country, has become a grave problem, with between 20 and 45 tonnes of topsoil being lost per hectare per annum on many cereal farms, whereas the loss from grassland and other uncropped land is no more than 0.1 tonne per hectare. Without question we are eroding our food base for the future. In more vulnerable parts of the world, in the tropics for instance, erosion of soil from farmland may amount to several hundred tonnes per hectare per annum.

Modern farmers counteract production losses caused by soil erosion by increasing fertilisers and using an array of chemicals to combat vulnerability to pests. While the additions of such chemicals maintain or even improve yields in the short term, they uphold a system which cannot last. They also affect the quality of the product itself which may be far poorer in important nutrients – vitamins for example – than food produced under less forcing circumstances. In general, quality has been sacrificed for quantity and as a result, through subsidies and price guarantees, in much of the industrialised Western world we have generated enormous surpluses of unwanted food. It must also be appreciated that a significant proportion of the fodder fed to our livestock is imported from developing Third World countries – for example, oil seeds from India and tapioca from Thailand – which have turned over vast acreages of land to the export of cash crops. Meanwhile, their own populations find themselves increasingly on the bread line.

The Green Alternative

A country's ability to feed itself should be evaluated not by the food coming off its farms but by the total number of acres required to produce that food. For instance, Britain depends on the United States, South America, Argentina, Africa and India for a large proportion of its annual feedstuffs. In the United Kingdom these non-visible acreages represent in terms of domestic yields 0.75 acre per person or more than twice the tilled land of England.[1]

Because of the degradation of land brought about through modern, intensive monoculture – the growing of the same crop on the same land year after year – and the increased costs of struggling to improve yields, farmers are beginning to look for alternatives. Organic 'biological' farming is a viable alternative. At the Centre for the Biology of Natural Systems in Illinois it has been shown that the net income on commercial organic farms growing similar crops to non-organic conventional farms is, if anything, higher. And as costs for fuel and chemicals rise, organic farming is likely to become more economic compared with conventional farming. In Britain more farmers and growers are converting their farms to 'organic' ones.

In the following questions and answers, we have looked at the state of the land in Britain and elsewhere in the world to give us some idea of the kind of farming practices that we should encourage and the size of the world population that we might be able to support. How we feed ourselves is critical to what we expect from our land. A healthy nutritious diet should increase rather than diminish our food base.

Is there enough land in the world for growing crops to feed the world's present population?

There is quite enough land to feed the world's population now. But if present agricultural policies are continued, this will not be the case for long because the world's soils are eroding at a fast and increasing pace.

The land surface of the world is said to be 13 thousand million hectares. Of this about 10 per cent is used for

74

agricultural purposes, much of which is under terrible pressure.

At the United Nations Environmental Conference on Desertification in 1977, it was shown that about one-third of the world's remaining agricultural land was threatened by desertification. A programme of soil conservation was proposed and member governments were asked to contribute towards financing it. Unfortunately, very little finance was obtained. Governments simply were not interested.

Meanwhile Africa's soils are disappearing before our eyes, and official estimates in the USA give much of the mid-west only fifty years more productivity; another 'dust bowl' could occur at any moment. Two drought years could trigger it. The black soil of Russia is disappearing fast and the new irrigated lands of drier areas in the USSR are becoming salt-encrusted. Salinisation is cancelling out the benefits of irrigation in many parts of the world. Whatever developments are made by science in increased crop production will be more than offset by the inexorable loss of soil. Also, the population is rising.

Is there any way we will be able to feed the coming billions?

If the billions come, the answer is unquestionably no. How can we possibly feed the 9 billion people who are supposed to inhabit this planet by the year 2100, let alone the 30 billion which the Food and Agricultural Organisation of the United Nations (FAO) assures us we are capable of feeding, if every year we are less capable of feeding the 4.5 billion people alive today – nearly a quarter of whom now live on the verge of starvation? Paul Ehrlich, Professor of Biological Sciences at Stanford University, California, considers the idea that the world can feed 8 billion people to be 'the most frequently repeated imbecility of all time'.

The Green Alternative

Can we afford not to exploit every possible short-term measure to produce enough food for the growing world population, even if the quality is suspect and the long-term health of the environment is endangered?

If we wish to avoid disaster by the end of the century, we must change our whole outlook from short-term to long-term and develop a sustainable system of farming based on the true potential of the land. To do otherwise merely postpones the calamity for a little time and ensures that it will be worse and even less reversible. We must farm for posterity.

What brings about today's starvation?

To produce food is not enough. It has to be made available where it is required and this cannot be done via the market system which makes food available to those who can pay the most for it. Hence, much of the best land in countries whose populations are suffering from malnutrition and starvation is used for growing cash crops for sale to the rich in the big cities or in the industrial West. Thus in the Philippines something like 55 per cent of the best land is used for that purpose. In Mauritius, the figure is said to be 80 per cent. Meanwhile, the peasants who produce food for local consumption are pushed on to marginal land – such as the mountain slopes which are unsuitable for cultivation. The result is erosion and desertification of those lands, resulting in increased malnutrition and famine.

Government food assistance will only be palliative and have no long-term effect in relieving the hunger of poor people unless the governments of the countries concerned institute soil conservation and land restoration practices. Otherwise, the only long-term effect is negative: food aid draws people into the towns and food distribution centres and prevents them cultivating their own lands. Even though we are much to blame for their condition there is a limit to the number of deprived the world will be either willing or able to support into perpetuity.

Isn't there much more land to bring into cultivation?

Bringing marginal areas into cultivation is destroying them in many parts of the world. In dry countries it can lead to galloping erosion. Controlled grazing of marginal areas can produce more food without degrading the soil but it requires a discipline on the part of the graziers that is extremely rare. Very few areas in the tropics are suitable for commercial agriculture and it is probable that all that can be used for that purpose has already been brought under the plough.

But surely we could use technology to make the deserts bloom?

It could probably be done in a small way, using traditional methods, but on a large scale it is simply not practical. The experience in Egypt is illustrative. There, using the energy and water made available by the Aswan Dam, a massive campaign launched to reclaim desert has proved a disaster. The quality of the soils reclaimed is extremely low and the cost of reclaiming them very high. Also, such land rapidly reverts to desert under the impact of modern intensive agriculture.

If we want to increase food production, shouldn't we irrigate more land?

Irrigated agriculture is certainly one of the most productive farming systems known to man. Not surprisingly, many agronomists argue that more land must be brought under irrigation if we are to have any chance of feeding the world's hungry. At present, some 220 million hectares of farmland are irrigated – but the UN Food and Agriculture Organisation (FAO) hopes to increase that figure by 100 million hectares before the turn of the century. Some experts argue that even that rate of expansion will leave many starving or malnourished. Bruce Stokes of the Washington-based Worldwatch Institute, for example, estimates that 70 million hectares will need to be brought under irrigation within the next decade to keep pace with food demand.

But, irrigation is a two-edged weapon. In arid areas, large-scale irrigation schemes have destroyed thousands of acres of land by salinising the soils and turning the land into salt deserts. Moreover, little of the food grown in such schemes is consumed by the local population, let alone the farmers who work the land. Most of it is exported abroad to earn foreign exchange.

You mentioned that irrigation causes salinisation. What does this mean?

All soils contain salt, the result of what geologists call 'weathering'. But if salt levels become too high, the land becomes toxic to plant life. The problem is particularly serious in the dry tropics (where the demand for irrigation is highest) because there is simply not enough water to flush out the salts which accumulate in the soils.

If arid lands are not to succumb to salinisation, it is essential that the 'water-salt balance' of the soil is maintained. In particular, water must not be allowed to accumulate in the soil, since this will lead to a rise in the water table. Where the water table is allowed to rise, groundwaters are drawn to the surface through capillary action. On the way up, they add to their own salt load by dissolving the salts in the soil. The land thus becomes waterlogged with increasingly saline water. That water quickly evaporates as it approaches the surface and the salts it contains are thus left behind to accumulate in the soil. It is not long before the whole area becomes covered with a white saline crust. The land is then said to be 'salinised'.

Why does irrigation cause land to become salinised?

Traditional irrigation schemes, where the land is allowed to lie fallow for sufficient time to recover before being irrigated again and where adequate drainage is ensured, rarely succumb to salinisation. But perennial irrigation schemes – that is, schemes where the land is irrigated year-in, year-out – are notorious for causing salinisation. The reason is that perennial irrigation schemes throw the delicate water–salt balance of arid lands out of kilter. Thus, perennial irrigation invariably raises the water table. In some areas, groundwater tables are rising at a rate of 3 to 5 metres a year. That rise in groundwater levels is caused primarily by water losses due to seepage from irrigation channels.

Large-scale irrigation schemes also add directly to the salt load of soils by increasing the rate of evapotranspiration. Not only does irrigation increase the extent of vegetative cover – and hence the rate of transpiration – but it also requires water to be spread thinly over a wide area, thus raising direct evaporation losses. The result of such evapotranspiration is that the natural salts in water become concentrated in the soils. According to Professor Arthur Pillsbury of the University of California, three-quarters of the water applied each year to irrigate land in the United States is lost to evapotranspiration. The result is a four-fold concentration of salts in the remaining water.

High evaporation rates also increase the salt burden of reservoirs and rivers. As a result, the water used to irrigate many areas is now in itself a significant factor in the spread of salinisation. According to Professor Victor Kovda of the University of Moscow, the best irrigation water from rivers now contains 200 to 500 milligrams/litre of salts. 'Supplying 10,000 cubic metres on 1 hectare of land during the irrigation season thus deposits 2 to 5 tons per hectare of salts in soils,' he notes. 'After 10 to 20 years of irrigation, this amount becomes enormous – amounting to dozens and even hundreds of tons per hectare.'

How serious is the problem of salinisation?

Very serious indeed. According to Professor Kovda, between 60 and 80 per cent of irrigated land is salinised, with 1–1.5 million hectares succumbing to salinisation every year. Significantly, much of that land is 'in irrigated areas of high potential production'. In India, according to one recent study, as much irrigated land is now being taken out of production owing to waterlogging and salinisation as new irrigation schemes are bringing into production.

In Iraq, more than 50 per cent of the 3.6 million hectares under irrigation now suffer from salinisation, and vast areas of South Iraq now 'glisten like fields of freshly fallen snow'.

If irrigation schemes were better drained, could salinisation be avoided?

Drainage is certainly a prerequisite to the avoidance of salinisation, but drainage only serves to flush salts away from irrigated lands. Those salts must go somewhere. Generally, they end up in the nearest river, thus increasing the river's salt content. For farmers downstream, the problem is obvious. They must irrigate their own fields with increasingly saline water. Indeed, many farmers in arid areas now find their livelihoood threatened by developments upstream of them. Northern Mexico, for example, is partly dependent for its water on two 'shared' rivers – the Rio Grande and the River Colorado. The water from both rivers is now so saline that it can only be used twice before it becomes too brackish for agriculture.

America has agreed to reduce the salinity levels of waters entering Mexico. To that end, a massive desalinisation plant is being built on the Mexican border at Yuma in Arizona, which is now expected to cost more than $1 billion. At that price, irrigation water provided by the plant will cost some $800 per acre-foot (one acre in surface areas to a depth of one foot), more than thirty-five times the current cost of irrigation water in the Imperial Valley of California.

Won't the various schemes to transfer water from other parts of North America solve California's salinisation problem?

Three major schemes have been proposed in order to provide water to flush excess salts from the soil of the US south-west and – more important from the government's point of view –

to extend the amount of land under irrigation. All three schemes involve importing vast quantities of water from other parts of the US. Two have run into financial difficulties and the third looks unlikely ever to get off the ground.

The North American Water and Power Alliance scheme is the most ambitious. It would divert water from Alaska and northern Canada to various parts of Canada, the US and Mexico. The drainage area of the scheme would be 1.3 million square miles and 160 million acre-feet of water would be diverted southwards for irrigation and 'waterway control'. The estimated cost of the project is $200 billion. Although, if the experience of similar projects is anything to go by, the final cost could well be three or four times higher. The scheme is likely to be strenuously opposed by environmentalists and by Alaska and Canada, neither of whom take kindly to the idea of their waters being diverted to the American south-west. Indeed, it seems that there is little chance of the scheme ever coming into operation.

Without the NAWAPA scheme, the future of the south-west is extremely precarious. Professor Arthur Pillsbury describes the project as 'the only concept advanced so far that will enable the lower reaches of western rivers to achieve the salt balance necessary for the long-term health of western agriculture, on which the entire US and indeed the world has much dependence.'

He goes on to warn: 'Unless the lower rivers are allowed to reassert their natural function as exporters of salt to the ocean, today's productive lands will eventually become salt-encrusted and barren.'

Is irrigated land mainly used to grow cash crops?

Yes. Setting up large-scale irrigation schemes is exorbitantly expensive – in some areas it costs as much as $10,000 to irrigate a single hectare of land – and in order to earn the foreign exchange to pay the bills, irrigated land is invariably used to grow cash crops for export, generally to the industrialised world. The rural poor have thus been the last people to benefit from large-scale irrigation schemes. Iran's

Dez Dam, for example, was intended to provide over 200,000 acres of irrigated land to small farmers in Khuzestan. In the event, however, the land went almost exclusively to foreign-owned companies which cultivated crops for export.

It is a story which has been repeated time and again the world over. In Senegal, over 370,000 hectares are to be irrigated under a massive scheme to develop the entire Senegal River basin. Officially the scheme is intended to promote 'communal rural development'. In reality, the setting up of small farms in the Manautali area will have ceased by 1987; after that date, all resources are to be devoted to expanding the area under large farms, which will produce crops for export.

But surely it is a good thing if irrigated land is put under cash crops?

As prime agricultural land is taken over for the production of cash crops, so peasant farmers are invariably pushed on to marginal lands. Those lands then become over-exploited. Many now ascribe the disastrous famines which have ravaged the Sahel since the late 1960s to the expansion of cash crops and the consequent pressure on local pastoralists to graze the arid and inhospitable margins of the Sahara desert. Moreover, the intensive nature of modern agriculture has resulted in the over-exploitation of that land used to grow cash crops. In Africa, for example, vast tracts of land which are suitable for growing grazing grasses or trees, but little else, have been torn up to make way for cotton or peanut plantations.

'The soil becomes rapidly poor in humus and loses its cohesiveness,' report Frances Moore Lappé and Joseph Collins of the Institute for Food and Development Policy. 'The wind, quite strong in the dry season, then easily erodes the soils. Soil deterioration leads to declining crops and, consequently, to an enormous expansion of cultivated land, often on to marginal soils.' In the Sahel, many peanut-growing areas are now so over-exploited and under-fertilised that there has been a rapid deterioration in the soil quality of the region. According to the Prefect of the Maradi District of Niger, some soils in his area 'can be considered totally depleted'.

Some soil erosion is inevitable through agriculture. Is such erosion of any consequence?

Erosion can be drastically reduced by polyculture and crop-rotation, and by assuring, in particular, that the land has vegetation cover during the rainy season. Sloping land, particularly prone to erosion, was traditionally terraced, but many modern farmers have abandoned the practice. Erosion can also be reduced by returning all available organic matter to the soil.

The extent to which this type of agriculture is sustainable is well illustrated in *Farmers of Forty Centuries* written by F. H. King, director of the American Soil Conservation Society in the year 1904. In it, he notes that the USA had already lost about a quarter of its original topsoil – whereas in China, Japan and Korea, which he visited, he found farmers who, by using traditional methods, had maintained the fertility of their soil for millennia.

Soil erosion is of great consequence, and it must lead to a steady reduction in crop yields. Artificial fertilisers cannot conceivably replace soil. Besides NPK (nitrogen, phosphorus and potassium) the soil requires all sorts of trace elements, of which it is deprived by over-cropping. Its organic content (which in much of the tropics is already very low) and hence its structure must also be maintained, otherwise its water-retaining capacity will be reduced and it will become much more vulnerable to erosion.

Could the 'dust bowl' of the American mid-west happen in Britain?

No. The soils in the southern plains, where the dust bowl occurred in the thirties, were very delicate and should never have been ploughed. That was pointed out by ecologists at the time. Erosion is, however, undoubtedly a serious problem in

The Green Alternative

Britain, as has now been well documented by two recent reports, one from Silsoe College in Bedford, the other by the Soil Survey of England and Wales. East Anglia, much of which is used for intensive prairie-type cereal production, is worst affected. If present methods of agriculture are allowed to continue for another few decades there is no doubt that agricultural yields will be seriously affected. However, the process of soil degradation is much slower than that which occurred in the southern plains in the thirties.

Is the United States losing its potential to generate food surpluses through soil erosion, salinisation and chemical contamination of groundwater?

At the rate North America is losing its topsoil and wasting its water resources, it is but a matter of a few decades before it ceases to be a food-exporting country. That will be very serious for many of the richer food-deficit countries, since about 50 per cent of world cereal imports and 75 per cent of the world's soya bean imports are derived from the USA.

Russia will clearly be among those affected. Soviet agriculture is far too highly centralised and bureaucratised and there tends to be a food shortage every year, which is largely made up by importing food from the USA. Although it once had plans to make its major Siberian rivers flow southwards so as to boost cereal production, the USSR has decided (in March 1986) not to go ahead with such plans on the grounds of the major ecological perturbations which might ensue.

Are deserts spreading? Can we stop them?

Deserts are spreading throughout the dry tropics, and at a dramatic rate. In 1977 the UNEP Conference on Desertification in Nairobi concluded that one-third of the world's agricultural land would probably be desertified by the end of the century. That is a terrifying statement for a conservative body like the UN to make. The trouble is that everything we are doing today must increase desertification. Deforestation, for instance, is occurring at an unprecedented rate and once the forests go there is nothing to protect the soil from wind and water erosion. Rainfall patterns are also affected. Thus much of the desertification in East Africa today has been caused by cutting down forests in West Africa. Previously the winds would blow across the forests, from which they would pick up moisture, which would then be deposited further inland. Now that the forests have gone there is little moisture to pick up. Intensive modern agriculture and livestock rearing must also create erosion and desertification when conducted on the very vulnerable soils of the dry tropics.

Drought is also occurring in areas where rainfall patterns have scarcely changed at all. What has in fact happened is that the soil has become so degraded by present agricultural practices that its water-retaining capacity has been drastically reduced, which means that when it rains the water simply passes straight through into the subsoil.

Hasn't the 'Green Revolution' been a boon to mankind?

In the 1960s the UN set out to solve the problem of starvation in the Third World by starting the Green Revolution. This involves making available high-yielding varieties of cereals such as rice and wheat. However, these are only high-yielding because they are much more receptive than traditional varieties to artificial fertiliser.

Fertiliser decreases the resistance of crops to pests, producing sick plants. As a result, in addition to fertiliser, farmers must also buy pesticides. To produce high yields the hybrids also need irrigation water, which provides the pretext for putting up vast capital-intensive water development schemes. Only big farmers can afford fertilisers, pesticides and irrigation water. Big modern irrigation schemes can cost up to $15,000 an acre to install, so the Green Revolution leads to the virtual elimination of the small farmer who is condemned to become a casual labourer or else migrate to the slums of the nearest large conurbation. The farmer who pays for all these inputs can no longer afford to sell locally, selling instead to the large cities or exporting abroad. So the Green Revolution, rather than helping to feed local people, has the opposite effect.

The Green Alternative

Apart from desertification, salinisation and erosion, the use of fertiliser and pesticides leads to the contamination of waterways. This, in many areas, has led to the virtual disappearance of fish life, which is particularly serious in south Asia and other parts of the world where rural people often depend entirely on fish for their animal protein.

Who should own the land?

Land should be held in trusteeship by the people who cultivate it. The cultivator – the husbandman – should consider him or herself the trustee of all the living things that have a right to live on that land. The only satisfactory concept of land ownership is to accept that all land belongs to God. Humans have a right and a duty to husband it for the benefit of all life and for future generations.

A farmer is surely justified in spraying his crops when they have infestation or disease?

From time to time emergencies arise where the choice is either to use lethal pesticides or lose the entire crop, and the farmer may be justified in spraying. In such circumstances it should be asked, 'Why has the pest appeared? Why has the crop failed to resist it? What could have been done to prevent it? What is the least harmful method of overcoming the problem – particularly in the long-term effect?' Insect, bacterial, virus or fungal infections tend to attack weak crops and are themselves the result of imbalances in the soil flora and fauna which can be caused by modern farming methods. The need to use pesticides should always be recognised as a sign that one's husbandry has been faulty. In the long term the aim should be to build up a healthy, living soil which will produce healthy, strong crops that are largely immune to pests and, even if attacked, will 'grow through' the crisis.

To be a farmer's boy

Should a farmer who doesn't treat cattle with pesticides against warble fly, or use similar pesticides against sheep scab, be fined?

Treating livestock with dangerous pesticides is irresponsible. The meat is bound to contain residues. British lamb, for instance, has been found to contain very high levels of lindane – a known carcinogen on whose use the Ministry of Agriculture, Fisheries and Food has, until very recently, insisted. It is on these grounds – although there may be other more commercial reasons – that the French have refused to import British lamb.

The Green Alternative

The Integrated Pest Control Movement in the United States has shown that an intelligent and non-simplistic approach to pest control can be extremely effective in the long run. Nature is not simple, it is infinitely complex, and we ignore the complexity at our peril. The farmers, bereft of help and each trying to do the work that should be done by ten, are forced into dangerous practices.

And what about clearing the tsetse fly from the African savannah with pesticides so that cattle can replace infected wildgame?

The big experiment in trying to clear tsetse fly from the Okavongo Swamps area of northern Botswana has proved to be the disaster that anybody could have predicted. The only reason why there are still some areas of Africa which are being protected from the ravages of rapacious farming methods is that there are fly areas where wildlife flourishes, thus protecting the soil from erosion and desertification. To clear fly areas of fly so that cattle can be introduced will be merely to destroy the land. People will swarm in, over-graze and plough unsuitable areas, erosion will follow and the wild animals that formerly lived there in peace, and which at least provided some human food, will be totally destroyed – as will the land itself. Ultimately it will benefit nothing and nobody.

Do farmers have to use pesticides?

They say that they do since otherwise crop yields would be lower, costs higher and produce less attractive. They argue that sprays are used with care and concern and that modern chemicals are less toxic than earlier remedies such as arsenic, tar, oils and nicotine.

While these arguments may be true in the short-term, they neglect the longer-term effects of pesticides on the local ecological balance: on the bacteria in the soil, animals and birds in the hedgerows – and on humans who eat the food and live in the neighbourhood. Many toxic pesticide sprays are borne by air currents way beyond their target areas, especially with aerial crop-spraying. There are some 200 licensed operators in the UK, but controls may be tightened with implementation of the Food and Environment Protection Act (1985).

If you are concerned about the use of pesticides in your area, write to your MP, the secretary of your local National Farmers' Union or your local branch of Friends of the Earth and press for implementation of the new Act.

Research shows that the use of pesticides, far from controlling pests, actually increases infestation. Is that true?

The numbers of infestations and pests have increased in step with the use of pesticides, and the usual reason given is that more land has been turned over to monoculture. It has also been pointed out that pesticides are indiscriminate in their action and very often predators which control pests are more vulnerable than the pests themselves, one reason being that pests have a far greater reproductive potential than predators, and so can develop resistance more quickly. But research, particularly by French agronomists such as Francis Chaboussou, until 1976 director of the Institute for Agronomic Research at Pont-de-la-Maye, indicates a far more important reason for the relative inefficacy of modern pesticides. These substances derange the metabolism of the crops they are supposedly safeguarding, and instead of producing cell proteins for healthy growth, the crops, under the influence of pesticides, produce soluble amino acids which are easy food for the pests. As a result of modern agronomic practices the pests are therefore having a field day.

Meanwhile, all over the world tens of thousands of farmers and their families suffer the effects of exposure to pesticides each year and a great many die, disasters such as Bhopal aside. The continued use of pesticides as currently applied is an iniquitous and unnecessary practice.

The Green Alternative

How dependent on pesticides are British farmers?

Each year British farmers now spend some £200 million simply on agrochemicals to kill cereal pests. An average field of wheat gets two or more applications of herbicides, two of insecticides and four of fungicides in one growing season. Some twenty years ago they would have received one herbicide dressing and nothing more. According to the Game Conservancy wildlife has declined substantially because of the spraying – indeed, evidence now suggests that game species such as the grey partridge have much reduced broods when in contact with sprayed headlands.

Further information can be obtained from the Game Conservancy (see p. 347).

What policy should we have in Britain for getting people to live and work in the countryside?

(a) Alter the planning laws in order to make it easier for people to live and work in the countryside

(b) Put a graduated tax on land ownership by corporations to prevent them using land purely for investment purposes

(c) Arrange training for people wishing to get back to the land. This training should include ancillary money-making activities as well as agriculture and horticulture

(d) Provide cheap credit

(e) Adjust tax laws and tenancy laws to encourage landlords offering small farm tenancies. Many would welcome the opportunity but are prevented from doing so by quite unacceptable tenancy regulations

What should the government do for young people wishing to become farmers?

In theory the government (through county councils) is obliged to provide garden allotments to all citizens and smallholdings for young aspirants who show that they are capable of becoming farmers. In fact the waiting lists for both allotments and smallholdings are terribly long. Many county councils have been selling off their smallholdings and have made the rent so high on the rest that only by intensive husbandry can the tenant make a living. At present it is not the policy of the government to increase the numbers of small, family farms, but rather the reverse.

Is it not true that we have taken jobs away from those on the land and given them to people who work in agro-industries?

Yes. It would be far preferable if the people now employed in the agro-industries making heavy and complicated machines, and above all making agricultural poisons, were employed on the land helping to make the use of these damaging things redundant. Agro-chemicals and excessive mechanisation are simply a substitute for people working on the land – and very dangerous and damaging substitutes too.

Should we each strive for self-sufficiency?

Complete self-sufficiency is not possible for an individual or family in an industrialised nation. Limited self-sufficiency for individuals or families who choose it can make for happier, more self-fulfilled people. But a large degree of regional and village self-sufficiency is most desirable. It leads to a more varied and interesting environment, people leading less boring lives, less shunting around of goods and services all over the planet, more local self-respect and less restlessness and dissatisfaction generally. Regional self-sufficiency should be accompanied by a determination by people to lead simpler lives and make less demands on the planet's non-renewable resources.

Could we produce enough food in the UK to feed ourselves?

We certainly could, provided we adjusted our ideas as to what we need. Obviously we cannot grow tea, coffee, citrus fruits or many other exotic foods, but we can grow enough cereals, pulses, vegetables, fruit, nuts, eggs, meat and dairy products to sustain our population in good health. A shift to less meat and more cereals and vegetables would not only be better for our health, but would be a more efficient way of producing the quantity of food that we need. We normally measure our yields in quantity only; quality (i.e. real food value) is far more difficult to estimate. If the quality can be improved, we shall need less quantity. The present vast surpluses produced in Europe result from EEC subsidies and guarantees, which have twisted farming practice from good husbandry into pure speculative business, with potentially disastrous effects on the land and the farmers' pockets. Every field in the land has a potential for growing crops. If we force it to yield above its potential today, we shall eventually have to take less later. Our aim should be to devise a *sustainable* system of husbandry that will make every field yield its true potential.

What about meat-eating

Britain has become a meat-eating nation *par excellence*. Out of a total of 19 million hectares of agricultural land in the UK, 15.3 million hectares, or more than 80 per cent, is used either directly or indirectly for meat and dairy production. The annual UK consumption of meat is 3.5 million tonnes, of which 3 million tonnes is home-produced. To produce the meat produced in the UK some 11 million tonnes of concentrates such as barley are required; indeed, more than 50 per cent of all UK grain is fed to animals.

What would happen if the UK opted for a diet that was more vegetarian-oriented? Would that help provide more food for human beings?

This needs careful thought. Sound farming practice demands that we use crop rotation involving, at some stage, putting the land back to grasses and clovers. However, the only way we can turn pasture into food for humans is to put them through an animal first, for we are not 'omnivorous' – we cannot digest cellulose. Cows and sheep can. *Controlled* grazing by herbivorous animals is a sensible way to produce good human food from much of the world's surface. Moreover, the only way to maintain the fertility of arable soil without resource to massive chemical input (and thus a poor energy input–output ratio) is by using animal dung. It has been the divorcing of domestic animals from the arable land that has forced farmers into the complete commitment to chemicals that is ruining the land and leading to erosion, pollution of the environment and many other evil effects. If we get the animals back on the arable land we will improve the heart of the land again and improve the soil instead of degrading it.

What size dairy herd should we have?

For good health and a sound nutrition the UK would still need a relatively large dairy herd. Apart from providing dairy products the herd would also help maintain soil fertility, and a by-product of a large dairy herd would be the production of surplus animals, either males or animals to be culled from the herd. Altogether some 27,500 million litres of milk would be required each year.

At present dairy cattle are expected to yield on average (two cows per hectare) some 10,000 litres per hectare each year, with each cow producing 5,000 litres. That production level depends on high inputs of fertilisers and imported feed concentrates. On the basis that farms would return to the use of organic manures and would sustain milk production levels from locally grown inputs milk production would inevitably fall, perhaps to little more than one-quarter the present output per hectare. Farmers would therefore return to stocking levels of one cow per hectare and 11 million cows on 11 million hectares would provide the UK's dairy requirements.

Such a low stocking rate and yield per cow – some 2,500 litres per cow per hectare, down to one-quarter of present levels – would allow all winter feed requirements to be easily met by home-grown hay or silage. It would also allow each cow to remain productive for longer – say five years instead of the present four – though each cow would still have to produce one calf each year. With a five-year lifespan, 20 per cent or 2.2 million cows would be replaced each year. Meanwhile, 11 million calves would be born of which 20 per cent would be kept to replace the culled animals, leaving 8.8 million for slaughter.

Since each adult yields 135 kg of meat and each calf 11 kg, a total of 394,000 tonnes of beef and veal are produced per year. Present consumption of beef and veal is 220 grams per person per week; the above production would allow a consumption of 137.5 grams or 62 per cent of the present level.

But what would Britain require in the way of food and land if it were to become more self-sufficient in food?

For a sound diet, it is not necessary to eat meat. With a population of approximately 55 million the total requirements would be roughly as follows:

Food	Quantity (million tonnes)	Quantity (million litres)
Grain	0.45	
Vegetables	27.5	
Fruit	7.7	
Nuts/Seeds	2.2	
Sugar/Honey	0.6	
Milk		27,500

In broad terms the land required for meeting those requirements would be as in the first table on page 95.

Hazel nuts grown in hedgerows were once a major part of the British diet. The re-establishment of hedgerows with hazels would make up some of the UK requirement without taking up valuable land. In fact hedgerows help farmers maintain fertility.

The actual land use would be as in the second table on page 95.

Thus when compared to the figures for land in the UK of 9 million hectares of grades 1,2, and 3 and 9.9 million hectares of grades 4 and 5, it can be seen that the UK could produce more than enough food for its own population. This could,

Food	Land (million hectares)	Land grades
Grain	0.1	1,2,3
Vegetables	3.5	1,2,3
Fruit	0.8	1,2,3
Nuts/seeds	2.0	
Sugar	0.1	1,2,3
Milk	2.8 ⎫	1,2,3
Milk	8.4 ⎭ = 11	4,5

Total: Grades 1,2,3   7.3 million hectares
       Grades 4,5   8.4 million hectares

(MAFF classifies land according to its quality, Grade 1 being prime quality arable land and Grade 5 marginal rough grazing land.)

Usage	Productive (million hectares)	Fallow (million hectares)
Arable	3.7	0.8
Fruit	0.8	
Dairy (grade 1,2,3)	2.0	0.8
Dairy (grade 4,5)	8.4	

moreover, be done while reducing the levels of non-organic inputs. Indeed, the rotation of a good mix of crops, including legumes and the grazing of fallow fields one year out of every five, would reduce the incidence of soil-borne diseases of plants and animals while the regular input of manure from dairy animals and nitrogen from legumes would reduce the need for inorganic fertilisers.

The Green Alternative

What in fact were the yields assumed per hectare in the table on p. 95?

Grain	4 tonnes per hectare	
Vegetables	8 ,, ,, ,,	
Fruit	10 ,, ,, ,,	
Nut/seed	1 ,, ,, ,,	
Sugar	3 ,, ,, ,,	
Milk	2,500 litres per hectare	

And what would a vegetarian consume each year?

Food	Kilograms per year
Grain	86
Pulses	14
Nut/Seed	38
Vegetables/Fruit	625
Sugar	11
Milk, including products	500 litres per year

To produce that food would require some 0.7 acres per person or, for the entire population, some 15.5 million hectares – hence 3.5 million hectares less than the total of agricultural land of all grades. With some meat consumption – since not everybody is going to become vegetarian – from the culling of the dairy herd, the level of nutrition should be high.

What about pigs and poultry? And sheep?

As we have seen, a significant reduction in the amount of land dedicated to the production of meat releases land for other purposes. To some extent sheep, including milking sheep, can replace cattle – such a mixed system helping to improve overall soil fertility, and of course providing other benefits such as wool production.

Clearly, more traditional methods of keeping pigs and chickens could never match the numbers of such animals now produced through intensive battery methods. The nutritional quality of intensively raised animals and the effects on human health suggest that we would be far better off consuming less food but of a much improved quality. Both pigs and chickens allowed some freedom to 'free-range' can make good use of vegetable waste and scraps while improving soil fertility. They are an important component of a mixed farming system.

Are our farmers more efficient today than were their predecessors using horses and labour?

That depends on how you measure 'efficiency'. If you take productivity per person employed *on the farm*, we are obviously far more efficient. If you count in the factory workers making tractors and machinery, the people in the fertiliser and pesticide factories, the animal-feed makers and many others on whom the farmer depends, it is another story.

Why are farmers going bankrupt (in Britain and in the US)?

Western civilisation has become used to cheap food, produced on recently exploited lands such as the north American prairies and in developing countries. Land was once cheap and fertile, and there seemed no end to its availability. To produce cheap food today, when so much of the earth's latent fertility has been squandered and there are so many more mouths to feed, modern high-capital, low-manpower farming has put the farmer, his land and his finances under very severe strain. Practically every farm in the land is grossly over-capitalised and mortgaged. It has been possible to service growing mortgages and ever increasing mechanisation so long as the price of land has been increasing and grant subsidies have been maintained for produce. Should the support system fail – as is happening because of finance problems in the EEC – and land prices fall, bankruptcies are inevitable.

£500,000 BANK LOAN AND 3000 TONS OF WHEAT TO SUPPORT

Would it help farmers' financial difficulties if they went 'organic'?

In the short term, no. Like an alcoholic being dried out, land suddenly deprived of chemical fertilisers after years of over-use will develop withdrawal symptoms and take some years of careful nursing back to health before reasonable crops can be achieved. To build up a healthy balance of soil flora and fauna, and through them a good soil structure, is a slow process which would require a deep pocket or outside financial support to keep the farmer solvent during the changeover. Some large, chemicalised farmers are making the change successfully by converting a portion of their land to organic husbandry every five years and accepting the loss on that portion. Ultimately, it is probable that we will be forced to farm organically because the land will not continue to yield good crops through intensive, chemical methods.

Why is food production subsidised when there is a surplus?

This is a political matter tied to the public's demand for cheap food. The modern farmer has been tied to quotas and sub-sidies, to improvement grants and government arm-twisting for so long that it would be quite disastrous to remove the supports overnight. Nevertheless, the long-term need could well be for a gradual change of emphasis from large-scale cash cropping to a more decentralised local economy. In the meantime some support must be given, particularly to small and marginal farmers, and money should be spent on research into sustainable organic systems of husbandry.

What is happening to all the old varieties of vegetables? Is it true that seed merchants may sell only those that have been patented? And who is patenting the seeds?

The adoption of the 'Green Revolution' has led to a tremendous reduction in our genetic resources. Consider that there were once something like 10,000 different varieties of rice cultivated in India which have now been reduced to about 50. The fact is that once agriculture is commercialised, only those varieties are grown that are economically viable under the present intensive regime – basically those that are receptive to artificial fertiliser – while all other varieties are simply abandoned.

Much the same thing has happened to vegetables; recently, the large oil companies have been buying up seed companies, and legislation has been passed which makes it possible to patent seeds. The seeds patented are, needless to say, those that are receptive to fertiliser and require the use of the pesticides that the oil companies themselves produce. In this way they are creating their own market. The oil companies have recently pressured the EEC to ban the use of many traditional varieties of vegetables in order to provide themselves with a virtual monopoly of the market.

4 Nutrition

In 1984 the Food Policy Unit of Manchester Polytechnic examined the diet of those on low incomes, including the unemployed. The results were an appalling indictment of what we eat. Practically without exception those interviewed ate no fresh food whatsoever, preferring convenience, pre-packaged food with its concoction of additives.

In recent years, a growing number of doctors, both GPs and specialists, have been making the connection between general ill-health and diet. Such 'clinical ecologists' claim that such widely disparate health problems as allergies, heart problems and mental illness can be triggered by food and the kind of residues and additives it contains. Indeed, the enormous toll of degenerative disease in our society, of cancer, cardiovascular disease, respiratory disease and intestinal problems, suggests that we are the victims of what we eat and how we live. And in many instances the evidence suggests that avoiding certain foods while selecting others may have an extremely beneficial effect on health.

In his book *Not All in the Mind* (Pan, 1976) Dr Richard Mackarness popularised the concept that modern highly processed food was the basis of underlying debilitating disease, and he suggested that a diet which avoided food contaminated with additives and residues could lead to improved health. According to Drs Lewith and Kenyon in their book *Clinical Ecology*,[1] violent, aggressive behaviour among the inmates of prisons and mental hospitals increases in proportion 'to the amount of fast carbohydrate-filled or junk food in the diet'.

But in our day of profits and productivity the changes to basic foods do not begin with the food-processing industry but down on the farm. The recent EEC attempt to ban the use of hormones for beef production has been opposed by the British government on the grounds that scientists had discovered no ill-effects. However, as we have come to know from the studies of radiation and cancer, or of smoking and the use of asbestos, scientific facts too often reflect the prejudices of those who call for them to be made public. But the EEC has responded to growing consumer concern and, as Frans Andriessen, the EEC's agriculture commissioner, stated about the hormone ban: 'It was wholly proper to pay more attention to political realities than to scientific facts.'

The pharmaceutical industry claims that the extra weight gained by livestock in Britain through the use of growth promoters is worth £35 million a year. But the EEC now has thousands of tons of beef in refrigerated storage, and the problem we face is not one of a shortage of meat. And although certain scientists are unable to detect harmful changes brought about through growth promotion, whether in vegetables or livestock, that does not mean they do not occur. On the contrary, the nutritional quality of meat is likely to be radically altered through growth promotion, whether hormonally induced or through the feeding of concentrates. A large consumption of such meat may well contribute to some form of degenerative disease later.

Concern is increasing about food additives, which according to one EEC report are causing allergic reactions in some 82,000 people in the UK. Indeed, 41 additives approved for use in Britain are suspected of being carcinogenic, and almost half that number are banned in other EEC countries. To pressurise Parliament to control the use of additives in food and to remove the secrecy which surrounds their regulation, a new body called FACT (Food Additives Campaign Team, see p. 346) – encompassing consumer and health organisations, as well as members of trade unions and representatives of the major political parties – has been launched.

In fact, we need a revolution in the way food is produced on the farm, in the way it is processed when processing is necessary, and in the way we prepare and consume food. Our food habits in the UK and Europe have a controlling effect on what is grown elsewhere in the world and on the resultant rate of destruction of forests, of soils, or indeed of traditional methods of food production.

The Green Alternative

Food additives – are the risks worthwhile?

We each eat about half a ton of food a year. Much of that food has a selection of some 3,000 chemicals added to it. These chemicals are known as additives. Some additives are added intentionally, whilst others, like pesticide residues, chemical pollutants and natural moulds are there unintentionally.

Official controls on additives do not include studies on the long-term effects on us. Yet some are known to be harmful and many others are under grave suspicion. Most of the added chemicals are for the producer's benefit and profit, not ours. Some are almost certainly poisoning us. It is up to us, the consumer, to halt this process and to do so now.

Is the use of additives on the increase?

Their use is increasing rapidly, reflecting the growth of supermarkets and convenience foods which have increased tenfold in thirty years. Convenience foods necessarily rely on additives: the average Briton ate about 1.5lb of additives in 1955, and will eat no less than 5.4lbs this year, equivalent to 22 aspirin-sized tablets every day.

The food industry argues that without additives its products would spoil more quickly, would be less nutritious, and might taste and look 'less attractive' and be less likely to sell. Additives can also permit less careful storage procedures.

Chemicals can transform soya, maize and sugar beet into 'cheese', 'tomato paste', and 'salami' with the right 'mouth feel'. Of the 3,000 additives in use over half are cosmetic, and it is these flavours and colours, of unproven safety, which are used to make foods look or taste either better than they really are – or like something else entirely.

But doesn't the testing process protect us?

Chemicals can cause a wide range of adverse effects and it is essential that food chemicals be tested as carefully as medicines, since both are swallowed. But the problems are overwhelming. The variety of effects a chemical can have on different animals makes the guessing of effects between different species unpredictable, as was shown by thalidomide. Later tests showed that a woman was 60 times more sensitive to the drug than a mouse, and 200 times more than a dog. The present testing systems cannot possibly be sure of showing up the harmful additives. Testing an additive already costs the industry up to £500,000.

But if the additives had adverse effects, surely we would have felt them by now?

Most human cancers are caused by something in our surroundings – but can take many years to develop. For example, lung cancers produced from contact with coal dust, asbestos dust, or smoke, may take ten to twenty years to show up. This makes testing the long-term results of additives almost impossible. Had thalidomide been a slow-acting cause of cancer, for instance, it would still be used today – and even though the drug produced gross malformations it took almost five years of concentrated research to establish the cause–effect relationship of this one chemical. Few additives are researched in such depth.

Are food preservatives bad for you?

In excess, yes. Food preservation has been practised for centuries. Butter, cheese, wine, dried or pickled fruit and vegetables, salted and cured meat and fish are all preserved foods. Such foods tended in the past to be consumed sparingly since most people had access to fresh locally grown food or game and varied their diet according to the seasons.

Modern urban industrial populations, divorced from the land, eat a much higher proportion of preserved foods than their ancestors. In addition to the old methods of preservation, new ones have been developed. These include sterilisation by heat and canning, freezing, preservation through various chemical additives, and sterilisation through irradiation.

All methods of preservation can be harmful in excess, and some more than others. Excessive salt can cause high blood pressure, while refined sugar-based syrups are high in calories, detrimental to teeth and contribute to various degenerative diseases. Little is known so far about the medical effects of irradiation, and many chemical additives are now known to be carcinogenic or to cause allergies. We should try to eat produce that is fresh and produced in a 'natural' organic way, deriving at least 60 per cent of our diet from raw fruit and vegetables.

The Soil Association has now set up an inspection system for farmers and horticulturists who wish to market their produce as *bona fide* organic. Such produce is now stamped with a Soil Association guaranteed organic label. Other organisations with similar objectives and schemes, are the Biodynamic Agriculture Association and Organic Farmers and Growers Ltd. No organic symbol is fool-proof, but the efforts being invested in them are well motivated and increasingly well organised. If you doubt the probity of a particular claim, ask for the identity of the grower and have him checked through by the Inspector of Weights and Measures, who will refer your enquiry to the Soil Association.

Are food colourings a particular problem?

There are now 46 food colours, many of which are derived from synthetically produced dyes. When the UK joined the EEC we had 24 permitted food colours while the EEC had 19, only 10 of which were allowed by both. Subject to the existing food-colour directive, we had to accept the extra 9 colours at least for a review period, which means that the UK now allows 33. The USA has only 10 permitted artificial colours and the USSR only 4, so many of our cosmetic food colours have been rejected as unsafe by other countries.

Tartrazine (shown on labels as E102), a yellow dye put into buns, medicines, sweets and many other foods is strongly suspected of causing hyperactivity in some children, and allergies in some adults and children, particularly people intolerant to aspirin. Some US researchers recommend that children avoid all artificial colours.

What is the difference between modern and traditional methods of food-processing?

Take flour refining. It is not just mechanisation that sets the modern bread factory apart from the traditional bakers, it is also the fact that manufacturers now use chemicals to 'trump' nature. Matured flour is easier to bake because it is stiffer, but maturing flour naturally means storing it – and storage costs money. Today flour in Britain is 'matured' by adding chemical oxidising agents, notably chlorine dioxide, which also bleaches it. Most other countries do not permit the use of chlorine dioxide in flour. Another additive called BHT (butylated hydroxytoluene) is also barred in many other countries. The Food Standards Committee has twice recommended that alternatives be found to BHT in food; it has been barred for baby and young children's food because it is felt to be unsafe, yet it is used in many processed foods. Around 34 additives are permitted in bread, which is why you should bake your own, preferably from organically grown wholewheat flour, from which additives are prohibited. The British government has now taken some action, however, and the Bread and Flour Regulations of 1984 call for a maximum limit of chlorine dioxide and of benzoyl peroxide, another bleaching agent.

Both bran and wheatgerm are removed from grain during its milling to produce white flour, and with the wheatgerm go many important nutrients, including vitamins. Such losses are not made up with the additives now incorporated into white flour, and even those which are will not be in the balanced form found in the natural grain.

Is wholemeal flour necessarily from an 'organic' source?

Unfortunately not, and if one is looking for wholemeal flour one should try if at all possible to find an organic source. In fact flour from wheat that is 'chemicalised' through the use of artificial fertilisers and pesticides may be more damaging to health when wholemeal than when refined since the bran accumulates the greater part of the chemicals used. Indeed, bran from a non-organic wheat source can be a particular liability to chemical-sensitive people.

Can the additives market really expand any further?

Yes. Manufacturers are drawing away from agriculture and seeking closer ties with the chemical industry. The British market is worth some £200 million.

It is predicted that there will be a 100 per cent increase in the use of flavour enhancers and anti-oxidants, a 70 per cent boost in sweeteners, a 60 per cent rise in preservatives, a 50 per cent increase in stabilisers and flavours and a 40 per cent rise in the use of foam controllers (which stop scum forming and prevent liquids boiling over) over the next ten years.

Can't you just avoid additives by looking at the label?

Not easy! Additives are often just given code numbers and some are just called 'preservatives' or 'colourings', although this option may soon be closed. The consumer must write for the 'Look at the Label' leaflet[2] or check the code against its chemical name at the public library. But even then no information is given about the purpose or the possible hazards of the chemical, whether it has been banned outside Britain, or how fully it has been tested.

In any case, the leaflet implies that we have to put up with these additives. We certainly do not – for example public pressure has caused a major US cereal manufacturer to remove added sugar from its leading brand. In Britain sugar is still added to the same cereal. The same pressure would also work for those additives used for purely cosmetic reasons and indeed is beginning to have some effect, as can be seen from the growing number of supermarkets with 'health foods'.

What are the E's in food?

The E Code is a European system for identifying chemical additives permitted in manufactured foods. Some additives are nutrients but most are not, and some are toxic. From

1 January 1986 the producer of the final packaged article must declare the additives introduced, listing them in rank order of quantity. He is not obliged to list additives introduced by his suppliers, which may be important ingredients in the finished product.

The maximum concentrations of some additives are controlled by law, but many are left to the discretion of the manufacturers. All of them are there primarily for the manufacturers' benefit, for instance to increase sales through enhancing shelf-life and appearance.

How widespread is the use of pesticides?

Britain permits the use of pesticides such as dieldrin and aldrin amongst others which are banned in the US.

Farmers say pesticides are safe for human consumption. Is this true?

No. Many fruit and vegetables, even when washed, are impregnated by pesticides. A MAFF survey states that nearly all UK fruit, cereals and vegetables are sprayed with pesticides *at least* once. These also get into milk and meat via livestock feed.

There is increasing evidence that many illnesses – such as stomach ailments, asthma, cancer, Parkinson's disease, and also birth defects and cell mutations – can be caused by the regular intake of pesticide residues.

Pesticide use is increasing rapidly. Voluntary codes exist between the pesticides industry and farmers but there are no statutory controls against harmful spraying of food produce, no legal limits on residues and no adequate monitoring.

Friends of the Earth have produced a report called 'The First Incidents Report', 1985 giving evidence presented to Parliament on the harmful effects of pesticide poisonings. They have also launched the 'Dirty Dozen' campaign, highlighting twelve of the world's most dangerous pesticides – many produced or traded in the UK. You can contact Friends of the Earth at the address on p. 347.

But surely foods that contain high pesticide residues are not allowed to be sold in Britain?

It is the view of the Ministry of Agriculture, Fisheries and Food working party on pesticide residues that 'in most circumstances occasional exposure to higher-than-average levels of a pesticide in a foodstuff has no public health significance'.

Are the permitted levels for other additives set on the same basis?

Yes. The permitted levels for mercury in fish, for instance, assume that an average serving weighs between 150 and 200 grams – no more, no less. Moreover, by averaging out the total amount of fish consumed in Britain, the government has been able to justify the sale of fish contaminated with higher levels of mercury. In the early 1970s it was discovered that tinned tuna contained high levels of mercury. In America, sales of the fish were banned, resulting in the withdrawal of 900 million cans of tuna from the market. In Britain where similar mercury levels were found, the government gave assurances that all was well.

How can we tell whether there are pesticide residues in the food we consume?

Unless tests are carried out on each food item – an impossible task – we cannot know whether pesticides are in our foods. However, the chances of contamination are high given that pesticides are widely used for treating seeds and preserving foods in shipment and storage. In some instances we *can* detect them – for example, chemically treated apples may cause a burning or tingling sensation on the lips. Sometimes people get allergic reactions as well, but all too often the direct association with chemicals goes undetected. Ultimately, pesticides are toxic to humans, tending to be deposited in fat tissues and released when the fat is broken down, for example when dieting.

Pesticides are not the sole problem; numerous other chemical substances in the form of stabilisers, food colourings, artificial sweeteners, can increase our sensitivity to other chemicals.

Instead of constantly worrying about all these substances, the best path is to avoid them, by eating food which comes from organic farms and often carries the Soil Association mark.

In some places mothers are advised not to breastfeed because of the chemical residues in the milk. Is it as bad as that?

It is true that chemical residues have been found in mothers' milk, but that should not deter mothers from nursing their babies. There are many advantages to breastfeeding which go beyond the nutrient value of the milk and which are too important to give up. For example, the psychological value of the strengthening of the tie between mother and child contributes as much to the emotional health and security of the child as to its physical health. Over and above that, the various substances a child needs (proteins, minerals, sugars) are present in the proper proportions in human milk – a ratio that is highly species specific – and the antibodies that are passed on with milk provide resistance to many diseases. However, if for some reason breastfeeding is not possible strongly treated milk forms, such as powdered milk and ultra-high-temperature-treated milk, should be avoided, as well as milk with added sugar.

We should peel vegetables and fruit to get rid of any residues, shouldn't we?

Instead of asking about peeling vegetables and fruit we should be avoiding contaminated foods. Buying foods from sources such as organic farms which don't use pesticides and other artificial chemicals is of course the most direct way.

But back to the main question – peeling foods. Actually, it doesn't help as much one would like to think. Pesticides used during the growing of foods are distributed throughout the

The Green Alternative

product, and peeling does not eliminate the problem. Many valuable nutrients are found in the peel and outer layer, and peeling therefore leads to nutritional loss.

Are we all equally susceptible to pollutants?

No. The irresponsible but convenient assumption that we are, is contradicted by biological evidence which shows that we are all different and that children are more susceptible to some pollutants than adults – and that the unborn child is even more vulnerable. For example, adults excrete almost 90 per cent of the lead that contaminates our food – children only 50 per cent. And children are more vulnerable to lead pollution than adults because it affects brain development. When setting the permitted levels of lead in food, the government ignores this.

Can you give us some practical hints for sound eating?

Additives. Examine the label carefully and buy food with the least number of harmful additives.

Pesticides. We spray around £4 billion worth of chemicals on to our plants annually. Many are banned in some countries but used in others. Few have been fully examined for health, environmental or ecological side effects. Most are unnecessary. Buy locally grown food from farm shops etc. whenever you can, and ask if it has been sprayed. Wash all fresh fruit and vegetables thoroughly. Better still, grow your own or buy organic food. A very useful 'Organic Food Finder' listing over 400 suppliers is available from the Henry Doubleday Research Association.

Fertilisers. Buy organically grown foods. Nitrate pollution from artificial fertilisers now threatens one-third of this country's water supplies, leading to potential cancer hazards and particular danger to babies and unborn children. The use of fertilisers is increasing, so the problem will get much worse in the next few years as the residues enter the water table.

Wholefoods. It is advisable to eat more wholefoods – wholewheat bread, beans, fresh fish – and increase your

110

consumption of fresh fruit and vegetables. Raw organic
vegetables are particularly nutritious. Visit your local wholefood shop. A wholefood diet may well be cheaper.

In general, you should be a vegetarian for two days a week
and select home-grown seasonal fruit and vegetables, instead
of imported produce. Avoid processed products including
sweet drinks and white flour and sugar. Remember that one
calorie of meat requires 3 to 12 calories of cereal: 3 for pork,
10 for beef, 12 for chicken. However, free-range hens scratching for their food in yards and meadows use plant and animal
matter otherwise wasted and return their dung to the soil;
they also clean the fields of parasites. The same holds true for
traditional methods of pig-rearing.

'Since we've also eliminated the
steroid steak, the oysters with
methyl mercury, the broccoli
dioxin di Seveso, the Château
ethylene glycol and the Caesium
135 sole – we'll have to settle for
an organic roll and a bottle of
Perrier water.'

**Wouldn't irradiating foods avoid questionable chemical
additives?**

International and national committees have evaluated what
changes, if any, take place in foods that have been irradiated
to preserve them. Their conclusion is that foods irradiated
with doses up to 10,000 grays (1 million rads, i.e. the

equivalent of several million X-rays) are safe, although with such treatment up to 10 per cent of the vitamin content may be lost. The Advisory Committee on Novel and Irradiated Foods reported to the UK Health Department in April 1986 that 'radiation treatment at average doses of up to 10 kilograys presents no toxicological hazard and introduces no special nutritional or microbiological problems'. When asked to provide references, the Committee refused. It did admit, however, that radiation damages vitamins A, B, C and E and essential polyunsaturated fatty acids. Public comment on the report was invited by July 1986, after which the Advisory Committee would make recommendations.

Radioactivity induced in the food under the conditions stipulated is very short lived. The irradiation is carried out using gamma rays emitted from isotopes such as cobalt-60 and caesium-137. Killing bacteria and viruses by such treatment sterilises the product and can extend shelf-life by weeks, months or even years. At present irradiated foods cannot be imported or sold in the UK, except under special medical circumstances, where patients are on sterile diets. However, some irradiated food has been illegally imported.

The purported advantages of food irradiation are:

(a) that it is a cold process with only a slight rise in temperature of the food and with few changes in the colour, flavour and texture

(b) that it can be used to treat food without altering packaging or equipment

Nevertheless, there must be changes in the food, even if to date they have not been detected. How much radioactivity is induced, for instance, and will the nutritional value be altered? Some long-term feeding experiments have been carried out on animals without signs of ill-effects, but few foods have been tested.

Because irradiation is a process rather than an additive governments have decided it is not obligatory to label food so treated. Various consumer associations have, however, argued that such labelling should be mandatory.

Professor Konrad Pfeilsticker of Bonn University has argued against food irradiation for the following reasons:

Purity. Irradiation does not imply a 'purer' product than food preserved by traditional techniques. Chemicals such as hydrogen peroxide often need to be added to irradiated food to alleviate the damage caused by the irradiation process.

Taste, texture, colour, quality. Because irradiation increases cell permeability, undesirable changes in the taste, texture, colour and quality of food may occur (red fruits become yellow, for instance). Often these changes do not show until some weeks after treatment. There is a danger that if irradiation doses are reduced so as to avoid these changes, the lower levels may not be adequate to deal with the health risks.

Health. While certain doses of irradiation may kill pathogenic micro-organisms such as bacilli which cause food to rot, they will not be able to kill others, e.g. those causing botulism. There is a danger that certain organisms could develop immunity to irradiation. In addition we still do not know what genetic changes in pathogenic micro-organisms might occur by being damaged, but not destroyed, by irradiation.

Expense. The process is uneconomic: the food industry prefers the alternative cheaper methods already available. (However, the International Atomic Energy Agency in Vienna, a UN body, is strongly promoting the technology.)

It will not solve the world's food problems. Irradiation of food is sometimes advocated as a way of reducing starvation in the Third World. It would not do this. The world's food problems are primarily economic and of distribution, and will not be solved by improved food preservation techniques.

The process is not necessary. We already have adequate food-preservation technology. While there may be room for improving existing methods, such as heat treatment, there is no need for a new one.

Nutrition. Vitamins C, B1 and others can be badly affected by irradiation. The normal appearance of some irradiated fruit could therefore be quite deceptive.

Undoubtedly the safest bet is to buy foods that do not need any kind of treatment – such as foods that can be used in a short time (like vegetables and fruits) or ones that are known to have a long shelf-life (grains, dried beans, rice, etc). Processed foods (including such items as egg powder), are much more susceptible to storage problems – and most treatments are likely to have adverse results.

. For more information contact: The National Housewives Association and the London Food Commission (addresses on pp. 348–9) see also Tony Webb and Angela Henderson's *Food Irradiation – Who wants it?* (London Food Commission).

What about disposal of equipment used in irradiating food – will this add to 'low-level' radioactive waste?

The irradiation of food is an offshoot of the nuclear industry, the source of irradiation being gamma-emitting isotopes extracted from nuclear waste. Therefore food irradiation is one more attempt to justify the use of nuclear power and the reprocessing of spent reactor fuel. The equipment used for irradiating will also become contaminated over time through the generation of activation products. Both the source of irradiation and the equipment will need to be disposed of so that environmental contamination is avoided. That cost must be taken into account when evaluating the use of irradiation.

How and where is irradiation used?

Here is a partial list of the countries where irradiation is allowed and/or used. Note that no country allows the complete and unchecked use of irradiation in doses of 5 million rads (50 kilograys) or more. (Further information is available from the Ministry of Agriculture, Food and Fisheries, London.)

Australia: use is authorised on imported meats, fish, shell fish and molluscs (fresh or frozen).

Belgium: use is authorised on imported spices, gelatine, dehydrated vegetables and food colouring. Also allowed for imported fresh fruits and vegetables.

Bulgaria: allowed for wheat, rice and other cereals and on dried fruit and vegetables imported into the country.

France: allowed for imported dried fruits and vegetables. Being considered for imported meat, fish and shell fish.

Israel: used on fresh fruits and vegetables. Permitted for imported meats and fish.

Italy: used on bulbs and tubers (potatoes, onions, etc).

Japan: used on bulbs and tubers.

Netherlands: authorised for imported wheat and cereals, meats, fish and spices. Used on fresh fruits and vegetables.

South Africa: used extensively on fresh fruits and vegetables. Permitted for imported dried fruits and vegetables, meat, fish and shell fish.

United States: used on food for the space programme. Being seriously considered as a quarantine measure for imports and exports (fruit, vegetables, beef, pork and prepared meats).

Does treating milk with ultra-high temperatures for long-life storage provide us with a valuable way of making use of a product that would otherwise spoil?

Users of high-temperature-treated milk know that its taste is altered and that it no longer behaves like milk: it can be kept over long periods until the package is opened – then it goes off very quickly. Because treatment alters the milk some people get low-grade fevers from drinking it, their bodies reacting to it as an 'alien' product. Infants fed on a formula made up with milk treated in this way can be harmed.

Why are people worried about the increase of diabetes? Don't we have it under control with the use of insulin?

Most people think that diabetes is inherited and that little can be done to prevent it. Yet in those predisposed to the disease, adult diabetes is more often acquired by eating an excess of refined, processed foods, in particular those with a high sugar content. Schoolchildren in Britain are now being warned that eating the present high amounts of fatty foods, crisps, cakes, etc for school lunches may result in adult diabetes.

Nor is the use of insulin totally benign. It can cause

blindness and affect blood circulation. Far better to avoid such complications whenever possible through eating a wholesome diet and making sure that that applies to one's children.

Are hamburgers bad for us?

Hamburgers from fast-food shops may lead to general ill-health beyond any nutritional deficiencies of the hamburger itself. Apart from the fact that the meat may have too high a fat content for health, hamburgers are usually packed in white bread buns, and we usually add to the problem by drinking sugar-laden beverages such as coca-cola, or milk shakes.

Beyond the health effects to individuals, however, the rapidly growing hamburger industry is leading to environmental disaster, particularly in Central and South America, but also increasingly in Africa, where vast areas of tropical forest are being destroyed for raising cattle. One-quarter of the forests of Central America have already gone and enormous inroads are being made into the tropical forests of the Amazon in Brazil.

Is cholesterol the danger to health we've heard about?
Should we give up butter? milk? cheese?

Cholesterol is the product of the digestion and use of fats in the body. It probably contributes to heart disease – but what causes a high level initially is still not clearly known. The culprit seems not to be the quantity of cholesterol ingested via food, but rather more a consequence of one's general diet (including sugar and alcohol) and the type of life one leads (stress factors) which can increase the body's cholesterol level, partially from the body's own production of cholesterol. Apparently a well-balanced diet, which *includes* dairy products, and a well-functioning digestive system with a minimum of refined carbohydrates – white flour, sugar etc – and fatty meat, are important in keeping the cholesterol level down.

Why is cholesterol a health problem? Wasn't it always?

One reason is that our diet is no longer balanced. For instance, the high incidence of heart disease appears to be associated with the advent of highly processed foods which through processing have lost at least three important B vitamins – choline, inositol and vitamin B6 (pyridoxine). In addition, intensive farming has changed the nature of meat, and although today's meat looks leaner it is impregnated with saturated fats. A study by Professor Michael Crawford at the Nuffield Institute for Nutrition in London has shown that the carcass of herbivorous animals such as wild African buffalo contains 75 per cent muscle and 5 per cent fat, while that of fattened domestic cattle may have only 50 per cent muscle and as much as 30 per cent fat, much of the fat closely associated with the muscle, causing it to be 'marbled'.

But the story doesn't end there. Fats can be basically divided into two kinds: essential and non-essential. Essential fats are polyunsaturated fats which the body needs for making cellular components such as membranes; they are particularly associated with nervous tissue. Animals cannot make essential fats from scratch and must derive them from plants, in particular from leafy material. In the green plant such polyunsaturated fats are always associated with anti-oxidants such as vitamin E, otherwise they would quickly become saturated and lose their essential properties.

Non-essential fats, on the other hand, are important in providing us with an energy store and with a layer of insulation against cold. But excess of them can unbalance our metabolism; indeed stress has been shown to cause the release of a stream of fatty material into the blood. If stress led to energetic activity – part of the fight or flight response needed for survival amongst traditional hunter-gatherer societies – then the release of such free fatty acids would not necessarily put our health at risk. But in our stress-laden sedentary society those fats can put considerable strain on the circulatory system, including the heart. The production of cholesterol is one result.

Reducing our consumption of meat from intensively reared

117

The Green Alternative

animals will certainly improve our health: indeed it must be appreciated that the ratio of non-essential to essential fats in domesticated animals is 50 to 1 compared to about 2 to 1 in the free-living animal – a twenty-five-fold difference. Fish is rich in polyunsaturated fats and the consumption of fish is highly beneficial, leading to a reduction of blood cholesterol.

Doesn't exercise help?

Life in the past was more physically demanding for most people and from that point of view more healthy. Indeed, the current epidemic of cardiovascular disease is a relatively new phenomenon associated with our modern industrialised lifestyle. Until recently most of the people affected have been men, but the rate of heart disease and associated disorders in women is now on the increase. At the same time women may naturally be better able to cope with a high fat diet than men, inasmuch as they need to store fat for reproductive and breastfeeding purposes.

The Cordon Bleu Cookery Diploma is generally recognised throughout Europe. This relies heavily on ingredients such as meat, cream, fats and sugar which are increasingly discouraged by dietitians since this may contribute to the risk of heart disease. Are there alternatives?

Yes. The Vegetarian Society has introduced a Cordon Vert Diploma and a range of other shorter courses for vegetarians in London and Manchester, which also include sugar-free baking and vegetarian meals for special ocasions.

For further details contact the Vegetarian Society (see p. 351).

What diseases may result from eating meat?

Probably the effect of very occasional meat-eating (monthly or less) is indistinguishable from total abstinence. Weekly or daily meals would affect people differently, according to individual susceptibility and what else is eaten. Anyone eating meat more often than once daily faces a wide range of possible hazards. Even organically grown meat is easily over-consumed. Our digestive system has been adapted to deal with it, but finds it difficult and expensive – particularly as juices for digesting meat can easily make the mistake of digesting your body. Duodenal and gastric ulcers can be the result. The abnormal burden of the extra fats in the blood stream, which can be seen in the serum with the naked eye, directly affects the nourishment of blood vessels. Those under most physical stress (i.e. near the heart) tear more easily and often, and heal less well. Atheroma (hardening of the arteries) results, which is the basis of heart attacks and many strokes. Meat residues in the bowel, and toxic digestive by-products from them, irritate the bowel wall excessively. Additive residues, prone to accumulate in the muscle ligaments and joints of the frequent meat-eater, may later give rise to rheumatism, rheumatoid arthritis and gout.

Abstinence from meat has enormously improved health in many individuals prepared to make that change.

Do we need to eat meat?

Meat is not essential. However, we need a balanced diet with the correct proportion of amino acids. Although these are most readily available from meat, fish, eggs and such dairy products as cheese, they can also be obtained from vegetable sources such as brewer's yeast, soya beans, cotton seed, nuts, wheatgerm, wholewheat or whole cereal grain including brown rice. In general, however, we need to mix our vegetables if we wish to procure all our amino acids from a vegetarian diet since different vegetables vary in their amino acid content, some lacking essential amino acids which others contain. For instance, to ensure a good diet pulses such as haricot beans or peas should be eaten with a wholegrain such as rice or wheat.

Undoubtedly, by using more grains and pulses, eating fewer processed cereal products and more wholegrain-based products we can cut down on our meat intake. Meat is an expensive source of protein, not only in terms of cost to the consumer but also at a cost to others living on the planet.

Meat-eating today is really a luxury associated with the affluent society. In the United States the average consumption is some 110 kilograms per person per year, in the United Kingdom 75 kilograms, in the USSR 51 kilograms, in Brazil 32 kilograms, in China 21 kilograms, in Nigeria 6 kilograms and in India 1.1 kilograms.

What can safely replace meat?

In the rich countries, protein excess rather than shortage is the problem. These people need simply to cut down drastically on meat consumption of all kinds. Even in poorer countries where there is a genuine protein shortage, adequate quantities can be found in ordinary cereals, beans and vegetables. There is no imperative need to invent new protein sources from such organisms as algae, bacteria and yeast, and we incur risks in doing so. Whenever something entirely novel is introduced into the diet of millions, we can only hope no dire results will follow.

The increased toll in cancers and degenerative disease in our society is, in fact, a response to our modern way of life, including dieting. Yet it may take thirty to fifty years for the health problems caused by a novel food to manifest themselves. And how can we pinpoint precisely what has caused what after such a passage of time?

What about chemicals contained in meat?

Chemicals cannot be easily disposed of. Heavy metal contaminants of soil are consumed by grazing livestock in herbage, or direct by rooting animals. Livestock feeds may be contaminated by processing chemicals or packaging.

The animal attempts to excrete these but fails, and its milk, fat, liver and kidneys accumulate residues which are passed on to human consumers. In addition the marbling of meat with streaks of fat, prized by some consumers, is a sign of ill-health in the animals.

What additives are in the meat we eat? Should we be concerned about them?

Antibiotics and hormones are now well established as aids to livestock production, and insecticides are used freely to control pest diseases. Many less obviously pharmacological changes have been introduced to animal feedstuffs to make them more 'efficient'. Britain, alone of EEC members, insists that growth-promoting hormones should still be permitted in the production of beef – the Minister of Agriculture claiming that no hazard to health has been noted.

The butcher may then use nitrates or smoke to cure and colour pig meat, or polyphosphates to texturise chicken and solidify cooked meats, to name but two of the techniques at his disposal.

All of these practices are open to abuse or overuse, and none have been tested rigorously enough to establish their effects on long-term consumers of meat products. In many instances no adequate scientific basis exists for such tests. Meat-eaters are, in effect, life-long subjects in a toxicity trial of these post-war technologies.

Studies comparing Seventh Day Adventists, who are vegetarians, with their neighbours indicate that people who do not eat meat may live as much as ten years longer on average than people who do.

Why do we need fibre in our food?

Vegetable fibre cleans teeth and tones gums when it is chewed, then swells with water to give a jelly-like texture to the intestinal contents. This conditions digestion very favourably, moderates the rate of absorption of digested nutrients into the body, transports the residues rapidly outwards and by wrapping toxic residues in a fibre web reduces the irritation they can cause in the lower bowel. Passage of a fibrous stool is easy and frequent, so that the pressure effects of straining do not occur. These effects include piles, varicose veins and diverticulosis – pouches of skin pushed out through weak points in the large bowel muscle, like Brussels sprouts on a stalk. Filth stagnates in these pouches, which become liable to a painful and dangerous infection known as diverticulitis. A large minority of elderly people accustomed to a refined (low fibre) diet will encounter this uncomfortable, chronic condition.

Everything is made of chemicals, so why should artificial ones be worse than natural ones?

The body lacks enzymes to break down many synthetic chemicals, like DDT, which when taken in with food may then accumulate in our tissues where they can cause chronic damage. In addition, many substances have different forms, mirror images of each other, only *one* of which is part of living systems. Thus, whereas in nature only one of several forms or configurations is synthesised, when these substances are made chemically, usually all the forms are produced simultaneously, and those which cannot be metabolised actually block reactions in the body.

Another factor, which often gets forgotten regarding natural versus chemical substances, particularly when they are identical from the analytical standpoint, is that nutritional balance may be lost. For instance, if we eat sugar coming direct from the plant in which it occurs, that is very different from consuming refined sugar free from any other substances normally associated with the intact plant. Minerals, vitamins and trace elements which the body needs to metabolise sugar occur in the sugar cane or beet, but are removed from refined sugar. Thus the body has to use its own supply of calcium (from tissues and bones) or B-vitamins to metabolise the sugar, and as a 'calcium robber' sugar can drastically affect the mineral content of teeth and bones. Likewise with nitrate. Although organically grown foods may, like conventionally grown crops and vegetables, also have nitrate in them, implying that they are no different, the higher vitamin C content of organic fruit and vegetables may help block the dangerous conversion of nitrate into the carcinogen nitrosamine.

As long as we eat essential ingredients, does it matter how we eat them?

No one thrives on a diet of pure nutrients out of packets, however well balanced. One's diet should be combined in sensible proportions in the right physical phase (usually colloidal or gel-like), and preferably in a vital condition (with enzyme systems and metabolic processes still operating).

And what about what we drink? Are we running out of fresh water?

We have made tremendous inroads into available water, either by irresponsible consumption or by contamination. When one considers that we use drinking quality water for everything in the household and garden it becomes apparent how much high-quality water we are wasting. In industry, water recycling (which also provides the opportunity to recover mineral resources) is done to only a fraction of its potential.

Pollution also decreases the amount of usable water. Today, groundwater contaminated to the point where it can no longer be used for drinking has already become a major problem in some areas.

One frequently heard suggestion to alleviate water shortage is to dam up valleys. Few realise, however, how this can change overall groundwater levels. Although the effects undoubtedly depend on the geological structure of the area, a dam will often mean the groundwater table is lowered below the dam. Water, like energy, should be used ecologically and economically.

Why all the fuss about the fluoridation of water supplies?

In 1985, after a cursory debate, the British government passed a Bill allowing fluoride to be added to water supplies. Britain had therefore moved one stage closer to the mandatory fluoridation of public water under the authority of the various Water Boards.

The Green Alternative

The aim of fluoridation is to reduce tooth decay, particularly in young children, evidence from the United States suggesting that levels of up to one part per million of fluoride in drinking water reduce dental caries by as much as one half. The United States Public Health Service has been advocating fluoridation of water supplies since the 1940s, and many towns in North America now have fluoridated water. However, countries such as Holland and West Germany have banned the practice as an infringement of human rights. In Britain the National Anti-Fluoridation Campaign has been active since 1963 in campaigning against moves in the UK to fluoridate water supplies. The Campaign points out that public water fluoridation creates a dangerous precedent for compulsory medication and bodily treatment without the consent of either adults or children. It is opposed to the practice on principle, whether or not fluoridation is beneficial to health.

As it happens, there is a growing body of evidence that fluoride, as supplied artificially to water supplies, is a major cause of disease in the recipient population. Dr Dean Burk, former head of the Cytochemistry Division of the US National Cancer Institute, and Dr John Yiamouyiannis, science director of the US National Health Foundation, claim that fluoride added to drinking water results in as many as 35,000 cancer deaths each year in the United States. That is one in ten of all cancer deaths in the country. Fluoride is also increasingly implicated in cot deaths, in causing stiffness in joints, bone fractures and even blindness. One of the earliest signs of fluoride poisoning is the appearance of mottled teeth. Many children in the United States now show some signs of such mottling.

How is fluoride harmful?

Since the turn of the century, the dangers of fluoride have been realised. It was known, for instance, that livestock as well as human beings in the vicinity of such industrial plants as aluminium smelters, iron and steel works, phosphate fertiliser factories, and brick kilns could suffer from the disease fluorosis (fluoride being emitted in the stacks). One of the main symptoms, apart from crumbling bones, was respiratory distress. As a poison, fluoride works by binding with essential minerals, such as magnesium, that are a vital component of certain enzyme systems in the body, in particular the cytochrome oxidase system which enables respiration to take place. Only a minute amount of fluoride will have toxic effects even though they may not be immediately apparent.

Fluoride is a relatively common element in nature, but it is safely bound with calcium to form fluorspar and most natural waters have extremely low levels of the mineral. When added to water supplies, it is in soluble form, usually as sodium fluoride and is much less tightly bound to sodium than it is to calcium. It is therefore free to act on the tissues of the body and bind with magnesium and calcium, thus depleting the body of its minerals and destroying enzymes.

Why should anyone want to put fluoride in the water supply?

The aluminium industry has been the most active of all industries in wanting to doctor public water supplies with fluoride. That outlet provides a convenient way of getting rid of otherwise extremely toxic and intractable wastes that build up in the industry. Much fluoride-containing waste has been dumped in the sea, as well as discharged into the atmosphere.

One major problem with adding fluoride to water is that a great many people have been persuaded by propaganda from the medical and dental profession to take fluoride in other ways, in toothpaste and sometimes even in the form of pills. In addition to symptoms of fluorosis evidence is again building up that children using fluoride mouthwashes and fluoride medicated toothpaste are showing increased incidence of cancer.

One of the most disturbing aspects of the fluoridation controversy is that the evidence for the efficacy of fluoride in preventing tooth decay is extremely circumstantial. Indeed, the original observations in the United States were all on water supplies that contained, in addition to fluoride, relatively large concentrations of essential minerals such as magnesium and calcium. Those high levels of benign salts may well have counteracted the harmful effects of a raised concentration of fluoride while themselves providing some protection against tooth decay.

As the national Anti-Fluoridation Campaign pointed out, the debate on the fluoridation of water supplies in the House of Commons was of mediocre quality, without any full or proper discussion of the hazards associated with fluoride. The British government, on the basis of half-truths from the Ministry of Health has therefore put a stamp of approval on a practice which is irresponsible and based on mediocre science.

And who foots the bill for fluoridation?

The Department of Health is pledged to supply 60 per cent of the capital costs of implementing fluoridation of water supplies but has only £500,000 available for the whole of Britain. The fluoridation of just one county's water supply – Dorset – would cost £3 million to set up and £480,000 a year to operate. Fluoridation may therefore never get off the ground.

For more information contact the National Anti-Fluoridation Campaign (see p. 348).

Are our freshwater lakes deteriorating? Why?

A number of our freshwater lakes are deteriorating, although often for different reasons. One of the main causes is eutrophication, where lakes receive too many nutrients which then cause the growth of algae. When such blooms of algae sink to the bottom, they decompose and use up available oxygen, causing fish to die. The nutrient responsible is often phosphate, sometimes present through waste waters containing sewage and detergents and sometimes via agriculture, but generally from the excessive use of phosphate fertilisers or manure from intensive animal production.

Biocides from agriculture can also run off into freshwater lakes. These biocides can disturb the ecological balance of the lake, for example by poisoning zoo-plankton, which normally eat the algae. The algae then accumulate even without a major excess of nutrients.

By removing nutrients water treatment plants can improve the situation, yet increasing quantities of nutrients from agriculture are flowing into the rivers and groundwater. As consumers we can influence the situation by buying from farmers producing in an environmentally compatible way.

River silt in industrial areas has also become severely polluted. In Holland, where Rhine silt accumulates and has periodically to be removed from Rotterdam harbour, the silt is so polluted that it cannot be used on the land. The problem has two aspects: firstly, the loss of fertile silt and, secondly, the problem of what can be done with the vast amount of contaminated materials other than dumping them in landfill sites or in the sea.

What does fertiliser run-off do to our drinking water?

Fertiliser run-off *is* causing a number of problems to surface and groundwater. The major ones are the run-off of phosphates which contribute to lake eutrophication, and the contamination of groundwater through leaching nitrates. Nitrates endanger infants by blocking the oxygen-carrying capacity of blood haemoglobin, leading to a 'blue baby' syndrome. Nitrates are considered a health hazard because the body can convert them into carcinogenic nitrosamines. In many parts of Europe today, especially in Holland, the groundwater is no longer considered safe to drink owing to nitrate contamination: and drinking water has to be brought daily by truck or bought in bottles.

What about heavy metal contamination of foodstuffs?

Heavy metal contamination of soil and thus of foods is a growing problem. The load of heavy metals in soils is continuously increasing, partly from the use of contaminated sewage sludge in agriculture and partly from atmospheric pollution like lead from leaded petrol or from emissions of lead, cadmium and mercury from waste incinerators. We cannot immediately stop this pollution but we could start reducing it by eliminating from refuse contaminants such as batteries (which should be collected separately) and certain plastics which contain, for example, cadmium in colouring pigments.

In Japan, since 1980, a full scale recycling system has been in operation for nickel-cadmium batteries used in security equipment such as emergency lighting and automated alarm systems. In 1984 just under 300 tons of these batteries were recycled, amounting to some 11 per cent of total production for the domestic market. These batteries last some 5 years, so, given the growth in the market, that figure of 11 per cent represents 20 per cent of the amount marketed five years previously.

In 1977, Sanyo Electric failed in a campaign to recover nickel-cadmium batteries encased in plastic, such as were used in the home, due to the poor public response. However, there is major concern in Japan over the discarding and dumping of home-use dry cells that are based on mercury, and half of the nation's local authorities have begun their own dry cell collection programmes. It may therefore be possible for the local authorities to act as collectors for all types of batteries and then forward the waste batteries to the correct destination for recycling, for which they would be properly recompensed. Cadmium and mercury in particular are highly toxic metals, and their recycling is therefore an important way to prevent pollution of the environment.

In the long term we in Britain must also press to keep heavy metals from being treated in sewage works to prevent sludge contamination. This means better waste-water treatment by industry itself, but also gradually replacing heavy metals in many products where alternatives are available. For instance, selenium sulphide should not be put into dandruff shampoos.

Sewage sludge may be excellent organic fertiliser, depending on its source, but if industrial chemical effluents are mixed with it problems can arise. Among these are heavy metals such as lead, cadmium and mercury, and other elements such as fluorine. These are toxic to plants and humans and accumulate in soil. Gradually levels build up in plants and their consumers, interfering increasingly with their metabolism and leading to disease, including mental disorders and kidney failure. In West Germany heavy metal contamination of soil has become a major problem.

Sewage should therefore be applied to land only so long as the heavy metal content of the soil remains below the accepted minima. After that only sewage or compost devoid of these metals should be used. Unfortunately, many chemical fertilisers also tend to contain cadmium and fluorine, and no limits have been set to applications of these.

Lead in any form tends to attack the nervous system selectively; evidence from reputable sources associates raised lead levels with dulled mental performance and irritability. Where this affects children during the phase of rapid brain development (up to three years), effects are permanent.

What link is there, if any, between nitrate use as fertiliser and human health?

Professor Helmut Vogtmann of Kassel University in West Germany, has shown that the addition of nitrates in artificial fertilisers leads to an increase of water in the crop without any increase in the fibrous matrix. The vitamin C content of highly fertilised vegetable crops is also reduced. Others have found that the storability of fertilised crops such as potatoes and even grains is also impaired, and what may seem like a large crop at the time of harvest deteriorates after a few months of storage to one that is smaller and less nutritious than a correspondingly organically grown crop.

If nitrate gets into the gut, there is a chance that some will become reduced to nitrite, especially in those people who suffer from a condition known as achlorhydria in which there is little or no hydrochloric acid. Ruminants such as cattle, on account of microbial action in their rumens, are even more likely to convert nitrates to nitrites. Nitrite destroys vitamins A and E and can give rise to hormonal imbalances in affected animals leading to toxaemia and a fall in productivity. A particular danger to humans arises from nitrites converting to nitrosamines, which are known to be carcinogenic. In the Transkei for instance, a high incidence of oesophageal cancer has been noted in the Bantu who use the fruit of a solanaceous plant (related to the potato and deadly nightshade) to curdle milk. The juice of that plant was found to contain dimethylnitrosamine. In Zambia, too, a high incidence of oesophageal cancer has been related to the drinking of spirits containing nitrosamines.

Infants are at particular risk from nitrites and hence from nitrates, insofar as their blood haemoglobin can react with nitrites to form a non-oxygen-carrying methaemoglobin. The World Health Organisation has recommended an upper limit of 50 milligrams per litre of nitrate in drinking water on account of the danger to children and adults. In certain areas, in parts of East Anglia for example, these levels are already exceeded and mothers are advised to give bottled water to their infants.

Certain vegetables such as spinach tend to concentrate nitrates, and although levels of nitrite are relatively low at the time of harvest, after a few days of storage they have increased substantially. The degree of nitrite formation is contingent on the quantity of nitrogen fertiliser used. When no fertiliser is used the nitrite level in spinach after four days of storage is 13.6 mg/kg (i.e. 13 parts per million). When 160 kg of N per hectare are applied, hazardous amounts of nitrites, greater than 200 mg/kg, can concentrate in spinach after four days storage.

What about other effects of nitrogen from fertilisers?

Apart from getting into waterways and contributing to the growth of algae, some nitrogen from fertiliser evaporates into the atmosphere, usually in the form of ammonia or ammonium hydroxide. Manures are particularly prone to evaporation, and research suggests that as much as 10 per cent of the nitrogen in fertiliser may get into the atmosphere. High levels of ammonia and ammonium in the atmosphere close to intensive farming are probably contributing to the death of spruce and pine in southern Sweden by oversaturating the trees with nutrients. One effect of excess nutrients is that the trees become covered in an algal slime and are prone to secondary disease and infestation. The large surplus quantities of manure produced in animal feedlots – large concentrations of animals in a confined space – have become a major environmental problem in countries such as West Germany and Holland.

5 Health

The classical determinants of health were summarised by Professor Thomas McKeown in *The Role of Medicine*:[1]

> Those who are fortunate enough to be born free of significant congenital disease or disability will remain well if three basic needs are met. They must be adequately fed; they must be protected from a wide range of hazards in the environment; and they must not depart radically from the pattern of personal behaviour under which man evolved – for example by smoking, overeating, or sedentary living.

This understanding is a continuation of the tradition established by the philosopher-healers of Ancient Greece. It fails today because our understanding of its meaning has been distorted by the assumptions of our culture. Our assumptions, and the misguided actions which follow them, damage our state of health.

Throughout the world there are massive inequalities in health. In general the poor suffer the worst health and have the shortest life expectancy. This remains true whether we compare rich and poor nations or the rich and poor within any nation. Indeed, recent public health data for the UK shows that infant and perinatal mortality among those of the lowest social class is double that of the highest social class. The relationship between health and poverty breaks down only in those rare communities where money and the values based upon it are unimportant.

What is the current state of human health?

In Western industrialised nations the picture is remarkably consistent and depressing. Reductions in child mortality achieved during the course of this century have not been matched by improvements in the quality of life, nor by any significant increase in life expectancy for mature people.

Fewer than 10 per cent of the population enjoy a high level of health. In Britain, the *General Household Survey* revealed in 1977 that 56 per cent of men and 70 per cent of women suffered chronic health problems. Of these around 70 per cent had to have some form of medical treatment all the time because of their chronic ill health. Within this group are 15 million people who daily rely on prescription drugs.[2]

There has been little monitoring of illness levels but the evidence of recent decades suggests a continuing deterioration. One study headed by Mike Wadsworth at Bristol University shows that today's children are markedly more likely to suffer a wide range of chronic forms of illness than their parents did at the same age. In particular, allergic conditions have increased many-fold and diabetes is six times more common.

Patterns of illness vary between cultures but the Western ways of sickness and death are increasing as the Western way of life dominates other cultures.

What contribution does medicine make to our health?

There are three areas where medicine is of positive benefit. First, in crisis care of injury. Second, in providing immunisation and antibiotic treatment against infection by certain pathogens. Third, in providing replacement therapy for metabolic and other body system malfunctions. However, uncritical assumptions about the benefits of medical care have led to an enormous overuse of hazardous forms of treatment, especially drug therapy. The result is that much modern medicine has become part of the ill-health problem – documented by Ivan Illich in *Medical Nemesis*.[3] Research by Professor Archie Cochrane, director of the Medical Research Council Epidemiological Unit at Cardiff, has demonstrated the 'doctor anomaly' – that, all other things being equal, more than 1 doctor per 1,000 of population produces an increase in mortality among that population. Yet our cultural response to health problems is still a demand for increased spending on medicine.

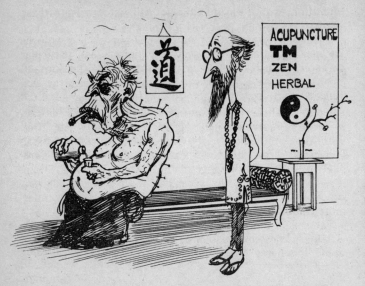

'Just cure the symptoms, doc, but for God's sake
don't ask me to change my way of life.'

What is going wrong?

If something fails, more of the same is applied despite its
failure. For health this has resulted in the creation of massive
additional burdens of iatrogenic (doctor-caused) disease.
Specifically, modern health care with its overuse of drugs,
surgery and technology fails to deal with those conditions
which have become the major killers of our time – the
'diseases of civilisation' such as heart and circulatory disease
(60 per cent of deaths), cancers (25 per cent), immunological
failures, and many chronic debilitating conditions. In the
simplest terms these conditions cannot be 'cured' by medicine because they are products of our way of life and this in
turn is a product of our philosophy. Without a change in
philosophy leading to a different culture and a subsequent

alteration in our way of life, we will not eradicate these modern diseases.[4]

A second aspect of the conventional approach is its focus on specific diseases, their precise symptoms and particular therapies, which dominates Western medical training and health care. Any comparison of the healthy with the sick reveals that susceptibility to illness is a generalised phenomenon; conditions such as poverty, social isolation, stress, bereavement and unhappiness are precursors of all forms of disease. We are naturally highly resilient creatures but many of the things we do break down our resistance to disease and stress our body systems beyond their capacity to adapt.

Can we identify causes of disease and thus avoid them?

To do this we must be prepared to move beyond the classical determinants of health. While retaining the worthwhile insights produced by traditional clinical methods, we need to build a holistic view of our life upon it, creating an understanding of human ecology within the wider context of a planetary ecology. To tackle our current disease problems we have to look critically at our culture and learn how to reject or control those elements which generate disease.

Cancers provide a good illustration. Our bodies produce faulty, potentially malignant cells all the time, and we have mechanisms which deal with them. The question we have to ask is what causes those mechanisms to fail. About 80 per cent of the cancers we suffer are triggered by environmental factors. Our attitude to the environment contributes directly to our growing cancer problems – we treat the planet as an infinite dustbin without regard to where the substances we dump end up. Many cancers are actively stimulated by the effects of radiation; in addition, we have cancers which occur because our body's defences are both overloaded by molecular pollution and reduced by lifestyle and social conditions which undermine resilience.

The modern approach to the cancer problem is to pour untold millions into searching for a 'cure', while upholding the right, for example, of the French government to pollute more of the Pacific with radioactive substances. The holistic approach is to remove the cause, to cut off the pollution at its source, to deny 'rights' which will produce predictable sickness and death.

The combination of attitudes and assumptions which we take from our culture creates disease. Different people have different patterns of strength and weakness which make them susceptible to different forms of illness. Moreover, we suffer the simultaneous effects of a variety of hazards – including poor diet, unsuitable social conditions, environmental pollution, unbalanced and inadequate use of our bodies. The overuse of medicine inevitably worsens the problem because it further disrupts our ecology and lulls us with an illusion of combined hope and helplessness.

How can we create the conditions for human health?

To stop the rot among the human species and re-create health we need an integrated picture of the way humans are intended to live, how they should relate to the biosphere as a whole, and what limits we have to accept because of our intrinsic nature. There are two immediate obstacles to this goal. Firstly, we have not yet evolved the language to describe concepts of health (we universally discuss health in terms of its opposite, illness). Secondly, the wide individual diversity among humans, springing from a resilient, highly adaptable nature, makes simplistic solutions inadequate. With a foothold on outer space, the most important journey of exploration is still within ourselves.

How can individuals maximise their health?

The Greek philosophers provided a sound starting point: 'know thyself'. Our culture encourages us to understand the fine details of many things, but to neglect ourselves. In addition to knowing ourselves, we also need to be able to say 'I understand what is happening to me'; then we can begin to make realistic choices and exert positive control over our lives. Until we can do this we remain random victims, both of causes we initiate and of other factors which are potentially damaging to us. While fulfilling the requirements of the classic determinants of health by changing our lifestyle as necessary, we must then go on to contribute actively to the creation of a sustainable planetary life dynamic. Ultimately, as Theodore Roszak, author of *Beyond the Wasteland*,[5] put it, the health of the person is the health of the planet. They are indivisible, and the further they are apart, the less healthy both will be.

What is holistic medicine? Surely we must have conventional medicine as well?

Holistic medicine looks at the whole person, not just that part apparently causing problems. Conventional doctors are beginning to realise that treating only the symptoms *per se* is not the way to good health. We can see from the way health costs have risen exorbitantly that, despite the knowledge we have accumulated and the tests, treatments and medicines we have developed, we are not healthier.

The two approaches to medicine – the conventional and alternative – can complement each other. But unfortunately, research funding for complementary medicine is desultory, and alternative approaches to conventional medicine are not receiving the recognition they should. Instead they are only available 'privately'.

If we are to create a Green perspective of health we must avoid the medical mentality: perpetually mopping the floor without thinking of turning off the tap that causes the flood. There will always be a variety of choices in dealing with illness, disease and incapacity. Our aim should be to minimise the need for them, rather than making them our priority concern. As individuals we must seek knowledge that will enable us to live in ways which promote rather than degrade our health. Human institutions currently direct their energies towards the accumulation of quantity; in the future we must concentrate on achieving quality in every sphere of life.

The Green Alternative

Will we be able to eradicate all infectious diseases? Won't we in time get the better of AIDS?

We are not eradicating infectious diseases. The World Health Organisation once insisted that malaria had been eradicated, but in the late sixties it staged a dramatic come-back. Schistosomiasis is spreading throughout the world wherever we build large-scale water development schemes, as they provide the ideal habitat for the snails which transmit the disease. Dengue fever and filariasis are spreading to areas where these diseases were previously unknown and in the Western world gonorrhoea is now completely out of control. Even TB is staging a comeback. The only disease that has been eradicated is smallpox.

It is unlikely that AIDS will exterminate mankind. It may well kill off many people but, at present, it seems that only about a fraction of those exposed to the virus actually develop the symptoms that must eventually kill them. Perhaps once the most vulnerable people have been killed off the disease will slowly disappear. This has been the case with other epidemics. In the meantime I doubt very much if we will be able to deal with the AIDS virus by waging chemical warfare against it. The devancement of an effective vaccine is a remote possibility.

Haven't life expectations increased with modern living?

Life expectancy for those who have reached the age of forty has scarcely changed in recent decades, for men or women. Some degenerations seem now to be penetrating younger age-groups than before – you probably know someone under forty who's had a coronary. The next twenty years could easily show a fall in life expectancies.

But quality of life matters too. Old people increasingly exist only as degenerate wrecks of their former selves, whose survival depends on shelter and service provided by younger people. This can scarcely be thought of as human life, and is a highly unsatisfactory end result of social policy. Poor life-long nutrition is very likely a major cause.

Isn't the rate of cancer increasing in our society?

One out of every four or five people in industrialised nations will die from a cancer, and the overall rate of cancer mortality appears to be increasing. We now subject our bodies to a host of chemical poisons, including those in our food; indeed some nutritionists claim that as many as one-third of all cancers can be linked to what we eat. A diet based on wholesome, organically produced food should go far in militating against cancer, as well as against other degenerative diseases of modern civilisation.

Could there be a link between acid rain, aluminium and Alzheimer's disease?

Some 2.5 million Americans suffer from Alzheimer's disease, a form of senile dementia. This degenerative disease, which causes severe loss of memory and mental disorder, now affects 13 per cent of those aged between 75 and 84, and 30 per cent of those older. Proportionately a similar number are affected in Britain. Although originally not considered a hazard to health, aluminium became implicated as a toxin after those who had been on kidney dialysis for several years began to develop mental disorders that paralleled those found in aged people with senile dementia. The large quantities of water used during dialysis had left high amounts of aluminium in the bodies of those treated.

Meanwhile, Dr Daniel Perl, a neuropathologist at the University of Vermont in the USA, found abnormally high concentrations of aluminium in the brains of those who had succumbed to Alzheimer's disease, the aluminium being found in association with abnormal clumps of nerve-cell fibres known as neurofibrillary tangles. Corroborating evidence for aluminium's role in the disease came from Perl's studies of the native Chamorro population of the island of Guam. These people, Sandra Postel of the US Worldwatch Institute points out, suffer a high incidence of neuro-degenerative disorders, and Perl found three to four times more aluminium in the neurofibrillary tangles of diseased islanders compared with tangle-free specimens. Parts of Guam are rich in bauxite, an ore of aluminium.

Acid rain, brought about through the burning of fossil fuels, has lowered the pH of soils and lakes in vulnerable areas. Aluminium is normally insoluble and as such it remains tightly bound up in the soil matrix. Therefore, even though it is the most abundant metal in the earth's crust, it is kept out of harm's way. However, as acidification proceeds aluminium becomes increasingly soluble and mobile, flushing into streams, rivers, lakes and groundwater and into the root system of plants. Some Canadian lakes now have concentrations of aluminium that are three to four times higher than those known to be toxic to fish, while in the Nanticoke river which feeds into the Atlantic from the US east coast aluminium concentrations have been found that are forty times the toxic level for fish.

Should one avoid cooking in aluminium pans?

Anyone who has used an aluminium pan will have come to appreciate how reactive this metal is: various foods, mainly those containing acid like rhubarb or tomatoes, when cooked in aluminium pans take off enough metal to leave a polished surface in the pan, or even to pit it. Another sign of the metal's reaction with foods is that many sauces change colour when left in aluminium pans.

A number of reports indicate that the reaction between aluminium and foods causes, amongst other health effects, diarrhoea in infants. And given the link with Alzheimer's disease, we may have to consider whether aluminium pots should be banned. Even though aluminium pots are not necessarily used in homes, they are widely used in catering.

Is it true that other people's smoking can affect one's own health?

In a closed room non-smokers are subjected to the same toxic substances as the smokers, without the advantage of some toxins being filtered through a cigarette. Sharing a house with someone who smokes twenty cigarettes a day, causes the non-smoker to inhale the equivalent of two cigarettes per week, according to *Which?* magazine. Non-smoking areas of trains, restaurants and work places are on the increase. Children are vulnerable, and have a higher cancer rate than the children of non-smoking parents. Smoking while pregnant is known to be a major risk factor for newborn babies. Not only is the birth weight lower, but the influence of smoke during embryonal development can lead to congenital birth defects.

Are clothes made of artificial fibres bad for us and if so why?

Artificial fibres can actually have a considerable effect on us. This should not come as a surprise, since most of us have noticed how different they feel on the body and that they rapidly acquire an unpleasant odour. Indeed, 'synthetics' engender unpleasant reactions between the fabric, skin and skin bacteria to the point where some people even break out in rashes and eczema. All too seldom is the cause recognised, and the rash alone is treated, usually with cortisone – which then has further harmful impact on the body.

141

The Green Alternative

What do detergents do to us? Are there alternatives?

Some people are allergic to the additional substances which are put into them, such as fluorescent whitening agents. The environmental impact is more direct. Phosphates in detergents have added to the already excessively high load of phosphates entering lakes, thus contributing to algae bloom and to oxygen problems, associated with eutrophication. Some of the new chemicals already being used, like NTA, or being considered to replace phosphates may also be problematic. Some degrade slowly and thus enter the environment either through effluent or through sludge used in agriculture.

Alternatives? Washing products can be bought which minimise the environmental impact – having either little or no phosphate, and a low concentration of other chemicals.

Do we need humidifiers to freshen the air in centrally heated buildings? Or do they use large amounts of electricity?

Humidifiers are required only when rooms are heated so much that the air is dried out. By keeping houses at a reasonable temperature (no more than 20°C) energy demands are reduced and we stay healthier. Plants in a room provide moisture (through photosynthesis) and, surprisingly, help remove smells (a candle burned also gets rid of smells, especially that of tobacco).

Is looking at video screens bad for health?

Television can affect our health in several ways; for example, children tend to sit too close to the television set, certainly exposing themselves to X-rays. Sitting very close to screens, as with computer terminals, for prolonged periods of time has also been associated with a number of problems with eyes, causing headaches, and an increase in mutagenic birth anomalies in children of women working under such conditions during their pregnancies.

Are neon lights bad for health?

Neon lights have been around for a long time, yet there are good reasons for not using them in homes. They give off light in a different way: one to which our eyes respond badly. Such lamps increase adrenalin levels and even lead to skin problems, by affecting hormone levels via eye receptors. Headaches can also be caused because neon lights eliminate shadows and the eye has difficulty adjusting to its surroundings, since it uses shadows for orientation. People working in offices with such lighting often fail to realise what causes their headaches, and end up taking pills for them.

What practical steps can we take now to safeguard our health?

Know yourself. Acknowledge the central importance of a way of life which promotes health. Develop a positive appreciation of yourself. Explore your needs, potential and limitations. Avoid pushing yourself into chronic exhaustion. Be selfish enough to take time, space, and facilities you need to be healthy and fulfilled, to maintain your emotional and spiritual integrity. Unless you know yourself, realistically and honestly, you will find it difficult to love others, and impossible to achieve a love of life in all its forms.

Fulfil and maintain your potential. Technological society has encouraged us to ignore first our emotions, then our bodies, and finally our spiritual needs. For many people intellectual development has taken precedence; each of us needs to redress the balance in the light of a critical self-assessment. The most immediate need for most people is to use their bodies to be physically active and competent. The epidemic of heart disease could be drastically limited if each of us were to walk a couple of brisk miles every day, instead of slipping easily behind the wheel and into degeneration.

Satisfy the requirements of the classical determinants of health. In our society this depends on a blend of political and personal choices. Nothing stops you acting in both spheres.

Learn to trust and rely on nature. Specifically, eat organically grown foods, campaign for clean air and pure water. Deal with illness by seeking to improve health through positive action rather than suppressing symptoms with medicine. Generally support and assist those who provide for human need by working with nature, rather than fighting against it.

Minimise your resource demands. Create your own energy, either by walking or biking for transport, and by improving your metabolism so that you avoid disease and do not need to be expensively heated. Wherever possible return your wastes to the soil as useful components of the interrelated cycles of life.

Clarify your expectations. Our society rewards us with material goods, status and the chance to show off. To minimise stress and dissatisfaction you must examine the validity and value of what you have been led to expect from life. Many of us wonder why our parents devoted themselves to the system of their day, for so little of substance or happiness, without being able to apply the same critical eye to our own situation. Would those 1 million people who died of avoidable heart and circulatory disease in the last three years in Britain follow the same life pattern to early disease and death if they could choose again? Your time of choice is now. The final aim should be a re-orientation of your life goals.

Accept that your freedom ends where that of others begins. The most unacceptable face of mechanistic philosophy is the way we exploit animals, frequently to extinction. If we can extend loving ourselves into a liberalisation and tolerance towards others of our own species, we may pave the way to accepting the 'right' to life of other species. Eventually we may encompass the needs of the planet within our consciousness, and behave accordingly.

Achieve a conceptual shift. For positive health we need a species-wide shift in consciousness. This major undertaking begins with the many small details which make up our picture of the reality of our own existence. The way you think about everything is very important, because in changing the way you think you help to change the minds of others; you contribute to an alteration in our species which will in turn change our cultural base. Changing human culture is the only long-term answer to the diseases that originate in that culture, those 'diseases of civilisation'. Your change to a healthy way of thinking is the most positive action you can take.

Improve the world on a day-to-day basis. Everywhere in the environment we have created humans are in retreat. Our predominant state of non-health is itself a symptom of this. In the pursuit of health we must avoid the trap of improving ourselves to become better servants of the processes which are causing the retreat. Our need is a restoration of human values and human scale in our day-to-day affairs; we need to re-create the sense of our own value, not in relation to what we can dominate or command, but for what we actually are and can be.

6 Energy

Through industrialisation we have created societies with far greater demands for energy and other basic resources such as metals, minerals and oil, than at any other time in history. In the Stone Age each individual probably consumed on average some 10,000 to 12,000 kilocalories of energy per day, one-third of which would have been taken in as food, the remainder being used as fuel for cooking and warmth. By the end of the Middle Ages total energy consumption per individual had doubled, the smelting of metals and forging of iron implements and weapons leading to considerably greater demands on resources, including wood for charcoal, compared with a Stone Age lifestyle. Today the average individual energy consumption in an affluent consumer society is some fifty times greater than one of our neolithic forebears and at least twenty times greater than someone in a country such as India. And of course high-spending, affluent people can use two or three times more energy still.

In the early 1970s, energy planners in the industrialised nations anticipated that world energy demand would continue to double every decade as it had since the Second World War. Indeed, they talked of meeting a world energy demand by about 2020 of at least fifty to sixty times that of the 1970s. To achieve this growth we are faced with the problem not simply of finding the resources to fuel future demands, but of laying down the infrastructure for producing and utilising the fuel, especially when, as with power stations, the utilities have a life of only a few decades at best. Thus, should the world double its energy needs every decade, then after sixty years not only would sixty-four times more energy be used, but in the last ten years of that period more energy would be consumed than in all the previous five decades put together. Such is exponential growth. And the same problems would apply to the infrastructure -- as many new power stations, oil rigs, refineries, coal mines, transportation systems having to be built up in one decade as had ever operated before. All the same, energy demand did not, in fact, increase but reached a peak in 1979 and has fallen since. It is now back to 1973 levels.

Despite the insuperable problems of growth, we in the UK, in common with many other countries, have still been told that our standards will fall unless we continue the drive to consume more energy. Such was the evidence given by the Central Electricity Generating Board at the Sizewell Public Inquiry.

Meanwhile, the UK Atomic Energy Authority has pleaded for a rapid deployment of nuclear power insofar as: 'Energy provides the power to progress. With a sufficiency of energy properly applied a people can rise from subsistence level to the highest standard of living.'

Have we in Britain not yet reached that sufficiency? Is that why our society is increasingly impoverished? And how is it that in Africa, where there has been a steady growth in energy use over the past few decades, more misery and starvation exists than ever before?

In Britain we should be setting out to improve the efficiency of energy use through energy conservation. An Earth Resources Research study shows that gross national product in the United Kingdom, which is one measure of the standard of living, could improve significantly in terms of human well-being while overall energy consumption is substantially reduced. ERR believes it practical for energy to fall from a consumption of 369 millions of tonnes of coal equivalent (mtce) in the year 1979–80 to 259 mtce by the year 2000. Moreover, electricity demand in ERR's analysis could be reduced to just over half that of 1979–80, with no fall in standards, through energy conservation and improved efficiency of use. Still hooked on growth, the CEGB anticipates a rise of at least 10 per cent by then.

Sweden has shown that where there is a will, there is a way. There the government has called for a 30 per cent cut in the energy used to heat buildings without any reduction in standards, and Swedish city councils have embarked on a programme to insulate the existing housing stock while laying down strict standards for new buildings. The policy is working well, even ahead of target. Sweden is also cutting back on oil as a heating fuel, and in less than 10 years cities such as Malmo have switched from almost total dependence on oil-fired boilers for their district heating systems to a combination of coal-fired plants, geothermal energy, biomass energy from coppiced willow, industrial waste heat, heat extracted from sewage and upgraded with heat pumps and refuse incineration.

Undoubtedly, cheap petroleum lulled us into a false sense of security and we now expect new forms of energy – nuclear power for instance – to take the place of crude oil. Yet electricity generated by nuclear power is five times more costly in conventional economic terms than energy from oil, and is far less versatile. Moreover, cheap uranium is a limited commodity and only by generating plutonium in sufficient quantities for burning in fast-breeder reactors can uranium resources be expanded to make a proper dent in the future energy demands of an industrialised world. And should we dare pin our faith and energy security on a machine that uses tonnes of plutonium for fuel – enough for a thousand warheads at a time?

If we opt for the nuclear pathway to solve our energy problems we will face the prospect of accidents far worse than Chernobyl. While thermal reactors like those at Chernobyl or at Three Mile Island in the United States can suffer massive hydrogen or steam explosions – enough to breach any containment – a fast reactor has the potential to explode like an atomic bomb. No sane society would ever accept nuclear power.

On the other hand we cannot continue to release carbon dioxide and other exhaust gases into the atmosphere without harmful consequences. Evidence is accumulating that the greenhouse effect of such gases is beginning to manifest itself, and global temperatures are rising. If they rise several degrees (centigrade) it could well be devastating for world agriculture. Meanwhile, acid rain is causing problems for Europe's lakes, forests and soils.

The alternative is one we have to grasp: of reducing our

overall energy demands while improving energy efficiency and developing more benign technologies. Otherwise the future of mankind may be bleak indeed.

Could we run out of energy?

No. As energy resources become scarcer, prices will rise and consumption will fall, as happened following the 1973 Arab oil embargo. We still have considerable reserves of fossil fuels: at present consumption, enough commercially exploitable oil to last 100 years. Geologists in the oil industry evaluate ultimate worldwide reserves of petroleum from conventional sources at some 250 to 300 billion tonnes, therefore at most some 2,000 billion barrels. Despite improvements in the percentage of petroleum recovered from 25 per cent in 1977 to an anticipated 40 per cent in the year 2000, the expectation is that production will peak in the 1990s at between 4 and 5 billion tonnes of oil per year and then will decline to approximately half that value by the year 2030, to dwindle away still more over the remainder of the twenty-first century.

But fossil fuel reserves, such as North Sea oil, should be exploited gradually. However, the oil companies need a high rate of oil flow from the wells to make them profitable, and the current rapid exploitation of these reserves is politically and economically disastrous.

Annual consumption of natural gas is just over the equivalent of 1 billion barrels of oil; meanwhile proved reserves are some fifty times greater at 50 billion barrels, with remaining undiscovered reserves estimated at more than three times that – some 185 billion tonnes of oil equivalent. Unconventional sources of natural gas, from coal beds, from shales, biomass and geo-pressured resources could conceivably double the production potential again. Therefore natural gas supplies should be available for another century at least, possibly as much as 300 years. Petroleum too could last several centuries at more modest rates of consumption than are currently experienced.

The Green Alternative

Annual world coal production is some 2.6 billion tonnes. While present-day world coal resources are estimated at more than 10,000 billion tonnes, exploitable reserves are put at a much lower figure of 640 billion tonnes, giving some 250 years of production at current rates. In the mid 1970s various energy analysts predicted that coal production would triple over the next thirty years. Given the economic conditions prevailing in the 1980s and likely to continue into the next century, it seems most unlikely that coal production will ever need to reach such high levels. At the same time the environmental consequences of producing and consuming that volume of coal would be immense, whether through degradation of the land from mining or through atmospheric pollution.

Could we reduce energy consumption without affecting our quality of life?

There is no simple relationship between energy consumption *per capita* and quality of life, nor between energy consumption and gross national product (GNP), or economic activity generally. For example, West Germany uses about half the energy for each unit of industrial output as Britain. It is becoming clear that reduced energy consumption can equate with increased economic activity and greater comfort.

In the first place, reduced expenditure on energy takes less of one's disposable income. Secondly, national energy conservation can increase the quality of life for many thousands of people by providing them with jobs, can reduce pollution and road traffic, result in better health and – if small-scale renewable energy schemes are developed – increase self-reliance and community participation.

What contribution should electricity be making to our overall energy needs?

The point is that electricity is inappropriate for many purposes. The need for it would be substantially reduced by a commitment to energy conservation and a sensible energy strategy, using, for example, coal and gas for most heating purposes, geothermally heated water for space and process heating, and developing combined-heat-and-power schemes wherever possible. At present electricity accounts for about 15 per cent of our energy needs; this could be reduced to 8 per cent, with most of it coming from a few large tidal and wave-power schemes.

Would it be possible to decentralise our energy supply system?

The present trend is towards a capital-intensive and central control of gas and electricity grids, with the coal industry managed in an increasingly autocratic way by the National Coal Board (now British Coal) and the oil industry controlled by a few large multinational companies.

While other countries, like Denmark and Austria, are moving towards decentralisation, the CEGB remains blind to the merits of an electricity grid fed by many small supply units. But such a grid would be far safer from industrial disruption and far more flexible to operate than the present British grid. Also, it is more economical to generate electricity as close as possible to the point of consumption.

Ought we to retain a sizeable coal industry?

Coal is an efficient fuel since very little energy is lost when converting it to useful heat. In comparison, when we heat by electricity we lose over 90 per cent of the fuel's primary energy because of the inefficiency of the transmission systems and electrical appliances. There are considerable UK coal reserves and Britain has indigenous expertise in both coal recovery and utilisation. We would be foolish to pretend that there are no hazards connected with the mining and burning of coal, but many of these hazards can be substantially overcome with existing technology. At present some 100 million tonnes of coal per year are produced in the UK, with the CEGB taking between 70 and 75 million tonnes. Should the CEGB's new power stations be nuclear, then the coal consumed would be greatly reduced, thus having a major effect on the coal industry.

A sensible UK energy strategy should include an output of about 90 million tonnes per year, including the continued mining of low-sulphur coal from Scotland and south Wales.

Can we really risk being dependent on the coal mines? Isn't the CEGB right to seek diversity of fuel in its strategy?

In 1983 coal was the single most important fuel in the UK, marginally displacing oil. The reason for the mild resurgence of coal is that it is economically attractive. In comparable, measurable units, coal is the cheapest fuel on the market. Its price is more likely to hold down than that of other fossil fuels because of the abundance of very good quality coal.

In fact, diversity, to the CEGB, means either oil, which is finite and will become expensive again (it added £2.2 billion to the CEGB bill for 1984); nuclear, which will become increasingly unacceptable; or imported coal. This latter was attractive in 1981 when the sterling exchange rate was high but at present the only cheap coal that is attractive is South African, and some Australian strip-mined coal. Denmark no longer imports coal from South Africa, partly for political reasons but also because of uncertainty of supply, for which reason it also cut off coal imports from Poland. Alternatives are Colombia and India, although political instability in both countries could disrupt supplies. So why abandon our own coal industry when we are likely to run into problems importing from other countries?

Really the issue is one of long-term strategy. Because of the nature of the industry a short-term run-down like that in the late sixties, which had to be reversed, could prove very costly. Consumers have good reason to prefer putting their trust in the UK coal industry because it is a high-tech industry with a skilled body of men, who deliver fuel at a lower cost than any competitor. Diversity into nuclear or foreign coal increases risk, uncertainty and cost.

What really then is the cost of importing coal?

The cost of importing coal is likely to remain relatively high, although sellers have been losing money. The cost of imported coal also depends on the exchange rate and unless it rises to $1.70 to the £ imported coal does not look economically attractive to Britain over any reasonable length of time. For example, coal mined in West Virginia at $25 a ton costs $60–70 to the UK buyer. Indeed, the cost of American coal doubles by the time it reaches Rotterdam and to that has to be added the cost of shipping to the Thames and then inland. At present the UK has little capacity for berthing ships of over 100,000 tons – and probably no more than 10 million tonnes a year can be brought in that way.

Can pits be re-opened, once closed, if the nation needs their coal?

Once closed, a pit rapidly deteriorates through flooding and shaft and tunnel collapse and becomes impossible to re-open: indeed, for safety purposes, most old mines are deliberately flooded and collapsed. Hence coal reserves in many of the older, traditional coalfields have been effectively sterilised. It now appears likely that all pits with a productivity of less than 1,000 tonnes per man per year will be closed, leaving hardly any deep mines in Scotland, Wales or the north-east of England and concentrating British coal production in Yorkshire and the Midlands. Reserves in these areas will be exhausted relatively rapidly and, because sizeable reserves elsewhere have in effect been written off, British theoretical reserves of over 300 years at current production levels will be reduced to less than 60 years.

Shouldn't we applaud the use of new mining techniques using machines rather than men?

In general, we should welcome the increasing use of mechanisation in unpleasant, unhealthy and dangerous workplaces. Improving pit working environments also tends to increase their productivity, and the mining unions have generally co-operated in the introduction of new technology. However, we must recognise the consequences of a labour-intensive industry being transformed into a capital-intensive one. Coal miners lose their jobs and those who remain lose the camaraderie of coalface work. The new automated system (MINOS), which controls mechanical coal-cutting, conveying and loading, is seen as essential for the efficiency of the new super-pits, such as Selby. But mines using such systems share the major disadvantage that they lack flexibility and therefore fail to exploit fully their potential.

Are there any clean, efficient methods of producing coal-based electricity?

Pressurised fluidised-bed combustion (PFBC) takes place in a furnace when the coal fire bed is fluidised by the combustion air blown upwards through it. This type of combustion is extremely efficient. It can be used for the desulphurisation of coal by using a suitable material, such as powdered limestone to make up the bed of the furnace. The lime reacts with the sulphur in the fuel, forming solid calcium sulphate, so preventing the emission of sulphur oxides. Moreover, because of lower combustion temperatures, nitrogen oxide emission is acceptably low. PFBC, when used for combined heat-and-power (CHP) would be about 40 per cent more efficient than a normal coal-burning, electricity generating station, with greatly reduced pollution. However, a large investment would be required to install PFBC equipment into present coal-fired power stations and, although the technique seems well-suited for stations up to 100 megawatt (the CEGB are now building stations in the 1000-megawatt range) or for CHP schemes, it may not be for large power stations.

It is another nettle the CEGB refuses to grasp. During the current outcry over acid rain the authorities could, instead of promoting nuclear power, tackle the problem at source and introduce PFBC. In Stockholm, Sweden, the Värten CHP plant is to be fitted with two coal-fired pressurised fluidised-bed combustion modules. Altogether these will deliver 131 megawatt (MW) of electricity and 215 MW of heat to the city. Sulphur emissions from the plant will be reduced by 80 per cent compared with the present oil-fired plant and nitrogen oxides by 50 per cent. Moreover, being efficient and compact, it will not disturb the Stockholm skyline. It can be done.

Wouldn't a few large power stations make electricity cheaper than lots of small ones?

In theory, the economies of scale involved in a 2000 MW power station should make it produce cheaper electricity than a small power station could. However, costs, per kilowatt, are notoriously difficult to calculate and the CEGB has been accused (even by bodies such as the Monopolies and Mergers Commission) of manipulating its figures to make an expanded nuclear power programme look attractive. A strategy of having a few large power stations means that the national grid cannot cope with an unexpectedly high electricity demand if several of these are out of commission at once – hence the CEGB has opted for great over-capacity. They actually need about 22 per cent, but at present they have more than 40 per cent over-capacity. Scotland has the capacity in its power stations to produce almost twice as much electricity as it needs.

We also have to consider power station efficiency. Large power stations typically operate at about 30 per cent efficiency, wasting between two out of three and three out of four tonnes of fuel burned. In contrast, small combined-heat-and-power stations can be 75 per cent efficient through combining electricity production with useful heat. Furthermore, CHP plants have low construction costs, can burn waste materials and produce cheap heat for sale to industry or to domestic consumers. The CEGB would have far greater security of supply and greater flexibility if it incorporated electricity from a large number of small generating alternatives using tidal, wave, wind and geothermal power in addition to fossil fuel.

The Green Alternative

If we choose liquefaction or gasification of coal, what will be the environmental consequences?

These are both options being seriously considered by the fuel industries: liquefaction as a substitute for oil, and gasification in place of natural gas. Most research is being done in the USA, but as North Sea oil and gas production begins to diminish, there is an increasing motivation for UK research and development. Coal can be gasified before being burned in a power station (as in the Texaco gasification process being tried out in California) or *in situ* in coal mines. However, when a primary fuel such as coal is converted into something else before being used by the consumer there is a huge loss of energy. For example, the extraction efficiency for *in situ* coal gasification is at most 30 per cent and often as low as 5 per cent, and the space left in the ground after the coal has been gasified is likely to lead to subsidence problems. This is therefore not an environmentally acceptable option.

With all the fuss about acid rain isn't it sensible to phase out the burning of fossil fuels in power stations?

No energy source is completely benign. Thus we have to compare the costs and benefits of fossil fuel burning with an energy strategy involving no fossil fuel use. About 97 per cent of the industrial energy consumed in the world comes from fossil fuels and in the UK 87 per cent of total energy consumption comes from oil, coal and gas. Electricity consumption accounts for 15 per cent of our total energy use, but about 83 per cent of our electricity comes from fossil-fuel power stations. Thus it would be quite unrealistic, even in the long-term, to phase out fossil fuels.

Dependence on fossil fuels can be reduced by increasing fuel efficiency and conserving energy in industry, commerce and houses. In addition, toxic emissions from power stations can be reduced to negligible levels by the introduction of readily available cleansing techniques. Many of the problems associated with acid rain arise out of the strategy of dispersing emissions from power plants and industry through very tall stacks. The Green answer is to control pollutants before emission.

Carbon dioxide, however, remains a problem because nearly as much energy would be required in entrapping it as is released from fossil fuel burning in the first place. CHP, by doubling the efficiency of energy end-use would reduce by a substantial amount the carbon dioxide problem in countries such as the UK.

The problem of transport emissions would only be solved by improved vehicle efficiency and a reduction in movement.

What is the problem with carbon dioxide?

The greenhouse effect of carbon dioxide has now become a major issue. Over the next century the carbon dioxide (CO_2) content of the atmosphere is likely to double from its pre-industrial levels of some 260 parts per million. Such a rise will probably lead to a 2 to 3 degrees centigrade increase in the global average surface temperature. That increase will be the biggest change to climate in many millions of years. Apart from dramatic disturbances to weather and rainfall patterns, the temperature rise will lead to the sea rising by one metre or more just through the thermal expansion of water. Once ice-melting over the Poles takes place, the sea will begin to rise rapidly possibly by as much as 30 metres or more and many of the major cities in the world – such as London and New York, as well as most of the Netherlands – would be submerged. To put the energy effect into perspective, doubling atmospheric CO_2 will have an 80 times greater effect on the global energy balance than the heat generated by the burning of fossil fuels and biomass that has given rise to the increase in CO_2 in the first place.

The burning of fossil fuels is undoubtedly a prime cause of the perceptible annual increase in carbon dioxide. But the destruction of forests, both through burning and decay are also adding to the CO_2 burden, the contribution from that source being almost as great as that from fossil fuel burning – in the range of some 5 billion tonnes of CO_2 per year.

The Green Alternative

Coal and oil pollute and are finite whereas nuclear power is clean and perpetual. So why are Greens opposed to nuclear power?

Coal and oil produce toxic substances only because we do not burn them efficiently. Strict pollution controls would reduce the environmental effects of burning hydrocarbons to less than 20 per cent of their present level. The CEGB and the Atomic Energy Authority (AEA) spend much public money promoting nuclear power.

In reality, nuclear power stations are extremely hazardous, as are the installations for mining, handling and reprocessing nuclear fuel. Radiation is continuously released from nuclear plants, with long-term health effects such as cancer, which may not show for many years. The plutonium released into the Irish Sea from Sellafield has made this the most radioactive sea in the world. The unsolved problem of disposal of long-term nuclear waste causes great public concern. We have seen the first results of the Chernobyl accident. A major nuclear power station accident, hi-jack or sabotage in Britain or France could happen and could result in the deaths of many thousands of people and the 'sterilising' of many square miles of British land for centuries to come. Also, although uranium is relatively plentiful at the moment, the richest ores being located in Central and South Africa, Australia, Canada and the USSR, it will become politically more difficult to obtain as demands grow for fuelling the increasing numbers of nuclear power stations.

Isn't nuclear power a cheap and effective alternative to coal?

Both the government and the nation have been misled by propaganda and creative accounting. The nuclear industry pretends that its electricity costs less than coal- or oil-produced electricity, but many independent studies of nuclear economics, including those done by the Monopolies and Mergers Commission and the House of Commons Select Committee on Energy, have revealed serious shortcomings in CEGB accounting practices. It is now beyond dispute that nuclear-generated electricity is about one-third more expensive than electricity from coal-fired stations. There is certainly no economic case to be made for the development of nuclear power.

What exactly is nuclear power?

Nuclear power stations produce heat which is used to generate steam for turbines. In principle, nuclear reactors use uranium as fuel. Uranium, like other minerals, is associated with rocks (in particular igneous rock such as granite), which are mined when an ore of sufficient richness is found. Uranium also leaches out of rocks and can be found in alluvial deposits, as well as in low concentrations in the sea. Uranium exists in several isotopes, by far the most common being uranium-238 (99.3 per cent). Uranium-238 is mildly radioactive, having a rate of transformation (or half-life) of some 4.7 billion years. For mankind, the important isotope of uranium is uranium-235 which therefore has three neutrons less in its nucleus and comprises some 0.7 per cent of uranium found naturally. Uranium-235 has a half-life indicating that it is intrinsically less stable than uranium-238. When a U-235 atom spontaneously undergoes transformation, neutrons and energy are released. In naturally occurring uranium, uranium-235 atoms are widely separated from each other in terms of atomic distances and the neutrons released from one spontaneous transformation of uranium pass through the ore material, gradually losing their considerable energies but without, in general, effecting any further transformations. Should, however, a released neutron strike another uranium-235 atom, there is a chance that fission will take place, and the already unstable U-235 atom will itself transform, releasing more neutrons in its turn.

The idea behind a nuclear-fission reactor is that it uses those released neutrons to keep a chain reaction going. The chain reaction is kept strictly under control because otherwise an atomic bomb, where the aim is to achieve as much fission in as short a space of time as possible, could be created. The reactor therefore extends over its twenty-thirty year operating life that which takes place in milliseconds in an atomic bomb.

How is controlled fission achieved?

When released, neutrons travel at speeds up to 10,000 miles per second. In developing nuclear reactors, physicists realised that a chain reaction would be more easily achieved if those neutrons could be slowed down. It is rather like crossing a busy road with one's eyes shut – the faster one runs, given the same volume of traffic, the less likely one is to be struck, and if one could go very fast, then the chances of being run down become increasingly improbable. The nuclear engineer wants to get as many collisions as possible for the number of neutrons released, and he achieves that by placing a material such as graphite or heavy water between the finely divided uranium fuel. Those materials slow the neutrons down without absorbing them to any degree; the neutrons are thus moderated and the materials used are moderators. Some moderators are better than others. Water containing heavy hydrogen (deuterium) is, for instance, better than ordinary 'light' water. Yet 'heavy' water is expensive to produce while 'light' water is bountiful and cheap.

Another way to achieve the chain reaction is to increase the proportion of U-235 in the uranium fuel – in other words to enrich it. To use the traffic analogy again, it is like increasing the volume and density of traffic on the road. Therefore, in light-water reactors the fuel is enriched in U-235 from its natural level of 0.7 per cent to some 3 per cent. Enrichment will also enable greater power densities in the reactor core, making the machine more compact and enabling higher coolant temperatures so that the thermodynamic efficiencies of electricity generation are improved. Britain's Magnox reactors use natural uranium fuel, carbon dioxide as coolant gas and graphite as moderator. The advanced gas reactors use slightly enriched fuel and therefore operate at higher temperatures.

If the fuel is enriched to more than 15 per cent with fissile material, then no moderator is needed. The fast reactor operates on that principle, the designation 'fast' referring to the speed of the neutrons, which keep a speed of 10,000 miles per second. The uranium-238 isotope also plays a role in the operation of nuclear power. When U-238 is struck by a neutron it does not undergo fission – instead it absorbs the neutron into itself and transforms into plutonium-239, which itself is a fissile material like U-235. Plutonium is therefore gradually produced in a nuclear reactor. It can be extracted from the fuel taken out of the reactor core by chemical means in a 'reprocessing' plant.

The fast reactor is designed to operate on plutonium-based fuel. The idea is also to surround the plutonium-rich core with a 'blanket' or covering of uranium-238. Neutrons which escape the core without having brought about fission are absorbed into the blanket and cause more plutonium to be made. In principle the fast reactor should be able to produce as much fuel or more than is consumed, so that all the potential energy in uranium, both in U-235 and U-238, is used, multiplying the total energy by at least sixty times, although that energy will not be released in one go, but over many centuries of nuclear power operation.

Another possibility is to use thorium, another naturally occurring radioactive substance, as blanket material. The thorium transforms to uranium-233 which is also fissile. However the U-233 is more difficult to handle (though not more dangerous) than plutonium, and the uranium–thorium cycle has not been pursued so vigorously as the uranium–plutonium one.

What about Chernobyl – has that made a difference to the public's perception of nuclear power?

The accident which began just before midnight (GMT) on Friday 25 April at the Chernobyl Number 4 reactor in the Ukraine, some eighty kilometres north of Kiev, was undoubtedly the worst ever to hit a large nuclear reactor. Yet that accident was by no means unique in that other reactors have suffered serious accidents, including that at the Three Mile Island Number 2 reactor at Harrisburg, Pennsylvania in 1979.

The Green Alternative

The fear, particularly with reactors such as the pressurised water reactor (PWR) at Three Mile Island, which have high power densities, is that if coolant is lost the exposed core will melt its way through the pressure vessel and concrete containment and will contaminate groundwater, the so-called 'China Syndrome'.

The waste radioactive material – amounting to millions of curies – generates considerable quantities of heat. That heat is sufficient to cause meltdown in the absence of a coolant circulation. In fact, the possibility of molten fuel burning its way through the bottom of the reactor was considered by the USSR scientists and engineers called in to deal with the Chernobyl accident, and was a prime reason why the water was drained from around the base of the reactor and a new concrete containment constructed. On the other hand, the USSR reactor known as RBMK has a much lower power density than the PWRs of the USA, and it may be that a loss of coolant cannot lead to high enough temperatures to cause the zirconium-niobium alloy that contains the uranium fuel to melt. To that extent at least the RBMK might be safer than a PWR.

Yet whatever the relative safety of the USSR reactor compared to other kinds of reactor, the explosion which ripped open the concrete reactor encasement and blew a cloud of radioactive material through a hole in the roof of the reactor building produced a coating of radioactive material through much of the northern hemisphere which in some areas, such as Bavaria in West Germany, equalled the fall-out from all the atmospheric weapons testing of the 1950s and '60s. Over the next few years people in those places which received the worst fall-out from Chernobyl will be exposed to a radiation dose which will effectively double the dose they would normally receive from natural background radiation.

Unless one has a complete map of the fall-out it is hard to estimate the precise numbers of people who are likely to suffer premature death from cancer as a result of the radiation. Barry Lambert, a radiobiologist at St Bartholomew's Hospital in London, for instance has calculated that Chernobyl will cause some 500 additional cancers in the UK over the next thirty to forty years. Yet those 500 must be put into perspective against 7 million who will die of cancer in Britain over the same period. Over the northern hemisphere as a whole many thousands will be affected, and that without taking into account the foetal deaths and congenital abnormalities.

The main lesson for people in Europe is that a nuclear accident on the scale of Chernobyl, and it is possible to envisage much worse accidents, can heavily contaminate areas thousands of kilometres away to the point where it is no longer safe to eat local produce. Gävle, to the north of Stockholm in Sweden was some 1000 kilometres away from Chernobyl, yet it received a level of contamination that made it unsafe to let animals out to graze several months after the accident. The lambs of North Wales, Cumbria and Scotland, which were found to have unacceptable levels of radioactive contamination were even further away from Chernobyl.

After the accident, the reluctance of the government to release precise information about fall-out and contamination of air, soil, water and food, made the public become increasingly suspicious that the truth was being withheld. Not surprisingly perceptions of nuclear power have shifted. Whereas before Chernobyl the public was more or less equally divided for and against nuclear power in Britain, after Chernobyl some 64 per cent of those asked in a poll commissioned by the Central Electricity General Board were against a continuation of the nuclear power programme, with 53 per cent wanting a complete ban. Farmers in particular have realised how vulnerable they are to a nuclear accident: they can be put totally out of business as the public turns away from their products through fear of radioactive contamination.

What other accidents have there been?

In October 1957 one of two plutonium-producing atomic piles at Sellafield caught fire and released a cloud of radioiodine which swept across Europe – some 20,000 curies (3.7×10^{10} becquerels per curie, each becquerel representing one transformation per second of a radioactive element into another element with the release of energy and radioactive particles) went into the atmosphere. Because the thyroid gland takes up iodine, over the following years there will have been an inevitable increase in the incidence of thyroid cancer, although barely detectable given the size of the population concerned.

When radioiodine undergoes radioactive transformation, it releases energy in the form of gamma rays (like powerful X-rays) as well as beta particles, which are energetic electrons. Some radioactive elements, such as plutonium, release alpha particles on transformation. Compared to other radioactive particles, alpha particles are extremely heavy, and although they cannot penetrate far, once inside the body they are between ten and twenty times more likely to cause cancers. Polonium-210, a particularly toxic and carcinogenic element because of its alpha particle emissions, was also released by the Sellafield fire. Because polonium was being used as a trigger for nuclear weapons, for defence reasons the escape of polonium was not admitted by the government, and it took a discerning statistician, John Urquhart at Newcastle University, to dig out the evidence more than twenty years later. Because of polonium's virulence, Urquhart estimated several thousand people might have contracted cancer.

The USSR also suffered a disastrous explosion at Kyshtym in the Urals during the winter of 1957. Some thirty villages had to be evacuated and there were a great many radiation victims, although precise numbers have never been revealed. Like the USSR, the West, including Britain and the USA, kept silent over the disaster; the USSR was probably embarrassed, the Western powers were probably intent on building up an arsenal of nuclear weapons and did not want the public to realise the real hazards of radioactive fall-out.

At Three Mile Island, a pressurised water reactor (PWR) in America, there was a partial core melt-down and a hydrogen explosion which, fortuitously, did not breach the concrete containment.

Lord Marshall, chairman of the CEGB, called the Chernobyl reactor 'a hybrid . . . a chimera'. Does that mean it was particularly unsafe, compared with the reactors in the West?

The Chernobyl reactor has many features common to Western reactors. All reactor designs are a compromise between safety and economics, although some – like the Chernobyl reactor, the Hanford reactors in Washington State, the Magnox reactors in the UK and the CANDU reactors in Canada – were originally designed to generate weapons-grade plutonium as a by-product. The Hanford and Chernobyl reactors are very similar in design, using graphite as a moderator and light water as coolant. While the Chernobyl and CANDU reactors use similar pressure tubes to carry coolant through the uranium oxide core, the nine Hanford reactors take water directly from the Savannah river, which has been seriously contaminated on a number of occasions. The Hanford reactors, all built for military purposes, date from the 1940s and the Manhattan project, in which British and American scientists cooperated in the development of the atomic bombs later dropped on Japan.

None of these early reactors, any more than the early British Magnox reactors at Calder Hall and Chapelcross, have adequate containment. The features shared with Chernobyl are sufficient for grave concern.

Do particular problems arise from using graphite as a moderator?

Moderators slow down the neutrons released during the fissioning of uranium so that the neutrons are more likely to 'hit' another fissile uranium atom and the chain reaction can be sustained. A moderator enables either natural or fissile fuel partially enriched with uranium-235 to be used. Graphite makes a good moderator because relatively few neutrons are lost through absorption during their slowing. However, should oxygen find its way into the reactor, and air comes into contact with graphite, this will burn at low temperatures.

The Green Alternative

Graphite warps through neutron bombardment and has to be allowed to regain its shape by being heated up carefully so that the stored energy – Wigner energy – is released.

Besides a Chernobyl-type accident, are other kinds of explosions conceivable in reactors?

During the Three Mile Island accident, hydrogen built up in the reactor, but luckily, a second large hydrogen bubble shrank of its own accord without exploding. Another type of explosion which is theoretically possible is a steam explosion, brought about when molten metal plunges into water. This could happen in any reactor containing water either as coolant or moderator, or both, and could be large enough to breach the most rugged concrete containment. Pressurised water reactors in particular are susceptible to pressure vessel failure and to accidents through loss of coolant. Meanwhile experiments on pressure vessels and steel containment structures indicated that in an explosion they are likely to fragment into relatively small pieces. France has built two fast reactors, one of which has shut down. They use large quantities of plutonium – some 5.5 tonnes in the French Super-phenix fast reactor. Theoretically these could explode like atomic bombs, with yields of 3 kilotons of TNT or more.

What happened at Chernobyl?

A hydrogen explosion severely damaged the reactor. Control was lost, overheating occurred, and a major release of radiation entered the atmosphere. It was the largest nuclear accident in the world. According to the official Soviet report delivered to the International Atomic Energy Agency in Vienna during mid-August 1986, the prime cause of the accident was an unauthorised experiment being conducted on the Number 4 reactor in which the emergency cooling system and other safety systems were shut down purposely. Those present in the reactor control room were interviewed on their deathbeds by the authorities. The authorities gleaned that the operators were trying to determine whether the residual heat in a reactor operating at minimal power would be sufficient to keep a turbo-generator going so that it could provide on-site electricity for the vital control systems that reactors need. A back-up electricity supply is required in case there should be a power failure or emergency shut-down, and all nuclear power stations have several sets of diesel generators. The operators were trying to establish, therefore, how long they would have before they needed to get the diesel plant in operation.

Within minutes of the experiment starting the reactor was, said the leader of the Soviet delegation, Academician Valery Legasov, 'without any means of control, and free to do as it wished'. Ironically, as the test began, power in the reactor dropped below the levels predicted and more cooling water entered the reactor core than was needed. With core pressure dropping, air bubbles formed in one of the intake pumps and stemmed the flow of cooling water. The original situation was suddenly transformed from one of excess coolant to a shortage, and temperatures in the core began to rise rapidly. Yet, in trying to raise the power when it had dropped, the operators had pulled out the control rods. The reactor was now in a runaway state where everything conspired to make it become hotter and hotter.

What are the particular dangers of the Chernobyl-type reactor?

RBMK reactors such as those at Chernobyl suffer from one inherent fault. If too much steam is generated in the core, either because of insufficient coolant getting to the reactor, or because of a pressure drop, then the rate of the chain reaction of the nuclear fuel speeds up. That in turn raises the temperature still more, which leads to greater reactivity in its turn – and so on. By the time the Chernobyl operators dropped the control rods into the core, to try to bring down the reaction, it was too late – power in the reactor had surged to some 100 times maximum operating power in a matter of seconds.

Enormous steam pressures were generated, fracturing pressure tubes within the reactor core. Then the steam itself began to interact with the zirconium metal used in the construction of the pressure tubes and the cladding for the uranium oxide fuel, generating hydrogen gas. The huge build-up of hydrogen and steam inside the Number 4 reactor caused a two-foot thick steel liner surrounding the core to give way, followed by the six-foot thick concrete containment. The escaping hydrogen now mixed with air, and exploded, hurling massive chunks of concrete through the reactor hall and toppling the 200-tonne refuelling crane. This in turn crashed down on the core, smashing it open and exposing the 1,900-tonne assembly of graphite blocks and uranium oxide fuel to a mixture of superheated steam and air. In the aftermath of the explosion, the graphite burst into flame and, like coke in a steel furnace, began to burn vigorously. The initial steam and hydrogen explosion brought about the first release of radioactive debris, sending it higher than 1,500 metres into the atmosphere through the destroyed reactor containment and the station roof, from where, carried by prevailing winds, it reached Sweden some thirty-six hours later. Meanwhile the graphite fire, with flames shooting some 500 metres into the sky, released an enormous quantity of radioactive substances, particularly radioactive iodine and caesium.

Over the next week the Soviet authorities battled desperately to extinguish the blaze, and to shut off the release of radioactive debris, by dumping some 5000 tonnes of lead, boron, clay, sand and dolomite from helicopters. Meanwhile the winds carried their radioactive burden westwards, first over Eastern Europe and then over West Germany, Southern France and Italy as well as southwards over the Balkans and Greece. Wherever it rained, a deadly shower of radioactive particles was brought down to earth, contaminating land, buildings, vehicles, livestock and unsuspecting humans, such as the shepherds of Corsica and Greece. Because the French government failed to take action to warn Corsican farmers about the level of radioactive contamination many Corsicans, in particular children, received radiation doses to their thyroid glands well over the maximum levels recommended as safe by authorities such as the International Commission on Radiological Protection.

But were there not doubts as to whether the Chernobyl reactor had any containment?

After the explosion at Chernobyl, Western reactor experts quickly claimed that the consequences of the accident were made worse because the reactor had inadequate containment. They suggested that if it had had a containment like that of the pressurised water reactor at Three Mile Island, practically all the radioactive debris would have been kept within its containment. The truth is somewhat different.

In fact the containment at Chernobyl, instead of being the familiar dome shape of French and many US PWRs, is of a type known as a pressure suppression containment system. Such containment is used for boiling water reactors (BWRs) in the West as well as for some PWRs. The United States has 49 plants either licensed for operation or under construction with pressure suppression containment, West Germany has 7, Switzerland 2, Sweden 9, the Netherlands 1 and Finland 2. The concept of the system is that internal pressures are kept low enough to prevent breaching the relatively weak containment shell, any pressure rise being suppressed by bubbling steam either through an 'ice basket' or a pool of water. However, according to the Union of Concerned Scientists in the United States, dangerous overpressures can easily develop in reactors with such containment. In his book, *The Accident Hazards of Nuclear Power Plants*[1] the nuclear engineer, Dr Richard Webb describes a situation in a boiling water reactor in the United States, where pressure built up to levels approaching the maximum design pressure of a containment system before the reactor could be brought under control. A Chernobyl-type accident may be far less unlikely than hitherto accepted by the nuclear authorities.

Even so, operator mismanagement was the downfall of Chernobyl. Surely that situation could not occur here, or elsewhere in Western Europe?

Operator errors or errors in maintenance are almost invariably to blame when reactors go seriously wrong whether the reactors are in the West or East. The problem is that despite intensive safety training, there are still many unknowns in reactor operation, and it is impossible to account fully in training and in design for all potential accident modes.

Inevitably, supporters of nuclear power like Lord Marshall of the CEGB will play down the likelihood in Britain of a Chernobyl-type accident, or will say that even though Chernobyl was bad, it did not kill all that many people – only two outright and a few dozen others over the next few months. As for the cancer cases, they are pure speculation, and who is to know? Indeed, radiation experts in the USSR and elsewhere are now saying that Chernobyl will cause only 2,000 extra cancer deaths at most among the population of the USSR. The reason that figure is ten times lower than they originally forecast is that levels of radioactive caesium found in the evacuated population in a thirty-kilometre zone around the reactor were ten times less than originally anticipated. Yet these scientists are failing to point out that much of the radioactive debris was carried far further afield and fell outside the Soviet Union.

Much of the burden of the extra cancer cases will fall on to the populations of countries to the west and north of the Soviet Union. In Lapland, for instance, measurements of caesium in reindeer indicate sixty times and more of the radio-isotope caesium than the absolute maximum accepted as permissible for human consumption. The Lapps, whose livelihood depends to a great extent on reindeer, are likely to be economically devastated by the accident at Chernobyl. And what about their health?

In fact Chernobyl *was* bad, and the tally of cancer cases is more likely to be in the hundred thousand range than the couple of thousands stated by official nuclear experts. Moreover, it could have been far worse: the initial explosion could have been even greater, causing the release of more radioactivity and making control of the fire over the next few days even more of a deadly task. And what would have happened if the next-door reactor had been affected as well? Nuclear engineers such as Dr Richard Webb and others in the Union of Concerned Scientists believe the explosion potential of a light water reactor is as great if not greater than the RBMK reactor at Chernobyl. And at the present accident rate we can expect a runaway reactor every ten to twenty years.

And the probability of such accidents?

Both the probability and consequences of a reactor accident in which containment is breached have been studied theoretically in the United States. According to the scenario of the 'maximum credible accident' a large radiation release could kill several thousand people downwind 'promptly' through radiation sickness. Radiation sickness is the result of being subjected all at once to a sudden large radiation dose to the entire body – a dose in the range of 100 rem and upwards (chest X-ray, for example, is about one-tenth of a rem, and the annual background radiation dose in the UK is approximately 0.15 rems per year). The several hundred firefighters and technicians who fought the Chernobyl fire suffered radiation sickness, some thirty dying over the first couple of months after the accident, and more than two hundred remaining in hospital months later.

Other than death from radiation sickness and burns, many thousands more would suffer premature death from cancer or would pass on genetic defects to their children after a large radiation release. Meanwhile, thousands of square kilometres would be heavily contaminated with radioactive fall-out, severely curtailing agriculture in those areas for years, if not decades. The probability of such an accident was put in the range of one per 100,000 reactor years or even less – hence a negligible risk according to official estimates. Prior to Chernobyl, the CEGB believed the probability of a serious accident was one in a billion years of reactor operation. Since Chernobyl, the CEGB, particularly through its chairman, Lord Marshall, has tried to distance British nuclear technology and operating management from that of the Soviet Union.

Critics of the official figures maintain a much higher accident rate is likely, a view that is increasingly accepted within the United States by officials in the Nuclear

Regulatory Commission. They now claim that there is a one in two chance of another Three Mile Island type accident in the USA over the next twenty years.

And the consequences of Chernobyl?

Having pilloried the USSR for its secrecy during the first week following the Chernobyl accident, the West followed suit by clamping down on information regarding the fall-out in their own countries from the radioactive cloud. As non-official scientists have shown through their own measurements, fall-out over many areas in Western Europe and Scandinavia was considerable. Because it is volatile like radio-iodine, radioactive caesium was released in large quantities from the stricken Chernobyl reactor. But whereas radio-iodine (iodine-131) decays rapidly, half of it transforming every 8 days so that at the end of 16 days only one quarter is left, and after 24 days, one eighth, radioactive caesium (a gamma and beta emitter) has a half-life of 30 years. Therefore it will take 30 years for the first half to vanish, 60 years for three-quarters and some 600 years (20 half-lives) for it to have been transformed to harmless levels. In fact food (such as lamb or Scottish grouse) contaminated with high levels of radioactive caesium (more than 1,000 becquerels per kilogram of meat) will not lose its radioactivity to any degree if put in the deep freeze for a couple of years, as suggested by a spokesman from the Ministry of Agriculture, Fisheries and Food when the grouse shooting season began on 12 August 1986.

Close to Munich in Bavaria, for instance, radiation from caesium went up to 35,000 becquerels per square metre of ground, thirty-five times that of uncontaminated soil. The contamination by caesium will therefore be longlasting. In Britain MAFF has assured farmers and the public that caesium passes fairly rapidly through the bodies of contaminated animals, having a biological half-life measured in days rather than years. However, MAFF has not pointed out that the radioactive caesium passes out with the faeces and can then re-enter the food chain through pasture.

What about the French nuclear power programme?

France embarked on a major nuclear power programme in the 1970s to reduce French dependence on oil imports following the Arab-Israeli war in 1973, and to meet an anticipated doubling of electricity demand by the 1980s. Initially, work was begun each year on some five or six large nuclear power units. The first reactors built were 900 megawatt. By the end of 1985 nuclear power stations – based on a modified Westinghouse pressurised water reactor design – generated nearly 65 per cent of French electricity, giving France the highest proportion of nuclear power in the world. During 1985 France had thirty-two PWRs in operation and a further twenty-one under construction.

And is the French nuclear programme a success?

Despite active encouragement by government and the electricity supply industry, electricity demand has not risen as foreseen. Moreover, oil consumption is only marginally affected – transport still being the main consumer of oil in France. But the nuclear policy has virtually killed off the French coal-mining industry. Hydroelectric power, which had been providing up to one-quarter of France's electricity relatively cheaply, has come to be used solely for peak demands, nuclear power replacing it as a base-load producer. Thus, to justify the enormous capital expenditure on nuclear power, the usual economic strategy of utilising the cheapest source of electricity for base-load (namely hydroelectric) has been abandoned. In fact, because of their numbers French nuclear plants are increasingly having to be used below their optimum capacity and even for following peaks in demand resulting from fluctuations in electricity consumption during the day, a task for which they are not well designed.

Isn't French electricity very cheap?

Electricité de France (EDF) claims that its nuclear power provides electricity considerably cheaper than its coal- and oil-fired plants. However, electricity prices have been rising rapidly and are now higher than those of Holland, which has a very small nuclear programme. The real cost of the French nuclear programme is not properly known as the government is subsidising it, but we do know that EDF has had to borrow extensively from overseas, mainly US, banks and owes more than £20 billion, creating serious balance-of-payment problems for France. France is now dependent on nuclear power (which has no long-term supply option without the fast-breeder reactor) and is therefore dependent on politically controlled supplies of imported uranium. The fast-breeder reactor is supposed to produce fuel but is unlikely to do so *and* remain an economic producer of electricity. Extraction of plutonium through reprocessing fast-reactor fuel on a commercial scale is also fraught with technical problems.

The fast reactor is supposed to produce more fuel than it consumes by generating plutonium in the blanket surrounding the core. That blanket plutonium would make excellent material for nuclear weapons. How do we know that this is not France's intention?

The Superphenix FBR was to have been commissioned by France in October 1983 but was finally started up two years late in 1985. In 1980 the authorities announced that its cost would be twice that originally stated. In fact, the cost is likely to be at least three times that of an equivalent pressurised water reactor. It also needs plutonium fuel. Where will this come from? From UK reprocessing plants? How can the French accept that dependence given that Superphenix is not a serious commercial venture at all? Had the French put the same amount of money into solar power they would be a leader in that field, with a large export potential. There is no export potential for Superphenix.

The sole justification for such a costly 'white elephant' is if the blanket plutonium, which is very good fission material, is used to make nuclear warheads. And that is probably where it will go, especially if the UK can provide the lower-grade plutonium for fuelling the fast-reactor core. In return, France is now exporting its surplus electricity via the newly laid 2,000 MW cable linking Britain and France across the Channel.

Why are the Americans abandoning their nuclear power programme?

Partly as a result of the public outrage following the Three Mile Island accident and partly because of the harsh economic realities facing the American nuclear industry. None of the nuclear plants ordered within the last decade has been built and no less than ninety-eight plants previously ordered have been cancelled. Plants in the course of construction have been abandoned or moth-balled and large investments written off. Among the reasons for the spectacular decline of the American nuclear industry are high inflation and interest rates, a sharp slow-down in electricity demand growth, the long lead times between beginning construction of the plant and its production of electricity, the huge cost, and the soaring budget over-runs which have frightened off the investors who fund the US energy utilities. Not surprisingly, the utilities are now investing in renewable energy, coal-fired generating plant with pollution-control devices and energy conservation measures as much more cost-effective and acceptable options.

Why are nuclear plants not located in cities where the energy is needed?

In the West nuclear power stations are still located in sites relatively remote from the main centres of population because nuclear power has not proved safe. Radiation leaks, radioactive waste storage and transport and the need for tight plant security are still problems. In the public mind, in the aftermath of the Three Mile Island accident in the United States and that of Chernobyl in the Ukraine, an urban nuclear power station would be totally unacceptable. Indeed, the widespread contamination following Chernobyl, with dangerous levels of radioactive fall-out hundreds of miles away from the stricken reactor indicate that no nuclear site can be made sufficiently safe to justify its use.

Can one insure against a nuclear accident?

No. The consequences of such a disaster are so great that no insurance company could provide adequate compensation, therefore insurance policies always specifically exclude nuclear risks. In fact, a report produced for the US Nuclear Regulatory Commission in 1975[2] indicated that a major accident to a 1,000 MW reactor could result in 3,300 to 45,000 deaths, 45,000 to 248,000 injuries, and property damages from \$14 billion upwards. The CEGB indemnifies itself against a reactor accident to a total sum of £20 million, with the government guaranteeing another £210 million.

Is nuclear waste disposal really such a problem?

This is the Achilles heel of the nuclear industry. Each year more than 1500 tonnes of spent British reactor fuel, containing 600 million curies of highly radioactive waste, go to Sellafield for reprocessing. The amount of radioactivity locked up in Sellafield is astronomical and any large-scale release (for example through accident, war or sabotage) would render thousands of square miles uninhabitable for decades and lead to the deaths of thousands of local people.

Sellafield discharges radioactive effluents into the Irish Sea from three pipelines. No one knows how many 'accidental' discharges have occurred above permissible limits. Meanwhile, permissible limits at Sellafield are 400 times higher than at the French equivalent reprocessing plant at Cap de la Hague in Normandy (for alpha-emitters such as plutonium and americium). So far at least a quarter of a tonne of plutonium has been released into the Irish Sea, helping to make it the most radioactive sea in the world. Some of the radioactive nuclides are dispersed as far away as Denmark, Norway and Arctic Russia, meanwhile some 250 kilos of plutonium is concentrated in silt, sand and living organisms close to the outfall pipes – a millionth of a gramme of plutonium inhaled gives a high risk of lung cancer.

Can't the waste be dumped in the deep ocean?

Dumping is under severe attack. Following a refusal to co-operate in sea dumping by the National Union of Seamen and other British trade unions, the UK government had to accede to the two-year moratorium on ocean dumping agreed at the London Dumping Convention of 1983, having initially announced that it would ignore the ban. Since 1983 pressure has been building up to a permanent ban on all dumping of radioactive materials in the Pacific and Atlantic oceans. Indeed, a continuation of the ban was voted for by a majority of nations at the 1985 London Dumping Convention.

Why do we in Britain import other countries' spent fuel? Aren't we truly becoming the world's nuclear dustbin?

Spent nuclear fuel is extremely hot and highly radioactive when it is removed from the reactor core. Exposure to the rods would give a lethal dose of radiation within microseconds. To carry just two tons of fuel rod assemblies one needs massive 14-inch thick steel casks, lined with lead, which weigh anything between 50 and 90 tons. Each cask contains the same radiation inventory as three Hiroshima-sized bombs. If even a small amount of the radioactivity were released, huge areas of land would be rendered uninhabitable for decades and thousands of prompt and latent cancer deaths would result.

Some 1,000 tonnes per year of spent fuel are imported into Britain from countries such as Japan, Italy, Sweden and Holland. These countries export this dangerous material because of its danger to the environment and because it is a hot political issue within their own countries. And the UK opens its doors to wash the world's dirty nuclear laundry. British Nuclear Fuels hopes to make a modest profit in reprocessing the imported spent fuel as well as the fuel from Britain's own reactors, but that profit has to be weighed

After J. Hassall

against the cost to the UK of a devastating release of radioactivity and grossly polluted seas.

Is it likely that nuclear fusion will provide the world with a cheap and inexhaustible source of energy?

Nuclear fusion is the process by which small elements such as hydrogen and its isotopes are fused under extraordinary conditions of pressure and temperature to form larger elements such as helium. Because there is a mass loss during fusion, enormous energies are potentially released. Cheap and inexhaustible energy supplies, if such things are possible, are mixed blessings. Although, in the 1950s, we were promised that conventional nuclear power would meet most of the UK's energy needs in the future, by 1985 it still only provided 17 per cent of our electricity production and therefore some 3 per cent of our total energy needs given that electricity is some 15 per cent of the whole. Fusion research has been conducted in at least six different countries, at great expense, but with no real technical breakthrough. The difficulties involved in maintaining temperatures in a controlled reaction (higher than those in the centre of the sun and, in close juxtaposition, temperatures colder than anywhere else on earth) have proved to be enormous. Even if the required breakthrough comes tomorrow, commercial fusion reactors could not contribute to our energy supplies before 2025. Many people, even Lord Marshall of the CEGB, himself a nuclear physicist, believe that fusion research is a very expensive blind alley.

Is there really a link between nuclear power and nuclear weapons?

The government has consistently told the public that the nuclear programme is limited to the production of electricity. In fact, the Calder Hall and Chapelcross Magnox reactors were specifically designed for military plutonium production. The electricity produced is sold as a by-product to the grid, so we are paying a direct subsidy to the nuclear weapons programme through our electricity bills. The Hinkley Point A station in Somerset and Hunterston A station in Ayrshire were also designed so that they could supply weapons-grade plutonium to the Ministry of Defence. Indeed, all Britain's Magnox stations will have been producing perfect weapons-grade plutonium for some of their operating time.

No figures have been released for the amount of plutonium which has passed from the British nuclear power programme into the nuclear weapons programme but the evidence is growing that some 6.5 tonnes of plutonium have probably been exported to the USA 'for mutual defence purposes', a sizeable proportion of which has been used in the manufacture of American nuclear warheads. In April 1986, after continual denials from both the CEGB and the government, Mrs Thatcher admitted that some of the plutonium from the electricity board's reactors had in fact been exported to the USA, although not during the present government's term in office.

Is there any organisation which can prevent the plutonium from civil reactors being diverted for weapons-making?

The International Atomic Energy Agency was set up by the UN in the late 1950s on President Eisenhower's initiative to promote the worldwide 'peaceful use of the atom'. It was intended to oversee nuclear programmes and ensure, within its power, their peaceful intent. The Non-Proliferation Treaty (NPT) was established in 1970 by the superpowers who already possessed nuclear weapons. They wanted to prevent the technology and hardware spreading to those countries without nuclear weapons, which still today means the great majority. The idea was that surveillance and therefore compliance would be under the aegis of the IAEA and, in Europe, of Euratom, the equivalent organisation for the EEC.

However, the IAEA does not have mandatory powers to inspect. Most countries that are using the commercial route to nuclear weapons have not signed the NPT and, although some do enter into IAEA agreements, these are carefully circumscribed. Anyway, all such agreements, including the NPT itself, can be terminated at short notice and unilaterally. The route from civilian nuclear power to nuclear weapons is the normal one and was taken by France, India, China, Pakistan, Argentina, Israel, Iraq, Brazil, South Africa, India and, not least, the UK itself. The UK has never agreed to put Sellafield and Dounreay (the site of Britain's only fast breeder reactor) under international inspection or control. Indeed, there is no effective international control. The only remedy is for each country to stop engaging in such activities – and we must appreciate that Britain and France are two of the prime culprits in the world.

Should we be concerned about the link between nuclear energy and civil liberties?

Unfortunately, nuclear technology and true democracy are incompatible. Because the nuclear programme is so intimately connected with the production of nuclear weapons, nuclear employees are politically vetted and then made to sign the Official Secrets Act. Nuclear plants and nuclear materials are vulnerable to terrorist attacks, theft and 'nuclear blackmail' and armed guards are considered essential. These guards accompany the road and rail transport of nuclear fuel and radioactive waste and elaborate precautions are taken against the threat of armed attack. The Atomic Energy Authority constabulary (the industry's armed police force) has increased to its present level of 646. Expenditure doubled between 1979 and 1984. Files are kept on anti-nuclear activists and telephone-tapping, surveillance and interference with mail are commonplace. It is clear that the government sees the anti-nuclear movement as a threat to the security of the state. In other countries many repressive measures such as riot police, legal measures and even murder have been used by the nuclear establishment in its attempts to suppress the nuclear protest movement. Inquiries into the murder in 1984 of Hilda Murrell, a prominent anti-nuclear campaigner in Britain, have suggested that she, and possibly others too, are victims of nuclear 'security'.

Your friendly neighbourhood policeman

Parliament is constrained from debate on the nuclear issue because of the industry's need for secrecy. The report of the Royal Commission on Nuclear Power and the Environment, 1976, stresses the serious implications for society that would arise from a 'plutonium economy'.

Wouldn't nuclear power solve the energy problems of the world's poorer nations?

In 1974, the International Atomic Energy Agency forecast that by the year 2000 the developing countries between them would have 400 GW (1 GW = 1,000 MW) of nuclear power (some 400 large reactors). The expectation now has been reduced to 13 GW at most. The reasons for that extraordinary decline are essentially economic and not safety. The cost of marginal nuclear electricity in heat terms is between ten and twenty times greater than that provided by a barrel of oil costing US $17.

Many nuclear protagonists argue that Third World energy crises will lead to international unrest. Global peace, they say, can only be maintained if we make nuclear technology freely available to countries in greatest need. This is at best naïve and at worst a cynical and immoral promotion of Western commercial interests. The gigantic cost of nuclear technology, the technical complexity of its station construction, the highly sophisticated skills required in reactor control and maintenance and the problems related to nuclear fuel supply and waste-handling all combine to offer developing countries an energy option which has all the characteristics of a Faustian contract.

Furthermore, its centralist nature and the need for secrecy and security make a nuclear power system the exact opposite of a developing country's needs. Developing countries need labour-intensive and relatively simple technologies which can utilise indigenous energy resources, such as solar radiation, wind power or methane gas derived from organic waste such as manure (biogas).

The Green Alternative

After Chernobyl, Britain's Energy Minister, Peter Walker, in line with others such as Dr Kohl, Chancellor of West Germany, stated that we had no alternative in meeting our energy needs but to proceed with nuclear power. Are they right?

Just two months to the day after the Chernobyl explosion, Peter Walker told the Engineering Employers' Federation in London that: 'If we care about the standards of living of generations yet to come, we must meet the challenge of the nuclear age and not retreat into the irresponsible course of leaving our children and grandchildren a world in deep and probably irreversible decline.' A few days later, on 31 July 1986, Lord Marshall, the CEGB chairman, proclaimed that without nuclear power Britain would be plunged into power cuts and shortages in the years to come.

But who is being irresponsible? The idea that the world will suffer an energy famine unless nuclear power provides between thirty and forty times more energy than it does today (those being the figures given by Peter Walker) is patent nonsense, quite apart from the increased dangers we would face from Chernobyl-type catastrophes – and worse.

In fact, in Sweden, which at present generates 50 per cent of its electricity from nuclear power, the government is committed, as a result of a public referendum taken in 1982, to phase out nuclear power completely by the year 2010. It will be replaced by energy-efficient conservation practices and alternative energy sources, including the renewables.

And in the United States, where economic criteria play a far greater role than in countries such as Britain, France and the USSR (in which a state monopoly is responsible for electricity generation), almost a hundred nuclear power stations ordered in the 1970s *have been cancelled or abandoned* because energy conservation and alternative modes of electricity generation are proving far more economic. Between 1981 and 1984 cancellations of new coal and nuclear plants in the United States actually outweighed orders by 65 GW – a generating capacity larger than the UK's total. At the same time, net orders for industrial cogeneration

184

(larger CHP stations), in which both heat and electricity are produced, exceeded 25 GW, and for small hydropower, windpower and other alternatives another 20 GW.

Since 1979, more than 100 times as much energy has been available in the US from savings as from all new orders for plants – and of those new orders, more new energy from sun, wind, water and wood than from oil, gas, coal and uranium. Renewable sources now supply a tenth of all US energy, and the fastest growing part.

If nuclear and fossil fuel energy sources are so harmful, what are the alternatives?

Energy can be geothermal, or derived from wind, sun, tides, waves and biofuels (including domestic waste). The CEGB scoffs that these 'renewables' would signal a return to the 'Ice Age', yet current standards of comfort are rising as a result of improved consumer products, while energy demand is falling, both because of energy conservation and because of technological improvement. Far from being a step backwards, an energy policy involving widespread use of renewable resources would provide more jobs, assist in the diversification and security of electricity supply, reduce pollution and stimulate local economies in rural areas. Furthermore, the removal of the nuclear power shadow would help substantially to reduce the alienation of many British people from the government, greatly reduce accident and security risks and provide a series of exciting technical challenges to the engineering and electrical industries. A highly developed renewable energy sector in the British economy would be accompanied by export prospects far brighter and far more honest than those of the nuclear industry.

But surely renewable energy sources cannot supply anything like all our needs?

This is certainly true for the near future, but the Department of Energy estimates that the total contribution of renewables to Britain's energy needs could be 2 million tonnes of coal equivalent (mtce) by 2000 AD with an ultimate potential of about 200 mtce. Other detailed studies and projections suggest that Britain could be supplying up to half its needs from renewables by the year 2025.[3,4] These studies are based largely on currently available technology and do not assume any major technological breakthroughs. In the even more distant future this fraction of renewables could be increased further through known technologies becoming cost-effective as conventional fuel prices rise, through new discoveries and possibly international trade in fuels manufactured from renewable sources. There seems little doubt that (given the political will) Britain's current energy requirements of 313 mtce could be reduced by 28 per cent by effective energy conservation methods, with more than half of our primary energy needs being met by renewables. The renewables, comprising wind, biofuels including domestic waste, geothermal, tidal, wave and solar power, could provide some 20 per cent of total requirements over the same period, given a commitment by the government and local authorities. That target would require the building of some fifty to sixty small (100 MW) refuse-burning CHP plants, 230 geothermal installations and 6,000 wind-turbine generators, one-third of them offshore, in addition to some 3 GW of tidal energy and 1.5 GW of hydroelectricity and wave.

Some 400 small wind turbines were installed in 1984 in Denmark, which now has 1,400 linked to a grid system, while France has been installing hot aquifer geothermal schemes at the rate of twenty or so per year, and has built up some forty schemes over the past two years.

To meet the equivalent energy produced by the renewables, some thirty-five large nuclear power stations would have to be built, each one costing some £1,500 million, and taking at least ten years to complete. And because of their energy inefficiency with some 70 per cent of the energy lost as heat to the environment, more nuclear power stations than that would be required to meet the scenario suggested above.

Will renewable energy become competitive with energy from fossil fuels?

It already is, and the balance will tip more towards renewables as fossil fuels become scarcer and more expensive and as the cost of nuclear power continues to escalate. As far as electricity-producing systems are concerned, government estimates of costs per unit are as follows: onshore wind machines approx 2.4p/kWh (kilowatt hours), offshore wind machines 4.7p/kWh, tidal power 3.7p/kWh, hot rocks 3.6p/kWh. Electricity from the Magnox stations cost 3.37p/kWh, and from coal-plant 2.28p/kWh (in March 1982). Researchers invariably claim that lower costs can be achieved but that their research programmes are hamstrung by official antagonism and lack of funding. A particularly furious debate centres on the cost of wave power, which the government has apparently written off; government figures suggest that electricity from wave-power devices will cost 9–15p/kWh, whereas researchers claim that 3p/kWh is easily attainable.

In the meantime, the Norwegians completed in 1985 a commercial wave-power device producing 500 kW at a cost of 3.4p/kWh. At Lund in Sweden an increasing proportion of heat for the district heating scheme, which meets 80 per cent of the space heating and hot water needs of the city, is derived from shallow geothermal sources, the heat being upgraded by means of heat pumps. For technologies not involving electricity, biofuels (such as straw briquettes) and refuse-derived fuel (RDF) are already competitive with coal, and methane is an excellent and cheap substitute for North Sea gas.

If renewable energy is so good, why don't we hear more about it?

Renewable energy technologies are suppressed in the UK because their research programmes are starved of funds; funding for renewables is currently about £14 million per year, as against an annual budget of well over £225 million for nuclear research and development.

The nuclear industry, at least until recently, has had a

decisive influence on the government's energy advisers. The Energy Technology Support Unit (ETSU), which controls and administers renewable energy research, is based at the Atomic Energy Research Establishment at Harwell, the headquarters of the nuclear establishment. Its proposals and decisions are filtered by the nuclear hierarchy. The Advisory Committee on Research and Development (ACORD), which advises the energy minister on energy research priorities, does not have a single member with detailed knowledge of renewable technologies, so it is not surprising that its priorities lie elsewhere. The part of British industry concerned with civil engineering and power station technology obviously has a vested interest in continuing the nuclear power programme. There are also powerful political pressures for the continuous production of plutonium for the nuclear weapons programme and hence the continuous expansion of the nuclear power programme.

Are there exciting technical challenges in the renewables?

The design, construction and testing of renewable energy devices (such as wave-power convertors, tidal power stations, large aerogenerators, small water turbines, solar-cell arrays, geothermal generating systems, methane-digester plants and even solar-power stations) are already stimulating a whole range of innovations throughout the world. Sadly, Britain lags behind and British innovations in this field have been taken over for development, manufacture and marketing by other countries, such as Japan, Sweden and Denmark. Much work remains to be done on the efficient combustion of fossil fuels and biofuels, and pollution control research has to go hand in hand with work on energy crops, combined-heat-and-power schemes and the burning of wastes as fuel. In the field of microchip technology, the CEGB could face a whole set of new challenges if it would abandon its 'big is beautiful' philosophy. The incorporation of electricity supplies from a multitude of small-scale generating plants (using wind, wave, tidal, hydro and solar energy) into the grid is no real problem to engineers, given the incentive to succeed.

'The trouble started when they cut back the trees for the dam and diverted the river.'

What are the employment prospects in an economy run on renewable energy?

A proper energy policy, emphasising energy conservation and renewable energy use, would create many thousands of new jobs. In energy conservation alone, an expansion of draught-proofing, insulation, double-glazing and energy-control work to take in half a million dwellings per year would create almost 30,000 new jobs. A crash programme of research, development and manufacture of wave-energy devices, wind machines, hydro plants, methane digesters and so forth could create at least 100,000 new jobs, many of them involving the traditional skills of shipbuilding, steel fabrication, light engineering, building construction and electrical engineering. They would go some way towards alleviating the terrible hardship currently experienced in our older industrial areas. A single large, civil engineering project, such as the tidal barrage scheme for generating more than 5 per cent of

The Green Alternative

the CEGB's electricity proposed for the Severn Estuary, could create 21,000 jobs over a period of ten years. Because renewable energy projects are labour-intensive rather than capital-intensive, they make good sense as part of a strategy to defeat unemployment.

Can I use renewable energy if I live in the centre of a town?

Although rural dwellers have much greater opportunities, the urban dweller can become more self-reliant in energy. For example, space heating accounts for about 64 per cent of most people's annual energy requirements. An annual gas heating bill of £640 could be reduced to around £80 if a house were well insulated, built to take full advantage of solar heating potential (by 'passive' solar methods), and used a supplementary gas-fired heat-pump. Solar water-heating systems can be installed for under £800 and can provide most hot water requirements between May and October. Small roof-mounted wind-chargers are perfectly feasible in urban situations, although care must be taken over planning rules and regulations. Biofuels can be used as substitutes for coal, gas or oil and some enthusiastic urban dwellers even have their own biogas plants!

Wouldn't windmills and water turbines make an unsightly impact on the countryside?

We have to recognise that all energy systems have detrimental effects upon the environment. But the Green movement has to choose which systems to support. If we decide that nuclear power must be opposed absolutely and that fossil fuel use should be reduced wherever possible, we must accept the small amount of environmental damage (and the small risk of accidents) arising from renewable energy use. There is no need for miles of closely packed wind machines across the British landscape; neither do we need endless chains of wave-power devices anchored just off the western coastline. We can, however, envisage a pleasantly varied landscape with occasional wind machines in exposed locations, occasional hydro plants in river valleys, methane digesters on dairy farms, tidal power stations in certain river estuaries and wave-power devices in strings off some of our exposed coastlines. Swedish research shows a positive response among people even to very large (2–3 MW) wind machines.

Large projects, such as the Severn Barrage, are more controversial and some environmentalists are concerned about its likely ecological impact. However, in opposing the plans for a Severn Barrage and the plans for new heat-and-power schemes in Scotland, environmentalists are in danger of killing off any hopes we may have for a safe, sustainable and non-polluting energy future.

Are solar panels economic?

Averaged out over the year, solar panels on their own can supply around 40 per cent of a family's hot water requirements; this percentage is likely to rise to perhaps 60 per cent with future technical improvements. In Sweden solar panel arrays are connected to large subterranean storage systems which in the course of the year will capture enough heat to supply almost all the hot water and space heating requirements of well-insulated housing blocks or estates.

Many of the 20,000 UK installations are not cost-effective in simple terms, i.e. the annual energy savings are often less than the interest on capital. This is mainly due to the early stage of development of the UK solar industry and the resulting high cost. In countries with a well-established industry, and that includes Sweden, commercial hardware and installation costs are much lower – low enough to make systems economically attractive, even in the UK climate. The UK industry needs government help, perhaps in the form of subsidies, to get over the initial hump and bring costs down. Cost-effectiveness is likely to improve anyway because of increasing conventional energy costs: many of the present installations may become quite profitable before the end of their useful life. DIY installations can certainly be made cost-effective now.

The Green Alternative

What is passive solar heating?

This involves designing buildings to make the best use of the solar energy falling on them by carefully balancing the area of south-facing window, insulation level and heat storage in the walls and floors. A very useful saving in annual heating energy requirements can be made compared to a conventional building at something like 10 per cent of conventional fuel costs (0.35p to 0.5p/kWh are quoted for a recent project in Milton Keynes). Estimates suggest that around 10 per cent of the UK's space heating requirement could be met by passive solar techniques. To meet all of the annual heating needs of a UK house from solar energy, long-term storage is necessary. Research and development has shown this to be feasible, but costs are still high.

Would the firewood problem of developing countries be overcome by the use of solar cookers?

Certainly cooking is a major use of dwindling wood supplies and a waste of dung which would be valuable as a fertiliser. However, solar cookers are not an easy answer. They are relatively simple to make, concentrating the sun's rays onto a focal point at which the cooking pot is located, but many development experts refer to solar cookers as 'inappropriate technology' devices since they work best in the middle of the day, whereas in many societies the main meal is cooked and eaten in the evening.

Cooking is often an important ritual and radical changes are therefore difficult, even when the need for change seems overwhelming to the outsider. Many of the technical difficulties could be overcome and research is progressing well on solar cookers which incorporate heat storage, but keeping the cost low enough to encourage widespread use will still be a problem. A more immediate low-cost approach is the introduction of locally made enclosed cooking stoves which make more efficient use of the traditional fuels. Solar crop driers are a different matter and have widespread applications where food storage and grain drying currently present problems. Solar water heaters are also simple to make and extremely useful to rural communities in arid and semi-arid regions.

Or would wood-burning stoves be a solution?

Using woodstoves in the Third World is no solution to the firewood problem: many of them are crude and actually less efficient than open fires for heating and cooking. Really efficient woodstoves are too bulky and too expensive to be widely adopted by peasant communities.

And in Britain?

Here, the wood-burning stove could become a real threat to our woodlands, its greatly increased use leading to a huge growth in the demand for timber. The supply of dead elms is now virtually exhausted and timber merchants are seeking other sources of fuel wood. Indirectly, this demand for timber could encourage the denuding of hedgerows and the removal of valuable areas of woodland. Timber can be used where supplies are abundant as long as every tree taken is replaced by at least two new trees for use by future generations. Good woodland management in rural areas can ensure a more or less inexhaustible supply of timber so long as the resource is not used by too many people.

A wood-burning stove used for space heating, cooking and hot water can consume seven tonnes of wood per year; this timber may have to come from more than a hectare of mature woodland. Combined with coal-burning, timber resources can be extended threefold and coal consumption cut by half. If the age-old technique of coppicing is used, however, there need be no woodland denudation. Many farms could be virtually self-sufficient in energy for heating and cooking if they coppiced 100m of hedgerow each year on a ten-year cycle. Three hectares of well-managed woodland can supply the energy requirements of a family dwelling *ad infinitum* if a quarter of a hectare is cut and dried each year.

However, the more efficient the woodstove and the lower

the combustion temperature, the greater the proportion of toxic materials produced – more than from coal- or oil-fired boilers. While it is true that woodstove pollution is localised and very small in scale, for those who do not have their own wood, it is cheaper to buy coal and the pollution generated is less harmful.

What about straw as fuel?

Currently Britain's farmers burn about 6 million tonnes of straw on the fields every year, leading to smoke hazard, road accidents, accidental damage to adjacent property and a great deal of public irritation. Although the soil surface is temporarily sterilised by burning, burning brings no real agricultural benefits and straw is a wasted fuel resource. Straw can be burned within the farm: chopped and fed into a boiler via a hopper, in conventional bales, or compressed into fuel briquettes. The first two methods are best suited for large-scale straw burning to heat factories, public buildings or large farms.

There are now many straw-processing and straw-burning plants on the market. The technology has been widely adopted in Denmark, where about 25 per cent of all farms are heated by straw. Straw fuel briquettes, which are clean, easy to use and come packaged in handy 20 kg or 25 kg bags, are suitable for domestic consumption. They are slightly more expensive than coal in terms of calorific value per kilo but they are less polluting. They are now widely available and many farmers and farm co-operatives are setting up manufacturing facilities for the processing of this valuable waste resource.

Should we aim to get biogas from all sewage and accumulations of animal manure? How much energy would that be worth?

Sewage and manure can certainly provide a useful amount of energy. From sewage, biogas (two-thirds methane, one-third carbon dioxide) with an energy content of 10–15 PJ/yr (petajoules)* could possibly be produced – but this meets less than 1 per cent of the UK's present gas consumption. The energy available from farm animal wastes is more substantial – around 110 PJ/yr gross – and digesters on farms using waste from penned animals only could possibly provide up to 60 PJ/yr of biogas. This is almost as much as the entire energy requirement of UK agriculture (73 PJ in 1976). (In addition, the residue slurry from digesters is a very good fertiliser.)

Biomass fuels derived from vegetable and animal matter are all right in principle but surely they use land which would otherwise feed people?

This is a complex question. In the Third World, it is indisputable that the real energy crisis of today is that of fuelwood. Nearly half the world's population is dependent to some extent upon fuelwood for cooking and heating. In India, it meets 93 per cent of the country's total energy need; in Africa 60 per cent. More than 100 million people cannot obtain enough fuelwood to meet their minimum energy requirements and a further 1,000 million are affected by shortages. Fuelwood is being harvested far faster than it is being replaced and in semi-arid regions desertification is an inevitable consequence.

As pointed out by the FAO and other bodies, the current famine in Ethiopia and Sudan is by no means simply the result of climatic change and over-grazing by domestic animals; over-population and the inexorable removal of scrub and woodland cover for heating and cooking are major contributory factors. In many areas it is vital that at least some of the land currently used for agriculture should be planted with fast-growing trees and shrubs as energy crops; if this is not done quickly the process of desertification will be accelerated. In countries such as Britain there is also a case for changing some agricultural acreages to energy crops. Instead of producing food mountains it would be wise to turn much marginal land over to coppiced timber and 'plant power' crops such as willow, alder and poplar.

* 1 TWh = 10^{12} Watt-hours = 3.6 petajoules.

The Green Alternative

Or we could grow energy crops in this country?

Countries like Sweden and Austria have already allocated a
great deal of marginal land to energy crops and Britain could
do the same. Energy crops can be used for direct combustion,
for fermentation to produce fuel alcohol, for the production
of biogas, for pyrolysis and the production of gaseous and
liquid hydrocarbons, and for the extraction by crushing of
fuel oils. In Britain, an expansion of woodland, especially of
native deciduous tree species which can be coppiced, should
be a part of any sensible energy policy. Methanol, which is a
viable liquid fuel with similar uses to petrol, can be produced
from wood wastes and ethanol or 'power alcohol' from
potatoes and many other plant crops.

Energy forests hold the greatest promise. Experiments
currently in progress in Sweden and the UK suggest that
tightly packed clones of willow, poplar and alder can be
grown in boggy areas. With a growth rate of over 4 metres per
year the productivity of an energy forest can be as high as 20
tonnes of dry matter per hectare per year. This is many times
the productivity of a normal mixed woodland and with careful
management a new energy forest may be even more profitable for a farmer than various forms of agriculture. However,
in the UK a much greater amount of energy is potentially
available from the combined use of farm crop residues,
forestry residues and refuse, which need no additional land
area.

It is estimated that around 550 PJ/yr could be available
from these sources (around 7 per cent of UK total energy).
Such waste materials can be burned directly or converted to
biogas or methanol. Some of these processes are already
economically attractive. Technically, there seems to be no
reason why we should not be able to run most of the UK's
transport system on methanol by early next century.

What about the Third World? It too needs energy to develop. Hydro-power surely can make a useful contribution?

On the face of it hydro-power seems extremely cheap. At $1,000 per kilowatt of installed capacity, it costs far less than power from a thermal plant, let alone a nuclear reactor. Worldwide just over 123,000 megawatts of hydro-electricity plant is currently under construction. Dams capable of adding a further 239,000 megawatts are in the planning stage, equivalent therefore to 400 large nuclear power stations.

According to experts at the World Energy Conference it should be possible to tap 19,000 terawatt-hours a year – as against the 1,300 terawatt hours produced today. (One terawatt hour is 10^{12} watt hours.) Third World governments have embarked on massive schemes to exploit the energy of their rivers. In Brazil, the Itaipu Dam on the Parana River will alone generate 12,600 megawatts – the equivalent output of thirteen large nuclear power stations – and China's Sanxia Dam on the Yangtse River is to generate 40 per cent of the country's current electricity output – equivalent to the output of twenty-five nuclear power stations.

So dams are a good thing?

Everything has its price. And that paid for hydroelectricity from large dams in the developing world is high – particularly if you live in the area to be flooded. The number of people that may have to move is often very large. Ghana's Volta Dam caused the evacuation of some 78,000 people from over 700 towns and villages. Lake Kainji in Nigeria displaced 42,000 people. The Pa Mong project in Vietnam uprooted 450,000 people. In the Philippines proposals to build forty new large dams over the next twenty years could affect the homes of over 1.5 million people.

The Green Alternative

But surely those who are resettled are adequately compensated?

No. Inadequate compensation (and in many cases, no compensation at all) is common. At least 45,000 people lost their homes when Sri Lanka's Victoria Reservoir was flooded; each received just £90 in compensation. And by international standards they were lucky. Landless squatters, of whom there are millions in the Third World, often receive no compensation at all. In Brazil, for example, between one- and two-thirds of those squatters affected by the Tucurui Dam will be unable to claim compensation, provoking enormous hardship for the large numbers – possibly 10,000 – of already impoverished people, and the land to which they are moved is frequently inferior to the valley land which they have left. Alternative housing is usually inadequate, or non-existent.

And what about problems with disease?

Dams have also given rise to a serious increase in water-borne disease, including malaria and schistosomiasis (Bilharzia). In Africa, water projects have led to a proliferation of *Anopheles gambiae* and *Anopheles funestas*, the former breeding in rice paddies, the latter in drainage and irrigation canals. *A. gambiae* has the reputation of being the most efficient of all the malarial mosquitos, biting humans in preference to other animals. In South Asia, irrigation schemes have favoured the mosquito, which acts as the vector for both the *Plasmodium vivax* and the *Plasmodium falciparum* parasites.

Perennial agriculture makes possible two crops a year, correspondingly increasing the mosquito breeding season. Irrigated agriculture also changes the biting habits of mosquitos. As the local human population increases and crops take over from livestock so the mosquitos switch from biting animals to biting humans.

Unfortunately, once the conditions for malaria have been established, the disease is virtually impossible to control. In 1981, the World Health Organisation reported that fifty-one species had developed resistance to one or more insecticide. As a result, there has been a resurgence of malaria in many countries in which it was once thought to have been practically eliminated.

What about diseases other than malaria?

In 1947, an estimated 114 million people suffered from schistosomiasis. Today, 200 million people are affected – the equivalent of the entire population of the USA.

In Kenya, schistosomiasis now affects almost 100 per cent of those children living in irrigated areas near Lake Victoria. In the Sudan, the massive Gezira irrigation scheme had a general infection rate amongst schoolchildren reaching over 90 per cent. All in all, 1.4 million people were affected. After the building of the Aswan High Dam, the infection rate rose to 100 per cent in some communities.

Is it true that dams can cause earthquakes?

The pressure applied to often fragile geological structures by the vast mass of water impounded by a large dam can – and often does – give rise to earthquakes. By 1968, major earthquakes had occurred at four large reservoirs: At Hsingengkiang in China (magnitude 6.1 on the Richter scale) in 1962; At Kariba in Rhodesia (magnitude 5.6) in 1963; At Kremesta in Greece (magnitude 6.3) in 1966; And at Koyna in India (magnitude 6.5) in 1967. Originally it was thought that earthquakes could only be induced when a reservoir was being filled – or immediately after it reached its maximum height. But earthquakes can also occur when a reservoir is emptied and then refilled.

But we need dams to control floods?

In India, nearly a billion dollars was spent on structural controls between 1953 and 1979. Yet the National Commission on Flood Control estimates that the area ravaged by floods has almost doubled in the last thirty years.

The Green Alternative

Are you saying that dams actually cause floods?

In some cases, yes. When dams are used to control floods, there is often a conflict between the need to keep reservoirs low for flood-control purposes and high in order to generate electricity and provide water for irrigation. The results are frequently disastrous.

In 1978, the authorities of a dam in West Bengal maintained the reservoir practically full even during the rains of May and June to generate the maximum hydroelectricity. The river's flood waters could not be contained within the reservoir and vast areas of West Bengal were flooded. In 1983 disastrous floods ravaged California. Heavy snowfall during the winter led to increased run-off from the Rocky Mountains in the spring, swelling the river Colorado to almost unprecedented heights. Under pressure from the tourist industry, the farming lobby and the hydroelectricity authorities, the reservoirs along the Colorado were kept filled to the brim. When a decision to lower the reservoirs was eventually taken, it was too late. Officials admitted that by releasing the flood waters, they were unleashing a controlled disaster on the South-West. Altogether, 55,000 acres of farmland were flooded and an estimated $100 million worth of property destroyed.

Great loss of life and material damage has occurred through people building houses on flood plains – lulled into a false sense of security by the dams upstream. Significantly, the 1969 UN Conference on Floods singled out the intensified use of flood plains as a major cause of the increased costs of floods in North America and Western Europe.

Furthermore, the useful life of dams in the tropics is adversely affected by becoming filled with silt and other detritus which the dam prevents from flowing downstream. Trying to clear that sediment by emptying the dam is ecologically disastrous, killing all fish for hundreds of miles downstream through clogging their gills and depriving them of oxygen. Even so, much of the silt is left behind. In temperate areas, the sedimentation of a reservoir is slower than in the tropics.

200

In India, the expected siltation rate of the Nizamsagar Dam in Andhra Pradesh was 530 acre-feet a year. The actual rate was closer to 8,700 acre-feet a year: the dam's reservoir is already estimated to have lost 60 per cent of its storage capacity. In China, the Sanmenxia Reservoir, which was completed in 1960, had to be decommissioned in 1964 due to premature siltation. Worse still, the Laoying Reservoir actually silted up before its dam was completed.

If a dam's reservoir silts up several times more rapidly than predicted (or worse still, as at Laoying, before the dam even has a chance to function) the time over which the costs of the dam must be amortised is inevitably decreased. Few dam projects in developing countries make economic sense, given the hidden costs of premature silting, structural failure, expulsion of local people, loss of valley farmland and surge in water-borne diseases.

So electricity from dams isn't as cheap as dam promoters make out?

No. It is also important to remember that the rural poor seldom benefit from the electricity produced by dams. Mainly that electricity is used by industry or exported to the cities. Worse still, the industries using the hydroelectric power are often highly polluting.

Polluting? Why?

One reason is that pollution controls are almost non-existent in most developing countries. Indeed, 'permission to pollute' is one of the major concessions granted by Third World governments to attract foreign industries. As a result, many companies, particularly Japanese ones, have exported their 'dirtier' operations to the developing world. The Australian environmental group International Development Action points out that one of the major reasons that Japan finances the construction of hydroelectric plants in South-East Asia and Oceania is that the small, densely populated and heavily industrialised islands of Japan can no longer accommodate further pollution.

So if not dams, what? You cannot deny the developing countries some electricity?

Rural electrification schemes in developing countries have in general been a disaster. The poor cannot afford either the electricity or the gadgets that go with it, and countries which have embarked on massive schemes to supply electricity – using dams for instance – have found themselves with surpluses, such as in Brazil, simply because the market is not there. The temptation then is to entice in overseas corporations, to exploit electricity at giveaway rates. The manufacturing concerns, as pointed out, are often ecological disasters. The priorities for the poor and needy in developing countries are not plentiful electricity, but adequate land and the means to work it.

It is becoming clear that dams are not the most benign way to generate electricity: thermal stations with proper pollution control, of the right size to fit reasonable demand, may be less ecologically destructive in the end than the sterilisation of vast areas under flood waters.

Instead of finding ways to generate more power, could energy be saved?

Nine million people live in the 130,000 square kilometres of territory supplied by the Southern California Edison Company. Since 1983 this utility has made savings from projected 1994 peak demand at a rate of nearly 1.2 GW (approximately 8.6 per cent of 1984 peak load) per year. The utility's cost: a few tenths of a cent per kWh, and falling. In contrast, US nuclear power, after $200 plus billion in private and public investment (current subsidies exceed $15 billion per year) now delivers about half as much energy as wood and is so uneconomic that, once built, the plants cost less to write off in favour of efficiency investments than to operate.

How can savings be achieved?

Houses and buildings can be major consumers of energy, yet
with careful design and the use of energy-efficient appliances,
energy consumption can be reduced by 90 per cent, and with
general improvements in comfort and warmth. Amory
Lovins, an exponent of alternative energy, lives in Colorado.
His house is a showpiece of energy efficiency, its central
heating plant consisting of a special greenhouse set right in
the heart of the house. The greenhouse, in which tropical
fruits grow, collects sufficient solar energy to keep the inside
temperature of the house at 21°C even when the outside
temperature has fallen to minus 8°C. The electrical
appliances in the house, meanwhile, consume one-fourth the
electricity of older conventional equipment. Altogether, the
house uses between one-tenth and one-twentieth the electricity of a conventional house of the same size. According to
Lovins, the extra cost of the energy-saving equipment was
paid back in one year. Over forty years the energy savings
alone will have paid off the cost of the entire house.

What are the prospects of energy saving and use in Britain?

In Britain, some 60 per cent of the energy dug out of the
ground is lost as heat into the environment during conversion,
distribution and use. One way of conserving that energy is to
combine as much as is practicable of thermal electricity
generating stations with district heating schemes. These combined heat and power plants can burn cleanly a variety of
different fuels such as oil, coal, natural gas or even biomass
fuels such as domestic refuse. And as long as the CHP plants
are kept small, then there need be few problems in building
up a district heating scheme to go with them. The reluctance
of CEGB to build CHP schemes stems from their attitude that
power stations must be in the gigawatt range. In fact, over the
past couple of years several hundred small CHP plants, all in
the 40 kW electricity range, have been installed, all of them
privately. Holland already has some 600 small plants and

'Well, it's only taxpayers' money.'

many thousands are planned for the United States. The capital costs per unit of energy delivered are no more than one-third that of the proposed Sizewell B nuclear power station. They also produce power at one-third the cost of nuclear-generated electricity. The Open University Research Group suggests that one 40 kW/CHP unit could be installed for a grouping of up to forty houses. Without any reduction in the standard of living as measured by comfort in the home and access to goods and transport, Britain's primary energy use could be reduced by 30 per cent or more over the next forty years – down from some 313 millions of tons of coal equivalent in 1984 to 219 mtce in 2025.

Would a heat pump cut fuel bills?

Heat pumps transfer energy from a cold place to a hotter one. For building heating they usually run on electricity and give out three times as much heat as an electric fire consuming the same power. The additional heat is extracted from outside air by cooling it. They can be cost-effective, particularly for buildings with no mains gas supply and where they can usefully be reversed for summer cooling. A particularly cost-effective application is swimming-pool heating using off-peak electricity.

Nationally, the energy saving is not clear-cut because 1 kWh of electricity has to be generated by burning 3–4 kWh of fuel. If the fuel were burnt directly, it would give about the same heat output as the electrically powered heat pumps. With hydro, wind, wave or nuclear electricity, of course, this argument does not apply. Any future system which must use electricity for low-temperature heat should use heat pumps. Less common are gas-powered heat pumps, which use an internal combustion engine instead of an electric motor to work the compressor. The waste heat from the engine combines with the heat pump output to give up to twice the heat output of a conventional gas boiler using the same quantity of gas. They are best suited to large buildings, swimming pools and commercial glasshouses.

The Green Alternative

What effect does insulation have on heating bills?

Insulation does not automatically reduce heating bills, since one can continue to use the same amount of fuel and live in greater comfort (at a higher temperature!). Something like 64 per cent of energy used in the home goes for space heating and 22 per cent for water heating. Government figures show that as much as 25 per cent of domestic heat may be lost through an uninsulated roof – so insulating the loft is paid for in three to five years.

Fitting a good, thick insulating jacket on a hot-water tank can cut heat loss by 75 per cent and can pay for itself in only a few weeks; fitting draught-proofing to windows and doors can save 15 per cent heat loss and pay for itself in less than one year; in some cases, 15 per cent of domestic heat loss can occur through floors and a further 15 per cent through uninsulated cavity walls – cavity-wall insulation pays for itself in five to ten years.

Annual fuel bill savings – in return for investments in energy-saving measures – can be anywhere between £100 and £400. With both insulation and better energy management it is not too difficult to reduce your energy consumption by two-thirds. Countries with an overall energy policy, such as Sweden, have embarked on a programme of extending the number of buildings connected to district heating schemes in towns and cities and, tied in with that, of insulating poorer housing in 'slum' areas. The aim, which is being achieved, is to reduce heating requirements for all buildings by a total of 30 per cent. That will reduce overall energy consumption by 15 per cent compared with levels of 1978. People can now live in greater comfort with reduced energy demand.

Is double-glazing really as effective as the salesmen claim?

Double-glazing can reduce heat losses through windows by 50 per cent, but it is still far more important to give priority to the insulation of walls, roof and floor, and eliminate draughts through doors and windows. It is not uncommon for a secondary double-glazing system installed by professionals to cost more than £750 and it may take twenty years for the householder to recoup this investment through savings on fuel, but we should not begrudge the double-glazing industry's success in the market-place – any insulation work is better than none!

How can we best conserve energy at home?

Keep the temperature at 20°C (70°F) by day and turn off the heating at night. This saves energy but also causes less pollution from burned gases, which contribute to acid rain. Make sure your house is well insulated and draught free. Don't let the hot water temperature rise above 70°C if you can help it.

Surely my own efforts at energy conservation will be insignificant since so much of Britain's energy is used in industry and transport?

Well over a quarter of British energy is used in the domestic sector. Furthermore, whilst transport and the industrial sectors have become more energy efficient over the past few years, this has not happened in house and home. Many of us can reduce our energy bills by three-quarters by the implementation of relatively simple measures and by making relatively small investments in insulation materials. Clearly there are many British households which are cold and damp and where means must be found to enable house-holders to use more energy, but even if fuel shortages and hypothermia can be eliminated, the implementation of energy conservation measures throughout the British housing stock could lead to a total saving of more than 8 per cent of total UK energy use. If we are concerned about energy issues, such as the depletion of fossil fuels, pollution and the threat of nuclear power, we can all do our bit to achieve a safe and sustainable energy future.

The Green Alternative

What are the priorities for achieving comfortable living at home while reducing energy use?

In striving for a reasonably warm, comfortable house while conserving energy, a priority must be to eliminate dampness in the floors and walls, since considerable energies are required to evaporate water. The use of a membrane and other damp-excluding materials in a basement or ground floor is therefore mandatory, as well as sound roofing and drainage. Once a dwelling has been made dry, the use of loft and wall insulation will achieve great reductions in the heating required to maintain a comfortable temperature. For comfort and health the inside room temperature need be no higher than 20°C in the living-room areas. Greater energy reductions can then be achieved through double or triple glazing, through adding a conservatory which traps the heat from the sun, and finally through solar panels to provide hot water.

Is there a link between energy conservation and jobs?

Indeed there is. An energy strategy based upon energy saving rather than upon energy production would create many thousands of jobs. For example, manufacturing and installing energy-saving materials (such as cavity-wall insulation, loft insulation and draught-proofing materials) for half a million homes per year would create over 27,000 steady new jobs. Moreover, these jobs would cost less than £30,000 per job, compared with over £2 million to create one job in the nuclear power industry. A measure of 'job effectiveness' is to compare the effect of £1 spent on saving 1 kW of delivered energy with £1 spent on producing 1 kW by new nuclear generating capacity. It turns out that draught-proofing, loft insulation, wall insulation and improved heating controls all represent far more cost-effective investments than new generating capacity. In some cases, insulation measures are five times more effective than building and operating new generating plant. In these days of very high unemployment, it is also worth noting that jobs in energy conservation work require relatively little prior training, taking people straight from the pool of unemployed, unskilled labour.

So what then should our energy future be?

In broad terms the world is not suffering an energy shortage, nor is it likely to in the immediate or distant future. The fossil fuels are available in sufficient quantities to provide a useful energy base for several centuries or more, especially if used wisely and not profligately as is the present tendency. Moreover, the pollution problems associated with the burning of fossil fuels can be virtually eliminated by using readily available technologies such as fluidised-bed combustion.

In fact, we are surrounded by energy and systems, whether inanimate or living, that can trap that energy and make it available for us. Both through a less profligate approach to energy consumption and through the application of energy-efficient technologies we have the opportunity to live well without endangering the existence of millions of people, either through energy deprivation or through pursuit of energy from the atom.

7 Transport

Movement cannot be divorced from the type of society of which each of us is a part – our own aspirations and behaviour have determined the transport systems which increasingly encumber our lives. Towns and cities grew as people wished to live close to the new industrial work places. Then, in the nineteenth century – with the arrival of the horse bus and the development of railways, trams, motor-buses and cars – it became possible to live beyond walking distance of one's work. As a result population densities fell and urban areas became more dispersed. The growth and dispersal of urban areas has gone on ever since; road and rail systems were an all-important shaping influence of our physical environment.

Modern industrial society may have made spectacular improvements in the speed and efficiency of transport systems, and have created complicated commuter service networks, but the overall result is to create a highly mobile society which consumes enormous quantities of energy on traffic movements. Roads and motorways are also voracious consumers of land: a motorway, with its intersections, flyovers and multi-lanes swallows some twenty acres per kilometre of road. As population pressure on land grows such losses will become increasingly hard to justify; yet road traffic continues to grow at the expense of rail. In terms of pollution, land-use and worker inefficiency, modern society has in fact taken a step backward from the past, when society was less mobile.

Our priorities – at present based on short-term destructive development – will have to change. Somehow a new balance must be achieved in which work, as well as leisure activities, become again integrated into local communities, in which the need for daily travel over distances of tens of miles no longer becomes necessary.

'I'm at Junction 1806B . . . Where should I be?'

What has urbanisation got to do with solving today's transport problems?

Everything. We have to understand the cause of today's problems to avoid similar problems in future. For example, we criticise the sometimes disastrous effects of road building but it was inevitable, when Victorian governments began to fund road maintenance and then took them over, that bureaucratic empire-building would result in more roads. Likewise, when county councils became responsible for local roads, their planning and construction became part of the industrial-society hierarchy. If we want fundamental change we must find new ways of getting around that are not dependent upon bureaucracy.

The Green Alternative

In fact, isn't Britain moving into a post-industrial era, in which the old ways of doing things will be inappropriate? For example, private cars cause congestion, whereas public transport is more efficient in moving people; would it not be more sensible to expand bus and train services?

Yes, our society is changing, although there is no agreement about what the future will hold. Towns in Britain are more spread out than in any other developed country and although more people used public transport in the early 1980s in Britain than anywhere else, its use has declined since around 1950. This will continue as urban areas become even more dispersed. It is possible to boost public transport by subsidy, but that does not seem to reduce overall car use and may accelerate urban dispersal by making it easier for people to commute further by bus or train. Subsidy results in more travel, whether it is cheap public transport or the 'free' use of roads. Thirty people in one bus is certainly more efficient than the same number in twenty cars, but if we are simply putting more buses on the road and the use of cars hardly changes, then more energy is consumed. It makes sense to reduce the need to travel.

Can information technology help to reduce travel?

Some people already work from home, using computers connected to their telephone lines to send and receive electronic mail. Telecommunications may shape our physical environment as much as railways did during the industrial era, but with quite different results. Telecommunications costs depend upon the amount of information sent, not the distance – so tele-workers can choose to live wherever they wish to. There is already a trend towards self-employment, and telecommunications will make this feasible for many who at the moment are desk-bound in cities. The notion of working at home is very attractive, particularly to those wanting to escape the hierarchies of big organisations, and some companies such as Rank Xerox, now see tele-working as commercially worthwhile.

Should we stop building more roads?

Yes. New roads and increasingly sophisticated traffic-control systems have hardly changed urban traffic speeds – people adjust their behaviour to the road space available. And now there is a financial crisis. Over the last fifty years resurfacing of minor roads was undertaken on a ten to fifteen year cycle, or less. Now, maintenance cycles of more than a hundred years long are being considered. With the realisation that some roads cannot be kept up, new options open up. The problem then will be to choose which roads to keep in good condition. Local people should be allowed to make these decisions. In some areas it may be decided to close ends of streets, to reduce the damage caused by heavy vehicles and eliminate through traffic or to change some roads to single-track gravel roads with passing places. More money could then be spent on footpaths and cycleways and the remaining roads.

The end result would be that the past tendency towards standardisation would be reversed and solutions which are wanted locally would be adopted.

What can I do?

Individuals can work to achieve sensible transport solutions by putting pressure on local or central government authorities. A government could impose higher taxes on energy resources, such as petroleum and natural gas, which also cause pollution, to encourage fuel conservation. A government could give people back the power to decide which streets they will maintain and which to close. That would be a marvellous way to regenerate real community co-operation – reorganising local streets so that motor vehicles were no longer dominant. So why not campaign for it? Already some towns have pedestrian-only areas.

WOONERF, a scheme in The Hague, Holland, has been running for six years. To improve the quality of life in a residential part of the city both the movement of vehicles and their speed have been restricted by landscaped obstructions.

The Green Alternative

Instead of segregating traffic from pedestrians through the use of pavements and kerbs, with the road being a danger area, pedestrians, cyclists, children and cars have equal rights over the entire road surface, and none may intentionally hinder the others. The speed of vehicles is kept very low by the short distances between the obstructions and parking is restricted. The scheme appears to have worked, with all age groups benefiting from the relative tranquillity and safety.

The key to the future is to decide what sort of society we want, and transport solutions will then follow. If we want a more self-sufficient local economy, it makes sense that we should concern ourselves with roads and locally oriented public transport services, as well as perhaps a local tele-work centre. People working locally put their money into the local economy and reduce motorised travel. Buying things locally not only benefits the local economy, but also cuts down our trips to the hypermarket. We are not then spoiling other people's environment with motorcars and are helping to keep local prices down, to the benefit of those without cars.

What about those who do not have cars?

We tend to forget that many non-car owners also cannot or

will not use conventional public transport. Old and handi-
capped people may be physically unable to climb bus steps or
be unwilling or incapable of travelling unaccompanied.
Mothers with children, no matter how good the service,
cannot carry heavy shopping on a bus.

From October 1986 taxi operators will be able to obtain, for
the asking, a special licence to run scheduled services, like
buses, collecting individual fares. Local co-operative efforts
could provide a local transport service which meets individual
needs in a way which is impossible with conventional public
transport (a small minibus can also be licensed as a taxi).

To keep money within communities we need to develop
local co-operative arrangements. Thus, markets which are
both ecologically sensible and reduce long distance transport
will be created. Local transport will be an essential part of a
locally based economy.

Is there a role for the transport 'expert'?

One problem is our inability to predict human behaviour – we
cannot be certain about all outcomes of our options. For
example, to what extent have city-centre parking restrictions
contributed to the decentralisation of businesses, or is the
phenomenon just part of the inevitable process of urban
dispersal and de-industrialisation? We may never know.
Most transport experts, working for national and local
government, who claim to understand travel behaviour have
a vested interest which rarely coincides with the best interests
of a locality; their so-called knowledge consists of many
unproven beliefs. Pehaps unconsciously they are motivated
to protect and expand their own bureaucratic empires, but
they also work within separate departments and are unable to
take a view of transport within the whole of society. Whilst it
may be natural for bureaucrats to behave in the way they do,
this should not prevent our advocacy of the need to return
decision-making to the street, the neighbourhood and the
village.

The fact that 'they' know no better than we do should
encourage us to take back responsibility for our own locality

and develop our own local expertise. The transport and communications systems we have reflect the lives we each live and the values of our society. The values underlying an ecological/holistic view of life are equally applicable to all kinds of communications. If we believe in organic development, local self-sufficiency, diversity, ecological responsibility and co-operation and are motivated to act accordingly, then – and only then – can we begin to find a sensible approach to transport and communications.

How much energy does transport use? Could we reduce this and still meet our requirements efficiently?

Some 20 per cent of the energy used in Britain goes on transport, nearly all as oil. Fuel efficiency in transport is no more than 25 per cent and with finite oil resources improving energy efficiency should be a policy priority. A car with one driver achieves between 20 and 50 mpg per person; a fully loaded car is four or five times as efficient, while fully loaded buses and trains can achieve 500 mpg per person. Indeed, a car with just the driver in it is five times less efficient than an urban bus, at one third capacity, while a bus is half as efficient as a tube train. In Singapore cars without passengers are now forbidden to enter the inner city.

We can reduce energy consumption dramatically by altering our travelling habits. We could use bicycles for short journeys, though a problem with cycling, particularly in urban areas, is the risk of being knocked down as well as suffering the ill-effects of breathing in traffic fumes. Part of this problem could be overcome by creating cycle-ways. There would be up to 60 per cent energy savings by switching freight transport from road to rail. There is great scope for increased efficiency in vehicle design by streamlining body shapes, making engines work with less friction, using microchips to ensure optimum automatic performance. The construction of cars with a 90 mpg capacity is possible, and better construction standards could double the average life of British cars, halving the energy consumed in car construction.

The Daily Sacrificer

The Green Alternative

Isn't the 'journey to work' a major consumer of energy?

Yes. Motor vehicles such as buses and cars are wasteful and inefficient at slow travel speeds, especially when vehicles stand still with engines idling. There are many partial solutions to the problem, including the greater use of buses, and ensuring that buses have priority over other traffic. Other improvements can be achieved through having express buses which use direct routes, for suburban commuters, as in Montreal, staggered working hours or 'flexi-time' and wider adoption of car-sharing schemes (although such schemes can run into problems with insurance and licensing).

Is subsidising buses just throwing good money after bad?

Besançon, in France, has doubled the use of buses by a carefully thought-out, consistent programme of support. Half the increase is from former car-users. In Britain, Sheffield increases its bus passengers every year and the Greater London Council fares integration policy (beween bus, tube and train) had a dramatic effect on passenger numbers. Where the political will exists, it can be done.

Even though walking and cycling are energy-efficient, aren't they just too slow?

We walk a third to a half of all trips, and motorised trips often involve walking – from car parks and tube stations, for example. Short trips are often quicker by foot. Cycling in urban areas is as fast as driving for slightly longer trips (up to two miles).

Can walking and cycling be effectively encouraged?

If local shops close down, if the school serves a huge area and is built on a 'green field' site, then non-motorised transport suffers. So it is vital to 'localise' activities – encouraging local schools, health centres and workshops, bringing interest and vitality back into villages and estates. At the same time we should create footpaths and cycleways that are really convenient and pleasant.

That all seems very long-term?

Long-term planning of cities is vital. But for quick results we can create cycle-ways along main commuter routes, with cyclists given priority at junctions, short cuts through parks, and so on. The results of government experiments are promising. In the London area, 1 per cent of the transport budget (*just* 1 per cent) has been put aside for cycling schemes: more people are now on their bikes, and more people are using public transport, while the increase in car use has slowed.

Would electric cars help to reduce both pollution and energy use?

Their use would help reduce exhaust emissions, but electric cars are inefficient because they require very large batteries to store electrical energy which have frequently to be recharged from mains electricity. Also, the 'energy budget' of an electric vehicle may be similar to a petrol-driven car when one counts up the energy used in the manufacture of batteries, the engine, transmission system and interior. For low speeds and frequent stopping and starting (as with a milk-float) an electric motor is very cost-effective but for family motoring the relatively low top speeds, the weight and size of battery-storage systems and the limited travel range militate against it. But new batteries and new vehicle designs are on the way and if petrol costs rise steeply, battery-driven cars may come into their own.

Bicycles, tricycles (and assorted electric vehicles for the old and disabled) should become available with all-weather protection. Some urban cycleways could be covered and well lit for far less cost than roads can be provided for cars. It might even be possible to add a safe – say 24 volt – electric rail (supplied from high voltage lines via transformers every mile or so) on to which people could put flexible leads from electric vehicles – since batteries seem to limit transport otherwise. A safe top speed of 20 mph would be sensible for such a system, and quite adequate.

What is the case for railways?

Railways are kinder to the landscape than roads or airports. They can also be less intrusive in towns and they can operate at high speed with safety between city centres. They are cleaner in the environment as electrification spreads and they are not dependent upon a specific fossil energy source. Heavy lorries, motor coaches and aeroplanes are tied to petroleum-derived fuels and certain to remain so, whereas electric trains could be driven by wind or wave power if necessary. In the meantime the trains can use 'coal by wire' as Lord Robens used to put it, and coal will not run out in the foreseeable future. North Sea oil, for example, is expected to peak this year and will run out, for all practical purposes, in the early years of the new century. After that we will be dependent upon imports, the price of which will be outside our control.

There are, then, good reasons for favouring a rail-based transport system for mainland Britain, although railways need not be ruled out on the bigger islands in the longer term. Electric main lines could connect *all* main centres – north, south and cross-country. Routes still exist, or could be relaid, or even built from scratch. A far-seeing and imaginative society would be aiming in this direction and making plans accordingly.

Sparsely populated areas could reasonably be served by diesel-powered buses or mini-buses running in connection with the trains at strategically located railheads. This would be better use for scarce oil fuel than belching it out on fast motorways which only duplicate main rail routes anyway.

Our railways could have the capacity to move *all* the heavy freight between major centres, which would largely remove the juggernaut from the system, and certainly from urban areas. With the profits so realised – for freight is profitable even on the railways as they are – a much reduced subsidy would be required for the passenger network. It would also be more comfortable for the private motorist who would not have the juggernauts to contend with. In addition, the roads' maintenance bill would be much less since cars cause little damage to the infrastructure.

Clearly our Western ideas of individual freedom could encroach here. Any such centrally directed policy would run up against the powerful lobby of the transport hauliers. However, if the plan included a good deal for the private motorist, then any vigorous and committed administration could sell it to the populace at large.

Railways are held in some regard – all the polls on the matter confirm this. A positive policy which organised public transport along the lines suggested would not be opposed by the generality of the people. It is all a question of political will.

Should all the railways be electrified, making use of centralised power production?

There are certain attractions in an electrified rail system, especially since electric trains are cleaner than diesel-driven trains. For underground or suburban rail networks, electrification can lead to reduced pollution, reduced noise, greater stopping and starting flexibility and greater comfort for travellers. However, electricity has to be produced somewhere and the environmental cost is paid by those areas that lie down-wind of major power stations. Two-thirds of the energy stored in fuel is presently wasted during the generation of electricity. Even if an electric train is 30 per cent efficient, the overall loss of converting the energy stored in fossil fuels into forward movement is huge and total atmospheric pollution is not necessarily reduced. It may be more efficient to burn fuel directly on a train (even allowing for the train having to carry its fuel) than for a train to use electricity transported on live tracks or overhead cables. There is also the high energy cost of installing the electrical gadgetry required along every inch of an electrified railway network. Calculations suggest that only a train drawing its electrical energy from a CHP generating plant has greater energy efficiency than a bus or diesel train.

The Green Alternative

Could we use our canals better or are they too small?

A small but vociferous canal transport lobby in Britain argues effectively for the transfer of much bulk freight transport to the inland waterway system. At one time the canals were very heavily used, but once door-to-door transport was required freight was increasingly carried by road. Today 90 per cent of Britain's freight traffic goes by road, even though freight costs per tonne per mile are more than three times greater by road than by water. So great savings are possible through the use of Britain's 1,500 miles of navigable rivers and canals. Freight such as coal, cement, sand, grain, semi-finished manufactured goods and chemicals can travel slowly and canal barges can carry them at a price of 250 tonne-miles per gallon of fuel consumed. British canal barges seldom exceed 500 tonnes carrying capacity, but the larger waterways can take self-propelled barges carrying 2,000 tonnes; vessels can also be adapted for special cargoes. The Inland Waterways Association presses for much greater inland waterway use; the care of canals deserves support, for canal use brings with it both reduced pollution and reduced energy use.

Why do we need to transport so many goods anyway?

The milk produced in the dairying region of West Wales is turned into butter and cheese and sold all over Britain. The people of West Wales drink, however, not their own milk but milk produced in Glamorgan (South Wales) which is bottled in Swansea and then transported sixty miles by road to the main distributors in Pembrokeshire. This little saga is repeated a million times, with a million different products, daily in every part of Britain. The separation of producer and consumer is one of the absurdities of modern life. Although many regions could be self-sufficient in many of the products needed for life today, they are caught up in a system of export and import, and endlessly complicated transport linkages. The energy costs of all this are difficult to calculate, but one small example of the scale of energy wastage lies in a single loaf of white bread which requires an energy input equivalent to about 6 units (kWh) of electricity from farm to kitchen table if it is produced in a centralised mass-production enterprise. A wholemeal loaf made from organically produced wheat which is milled locally and baked at home uses only 3 kWh of energy. We do not need to transport raw materials, partly finished goods, manufactured products and packaging materials furiously across the length and breadth of Britain. Given the political will, huge energy savings (and greater self-reliance, social harmony and economic stability) can flow from decentralisation and simplified and smaller-scale production of the things we need.

8   Land use and urbanisation

People in the world are increasingly living in cities. In 1925, when the world population was less than half that of today, 28 per cent lived in cities and conurbations. Now the urban population worldwide is over 40 per cent, with 80 per cent in the developed industrialised countries living in cities. Moreover, the world population is increased each year by 80 to 90 million people and the drift to the cities is accelerating. Should the trends continue, by the end of the century half of the world's projected population of 6.13 billion – massive disasters aside – will live in cities, some of them like Mexico City and São Paulo in Brazil with populations of over 25 million. Most of the new mega-cities will be in the developing countries, where facilities for housing, sewage and waste disposal, clean water and transport will be grossly inadequate. Already in São Paulo some rivers have become little more than moving cesspools.

Much of the present drift to the cities results in shanty slums – like the favellas of São Paulo – and in poverty and disease. Such a process can hardly be called 'development', yet it is an inevitable consequence of the transformation of society from being agrarian-based to one concerned with consumerism and manufacture.

The civil engineer Ken Newcombe claims in the journal *Ambio* of the Swedish Royal Academy (January 1978) that to provide the new mega-cities expected by the turn of the century with the facilities and standard of living prevailing today in a city such as Hong Kong would require at least five times the total energy consumed by the world in 1973 – a peak year in energy use. Meanwhile the average energy consumption per individual in today's Hong Kong is several fold less than that found in most cities in industrialised countries.

Cities and the infrastructure to support them engulf a great deal of land, often of prime agricultural quality – some 130,000 square kilometres having been lost to urbanisation in

224

the United States over the past decade. Worldwide, the loss between 1980 and 2000 is likely to amount to 10 million acres, enough to feed 84 million people. Indeed, in Egypt the equivalent of all the agricultural land gained through irrigation from the Aswan Dam has already been lost to urban growth, itself the result of the displacement from the land brought about through mechanisation of agriculture and the displacement of traditional farming practices.

In Britain less than 2 per cent of the population are now actively engaged in agriculture and horticulture, and with the longest history of industrialisation in the world, it is not surprising that a large proportion of the population lives in cities, towns and suburbs. Yet the British have a long history of enjoying nature and the countryside, the idea of the 'Garden City' being one way in which nature – admittedly highly regulated – and the town may be brought together into a wholesome compromise.

Are there any examples of modern Garden City developments?

The Town and Country Planning Association, together with the Rowntree Trust, have set out to keep alive the concept of the Garden City as first expounded by Ebenezer Howard. To work out what might be the modern equivalent of Howard's concept, the TCPA and the Trust set up nine working parties which have resulted in what have been called the Lightmoor New Community Project in Telford New Town in Shropshire and the Conway Inner Cities Project in Birkenhead.

Tony Gibson, who developed the Education for Neighbourhood Change programme at Nottingham University's School of Education, took part in two of the nine working parties, and compiled a book on the findings of the working parties, *Counterweight: the Neighbourhood Option*, recently published by the TCPA. He is currently Development Officer for the TCPA for both the Lightmoor and Conway Inner Cities projects.

The Green Alternative

So what's new about the Lightmoor New Community?

Nothing much, if you go far enough back to the days when the first settlements took shape. Then people were looking for land to build their own homes and workplaces on, partly by individual effort and partly by working together. More recently, the sequence of people–land–development has become twisted around. Outside developers find the land and develop it to suit their interests. Then they offer it, with strings, to the people who are going to live there. The Lightmoor New Community is an attempt to get the sequence right again.

How are they going about it?

They set out to find people interested in making a new settlement, and were able to obtain and offer land, 22½ acres in the first phase, with a possibility of 250 acres in all eventually, from the Telford Development Corporation. It's low-grade agricultural land seamed with nineteenth-century family mineworkings, plenty of trees and grass and other wildlife, lovely to look at and walk over, but needing a 'one-off' approach to make the most of its possibilities. Suited to pioneer settlers, rather than to conventional developers and builders.

What sort of people have come forward?

So far it is a good cross-section. All want somewhere to live where they are at home with each other and can enjoy the countryside and improve it, and can use their skills to make a modest living on their own or together. There is a bricklayer and his wife who keeps goats, a computer technologist, a local government planner taking early retirement and his wife who is a skilled cook, a craft-design teacher, a civil engineer. They are mostly people who want two strings to their bow, combining a bit of cultivation in the back garden and keeping a pig or two, with another skill. This may be home-based, say computing, or baking or architectural design – or it might be a local teaching job. The point is that it is the combination of the skills – the computer in the kitchen and the pig in the backyard, which makes up the livelihood.

Why such a fuss about the belt-and-braces economy?

Space-age technology is making it much easier to store power and use sophisticated tools, whether it is a knitting machine or a word processor, and to tap into the outside world from a home base. More important, change is being forced upon people at an increasing rate. No single generation in the history of mankind has experienced so many and so various changes as the generations which are living now. To cope with our future depends on being able to adapt, to take advantage of changing circumstances.

You mean each one for himself or herself?

No. The other side of the coin is the need which is being forced on us (and which many of us accept with enjoyment) to co-operate in order to make the most of slender resources. So the point about schemes like Lightmoor is that there is a sort of balance between what you do on your own and what you decide together.

For instance?

They put a big contour model of the first phase of the site in the middle of the field where the buildings might go, as a focus for the group of prospective residents, with one or two planners from the Telford Development Corporation in attendance. Between them they worked out where the access road and the different building plots could go to suit the lie of the land. They established a group policy on the building area and the maximum size of the plots. Each family then worked out what kind of house they could afford and had long consultations with individual architects (now there is also an off-the-shelf basic design available if people want to save architect's fees, and still leave themselves room for variation on the basic design). The group decided on how to share the cost of the soil investigation and the access road. Individuals work out how they are going to develop their own livelihoods, and if they choose they can club together to form a small co-operative.

How much do they leave to the professionals?

They have been able to develop a very good working relationship with officers in the Development Corporation and the district and county councils. This is partly because all three bodies are represented – along with the Town and Country Planning Association and representatives elected by the prospective residents – on the non-profit-making company, Lightmoor New Community Limited, which holds and allocates the land. Because these professionals have taken part, with prospective residents, in most of the formative discussions they have firmly grasped the idea that they are there to explain the possibilities and the constraints – to set out the options but then to leave it to the residents to choose. So the experts are on tap, not on top.

Isn't Lightmoor rather a special case? Would it work anywhere else?

They are lucky in that under the New Towns Act a Development Corporation can obtain and pass on a more flexible planning system – for instance, having work areas integrated with housing areas. But most public authorities have discretion if they choose to use it, when it's a question of recovering resources that would otherwise be unused.

All over this country there is land which has lain unused or underused because its former uses are obsolete: low-grade agricultural land, condemned pit heads, docklands, the vandalised and neglected demolition areas of the inner cities. They have not been developed so far because the traditional centralised planning system is top-heavy. Working from the top down seldom provides for the imagination and the flexibility which is required in order to make the most of such resources. And besides, even when a top-down scheme is developed, directed by an outside body, commercial or governmental – its prospects for survival in these days are dim. It is probably going to get vandalised, because the people who are brought in to live on the ready-made estate have no real commitment to it, they can take no credit for it, and recent history has shown that when it gets vandalised by some members of the community the others will look on.

People are likely to safeguard what they have had a hand in creating. The act of creation itself begins to bring about a change in mutual self-confidence and in the quality of life, a tiny cluster at a time. It is like growing many small tree plantations. In the end they change the climate.

Anyone interested in joining the Lightmoor Project, or adapting the idea to their own neighbourhood, should contact the Project Office at 10, Helton Terrace, St Georges, Telford, Shropshire.

Should we try to create land-based communities?

The kibbutzim in Israel, as well as various nineteenth-century communities in America, mostly religiously oriented, such as the Shakers, have demonstrated quite effectively the possibilities of a move towards self-sufficiency. There is much to commend similar experiments in Britain today. However, intended communities seldom seem to get beyond the planning stage, and it might be better to work with natural communities towards more ecological and self-sufficient economies. This was done at Dartington in Devon, over many years, with a large input of capital. In the United States experiments have been tried with land trusts, as a form of communal ownership that can provide continuity. These are based on the concept that the land should be used in the best interests of the whole community, present and future.

Naturally, there are difficulties in getting full or even majority agreement to major community decisions. It is this 'political' problem that has made village-scale 'utopias' so difficult to get off the ground – or rather, on to the ground! In the early nineteenth century, the utopian writer Charles

The Green Alternative

Fourier worked out the ideal community down to the last pear tree, and had many brilliant ideas, alongside some more controversial ones. His theories inspired several practical attempts in America. None of these ideas should be dismissed as impractical in a world where industrialism has brought such ecological and political chaos. A lead could still be made in the direction of ideal communities. Some research on their present-day needs is being done at the Food and Energy Research Centre (see p. 347).

Is it legal to issue a local money? If it were, what ecological advantages might it have?

It is unlikely that any kind of local money would be legal in Britain today. But during the depression in the United States, a few communities were able to 'pull themselves up by their bootstraps' by using a local medium of exchange to get economic activities going.

The main objection is likely to come from tax collectors, who want to be able to benefit from any trade that takes place. Nevertheless, a sizeable amount of barter takes place in any case as people realise its tax advantages but, in theory, and occasionally in practice, the authorities can clamp down on this too.

A kind of money that can be used only within a certain community would bring about more local self-sufficiency and, in many instances, this could be ecologically beneficial in reducing unnecessary trade and transport and thus increasing the variety of production in a region or community.

How can I store my savings in a way that will help the world become Greener?

You can put your savings into a Green project – such as buying land for trees and conservation, or for self-sufficient or commercial organic growing, or into other ecological projects, for instance special energy projects.

The Mercury Provident Society Ltd (Orlingbury House, Lewes Road, Forest Row, Sussex RH18 5AA) has been developed in recent years to bring together those who wish to invest money in projects of an ecological nature and those who are running or planning such projects. More recently, the Stewardship Unit Trust (Freepost, Stewardship Dept, Friends' Provident Life Office, Dorking, Surrey RH4 1BR) has been started to try to steer regular market investments away from the more noxious products and business practices. As a general adviser in this field, there is EIRIS (Ethical Investment Research and Information Service, 266 Pentonville Road, London N1 9JY). Many other ecologically oriented charities now exist, contributing to which may confer tax advantages.

The Ecology Building Society was set up to lend money on energy-saving properties and other ecologically sound projects. The Society's assets have risen from an initial £5,000 in 1981 when it was formed, to over £1,275,000 in December 1985 with over 1,000 investors and depositors. The Ecology Building Society is able to help where other societies will not. In lending on ecologically sound properties they feel that they are making a contribution to the sort of lifestyle for which an increasing number of people are looking. During 1985 the Society provided advances on smallholdings, terraced houses, small craft enterprises, an organic farm, a wholefood shop and some woodland.

9 The nuclear arms race

The two superpowers, the USA and the USSR seem implacably caught up in a nuclear arms race. The SALT 2 Strategic Arms Limitation Treaty of 1979 does not appear to be working and despite summit talks between Ronald Reagan and Mikhail Gorbachov, is in jeopardy. Britain and France too, with their own nuclear strike force, are an added complication in any move towards disarmament by the two superpowers. Britain, as a member of NATO, has American bases and cruise missiles in addition to its own nuclear force; France, with its *Force de Frappe*, is independent and has not signed the Non-Proliferation Treaty of 1969.

It would seem that the world is moving inexorably towards Armageddon. Even a limited nuclear war would make the earth uninhabitable for most, if not all, human beings. Indeed, the nuclear winter scenario in which dust, ash and smoke sucked up into the atmosphere blot out the sun and cause a precipitous decline in surface temperatures is now for American and Russian scientists alike the accepted outcome of nuclear war.

And what about 'Star Wars', Reagan's Strategic Defense Initiative? Star Wars is based on the firing of powerful laser beams against incoming enemy missiles. It will depend on a highly coordinated, all-encompassing network of monitoring devices that will be able to detect and distinguish real targets from every other kind of object in space, including one's own defence system. The decision to fire the lasers will have to be taken automatically, as there will be no time for human intervention. To be effective and provide the necessary protection the automatic scanning of space against attack will have to work to perfection, as will the missile destroying lasers. No one can guarantee that Star Wars will work, and computer scientists in particular are sceptical. Nevertheless, the contracts to be won for participating in Star Wars will entice many scientists to work on something in which they do not wholeheartedly believe.

232

The new trends in nuclear defence and deterrence have deeply worrying implications for the future of the human race. The following terms are used in this chapter:

strategic weapons – those with predestined targets that are deployed in advance as part of a defence strategy

tactical weapons – those for which decisions on targets are taken during the course of battle manoeuvres

Star Wars – Strategic Defense Initiative

MAD – Mutual Assured Destruction

CEP – Circular Error Probability

MIRV – Multiple Independently Targeted Re-Entry Vehicles

ICBM – InterContinental Ballistic Missile

SLBM – Submarine Launched Ballistic Missile

ASW – Anti-Submarine Warfare

The Green Alternative

NUTS – Nuclear Utility Targeting Strategy
NAVSTAR – the American 18-Satellite navigation system

Isn't Star Wars a good advance from MAD – Mutually Assured Destruction?

When, on 23 March 1983, President Reagan introduced his 'Star Wars' Strategic Defense Initiative, he complained that Soviet and American nuclear policies relied 'on the spectre of retaliation, on mutual threat'. 'And', he said, 'that's a sad commentary on the human condition. Wouldn't it be better to save lives than to avenge them?' The President was referring to the superpowers being engaged in a policy of nuclear deterrence based on mutually assured destruction, a policy commonly known as MAD.

'What if', President Reagan asked, 'free people could live secure in the knowledge that their security did not rest upon the threat of instant US retaliation to deter a Soviet attack, that we could intercept and destroy strategic ballistic missiles before they reached our own soil or that of our allies?' He asked the scientific community 'to give us the means of rendering these nuclear weapons impotent and obsolete'.

Some Star Wars advocates claim that a less than perfect strategic defence will be worth having even though a perfect defence is unattainable because it will make the other side, i.e. the USSR, less inclined to risk MAD in so far as its missiles would be vulnerable and those of the US less so. They also argue that new American strategic offensive weapons should be deployed 'to safeguard stability during the initial phase of a defensive transition'. Star Wars advocates want no slackening of the pace of the development and deployment of new offensive strategic nuclear weapons while defensive strategic nuclear weapons are being developed and deployed.

Are the superpowers now really operating MAD policies?

The USA is set to produce, during the 1980s and up to the mid-1990s, some 30,000 new warheads. Of these about 14,000 are for weapons in current research and development programmes. The US will probably deploy – i.e. have ready to fire – 23,000 or so new nuclear warheads during the 1980s. About 17,000 nuclear warheads will be withdrawn from the stockpile or replaced during this period. And by 1990 the American nuclear stockpile will contain about 32,000 weapons. Today, they have about 25,000 nuclear weapons. We must expect the Soviets to increase their nuclear weapons to a similar extent. Today's Soviet nuclear arsenal contains about the same number of nuclear weapons as the Americans'.

Huge though these increases in the numbers of nuclear weapons are, from the point of view of world security, they are much less important than qualitative improvements in the weapons. There is already so much 'overkill' in the nuclear arsenals – there is no rational reason, military, strategic or political, for having 25,000 nuclear warheads – that even large increases in numbers are of little relevance to the nuclear policies of the superpowers; they simply make an irrational situation somewhat more irrational.

At most there are 200 cities in each superpower containing more than about 100,000 people. Assuming two nuclear warheads are needed to destroy a large city, about 400 warheads would be an adequate nuclear deterrent, more than enough, in fact, to kill roughly 100 million people in each superpower and destroy about a half of its industrial capacity.

And what about qualitative improvements in nuclear weapons?

The most crucial qualitative advances in nuclear weapons are those which improve their accuracy and reliability. The more accurate a warhead is, the smaller the target that can be destroyed. This means that, as nuclear weapons become more accurate, more military targets are chosen. Many of the new strategic nuclear weapons being deployed may, therefore, be seen as more suitable for actually fighting a nuclear war than using MAD as a deterrent.

The accuracy of a nuclear warhead is normally measured by

235

its circular error probability, or CEP. This is defined as the radius of the circle centred on the target within which half of a large number of warheads of the same type would fall. Both the Americans and the Soviet are reducing the CEPs – and, therefore, increasing the accuracy – of their nuclear-weapon systems, including their ICBMs, SLBMs, strategic cruise missiles, and tactical nuclear weapons. The Americans have improved the guidance system of the Minuteman ICBM, and these improvements have reduced the CEP from about 400 metres (its value at the end of the 1970s) to about 200 metres (its current value). At the same time, the design of the Minuteman warhead has improved so that for the same weight, volume, radar cross-section and aerodynamic characteristics, the explosive power of the warhead has increased from the equivalent of the explosive power of 170,000 tons of TNT to that of 330,000 tons of TNT.

The Hiroshima bomb, weighing 4 tons, exploded with a power equivalent to that of about 12,000 tons of TNT. The ratio of the explosive yield to weight was 3,000. The new Minuteman warhead has an explosive power equal to that of 330,000 tons of TNT and a weight of about 300 kilograms, giving a yield-to-weight ratio of more than 1,000,000. This vast increase in the efficiency of nuclear weapons, achieved in just over thirty years, is only one indication of the incredible rate at which military technology advances.

How do these developments come about?

About 500,000 of the world's 2,250,000 scientists work world-wide on military research and development. Counting only physicists and engineering scientists – those at the forefront of technological advances – more than a half are working on military research and development. Governments are funding military science to the tune of nearly $100,000 million a year, far more than they give for peaceful research.

What are the latest developments?

The new higher-yield Minuteman warhead, delivered with the increased accuracy, has more than a 50 per cent chance of destroying a Soviet ICBM in its silo (hardened to withstand an over-pressure of about 2,500 pounds per square inch). If two Minuteman warheads are fired at a Soviet missile silo the probability of destroying it is about 90 per cent.

The American new ICBM, the MX, will be even more accurate than the Minuteman. The guidance for the MX uses a new all-altitude guidance system, called the advanced inertial reference sphere, that can take account of the missile being moved from its base before it is fired. A CEP of about 100 metres, half that of the Minuteman, will be achieved with this system. The MX warheads may also be fitted with terminal guidance, in which a laser or radar set in the nose of the warhead scans the ground around the target as the warhead travels through the earth's atmosphere. The laser or radar locks on to a distinctive fixed feature in the area, such as a tall building or a hill, and guides the warhead with great accuracy onto its target. With terminal guidance, MX missiles will have CEPs of 30 metres or so. The Americans are also developing a new small, mobile ICBM, carrying a single warhead, to replace the MXs in the 1990s; it will be called Midgetman.

The most formidable Soviet ICBM is the ss-18. The CEP of the ss-18 is, or soon will be, about 250 metres. A typical ss-18 warhead probably has an explosive yield of about 500 kt and would have about a 50 per cent probability of destroying an American ICBM in its silo. Two warheads fired in succession would have about a 90 per cent chance of success. The USSR has ss-18s in service, most, if not all of which, carry 10 MIRved warheads each. The ss-18 ICBM force, 3,000 or so warheads strong is, therefore, a significant threat to the American 1,000-missile strong ICBM force. In theory, three ss-18 warheads could be targeted on each American ICBM. The Soviet ss-19 ICBM may carry 6 MIRved warheads so that the total force of 360 missiles may be able to deliver 2,160 warheads, though the CIA claims that the ss-19 is not accurate enough to be a serious threat to American ICBMs.

And submarines?

Both superpowers are busily modernising their submarine fleets. The USA, for example, plans to deploy about one new Trident submarine a year for the next few years, at a cost of about $2,000 million per submarine. The US Navy envisages a fleet of some twenty-five Tridents early in the twenty-first century. Seven Tridents are already operational and the eighth began sea trials in May 1986.

The first eight Tridents will be fitted with Trident C-4, also called Trident-1, SLBMs. But the ninth Trident, currently due to become operational in 1988, will be equipped with the Trident-2 SLBM. The Trident-2 will have a longer range than the Trident-1 and will therefore be less exposed to Soviet anti-submarine warfare (ASW) systems. If the US Navy's plan to operate twenty-five Trident submarines early in the next century comes about, they will carry 600 Trident-2 SLBMs equipped with about 6,000 nuclear warheads. Each warhead will probably have an explosive power of about 500 kt.

Trident-2 warheads will be very accurate. Whereas the CEPs of the new submarine-launched Poseidon c-3 and the Trident-1 missiles are about 450 metres, the CEP of the Trident-2 will be about 200 metres. The improved accuracy will be achieved by mid-course guidance and more accurate navigation of submarines through NAVSTAR, the American 18-satellite navigational system due to become operational in 1988.

The use of terminal guidance will increase the accuracy of Trident-2 SLBMs even more. With it, CEPs can be expected to come down to roughly 50 metres, which is probably the best attainable in practice for ballistic missiles. Within a few years, then, American SLBMs will be as lethal as ICBMs.

The USSR is also improving the quality of its SLBM force although Soviet SLBMs are thought to be less accurate than their American counterparts. The CEP of the ss-n-18, for example, is probably about 600 metres, although the ss-n-20 and the ss-nx-23, now under development, are almost certainly more accurate.

Once the 50-metre plateau is reached by the USA, it is only

a matter of time – probably three to five years – before the USSR catches up.

And what about tactical nuclear weapons?

Both superpowers are modernising their tactical (for use on battlefields) nuclear arsenals. Tactical nuclear weapons generally have a shelf-life of twenty years, after which they must be replaced or withdrawn. The weapons deteriorate because the fission and fusion material in them, particularly tritium, decays and some of the non-nuclear materials deteriorate. Modernisation is, therefore, inevitable if nuclear weapons continue to be deployed.

Among the new types of tactical nuclear weapons being deployed by the USA in NATO countries are Pershing-2 ground-to-ground missiles and ground-launched cruise missiles (designed to hug the ground and avoid detection). Both types are fitted with terminal guidance and are extremely accurate, with CEPs of about 50 metres. The Pershing-2 missiles have a range of 1,800 kilometres and the ground-launched cruise missiles have a range of about 2,500 kilometres. Both carry warheads with explosive yields of a few kilotons. The deployment in Western Europe of 108 Pershing-2s and 464 cruise missiles is now being carried out.

These American missiles have been deployed in NATO European countries in response to the Soviet deployment of the ss-20 missile. In turn, the Soviets have deployed new ground-to-ground missiles, the ss-21, ss-22 and ss-23, in response to the American deployment of Pershing-2s and cruise missiles. The Soviet missiles are, however, less sophisticated and accurate than the American ones. The ss-20, for example, a mobile missile with a range of about 5,000 kilometres and carrying three MIRVed warheads each with a yield of 150 kt, has a CEP of about 400 or 500 metres. The probability of the ss-20 destroying a target of a given protective hardness is about the same as that of an American Poseidon SLBM. Pershing-2, missiles, however, are many times more lethal than the ss-20, and the two weapons cannot be regarded as comparable. The Soviets have deployed about 400 ss-20s, about half of them west of the Urals, targeted on Western Europe, and the others east of the Urals, aimed at targets in Asia.

Is NUTS (Nuclear Utility Targeting Strategy) better than MAD?

Until the early 1960s, NATO's official military policy was massive retaliation. If the Soviets attacked Western Europe, NATO would respond by dropping nuclear weapons on Soviet cities and destroying Soviet society. But in the early 1960s the policy was abruptly changed to 'flexible response' because the Soviet nuclear arsenal had grown to make massive retaliation no longer sensible. The idea of flexible response is that if the Warsaw Pact attacks NATO then NATO would try to beat off the attack, and win the war, with conventional weapons. But if the Warsaw Pact broke through into West Germany, NATO would stem the advance by using tactical nuclear weapons. There may then be a nuclear exchange but, hopefully, one limited to low-yield nuclear weapons.

Flexible response advocates argue that at this stage sanity may prevail and NATO and the Warsaw Pact might negotiate an end to war. But if the fighting continued NATO would be prepared, if necessary, to escalate the conflict and use higher-yield nuclear weapons. The final stage in this ladder of escalation would be the use of strategic nuclear weapons against the homeland of the superpowers. Massive retaliation has not been abandoned, just delayed. And since both sides can now do it, it has become mutual.

The theory is, of course, that the threat of mutual massive retaliation is enough to prevent one side from attacking the other in the first place. Hence, the policy of flexible response depends upon a strategy of nuclear deterrence based on mutual assured destruction. Morton Halperin, who served on the US National Security Council under Henry Kissinger, summarised NATO's policy of flexible response as follows. 'First, we will fight with conventional weapons until we are losing. Then we will fight with battlefield nuclear weapons until we are losing. Then we will blow up the world!'

A paradox of MAD is that it only works with inaccurate nuclear weapons. When a large number of nuclear weapons are deployed, the enemy, knowing they are accurate will assume that they are targeted on his military forces and not on his cities. The cities then cease to be the hostages. Accuracy, in other words, kills deterrence. With accurate nuclear weapons, nuclear war-fighting based on the destruction of hostile military forces becomes the preferred policy.

Current American nuclear policy, Russian also, is a confusing mixture of MAD and NUTS – nuclear-war fighting. SLBMs provide the MAD element, being still inaccurate enough to be targeted on cities, while ICBMs are nuclear war-fighting weapons, accurate enough to be targeted on enemy strategic nuclear forces and other military targets. But when Trident-2 SLBMs are deployed in the late 1980s they will be accurate enough to be targeted on military targets in the USSR, and American nuclear policy will go totally from MAD to NUTS.

The Green Alternative

Nuclear war will surely destroy the world, won't it?

A range of military technologies is being developed that will strengthen the belief that a nuclear war can be fought and won. The most important of the 'war-winning' technologies now under development are those related to anti-submarine warfare, anti-ballistic missiles and anti-satellite warfare systems. The aim of strategic ASW is to detect and destroy within a short time all the enemy's strategic nuclear submarines within range of one's homeland. There is much secrecy about ASW developments. For example, the US Navy is working with blue-green lasers, possibly deployed on satellites, to detect submarines, but little is known about the results of this work. From time to time statements are made by, for example, US Naval spokesmen implying an existing capability to detect and destroy Soviet strategic nuclear submarines, at least those close to the US coast.

When one side can severely limit the damage caused by the other side's strategic nuclear forces in a retaliatory strike, and believes it can destroy any enemy warheads that survive a surprise attack by using ballistic missile defences, then the temptation to make an all-out first strike may become irresistible, particularly during an international crisis. And the side that first perceives that it has a first-strike capability may well believe that it should use it to prevent the other side from building up its defence capabilities and thinking that it is ahead and can afford the risk of first strike.

The first action in a nuclear surprise attack would be to destroy the other side's military satellites, the 'eyes and ears' of the military in space. This is why great efforts are being made to develop effective anti-satellite weapons. The current developments in weapons guidance systems and the increased possibility of breaching the other side's defences are much more likely to lead to an offensive nuclear first-strike capability than to the nuclear defence advocated by President Reagan. The President's dream of the perfect defence against nuclear attack may well become a nightmare.

'Look at it this way: we annihilated the Ruskies ten times over; they annihilated us only nine times over – technically, WE WON.'

Can we control the nuclear arms race?

Since the Second World War great efforts have been made to control the nuclear arms race and achieve some nuclear disarmament. But these efforts have failed. We have learnt that whereas military technology advances very rapidly, diplomacy moves very slowly. By the time arms control treaties can be negotiated they are out of date.

Given this situation, the best way forward would be to negotiate a nuclear freeze in which the nuclear-weapon powers would agree to stop the testing, production and deployment of nuclear weapons. The most important elements of a freeze are:

- A comprehensive ban on all nuclear-weapon tests
- A ban on the testing of ballistic missiles
- A cut-off in the production of fissile material for military use

The Green Alternative

Of these measures, which could be negotiated separately, a comprehensive nuclear test ban is the most urgent. Such a ban would prevent the further modernisation of nuclear weapons since testing is vital to check that they work effectively.

A nuclear freeze should not be seen as an end in itself but the first step to ending the nuclear arms race and beginning the progress of nuclear disarmament, starting with the destruction of tactical nuclear weapons. Only when we all begin to understand the mad logic behind the arms race can we hope to succeed in getting rid of these weapons before they get rid of us.

Where does the plutonium for weapons come from?

All nuclear reactors produce some plutonium as a result of using uranium as fuel. If the plutonium is left in the core for a short time, the fuel will contain a high proportion of the plutonium isotope most useful for weapon-making – plutonium-239. Leaving the fuel in for longer causes a build-up of other plutonium isotopes such as 240 and 241 which are less fissile. Many reactors are dual-purpose, the aim being to generate electricity and good quality plutonium at the same time.

If we wanted to dismantle nuclear weapons, what should we do with the plutonium?

Even supposing the superpowers were persuaded to disarm, the world would still be left with the nuclear weapons. It has been suggested that the safest way to dispose of the plutonium would be to incinerate it in nuclear reactors, thereby generating electricity at the same time. The problem with that proposition is that only a small proportion of fissile fuel gets consumed during its stay in the reactor core, and, since uranium is still present, more plutonium is generated all the time. The fuel would therefore have to be reprocessed to extract out the unused plutonium, and whatever one's feeling about the safety of reactors, reprocessing is potentially the most risky part of the nuclear fuel cycle since solid spent fuel has to be dissolved chemically in hot nitric acid. Containment of all radioactive debris and waste from then on becomes a major environmental problem.

Having incinerated and reprocessed the plutonium, the next stage would be to manufacture new fuel. Reprocessed material is, however, contaminated with radioactive poisons – some of them gamma-emitters and some of them neutron-absorbers. The fuel can no longer be handled by hand as can fresh fuel manufactured from natural uranium; moreover, the build-up of neutron-absorbing poisons spoils the chain reaction and over several generations makes the reprocessed material useless as fissile fuel.

It must be appreciated that an attempt to incinerate all the plutonium that now exists in the world would take many fuel changes and have to continue over a century or more. Such a policy, therefore, would not be a short-term solution, nor in all probability, given the risk of reactor and reprocessing plant accidents, a long-term one.

So what then is a solution?

It would take at least 250,000 years for the plutonium we have already produced to disintegrate naturally to harmless levels, so we probably have no option left but to live with it. That, however, does not mean that nuclear weapons are justified. We must work for the dismantling of all nuclear war-heads and the safeguarding of fissile material which can be used for explosive purposes. The plutonium will have to be kept in lead-lined stores that are sealed in such a way that they cannot easily be breached. In fact, such stores will have to be guarded in perpetuity.

10   The developing world

Since the Second World War, and fuelled largely by cheap petroleum, the world has seen a spate of hugely expensive development projects in the Third World funded by the multinational aid agencies, including the World Bank, and also, since the 1970s, by Western private banks, including the main British ones. These schemes, which involve the establishment of industries and large agricultural projects, are intended to give greater prosperity to the populations concerned because poverty is seen to be a consequence of inadequate development and much environmental damage in developing countries to be the result of poverty.

The development model used by the International Monetary Fund (IMF), the World Bank and others such as the Inter-American Development Bank, exhorts the recipient country to unleash an export-oriented drive based on rapid industrialisation of the manufacturing and agricultural sector. This means that cash crops replace the local population's food crops, and self-reliance is replaced by the necessity to pay off loans and pay for high technology imports and inputs. By the law of 'comparative advantage' countries are directed to move away from manufacturing goods that are produced more cheaply elsewhere and open their doors – by removing import quotas and tariffs – to goods from abroad, producing only what they can to their own advantage. The IMF and the development banks still base their philosophies on the economist Adam Smith and his nineteenth-century follower David Ricardo. According to Ricardo in his *Principles of Political Economy*, 'It is quite important to the happiness of mankind that our own enjoyment should be increased by the better distribution of labour, by each country producing those commodities for which, by its situation, its climate, and its natural or artificial advantages, it is adapted, and by their exchanging them for the commodities of other countries.'

Already billions have been spent in pursuit of free trade

and the notion that all will benefit from the shipping of goods across the globe. But is the world really a better place for all that intense economic activity? Edward Goldsmith of the *Ecologist* argues that, on the contrary, the process of development has led to the impoverishment of the many to the benefit of the few by destroying traditional societies and disrupting family and social bonds, and that it is the main factor behind the growth of urban slums and the massive degradation of soil and land. His view stands in sharp conflict with that of the people who promote further development. For instance, A. W. Clausen, President of the World Bank, insists that 'a better environment more often than not depends on continued economic growth', and that 'all development can enhance the conditions in which we live'.

There are many examples to show that Clausen and others who believe in conventional development as fostered by the industrialised nations are fundamentally wrong. Development has become little more than a guise for colonialism, with the multinationals moving in to employ cheap labour and remove resources for profits to be made elsewhere. Meanwhile, the banks, especially the private ones, reap the interest of massive loans that the developing countries can no longer afford. And while the leaders of these countries wish to enjoy the luxurious benefits of modern living, they continue to milk the land and its people of basic resources.[1]

Sri Lanka is a telling example. In 1977, after defeating the United Front government, Julius Jayawardene's United National Party decided to accept 'the conditionalities' of 'export-oriented industrialisation' as laid down by the IMF. In its 1978 *Annual Report* the Central Bank of Ceylon spoke of the new government policies as 'a sweeping departure from the tightly controlled, inward-looking welfare-oriented economic strategy to a more liberalised outward-looking and growth-oriented one'. Until then, Sri Lanka had built up a tradition of social welfare policies which enabled the population to live in relative health and well-being, despite low economic growth. In terms of life-expectancy, infant mortality, fertility and literacy Sri Lanka was among the top of fifty-nine developing countries and even the *World Bank* had to admit in its 1982 report that: 'Throughout the post-war period, Sri Lanka was exceptionally successful in protecting the poor from the worst effects of falling consumption and in improving, albeit slowly, the high quality of life as measured by various social indicators.'

By July 1977 the total expenditure on welfare services, including food subsidies, had reached 41 per cent of government expenditure and considerable efforts were made to achieve self-sufficiency in food through land reform, guaranteed prices for produce, subsidies for inputs and rural credit at reasonable terms. At least until 1974 the government was able to maintain relative price stability through regulating the economy, imposing constraints on luxury imports, and conspicuous consumption was kept down. American sociologist Garry Fields has pointed out that 'the poor in Sri Lanka are gaining absolutely and relatively: the reverse is true of the rich'.

All that was 'reformed' by Jayawardene's government. It established a 'free trade zone' to bring in overseas investment and create some 50,000 jobs, but by 1983 only 20,000 jobs had been created, most in the garment manufacturing sector. Meanwhile, according to Dr Wickremashinghe, a leading adviser to the government, the invitation to foreign investors took a very different turn from that expected, and many foreign firms took over completely from domestic companies, 'who due to unrestricted dumping have been faced with the alternatives of bankruptcy or selling out to multinationals'.

As for the large dam projects – the Kotmale, Maduru Oya and Randenigala dams – which were supposed to provide peasants displaced by the flooded reservoirs with some 300,000 acres of irrigated land, these are to be used instead for 'agro-based industrial development' involving foreign companies. The All Ceylon Peasants Committee appealed to the government: 'The peasantry who comprise a large proportion of the population face ruin. They are being turned into a reservoir of cheap labour to be exploited by foreign companies. . . . We are being deprived of our land, of land which has been cleared, irrigated and settled from public funds for development by our farmers. We are enslaved once again to foreign capital.'

As a result of the new government's attitude to trade, Sri Lankan imports increased by a factor of five between 1978 and 1981 compared to the years from 1974 to 1977. And while export prices increased by 29 per cent between 1978 and 1981, import prices rose by 182 per cent. Not surprisingly, the foreign debt grew by a factor of seven between June 1977 and 1982. The World Bank has now warned that 'Sri Lanka will soon find itself undertaking a new commercial borrowing mainly to pay interest on the existing debt' and calls for 'adjustment measures' in which the relics of the welfare state will be further dismantled. Indeed, the IMF asked the Sri Lankan government to abandon its 'Food Stamps Scheme' brought in to replace the food subsidies and welfare policies of the previous administration.

Compared with a decade ago the average Sri Lankan family now finds it increasingly difficult to support itself. One consequence of this is the growing export to the Middle East of Sri Lankan women to work as housemaids; this 'export' has become the second largest exchange earner for the government. Infant mortality has begun to rise and one-third of schoolchildren now show signs of malnutrition. Undoubtedly too the economic situation has helped to fire the Tamil separatist movement.

Examples from Africa, Latin America and Asia demonstrate conclusively that development has left many people worse off than they were before. People have become 'marginalised' through the very process of having to take part in the cash economy and have been forced off their traditional lands when they are taken over for cash crop plantations. Clearly the model of development espoused by development economists and promoted by most governments, both donor and recipient, is manifestly flawed and must be replaced by fundamentally different alternatives. Nor is it simply a matter of the developing countries learning from the mistakes of the industrialised world and avoiding the pitfalls.

At the World Industry Conference on Environmental

The Green Alternative

Management in November 1984, the Indian Anil Agarwal stated:

> What is there to learn? If the affected poor could be absorbed by the industrialisation process then there would be little to quibble about. But the last three decades of industrialisation in the Third World have shown that this is not so. With the growth of slums in unmanageable proportions there are any number of economists and politicians who are saying that we need to keep people on the land. The needs of the Third World can only be met if the industrialisation process, together with the overall development process, is firstly people-oriented – that is truly employment creating and human-need oriented – and secondly environment-oriented, so that it conserves and improves the environment of those vast numbers of people who are crucially dependent on the environment.

Once one has cut down the forests, diverted and polluted waters, broken community ties and destroyed the relationship between population and the land on which it resides and from which it derives its sustenance, it is hardly surprising that people should find themselves utterly impoverished.

What is meant by Third World countries?

The United Nations has defined the three worlds in the following terms: capitalist, industrialised and democratic countries such as those of Western Europe, North America, Japan, Australia and New Zealand are bracketed as first world; socialist, industrialised countries including the USSR, and those of Eastern Europe are bracketed as second world; the Third World is a mixture of socialist and capitalist countries fast industrialising but still far behind in the industrial race (this includes countries like China, India, most African and South American countries and the Middle East); the Fourth World comprises the poorest of the poor countries.

However, we must take this categorisation with a pinch of salt as within the so-called industrial nations pockets of severe poverty, malnutrition and the reign of ignorance exist while in the so-called Third and Fourth World there are pockets of very rich and industrialised communities which may be richer than those in countries higher on the GNP table.

Aren't the problems of the Third World insoluble?

The primary cause of Third World poverty is not overpopulation or ignorance but maldistribution of land and other means of production, exploitation by the rich of their own country as well as by the First and Second World, and the wrong kind of values governing society. Values of materialism, money and military might are considered supreme, while countries with a simpler way of life which are less strong militarily and more spiritually orientated are considered backward, under-developed and poor. If we of the First World want to see the problems of poverty, hunger and exploitation solved we have to change our values as well as our own way of life. As long as we try to impose our materialistic culture on the world we have responsibility for the chaos caused.

Is it better to provide technological know-how so that the Third World can produce things for themselves and also improve their agricultural output?

The advanced technology of the West is totally unsuitable for the Third World. In fact, the gigantic scale of technological advancement has brought undesirable environmental consequences in the West itself. Therefore we do not need to export our technological know-how. E.F. Schumacher coined the term 'intermediate technology' which in fact exists already in the Third World. If we can restore the values of respect for the environment and the land and respect for a less materialistic life and stop exploiting the Third World, the Third World might, once again, become capable of feeding itself adequately. At the moment food is imported from the Third World to feed cattle in the West for our meat consumption. If we reduce our meat intake and import less grain from the Third World there will be more food for the people of

The Green Alternative

those countries, provided they can readjust to local economic self-reliance.

In Africa, economic success and the well-being of the people do not necessarily coincide, do they?

No. For example, it has been noted in Tanzania that during national economic recession, when the distribution system breaks down, villagers cannot get cash and food crops to market, so they eat the food they have grown themselves. They also use land that grows cash crops to grow food instead. Recession in the national economy has meant that many villagers in Tanzania today have more to eat. Malnutrition does at least seem not to be getting worse.

Is it better for the Third World to industrialise and cure its poverty or maintain its traditional cultures?

There can be no black and white opinion as to whether it is better to industrialise or to stick to traditional ways. Rapid and sudden industrialisation has caused many problems, such as large-scale unemployment, because the tasks people could at one time do with their hands are now being done by machines. Also, pollution and resource depletion are being caused by the process of industrialisation while natural resources have been used up much faster than they would ever have been by human hands.

In order to improve the quality of life it is important to introduce cottage industries, small-scale industries and appropriate industries, and make a marriage between traditional culture and modern inventions.

Should the developed countries continue to manufacture industrial goods for export to the Third World?

No. We must not depend on the fragile links and impermanent economics of export. Every country at the moment is trying to stop importing and increase exporting. With every country trying to do that not all can succeed because only a

252

few clever countries will manage to manipulate the market forces to export their goods. Therefore we must never treat the Third World as our market. The permanence and sustainability of economies can only be achieved if we attempt to manufacture and produce goods for local consumption and see the export part as a luxury, only limited to things which cannot be made or produced locally. The export element should be like the icing on the cake, but at the moment we seem to be longing for the icing and will be left with no cake.

How fair is world trade? Aren't developing countries getting a good deal obtaining finished products and technology in return for basic resources?

In the present pattern of world trade, developing nations are generally trading primary products, which are plentiful and which tend to be of a uniform nature, for manufactured products which vary according to who makes them, and which allow the manufacturer more freedom to recoup costs than the primary producer. World trade is unlikely ever to bring a fair deal to producers unless producing countries co-operate together to regulate the amount of primary products coming on to the market. Trading fewer goods with Western countries could ironically bring developing countries a higher return and release resources, including land, for other uses, especially growing more food.

By importing foods from Third World countries such as Africa, aren't we helping their economies?

Third World countries are run by Western-educated élites whose policies are indistinguishable from those of their colonialist predecessors. They are necessarily committed to economic development – in order to maintain their Western lifestyle – and because it has become axiomatic that it provides the only avenue to progress and prosperity. To finance economic development, a vast amount of foreign exchange is required – and to earn it means selling off everything that is saleable, which means above all timber – for which purpose native forests are systematically destroyed – and cash crops such as sugar, bananas, coffee, cotton. Only in that way can such countries earn the foreign exchange required for development.

By growing crops for export, Africans earn money which can increase their wealth – provided the return they receive covers the cost of producing those crops. Prices of most cash crops are low because there is a glut of them on world markets. A key question is whether land which now grows such crops would not be better employed growing food for local consumption. Hunger in Africa is rampant, food output per head is generally falling and cash crop prices are low. This should be a clear sign to policy-makers that some switch from cash to food crops is needed. Governments of cash crop producing countries need to co-operate with each other to agree on reducing acreages of these crops.

Is climate the root cause of the present crisis in Africa?

Drought is a popular scapegoat for the African famine; it hides deeper reasons. Rainfall was low in many countries in 1983 and 1984 but whilst this exacerbated problems it did not cause them. Africa's capacity to produce food has been damaged by many factors, including the inadequacy and sometimes incompetence of government agricultural policies, neglect of the poor in official policies, insufficient attention to rain-fed crops for local people, the encouragement of cash crops on land where food could be grown (and which often makes it harder for soil to cope with dry weather) and the spread of desert and soil deterioration.

What is the extent of malnutrition in Africa?

In Africa today some 30 million people are threatened with death through starvation out of 100 million or more who are malnourished and hungry. We have now become horribly accustomed to the spectacle of bare soils, denuded hillsides scarred by erosion gullies, withered trees, dead carcasses and the faces of emaciated, dying people. We saw it in the 1970s when drought hit Mali, Niger, Chad and other Sahelian countries, and before that in Biafra. But nothing in African history can compare with the present crisis, in which famine and devastation now stretch right across the continent from the Atlantic to the Indian Ocean and down beyond Mozambique into South Africa.

'Africa is dying,' said Edem Kodjo when secretary-general of the Organisation of African Unity in 1978. 'It is clear that the economy of our continent is lying in ruins. . . . Our ancient continent . . . . is now on the brink of disaster.'

But who is to blame?

It is we in the Western industrialised nations who, through centuries of colonialism and exploitation, have laid down the foundations of what must surely be one of the worst ecological crises to strike our planet in many thousands of years. By using Africa to grow cheap cash crops, to produce beef and animal feedstuffs and to provide hardwood timber, we have helped transform a country rich in forest and fertile savannah lands into barren wilderness.

Throughout sub-Saharan Africa available food has been steadily declining: today people have on average two-thirds of the amount they had twenty years ago. Rapid population growth is certainly partly to blame, but another major reason is that the best land is being increasingly used for exportable cash crops. In Niger, for example, one of France's Sahelian ex-colonies, peanut-growing expanded six fold after the Second World War to provide Europe with a cheap vegetable oil in place of American soya bean products. Inevitably, farmers used their best land for peanuts and, despite the rapid loss of fertility, abandoned the traditional period of fallow. Simultaneously, nomadic herdsmen who used to graze their cattle, goats and sheep on the fallow land, thus manuring it in preparation for the cultivation of staple foodstuffs such as sorghum and millet, found themselves fenced out.

Notwithstanding the fact that land available to the nomads had shrunk, the experts came with their plans to eliminate disease in the animals, increase the breeding and, to make up for the apparent shortage of drinking water, drill hundreds of boreholes. The nomads, whose status had always depended on the numbers of livestock, responded by increasing their herds by at least a third between 1960 and 1970, by which time the groundwork for the Sahelian drought tragedy had been well laid. Nevertheless the IMF experts still had the gall to proclaim that, in Niger 'growth of the livestock population has been hindered by insufficient watering points and pumping equipment in the dry season, improper use of pastures and by epidemics.' What the IMF sages had failed to learn was that livestock in drought-ravaged areas do not die from lack of water; they just do not have the strength to find the grass which over-grazing round the boreholes has put out of their reach.

The developing world

What could be done in these drought-ravaged areas?

The break with tradition throughout the Sahel and Sudan has meant that the use of the acacia tree has been increasingly neglected. The acacia is an integral part of traditional farming in the arid sub-tropics, providing shade and highly nutritious fodder for livestock while increasing the fertility of soil and preventing wind erosion. In Senegal, for example, the yields of millet and sorghum grown under *Acacia albida* are more than double the yields from open fields. The acacia is particularly drought-resistant, sending tap roots down some thirty metres in pursuit of groundwater. One of the priorities in restoring the drought areas to something of their previous fertility will be through planting and nurturing the acacia tree.

Is it true that people are starving while food is exported?

While millions face starvation, countries like the Sudan, Chad, Niger, Senegal and Mali have been achieving record cotton harvests. Nor has Ethiopia turned from growing cash crops like melons to feeding the hungry. In some respects, things do not change; during the potato famine in Ireland, Britain actually had troops in the docks protecting boats being laden with food for export.

In addition, beef for the EEC, despite its own beef mountain, has caused the decimation of wildlife and terrible destruction of the environment in Africa. Botswana, for example, exports 19,000 tonnes of beef each year into Western Europe at subsidised rates. With such a ready market available it has, not surprisingly, increased its total cattle numbers by more than twenty times over the past couple of decades. Consequently the carrying capacity of the land has been far exceeded, and the cattle ranchers, particularly the more wealthy ones, have been encroaching into the Kalahari wildlife reservation.

The Green Alternative

What can or should we do to help those suffering from poverty and starvation in the world – surely aid is vital?

Often the poorest communities in the world have little to trade, and are ignored by their government. Aid from abroad has the potential to help the poor, but at present rarely does. Countries who are sincere about wanting to help could stipulate that they will give priority to requests for aid that are directly geared to the poor, who would then have a say about what they want. Small amounts of money for many different community projects would probably be most helpful.

It's not aid that is wrong – just the people who siphon it their way and stop it getting to its target?

Aid works in this way: a government requests aid for a project, the request is vetted and, if approved, money is allocated. But financial aid is generally tied to the purchase of goods. Most British aid does not leave here in the form of money – goods go instead. There are few opportunities for aid money to be siphoned off, as any money that does go tends to be tightly controlled. But just because a project satisfies economic criteria does not mean it is good for the poor.

Africa, in fact, is littered with the relics of capital intensive development schemes that have misfired. Yet the governments of African countries still request more loans and multinational aid. Even the World Bank admits that much of the money loaned to Africa has gone into financing large public investments such as enormous government buildings or motorways, which have had more to do with the self-aggrandisement of those in power than in serving the real needs of the African. 'Genuine mistakes,' it says, 'cannot explain the excessive number of white elephants.'

Indeed, money poured into the Sahel after the 1968–73 drought, increasing from $756 million in 1974 to $1.97 billion by 1981. Yet only 4 per cent of all that money subsidised the growing of rain-fed crops and just 1.5 per cent was spent on tree-planting and soil and water conservation – the very basis of recovery. Unfortunately much of the food aid finished up in the hands of middle men who, by controlling the market, made it economically impossible for farmers to go back to growing staple foods for the indigenous population.

Shouldn't we applaud the development banks for their contribution to alleviating injustices?

The World Bank is the world's largest multinational aid organisation but it acts like a commercial bank, concerned with rates of return, rather than necessarily with meeting people's needs. The poorest, who most need aid, are often left out of World Bank aided projects.

What are the objectives of the International Monetary Fund?

Like the World Bank, the IMF was created at Bretton Woods in the United States in 1944. Although both are international organisations, they were conceived to help the US – the strongest economy then as now – foster free trade and spread the sphere of its influence through an economic strategy. Indeed, one of the six objectives of the IMF is 'to facilitate balanced growth of international trade and, through this, contribute to high levels of employment and real income and the development of productive capacity'. Another of its aims is 'to seek the elimination of exchange restrictions that hinder the growth of world trade'.

In overall lending terms how important is the IMF?

At the level of those supposedly most in need, the poor, less developed countries (LDCs), the IMF was not very prominent during the period 1974 to 1979, supplying less than 5 per cent of their financing needs. Indeed, in 1978 non-oil-producing LDCs repaid $900 million more to the IMF than they borrowed, while one year later the $1.8 billion loaned to such countries was only $200 million more than repayments.

The Green Alternative

Who then were the main lenders?

After 1973 and the first sharp rise in the price of oil, OPEC countries shifted their enormous cash surpluses to Western banks, and as a result the private banks embarked on a spate of lending to developing countries: between 1973 and 1981 the rate of lending to the Third World grew by 25 per cent per year. After the second sharp rise in the price of oil in 1979, the banks again increased their loans so that by the early 1980s between 55 and 60 per cent of the entire debt of the less developed countries was owed to private banks.

Hasn't the danger of defaulting on the loans put the banks into a dangerous position? If countries defaulted *en masse* – or even just those with the biggest borrowings such as Mexico, Brazil and Argentina – would that end the present economic system?

Having loaned such substantial amounts to Third World countries, amounts running into hundreds of millions of dollars, the private banks not only derive a significant proportion of their income from the loans – as much as 45 per cent in some instances – but the loans represent double or more of their total equity. The banks could not therefore pay off their depositors should those countries in debt default on their loans. The resulting run on the banks would indeed lead to bankruptcy and the possible breakdown of the Western economic system.

But isn't that when the IMF comes into the picture?

When in severe financial difficulties many countries call in the IMF, which usually advises on what measures must be taken to reduce the impact of the debt. The 'adjustment programme' in general requires that the country concerned sets out to increase its income and reduce expenditure. Governments are therefore asked to devalue their currency to encourage exports at the expense of imports and to cut back on social expenditure while controlling wages.

The developing world

'All this may sound eminently reasonable,' says Susan George, senior fellow of the Institute for Policy Studies. 'Countries cannot live forever beyond their means any more than families can. But who is living beyond those means? Who has to swallow the IMF medicine? What we know for certain is that the LDC élites, and more often than not the military, were responsible for incurring the heavy debts to begin with. It was they who borrowed in order to buy Phantom jets or large "development" schemes benefiting only themselves: they who sent the suitcases full of money north to private accounts, they again who maintained internal security force to keep their own people "in their place". If one principle of any "ethical economics" should be "Those who reap the benefits should also pay the costs," then IMF adjustment programmes aimed at insuring debt repayment take us farther than ever from that goal.'

What then are the results of adjustment programmes? Does anyone suffer from the austerity measures?

In her paper to the 1985 TOES (The Other Economic Summit), Susan George listed just a few of the ways people in different countries were affected by the IMF demands on their governments. In Brazil the removal of subsidies on food increased prices as much as seven fold. In the Dominican Republic similar price rises provoked riots in which 186 people were killed. And while the cost of living goes up, salaries for those lucky enough to be employed either go up by a smaller proportion or stay put. In Mexico, as a result of austerity measures, the majority of lower income Mexicans have stopped eating rice, eggs, fruit, vegetables and milk. Crime is up, and people are even robbed as they emerge from supermarkets. Investment in public health, meanwhile, has been cut by two-thirds.

The Green Alternative

Does the IMF take any responsibility for these consequences?

According to the Managing Director of the IMF: 'An international institution such as the Fund cannot take upon itself the role of dictating social and political objectives to sovereign governments.' Such a position is wholly untenable – the IMF must use its power to demand that countries pursue social objectives that enhance rather than ruin the chances of the poor. In fact, the Fund is not at all detached from the policies and political interests of the United States.

'Too many countries,' says Susan George, 'are using the IMF's programmes as a convenient excuse for more severe repression, for breaking the backs of trade unions or community organisations, for bringing their own working classes under greater control. The LDCs must improve trading and banking relations among themselves, develop a common attitude *vis à vis* their debt obligations and . . . why not? . . . create their own South Central Bank before this happens.'

The multinationals have also helped in the development process, haven't they?

The activities of multinational companies can create new jobs in developing countries and bring additional wealth. But a country that wants to attract multinationals has to devote resources to creating the conditions that attract them – it has for example to encourage a docile labour force, unlikely to strike, and one which is prepared to accept wages that are very low by the standards of developed countries. It may have to give incentives, such as charging no tax to the firm for five years or more. The flow of profits, interests and dividends now leaving developing countries to Western-based multinationals is considerable, and suggests that the cost of these corporations is generally greater than the benefits they bring.

Population growth in developing countries is surely one of the major ecological problems facing us?

In 1798 Thomas Malthus wrote his *Essay on the Principles of Population* in which he argued that population growth without control would, because of its exponential nature, quickly outstrip food production and supply. Although many have since argued that Malthus was wrong, since he failed to take into account the technological improvements that have made far greater yields possible than were ever imagined at the end of the eighteenth century, in principle he remains correct. Indeed, agronomists have had to go to extraordinary lengths over the past forty years, employing a host of chemicals, in the drive to double yields, and the chances of their being able to bring off another doubling without totally destroying soil structure are slim. Meanwhile, population growth in certain parts of the world, in many parts of Africa or South East Asia, for instance, is leading to a doubling of populations every fifteen to twenty years. In Africa food production can no longer keep pace with population growth and, even with food aid from the Western world, starvation is rife.

In fact, one of the arguments put forward in favour of industrialising the 'underdeveloped' parts of the world is that control over population growth will assert itself once people acquire, in Western terms, a decent standard of living. Inevitably the notion inherent in such thinking is that we of the Western world are somehow more civilised, and more capable of restraint and control, than are our brethren in the developing parts of the world.

What has caused this increase in population?

As it happens, it is the interference with traditional ways of life and the introduction of technology, including modern medicines, that has often caused an uncontrollable surge in population growth. We know that population growth over the past million years or so of human development was relatively slow until the eighteenth century and the coming of the industrial revolution. Admittedly there had been small spurts of growth after the neolithic revolution and the beginnings of agriculture, but the general trend was slow. Although there were famines, wars and plagues at various times in history which carried off a good number of the population, those were invariably among the more heavily populated regions of the world where there was already a substantial urban, mercantile class.

What we have tended to overlook is the situation prevailing among the indigenous tribal peoples of the world, who until faced with the impact of colonisation, led lives that did not threaten their environment with over-pressure of population and degradation. On the contrary, tribals lived for the most part well within the carrying capacities of the land, understanding the ecological subtleties of their environment, including the consequences of excessive population growth. Contemporary studies of hunter-gatherers, the Kalahari bushmen, for example, or of stone-age horticulturalists such as the Tsembaga of New Guinea, indicate that those peoples are rarely, if ever, short of food. The anthropologist Richard B. Lee spent considerable periods with the Kung bushmen and, from examples of food brought into the camp, was able to show that bushmen not only had an adequate and very varied diet, but a high percentage of protein, mostly from vegetable sources. Moreover, Lee made his observations during the second year of a severe drought which had seriously dislocated the pastoral and farming economies of the Bantu.

As long as peasant economies remain free of outside market forces, they also appear to generate their own stability. Alexander Chayanov, who was director of the Institute of Agricultural Economy after the Russian Revolution, but was later arrested and killed by Stalin, made the then challenging observation that the peasant was more intent on meeting his family's needs than in making a profit. The peasant therefore tried to find a balance between subsistence needs and his basic dislike of manual labour. Subsistence was a *goal and not the result of deprivation*, which has often been the modern interpretation.

The runaway growth in many peasant populations today is more than the simple arithmetic of births for once swamping deaths because of modern medicine and hygiene. Heinrich von Loesch, an economist specialising in demography for the United Nations Food and Agriculture Organisation, lays the blame on 'imported progress' which ' . . . offered an unexpected chance for social and economic improvement to the peoples of poor countries. Wholly inexperienced in matters of progress they react in a logical way . . . by sacrificing personal mobility and consumption to have more children for the better future of their families'. Von Loesch derides the current idea that peasants have increased the size of their families because they lack the psychological or physical techniques of restraint.

Is there a solution?

Whereas in the past people living in village and tribal communities would take responsibility for their offspring, ensuring continuity rather than change, today the breakdown in traditional life and social behaviour has led to state intervention. Indeed, the state in countries such as China or Indonesia offers, or even imposes, advice on birth control and sets out to regulate family size. In China couples are only allowed to procreate after they have reached a certain age, and then only to have one child.

It may be that rigorous birth control is preferable to an anarchic situation where unwanted children are born into slums. Through what is claimed to be a voluntary family planning programme, Indonesia has managed to reduce the growth in population to 1.8 per cent a year, which implies that the total population will double in size every thirty-eight years. Mexico with a 3 per cent growth rate has a population which will double every twenty-three years.

One result of rapid population growth is that the demographic balance shifts so that the majority of people are aged fifteen and under. If most of that youthful population survives into reproductive age the overall population will retain its impetus to grow. Therefore any attempt to curb population growth will only be successful if it can impinge on those still in their teens.

What alternatives are there for developing countries?

Alternative development strategies are urgently needed, especially for the poorest countries. One alternative is to promote the participation of the rural poor in a way that has so far been attempted in only a few communities, but where it has been attempted is paying off. In Sri Lanka, the Philippines, India and Bangladesh there are today examples of the poor taking initiatives, setting objectives and participating in development through an organisation which they manage and control. This is bringing new hope, releasing creative energies, increasing opportunities for the poor to develop their potential – as well as raising people's incomes and enabling them to provide enough food for themselves and their families.

What in fact is poverty?

We must distinguish between the lack of material possessions found in traditional societies and the poverty of those who, although they may possess gadgets such as transistor radios, live in a state of squalor and deprivation. The American anthropologist Professor Marshall Sahlins points out in a study of tribal peoples that they actively free themselves from material possessions in order to be affluent, their affluence being measured in terms of health and cultural integrity. Their life is not 'nasty, brutish and short', their health is usually good, their diet highly varied and nutritious, and culture and tradition play an important role in holding their societies together.

Such tribal 'primitive' people generate no gross national product and would therefore be rated as the lowest of the low by today's economic yardstick. Development may appear to raise their standard of living by raising their *per capita* income, but instead it too often relegates them to true poverty. The problem in our world of statistics and numbers is how to measure the value of stabilising cultures and traditions which are, without exception, the first victims of any programme of development.

Can the self-sufficient communities still in existence survive the onslaught of development?

In some countries, such as Brazil, the indigenous tribespeople are not given the choice over whether or not they want themselves or their environment transformed. In other parts of the world, however, peoples whose way of life has hardly changed in centuries will often, when exposed to industrial society, fall for its apparent benefits without seeing the drawbacks.

What has been going on in Ladakh over the past ten years is a case in point. Helena Norberg-Hodge has spent much of her time in Ladakh, that outpost of India, north of Jammu, wedged between China, Tibet and Pakistan across the Himalayas. She first went there in spring 1975, a few months after the Indian government had opened the border to tourists for the first time since independence. Over the past twelve years she has witnessed a slow transformation in Ladakh from a way of life that was totally self-sufficient to one increasingly dependent on the outside world: for cash, fuel, education and technological gadgetry including pumps and electricity. She is convinced that as dependence grows and as Ladakh's 100,000 population get gradually drawn into the cash economy so will the ancient traditions crumble, leaving a society, once happy and self-sustaining, vulnerable and disintegrating.

Just as the Amazon Indians blended their lives to the forest, not threatening the intricate balance of the ecosystem, the Ladakhis have adapted themselves to a harsh, difficult environment. About the size of Austria, much of the land is barren, arid desert with an average annual rainfall of some four inches; during the winter night temperatures can fall to −40°C. Most villages are at around 11,000 feet, the 300 or so houses built of thick stone walls and adobe. Crops, mainly barley, are grown at this altitude, using water brought down from the glaciers in small irrigation canals, made of mud and stone, running along the mountain slopes with carved-out logs to traverse the occasional gap. The pasture for goats, sheep, donkeys, yaks, cows, mules and the yak–cow cross – the dzo – is high, up at 15,000 feet or higher, and provides winter feed for the animals. The Ladakhis also grow apricots and walnuts, and willow and poplar for construction purposes, coppicing and replanting it. Wood is too valuable to use as fuel, and instead the Ladakhis traditionally burn animal dung. All human waste is composted and goes back on the land.

The Ladakhi way of life, at least up until 1975, was completely self-contained and sustainable. The population too, appears to have been remarkably stable, a feature of the social system which combines flexibility with an intuitive sense of environmental limits.

How about their health?

Overall, the health of the Ladakhis is good, except for the effects on the eyes and lungs of smoke from the burning of dung inside the houses. Medicines are based mainly on herbs: a blend of Chinese and Indian tradition that goes back to the eighth century, with a sound recognition of the importance of mind in the cause and cure of disease. Ladakh, although a separate kingdom from Tibet, having had its own monarch until the country was invaded and conquered by Dogras from Jammu in 1834, has always looked to Tibet and to the Dalai Lama for its religious traditions and culture. Being part of India, however, it escaped the Chinese invasion of Tibet in the 1950s.

Will tourism affect the traditional culture of the Ladakhis?

Tourism has now become a major industry in Ladakh and as many as 15,000 people, mainly Europeans, cross the Himalayas each year. Consequently, Ladakhis, especially the young, have the notion that modern life is one of riches and leisure. They see a tourist spend more money in a week than they would normally get through in a lifetime. The tourist comes with his modern gadgets, expecting Western food, hotels that provide some of the conveniences of modern life, including running water and a flush toilet. In the capital, Leh, it is not unusual to see boys clambering on to the roof to pour water into a tank. Pumps are increasingly used to get water in the houses.

India, meanwhile, is slowly developing Ladakh. More vehicles are on the roads, especially in the capital, and mass-manufactured goods are beginning to replace traditional ones. New houses are being built of concrete blocks and are provided with kerosene heating, while on the land agrochemicals are increasingly used. The demands for more water are being met through the construction of concrete irrigation pipes, despite problems with frost cracking in winter, and through pumping water from bore holes. Tractors are now being imported although most Ladakhis still plough, till and harvest using their traditional beast of burden, the dzo.

'Greater changes have taken place in the last twenty years than have during the last thousand', says Helena Norberg-Hodge, 'undoubtedly the most dramatic being the way that Ladakh is being drawn into the cash economy with all the growing dependence that goes with that kind of development. The problem is that once development starts almost everyone wants to get on the bandwagon with a subsequent breakdown of communal ties and co-operation.' And whereas in the past everyone participated in the maintenance and construction of irrigation canals, today Ladakhis see the government constructing permanent structures out of concrete and bringing in more water to increase productivity in the fields. On the face of things the new imported ideas appear better and it is not surprising that Ladakhis from one village, seeing the improvements carried out in a neighbouring village, want similar treatment. The paradox is that life in Ladakh has been totally free; whereas the slightest modern development requires money and creates a value for activities that previously have been taken wholly for granted. Ironically, Ladakhis will only remain in control of their own lives while they are outside the cash economy. Once in, despite the illusion that money confers freedom of choice, they will in fact find themselves on a treadmill.

The notion of poverty hardly existed before; today it has become part of the language. And the most damaging aspect of tourism has therefore been its psychological impact in giving young Ladakhis, in particular, a deep sense of the inferiority of their own culture and way of life. To redress the balance, Helena has started using the local radio and bringing in books and literature from the outside world to show Ladakhis that the reason tourists come to their country is because they hope to find there the very values that they have lost in their own societies and have come to cherish.

Is there a way in which Ladakh can avoid the pitfalls of development?

A Ladakh Ecological Development Group now exists, based in Leh, its members mainly made up of Ladakhis. To support it internationally, Helena has created an organisation called the 'Ladakh Project'. The Ecological Development Group is trying to raise the standard of living in Ladakh without sacrificing the essential values and resources. They are introducing 'appropriate' technologies – appropriate because they are small-scale and affordable, and tailored to meet specific, local needs, and rely largely on locally available materials and skills. For example, because Ladakh has an abundance of sunshine (about 320 days a year), solar technology offers a much more logical way to meet energy needs than expensive, pollution-producing fossil fuels which must be trucked across the mountains. As a result the Ecological Development Group has been building Trombe walls on Ladakhi houses. This passive solar method of space heating has maintained indoor temperatures in the 50s and 60s (Fahrenheit), even through the coldest winter nights. The Ladakhis are more comfortable, without becoming hooked on expensive fuels whose production and delivery they can't control. The group's approach is always to reinforce the traditional practices, such as the highly successful system of organic farming. When a new solution seems to be required, as in the area of energy, the Ecological Group seeks a technique that will not erode the Ladakhis' material self-sufficiency, culture or fragile natural environment.

Helena believes that certain principles have to be adhered to if a traditional society is to be sustained using its own resources. These principles are:

1 All basic needs must be met at the local level. Self-reliance is essential, although that principle need not exclude importing and trade. Much of the colourful stones and corals used as decoration by Ladakhi women have been imported over the centuries from Italy.

2 Decisions affecting the community should be made at the household level and not be delegated to some distant representative. In general in Ladakh some twenty households in a village community are involved in decision-making and organising their affairs. Boundaries themselves do not appear to be important. Indeed, village size and therefore the number of households reflects the resources available in the vicinity. In that respect the countryside can be divided into bioregions, each with its own group of decision-makers.

3 Small-scale units are essential for self-sufficiency. In such communities there is no waste, life close to nature being truly efficient.

4 Everything in a self-reliant community is free, and self-sufficiency can only exist outside the cash economy. Yet toil under such circumstances is not drudgery. Indeed, no rigid distinction is evident in such communities between work and play.

5 Finally, the decentralisation found in self-sufficient communities must be associated with a strong binding culture, completely accepted and respected by the people involved. That way decisions are likely to benefit all.

For Helena, one of the most striking aspects of life in Ladakh is the overall happiness of the people. Ladakhis seem to spend most of their lives with humour and laughter derived from an extraordinary peace of mind. 'That happiness is deep-rooted and sincere, and such a contrast to the way our own lives are ridden with stress and anxiety,' says Helena. Compared to many other peoples in the world suddenly faced with development, Helena believes the Ladakhis have as good a chance as any of accepting only those aspects that can be incorporated into the culture without destroying it.

Isn't it sheer sentimentalism to want to protect the way of life of these simple communities? Wouldn't they be better integrated into the modern world?

Viewing the options open to tribal peoples as being ones either of 'integration' or 'isolation' presupposes that it is up to us to decide what future they may have. They themselves however, reject both alternatives, wanting neither to be preserved in 'human zoos', nor to lose their social identities by being forcibly assimilated into the dominant societies. What they demand is the right to determine their own destinies.

Far from rejecting all change and development, tribal people are asking only that such change and development should be adapted to their needs and demands rather than that they should be forcibly changed to suit the goals of development.

Isn't conserving the rights of peoples in these societies not only a waste of time and resources, but doesn't it hold up useful progress?

Certainly there are real contradictions between development models and the needs and demands of tribal peoples. But they themselves are no longer alone in questioning the validity of such 'development'. Much of the world's recent 'progress' has in fact benefited only a small minority, being achieved at terrible social and environmental costs. These costs have been borne disproportionately by tribal peoples. To be 'useful' progress must be sustainable and acceptable to those whose lands and resources are being exploited to make it possible. The double tragedy of much present-day 'development' is that, apart from causing irreversible ecological ruin and mass human suffering, it is eliminating the very peoples who possess a wealth of irreplaceable knowledge about the effective management of their traditional environments.

If it really is true that we have a lot to learn from tribal peoples about conserving the environment, what can we do to protect them?

The survival of tribal peoples depends primarily on the recognition of their territorial rights. Once their inalienable rights to the collective ownership of their traditional lands and resources are defined and protected by law, invasion can be averted. If tribal peoples lose their land, they have no time to adjust to the outside world. With their land intact they can adapt slowly, secure in the knowledge that they can sustain themselves as they have done for millennia.

Who are we to tell them what to do?

Those who are active in the defence of tribal peoples' rights only echo the demands of tribal peoples themselves, who insist that it is arrogant and unwelcome of governments to impose their policies on them. Many governments do find international criticism of their 'internal' affairs embarrassing, which is why it is so effective. Tribal peoples are constantly appealing to international campaigning organisations, like Survival International, to take action on their behalf, denied as they are the legal, political and economic means of achieving redress for their problems themselves.

These developing countries are nation states. Don't they have the right to determine how they want to develop?

Emphasising the sanctity of nation states to manage their own affairs is to ignore the global social reality that the economies and futures of the entire world are now closely entwined.

The Green Alternative

Uranium for the bombs and electricity of the developed world is mined on tribal land. Our taxes provide the funding for multilateral development schemes that are flooding tribal villages and which are clearing the tribals' forests to provide wood to laminate our hi-fi equipment and to raise the beef to fill our hamburgers. Like it or not, every one of us is partly responsible for the invasion of tribal territory as the global economy digs deeper and deeper into the wilderness. The challenge for all of us is to develop an active moral concern as wide-reaching as the economies we depend on. Survival International is an expression of that concern.

Don't people adjust in the end to our civilised ways?

The abuse of tribal peoples' rights is far worse than is generally thought. The Indian population of the Americas has been reduced by an estimated 90 per cent since 1492. The forest Indians of Amazonia are now more threatened by uncontrolled development and settlement than ever before. According to one estimate by the World Bank, the lands of over 2 million tribal people are now menaced with inundation by hydropower schemes in India alone. Massive army-backed colonisation schemes are being carried out at gun point on tribal lands in places as far apart as Guatemala, Bangladesh, West Papua (New Guinea) and Ethiopia.

Denied their lands, their villages decimated by introduced diseases, their self-confidence and sense of identity shattered by the suddenness of contact and the imposition of racist and uncaring attitudes, tribal peoples find that they can only adjust to 'civilisation' at the lowest rank in society. Bonded labour, debt-peonage, prostitution and beggary become their way of life, leading them to be further reviled by the invaders of their lands. Alcoholism and suicide provide them with their only avenues of escape. Many tribal groups, despairing and shocked by contact with Western civilisation, cease reproduction. Whole peoples are vanishing from the face of the earth before outsiders can even learn to communicate with them in their own languages.

Civilisation has brought undeniable benefits to some, mainly the inhabitants of the First and Second Worlds and the ruling élites in the Third. It has won out through an assumption of power, through the control of economic and political processes, ultimately through military force. However, those who have experienced traditional societies find there a wealth of a different kind: a sense of human purpose, fulfilment and community that the alienated inhabitants of modern societies can no longer even imagine.

'This is the site, Crumberger – a penniless government, a simple, guileless people, an untouched island paradise and not an environmental regulation for 1,500 miles.'

If you want to help, contact *Survival International* – a human rights organisation that defends the rights of threatened tribal peoples to survival, self-determination and the use and ownership of their traditional lands. It has become the foremost international campaigning group active in the defence of tribal peoples' rights. Survival International is a membership organisation that relies on the active involvement of its members and supporters to achieve effect. Write to them for details of how you can get involved (see p. 350).

11 The Green philosophy

To create our modern world of skyscraper cities, of rapid global transport, our forays into space, our vast acreages of single crops, we have tucked into the resources of the earth, taking what we can and replacing the natural world of the biosphere with one of our own making. All has not gone quite as planned, as the sprawling shanty towns, congested highways and eroded landscapes testify, but the inexorable drive to conquer more and more of the natural world continues whilst the earth's beneficence is directed to a single goal of mankind's needs, whether real or professed.

Our world of artefacts and technological gadgetry implies that we have conquered nature – it has been subjugated to our cause. Today hardly an area of wilderness remains inviolate: we scurry across Antarctica with an eye on claiming the vast riches buried there; we criss-cross the Himalayas, we accelerate the process of erosion with our need for firewood, and within a generation we will have destroyed the great ancient tropical forests of the world. We designate areas as national parks, but for their recreational value or because they are good for tourism; we may even feel nostalgia for nature free and unsullied. What we have not done is to put aside such areas because we believe we need them for our own survival. To do so might be to admit that technology may not be enough to ensure that the earth continues to be able to support human life. But then we have been remarkably successful since the industrial revolution in isolating ourselves from nature, imagining instead that we can with impunity continue to replace with our own systems the far more delicate living ones that have evolved over several billion years.

Given the squalor and misery of millions of our people, ekeing out a wretched existence in the slums of swelling cities or scratching a few crumbs of sustenance from a baked, lifeless soil, the extraordinary miracle of life is not always immediately apparent. Yet, as our prehistoric and classical ancestors knew intuitively, life itself depends first and foremost on how we treat the earth. The ancient Greeks believed that the earth was a living organism able to reward mankind with her bounty for good treatment or, equally, to revenge abuse. The Greeks called the Earth goddess 'Gaia' or 'Ge', from which we derive the root 'geo-' as used in words like geology. In his *Economics*, the soldier/farmer Xenophon, who saved a Greek army from disaster in Persia, stated: 'Earth is a goddess, and she teaches justice to those who can learn: for the better she is served, the more good things she gives in return.' Plato blamed deforestation for causing erosion, climate changes and crop failure in the vulnerable Mediterranean environment. 'What now remains of the once rich land is like the skeleton of a sick man, all the fat and soft earth having wasted away, only the bare framework is left.' Clearly the problems of today, the savage erosion and devastation in the tropics and semi-arid lands of Ethiopia, have been seen before.

In their worship of Gaia, Greeks were well aware that the earth was not wholly at their disposal. They put aside sanctuaries where nothing of nature should be touched: no trees cut, no wood removed, no animals hunted nor fish caught. Truly the care taken to protect those *temenos*, chosen for their outstanding beauty, anticipated our own national parks.

But if Gaia was goddess, where did mankind stand in relation to the rest of creation? Plato was in no doubt that the world is 'that living creature of which all other living creatures, severally and generically, are portions'. Undoubtedly, our conception and awareness of the earth arises from our being part of the whole. Plato asked, 'Whence can a human body have received its soul if the body of the world does not possess soul?' These thoughts would seem to be echoed by the words of the Red Indian, Chief Seattle, to the US Government in 1854 at seeing his people betrayed once again by the white settlers and his land ravaged:

> Teach your children what we have taught our children; that the earth is our mother whatever befalls the sons of the earth. If men spit upon the ground, they spit upon themselves. This

we know, that the earth does not belong to man; man belongs to the earth. This we know; all things are connected, like the blood which unites one family. . . . Man did not weave the web of life; he is merely a strand in it. Whatever he does to the web, he does to himself.

The classical, tribal view of the earth has been repeated in our times not only among the Hippies, but also in the scientific theories of the atmospheric chemist, Professor James Lovelock. Although he has called his theory the 'Gaia Hypothesis',[1] he invokes no goddess in his proposition that life on earth is not only regulated by its environment but regulates the environment itself, gradually transforming it over aeons of time into, as far as possible, optimal conditions for life. The Gaia Hypothesis therefore implies that life is bountiful and rich not because it has luckily found a suitable planet, but because it has used the special resources of planet earth to create a planet capable of harbouring living forms. Lovelock's conception places humanity fair and square in its place among the rest of nature. If he is correct we certainly need nature for our survival, although whether nature needs us is an entirely different matter.

In the Gaia Hypothesis Lovelock and his collaborator Professor Lynn Margulis of Boston University contend that the interaction of living organisms during the history of life on earth – therefore encompassing some $3\frac{1}{2}$ billion years – has actually created the conditions which are now vitally necessary for life. The atmosphere, for instance, contains just the right mixture of gases – of oxygen, carbon dioxide, methane and nitrogen – not only to enable us to breathe and be active, and for plants to photosynthesise sugars, but also to keep the temperature of the earth's surface at levels where we neither freeze nor boil and bake.

Through intricate computer modelling Lovelock demonstrates how life has dumped masses of carbon dioxide in the form of limestone cliffs and coral reefs; from making up some 30 per cent of the atmosphere's composition at the beginning of life, carbon dioxide now forms a mere 0.03 per cent today, the main result of that being a life-engineered regulation of the earth's surface temperature. The sun is now at least 30 per cent hotter than when the earth began, so this reduction in the carbon dioxide 'greenhouse effect' has ensured that the temperature at the earth's surface has remained cool enough for life to flourish. If carbon dioxide and other like greenhouse gases such as methane had remained in their original concentrations, the earth would have become a dead planet – like Venus.

Lovelock also points out that if it were not for life forms getting rid of salts from the sea, and in particular common salt, the oceans would now be at least 35 per cent salt and thus intolerable to life. The coral reefs, the limestone cliffs, the enormous salt deposits now formed on land, are all testimony to life's extraordinary activities in making the planet habitable.

Lovelock deduces that living organisms act as the earth's sensors – the interplay between different species and types of organism adjusting the planet's global metabolism to the detection of change. Thus one organism's effluent is another's food, to the point where a complete cycle is formed and a balance established. At times the balance is disturbed – catastrophes do indeed occur – yet such has been the power of life and its grasp on earth that the equilibrium is soon restored and a new flourishing of organisms promoted. Evolution is therefore a response to the power of Gaia to re-establish some balance, new species arising to adapt to the gaps left by the demise of the old order of organisms.

The spiritual implications of Gaia are profound, as they were to the ancient Greeks, and it is hardly surprising that the resurrection of an ancient idea should have begun to influence a new wave of philosophers. 'Deep Ecology' is one such movement, Arne Naess of Norway being one of its first proponents. Deep Ecologists believe inherently in the importance of the entire framework of life, from the simplest micro-organism to the mighty whale. While living within that framework and enjoying its fruits we should not disrupt or destroy it, although with wisdom we might be able to guide and develop it.

The Green philosophy

How can ecology be a philosophy?

Ecology itself is the science covering the interrelationship of all species and matter. But it has come to have a far broader meaning which is now implicit in the Green use of the word. The basic philosophy underlying this wider meaning has been called Deep Ecology. This is an attempt to find a philosophy in ecology and is an attempt to find a way of rethinking the relationship between humanity and nature. Deep Ecology thus: tries to provide a philosophical foundation for environmental activism; encourages decision-makers to consider philosophical and religious assertions when deciding policy – present approaches do not do this; tries to get people to think about themselves and nature in a new way.

Here are seven basic points of Deep Ecology. They are derived from many sources, and are general enough to be interpreted in a variety of ways. They are meant to serve as a set of core values, a platform to guide discussion and action.

1 All life has intrinsic value.

2 Nature, in all its complexity and diversity, results from symbiosis. Diversity means the many different kinds of individuals, species, and ecosystems which the whole of nature contains and in itself implies the idea of 'many'. But in nature, instead of a multiplicity of detached entities, organisms are bound to each other through threads of symbiosis and depend upon interaction with others for survival.

   Symbiosis with diversity together form the complexity of nature – a vast world of relationships, connections, and possibilities. There is intrinsic value in this crystal web of complexity. Our species is but one strand in the web.

3 People are part of nature, but our potential power means that our responsibility toward nature is greater than that of any other species. Individuals of all species have a natural tendency to explore their environment and simultaneously create and fill an ecological niche. In defining our niche we have altered nature more than any other species has done.

The Green Alternative

This imposed change, carried out on a massive scale, detaches us from the earth, and neither furthers our own survival nor the well-being of the planet.

4 We have become estranged from the earth because we have interfered with the complexity of nature. Yet our species has more than the ability to destroy: it also has a potential for understanding.

5 We should change the basic structure of our society and the policies which uphold it. The idea of growth should be redefined so that it refers to the increase of our understanding and experience of nature. Comprehending should form the basis of our actions. We therefore need to rethink our policies on:

Economics. Economic needs are the factual needs of survival. But only individuals can have such needs, not organisations nor corporations. Present economic ideology tends to value material goods and the flow of goods and services, and industries try to create or increase the needs for products. We should instead identify the needs of people and those of other species, and develop ways of realising them.

Society and politics. Our world is largely controlled by massive organisations and it is unrealistic to assume that we could function without them. But to promote growth we must encourage local, participatory structures, based on the principles of self-reliance. Local autonomy does not imply isolation and decentralisation does not suggest a lack of co-operation and meeting. The movement towards smaller, more egalitarian and less hierarchical organisations cannot be done in opposition to the dominant system: it must come from within its depths.

Cultures. Different cultures have different needs – cultures must be seen as dynamic patterns, flows of change based on enduring values identified through history. For cultural diversity to survive demands that the basic aims of each culture should be sustained. No culture should impose upon another.

6 We must seek quality of personal life rather than higher standards of living, self-realisation rather than mere monetary gain. Measuring quantities in our lives is easy, but measuring quality is not. Statistics alone can never be the basis for decisions – underlying values must be considered. It is essential to establish principles of life quality before criticisms and paths for change are mapped out.

Ecological consciousness connects the individual to the larger world. It allows the full realisation of the possibilities open to any person in society and nature. No one's self-realisation can come about in isolation, however: compassion and altruism must be the foundations of a life that is truly one of quality.

7 We need to identify more with nature. Only then will we see our part in it again. Science can help us to do this, as the search for basic laws brings us closer to natural values.

The more we learn of nature, the more we see that we cannot accept as inevitable our present dangerously imperfect world. We can direct whatever abilities we possess towards change, both immediate action and the achievement of long-term goals. Four broad ways of involving oneself in change can be identified:

- Living according to ecological ideals of self-reliance, as an individual or in a small group. To do this at present requires some detachment from the dominant system.
- Encouraging compromise between the present and the ideal: a mix of centralised and local technologies and institutions, providing a realistic path of transition.
- Trying to change the system directly. This means talking to people, including 'experts' and decision-makers.
- Artistic and philosophical reflection on the closeness of man and nature for its own sake.

As we do not live in an ideal world, we require ideals to guide us.

The Green Alternative

Isn't our concern for nature and the environment actually concern for ourselves?

Many people see themselves as enlightened when they argue that the nonhuman world ought to be preserved: (i) as a stockpile of genetic diversity for agricultural, medical and other purposes; (ii) as material for scientific study, for instance of our evolutionary origins; (iii) for recreation and (iv) for the opportunities it provides for aesthetic pleasure and spiritual inspiration. However, although enlightened, these reasons are all related to the instrumental value of the nonhuman world to humans. What is missing is any sense of a more impartial, biocentric – or biosphere-centred – view in which the nonhuman world is considered to be of intrinsic value.

How should we relate to the nonhuman world?

Pre-scientific views saw humans as dwelling at the centre of the universe and located between the 'beasts' and the angels – or between matter and spirit – in a static hierarchy of creation. The development of modern science swept these views aside but not the assumption that underlay them. Descartes saw science as rendering us the 'masters and possessors of nature'. Even those modern philosophical and social movements most concerned with exposing discrimination have typically confined their attention to the issues of race, class and sex and have been only marginally concerned with the exploitation of the nonhuman by the human.

How can we avoid our self-centred view of reality?

We need an ethic that recognises the intrinsic value of all aspects of the nonhuman world. For example, the animal rights movement argues that, since it is always wrong to cause unnecessary suffering, we must consider any entity to be intrinsically valuable if it possesses the capacity to feel. This extension of intrinsic value to all sentient creatures demands that both they and their environment be taken into account.

284

The Green philosophy

Does the new awareness of nature demand vegetarianism?

The human chauvinist answer is either a flat 'no' or a 'yes', justified on entirely human-centred grounds, such as that more humans could be more adequately fed if we were all vegetarian. The animal rights answer is 'yes' on the grounds that meat-eating inflicts avoidable suffering upon animals in a factory-farm situation and/or at the time of their death.

In contrast, the Deep Ecology approach of minimising harm or limitation to the free flow of nature, using nature as economically as possible, means that animals have their place in the food chain and among certain groups of people (such as the Eskimo population and tribal Indians in the Amazon) eating meat is essential for survival. However, to conform with such principles we should certainly reduce the amount of meat we consume in the West.

Why are some people vegetarians?

Firstly, many now realise that meat is not necessary for human health. For example, Joyce Smith, one of Britain's foremost marathon runners, is a recently converted vegetarian who feels that her performance is improved by a non-meat diet. Secondly, many people feel concerned at the events in Ethiopia and other countries of the developing world, recognising that starvation is linked as much, if not more, to our excessive consumption of resources in the north as it is to population or climate in the south. Meat-eating, especially to the excess seen in the USA and increasingly in west Europe and Japan, typifies such over-consumption of resources. Thirdly, some people are worried about the anti-biotics, hormones and strong chemicals fed to animals.

So a vegetarian is more moral than a meat-eater?

It is not that a vegetarian is more moral, just that he or she has made this particular moral choice. Car-exhaust emissions are harmful to people and the environment. Is the vegetarian who drives more or less moral than the meat-eater who cycles?

Should scientists have a greater moral conscience with regard to their research or is the pursuit of truth a valid goal?

It is probably incorrect to state that scientists are involved in the pursuit of objective truth. Their research is mainly oriented towards gathering information of a specific type: that which can be exploited for military or commercial purposes. Very little, if any, research is conducted on the effects of scientific inventions on human health or on that of ecosystems in general. For instance, practically no research is conducted on the effects on health of pesticides, and when it is the results are almost always kept secret.

Modern science has now become indistinguishable from the technology that it spawns, and this technology is becoming increasingly destructive. Nuclear power, genetic engineering and microelectronics have an enormous potential for transforming life on this planet. It is totally unrealistic to say, as many scientists do, that science and technology are neutral and that it is not their fault if their inventions are used destructively.

Surely genetic engineering and other scientific advances will help us overcome disability and improve on nature?

Biotechnology is the most extreme instance of the modern, anthropocentric desire that we become the 'masters and possessors of nature'. The biotechnology debate has to do with the kind of beings we wish to be and with the kind of world in which we wish to live. As Jeremy Rifkin says in his book *Algeny*:

> Two futures beckon us. We can choose to engineer the life of the planet, creating a second nature in our image, or we can choose to participate with the rest of the living kingdom . . . an engineering approach . . . or an ecological approach. The battle between [them] is a battle of values. Our choice, in the final analysis, depends on what we value most in life.

The Green philosophy

Even if one accepts that the products of technology are capable of exterminating life on earth, isn't it extreme to argue that there is actually something wrong with the technological style of mind?

The technological style of mind views the nonhuman world as being there for humans. Dominated by this assumption, we treat the world as a 'resource' and continue to suffer an alienation from nature. The alternative is not to reject technology *per se* but rather to reject the ideal of technological control in favour of the ideal of ecological consciousness. This means rejecting the fantasy that we are charged with the responsibility for steering (and maybe speeding up) the future course of evolution. Instead, we should allow all beings to follow their own evolutionary destinies.

Technology is surely serving the real needs of mankind?

Human beings have biological, social, spiritual and aesthetic needs. They have neither material nor technological needs. It is only in specific and highly aberrant conditions such as those that exist in much of the industrialised world today that manufactured goods and technological devices are required to satisfy real needs. Even then, they do not do so satisfactorily. Technology in itself cannot feed the world. A tractor does not feed people, it just saves labour which is not a problem in the countries affected by famine today. Herbicides don't feed people either. They save people the trouble of weeding their gardens and fields by hand, and again shortage of labour is not a problem in the Third World. Fertiliser is only required because new hybrids are grown which require fertiliser. Man has lived for 3 million years without any sophisticated technological devices. He could not have survived that long without fertile soil and fresh uncontaminated water. So if we must desertify our soil and destroy our water resources in order to produce the technology, then clearly we are far better off without it.

The Green Alternative

Should women have a particular role in an ecologically oriented society?

Each person should be valued as an equal member of the community, and each community should see itself as being intrinsically connected to the natural environment. The idea of community should be the common social bond, and the idea of harmony with nature would be the common social concern.

Implicit in this concept is the achievement of an atmosphere free from the threat and actuality of violence. In this freedom from violence the women's and ecology movements have one of their strongest links, both recognising human and natural resources and rejecting the domination, humiliation and exploitation of any of these. At the same time the liberation of women – the chance to become free, equal and independent beings – should lead to the liberation of men and children.

But in the threat to our survival – from the ungovernable arms race, for instance – isn't feminism a subsidiary issue?

The failure to connect issues and the dividing of concerns is part of the problem itself. That separatist way of thinking has helped contribute to the arms race, to the present ecological crisis, to our inability adequately to feed or shelter the world's population, to our incapacity to provide the dignity of a job to every person who wants one and to our unwillingness to recognise the basic rights to existence of every form of life on our planet.

Accordingly, the need for change is all-encompassing and will not be lastingly achieved by selective alterations in some spheres at the expense of, or while ignoring the needs of, others. At the same time the 'good life' that we are all striving for is not simply a question of putting people physically or geographically closer to nature. With our current social and economic structures, any move to simpler living would increase rather than diminish the oppression and exploitation of over half the population – namely women. A simpler, more ecologically harmonious lifestyle might entail longer and harder labour, increased isolation and even greater economic dependency for women. We need, therefore, to think not only how we relate to nature, but also how we relate to each other, and to see all those relations as inherently connected and of equal importance.

Let us suppose that the good life lies at the centre of a web of interconnecting strands. Emanating from the centre are strands representing a variety of factors – social, political, environmental and economic – which are linked together. The idea of community is one cross-strand in the web, linking social relations to the other factors, as well as to the good life at the centre.

Surely we already have communities, both rural and urban, so what's the problem?

Yes, we do already have communities, but they're based by and large on the central unit of the nuclear family or its variations; therefore, single- and two-parent families, couples, or people living alone still retreat into their separate households to use their separate appliances and to find separate solutions to the tasks of childrearing, housework, and financial support. From a technical point of view, this means that each household owns or would like to own appliances or equipment (vacuum cleaners and grass cutters, for example) that could easily be shared and communally owned. The same goes for labour-intensive tasks. The isolation and the emotional frustration and exhaustion often felt by those responsible for housework and child-rearing are not efficiently or effectively solved by either a reversal of the traditional roles or, where applicable, by both parents taking full-time waged work. In the former, it simply means that men would in their turn become prone to the 'housewife blues', and in the latter, even if all unpaid work were shared, there would be little or no time left for relaxation or leisure, not to mention the additional financial burden of babysitters and child-minders. As long as we define the words 'family' and 'family ties, duties and responsibilities' as applying to a group of people biologically or legally related, we will only be paying lip service to the roles of mother, parent and family member, while in fact punishing those who assume those roles by excluding them from full and active participation in the life of the community.

To remedy this, we need free and universal daycare facilities, and not only at the workplace. Every child should be seen as the shared responsibility of each member of a community, and this means that every task, every social activity and event where children could not participate would have additional facilities where they could be fully and lovingly cared for. Responsibility for this could easily be arranged on a rotating basis, as could the tasks associated with housework, like cleaning, washing and cooking. These tasks, essential to

'We're just so terribly lucky that Gladys absolutely *loves* cooking, washing up, weeding the garden, looking after the kids, etc, etc.'

the survival of the community, need not, with very few exceptions, be gender-specific or assumed as part of a rigid role by one person for all of the time. Reassessing the concepts of 'women's work' and 'men's work', as well as communally shared essential tasks, would ultimately give everyone more free time to develop their own potential. Equality in the community means not only equal rights for females and males, it also means finding a balance between the needs of the community and the needs of the individual, so that none clash with the preservation of nature.

So we're all going to share the housework. What's that got to do with ecology?

Many of the labour-saving devices in our homes, which also happen to be wasteful from an ecological point of view, were designed for and are used by housewives and mothers; they include everything from electric blenders to disposable nappies. They are called 'labour-saving', yet they use valuable energy resources, make women dependent on technology and do nothing in substance to alter the roles of housewife or mother which still carry low social status and are financially unrewarded. If we took away the ecologically wasteful appliances yet retained the roles as gender-specific or as applying to one person for all of the time, that would mean that the household tasks which are menial, boring and repetitive would become even more so. Alternatively, if the essential tasks are recognised as essential and thus to be shared equally by the community, even the most humble job would be valued and the person performing it at any one time would not feel exploited or demeaned.

Have any communities on the lines you propose been successful?

One successful type of community is that of the commune or kibbutz in Israel in which work, income and the collective raising of children is shared. It means shared responsibility rather than sole responsibility or no responsibility, and may well be the best way to combat the isolation of the nuclear family and the inequalities built into it for women if they assume traditional roles or even share them. In Israel kibbutzim have been in operation for more than three-quarters of a century, providing a way of life for some 5 per cent of the population in 350 different communes. Most of the rest of the rural population in Israel live in moshavim, which are cooperatives sharing equipment and marketing facilities, while still retaining the structure of an independent family existence.

Although kibbutzim have undoubtedly changed with the times, many of them becoming well-endowed, with a comfortable lifestyle, they still adhere strongly to the collective, communitarian principles on which they were founded. In the UK it must be appreciated that fewer than 2 per cent of the population are now involved with farming and horticulture, and a negligible proportion of those are involved in any kind of collective or cooperative venture. That has to be compared with more than 10 per cent of the Israeli population. With the right political structure and support, community living need no longer be an aberration or a struggle against impossible odds.

And what about family planning in the community?

If the family is redefined as taking in all members of the community, then birth control becomes an issue of both individual responsibility and collective community concern. The aim is for a community in which no child is unwanted or unloved, and at the same time our limited natural resources are not overtaxed by unrestricted population growth. Again, it is important to stress the balance that must be achieved between the individual and the collective. For individual women, this means the right to control their own bodies, hence abortion on demand and free, safe and effective birth control, as well as a shared responsibility with men in its use.

For all members of the community, balanced family planning also means a programme of sexual education that includes an awareness of the natural dignity and autonomy of the human body and its sexuality, in addition to an awareness of how many people the resources of the community can support without straining the social or ecological balance. Overcrowding is unquestionably one of the factors leading to frustration, scarcity and violence among people, which in turn leads to a form of violence on the earth's resources and the natural environment. It follows, too, that if women had control over their own bodies, as well as the equal chance to develop their full human potential in any number of roles and pursuits, they would be unlikely to define themselves solely as mothers – just as, at present, it is rare to find a man who defines himself solely as a father.

What about violence? Does an equal and an ecologically balanced community mean there would be no rape, no pornography, no abuse or assault?

Again, learning not to exploit, degrade or harm one another is inevitably linked to learning not to exploit, degrade and harm our natural environment. The pornographic mind, the rapist mind and the violent mind is one divided from other people and the environment, as well as divided from a part of itself which it fears and denies.

As a result of that growing alienation it is hardly surprising that we live in a society that exploits, degrades and performs acts of violence against both women and nature. This condition will persist unless we learn to come to terms with ourselves, with each other and with everything that lives. If we learn to recognise and give equal value to the masculine and feminine within each of us, it follows that we will learn to recognise and value every human being in our society, free from the rigidly defined roles currently assigned to gender.

It follows, too, that if we value and respect all parts of ourselves, we will value and respect everyone and everything that contributes to our needs and our survival – enabled, finally, to see the links between individual and community and environment.

12 Education

One of the problems facing us in Britain today is that of the 'dispossessed' young – those teenagers and young people who have rejected the system, who, however successful they were at primary school, have dropped behind or dropped out of secondary school. Those who have decided that it is pointless to try to seek work or to join 'schemes' or who, having searched and failed to find work, feel totally rejected. Those who do not 'get on their bikes' as admonished by the government except, perhaps, to terrorise seaside resorts.

But what relevance has the Green movement to today's unemployed youngsters? Unfortunately, the answer has to be none, unless we can change the system enough to make the question irrelevant. There are no piecemeal solutions. We must change the kind of society which leaves children growing up without leadership from parents and teachers, leaving them without goals, without faith, without respect for traditions.

Unless we adopt a new approach, putting people's destinies and welfare before our technological way of life, our planet before 'progress', we will enter the next decade with a society so divided that the boundaries cannot be crossed. We must give these 'dispossessed' hope, and a future, by transforming the aspirations and values of society. That will entail fundamental changes in our education system.

What is the purpose of education?

The purpose of education is to bring out the potential qualities of a child, as well as of an adult, in the physical, spiritual, intellectual and psychological fields. In its broadest sense, education is the process of discovering the essential nature of our beings and our place in the universe. In that sense we all attend this earthly 'school of life'.

Education has, however, come more narrowly to mean the

294

preparation of the young for life in their particular culture. This is increasingly taken to be the role of the state through the provision of formal education structures, designed to prepare participants for a consumer society.

Who influences the nature of our schools?

Today schools reflect little of the hopes and real requirements of students or teachers and largely ignore the needs of local communities. A lack of consultation and participation in educational decisions has left teachers, students and parents without the skills and confidence needed to influence their futures. Indeed, most secondary-school teachers' work is largely determined by university requirements, as administered by the examination boards. The local education authorities and the Department of Education and Science are only just beginning to exert a direct influence on the school curriculum.

What should parents, teachers, administrators and students want from education?

'Preparation for life' is a commonly held overall aim, but what kind of life do we want to prepare for? To what preparation for life is every child entitled? What can society reasonably expect from an adult citizen? And what share of this preparation, what contribution to seeing that these expectations are met, properly belongs to the school? If 'education is not merely the acquisition of technical knowledge, but the understanding, with sensitivity and intelligence, of the whole problem of living', the state of health or well-being of our children, our societies, economies, political systems and natural environment should be a central concern of our schools.

What is the best way to achieve good student/teacher relationships?

The kind of learning that influences behaviour is most important; this is self-discovered, self-appropriated learning. The

most effective way to enable others to learn is for the
'teacher' to join the pupils, learning about what matters to
them and what influences their behaviour.

Research[1] shows how, where teachers are seen as
genuinely part of the class, where they in turn respect the
uniqueness of each student, where teaching goals help
students to think for themselves and to participate actively,
the following qualities develop: students learn reading, maths
and other subjects more quickly; they learn more eagerly,
asking more questions; they develop problem-solving and
decision-making abilities; and they become more creative.
Student absenteeism is reduced and students become more
self-confident and self-directing, less rigid in their perceptions
and adopt more realistic goals for themselves. They behave
more maturely, are able to change maladjusted behaviour
and become more as they would like to be; they become more
popular and more open to evidence of what is going on inside
and outside themselves. This is seen to be true for children in
a wide range of cultures, of all school ages and of all abilities,
from retarded to gifted.

Teachers engaged in the process of personal transformation recognise that this learning is not just healthy: it *is* health.
Like holistic medicine, holistic education is concerned with
the whole person. These teachers turn away from a curriculum that fragments knowledge into subjects, history into
dates and our relationships with the natural environment into
abstract geographical patterns. They work towards a system
of learning that emphasises the interrelationships and unity of
all forms of life.

Teachers who have tried out this approach successfully
insist that it is not enough to transform a classroom – the
whole educational administration needs to be changed. In an
early edition of *Freedom to Learn*[2] Professor Carl Rogers
outlines a week's residential course for the administrators:

> I think of administrators who have worked together for
> twenty years and discover that they have never known each
> other as persons; of negative feelings that wrecked planning
> work for years, which can now be safely brought out into the
> open, understood and dissolved; of positive feelings that have

always seemed too risky to voice . . . of the intense sense of
community which develops . . . the willingness to risk new
behaviours, new directions, new purposes.

The next step would be to run a similar course for teachers,
replacing the friction and inadequacy of hierarchies with the
co-operation of understanding and trust. At the same time
weekend groups for parents, possibly of one class, could be
held. Then vertical groups could be set up with, say, two
members of the board of governors, two members of the local
education authority, two teachers, two parents and four
students of widely differing abilities.

Is education producing crippled or healthy minds?

What has been called 'whole-brain knowing', emerging from
the discoveries of brain research, has revolutionised our
understanding of the learning process. Unfortunately this
news has hardly reached our schools: pupils continue to start
off as butterflies and end up in cocoons. The discoveries about
the specialisation of the left and right brain hemispheres
should be transforming our approach to learning.[3]

The left-brain mode is logical, abstract, objective, analytical, convergent, linear, sequential, and controls verbal
expression. The right-brain mode is intuitive, synthesising,
creative, and concerned with spatial awareness, imagination
and spontaneity.

Only an integration of both sides of our brain can enable us
to develop our true mental potential. We need the right brain
to generate new ideas and the left brain to organise the
information into the existing scheme of things. 'The com-
plementarity of these two modes underlies our highest
achievements', says Professor Robert Ornstein.[4]

Even a cursory glance at the Western model of education
would show an observer that 'the entire student body is being
educated lopsidedly'. Over ten years ago Dr James Hemming
showed clearly in *The Betrayal of Youth* how narrow
academic specialisation was crippling the personalities of the
young. All great educational innovators have accorded equal

weight to our two modes of consciousness: Neill of Summerhill, Curry of Dartington, Badley of Bedales, for example. Brunner noted how a child approaching a new problem would be paralysed without the use of intuition.

Conventional schooling splits the mental vision and goes a long way to explaining the dis-ease so many students feel in the classroom learning situation. Concentration on the left-brain mode of consciousness has made most people very poor learners. When both brain modes are used there is a spectacular acceleration in the speed and breadth of learning. Famous learning experiments with schoolchildren have been carried out in Bulgaria for the Ministry of National Education by Georgyi Lozanov. Slow learners found a joy in their work for the first time and the more gifted had up to 50 per cent more time for the purely creative and recreational activities.

Why isn't this more widespread?

For the same reasons which commonly prevent the adoption of many other improvements in education: over-worked teachers do not make time to read outside their narrow field; little time or money is available for teachers to develop new learning programmes even if they are aware of the possibilities; students fear innovation in competitive learning situations; parents dislike experimentation when this is undertaken by a teacher outside an official programme of research; governments lack interest in whole-brain learning and educational authorities prefer shorter-term and cheaper 'solutions'; pupils and teachers do not complain about the present situation; left-brain thinkers predominate among decision-makers. Teachers also, commonly believe they should teach the knowledge they were taught but rarely used themselves, and maximise the number of examination passes.

Every teacher could be involved in whole-brain learning, instead of splitting the roles between humanities, science and arts. Each learning area ('subject') could have components of: the intellectual, the social and moral, the aesthetic, the spiritual, the affective, the practical and physical, the creative and expressive. Teachers should be specialists in the dynamics of individual development as much as masters/mistresses of specific subject skills.

What is education for a healthy body?

Schools have always paid some attention to healthy bodies, providing sports facilities and training. However, in general they have not co-ordinated this with the provision of 'health education' and of various outdoor pursuits and leisure activities. The programme needs to be expanded to include awareness of body functions and senses, as well as the interplay of the body with the emotions, mind and spirit.

A healthy diet is a new element in health education. Particularly valuable work is taking place in schools which combine dietary education with changes in the school catering service, one of the best experiments being undertaken by Surrey County Council. Their 'Choosing Food for Healthy Living' programme details can be obtained from the Surrey County Council School Catering Service.

What is education for a healthy society?

Education systems tend to be administered by bureaucrats and run by professionals, with the emphasis on the authority of the text and the teacher. The head-teacher takes most of the responsibility for the school, with the teachers grouped in a hierarchical order below. If the lowest rank of teacher has little responsibility for the nature of the education system, that of parents and students is even less.

Pupils learn and memorise what society already knows. They compete against each other, tested by difficult examinations, in order to select the future decision-makers. The majority see themselves as unimportant members of their school 'community' whose opinions are never sought. The effects of this, found in all but the highest levels of the hierarchy, are feelings of inadequacy, inability to express themselves, or to influence anyone, feelings of being shut out, cynicism, and an increase in destructive feelings. People feel that they have to dominate or be dominated and need to conform. They feel that intolerance and prejudice are all right. And of course they feel that new ideas must come from the top.

There is a spiral in human development from alienation and anomie at the bottom to the fully creative being at the top. We are all either moving up or down this spiral. Most hierarchical organisations are driving people downwards.

Educationalist Elizabeth Simpson took up this point in the context of the classroom. She developed a scale to measure the position on this development spiral of children between five and seventeen years, relating this to democratic values and attitudes, choosing five fundamental beliefs to represent these values:

1 Belief in human nature – that human beings are basically good and trustworthy.

2 Belief that people have some power over their own lives.

3 Desire to think for oneself, rather than accepting the opinion of others as to what is right.

4 Belief in the validity of the experiences and opinions of others – they have the right to be different.

5 Belief that the rights of other people are to be respected, just because they are human beings.

Simpson argued that anyone who held these five views would want to live in a democratic system and that anyone who held the opposite views would prefer a strong leader to take all the decisions. She found that the more psychologically deprived the child was, the less did they tend to hold a democratic outlook.

What alternative models of society are there?

One is known as 'the populist model of an egalitarian society', characterised by decentralised, democratic decision-making, within co-operative forms of organisation. Here the oppressive hierarchy which reduces people to roles is absent. In such a society the local community must set the education goals in conjunction with the teachers and students. Parents and workers should come into the school as often as students go out into the community. Students should leave school with a wide range of useful skills, including the ability to make creative decisions over how to improve their lives and that of the community.

How would schools be affected by this kind of decentralised open and egalitarian society?

Schools would have to change profoundly. The results could be that feelings would be expressed honestly, rather than being suppressed; there would be more understanding between working groups; and teachers, students, parents and administrators would work more effectively together. Better methods of conflict resolution would develop. A more open problem-solving climate would emerge throughout the system, resulting in a wider sharing of responsibility and more trust. Competition would be made relevant to work goals and to increased co-operative efforts and the school would move towards a reward system which recognised the development of people. Everyone would feel an increasing sense of control over aims and objectives and increased self-control and self-direction within the organisation.

The process of change would involve a difficult and painful transfer of power for both sides. Nevertheless, the more power an élite sheds, the more power the whole organism gains. Few groups ever give away power and peaceful strategies are needed to relieve them of it.

Do 'healthy' school communities exist?

In *The Aquarian Conspiracy*[5] Marilyn Ferguson writes of the many new 'alternative-neighbourhood' schools that are springing up in the United States. These schools are similar to an extended family. Parents, teachers and students jointly decide issues of policy and curriculum and choose the staff. Teachers are more like friends than authority figures. Age groups are flexible, with enough structure to remind the pupils of the outside society. The curriculum is not dominated by the exam system but external exams are sat if needed. The curriculum knows only the boundaries of the school budget and the teachers'/pupils'/parents' energy. Parents and specialists in the community teach special subjects voluntarily. Pupils also teach each other.

The learning process involves the use of relaxation, meditation, guided fantasy and intuition to raise the level of consciousness. Music, drama, visual arts, festivals and physical exercises develop greater self-awareness and creativity. Pupils learn the use of power and responsibility by attending governors' and education authority meetings. The nature of inter-personal relationships is explored, identifying happiness, fear and conflict and their sources. Pupils learn how to act responsibly in 'their' school and how to communicate their thoughts and feelings. Autonomy, empathy and mutual support are emphasised. Working in groups is common, not only helping to eradicate the tyranny of dominant perception, but also to sustain change.

What is education for a healthy economy?

Economic reality – everyone's education should include a study in the basics of achieving and managing a healthy economy. Yet few students leave school with even an elementary understanding of either the nature of wealth – not only money and possessions but also the quality of life – or how it is achieved and lost in economic development.

Students are being educated for a work situation that no longer exists. After forty years of expansion the world labour market is now stagnating in the poor South, as well as in the rich North. Automation is now replacing workers everywhere. Between now and the end of the century, should trends continue, the world's population will increase by 31.5 per cent from 4,600 to 6,050 million. The adult labour force will grow from 2,400 million to 3,630 million – a 51 per cent increase. The number unable to earn a minimal living will increase, if present trends continue, from 900 million to 1,540 million – an increase of 71 per cent!

It is clear that for those not, or unhappy, in full-time

employment, a very different future has to be faced than that assumed by our present education systems. Fritz Schumacher was one of the first economists to show how a healthy economy could grow without harm and with dignity for all, depending on the use of 'human-scale technology', 'appropriate forms of ownership' and 'education for good work'. Brian Wren in his book *Education For Justice*[6] points out how 'knowing' is only a first step; 'doing' must follow and can do so through appropriate 'problem-posing education'.

A start is being made in the non-exam classes called variously 'Preparation For Adult Life' or 'Lifeskills', but this is not enough.

Can the formal education system adapt in time to economic reality?

In 1981 49 per cent of all boys and 44 per cent of all girls in the UK left school without passing an 'O' Level or a grade I CSE – in their own minds, failures.

Enlightened educationalists are trying to change the system. Professor John Tomlinson, director of Warwick University's Institute of Education, wants 'radical changes in traditional exams and school time-tables if the education system is to meet the challenges of the future structure of employment in the industrial world'. Professor Tomlinson, together with several headmasters, has warned teachers that many of the present curriculum changes are like 're-arranging the deck-chairs on the Titanic'.

Traditional exams do not allow the full development of the human potential needed to survive in the future. Traditional subject divisions must not dominate in the strait-jacket of the thirty-to-forty-period week of teacher contact for around ten subjects. Much longer study/work periods are needed, integrating traditional disciplines, to allow students to develop such skills as group co-operation, creative thinking and problem solving, to study reality, not just text-book fiction, and to make a contribution to community life.

Specialist-subject teachers must work together as a team to develop the full potential of their pupils and every teacher should be able to integrate several of the curriculum areas accorded equal importance in the HMI document 'Curriculum Planning 11–16'.

The present government-led top-down rather than grass roots reform of offering yet another academic exam system, leaving the necessary work of transformation to those teachers still willing to devote time freely in their weekends and evenings, is a tragic mistake. Money has to be spent in the right places; no amount of post-sixteen vocational training schemes can make up for damage done during the previous five years or more. The growing pressure to add technical, practical and vocational areas to the curriculum is merely adding just another narrow view of the world. The whole has to be changed and integrated.

Is the Western model of education proving a disaster for the development of the world's poorer countries?

Formal education is still mostly reserved for the planet's wealthy. Although the developing countries have over half the world's population, they only spent 9 per cent of the world's education budget (which was $36 billion out of a total of $294 billion) in 1975. Yet every country believes that its formal education system is essential for economic development. Despite evidence to the contrary, the belief that more of the same type of education will improve economies is as widespread as it was forty years ago – quite apart from the mistaken belief in the benefits of economic growth!

Basic literacy and numeracy have become an essential defence against losing what little people have and a vital element in any strategy for economic justice for the poor. These skills are also needed for learning new techniques in farming, manufacturing and services – though the promised increase in productivity may turn into a long-term decrease. In fact, education has come to mean just a way to acquire the paper qualifications for a better job.

Most under-developed countries began their system of formal education under colonial rule. The colonists needed clerks for their administration, technical assistants and foremen for their industries, and introduced their own form of education, together with their own language and culture. The newly independent countries (run by the educated élite) expanded this education system and enrolments increased until about 1975, when public spending cuts were forced upon the 'developing' countries by the rise in the price of oil and other foreign imports; the rise in interest rates on foreign debts and the fall in purchasing power of their primary exports.

The year 1975 saw 62 per cent of the 'Third World' children of primary age in schools, 35 per cent in secondary schools and 4.5 per cent in higher education. This compared to 94 per cent, 84 per cent and 16 per cent respectively for the developed countries. In 1980 a world total of 795 million adults were illiterate, 60 per cent of whom were women.

'An Honours Degree in X-ray Crystallography, huh . . .
a Witchdoctor's Degree in Rainmaking would have been more
to the point.'

The Green Alternative

What did this expenditure achieve?

This system of education has been called the 'alienation machine'. The result has been an increase in the inequalities of wealth in the world as the wealthy, who could pay for this expensive education improved their chances, but the poor, unable to meet this cost, did not improve their ability to provide a better diet or better conditions to bring up children. Malnutrition, poor sanitation and lack of stimulation left the poorer children with sadly underdeveloped mental potential. Many of those who did manage to finish primary or even secondary levels became 'drones', unwilling to take up 'inferior' rural work, unfit for manufacturing jobs and unable to find clerical work.

What alternative educational models are being developed in the Third World?

In Tanzania primary schools have self-contained courses, with students and parents involved in decision-making for democratic community development. Schools teach self-reliance by being self-reliant! They grow food, maintain buildings and participate in community projects. However, inadequate preparation of teachers and an unwillingness on the part of students to forgo status based on paper qualifications has weakened this programme.

This latter pitfall has been recognised in Papua New Guinea, in the Secondary Schools Community Extension Project, where academic qualifications are only awarded if the student has demonstrated skill at applying curriculum content to the solution of a practical community issue.

Education to benefit the poor was the focus of The People's School, Gono Pathshala, at Savar in Bangladesh. This arose out of Zafrullah Chowdhury's medical work as a barefoot doctor.

The school is only for poor families and has no fees or uniforms, the materials are free and the school closes on market days and during harvest. The local community built the school and benefits from the practical curriculum; farming, carpentry, health education, reading and writing are all learnt every day. The older and brighter children help the others. Work is done in self-chosen groups of ten and promotion to the next class has to be earned by the group as a whole. Once a week the children go out into the community to share their learning.

Many community education schemes, such as ACPO in Colombia, are based on the work of Paulo Freire, who ran Brazil's national plan for adult literacy until the right-wing coup in 1964.

Freire believed that peasants were held in poverty and semi-slavery by a 'culture of silence', lacking political power and economic resources. With no voice, there was no hope of change and so no motivation for literacy or numeracy.

He rejected Western education, which only led to dependence on the teacher and the employer, and developed a literacy programme which related directly to the lives of the peasants, enabling them to take control of their lives and recreate their world.

A final example is the work of Bhagwan Sri Sathya Sai Baba, who began an education programme in the region of Bangalore, in the state of Andhra Pradesh, Southern India in 1940. He based it on the values he considered fundamental to every society in the world:

1 The cultivation of *truth*, the cultivation of the mind [*Sathya*]

2 The adherence to *right action* or *conduct*, or the refinement and purification of the human will [*Dharma*]

3 The understanding of the emotional being, perfect self-control and the flow of spontaneous *peace* [*Shanti*]

4 *Love* or the sharpening of the *intuition*, the awakening of the psyche [*Prema*]

5 *Universal love or compassion*, the awakening of the spirit [*Ahisma*]

These 'human values' are the basis of any knowledge of how to earn a living, of respect for elders, service to the community and a love of all peoples and their faiths.

The Green Alternative

There are now over 2,300 instructional classes (*bal vikas*) for the six to fourteen age group all over India, and there are many Sathya Sai Schools and five colleges at university level in four states.

An integral part of the education of the college students is to learn how to use the benefits of their learning for the good of the community in the rural development and health education schemes. This includes the setting-up of primary schools, vocational training centres and adult education centres; the laying of rural link roads, village streets, pavements, drainage and sewerage systems; the provision of drinking-water facilities; the improvement of cattle and crop farming and of medical facilities. All this is free of any caste, religious or racial prejudices.

Shouldn't we in the developed world offer aid in the form of education?

Government to government financial aid is bad enough but government to government transfer of education would be even worse. The education of one country is frequently irrelevant to the needs and requirements of another. Such a transfer would also open up a new channel for the imposition of external, and in many cases alien, ideas. Indeed this has already been happening as a result of attempts to create a synthetic society in Third World countries, to boost unsound home economies and cash in on surpluses.

After all, the purpose of aid is to enable and facilitate the recipients to achieve their objectives, not ours. Who are we to say what they need and what is good for them? The Third World countries have a great cultural tradition, old civilisation and spiritual wisdom. Therefore in the West we need to be more humble and learn from the Third World as much as teach, take as much as give. Only through mutual respect, mutual co-operation and mutual aid on equal terms can we create a world from which will result peace and a harmonious relationship. Nevertheless, the education system in many developing countries (particularly India) is totally town/

examination focused and ignores the real needs of the mass of
of the (rural) people.

Should education be concerned with healthy environmental systems and relationships?

Just as studies on development are missing from the curricula
of most schools, so too schools are generally failing to educate
our young people in our planet's life sustaining systems, the
nature of human impact upon them, and the paths to sustainable futures.

Education must play a major role in the about-turn needed
to avoid the destruction of life itself on our planet, which is
now in progress through such acts as deforestation, soil
erosion, pollution, loss of genetic diversity and the threat of
nuclear war.

The Draft Final Report of the Intergovernmental Conference on Environmental Education organised by UNESCO
at Tbilisi, USSR in 1977 stated that environmental education
should:

● provide the necessary knowledge, understanding, values and
skills needed by the general public and many occupational
groups

● help create an awareness of the economic, political and
ecological interdependence of the modern world

● involve learning from the environment as well as about it

● be an integral part of the educational process

● represent a means of introducing a certain unity into the
educational process

Despite official words that all is well, at present
environmental education remains embryonic in the strait-
jacket of the reductionist approach, which has served scientific discovery reasonably well but has prevented us from
putting the academic pieces together to see just what is
happening to our world. For example, an issue like the
destruction of the world's tropical forests is not just the

concern of the environmentalist, as it concerns economic development, and human and animal rights.

You cannot properly explain any major world issues by reference to one academic discipline. The famine in Ethiopia is partly due to overpopulation, regional inequalities in development, environmental destruction, abuse of political power, violation of human rights, civil war and the super-power conflict.

Environmental education emerged in the 1960s with the re-birth of the science of ecology, but has remained confined to primary level nature study and relegated to a position of secondary importance in the current educational system.

13 Politics

We live in times of momentous change. We are seeing the demise both of traditional industries and traditional ways of manufacturing, while unemployment, currently affecting some 4 million people, has become a major issue. Indeed, the fabric of society seems to be disintegrating: our major industrial cities are decaying, the tax and rate base to support them having fallen away; the countryside needs fewer people, farmers using machines rather than labour. What can politicians do under such circumstances?

The total labour force in Britain amounts to some 27 million out of which, in June 1984, nearly 21 million were employed, including some 2.44 million self-employed and 300,000 in the armed forces. At the same time, 3.2 million were registered as unemployed. Barrie Sherman in *Working at Leisure*[1] assesses that the numbers of those likely to be in full employment by the turn of the century and beyond will fall from current levels to 14.8 million – a drop of 6 million. That prognosis is based on the number of jobs likely to be available. Meanwhile, an extra 1.4 million people should be seeking jobs as a result of the 1960s baby boom. Those who are self-employed are likely to increase to some 4 million.

We have created a society over the past two hundred years of industrialism in which to be jobless signifies failure. Not surprisingly those made redundant or who have failed ever to find a full-time job often become apathetic and depressed. But the jobs are not going to be there, at least not in traditional terms, and neither of the mainstream political ideas – monetarism, nor increasing state expenditure, are likely to solve the unemployment problem. One effect of monetarist, anti-inflation policies is to increase the pool of available cheap labour and to reduce the spending power of the unemployed. Meanwhile, with very low growth, increased spending by the state to create jobs will tend to depress the economy still further.

The Green Alternative

Competition, particularly from Japan and increasingly from developing countries such as Brazil, has undoubtedly whittled away Britain's manufacturing base, but the introduction of micro-chip technology, particularly in the manufacturing industries, of computer control and robotic fabrication has replaced thousands employed on production lines. The question has therefore arisen of whether the cost in human terms incurred through micro-chip technology more than outweighs the benefits. Yet the advantages of micro-chip technology in increasing efficiency of production at reduced costs offers us an extraordinary opportunity to reorganise the basis of employment in ways which would serve society to advantage and would conform to Green policies.

In a Green society the dual aim must be to enable people to work so that they gain self-respect and to earn enough to keep themselves and their families comfortably. Given that there are likely to be twice the numbers available for work as there will be jobs, one solution would be to share jobs through a reduced working week to some thirty hours. Free time could be devoted to leisure activities and to community work. But such a system would only succeed if each person working received an adequate wage, whether supplemented or not.

One important aspect of Green policy would be to foster people's pride in their community and surroundings. At present we are very much a divided society: the establishment of communities in which people actively participate should have the effect of clarifying the minds of politicians themselves, for whom Green ideas will have to become second nature.

All aspects of life and living will be affected by Green policies: what we do with the land, what we eat, what we manufacture, what sort of transportation system we have, how we educate our children, what work we do and how we get paid. In the end Green ideas mean, quite simply, concern for life on earth. Not just concern for one's own family, or friends, for a community or the whole human race, but concern for the process of life itself, and everything that nurtures and sustains that process. How we care for our environment and ultimately the earth will reflect on how we care for people and for the communities in which they live.

What are Green politics?

Green politics are the business of finding alternative ways of creating wealth and organising society that are compatible with Green principles.

It means combating at every turn the myths, lies and vested interests of industrialism, that system of wealth creation and social organisation that prevails in almost all nations today and which in many respects has brought us to the point of no return.

It means adopting Green alternatives wherever possible, through party politics or involvement in pressure group activities, by personal example or through one's spiritual beliefs.

What's it to do with me?

Everything! No man or woman is an island: we are all inextricably linked together and dependent on each other. So, even though we may think we are safe from the many threats to survival, we are not – it's an illusion.

It's not just our self-interest that is at stake, it's our interest in the future of our children and in the whole of humanity.

Some people have worries of their own, like unemployment. Why should they care?

Because the planet is the source of *all* our wealth; in destroying that, we destroy forever the chance of things getting better for all of us. But it is a lunatic system that allows minorities to get ridiculously wealthy at the expense of the rest. The politics of industrialism, right, left or centre, is based on the systematic exploitation of the world's weak by the world's strong, and of the planet by us all. The only way to stop being exploited is to stop being an exploiter – and that means thinking and doing things in a Green way.

The Green Alternative

Are things really as bad as the Greens say?

Things are actually worse than we say, but we don't dare say that because people won't listen. They tend to roll themselves up in a little ball like an armadillo and just hope they won't get stamped on. This was what happened in the sixties and seventies when the full realisation of the costs and dangers of our industrial civilisation began to dawn on people. But the warnings were just too dire and there wasn't enough easily visible evidence or a high enough pile of victims to convince the doubting Thomases.

The natural wealth of the planet is vast, but it is not inexhaustible. And the resilience of the planet in coping with the pollution of our waste is also extraordinary, but there are limits and these limits are being reached. Ethiopia, Bhopal, Sellafield, the Amazon forests, flooding, soil erosion, acid rain – it's a long, long list of causes and effects which reflect our exploitation of natural systems. Things are serious and it's a foolish person who pretends that they're not.

Are Greens living in the real world?

The real 'real' world is made up of earth and rock and coal and water and crops and grass – in contrast to the phoney world of money markets, capital transfers and petro-dollars, of hollow promises, political myths and notional levels of economic growth.

There are children in school today who don't know where milk comes from, or what coal actually is. There are politicians who don't understand the miracle of topsoil or the vulnerability of our natural life-support systems on which we all depend – and which, incidentally, affect our future survival far more than any presumed threat of Russian tanks appearing over the horizon.

To question and criticise the nature of what counts as reality today is to be the ultimate realist!

The Greens seem to want to go back to an idealised past rather than forwards. Is that true?

No, it's not. We do want to get out of the trap we're in, but *not* by going back. There was nothing particularly glorious about our pre-industrial history, and we can all count the blessings that progress has brought us since then. But that particular pattern of progress is simply not sustainable. So we say, 'Let's move forward in a different way, producing our food differently, creating our wealth differently and developing different technologies more appropriate to our circumstances'. But we don't write off the past. There is much that can be learned from how we once managed things. From this perspective, the Greens are rediscovering old wisdom made newly relevant in a very different age.

There's nothing wrong with being idealistic, and nothing wrong with having a model of a better future – we're surely not condemned to the increasingly drab banality of our industrial society for ever more?

But the Green movement is *not* promising easy answers: the future is going to be tough, however you approach it. People are going to have to work hard, share more readily, be more self-reliant and far more responsible in the use they make of the world's resources. Our quality of life, our real standard of living, could indeed be far, far better and we could indeed achieve this without trampling on the rights of future generations – but it won't be done easily.

But you can't change human nature, can you?

Human nature is not something fixed and immovable for all time; it's a collection of potentialities, a seed that will flourish or wither according to where it's planted. And at the moment we expect people to grow out of very stony ground, nurtured on images and models of violence, greed, envy and exploitation. The Green movement is not talking about changing human nature, but changing the environment in which the seed grows.

The Green Alternative

How can Britain become a Green society by itself? If other countries won't change too, won't Britain lose out?

It *is* difficult to imagine any one country opting out of the world economy to go it entirely alone. But as more and more countries move inevitably towards greater self-reliance and sustainable economies, the motivation for others to follow will be greatly increased. The transition will be difficult, but a transition there *has* to be, and all politicians with even an ounce of vision should be helping to get us geared up to it right now, not exhorting us to dwell in the past.

The pursuit of national self-interest at the expense of all other nations and global resources is the greatest threat we face today. We *have* to transcend nationalism, or perish.

So is there a credible alternative to the modern nation state?

The modern state has indeed become something of a disaster. For every 'winner' as nation state competes against nation state there has to be a loser, and by investing in weapons rather than people modern states undermine national security rather than enhance it.

There *are* alternatives. They involve on the one hand a genuine commitment to internationalism and the fairer sharing of our 'global commons', strengthening international organisations such as the United Nations, and on the other a radical devolution of many of central government's powers to the regional and local levels. 'Act locally, think globally' is a fundamental precept of the Green movement. The nation state makes both equally difficult.

Why should we care about the Third World?

Common humanity should be motivation enough to encourage us to care for the poor of this world. 'It's a small world', people say – and it is. Compassion and common sense today should be reinforced by ecological wisdom. When you look at the natural wealth of the planet, there's no such thing as the 'First World' or the 'Third World': there's *one* world, and all its people jointly share the responsibility for its maintenance and safe-keeping.

What are the political alternatives in Britain?

Disasters such as Bhopal, Chernobyl and the dying of forests and lakes have made us realise that environmental issues are important and should be tackled by politicians. All the major political parties, with an eye to catching votes, have been coming up with policies which they claim will protect the environment. During their term of office the Conservatives, for instance, have tightened the authorisation on discharges of radioactive waste from the Sellafield reprocessing plant, without, however, turning their back on nuclear power. Reluctantly, too, they have finally agree to curb sulphur dioxide discharges from the UK, and are forcing the CEGB to spend £600 million on installing desulphurisation flue-gas scrubbers at three of their main coal-fired stations. Attempts have also been made to protect wildlife and to create sanctuaries under the designation of Sites of Special Scientific Interest.

The Labour party too has begun to embrace Green policies, and in particular is set to halt the nuclear power programme – if not to phase it out altogether – although it is divided over what to do with Sellafield. And in vying with the Conservative party it has now stated that if it wins the next general election it will cut sulphur dioxide emissions from the UK by 60 per cent within a decade, thus making it mandatory for power stations to be fitted with desulphurisation equipment.

In the SDP/Liberal alliance, the Liberals have consistently paid a great deal of attention to environmental policies, having decided to phase out both nuclear power and nuclear weapons and build up an alternative energy strategy.

The Green party (formerly the Ecology Party) differs from the other parties in that its policies stem from the belief that a healthy environment must underlie *all* action. The Greens therefore accept the constraints of a planet with finite resources while looking for ways in which best to utilise its potential. In political terms the Greens have undoubtedly had their greatest success in West Germany, where they have some 5 per cent of the seats in the Bundestag – the Federal Parliament. They argue against the need for economic growth and they differentiate between what they consider work and employment. For the time being, radical policies are difficult if not impossible to put into practice, yet, as the numbers of unemployed increase and the obsolescence of the old system becomes exposed, then the Greens may well have their chance.

Where do Green politics fit into the political spectrum?

Green politics is at odds with both contemporary capitalism and mainstream socialism. Capitalism depends on the permanent expansion of the economy and on the ruthless exploitation of the planet to fuel that expansion. People are treated primarily as consumers rather than individuals in their own right. Socialism seeks to do much the same through the intervention of the state, with people treated primarily as units of production rather than individuals in their own right. The destruction of the planet, and the accompanying oppression and alienation of its people, are the inevitable consequences of both ideologies.

There is, however, an alternative, potentially Green, decentralist tradition of socialism, *and* a different attitude towards the entrepreneur – based on socially responsible, small-scale production. But at the moment, these alternatives are all but invisible.

Won't Green policies lead to something like Communism?

You mean, like tomatoes, we'll start off green and then turn red? Not so! Green politics has in common with socialism a commitment to redistribute wealth more fairly, to protect the weak and to use technology more wisely and responsibly. But we do *not* share their readiness to exploit the earth to achieve these goals, nor have we much sympathy with their dogged devotion to the centralised state, class warfare, perpetual wage-labour, hierarchical trade unions, and the creed of materialism. There is still a world of difference between red and green – though it's good that many are now seeking ways of bridging that gap.

What about local politics in a Green society?

Greens believe that many more decisions should be taken at the local level, encouraging greater participation and accountability. There's absolutely no reason why political parties should exist at all at a local level. Individuals should be elected on the strength of their own ideas and their own record of achievement and involvement in the community.

Won't a Green society need to impose a lot of controls to stop all the waste, pollution and over-exploitation of resources?

Yes, there will have to be controls – to be Green does not mean that one is an anarchist! But we're talking about establishing at the national level the *minimum legislative framework* necessary for the maintenance of ecological principles, leaving the details to be determined locally. By selectively wielding the stick and offering the carrot, much could be done in a very short time to change prevailing attitudes on both pollution and waste.

Won't the Greens become as bad as all the others if elected?

Quite possibly. Anyone, including the Greenest of the Green, who has to exercise power is open to corruption, greed and self-interest. But without sounding too sanctimonious about it, Greens are intent on representing the interests of *all*, not just a partisan few, and on promoting less selfish values as the only way of achieving this.

Moreover, though they like to claim that politics is 'the art of the possible', all mainstream politicians today are committed to achieving the totally impossible. That, at least, is one trap we shall not fall into.

Doesn't our political system generate apathy?

Yes, it generates apathy because, beyond putting an occasional cross in the box, ordinary people really can't participate any longer. Politics has become the preserve of professionals and experts – and with power concentrated at the centre people feel squeezed out even at the local level.

That needn't be the case, however; it is possible to have a democracy based on mass voting, but only if it is understood that voting is the *beginning* not the *end* of one's democratic commitment. And the introduction of proportional representation would do much to eliminate the absurdities of the present 'first past the post' system, and would revitalise politics at all levels.

Is there an economic system that has an ecological base?

The real complication arises over what we mean by 'economic'. For instance in today's world, it is economic to destroy virgin forest, but not economic to recycle paper. It is economic to spend billions on nuclear reactors, but not on cheaper, safer, more efficient and labour-intensive alternatives. In fact, economics literally means 'managing our earthly resources' – and it's about time we started doing just that, rather than creating fantasy worlds based on today's abstractions and illusions.

Wouldn't a Green future cost too much?

Quite the reverse. It is the present way of doing things that is exacting a terrible price from people and the environment. We are literally eating up the future with our industrial consumerism. We either start moving in a Green direction now, or we and our children will inherit a future that is poorer, uglier, less healthy and more dangerous than anything we have experienced so far.

Economics is about how we produce and distribute wealth. The essential points of the new economics are that it will seek first and foremost to satisfy human needs, material and non-material; it will enable people to do good work, paid and unpaid; it will foster self-reliance; it will treat health as part of wealth, so that health creation will be an important part of economic policy; it will conserve resources and the environment, which are the foundations of wealth and life itself.

How can we set about changing economic policy?

The only way is to develop new economic *theory*, *policy* and *practice* which is more in touch with reality than traditional economics. Many people are already doing this. There are new financial institutions which take account of social costs and benefits as well as financial return, and organic farmers are part of the real economy of food production, working with the natural forces on which we all depend, rather than undermining them. The recent growth in co-operatives, linking people who are seeking to do good, responsible work in a mutually supportive way, is another sign. Traditional economics will only stand aside when there is something better to put in its place.

The Green Alternative

How can we prevent money flowing out of the community?

In a country which is trying to achieve self-sufficiency there is simply no role nor interest for the multinational company nor the international banker. These can only thrive in the absence of any restrictions on the freedom of trade and the transfer of capital. The tax system will also need to be reorganised so that the major part of taxes raised are spent locally, with only the minor part going to support the co-ordinating foreign affairs and defence role of central government. In Sweden local government receives the bulk of taxes, with a consequent greater accountability to the local community.

What about the European Parliament? Isn't it a waste of time and resources?

It is certainly expensive, because of the conditions of work – because it has to work in several different languages and has to move around: from Brussels, to Strasbourg, to Luxembourg. But it does have an effect on some issues, the Spinelli Resolution, for one example – at one end of the scale – which led to the setting up of the Intergovernmental Conference which aims to revise the Treaty of Rome. Or, at the other end of the scale, some rather specific actions, like the seal product ban, which had a large impact both on public opinion and on the issue itself.

Wouldn't a Green Britain have to get out of the Common Market?

If the Common Market had not changed at all over the last twenty years, then a genuinely Green Britain might feel tempted to get out. But Common Market supporters feel there has already been massive evolution in its approach to environmental problems. There is now going to be a review of the common agricultural policy and perhaps the conflict between Common Market policies and the health of the environment will be less acute than it is today. Agriculture, certainly, is one of the key themes. It affects not only wildlife but also, through agricultural pollution, many other aspects of our life. One can argue that agricultural surpluses generated by the EEC make it both possible and necessary for the EEC to continue a food-aid policy in, say, parts of Africa, even after such a policy ceases to be justified by the realities of the situation; when it may indeed be positively harmful in the sense of adversely affecting the development of local food-crops.

The EEC is surely too slow and divided to deal effectively with serious environmental problems?

Of course the EEC is not responding quickly or far enough to environmental damage, but it has made some attempt. The European Communities Environmental Programme dates from 1973 and over the last ten or twelve years has introduced legislation dealing with the pollution of air, land and water. It is now trying to establish some other instruments, for example the Environmental Impact Assessment Procedure, which ought to help ensure that prevention becomes at least as important as cure. There are a number of major proposals still before the Council, for example the proposal relating to atmospheric pollution caused by large industrial plants. When these are passed, the Fourth Environment Action Programme will be prepared which, it is to be hoped, will build on the progress so far achieved.

Can public pressure on governments effect policy changes?

The environment is moving more and more to the centre of the stage. At meetings of the summit countries, whether these take place in an EEC context or more generally in the context of the industrialised world, references are increasingly made to environmental policy. The involvement of non-governmental organisations is crucial in achieving more official recognition of the importance of environmental policy. Individuals *can* make a difference: there will be no progress without a groundswell of public opinion.

Governments must come to realise that it is only the

environmental ethic – as expressed in a no-waste, no-pollution, 'conserving' society – that will provide the lasting basis of the modern society which they hope to promote. Increasingly the evidence is pointing in the direction of the unsustainability of current practices and – indeed – their public unacceptability. If governments want to stay in power, they have got to start paying attention to this.

Compared to other member countries has Britain been dragging its feet on environmental issues?

The EEC has had to force Britain to respond to environmental strictures. There has of course been a tension between the EEC approach, which, on the whole, relies on setting common standards for products and processes, and the British approach which maintains that different regulations should apply to different situations. But if Britain had to endure fully the effects of the pollution which it creates (in other words, if we were not an island surrounded by seas and blown over by winds), then it is possible that our approach to sulphur dioxide discharges and radioactive waste etc., would be every bit as rigorous as those of other EEC countries. We are no longer in a situation where air and water can be seen as 'free goods'. This is in any case contrary to the principles formulated and agreed upon at the United Nations Conference on the Human Environment held in Stockholm in 1972.

Would trade harmonisation (product, plant operation) agreements lead to fairer trade conditions and maintain better standards anywhere?

Harmonisation of trade conditions is an important element in environmental policy, but it depends on the level at which harmonisation is achieved. If we agree that before chemical products are traded they should be subject to an environmental scrutiny and that the details of this procedure should be known and internationally accepted, the result may be good or bad for the environment depending on the nature of the harmonisation involved. There may be a case for the operation of the 'law of comparative advantage', but that should never be to the prejudice of harmonisation measures and certainly should not involve the exploitation of an environment beyond a certain level. That is why the EEC has been concerned not merely to introduce product standards and process standards but also to ensure that certain environmental quality objectives for air, land or water are set and observed throughout the Member States of the European Community. There must not be a licence to pollute in a virgin environment, merely because it is virgin. On the contrary, our objective ought to be to preserve 'virginity' where we have it and to clean up elsewhere.

Surely the EEC ban on seal imports is irrelevant when there are real issues to face such as acid rain?

You can't separate out environmental policy from animal welfare policy. You can't separate out concern for the conservation of a species from other issues which may involve more directly ethical and humanitarian considerations. In any case, we spend a great deal of time – as we should – thinking about the protection of endangered species, but we ought also to be spending more time thinking how to protect and preserve abundance where we have it. That said, the seal issue was only one of a number of 'wildlife issues' which have to be tackled by the EEC and by Local Governments. We ought to be doing something about the trade in fur-bearing animals, kangaroos, frogs' legs, the Faroe Islands' whale-kill, bull-fighting, etc. These are all issues of concern from the point of view of both environment and animal welfare. And there are plenty of others too.

Has the EEC gone far enough with regard to legislation on lead in petrol?

When all lead is out of petrol, then that will be far enough. Considerable progress has recently been made on exhaust controls, and the present proposals about to be adopted by the EEC Council do represent a fairly important step in the right direction. We would not have got this far without the EEC Environmental Policy and, of course, without the pressure of public opinion. Of course the real problem is also that there are too many private and commercial vehicles on the road. It is perhaps one of the failures of the EEC that we have not managed to achieve any significant changes in the pattern of transportation. Our common transport policy never really got off the ground.

What is the Common Transport Policy?

Transport provides some 6.5 per cent of the gross national product of the European Community and employs more than 6 million people. Since 1957 the Community has been trying to organise a common market for land transport. After the enlargement of the Community an action programme was launched in 1973 which brought in sea and air transport as well.

The European Parliament has condemned the European Council for failing to achieve a Common Transport policy, and its case against the Council has now been upheld by Court decision. In essence the Common Transport Policy aims to eliminate distortions of competition and discrimination in the transport sector, the free movement of people, goods, capital and service being a fundamental principle of the Common Market. At present the European Parliament claims that the wide divergence between the national policies of member states is damaging the efficiency, profitability and productivity of the transport systems. The Community, it says, should be contributing technically and financially to projects straddling national boundaries.

What has been achieved to date?

Each year 50,000 people are killed and 1.5 million injured on roads in the Community. The European Commission is therefore drawing up an action plan to bring about road and vehicle safety improvements throughout the Community. A number of European directives are now in force with regard to harmonising standards for brakes, lighting and sound levels, as well as in limiting exhaust emissions from engines.

The Commission has also tried to equalise competition between road and other forms of transport, including waterways and railways. In 1984, for instance, it called for an improved capital structure for railway companies and better sharing of infrastructure costs – much of the available capital at present being spent on roads.

The report 'Limits to Growth' was wrong, wasn't it?

In the early 1970s the Club of Rome – a group of European industrialists – sponsored a study on the consequences of industrial and population growth on the availability of natural resources and on the state of the environment. The study, carried out at the Massachusetts Institute of Technology, indicated that not only would essential basic resources run out in the relatively near future – over the next 100 years – but that human beings would so pollute their environment as to put their own survival at stake.

The investigators underestimated two things: one, the extent to which new reserves and deposits would be discovered; two, the ability of 'the system' to cope. We have a little more breathing space in which to adapt. But since we show no more readiness to adapt now than we did then, the outlook is scarcely heartening.

Ultimately, whatever timescale you care to use, time is running out. The simple fact is that if we go on using up the earth's nonrenewable resources (its oil, coal, minerals) at the rate we are now, and misusing the earth's renewable resources (its fertile soil, clear water, forests) at the rate we do now, then at some stage in the future the whole system is going to fall apart.

Those who claim that the fact it hasn't done so yet is proof that it never will are dangerous idiots. Technological innovation may well postpone the final crunch, but not for long.

What about the unions? Don't they want change?

Most trade unions don't. And that's hardly surprising: theirs is a tradition of permanently having to defend the rights and interests of their members against a grudging, exploitative system. They have become as much the product of that system as those they oppose, and now that it's becoming defunct they feel they have to defend the system itself if they are to defend their members.

However, the days of full employment and industrial regeneration are over so they are defending an illusion. And that means they will either go down with it, as is clearly happening now, or they will adapt to become the protagonists of a new order of work and politics that embraces all people rather than the lucky few who happen to have jobs.

How could we achieve employment without inflation?

Inflation and unemployment are both unpleasant symptoms of the impending collapse of the existing economic system. The question is like asking whether it is better to have a pain in the head or in the stomach. In a sustainable economy neither problem arises. Because the goods and services necessary to support the population are maintained at constant levels, employment, supply and demand and the money in circulation also remain constant. Probably, the provision of the necessary level of goods and services will not require a full week's work from every able person, but they will all receive the same wage.

Does stopping growth mean fewer jobs?

No, because stopping growth does not mean simply maintaining the economy at its present level, but changing it fundamentally in order to achieve greater self-sufficiency. This will involve the creation of new industries in the fields of import substitution, energy saving, pollution avoidance, recycling and the like.

The Green Alternative

Should community work be found for those without a conventional job?

Community work isn't a long-term answer – it would certainly be considered second-class work unless everyone had to do it at some time in their lives. The answer to unemployment is not to invent a special sort of work for the unemployed but to take that work into the mainstream economy. Many policies would help to achieve this: a basic income for all, provided by taxes, which would enable people to do part-time work; a shift in the taxation burden from jobs (e.g. income tax, national insurance) to the use of resources (e.g. fuels, water); a commitment to conserve resources and the environment through developing industries of repair, recycling, reconditioning and re-use. These are far more labour-intensive than equivalent industries that just churn out new goods.

Since we are all members of the community, each one of us needs to do some work for the general good of everyone; for instance, maintenance of hedges and footpaths, general care of the woodlands and countryside, ensuring the cleanliness of public places, service to the elderly and so on. Perhaps each one of us should have to devote a period to community service.

We are now told that it isn't 'economic' to create such jobs, and even the caring professions are measured according to their profitability. But it is considered 'economic' to make more and more weapons, or endless varieties of cat food or video nasties – as long as there's a market out there for them.

It's absurd that we can't match up, on the one hand, people's desire to work and what they have to offer with, on the other, what society and our communities need. This is the one overriding challenge for politicians today – but they can't meet it because their antiquated, dehumanised, earth-battering economic theories blind them to alternatives based on human potential, ecological sustainability and production for need rather than production for exchange or profit.

In a just society, should people have equal incomes?

Equal pay is surely just. Those who do tedious or arduous jobs deserve as much as those who do interesting, skilled, responsible work, even if the latter have a scarcity value that raises the price of their labour in a market economy.

Equal pay can certainly not come about in a market economy, but the idea of a 'guaranteed income' makes considerable sense. If everyone were entitled to a basic minimum income, as a member of the larger community, some of the existing welfare administration costs would be saved.

If payment is dissociated from work, the motivation to do uninteresting but necessary work may be missing. In an ecologically sound society, such work could perhaps be done in rotation. In looking for a fairer and potentially ecological society, we should not be shy about examining alternative structures.

Isn't it the work ethic which is destroying the world?

There's nothing wrong with a work ethic that encourages us to use our abilities to improve our own quality of life and help others. But a work ethic that says you are worthless if you are out of a job in an economy that cannot possibly provide enough jobs is both defunct and dangerous.

Should we get people, especially the unemployed, back on the land to help restore our rural heritage?

Certainly we should ensure that those who want to work can do so, and reforming agricultural practice could provide many job opportunities. Britain has the lowest percentage in Europe of people working on the land, so there is the potential for hundreds of thousands of jobs there, just to bring us into line with other European countries. This could be achieved by changing the nature of public subsidies for agriculture – to encourage people to work on the land, rather than manufacture chemicals or heavy machinery – and to

The Green Alternative

place far more emphasis on conservation of the countryside, on farming *with* nature rather than against it.

How can job satisfaction be achieved at all levels of society?

Everyone will have their own definition of satisfying work. One definition is work that:

- is challenging and, for much of the time, at least, enjoyable

- uses and develops people's skills

- produces useful goods and services for the worker and for other people

There are two main elements in creating job satisfaction: *education* at all levels needs to show people that work can be useful and enjoyable; *technology*, and especially new technology, needs to be put firmly under society's control. While so much schooling is irrelevant, and until we start judging new technology by standards of work satisfaction, as well as for the cheapness of the goods it produces, satisfying work will continue to be limited.

Are Greens against computers and microelectronic developments?

Technology should only be used when it enhances the good work that is available rather than supplants it. Computers, and micro-electronics in general, *could* be used to benefit us all: by relieving us of dirty, dangerous and mind-bendingly boring work; by doing things more efficiently and more sparingly of energy and resources; by making information available in such a way as to give us all more influence over decisions.

But they could also do exactly the opposite: enriching the few at the expense of the majority, denying people access to good work and empowering those who seek to suppress and control others. Computer technology is very much a two-edged sword – so it rather depends who's wielding it.

What are the Greens going to do about the unemployed?

Stop pretending that we can get back to full employment. Those days are over. New technology, changing world markets, ecological restraints, market saturation – there are so many factors that tend to make today's economic ideas redundant. But Greens are in the business of promoting the kind of changes that will allow everyone to have access to psychologically rewarding work. By that we mean making the things we need and providing the services we require in a way that provides people with fulfilling work and a reasonable income, is ecologically sustainable, and emphasises the quality of the work involved.

Should market forces alone determine what is technologically sound?

The question assumes that all competition is healthy and that an all-socialist, and therefore an all-planned as opposed to a free market, economy will not be innovative. Neither assumption is justified. Competition can lead to the increasing refinement of unnecessary products, to the over-exploitation of resources and to the reduction of environmental protection, none of which is a healthy consequence. Innovation is not stimulated only by the profit motive. To sustain our population without diminishing or damaging our resources will require every ounce of inventiveness we have.

How can we give shelter and housing to the homeless?

Present economic policies force people to leave depressed areas, where there are houses, to look for jobs in prosperous areas, where there are not enough houses. Obviously, building more houses (and to much higher standards of insulation and heat-efficiency) is part of the answer to homelessness, but we also need to revive *local* economies around the country, to create jobs where people and houses already are, rather than forcing people to move to places where housing is expensive and in short supply. There's a real need, too, for a crash programme of housing repair, especially in inner cities, which would create a lot of jobs as well. To pay for this the government will need to pump-prime the local economic recoveries, but they should then be self-sustaining, as previously unemployed people start producing for themselves and for each other the goods and services – like houses – of which they were deprived before.

Can Britain avoid becoming complacent and parochial if it adopts a policy of self-sufficiency?

It would be highly desirable if this country could meet as many of its economic needs as possible from its own resources – i.e. without imports. This might well mean that in the short-term we would pay more for certain products, but in the long-term we would gain far more from the work created and the wealth generated through such import substitution. But there will always be some things we need to import (we're hardly likely to do without our coffee and tea after all these years!) and trade in certain commodities and products will no doubt continue.

There is therefore a difference between *self-sufficiency* (a state of absolute economic independence) and *self-reliance* (a state of relative independence). The first would be painful if not impossible to achieve, and would also be very damaging to many developing countries; the second is both achievable and desirable.

If we control consumerism excessively won't we generate a drab, forbidding society?

Consumer choice won't vanish, but neither will it make slaves of us. There is no question of forcing moderation or even asceticism on a reluctant consumption-crazed society, for once people have realised the full human and ecological costs of unrestrained consumerism, they will demand (as they are already beginning to do) a more responsible, discriminating pattern of production, with the emphasis on higher quality, more durable goods. The kind of wasteful, shoddy, short-lived, over-packaged detritus that features so largely in today's 'wealthy' societies will be scorned. Though choice will indeed be limited compared with today, there need be nothing drab about such a society.

Will people be able to have washing-machines and other gadgets?

Industry's primary role will be to meet people's genuine needs and to develop technologies appropriate to this task, rather than to go on making things and persuading people to buy them purely to make more money. Of course people will still have washing-machines (as long as they are energy-efficient). But electric toothbrushes and carving knives? That's another matter!

Does a Green future mean a reduction in our standard of living?

There's no one definition of wealth. It's a relative concept, determined by prevailing political ideas and cultural values. What we call wealth today is often an illusion, for we can create it only by destroying the natural wealth of the planet, by misusing technology and by wasting or abusing our own potential creativity. Monetary wealth and quality of life are often poles apart.

Judged by illusory standards of wealth we might well be 'poorer' in a Green future – but we would, *in reality*, have a higher standard of living, better food, healthier bodies, rewarding work, good companionship, cleaner air, greater self-reliance, more supportive communities and, above all, a safer world to live in.

And this would be for *all* people – not just the privileged few.

The developing countries are trying to improve their standard of living. How will Green policies affect them?

That it's utterly, indisputably impossible for every single person on this planet now (let alone the extra millions due to arrive by the turn of the century) to achieve anything like the standard of living of the average American is indeed a pretty clear indictment of the whole system – unless we are prepared *openly* to acknowledge gross injustice and cruelty as an inevitable part of that system. The gap isn't narrowing. Increased growth in the world economy still gives us more of the world's resources than it does the developing world.

If ways are to be found of narrowing that gap, we in the West will have to learn to use energy and raw materials far more efficiently, stop exploiting the resources of the Third World and find ways of 'living more simply that others may simply live'.

What does it matter what I do? How can I change anything if everybody goes on doing exactly as before?

What one does is, finally, a matter between one's conscience and oneself, but example is catching and, in fact, people do not simply go on behaving as before. Attitudes change as a result of the aggregate of individual actions. The extent of the Green movement and the acceptance of Green policies today would have been unimaginable as little as ten years ago.

Where is the best place to start building for a Green future?

The best, and only, place you can start building for a Green future is in and with your own life and work: how you interact with other people and your community; who you work for and with and on what terms; what you do; what organisations you join, their aims and objectives and how they seek to achieve them; how you relax and enjoy yourself, and how all of this relates to other people, to society and the whole environment. The only possible building blocks of a Greener future are individuals moving towards a Greener way of life *themselves* and joining together with others who are doing the same.

Postscript

In this book we have tried to cover an enormous amount of ground. Inevitably, many assumptions by which we currently live are questioned, while many solutions have yet to be tried. Where then does this leave us?

The way forward into a new land requires the creation of a map. We who call ourselves Green are standing on the high ground of environmental awareness and trying to make out the shape of the land which lies ahead. There is much which is obscure, much to be found out. But one thing is clear: if we do not go the right way forward we shall perish from the combined effects of all the environmentally destructive ways of living which increasingly characterise this age.

This, then, is a contribution to the making of a new map. If it stimulates others to evolve further the points we have made, it will have succeeded in its aim. The book is not a blueprint so much as an attempt to put between two covers the spectrum of Green thought which currently exists.

Glossary

ACORD	Advisory Committee on Research and Development
AGR	advanced gas reactor
AONB	Area of Outstanding Natural Beauty
ASW	anti-submarine warfare
BaP	benzo(a)pyrene
BNFL	British Nuclear Fuels Limited
BWR	boiling water reactor
CBI	Confederation of British Industry
CEGB	Central Electricity Generating Board
CEP	circular error probability
CHP	combined heat-and-power
CITES	Convention on International Trade in Endangered Species
CO	carbon monoxide
CO_2	carbon dioxide
CPRE	Council for the Protection of Rural England
DOE	Department of the Environment
EDF	Electricité de France
EIRIS	Ethical Investment Research and Information Service
ERR	Earth Resources Research
ETSU	Energy Technology Support Unit
FACT	Food Additives Campaign Team
FAO	United Nations Food and Agricultural Organisation
FOE	Friends of the Earth
GNP	gross national product
GW	gigawatt
IAEA	International Atomic Energy Agency (US) (Euratom is European equivalent)
ICBM	inter-continental ballistic missile

IMF	International Monetary Fund
kW	kilowatt
kWh	kilowatt hour
LDCs	less developed countries
MAD	mutual assured destruction
MAFF	Ministry of Agriculture, Fisheries and Food
MIRV	multiple independently targeted re-entry vehicles
m/Sv	millisieverts
mtce	millions of tonnes of coal equivalent
MW	megawatt
NAVSTAR	American 18-satellite navigation system
NAWAPA	North American Water and Power Alliance
NCC	Nature Conservancy Council
NO_x	nitrogen oxide
NPK	nitrogen, phosphorus and potassium
NPT	Non-Proliferation Treaty
NTA	nitrilotriacetic acid
NUTS	nuclear utility targeting strategy
PAHs	polycyclic aromatic hydrocarbons
PCBs	polychlorobiphenyls
PET	polyethylene trichloride
PFBC	pressurised fluidised-bed combustion
PICs	products of incomplete combustion
PWR	pressurised water reactor
SLBM	submarine-launched ballistic missile
SO_2	sulphur dioxide
SSSI	Site of Special Scientific Interest
Star Wars	Strategic Defense Initiative
SUDAM	Superintendency for the Development of the Amazon
TBT	Tributyl tin-based (anti-foulings for boats)
THMs	trihalomethanes
TOES	The Other Economic Summit
TPO	tree preservation order
TSCA	Toxic Substances Control Act (US)
TWh	terawatt hour
UKAEA	United Kingdom Atomic Energy Authority
UNEP	United Nations Environment Programme

Glossary

WEAP   World Ecological Areas Programme
WHO   World Health Organisation

one becquerel = one atomic disintegration per second
one curie = 37,000 million atomic disintegrations per second
one gigawatt = one million kilowatts or one thousand megawatts
one kilowatt-hour = 1,000 watts of energy used for one hour or
                                one unit of electricity
one TWh = 10^{12} watt hours = 3.6 petajoules
rem = measurement of radiation

Notes

1 Conservation and nature

1 Royal Society for Nature Conservation: British Wildlife Appeal.
2 Conducted in March 1983 by the British Market Research Bureau for the Country Landowners' Association.
3 Conducted by MORI for the World Conservation Strategy.
4 *A Second Look* (Countryside Commission, 1984).
5 'Pall of Poison', 1984.
6 The quantity of permethrin which in a standard test on male rats will kill 50 per cent is 430 mg/kg compared to Gamma HCH of 88 mg/kg and dieldrin which is 46 mg/kg.
7 Chemicals safe for use in bat roosts: insecticides – permethrin, cypermethrin, borester 7, polybor, boric acid; fungicides – copper naphthenate, zinc naphthenate, zinc acypetas, zinc octoate, borester 7, polybor.
8 *Focus on Bats, Their Conservation and the Law* (Nature Conservancy Council, 1985). *Bats in Roofs: A guide for surveyors* (NCC Publications).
9 Norman Myers, *The Primary Source* (Norton, 1984).
10 Ira Rubinoff, *Ecologist*, 1982, no. 6.
11 Catherine Caufield, *In the Rainforest* (Heinemann, 1985).
12 World Bank, Operations Evaluation Department (Loan 739 – Co 1978 A5).

2 Pollution of the environment

1 House of Commons debate on the EEC Directive.
2 Memorandum submitted to the House of Lords Select Committee on the European Communities' Environment.
3 Information from Dr Robin Russell-Jones, chairman of the Campaign for Lead-Free Air and a member of the Friends of the Earth Pollution Advisory Committee.

3 Agriculture

1 Georg Borgstrom, *Too Many* (Macmillan, New York, 1969).

Notes

4 Nutrition

1 (Thorsons, 1985).
2 (MAFF, 1984).

5 Health

1 (Blackwell, 1979)
2 See *Cured to Death: the Effects of Prescription Drugs* by Melville and Johnson (Secker and Warburg, 1982).
3 (Calder and Boyars, 1975).
4 Brian Inglis, *The Diseases of Civilisation* (Hodder and Stoughton, 1981)
5 (Faber, 1972).

6 Energy

1 (The University of Massachusetts Press, 1976).
2 The WASH 1400 report.
3 'Energy Efficient Future for the UK', ERR, 278 Pentonville Road, London N1.
4 'Alternative Energy Systems for the UK', the Centre of Alternative Technology, Machynlleth, Powys, Wales.

10 The developing world

1 *Ecologist*, 1985, Vol. 1/2 and 5/6.

11 The Green philosophy

1 James Lovelock, *Gaia – A New Look at Life on Earth* (Oxford, 1979).

12 Education

1 Dr Carl Rogers, Department of Psychology and Psychiatry, University of Wisconsin, USA, *Freedom to Learn for the Eighties* (Merrill Publishing International, 1983).
2 see note 1.
3 See *The Right Brain Experience* by Marilla Zdenek (Corgi, 1985), *The Betrayal of Youth* by James Hemming (Calder and Boyars, 1980) and *Drawing on the Right Side of the Brain* by Betty Edwards (Souvenir Press, 1981).

4 Robert Ornstein, *The Psychology of Consciousness* (Penguin, 1975).
5 Marilyn Ferguson, *The Aquarian Conspiracy* (Routledge and Kegan Paul, 1981).
6 Brian Wren, *Education for Justice* (SCM Press, 1986).
7 (HMI, 1977).

13 Politics

1 (Methuen, 1986).

Contributors

Preface
Fern Morgan-Grenville

Introduction
Peter Bunyard

1 Conservation and nature
Peter Bunyard, David Condon, Derek Eastmond,
Herbert Girardet, Richard Meyer, Fern Morgan-Grenville,
Peter Wilkinson

2 Pollution of the environment
Peter Bunyard, Joan Davis, Nicholas Hildyard, Brian John,
Stanley Johnson, Diana Schumacher, Colin Trier,
Peter Wilkinson

3 Agriculture
Peter Bunyard, Edward Goldsmith, Nicholas Hildyard,
Martin Mathers, John Seymour, Sedley Sweeny

4 Nutrition
Peter Bunyard, Joan Davis, Ros Fry, Colin Johnson,
Peter Mansfield, Arabella Melville, Miriam Polunin,
Diana Schumacher, James Thomson

5 Health
Peter Bunyard, Joan Davis, Edward Goldsmith, Ros Fry,
Colin Johnson, Peter Mansfield, Arabella Melville,
Fern Morgan-Grenville, Miriam Polunin, James Thomson

6 Energy
Peter Bunyard, Joan Davis, Nicholas Hildyard, Brian John,
Colin Sweet, Robert Todd

7 Transport
Hugh Barton, Barry Cooper, Roger Franklin, Brian John,
Fern Morgan-Grenville, ScotRail

Addresses

Most of the following addresses are of voluntary organisations which appreciate self-addressed, stamped envelopes with enquiries.

Agricultural Development
  and Advisory Service
Westminster House
Horseferry Lane
London SW1

Alternative Technology
  Group
Open University
Milton Keynes
Buckinghamshire

Amnesty International
5 Roberts Place
London EC10

Ancient Monuments Society
St Andrew-by-the-Wardrobe
Queen Victoria Street
London EC4V 5DE

Anti-Slavery Society
180 Brixton Road
London SW9 6AT

Apple and Pear Develop-
  ment Council
Unicorn House
The Pantiles
Tunbridge Wells
Kent

Bach Flower Remedies
Bach Flower Centre
Mount Vernon
Sotwell
Wallingford
Oxon OX10 0PZ

Bertrand Russell Committee
  Against Chemical Weapons
Bertrand Russell House
Gamble Street
Nottingham NG7 4ET

Biodynamic Agricultural
  Association
Broome Farm
Clent
Stourbridge
Worcestershire

British Butterfly Conserva-
  tion Society
PO Box 2
Compton House
Sherborne
Dorset

British Hay and Straw
  Merchants' Association
66a High Street
Potters Bar
Herts
EN6 5AB

British Homoeopathic
  Association
27a Devonshire Street
London W1

British Society of Dowsers
Sycamore Cottage
Tamley Lane
Hastingleigh
Kent TN25 5HW

British Society for Social
  Responsibility in Science
9 Poland Street
London W1V 3DG

British Trust for Conservation Volunteers
36 St Mary's Street
Wallingford
Oxon OX10 0EU

British Trust for Ornithology
Beech Grove
Station Road
Tring
Herts HP23 5NR

British Unemployment
  Resource Network
  (BURN)
318 Summer Lane
Birmingham B19 3RL

British Union for the Aboli-
  tion of Vivisection
16a Crane Grove
Islington
London N7

British Waste Paper
  Association
21 Devonshire Street
London W1

British Wind Energy
  Association
4 Hamilton Place
London W1V 0BQ

Building Research Establishment
Garston
Watford WD2 7JR

Byways and Bridleways Trust
9 Queen Anne's Gate
London SW1 9BY

Campaign Against the Arms
  Trade (CAAT)
11 Goodwin Street
London N4 3HQ

Campaign for Freedom of
  Information
2 Northdown Street
London N1 9BG

Campaign Against Lead in
  Petrol
68 Dora Road
London SW19 7HH

Campaign for Nuclear Dis-
  armament (CND)
22 Underwood Street
London N1 7JG

Cancer Help Centre
Grove House
Cornwallis Grove
Clifton
Bristol BS8 4PG

List of addresses

Centre for Alternative
   Industrial and Technologi-
   cal Systems (CAITS)
North London Polytechnic
Holloway Road
London N7 8DB

Centre for Peace Studies
St Martins College
Lancaster LA1 3JD

Chase Organics
Gibraltar House
Shepperton
Middlesex TW17
(*Commercial suppliers of
   untreated seeds, organic
   fertilisers, sprays*)

Christian Aid
240 Ferndale Road
London SW9 8BH

Civic Trust
17 Carlton House Terrace
London SW1Y 5AW

Common Ground
21 Ospringe Road
Kentish Town
London NW5
(*encourages links between
   nature, landscape conservation and the arts*)

Communes Network
Laurieston Hall
Castle Douglas
Kirkcudbrightshire DG7 2NB

Community Architectural
   Service
RIBA
66 Portland Place
London W1

Community Service Volun-
   teers (CSV)
237 Pentonville Road
London N1 9NJ

Compassion in World
   Farming
Lyndham House
Greatham
Petersfield
Hampshire

Concord Film Council
201 Felixstowe Road
Ipswich
Suffolk IP3 9BF

Conservation Society
12a Guildford Street
Chertsey
Surrey KT16 9BQ

Council for the Protection of
   Rural England
4 Hobart Place
London SW1W 0HY

Council for the Protection of
   Rural Wales
Ty Gwyn
31 High Street
Welshpool
Powys

Countryside Commission
John Dower House
Crescent Place
Cheltenham
Gloucestershire G150 3RA

Craft Council
12 Waterloo Place
London SW1Y 4AN

Cyclepath Project
35 King Street
Bristol

Directory of Social Change
9 Mansfield Place
London NW3

Dry Stone Walling Association
YFC Centre
National Agricultural Centre
Kenilworth
Warwickshire CV8 2LG

Earthlife
10 Belgrave Square
London SW1X 8TH

Earth Resources Research
    Ltd
30–31 Islington Green
London N1

Ecological Development
    Group
c/o Henbant
Llanbedr
Crickhowell
Powys

Ecology Building Society
43 Main Street
Cross Hills via Keighley
West Yorkshire BD20 8TT

Ecoropa
Henbant
Crickhowell
Powys NP8 1TA

European Court of Human
    Rights
Council of Europe
67000 Strasbourg
France

European Nuclear Disarma-
    ment (END)
Southbank House
Black Prince Road
London SE1 7SL

FACT (Food Additives
    Campaign Team)
25 Horsell road
London N5 1XL

Farm and Food Society
4 Willifield Way
London NW11
(*against pollution in
    agriculture*)

Farming and Wildlife
    Advisory Group (FWAG)
The Lodge
Sandy
Bedfordshire SG19 2DL

List of addresses

Fauna and Flora Preservation
  Society
c/o Zoological Society of
  London
Regent's Park
London NW1 4RY

Findhorn Foundation
The Park
Forres
Scotland IV36 0TZ

Food and Energy Research
  Centre
Cleeve Prior
Evesham Worcestershire

Friends of the Earth
377 City Road
London EC1

Game Conservancy
Fordingbridge
Hants

Good Gardeners Association
C.R.G. Shewell-Cooper
Arkley Manor Farm
Rowley Lane
Arkley
Barnet
Herts EN5 3HS

Green Alliance
60 Chandos Place
London WC2

Green Deserts
High Rougham
Bury St Edmunds
Suffolk

Green Party
36–38 Clapham Road
London SW9 0JQ

Greenpeace
30–31 Islington Green
London N1

Hawk Trust
Freepost
Beckenham
Kent

Henry Doubleday Research
  Association
Ryton-on-Dunsmere
Coventry
Warwickshire CV8 3LG

Inter Action Advisory
  Service
15 Wilkin Street
London NW5

Intermediate Technology
  Development Group
Myson House
Railway Terrace
Rugby
Warwickshire

The Intermediate Technology
  Publications
King Street
London WC2 EH10

International Court of Justice
Peace Palace
The Hague
Netherlands 924441

International Institute of Biological Husbandry
9 Station Approach
Needham Market
Ipswich
Suffolk
(*links with many organic
bodies*)

The International Institute
for Environment and
Development
3 Endsleigh Street
London WC1H 0DO

LESS (Low Energy Supply
Systems)
82 Colston Road
Bristol BS1 5BB

Life Style Movement
Manor Farm
Little Gidding
Huntingdon PE17 5RJ
(*offers a voluntary common
discipline to those committed to a more equitable distribution of the earth's
resources*)

London Food Commission
PO Box 291
London N5 1DU

The Marine Conservation
Society
4 Gloucester Road
Ross-on-Wye
Herefordshire

Men of the Trees
Turners
Hill Road
Crawley Down
Crawley
West Sussex RH10 4HL

Mercury Provident Society
2 Orlingbury House
Lewes Road
Forest Row
Sussex RH18 5AA
(*financial channel to encourage and facilitate socially
beneficial enterprises*)

National Anti-Fluoridation
Campaign
36 Station Road
Thames Ditton
Surrey KT7 0NS

National Anglers' Council
11 Cowgate
Peterborough PE1 1LZ

National Association of
Water Power Users
PO Box 27
Exchange Chambers
10b Highgate
Kendal
Cumbria

National Campaign for the
Homeless (SHELTER)
1 Macklin Street
London WC2B 5NH

National Centre for Alterna-
tive Technology
Llwyngwern Quarry
Machynlleth
Powys

List of addresses

Nature Conservancy Council
19 Belgrave Square
London SW1X 8PY

National Council for Civil
  Liberties
21 Tabard Street
London SE1

National Council for Voluntary Organisation (NCVO)
26 Bedford Square
London WC1B 3HU

National Federation of
  Badger Groups
16 Ashdown Gardens
Sanderstead
South Croydon CR2 9DR
Surrey
(*represents interests of local
  badger protection groups
  on national issues*)

National Housewives'
  Association
68 Somerset Place
Stoke
Plymouth
Devon

National Peace Council
29 Great James Street
London WC1N 3ES

Open Spaces Society
25a Bell Street
Henley-on-Thames
Oxon RG9 2BA

Organic Food Services
Ashe Churston Ferres
Nr Brixham
Devon
(*organic seeds and bee
  equipment*)

Organic Growers Association
Aeron Park
Llangietho
Dyfed

The Otter Trust
Earsham
Nr Bungay
Suffolk NR35 2AF

The Overseas Development
  Institute
10 Percy Street
London W1P 0JB

Oxfam
274 Banbury Road
Oxford OX2

Pax Christi
St Francis of Assisi Centre
Pottery Lane
London W11 4NQ

Peace Concern
113 Spetchley Road
Worcester
(*services peace movement
  with mail order literature,
  stickers, etc.*)

Peace Tax Campaign
1a Hollybush Place
London E2 9QX

Quaker Peace and Service
Friends House
Euston Road
London NW1 2BJ

Ramblers Association
1/5 Wandsworth Road
London SW8

Rare Breeds Survival Trust
4th Street NAC
Stoneleigh Park
Kenilworth
Warwickshire CV8 2LG

Royal Society for Nature
   Conservation
The Green Nettleham
Lincoln LN2 2NR

Royal Society for the Preven-
   tion of Cruelty to Animals
   (RSPCA)
Causeway
Horsham
West Sussex RH12 1HG

Royal Society for the Protec-
   tion of Birds (RSPB)
The Lodge
Sandy
Bedfordshire SG19 2DL

Save the Children Fund
17 Grove lane
London SE5 8RD

Scottish Campaign to Resist
   the Atomic Menace
   (SCRAM)
11 Forth Street
Edinburgh EH1 3LE

Sea Shepherd
12 Royal Terrace
Glasgow G3 7NY

Smallholding Supplies
Little Burcot
Nr Wells
Somerset DA5 1NG
(*mainly mail order for small-
   holding equipment*)

Society for the Protection of
   Ancient Buildings
37 Spital Square
London E1 6DY

Soil Association
86 Colston Street
Bristol BS1 5BB

Southalls (Birmingham) Ltd
Alum Rock Road
Birmingham B8 3DZ
(*recycled paper*)

Survival International
29 Craven Street
London WC2N 5NT

The Other Economic Summit
   (TOES)
2 Warriner Gardens
London SW11

Timber Research and
   Development Association
Stocking Lane
Hughendon Valley
High Wycombe
Bucks

List of addresses

Tools for Self Reliance
1 Little Anglesey
Gosport
Hampshire

Tree Council
Room 101
Agriculture House
Knightsbridge
London SW1X 7NJ

Trust for the Protection of
    Britain's Land Heritage
Wellington
Somerset
(*aims to acquire land to
    tenant to organic farmers
    and growers*)

United Nations Association
14 Stratford Place
London W1

United Nations Children's
    Fund (UNICEF)
55 Lincoln's Inn Fields
London WC2

Urban Centre for Appropri-
    ate Technology
82 Colston Street
Bristol

Urban Wildlife Group
11 Albert Street
Birmingham B4 7UA

The Vegetarian Society
53 Marlowe Road
London W8 6LA

Vincent Wildlife Trust
(Otter Haven Project)
Baltic Exchange Buildings
21 Bury Street
London EC3A 5AU

Wadebridge Ecological
    Centre
Worthyvale Manor
Camelford
Cornwall

Warmer Campaign
83 Mount Ephraim
Tunbridge Wells
Kent TN4 8BS

War on Want
1 London Bridge Road
London SE1 9SG

Welsh Anti-Nuclear Alliance
    (WANA)
PO Box 1
Llandrindod Wells
Powys LD1 5AA

Women's Peace Group
52 Featherstone Street
London EC1

Woodland Trust
Autumn Park
Dysart Road
Grantham
Lincs NG31 6LL

World Food Assembly
    Secretariat
15 Devonshire Terrace
London WC2 3DW

List of addresses

World Forest Campaign
6 Glebe Street
Oxford OX4 1DQ

World Information Service
  on Energy (WISE)
PO Box 5627
1007, AR Amsterdam
Netherlands

World Wildlife Fund
29 Grenville Street
London EC1N 8AX

Working Weekends on
  Organic Farms (WWOOF)
19 Bradford Road
Lewes
Sussex BN7 1RB

Bibliography

The Environment
Catharine Caufield, *In the Rainforest* (Heinemann, 1985)
R. Dassmann, *Environmental Conservation* (John Wiley, 1984)
Shelton Davis, *Victims of the Miracle* (Cambridge University Press, 1977)
J. Dorst, *Before Nature Dies* (Collins, 1970)
Rene Dubos, *The Wooing of the Earth* (Athlone Press, 1980)
Nigel Dudley, *The Death of Trees* (Pluto Press, 1985)
Paul and Anne Ehrlich, *Extinction* (Gollancz, 1982)
Edward Goldsmith and Nicholas Hildyard (eds), *Green Britain or Industrial Wasteland* (Policy Press, 1986)
Edward Goldsmith and Nicholas Hildyard, *The Social and Environmental Effects of Large Dams* (Wadebridge Ecological Centre, 1984)
Alan Grainger, *Desertification* (Earthscan, 1983)
J. Gribbin, *Carbon Dioxide, Climate and Man* (Earthscan, 1981)
A. Huxley, *The Green Inheritance* (Harvill Press, 1984)
A. King and S. Clifford, *Holding your Ground* (Templesmith, 1985)
Robert Lamb, *World without Trees* (Magnum Books, 1980)
John McCormick, *User's Guide to the Environment* (Kogan Page, 1985)
Norman Myers, *The Primary Source* (Norton, New York, 1984)
Norman Myers (ed), *The Gaia Atlas of Planet Management* (Pan, 1985)
S. Schneider and R. Londer, *The Coevolution of Climate and Life* (Sierra Club Books, San Francisco, 1984)
P. Selman, *Ecology and Planning* (Godwin, 1981)
John Seymour and Herbert Girardet, *Far From Paradise* (BBC Publications, 1985)
Peter Singer, *In Defence of Animals* (Blackwell, 1985)

Pollution
Murray Bookchin, *Our Synthetic Environment* (Harper and Row, 1974)

Jeremy Bugler, *Polluting Britain* (Penguin, 1972)

Rachel Carson, *Silent Spring* (Penguin, 1982)

Barry Commoner, *The Closing Circle* (Cape, 1972)

R. C. Denney, *This Dirty World* (Nelson, 1971)

S. Elsworth, *Acid Rain* (Pluto Press, 1984)

M. Frankel, *Control of Industrial Air Pollution Handbook* (Social Audit, 1974)

Nicholas Hildyard, *Cover-Up* (New English Library, 1981)

Nicholas Hildyard and Samuel Epstein, *The Toxic Timebomb* (Oxford University Press, 1987)

K. W. Kapp, *The Social Costs of Business Enterprise* (Spokesman Books, 1978)

R. Mabey, *The Pollution Handbook* (Penguin, 1974)

J. McCormick, *Acid Earth* (Earthscan, 1985)

Anthony Tucker, *The Toxic Metals* (Pan, 1972)

Food and Agriculture

Wendell Berry, *The Unsettling of America* (Sierra Club Books, San Francisco, 1977)

Georg Borgstrom, *Too Many* (Macmillan, New York, 1969)

David Bull, *A Growing Problem: Pesticides and the Third World Poor* (Oxfam, 1982)

Consumer Commission of EEC, *Food Additives and the Consumer* (HMSO, 1980)

Barbara Dinham and Colin Hines, *Agribusiness in Africa* (Zed Books, 1982)

R. Dumont and N. Cohen, *The Growth of Hunger* (Marion Boyars, 1980)

E. Eckholm, *Losing Ground* (Pergamon Press, 1978)

Susan George, *How the Other Half Dies* (Penguin, 1976)

Herbert Girardet, *Land for the People* (Crescent Books, 1976)

Frances Moore Lappe and Joseph Collins, *Food First* (Souvenir Press, 1980)

London Food Commission, *Danger, Additives at Work* (October, 1985)

M. Perelman, *Farming for Profit in a Hungry World* (Allenheld, New Jersey, 1978)

David Pimentel et al, *Food, Energy and Society* (Edward Arnold, 1979)

John Seymour, *Bring me my Bow* (Turnstone Books, 1977)

Bibliography

John Soper, *Biodynamic Gardening* (Biodynamic Agricultural Assn, 1983)

Sedley Sweeney, *The Challenge of Smallholding* (Oxford University Press, 1984)

Tony Webb and Angela Henderson, *Food Irradiation – who wants it?* (London Food Commission, 1986)

Nutrition and Health

T. L. Cleave, *Saccharine Disease* (Wright, 1974)

Peter Cox, *Why you don't Need Meat* (Thorsons, 1986)

Gail Duff, *Vegetarian Cookbook* (Macmillan, 1978)

R. Elliot, *Your Very Good Health* (Fontana, 1981)

Alan Gear (ed), *Organic Food Guide* (Doubleday Research Assn, 1983)

M. Hanssen, *E for Additives* (Thorsons, 1984)

J. de Bairacli Levy, *Illustrated Herbal Handbook* (Faber, 1974)

Sir Robert McCarrison, *Nutrition and Health* (McCarrison Society Publications, 1982)

Arabella Melville and Colin Johnson, *Cured to Death* (New English Library, 1982)

Arabella Melville and Colin Johnson, *The Long-Life Heart* (Century Publishing, 1985)

Miriam Polunin, *The Right Way to Eat* (Dent, 1984)

Miriam Polunin, *New Cookbook* (Macdonald, 1984)

T. G. Randolph and R. W. Moss, *Allergies: Your Hidden Enemy* (Thorsons, 1984)

Energy

Rosalie Bertell, *No Immediate Danger: Prognosis for a Radioactive Earth* (The Women's Press, 1985)

G. Boyle and P. Harper, *Radical Technology* (Wildwood, 1976)

Peter Bunyard, *Nuclear Britain* (New English Library, 1981)

William Cannell, *The PWR Decision: How not to buy a Nuclear Reactor* (Friends of the Earth, 1983)

Barry Commoner, *The Poverty of Power* (Cape, 1976)

David Elliot, *The Politics of Nuclear Power* (Polity Press, 1979)

Michael Flood, *Solar Prospects* (Wildwood, 1983)

Denis Hayes, *Rays of Hope* (Worldwatch Institute, Washington DC)

House of Commons Environmental Committee report on

Bibliography

Radioactive Waste, *House of Commons Paper 181–1* (HMSO, 1986)

Ivan Illich, *Energy and Equity* (Marion Boyars, 1973)

Gerald Leach, *A Low Energy Strategy for the United Kingdom* (Science Reviews IIED, 1979)

Howard Odum, *Environment, Power and Society* (Interscience, 1971)

Stan Openshaw, *Nuclear Power, Siting and Safety* (Routledge and Kegan Paul, 1985)

Walt Patterson, *Nuclear Power* (Penguin, 1983)

Walt Patterson, *The Plutonium Business* (Wildwood House, 1984)

Diana Schumacher, *Energy: Crisis or Opportunity* (Macmillan, London, 1985)

John Valentine, *Atomic Crossroads: Before and After Sizewell* (Merlin Press, 1985)

Resources, Economics and Limits to Growth

Alan Bollard and John Davis, *As Though People Mattered*, Intermediate Technology Publications, 1986)

Peter Chapman and F. Roberts, *Metal Resources and Energy* (Butterworth, 1983)

Paul Ehrlich et al, *Man and the Ecosphere* (Scientific American, 1971)

Paul Ekins (ed), *The New Economics* (Routledge and Kegan Paul, 1986)

S. R. Eyre, *The Real Wealth of Nations* (Edward Arnold, 1978)

Edward Goldsmith et al, *Blueprint for Survival* (Penguin, 1972)

Denis Hayes, *Repairs, Reuse, Recycling* (Worldwatch Papers, 1978)

Hazel Henderson, *The Politics of the Solar Age: Alternatives to Economics* (Doubleday, 1981)

F. Hirsch, *Social Limits to Growth* (Harvard University Press, 1976)

C. A Hunt and R. M. Garrells, *Water: The Web of Life* (Norton, 1972)

Herman Kahn, *The Next 200 Years* (William Morrow, 1976)

Denis Meadows et al, *Dynamics of Growth in a Finite World* (MIT Press, 1977)

E. J. Mishan, *The Economic Growth Debate* (Allen and Unwin, 1977)

Bibliography

Population

Lester R. Brown, *In the Human Interest* (Pergamon Press, 1976)

Paul Ehrlich, *The Population Bomb* (Pan, 1971)

J. Jacobsen, *Promoting Population Stabilisation* (Unipub, 1983)

T. McKeown, *The Modern Rise of Population* (Edward Arnold, 1977)

Ecophilosophy and Politics

Michael Allaby and Peter Bunyard, *The Politics of Self Sufficiency* (Oxford University Press, 1980)

Robert Allen, *How to Save the World* (Kogan Page, 1980)

R. Arvill, *Man and the Environment* (Penguin, 1969)

Frank Barnaby, *Future War: Armed Conflict in the Next Decade* (Michael Joseph, 1984)

Gerald Barney (ed), *Global 2000 Report to the President* (Pergamon Press, 1980)

C. Birch and J. B. Cobb, *The Liberation of Life* (Cambridge University Press, 1981)

L. Caldecott and S. Leland, *Reclaim the Earth* (The Women's Press, 1983)

Fritzjoh Capra, *The Turning Point* (Wildwood House, 1982)

Paul Ehrlich et al, *The Cold and the Dark* (Sidgwick & Jackson, 1984)

Erich Fromm, *The Sane Society* (Routledge and Kegan Paul, 1956)

Johann Galtung, *There are Alternatives* (Spokesman Books, 1984)

Teresa Hayter, *The Creation of World Poverty* (Pluto Press, 1981)

C. R. Hensman, *Rich Against Poor* (Penguin, 1975)

Sir Edmund Hillary (ed), *Ecology 2000* (Michael Joseph, 1984)

Jane Jacobs, *The Question of Separatism* (Random House, 1980)

Leopold Kohr, *The Breakdown of Nations* (Christopher Davies Publications Ltd, 1957)

Leopold Kohr, *The Overdeveloped Nations* (Christopher Davies Publications Ltd, 1977)

Peter Kropotkin, *Fields, Factories and Workshops* (1899) Updated version by Colin Ward (George Allen and Unwin, 1974)

F. M. Lappe, J. Collins and Kennley, *Aid as Obstacle* (Institute of Foods Development Policy, San Francisco, 1980)

Bibliography

James Lovelock, *Gaia: A New Look at Life on Earth* (Oxford University Press, 1979)

John Papworth, *The New Politics* (Vikas, 1982)

D. Pirages, *Global Ecopolitics* (Duxbury, 1978)

Jonathan Porritt, *Seeing Green* (Blackwell, 1984)

Jeremy Rifkin, *Algeny* (Penguin, 1984)

James Robertson, *Power, Money and Sex* (Marion Boyars, 1976)

Paul Rogers, Malcolm Dando and Peter Van den Dieren, *As Lambs to the Slaughter* (Arrow Books with Ecoropa, 1981)

Theodore Roszak, *Where the Wasteland Ends* (Faber, 1972)

Rural Settlement Handbook (Prism Alpha/Lighthouse, 1985)

Kirkpatrick Sale, *Human Scale* (Secker & Warburg, 1980)

C. Sanger, *Safe and Sound: Disarmament and Development in the Eighties* (Zed Books, 1982)

Jonathan Schell, *The Fate of the Earth* (Knopf, 1982)

Fritz Schumacher, *Small is Beautiful* (Abacus, 1973)

Barrie Sherman, *Working at Leisure* (Methuen, 1986)

F. E. Trainer, *Abandon Affluence and Growth* (Zed Books, 1985)

Richard Wilkinson, *Poverty and Progress* (Methuen, 1973)

The City and Urban Planning

Murray Bookchin, *The Limits of the City* (Harper and Row, 1974)

Paul Harrison, *Inside the Inner Cty* (Penguin, 1983)

Ivan Illich, *Tools for Conviviality* (Marion Boyars, 1973)

J. H. Lowry, *World City Growth* (Edward Arnold, 1975)

P. McAuslan, *Urban Land and Shelter for the Poor* (Earthscan, 1985)

I. L. McHarg, *Design with Nature* (Natural History Publishing Co., La Jolla, Ca., 1971)

Lewis Mumford, *The City in History* (Secker and Warburg, 1961)

K. Newland, *City Limits: Emerging Constraints on Urban Growth* (Worldwatch Institute, 1980)

Kirkpatrick Sale, *Dwellers in the Land: The Bioregional Vision* (Sierra Club books, 1985)

P. Steadman, *Energy, Environment and Building* (Cambridge University Press, 1975)

Barbara Ward, *The Home of Man* (Andre Deutsch, 1976)

Bibliography

This is by no means an exhaustive book list: indeed the number of books covering various aspects of environmental issues seems to be increasing exponentially each year: perhaps an indication of the seriousness of the current situation. Many magazines and journals now publish useful articles on the environment, and a list of useful journals and directories follows.

Armament and Disarmament
    Information Units (ADIU)
Science Policy Research Unit
Mantell Buildings
University of Sussex
Falmer
Brighton
East Sussex BN1 9RF
(*publishes bi-monthly report
    carrying articles and lists of
    publications*)

The Dendrologist
3 Arnett Close
Rickmansworth
Herts WD3 4DB
(*newsletter for tree
    enthusiasts, tree bank
    register, list of individuals
    and groups willing to give
    trees for amenity planting*)

Directory of Communes
Commune Network
Crabapple
Berrington hall
Berrington
Shrewsbury SY5 6HA

Directory for the
    Environment
Routledge and Kegan Paul
11 New Fetter Lane
London EC4P 4EE

The Ecologist
Worthyvale Manor
Camelford
Cornwall PL32 9TT

Food Policy
Butterworth Scientific
    Limited
PO Box 63
Westbury House
Bury Street
Guildford GU2 5BH

Gloucestershire Directory
15 St Anne's Terrace
Cheltenham (*good address
    list, £2.50*)

Golden List of Beaches
Coastal Anti-Pollution
    League Limited
94 Greenway Lane
Bath
Avon BA2 4LN
(*annually*)

Green Digest
Worthyvale Manor
Camelford
Cornwall PL32 9TT
(*monthly résumé of all
    important environmental
    news*)

Bibliography

Green Pages
Earthlife
10 Belgrave Square
London SW1X 8TH
(*list of people and resources
  in Europe available to
  Green movement; includes
  greener parts of industry*)

Green Pages
Urban Centre for
  Appropriate Technology
82 Colston Street
Bristol BS1 5BB
(*a directory of Appropriate
  Technology in Britain*)

Growing Concerns
3 Thorngarth Lane
Barrow-on-Humber
South Humberside DN19
  7AW
(*newsletter of Working Group
  on Agriculture, Food,
  Forestry, Fishing and
  Countryside. £1.50 p.a.*)

Home Farm
Broad Leys Publishing Co.
Widdington
Saffron Walden
Essex CB11 3SP
(*for smallholders*)

New Internationalist
42 Hythe Bridge Street
Oxford OX1 2EP

New Scientist
Commonwealth House
1–19 New Oxford Street
London WC1A 1NG

Resurgence
Ford House
Hartland
Devon

Turning Point
Spring Cottage
9 New Road
Ironbridge
Salop TF8 7AU
(*2 p.a.; focus for
  international network of
  people who feel mankind is
  at a turning point*)

*Working Weekends on
  Organic Farms (WWOOF)*
c/o S. Blethyn
10 Penn Lea Road
Bath BA1 3RA
(*directory of all organisations
  in UK directly or indirectly
  concerned with organic
  farming*)

Index

Index

Index

Index